"Epic in scope, a microcosm of Americana plotted by a gifted storyteller."
—*Columbus Dipatch*

"A powerful story of powerful people—avaricious, lusty, dynamic."

—*NBC News*

"Will keep the reader turning pages."
—*The Lewiston Daily Sun*

"For sheer entertainment *THINE IS THE GLORY* . . . is recommended. . . . the book's blend of history and fiction makes a fast-paced novel."
—*The Pensacola News-Journal*

"The fascinating saga of one family and the turn-of-the-century rise of Pittsburgh. . . . Besides producing such diverse people as Harry Thaw and Gertrude Stein, it was the place where Clay Frick began his career . . . Westinghouse . . . and the inimitable Carnegie. . . . This kind of book would be good reading anytime, but is especially appropriate now."
—*St. Louis Globe-Democrat*

THINE IS THE GLORY

A NOVEL BY

Samuel A. Schreiner, Jr.

A FAWCETT CREST BOOK

Fawcett Publications, Inc., Greenwich, Connecticut

To my wife, Dorrie, who first suggested
that I should do a novel about Pittsburgh,
the city in which I have my roots,
and who bore with love and patience
the deprivation of having her husband so long
and so deeply involved with a fictional family.

Prelude

It seemed truly blessed of God. In the long process of creation, it was given more than its natural share of wealth. For sixty million years of the Carboniferous period, great forests thrived in its tropical temperatures, grew old and subsided into the swamps at their feet and were pressed over another two hundred million years of time into the black rock men call coal. The fingers of glaciers receding from western Pennsylvania in what was only yesterday on the clock of creation clawed valleys to cradle swift rivers. Although withdrawing ice humped the land, it left a rich blanket of silt that lifted great forests into the air and, later, turned easily to the plow. It left limestone, capping vast pools of oil and gas, the distillates of millions of years of decay and pressure. It left clay, too, and sand and iron ore and, above all, water.

Flowing ceaselessly from the lakes and melting snows of the highlands, the water came down the valleys to Pittsburgh in two streams, named by the Indians who fished them and hunted their banks—the swift Allegheny River on the north, and the sluggish Monongahela River on the south. Meeting, they carved a point, sharp as an Indian arrowhead, and joined to flow on westward as the Ohio. It was this curious point of land that first caught the eye of Europeans pushing across the high Allegheny mountain divide to seek the riches of the West. Coming on it in 1753, practical George Washington wrote, "As I got down from the canoe, I spent some time viewing the rivers, and the land in the fork; which I think extremely well-situated for a fort. . . ." For the next five years, through a series of forts, it became the seesaw point of struggle between the French drifting down the rivers from Canada and the British breaching the mountains from Virginia. Finally secured

7

for the British and their American colonists, Fort Pitt and the little village that rapidly grew around it became a natural gateway to the West beyond; everything from nails to whiskey could be freighted cheaply down the currents of the Ohio to the Mississippi and on to New Orleans and the sea.

Into this pointed valley flowed pioneers, mostly of Scotch-Irish and German stock—traders, farmers, artisans. Cut off from the century-old cities of the east by the Allegheny range, they turned quickly to the riches at hand. From the forests they made barrels, boxes, barges; from the limestone and sand they made glass; from the coal, some of it lying naked to the eye, they made fire for iron forges; from the soil they grew grain for bread and whiskey. They were a stubborn lot, the first to rise up against the new government of the United States when it taxed their whiskey. For every distillery, they built a church, generally in the Scotch Presbyterian tradition of their heritage. It was said that John Knox prayed, "Oh, Lord, give me Scotland," and a gracious God answered him by throwing Pittsburgh in, too.

By the time the iron ribbons of the railway had been snaked through and over the mountains to end its isolation, Pittsburgh was ready. Into the great struggle between the states, it poured its metal and its men. By the end of the war, Pittsburgh was seen to be the foundry of a united and growing nation and had found, in the words of William Lucien Scaife, "its real meaning and mission; namely, the conquest of nature by intelligent energy directing suitable machinery, whose life comes from that smoke and dirt producer, bituminous coal." This story is the story of men and women who understood this mission and, for better and for worse, carried it forward.

A Look at General Grant

Mary Stewart slept lightly as she always did the night before any big event in the family. She wanted to be sure to see that Annie was up and the fires lit in time to have breakfast on the table for the doctor and their older son Scott by seven at the latest. So it was she who first heard in the pre-dawn dark the clank of harness and the creak of wagon wheels, then a knock on the front door. Quickly and quietly so as not to awaken the doctor, she slipped out of the warm envelope of their bed, threw a robe over her nightdress and ran down the stairs. The chimes on the clock in the corner of the hallway were throbbing out a quarter to some hour, probably five, she guessed, when she opened the door.

Until he fumbled off his hat at the sight of her, Mary didn't recognize the man standing there in the dim light as Scott McClure. She was accustomed to seeing him all starched up for church, but now he wore rough corduroy farm clothes; his hair was tousled and his chin was stubbled with half a week's growth of beard. There was a wild frantic look in his eye. "Ma'am . . . Mary . . . sorry to wake you—is Doctor in?"

"Yes, he's asleep. Here, come in, Scott, and let me light a candle," she said. When she struck a match to the candle she kept by the door, she noted that her hunch had been right: it was going on five. "What brings you out so early?"

"Nellie," he said. "I think it's her time."

"Nonsense, Scott. I talked to her last Sunday; she's not due for a week or more."

"It's the pains . . ."

"How fast are they coming?"

"Well, not so fast yet—an hour or two apart, maybe. But she's complaining it ain't like all the other times."

9

"I see. Sounds like it might be a false start. I had that with Lucinda days before. You wouldn't want to have the doctor sitting out there wasting his time, would you?"

"Well, I . . ."

"The doctor's been planning for weeks to go to Pittsburgh today and take little Scott with him. I'd hate to see him give it up for a wild-goose chase, and you know he would if I wake him," Mary said.

"I know, I know, God bless 'im. He was there nearly a week last time."

"I think your Nellie just gets frightened."

"She does that. That's why I'd hate to go back without . . ."

"I have an idea, Scott," Mary said. "Why don't you go get Mrs. Smith and take her back with you? The doctor would want her to be there anyway, and I promise you he'll look in tonight as soon as he gets back."

"All right, Mary, if you say so, but you'll see he gets to us tonight?"

Mary nodded. Watching McClure clamp his hat on and lurch out into the darkness in search of comfort for his wife, Mary had a twinge of doubt: what if her hunch about Nellie McClure was wrong? Well, Mrs. Smith was a capable midwife, probably better at delivering babies than Doctor if the truth were known. In any case, Nellie was a great one for false alarms. You'd think she was having her first instead of her fourth the way she carried on, but she was always that way. Doctor had sat out there on the farm for days at a time on each delivery; maybe it was all those idle hours of talking with Scott McClure that made the doctor come to like him so much that he named his own first son after him. No doubt Doctor would be angry with her for sending McClure away, but she was determined not to have anything ruin this day for both her husband and her son, so determined that she decided not to tell the doctor about it until evening.

It was too late to go back to bed, so Mary Stewart went out to the kitchen, called up the back stairs to Annie and began laying the fire in the big wood-burning stove herself. She hoped Doctor would get at least another hour's sleep to put him in a good mood for the day. The poor man never seemed to get enough rest, and for the life of her Mary couldn't understand why he insisted on sitting up in his office, nodding over his books until all hours, when he could have been in bed. If he were reading up on medicine, it might make some sense to Mary, but like as not he was dreaming over some poetry or philosophy or something. The thing he was excited about now was a book with a title so long Mary couldn't imagine anybody's even wanting to open it—something called *On the Origin of the Species by Means of Natural Selection, or the Preservation of Favoured Races in the Struggle for Life,* by a man named Charles Darwin. "Wait'll I nail old Gordon Wallace with this," he told Mary when he tried to explain to her Darwin's theory that men had descended from apes or some such. "Makes a lot more sense than that Adam and Eve story."

There were times when Mary wished that the doctor wouldn't tease the Reverend Mister Wallace so much. She knew it was all in fun, but she was afraid other people might get the wrong idea and think that Doctor Stewart was an atheist or something. There was enough talk already about all those books in the doctor's library, some written by people who actually *were* atheists, like that Frenchman Voltaire. Most people in the township, even Mr. Wallace and the schoolmaster and Mary herself, didn't have much need or time for reading beyond the Bible and what newspapers they could get from Pittsburgh, and maybe an occasional copy of *Harper's Weekly* or *Atlantic* or *Godey's Lady's Book* that might fall into their hands, and some were downright angry at the doctor for his habit of passing his books around so freely to young people without seeming to care what might be in them. Mary often worried a little about her own children, particularly Scott, who at twelve seemed to have his nose in a book all the time. She was afraid he was filling his head with foolishness reading novels the doctor brought home like *Ivanhoe* instead of concentrating on his lessons.

Where was Annie? Mary called up the stairs again and got an answer so sleepy that she knew the girl was just now waking up. Mary wasn't about to go out to the smokehouse in her nightdress to cut a few strips of bacon, so she put a large pot of water on to boil for oatmeal. The doctor didn't like it as well as his bacon, but it would fill him up until lunch. She knew he always indulged his odd taste for seafood on the rare days he went to the city, so she didn't feel so badly about the bacon. But she'd have to do something about Annie. The girl was honest and clean enough. but she was slow-witted. She'd sleep the day through if Mary weren't up and around to wake her; it would be almost easier keeping house without her, but Mary knew the doctor wouldn't hear of it. He'd brought Annie back with him after he delivered her mother's eighth child. "A miner doesn't make enough to feed all those mouths," he told Mary, "and you could use a hand around

11

here." Between Annie and Moses, another of the doctor's lame ducks, as she called them, she guessed she had two hands to help her—but certainly not four.

By the time breakfast was ready, Doctor Stewart was sitting at the head of the table in the dining room, which was suffused with the cheerful light of a bright October dawn. Scott's place was still empty, and Mary called up the front stairs to him before she went in to sit down herself. The doctor was dressed for the city in his best black broadcloth; the little diamond stickpin he had inherited from his father, the first Doctor Stewart, winked from the folds of his black cravat. With his wavy hair and full curly beard he was far and away the handsomest man in the whole South Hills, and, although she was often baffled by what went on behind his light gray eyes that could change in mood like a pond reflecting an unstable sky, Mary always counted herself lucky to be his wife even when, as now, he snapped at her.

"No bacon?" he grumbled when a drowsy Annie set the oatmeal in front of him.

"I couldn't get Annie up," Mary explained after the girl left. "That girl's hardly any use to me, you know."

"I don't know why not—she's strong as an ox."

"And dumb as one, too."

"Now be patient, Mary," Doctor Stewart said. "She'll come along; she's only eighteen. What was all that fuss at the door this morning?"

Mary Stewart couldn't lie outright. "Scott McClure. He thinks Nellie's time has come."

"Well, why didn't you wake me? I'll have to go."

"No you won't—not this time, Doctor," Mary said. "You know Nellie, she always panics."

"But she's so small. . . ."

"Small or not, she's had three children with no trouble. I sent Scott off to get Mrs. Smith, just in case. . . ."

"She's not a doctor."

"Come now, Doctor, how do you think women had babies around here all these years before you came along? You've got a promise to keep to your son."

"Mary, you know I don't believe in letting family affairs stand in the way of my duty. I also don't like your making decisions for me."

"I don't mean to be making decisions, Doctor," Mary said. "It's just that . . . well, you've told me many times yourself there's precious little a doctor can really do at a delivery but comfort everybody. If it were any other day, I'd say give up

12

your trip to town, but the boy has so looked forward to this, and so have you . . ."

"I know, Mary. Still, it would never leave me if anything happened to Nellie, and I weren't there. . . ."

"Daddy, what's the matter? Aren't we going?"

Neither the doctor nor Mary had noticed Scott standing uncertainly at the dining-room door. A solemn boy, small for twelve, he had his mother's black hair, deep brown eyes and dark brows. Just now he was having trouble controlling the corners of his down-turning mouth; his voice trembled and nearly broke into soprano range. Nobody looking at him, hearing him, could doubt for a moment the intensity of his disappointment. Today was going to be the most exciting day of his whole life, and now his father was calmly talking about calling it off. It couldn't happen. But he knew it might; he had seen his father too often go slamming out into the night or the rain or the snow, ignoring his mother's protests.

One look at the boy's face caused Doctor Stewart to stop and reflect. It *would* be a shame to ruin this day for Scott—for both of them. It was no ordinary day! in fact, it promised a once-in-a-lifetime experience, and babies came along in the countryside as regularly as calves. He smiled at Scott. "I guess your mother's already fixed it so we can go," he said. "Now sit down and eat, son, it will be a long time until lunch."

Scott sat down and tried, but the food was dry on his excited tongue. His mother's new idea was almost as entrancing as the prospect of seeing the city, of getting a look at the famous General Grant. "Doctor, as long as you're in there," she was saying, "I think you should buy Scott a suit and a new shirt. You know he's joining the church next month, and he'll be going to the Academy in a year."

Scott had never in his life owned a suit that hadn't been laboriously refashioned from an old one of his father's. "But, Mary," the doctor protested, "the boy doesn't have his growth yet; you can see it to look at him."

"Never mind. Just tell them to tuck some extra up the sleeves and pants, and I'll take care of that. Don't you think the doctor's son should look his best when he goes up before the church?"

Doctor Stewart sighed. "Very well, Mary, he shall have a suit. Anything else you need?"

"Not that I can think of . . . Oh, yes, if you're getting presents for the girls, Lucinda said she would like a pencil set and Sarah . . ."

Moses had the buggy harnessed and waiting at the door; he

was stroking Old Pat's nose. "Morning, Moses." "Mornin', Doctor; fine day for the General." "Yes, fine day. Maybe you ought to be going in to pay your respects instead of us, but then I guess you freed yourself, didn't you?" "Yes, suh!"

Riding anywhere in the buggy was always a treat for the Stewart children. It was a thing of beauty—ebony black with brass lamps and trim and a fringed top to protect the doctor from the weather. He used it only for business since it was a gift from the local coal-mine owner whose employes the doctor treated for the sum of five hundred dollars a year, which some years was almost the only cash he saw. The doctor took the view that his family could travel, if they ever traveled, in the farm wagon like the rest of their neighbors. But since one purpose of today's trip was the purchase of medicine, the doctor felt the use of the buggy was legitimate. For his part, Scott was delighted to go down to the city in style; he only regretted that it was too early for his fellow pupils to see him when they passed the school yard and envy him not only for his great adventure but for being allowed to have the day off.

When Old Pat settled into a steady trot on the road north toward the city, Doctor Stewart shrugged off the nagging worry in the back of his mind about Nellie McClure and began to think ahead to the day's events. Though Pittsburgh lay only some ten miles from their door, the doctor seldom went into town—not more than once a month or so to buy medicines, pick up supplies for the house they couldn't get in the South Hills, talk to a more learned colleague about a medical problem and, above all, get new books to read. He had never yet taken any of the children with him, though they begged him each time, because he felt the atmosphere and sights of the city could do little but harm to their tender bodies and still innocent minds. Time enough for the city when they had their growth. But when he learned that General Grant would visit Pittsburgh on Thursday, October 5, he decided that he should take Scott, the eldest, with him to witness this historic occasion. After all, Scott was about to join the church, a kind of rite of manhood, and his studiousness seemed to have prematurely aged his mind. Doctor Stewart noted, in fact, with some amusement that Scott had even brought along a book today. Well, if nothing else, it would give them something to talk about, a matter of some importance since Doctor Stewart suddenly realized he and his son had never spent more than an hour alone together, and he had no doubt the boy felt as awkward as he did.

"What's that you brought to read, son?" he asked.

"Plutarch's Lives."

"A good choice for today, though I doubt any of those lives could match the life of the man you are going to see today. Imagine in victory letting your enemy keep his sword, the way I hear Grant did at Appomattox, or telling your own troops not to cheer. They say General Grant said to his men, 'The war is over; the rebels are our countrymen again.' Those are the actions and words of a considerable man, and I guess I'm as excited about seeing him as you must be."

It was true. The doctor had read every word he could find about the great struggle between the states, and he'd found Grant, next to Lincoln, the most intriguing personality in the whole drama. He had been bitterly disappointed last spring when the Lincoln funeral train was routed north through New York, and he felt now that seeing Grant might at least partly make up for missing that historic event.

The book hadn't provided much for conversation, so Doctor Stewart tried a new subject. "You're going to be entering the Academy next year, son," he said. "You'll have to be making up your mind what you want to do, so you know what to study. Have you thought about that?"

"Yes, Father. I want to be a minister, like Mr. Wallace."

"Oh, my God."

Doctor Stewart hadn't meant to react so strongly. He had never before uttered anything like an oath in front of his children, but surprise took the words out of his mouth. He had just assumed Scott would want to follow him into medicine, the way he had his father. That was one reason Doctor Stewart never complained when Scott haunted the special office-library he'd had built with a side entry and no opening into the house to give his patients, and himself, privacy from the family. He didn't know what the boy read there, but he couldn't help absorb the atmosphere. True, Scott was a bit squeamish. Once when he took the boy along on call, he'd found it expedient to extract an old farmer's abscessed tooth right there by the buggy. At the sight of the blood Scott had thrown up all over the seat. But Doctor Stewart was sure the boy would grow out of that. Maybe he would grow out of this too.

"I'm sorry, son, you just took me by surprise. I thought maybe you'd want to be a doctor. You know it's sort of a tradition in our family. . . ."

"But, father, Great Uncle Karl was a minister. . . ."

Ah, so that was it—it was the Shallenberger in him coming out. Mary was always boasting about her Uncle Karl the minister—he was the only one in her whole connection who wasn't

15

just a plain farmer like her father. Of course, Scott inherited that blood; he was at least half German, and Doctor Stewart always felt there was something humorless and murky about the way Germans thought. They took naturally to the mythology of theology, finding angels and devils no harder to conjure up than the Lorelei they claimed to see along the banks of the Rhine. Given that turn of mind, if he had it, Scott was probably taking too seriously all the training Gordon Wallace was giving him in preparation for joining the church. At the moment Doctor Stewart, who himself was an elder of the church, didn't feel it right to raise any questions in his son's mind. Time and study might broaden the boy's view, but if it didn't he would certainly argue with him later. Doctor Stewart held most ministers, and especially Gordon Wallace, in low esteem. They had closed minds, and, worse, they always seemed willing to sacrifice people to doctrine—an abomination to a man who devoted his whole life trying to ease people's pain, never mind their beliefs.

"Don't forget you'll have to study Greek if you get to be a minister," the doctor teased.

"Oh, yes, and Mr. Wallace says I'll have to study Latin and Hebrew and . . . Father!"

Doctor Stewart had been so absorbed in his thought and so accustomed to the road that he had not been aware when they wound over the top of Mt. Washington, the great hump that separated their rural South Hills from the river valleys through which the city of Pittsburgh was spreading. Scott's exclamation prompted him to pull Old Pat to a halt, and he tried to look out over the panorama lying four hundred feet below them through his son's fresh eye. Hills to the east and north rimmed a bowl in which the Monongahela River at their feet and the Allegheny River beyond had carved the land into a sharp point whence they flowed together into the broad Ohio. Into this narrow triangle was jammed an unsightly collection of squat, square boxes of every size—houses, warehouses, business buildings, hostelries—and over them, particularly to the east, rose the spires of a dozen or more churches like fingers pointing toward God. A forest of tall chimneys sprouted from the flats along the rivers as far as the eye could see, and the black smoke torn from their tops by the breeze blended into a film of haze across the whole bowl. Along the Monongahela, their stern paddles churning the yellow water into wakes of white froth, twin-stacked steamers marked their progress with inky lines. From where they sat, high in the clear October air,

16

far from all sound, it was like peering down on a toy town laid out under smoky glass.

"What do you make of it, Scott?"

"It's . . . it's big."

"Yes, more than fifty thousand people they say now—and half again as many in Allegheny City, across the Allegheny River there, and Birmingham below us this side of the Monongahela. See all those stacks—there's more than thirty rolling mills and half a dozen or more steelworks. I'd venture to say there isn't a city like it in America, or maybe the whole world."

As they clip-clopped down the hill, they descended into ever denser layers of haze. There was an acrid smell to the air, and the sun became a curious copper ball in the darkening sky above them. The doctor stabled Old Pat in Birmingham, and they boarded a horse car to cross the Smithfield Street bridge into town. The smoke was so thick now that gaslights flared along the bridge and from the streets and windows of the city they were approaching. Scott had something of the same sensation he'd had when he opened his eyes under water in the weedy green farm pond where he often swam on a warm summer afternoon; everything was a little dim, a little fuzzy. But unlike water, the air here was alive with sound. As they swayed across the bridge, the driver of their car clanged his bell furiously at any man or beast careless enough to block his way. Whistles shrieked, and boats in the river below them moaned. Just across the bridge they had to stop for a steam engine, hissing and chuffing right down the middle of the street and belching such cindery smoke from its wide-mouthed stack into their open car that Scott could actually feel it grind between his teeth. People all around them were coughing and choking, and Doctor Stewart took out a handkerchief, wiped his own face and smarting eyes and handed it to Scott. "Now you don't wonder why I've always complained of the dirt here," he said.

"Yes, but it's real exciting," Scott said.

"I dare say—the first time. Let's get off and walk."

Everything seemed to close in around them as they walked. The narrow streets were like tunnels, walled with the lighted windows of shops and offices. More people than Scott had ever seen in his life—men in sober city frock coats with black stovepipe hats, women with their wide hoop skirts stirring eddies of dust behind them, young boys his own age but dressed like men weaving and darting through the crowds—jostled them for space on the sidewalk. The street itself was a dangerous

17

river of vehicles flowing in every direction—carriages that made his father's buggy seem an ancient relic of the past; wagons heaped with barrels, lumber, produce, jangling horse cars. Smells assailed them from all sides and mingled in a kind of heavy odor of steaming life. There was the delicious aroma from an open bakery door, the sour stench of a saloon, the familiar barnyard reek of the horse-manured street, a whiff of perfume or tobacco from the person of a passing stranger and over it all and through it all the rotten-egg smell of smoke. On one corner a man, blind by the looks of his eyes and wearing a frayed blue coat, was coaxing an off-key version of "Tenting tonight on the old camp ground . . ." from a battered violin. Doctor Stewart dropped a coin into the tin cup at his feet. "A veteran no doubt, poor beggar," he said.

When they passed by the *Pittsburgh Dispatch* building, they paused as others were doing to read the bulletin board hung from the arched windows of the news room on the second floor. The major event, of course, was General Grant's appearance, scheduled to take place within the hour. They hurried along to try to get a good position in the crowd gathering beneath the balcony of the Monongahela House, the same balcony from which Lincoln had spoken four years before on his way to Washington and a rendezvous with a tragic destiny nobody could have predicted. Dr. Stewart managed to maneuver against the wall of a building across the street, where he could prop his son up on a window ledge.

They didn't have long to wait. The hotel was astir, and people were already hanging out its richly curtained windows to get a better view of the flag-draped platform where the dignitaries were gathering. Suddenly a small man with wavy hair and a full beard lurched to the front of the platform. He wore a plain blue uniform—no medals, just the three stars of a lieutenant general on his shoulder bars. The crowd recognized Ulysses S. Grant at once. A great cheer went up, and the little man raised his hand in response. While people were still yelling and singing—someone had struck up the "Battle Hymn of the Republic"—Grant fell back among his frock-coated companions like a sparrow disappearing into a flock of crows. So that was the mighty General Grant? Dr. Stewart rather agreed with the comment of a rough-looking man near him—"Th' little fart don't look like any general to me"—but he hoped his son didn't hear either the crude language or the cynical observation. The boy's disappointment was evident, however, in a whispered question as to why the general wore no medals. The doctor tried to make the best of it: "It's part of the man's greatness, son. He doesn't believe in show. Why I read he wore only a private soldier's uniform the day he received Lee at Appomattox."

The crowd was beginning to quiet down now, and a portly, florid man with white hair and bushy mutton chops to match was trying to speak. "Ladies and gentlemen," he began, "the general regrets that he has prepared no remarks for this occasion, but he has asked me to speak on his behalf. Of all the cities in this great country there is none, according to General Grant, that played a more vital role in making possible his victory over the rebel states. From the shores of these great rivers came the superior force of armament that alone prevailed in the face of a fanatical resistance to the laws and the Constitution of these great United States. It was Pittsburgh that forged the guns for the mighty *Monitor*. It was Pittsburgh that . . ."

Obviously, General Grant who by now had sat down and was smiling and talking to the man nearest him, had no intention of speaking. Dr. Stewart lifted his son off the sill, took him by the hand and started edging out through the crowd. "We have too much business," he said, "to waste time listening to a political windbag like that. It appears the general really is a man of few words, as they've said."

When they were free of the crowd, he went on. "I suppose he didn't seem much of a hero to you, did he, Scott? Well, maybe it's just as well. You can see by looking at him that great things can be performed by very ordinary human beings."

It had been a long time since breakfast, and Dr. Stewart, hungry himself, knew that Scott, who had eaten very little in his excitement, must be starved. Perhaps the boy would be hungry enough to take to the exotic taste of seafood. At any rate he decided to try, even at the risk of shocking his son. Out in the South Hills, Doctor Stewart maintained for the sake of his practice and his family a front of somewhat rigid rectitude. He didn't drink or smoke, though he did, like most of his neighbors, including the preacher, keep a chew of tobacco discreetly tucked in his cheek most of his waking hours. He attended church religiously, regardless of what was going on in his mind while Mr. Wallace thundered from the pulpit, and, therefore, subscribed by implication at least to the minister's hell-fire-and-damnation views on alcohol. But on his rare visits to Pittsburgh, where he was not likely to be observed by friends or patients and where his services would

19

not be needed, the doctor liked to indulge himself with food, and drink. He regarded it as sound medical theory that such infrequent indulgence was beneficial to his nerves and spirit no matter what Gordon Wallace with his narrow Calvinistic vision might say.

So Doctor Stewart led Scott, without explanation, into his favorite saloon. It was his favorite because, along with drinks, free seafood was served across the wide bar. Fresh seafood—oysters, clams, mussels—was still an exotic taste to natives of the Pittsburgh region like Doctor Stewart; only improving train service in the last ten years made it possible to ice it down and bring it in from the coast before it spoiled. There was still some risk in eating it, as the doctor knew only too well, but he couldn't resist the temptation. There was something about its taste and smell that gave him just a touch of the one thing he longed to see before his life was over—the ocean. He was, in fact, accumulating a little secret fund with which he planned to take Mary to Atlantic City when the children were old enough to leave. Meanwhile he subsisted on occasional bites of seafood and great gulps of salty literature.

Scott's surprise when they entered the saloon was certainly as great as his father had anticipated. He'd read of saloons, of course, and heard of them often in the many temperance meetings held at the church. Their swinging doors were, in the view of Mr. Wallace and even more impassioned speakers, the very gates of Hell. Now his father was not only leading him into this iniquitous place, but it was immediately evident that he had been there often before. A loud and cheerful man behind the bar, a man with great bristling mustaches and a barrel belly swathed in a dirty white apron, called out, "Well, if it isn't the good Doctor Stewart himself! The usual whiskey, Doctor?"

"Yes, Brian," the doctor said. "Mr. O'Donnell, this is my son, Scott. I wonder if you might have a nice bowl of oyster stew for him. He's never tasted it."

"I do that, Doctor. 'Tis a fine young man you have here. Your first visit to the city, son?"

Scott couldn't risk speech, afraid his voice might break. He managed a feeble nod at the cheery Mr. O'Donnell, who bore no resemblance to the horned devil of his imagination. Meanwhile, his senses soaked up the forbidden atmosphere. Gaslights flared against the great mirrors back of the bar, the floor was strewn with damp sawdust, and the sweet-sour smell of the place was unlike anything he'd ever breathed before. When a small glass of evil-smelling brown liquid had been set before his father, the doctor took a sip and then smiled at his obviously distraught son.

"I wondered about bringing you here, Scott, but then I decided if you are old enough to make up your mind about joining the Church, you are old enough to make up your mind about other things too. I know this goes against all you've heard your mother and the preacher and perhaps even me say about the evils of drink. Well, drink can be evil if it really gets a hold of a man, and that's why I publicly urge everybody—man, woman or child—to stay away from it. On the other hand, as you'll find in your reading, a number of worthy men through all history have used drink with little harm to ease the pressures they face. General Grant himself is one of them. They say when someone complained to President Lincoln that Grant drank whiskey, Lincoln told them, 'Find out what brand he uses and send it to my other generals.'"

Doctor Stewart could see from the look on Scott's face that his son was still bewildered. Maybe he'd made a bad mistake. He tried another tack—self-defense. "I really need this little bit of relaxation, son," he said. "You may not understand now, but I hope you will when you grow up to face responsibilities, particularly responsibilities beyond your power to meet them. You know a doctor isn't like a preacher or a teacher or a farmer. A doctor buries his mistakes, as they say, and only he knows how many of them he makes. We have so little knowledge, Scott; we've just begun to understand something of how the human body works—and almost nothing of the mind. I'll confide in you, son—I feel pretty helpless when I can only guess at what's wrong with somebody or when I can't find anything in my bag to relieve their agony. I hope you can appreciate that, and I hope you'll keep this whole experience a secret between us, man to man. No use upsetting your mother or the other children with things they might not understand. All right?"

Scott nodded, and Doctor Stewart felt he'd at least managed the right note.

Scott didn't really understand all his father was trying to tell him, but he did get a warm feeling of sharing some kind of special moment with a man he hardly knew outside of his austere, doctor-father role at home. To hear his father confess to his own limitations made Scott feel more of a man himself, and a little scared, too. He knew his father was doing something Mr. Wallace would say was bad, and yet he enjoyed watching him relax, hearing him talk easy with Mr. O'Donnell, seeing him dig into the queer-looking seafood with such appetite. As his father had hoped, Scott made up his mind he wouldn't share this special secret knowledge of his father with anyone—it was, indeed, something that ought to be kept "man to man."

When the steaming stew came, Scott was ravenous and thought it the best thing he'd ever tasted. Though the blobs of oyster had a rather unpleasant gritty, stringy feel to them, the warm salty milk, streaked with golden butter, was just what his excited stomach craved. Seeing his son enjoy the stew, Dr. Stewart was glad now that he had followed his instincts. With the whiskey and food washed down by a foaming stein of beer, he was taking on a contented glow. He signaled O'Donnell for his last indulgence—a long, black Pittsburgh stogie that he puffed awkwardly, like an engine getting up steam, as they set out on a shopping expedition.

At the clothier's, the doctor insisted his son be provided with the best available broadcloth. "Good quality wears longest," he said. It was a real man's suit with double-breasted vest and a jacket in the new sack style. Looking at himself in the mirror, Scott felt he'd grown inches in the last hour. There was no way now to tell him from the natty young men he'd seen on the city streets, except for the fact that not so much as a hair had yet appeared on his full cheeks and dimpled chin. In the dark suit with tie to match, he did, indeed, look as his father said, like a "little man." Scott's was a serious face and it irritated him when the doctor would frequently tease, "Why so solemn, young man?" But on a growing day like this, he was proud he had a face to match the authority of his new clothes.

When they were through at the clothier's, Doctor Stewart set about getting presents for the other members of the family, as he always did on his trips to town. Six-year-old Lucinda was easy; he remembered about the pencil box. For Sarah, almost as serious and studious as Scott at eleven, he picked up a new book *Hospital Sketches*, by Louisa May Alcott, in which she told of her nursing experiences in Georgetown during the War. Maybe it would interest Sarah in the healing arts; better a daughter than nobody following in his footsteps. Doctor Stewart let Scott pick out something for two-year-old Reed—his namesake, John Reed Stewart, Jr. It was an ingenious, red-and-silver tin top that kept turning when you pushed down the handle. Every time he went shopping for the children, Doctor Stewart was reminded of the two small headstones in the little cemetery by the church where Mary, dead at three of scarlet fever, and Franklin, dead at two months of suffocation, lay. Though losing children was the melancholy experience of nearly every family, it was particularly galling to him, an awful proof of the professional lacks he was trying to describe to Scott. These deaths were even harder on Mary, and the doctor always felt that any present he could give her was too little. This time he found a new bonnet, bright with flowers and birds, for her to wear at the service when Scott joined the church. Usually she just covered her head with a simple scarf, but for her, at least, this would be a special occasion calling for a special touch of gaiety.

Just before he fell asleep to the rhythm of the jiggling buggy winding its way back up Mt. Washington and on homeward through the gathering dark, Scott said drowsily, "Thank you for a wonderful day, Father. Do you think General Grant saw me?"

"I've no doubt he did," the doctor said, without a twinge. "He may have a quiet tongue, but I'm sure he has a sharp eye."

"Can I say so in school?"

"Oh, I don't see any harm in it. . . ."

What a serious one, the boy was. The doctor hoped it wouldn't entirely get the better of him.

A Doctor's Dilemma

The United Presbyterian Church was filled as it always was for the taking in of new members. The Stewarts had come early to be sure to get their regular pew, halfway down the center aisle on the right. Despite the last-minute disappointment that the doctor couldn't come, Mary Stewart proudly wore the new bonnet he'd brought her from Pittsburgh. This was an occasion of such moment that she had decreed that even little Reed and Annie join them. She was peeved with the doctor. She really didn't believe him when he insisted that he had to look in on a miner who'd fallen down a shaft. In her opinion, an injury that had waited through the night could wait another hour, the most important hour in their son's life. But she didn't argue with the doctor, because, ever since Nellie McClure's death, he had been acting strangely. When he wasn't on call, he spent longer and longer hours in his office, sometimes the whole night. If he was in the house, he spoke only in monosyllables and often snapped at the children, or even her. It wasn't at all like him, but then Mary Stewart had lived through such periods before after he lost a case. She knew the least she could do for him was to hold her tongue.

As usual, the McClure family sat in front of them. Mr. McClure greeted them affably enough and even shook young Scott's hand in congratulation. If Doctor Stewart's real reason for staying away had been the fear of facing his old friend, he needn't have worried, Mary thought. Scott McClure was a strong man and a good Christian who never once brought up the fact that Doctor Stewart had not come until it was too late. He seemed to accept the fact that Nellie's death was God's will. Even at the funeral, he had been dry-eyed and dignified for the sake of his children, and it was then that Mary was especially glad they had used his name for their first son. To Mary, and she was sure to any good Christian, death was a normal expectation—the "valley of the shadow" the Bible talked about. What good was faith if it didn't arm you for the walk through this valley? In fact, to a real Christian, death was a kind of triumph. Right now Nellie McClure would be dwelling in one of the many mansions Jesus had promised His Father would prepare for true believers, just as Mary's own little children were.

Her own part in persuading the doctor into going to Pittsburgh had given Mary many a sleepless night until she worked up the courage to have a private talk with Mr. Wallace. He had persuaded her with numerous quotations from scripture and a comforting prayer that Nellie's natural time had come, that in the Presbyterian theology to which she had subscribed in faith, everything was indeed governed by predestination. It worried her that Doctor Stewart couldn't seem to feel this way about death. Was he really a man of little faith? When, as right now, she had these dark questions about the doctor, Mary reminded herself he was without question a good man and took for the text of a little sermon to herself that "faith without works is dead."

The service began with a hymn that Mary herself had suggested because it seemed to fit in with the studies the young people had just completed. As the congregation sang, "Oh, how love I Thy law, Oh, how love I Thy law; it is my meditation all the day," Mary caught a slight nod of acknowledgment from Mr. Wallace, whose baritone set the tune for them from the pulpit. For Gordon Wallace, singing hymns at all was a grudging concession to the more frivolous members of his congregation and his ignorance of the whole matter led him to rely on one of them, Mary Stewart, for advice. In fact, despite the rather regrettable leavings of a Methodist upbringing in Mary Stewart's thinking, she had become something of a sounding board for the minister. Besides, the Stewarts' big white house lay on the same hilltop just across the pike from the old brick church and its manse. Over the years, Mr. Wallace had developed a habit of dropping in on the Stewarts of a Saturday afternoon. He liked to pretend it was a ministerial duty call, but in truth it was more of a social pleasure.

The Stewarts had in their parlor the only piano in the whole congregation. It was an extravagant and thoughtful wedding gift to Mary from the doctor, who thought she might want to enjoy, at least in her home, some of the hymns of her Methodist childhood. Doctor Stewart knew that as long as Gordon Wallace held the pulpit it was unlikely that any musical instrument would profane the United Presbyterian Church. A pitch pipe to set the tune was the farthest Wallace would go in the direction of musical instruments. So it became a custom on those Saturday afternoons for Mary, and now her daughter Sarah, who was learning her way around the keyboard, to play the hymn for the coming Sunday so that Mr. Wallace could learn to sing it. After that Mary usually served tea with some bread or cake still warm from the oven out in the washhouse. There would be talk, and most of the time Mr. Wallace would manage to test out Mary's reaction to the thrust of the sermon he'd prepared for the next day.

Gordon Wallace was often a little disturbed in conscience that he preferred those visits to the Stewarts when the doctor was unable to join them. Although he would have trusted his life in Doctor Stewart's hands, he found it disconcerting to have those light eyes of the doctor's, with their webs of mirth lines running out from the corners, fixed on him. The doctor too often posed embarrassing theological questions, though in the politest way, and seemed to enjoy the minister's discomfiture. Mary was another matter. Gordon Wallace could tell that she had the utmost respect, if not for him, at least for his office. It was an attitude he'd come to expect from his congregation, particularly the women, and he did, he felt, everything possible to deserve it. Now in his sixties, he was blessed with the proper physical presence. He was tall—not quite as tall as the doctor, to be sure, but he had made up for that by letting his body assume a solidity just short of fat. His thick hair and beard had fortunately turned pure white, and he kept them that way with repeated washing and grooming. He dressed always in the darkest broadcloth with a gleaming shirt front to match his hair. Keeping his linen that clean had been the curse of all three of his wives, and their grumbling had been his cross to bear.

Every time Gordon Wallace visited with Mary Stewart, he was frankly a little jealous of the doctor. There was a sense of quiet order in the Stewart household that none of his wives had managed to achieve. Despite the fact that horses and wagons raised clouds of dust along the pike outside, not a speck of it ever seemed to rest on the gleaming dark wood of the furniture in the Stewart parlor. Mary was never heard to raise her voice to a rambunctious child, though Mr. Wallace well knew that the Stewart children, particularly little Lucinda, were full of life since each of them had a friend among his own ten. It would not be fair to say that Mary was a ravishing beauty, but she had a slim waist despite her six births, a straight back and delicate neck that gave her a look of gentle pride, and solemn dark eyes, like her son Scott's, that seemed to concentrate with special warmth on anyone she was listening to. She'd only attended a few years of country school and read little but the Bible, but she had managed to pick up many graces, like playing the piano and doing the fine needlework that made the seats on her sofa and chairs a delight to the eye. Altogether a fine woman, Gordon Wallace thought, and the chance to visit with her so regularly helped a little to make up for his own disappointments.

When the hymn singing ended, Mr. Wallace called the members of the communicants' class forward. There were six of them—four girls and two boys. Mary Stewart was proud of Scott, who looked so grown up, so stiffly elegant in his new suit. What if he did stand out from the others in their faded hand-me-downs? Her son was meant to stand out, like his father, like Mr. Wallace, who obviously saw no harm in a minister's dressing above his congregation. Scott had recently told her about his decision to become a minister, and nothing could have made her happier, since in memory the ministry was the distinguishing profession in her own lineage. Now as the boy repeated his vows and received the benediction, she was aware that he was crossing over into consecrated manhood. If only the doctor could be with her, not so much in the flesh as in the spirit.

The doctor didn't even join them for dinner after church, though Mr. and Mrs. Wallace were honored guests. He came back from his call to the mines and went directly to his office. "I can't see why he's carrying on so," Mr. Wallace said at dinner. "Nellie's death was surely God's will, and it is a blessing the baby didn't survive with no mother to feed him. Maybe I should go and pray with Dr. Stewart."

"I wouldn't, Mr. Wallace," Mary said. "Not that he doesn't need prayer. The thing is for all of us to pray for him, but to leave him alone. He has to work things out in his own mind."

When it was dark and the doctor still hadn't come into the house, Mary began to worry. She suggested that Scott take the new Bible, embossed with his name in gold on the leather cover, that he had received for joining the church and show it to the doctor. It would be an innocent thing for a son to do, and, although she didn't tell Scott, a way of finding out if the doctor was all right. While he didn't understand it fully, Scott felt caught in the middle of something. He was reluctant to go, knowing his father's strict insistence on privacy in his office. So he walked with pounding heart around the corner of the dark porch. Through the window, he could see by the soft light of the oil lamp on the desk that his father's head was bent over a book. Oddly, the door was slightly ajar, as if his father were silently asking for a visit. Scott slipped in and, even before he could say a word, knew something was terribly wrong. The place reeked of the sour smell of whiskey he recognized from his visit to the saloon in Pittsburgh. He just stared.

"Hallo, Schott," his father said in a voice that sounded like he had a mouth full of mush. "Well, well, you came to show me your Bible, I . . . let's . . . let's have a look there. . . ."

Scott stood, rooted with fear, and clutched the Bible like a talisman to his chest.

His father chuckled, a mirthless sound. "You figure I'll profane it? Maybe so, maybe . . . but she didn't have to die, you know that? She didn't have to die, didn't have to . . ."

Suddenly Scott found himself saying, "It was God's will, mother says that and just today at dinner Mr. Wallace said so too. . . ."

Suddenly the doctor straightened up and said clearly but in

a kind of hissing whisper, "Get out, Scott, just get out of here—"

Scott did and shut the door tightly behind him. For a long while he stood leaning against the wall, trying to think of what to say to his mother.

When Scott had gone, Doctor Stewart reached into a bottom drawer of his desk, brought out the bottle that had never before been used in this room except as medicine, and took another long swig. Damn them . . . all of them. How could people go around blaming everything on God when any fool could see it was *his* human fault? God's will. God's will. What kind of God would will the thing that happened that night? No God he could love. He had tried everything to blot it out of his mind. Now whiskey. Nothing worked.

Close his eyes, and Doctor Stewart was again in that cramped little bedroom in the upper corner of the old McClure farmhouse where Nellie McClure, her uterus torn beyond help, bled to white death in his arms while her husband, kneeling by the bed, alternately prayed, "Oh, God. Please God," and muffled his sobs in the mattress. Doctor Stewart knew he should have been there earlier, from the moment Mrs. Smith met him at the door . . . "I don't know what to do—it won't come out. I can see its face but it won't come out." Doctor Stewart had rushed upstairs. Nellie, bathed in sweat, was flopped with legs extended and moaning softly; she had ceased to labor. A look confirmed that it was what the doctor's books called a chin presentation with the baby's head cocked so that it couldn't be born. Mrs. Smith should have known enough to try to rotate the baby to get its head into the right position, but then she had probably never seen such a thing and assumed, just because the head was coming first, that it would be all right. The baby was already dead. Doctor Stewart took it with his hands and forceps, but the damage had been done. When his stethoscope told him Nellie's heart had stopped beating, he closed her lids, tried to say something to Scott McClure and couldn't, and went home feeling that at least now he did believe there was a living hell. . . .

Scott's mother met him in the hall. "Did your father like the Bible?"

"I guess so," Scott said, trying on the day he'd taken his Christian vows not to lie outright.

"Is he all right? What is he doing—reading?"

"Yes." It was only a half lie, because for all he knew his father might be reading—too.

"Well, then, I guess we might as well go up to bed. He's

28

been having trouble sleeping, you know, and sometimes reads the night away."

Going up to bed was one thing, sleeping another. Scott, his conscience churned up by lying and by the scary sight of his drunken father, tossed and turned as much as he dared without waking his brother Reed, who was wuffling like some contented little animal in his trundle bed in the corner. Only the demands of a youthful body finally dragged him into restless sleep. But there was no youth to help Mary Stewart. She didn't even try to close her eyes. Staring into the shadowed darkness, she listened vainly for sounds from below that would indicate that her husband was coming up to her bed. Once she thought she heard his footsteps on the porch, but he didn't appear. This was worse than ever before, and she knew now that she would have to try to do something—talk to him, get some help somewhere. . . .

Dawn was silvering the sky when finally there was a tread on the stair and, surprisingly, a knock at her door. "Yes?" she said.

It was Moses' husky voice that answered her. "Ma'am, come soon. . . . The doctor."

Something dreadful had happened; Moses, by choice, hadn't been beyond the kitchen, where he took his meals, in all the two years he'd been with them. Moses was another of Doctor Stewart's oddities. In all the township he was the only black hired man, but Doctor Stewart had insisted on finding another place for their old hired man Clem so that he could give Moses a job after Moses appeared one day on the road in front of their house—a half-starved escaped slave who'd made his way through the fighting lines in a year-long odyssey. His name wasn't even Moses, but the doctor had so christened him because he had "come up out of Egypt." Keeping him was the most dramatic way the doctor could show his violent feelings against slavery. From Mary's point of view, it had created problems, since a bullet that lodged in his hip during his wild night of escape had left Moses with such a limp that he literally dragged his feet on the chores Clem used to do in half the time. Not only that, but there was something deeply, disturbingly sad about him. He could sit in his room above the washhouse, crooning spirituals to himself by the hour and scaring the children half to death with the mournful sound. When she would complain to the doctor, he would only say, "Think what the man's been through, Mary. Time our children knew how some people have to suffer."

Moses was still at the door, and she cautioned him with a

finger not to wake the children. Silently she followed him down the stairs and out into the dew-chilled dawn. She had forgotten to put on slippers and the feel of the cold damp grass set her to shivering, but she didn't want to turn back. Moses was heading directly for the barn, and she continued to follow, still silent because she really didn't want to hear what he might have to say. Half the barn door had been swung open, and it let enough light into the cavernous haying floor that she could see quite distinctly the doctor's body swaying from a rope thrown over a high beam. Though she turned instantly away, the contorted, blackened mask of what had been her husband's face was forever photographed on her mind. She leaned against the outside of the closed door, shivering, gasping for air and finally vomiting repeatedly while Moses shifted nervously from one foot to the other and tried to look away from her anguish. When she felt literally emptied, Mary said, "Cut him down, Moses. Make a pine box and nail him in right now. The children must never see him this way, or even know about it. He died of apoplexy trying to harness the horse and you found him. Do you understand? Can you say that, Moses?"

"Yes, ma'am. You know I loved the doctor."

For the first time, Mary really looked at Moses and saw that his cheeks were streaming with tears. Well, she would cry, too, later; there was much to be done now. One of the things, unfortunately, according to Mr. Wallace who was summoned from his sleep, was to meet the legal requirement for a death certificate. So a physician from nearby Washington County with whom Doctor Stewart had often worked was sent for. The coffin was opened for his inspection only. When he had finished, he came into the parlor and said to Mary, "My God, I'm sorry, Mrs. Stewart. Do you have a drink?"

"You know we don't keep whiskey in this house, Doctor," she said.

The doctor gave her an odd look and then sighed. "No, I guess not."

"Must anybody know beyond your official report? The children . . ."

The doctor patted her. "Now don't you worry, Mrs. Stewart," he said, and went away with Mr. Wallace.

Because he had slept so poorly, Scott was the first of the children down. Mary led him into the parlor and told him solemnly that his father had died of apoplexy harnessing the horse; Moses had found him in the barn. Then, "Tell me, Scott, did he look sick to you last night? What did he look like?"

The shock of the news drove Scott to truth. "Mother," he said, struggling hard not to cry, "he was . . . he was drunk."

"Oh, thank God!" Mary Stewart said.

"But, mother . . . ?"

Mary Stewart had unexpectedly come to a difficult crossroads. Her reaction to Scott's news had obviously surprised and baffled the boy. Should she tell him more? She wanted to desperately, because she didn't know how she could go on bearing the burden alone. He was old enough and intelligent enough that he might put two and two together and begin suspecting something. If he ever discovered the truth, wouldn't her deception prove only another blow to him? Fortunately, Scott was a pious boy whose faith might just be strong enough to help him absorb the shock. She decided she would have to chance it. For his sake . . . for her sake.

"Scott," she said. "I . . . I didn't tell you the whole truth, just as you didn't tell me the whole truth. Something has been wrong with your father, you know, ever since Mrs. McClure died, and . . . well . . . he didn't die of apoplexy, he . . . he took his own life . . . and that's why I was glad to know he at least wasn't in his proper mind when . . ."

"How?"

It was only one word, squeaked out in a quivering treble, but it bore the freight of all the boy's astonishment, fright, curiosity. "Well, he . . . he hanged himself from a . . . from a rafter . . . Oh, Scott, I'm so sorry . . . so sorry. . . ."

Mary at last did start to cry. She sank into a chair and buried her face into its back to spare her son the sight and, as much as possible, the sound of her grief and shame. The boy stood there, fists clenched, having no idea what to say or do or think. Just then Mr. Wallace came into the room, went over to Mary, knelt beside her and put an arm around her shoulders. "You poor child," he said, "you poor child . . ."

Mary turned to look at him. "Then you know?"

Mr. Wallace nodded. "Perhaps I shouldn't, but that doctor was pretty shaken. I rummaged around home and found a little medicinal whiskey for him, and it loosened his tongue. Oh, my dear lady, what shame that such sin should fall upon your house."

"Sin?"

"Aye, the taking of one's own life. And I understand Doctor Stewart had been drinking, too."

"Yes, Scott tells me. He wasn't in his right mind, don't you see?"

"Oh, the wages of sin," Mr. Wallace said and, seeing Scott,

added, "You see now, lad, why I tell you that you have to be strong in the faith. If your father had only believed, had only submitted to the will of God. He always was a doubter. Remember how he taunted me, Mrs. Stewart?"

"Please, I don't think it is right to speak about him now like . . ."

"Yes, I'm sorry," Mr. Wallace said. "Come, pray with me."

Taking Scott's hand in one of his and Mary's in the other, Mr. Wallace brought them to their knees on the floor. Looking up toward God but with eyes tightly closed, he prayed, "Dear Lord: Thy will be done. Have mercy upon the soul of Doctor Stewart and give these, Thy true and troubled servants, the strength to carry the burdens thrust upon them by this grievous sin. Look down in mercy upon them, dear God. Let not their feet falter in Thy path and bless their every work that, through this tragedy, they may be strengthened to do Thy holy will. Guard them, keep them, feed them we pray in the name of Thy only Son, our Savior, Jesus Christ. Amen."

When they got up, Mr. Wallace shook each of their hands and said, "Now remember if there's anything I can do, anything . . ."

When he had gone, Scott asked his mother, "Do you think father was a . . . a sinner?"

"I don't know. . . . No, I don't think he was. . . . He just had more than he could bear. . . . Oh, Scott, if only I had let him go to Nellie McClure. . . ."

"It wasn't your fault, mother. Mr. Wallace said so himself; it was God's will."

"Yes, I guess I'll just have to believe it was . . . and this, too,"

"It was, Mother, it was. I know it."

She looked at him, startled by his firmness, and yet grateful for it too.

"Yes, well, bring the other children down, and we'll tell them. They needn't know yet any more than that their father dropped dead harnessing the horse. Yes, that will be all we'll tell them, or anybody. That will be all. . . ."

Despite the fact that a cold November rain swept in sheets across their hilltop, the funeral for Dr. John Reed Stewart was the biggest event in memory at the United Presbyterian Church. School was let out, and virtually every family in the township packed into the pews and spread up and down the aisles and into the vestibule in back. More than a dozen roughly dressed miners, who must have been on the night shift and some of whom were surely Catholics, came with their wives. Inspired by the crowd, the Reverend Mr. Wallace out-did himself with a long sermon some observers declared more an extolling of the healing powers of Christianity than a eulogy for the departed. It went on so long that three people fainted in the steamy sanctuary, and Mary Stewart, coming down with a cold as a result of going outside in her bare feet, wasn't able to concentrate on a word. She had to devote her whole attention to not joining the swooners by gritting her teeth and praying over and over again, "God help me through this . . . God help me through this."

The elders of the church, brave against the rain, bore their fellow elder's casket to the hilly little cemetery beside the church. It was lowered into a freshly dug hole just above the small headstones of the two Stewart children. Ashes to ashes, dust to dust. Mr. Wallace, his brushed mane of white hair turned to damp strings, intoned what probably was the shortest prayer of his career. But it was just long enough to let Mary indulge in the release of tears again. The bleakness of the day, the sight of the open muddy hole and the two little white markers of lost children were all in harmony with her mood. She wondered whether she would really find the strength to go on. Despite all of Mr. Wallace's calling on God, she no longer felt the sure reassurance she had when Nellie McClure died, when her own children died. In truth, it did seem to be ashes to ashes, dust to dust. Could God, would God, save a man who had done what Doctor Stewart did? If not, what kind of a God could He be? How could God let a man like her husband so suffer for his goodness and then consign him to hell fire? But if there was no punishment for sin, how could there be salvation? And if she couldn't believe in the Christian promise, then what would make sense of a life that came always here, to the grave? Doubt, and a sense of desolation, swept her like the rain. And then a hand took hers and she looked down to see little Lucinda, usually the pretty one, the happy one, the naughty one. Her face was streaked with tears and dirt, her skirt splattered with mud, her golden hair plastered like a helmet to her head. Mary gripped her daughter's hand and turned away from the graves. "We have to go home and get cleaned up, Lucinda," she said. "Our friends are waiting."

They were, indeed. Ladies of the church had taken over the Stewart kitchen to prepare a full buffet for the family and invited guests. The house Mary and Lucinda came into was warm and lively and full of delicious smells. Grandfather and Grandmother Shallenberger and Mary's sister, Kate, were there as were the aunts from Pittsburgh and the Wallaces and the McClures and Judge Shaw from the Allegheny County court who maintained a farm in the township and who'd handled whatever small legal affairs Doctor Stewart had. At first they spoke gravely of "old Doctor Stewart" and his many kindnesses but finally the talk drifted around to brighter recollections, such as the time the good doctor's horse took off and the doctor, standing in his buggy like a Roman charioteer, careened down the pike, scattering chickens and pigs and pedestrians from his path; about the time one of the naughty McClure girls dabbed her face with iodine and held hot water in her mouth to fool the doctor into diagnosing measles so that she could stay home from school; about the Sunday-school picnic when the doctor's class decided to make a proper Baptist of him and dunked him in the pond. Not an hour in his grave, the doctor was already becoming a kind of local legend and a source of pride to the family, even Scott and Mary. But after most of the guests had left, Judge Shaw called the family into the parlor, and the atmosphere turned somber again.

The will was short and simple—everything bequeathed to "my beloved wife, Mary Shallenberger Stewart." The problem was what this everything meant. "I'm really not sure what assets the doctor had," Judge Shaw said. "There is a small account—a thousand or so—in the Diamond Saving Institution in Pittsburgh that he kept mostly to buy medicines. You'll probably find some cash when you search his effects and surely many bills owing. We could sue on those if they are not paid, but they will all be friends and neighbors. I've spoken to the manager of the coal mine and he's willing to pay out the last quarter of the doctor's fee, which is $125, but that's the extent of his generosity. He would like to have the buggy back for the next doctor, whoever he may be, to use. You do, of course, have the land here—about six acres according to the deed—with only a small mortgage, and I'm willing to predict it will someday be valuable. Pittsburgh is growing and pushing out in every direction. When they put a tunnel through Mount Washington, as they surely will, this area will come alive. I suggest you get together everything about the doctor's business you can find, and I will be happy to go over it with you. And another thing—there will be no fees. Doctor Stewart was the finest man I've ever known."

That night when the family at last started up to bed, Mary held Scott back for a moment. "Scott, I'd like you to take over locking the house."

34

Scott nodded, and Mary started up the stairs. "Mother," Scott called after her, "Mother, I don't believe we are going to find anything. I'm going down to Pittsburgh to work. I saw lots of boys my age in shops and offices there. I hear they always need messengers for the telegraph service. They say it pays twenty-five dollars a month and sometimes tips. Can I do that, Mother?"

In a rare show of affection, Mary Stewart came back down the stairs, took her son's head in both her hands and kissed him on the forehead. "Bless you, Scott. Bless you," she said. "We'll talk about it in the morning."

A Message for Mr. Carnegie

Although Scott was impatient to get home and blurt out the news he let Old Pat set his own pace. For one thing, too fast a ride could be a bone-jarring affair in the little two-wheeled cart Moses had managed to put together from a couple of old wagon wheels and spare boards to replace the dispossessed buggy. For another, the weather was beguiling on this balmy Saturday afternoon in the early spring of 1866. The sun was warm on his back; the pussy willows were out, and the forsythia was aflame; the trees, clumped around farm buildings like oases in a desert of furrowed black land, were turning to a green lace of budding leaves. On any other spring Scott's skin would already have been browning from Saturdays spent helping Moses plow and plant the gardens to earn his dollar, or luckier, lazier days fishing the nearby streams and ponds. This year, though, he was fortunate to enjoy an occasional hour of country daylight late on a Saturday afternoon or on Sunday after church. So the slow ride was not altogether lost. While enjoying the sun and the landscape, he went over his amazing experience in every detail in preparation for telling the family.

Scott had been right about the telegraph service. Boys came and went rapidly at the Western Union Company at Wood and Third streets, and the manager had been only too happy to hire the solemn-looking lad in the fine business suit. The hours were long—eight in the morning until eight at night except for an occasional Saturday afternoon—and made longer for Scott by the fact that he drove his cart into Birmingham every morning and back home again at night. They were made tolerable, however, by the fact that there was plenty of time while waiting for messages to allow an ambitious young man to read or improve his skills and by the fact that there was a variety of experience in the streets. Most of the work was on foot, of course, in that narrow triangle between the rivers into which the newspapers, banks, business offices and stores of the city were squeezing themselves. Occasionally there would be a horse-cart ride over into Allegheny or out along the banks of the Monongahela, where the fiery plants of the iron makers were located.

Perhaps more than the other boys who had been raised in the city, Scott never tired of his trips into the streets when he could absorb the exciting atmosphere. Pittsburgh was, to his mind, exactly what a city should be—a bustling, crowded, noisy, dirty place where serious work was going on. Gritty smoke hung in such a pall above the buildings that gaslights were often needed to brighten the offices and streets even at noon on a sunny day and almost always in bad weather. Each night when he got home Scott would brush his suit carefully, and his cuffs, collars and shirts were so ringed with black they had to be washed. It proved such a chore for Annie that he took to buying cheap paper collars and throwing them away. Still, smoke was the inevitable price of making things, and making things was the purpose of the city. Nobody, least of all the bankers and iron masters in their stovepipe hats, seemed to care that the stone facades of their great new buildings blackened before the mortgages were paid. Living in Pittsburgh was living with smoke, and a man who wanted what Pittsburgh had to give would learn to tolerate it.

Scott badly wanted what Pittsburgh had to give. The search of the doctor's effects had turned up little but due bills, bills that could not in conscience be collected from hard-pressed farmers who honestly tried to pay, more often with a side of beef or a sack of flour than cash. Though the chickens and pigs and cows and vegetables from their gardens would keep the family in food, there was still a mortgage on the house— a grand house, Scott now realized, in comparison with the hovels he saw in Pittsburgh—that the doctor had built in 1860, and there was need for things like clothes and sugar and salt and tea. He simply had to earn hard cash—and fast. Luckily cash was abundant in the smoky city. Scott's rounds took him past the stores of Fifth Avenue, where the latest fashions from Paris at prices beyond the dreams of his mother and sisters were on display; elegant equipages with prancing, blooded horses nearly ran him down in the streets if he weren't careful; in the richly paneled executive offices where he sometimes delivered messages Scott would see well-fed men whose shirt fronts, spilling out above tailored vests, were studded with real diamonds. Though much of the money had come from supplying the insatiable demands of the late war, there was talk around that things would be even better for Pittsburgh now that peace was making it possible to start pushing the great railways with their iron tracks and bridges across the country.

Lacking any wealthy connections in the city, Scott knew only one way to get what he needed—work. Fortunately, he believed that anything was possible with work, just as anything was possible with God. Everything Scott heard from the pulpit or learned in school emphasized that work was next to godliness, or maybe the same thing. Once, in trying to explain to his congregation the paradox of wealth and poverty, Mr. Wallace had quoted the famous Reverend Mr. Francis Wayland of Brown University. Scott was so impressed that he asked for the book, *Elements of Political Economy*, and copied it down. "He who refuses to labor," Wayland had written, "suffers besides the pains of disease, all the evils of poverty, cold, hunger, and nakedness. The results which our Creator has attached to idleness are all to be considered as punishments, which He inflicts for the neglect of this established law of our being. And, on the other hand, God has assigned to industry rich and abundant rewards. . . . All that now exists of capital, of convenience, of comfort, and of intelligence, is the work of industry, and is the reward which God bestowed upon us for obedience to the Law of our being." Strong words—and true in Scott's young mind. One of the gems from McGuffey's reader that he had learned by rote for a school recitation carried the same message.

> Work, work, work, my boy, be not afraid;
> Look labor boldly in the face;
> Take up the hammer or the spade,
> And blush not for your humble place.

37

Feeling all this, Scott was shocked by the other boys who would sneak out in their idle hours to smoke stogies and swap gossip in the alleyway, or compete for the chance to rush growlers of beer to the men on the telegraph keys so they could steal sips on the way, or linger to watch the show if they happened to have a message for the theater. Instead, Scott studied the map of the city, memorizing streets and addresses and devising shortcuts for delivery. That done, he went to work on the Morse code and was soon able to sit in occasionally for any operator who wanted a break. By the turn of the year, there was little Scott didn't know about the operation of a telegraph office, and so he began immersing himself in books on accounting and penmanship, the tools he might need if the Lord chose to reward his industry. . . .

He was happily lost in what seemed to him an involved problem in mathematics this spring Saturday when the manager called him over to his desk. "I have a very important message here for Mr. Andrew Carnegie," the manager said. "He's at his house in Homewood, and you're the only boy who looks decent enough to send out there. I'd go myself if I could trust these rascals not to disappear into a saloon. Mind now, get a receipt from Mr. Carnegie himself; it would mean my neck, I'm sure, if he didn't get this. Here, take some money for train fare."

What had started out as a very ordinary day had suddenly become the most adventurous of Scott's career. Although still only thirty-one years old, Andrew Carnegie was already a legendary figure in Pittsburgh business circles. He was known to be involved in just about everything—oil, bridge building, sleeping cars, telegraph lines. A Scottish immigrant boy who grew up in Slabtown, the worst slum area of Allegheny City, he started out, just as Scott was starting, in the telegraph office. He moved to the Pennsylvania Railroad, where he rose so rapidly that at twenty-four he was made superintendent of the western division with offices at Pittsburgh. During the early years of the War, his old Pittsburgh boss, Thomas A. Scott, who was in charge of transportation for the War Department, summoned Carnegie to Washington to get the trains running. Back in Pittsburgh, Carnegie invested so shrewdly that he was able to leave the railroad in '65 and devote his time to managing his money. Nobody knew just how much he had, but Carnegie was supposed to have recently boasted to a friend, "I'm rich! I'm rich!" In any case, there was no doubt in young Scott Stewart's mind that whatever he was carrying to

Mr. Carnegie was of utmost importance.

As if the possibility of seeing Mr. Carnegie weren't enough in the way of excitement, the fact that he was in Homewood turned the job into an adventure. Lying some fifteen miles to the northeast of the city in the East Liberty valley, Homewood was rapidly becoming a community of Pittsburghers who were wealthy enough to escape the city's fumes. The place took its name from the estate of Pittsburgh's most famous citizen, Judge William Wilkins, whose long career of public service had included acting as President Jackson's minister to Russia and President Tyler's Secretary of War. Scott had read all about Homewood the year before when Judge Wilkins died at eighty-five, and he was eager to see the splendid homes of the rich. Not only that, but Homewood lay conveniently on the eastbound line of the Pennsylvania, and getting there would mean that Scott would have the first train ride of his life. He ran all the way to the station.

He got there in time to see the train pull in; the engine, a squat iron barrel with a high, flaring stack, wreathed the waiting passengers in white mist when it screeched and ground to a stop. As he boarded the first carriage, Scott saw a sweating man, his head turbaned in cloth, on top of the black pile in the coal car swinging great shovelfuls into the glowing mouth of the furnace under the boiler; the engineer sat casually by the wondrous wheels and levers of power, puffing a long stogie and cheering his fireman on. The carriage was one of the new types with plush seats swung on iron frames; the man he sat beside, evidently an experienced traveler, showed Scott how to lower the back so that he could stretch out. The train started off with a shrill whistle and a jerk and soon picked up speed until the telegraph poles along the line, turning into a soft blur, made him feel dizzy. The windows were open to the sudden spring warmth, and from time to time dense puffs from the engine curled in and drove all the choking passengers to grab for their handkerchiefs. But for Scott the ride was all too short; the power and speed of the train entranced him, and he wished he were going on East like the man beside him —to Harrisburg, to Philadelphia, to New York.

At the station platform nearest Homewood, Scott realized that he hadn't the slightest idea of where Mr. Carnegie's house was or how far it was. There was a farmer dozing on top of a wagon, and Scott, who had some change left over from the train fare his superintendent had given him, got the idea of hiring the man to take him to the Carnegie home. "Mr. Carnegie? Don't reckon I do know where he lives but I reckon for

39

fifty cents I can find out," the man said. "We can stop by the judge's for the directions."

It was a welcome detour. At the end of a drive that wound through lawns and shrubs just greening with spring, they came on the most magnificent house Scott had ever seen. It was what he would imagine a Greek temple to be: a central core two stories high with four fluted columns the height of the house supporting the front portico, two single-story wings of perfect symmetry on either end of the house, and a flat roof ringed with a carved cornice. It had to have twenty rooms or more. That anybody could afford to build such a thing for his own living was almost beyond Scott's comprehension. The Lord certainly did reward industry. Scott made up his mind that one day he would have such a house. He could just imagine himself of a morning, pacing back and forth under the high columns of the portico and gazing with contentment on the sweeping grounds while he awaited the shining carriage that would take him off to deal with important affairs in the city. . . . His important affair of the moment, it turned out, was moved along by Judge Wilkins' gardener, a friend of the farmer's, who was able to point out the way to Carnegie's.

Though large and comfortable, the Carnegie house was not so impressive after what Scott had just seen. And it was just as well, because Scott suddenly developed a case of very cold feet as he went up to the door. What would Mr. Carnegie say? What would he do? How could he get a big man like Mr. Carnegie to bother signing a receipt for him? A maid opened the door and, letting him stand on the porch, offered to take the message to Mr. Carnegie. He managed to explain about the receipt and held on to his message. The maid told him to wait and in a few minutes she was back, leading him through a hallway dim against the bright spring sunshine and on into a large, cheerful room. Seated at a desk in one corner was one of the smallest men Scott had ever seen; his feet dangling from the chair barely touched the floor. He waved Scott over.

"Well, young man, from Western Union, eh?" Carnegie said. "Must be an important message to send you all this way."

"Ye . . . Yes, sir. And I have a receipt."

"So I understand."

Carnegie stood up and held out his hand for the message. At five feet three inches he was no taller than Scott himself. In his quick motions and tone of his voice, though, there was an air of decisiveness and self-assurance. His hair and the fringe of beard along the line of his square jaw was so blond

40

that it was almost white, making him look far older than his true age. But there was an openness to his broad face, a merriness in his eyes and voice that invited response. No wonder his workers were said to refer to him affectionately as "little Andy." While he scanned the message, Carnegie asked, "What's your name, son?"

"Scott, Scott Stewart."

"A good name that, lad. You must be one of us. Well, sit down while I scribble an answer—and give me your precious receipt."

Carnegie turned back to his desk and began to write. Suddenly he stopped and handed Scott a small package. "While you're waiting would you open this for me?" It was bound with strong cord and tightly tied in a knot so small that Scott doubted his fingers could cope with it. "Mr. Carnegie, would you have a knife there?" he asked.

Carnegie erupted in a high, merry laugh. "Never mind, lad, give it back. It's a test I have. The dumb ones start fumbling with their fingers. So you're quick-witted? Tell me, why are you working so young?"

Scott told the story briefly—death of a father, family to support. Carnegie, studying him so intently that Scott had to shift his eyes away, said, "Your father was a doctor? I suppose you were planning to follow a profession?"

"Yes, sir, the ministry."

"Well, praise the Lord you were saved from that. I think you have the makings of a good businessman, and you are starting the right way. You know I got my start as a telegraph boy, but I was worse off than you—I wasn't a doctor's son. How much do they pay you?"

"Twenty-five dollars a month."

"More than twice what I got, but then there's more money to be had these days, thank God. And what do you do with all that money, Scott?"

"Take it home to my mother, sir."

"Good boy. But take a tip from me. Save some of it out, however little, to invest. It's money earning money that will get you ahead, lad; that's the way of the world. I still remember my first investment—it was just ten years ago. I'd been working for the railroad, and my employer, Mr. Scott"— he smiled—"gave me the same advice I'm giving you; in fact he even loaned me some of the money, six hundred dollars, to put into ten shares of Adams Express stock. Well, when I got that first dividend of ten dollars, I was so excited I ran to my 'Slabtown' friends who were all working a fortnight for less than that and told them I'd found the goose that lays the golden eggs. And so it has proved."

Scott was spellbound. Imagine a man like Mr. Carnegie taking so much time to talk to a mere messenger boy—and telling him so much about his own affairs. He already felt nobody would believe him when he told about his experience. Carnegie stood up in a gesture of dismissal, holding out his reply and the receipt, and Scott jumped to his feet too. Then Carnegie seemed to have a second thought and turned to his desk again. "I could give you a tip, lad, but I'm going to give you something more valuable," and made a quick jotting on a piece of paper. It was a note, reading, "To Whom It May Concern: Scott Stewart is a good Scots lad. I beg you give him every courtesy. Andrew Carnegie."

The note was proof that Scott had met and talked with the great Mr. Carnegie, but, more than that, it might some day open the right door to him. All the way back to Pittsburgh and now all the way home in the buggy he kept reaching into his pocket to touch it and assure himself that it was still there. When he burst into the house, full of his story, he found Mr. Wallace and a strange young man having Saturday tea with his mother and the girls. Although he was a bit impatient with the formalities of introduction—"Scott, this is Donald Sharp," his mother said, "he's a seminary student and is going to help Mr. Wallace with the church and board with us weekends"— Scott was glad the minister was there to hear his story. Since his father's death, he had grown close to Mr. Wallace, who had taken on himself the duty of comforting the unfortunate doctor's widow and children. There were some in the community who thought Mr. Wallace was seen too often going into a widow's house; malicious tongues recalled that he had already buried two wives in the course of begetting all those children and might be buying insurance in case the third Mrs. Wallace, who was looking pale these days, collapsed under the strain. When such talk came back to her ears, Mary Stewart ignored it; she felt grateful that her son had a man to advise him now that he was having to face the challenges and dangers of the city.

Mary regretted that Scott had been forced to postpone, or perhaps forgo entirely, his ambition to enter the ministry, but Mr. Wallace was reassuring. "You know, the boy can serve wherever he is. There's no sin in honest work, and I'm sure the Lord will reward his efforts if he keeps the commandments."

Whenever he had the opportunity, Mr. Wallace warned Scott

against the evils of drink—"It was the undoing of your poor father, I'm afraid"—and something called "loose women." Although he looked closely at women he passed in Pittsburgh streets, Scott couldn't figure out how you could tell a loose one from any other kind, but he didn't worry about it since living with two silly sisters made him wonder how a serious man would bother with women at all. "If you are ever tempted, pray for strength," Mr. Wallace would advise Scott. "If you need anything, ask it of God. Knock and it shall be opened unto you. Faith can move mountains, my boy. Remember, if you believe in Jesus Christ, you are among the elect of God; the very gates of Hell shall not prevail against you."

Mr. Wallace's booming faith was just the tonic serious-minded Scott needed as the enormity of what had happened to his father began to sink into his consciousness. When fears of suffering a similar fate would come at him in the night, he found that he could pray them away. He decided, with some not so subtle prompting from Mr. Wallace, that his father's doubts and uncertainties had arisen from all that reading of ungodly philosophy that weakened his faith. Otherwise he would have seen his limitations as a doctor as the will of God and been able to accept them. If he had been able to "take it to the Lord in prayer," as the hymn said, he would never have needed the solace of whiskey or the release of death. So Scott began to "put on the whole armor of God," as Mr. Wallace phrased it, by kneeling at his bedside morning and night and reading a chapter of the Bible every day. He was in church every time the doors were open, and, despite his youth, he was entrusted by Mr. Wallace with a Sunday-school class of the youngest children.

This piety did not go unnoticed by the younger Stewart children, and Lucinda particularly would often tease Scott about it. Knowing what they didn't, Mary Stewart would always intervene on Scott's behalf. "Leave your brother alone; he's just doing what you all ought to be doing if you paid any attention to your Sunday-school lessons." Mary would say. Occasionally, she would worry that Scott was too intense, too serious, but she was aware that he had a strange kind of strength for a boy so young, and she didn't dare tamper with whatever might be its source. And far from interfering with his work in town, his piety seemed to be helping. He'd already received a much-needed raise, and Mary was beginning to feel confident that somehow the family would be able to go on

43

living and even hold on to their home. Perhaps it was, indeed, the blessing of God.

As soon as he decently could, Scott blurted out his story about meeting Mr. Carnegie and passed around the precious note. It brought satisfying oohs and aahs, particularly from the young seminary student. A strikingly handsome man of about twenty with dark curly beard and hair and a dark complexion that emphasized the bright blue of his eyes, Donald Sharp had recently come to Pittsburgh from Virginia. He'd been called up to serve as a private soldier in the last days of the war. It was in the hell of the battlefield, as he told it, that he found God and determined to serve Him—and to serve Him in the North where he would be forced to learn to love his enemies and, hopefully, to make them love him. Now, looking at the note, he said, "Well, Mr. Andrew Carnegie, I do declare! That is a prize. From what I hear he must be the richest man in all of Pittsburgh."

Only Mr. Wallace seemed a bit disturbed. "I hope you'll pray over this before you use it, Scott," he said.

"Why?"

"Because Mr. Carnegie, however rich he might be, is not a Christian. . . ."

"What makes you say that, Mr. Wallace?" Don Sharp asked.

"Oh, it's well known—ask anybody at the seminary. He comes from people who began speaking against the true church back in Scotland—in Dunfermline or wherever it was they lived," Mr. Wallace said. "You know, the story is that Carnegie's father was in church when the minister was preaching on infant damnation which, as you know, Mr. Sharp, is good Presbyterian doctrine. Well, he jumps right out of his seat and says loud enough for the whole church to hear, 'If that be your religion and that your God, I shall seek a better religion and a nobler God.' "

Mary Stewart, whose Methodist background had made her a little skeptical about some of the harsher bits of Presbyterian doctrine, was more intrigued than alarmed. "But did the poor man find a better religion?" she asked.

"Why, Mrs. Stewart, I'm surprised," Mr. Wallace said. "Do you think there is a better religion?"

"Well, I was a Methodist. . . ."

"Yes, and I'm grateful for it when it comes to the hymns. But, as to Mr. Carnegie's father, I'm afraid he followed false gods. He joined the Swedenborgian church when he came to Allegheny," Mr. Wallace said. "Young Andrew may have tried it, too, for a while—I don't know. But my friends over Allegheny way say he used to profane the Sabbath for all to see by skating on the river while everybody was going to church."

All this unexpected talk about Mr. Carnegie's religious views was taking considerable wind out of Scott's sails, and he was grateful when Don Sharp asked, "But, Mr. Wallace, why would all this matter to young Scott here in a business way?"

"Even in business, the Lord's blessing is upon those who serve Him, Mr. Sharp. If you haven't learned that already, I hope you will before you come into the pulpit. . . . Well, we must go, we've overstayed our time . . ."

"Not at all," Mary Stewart said, but she rose to see them out. She thought it was rather unfortunate that Mr. Wallace had brought up that business to spoil Scott's excitement.

When they'd gone, the girls, who had sat in silence through what must have been a boring discussion for them, revealed what had truly enthralled them. It was the Southern drawl that made Don Sharp draw his words out as if he were pulling taffy. Lucinda began prancing around the room, piping, "Ah declaaa, maa'aam" and "Mistah Caahnegie" in such perfect imitation that her mother laughed until her sides ached, and told herself she'd need to keep an eye on Lucinda so her lively girl wouldn't insult their guest. Mary could confidently picture in her mind how Sarah would turn out as she grew to womanhood, but Lucinda was a puzzle. Wiggling her way through church and school, biting her lips to keep from giggling at the wrong time, mocking her elders (she could deliver a perfect soprano imitation of a hell-fire sermon by Mr. Wallace), Lucinda seemed destined to resist in her fashion the duller side of life. Even now she was able to talk Moses into taking her turn at wringing the wash, or get Annie to mend her skirts and petticoats that were so often torn in climbing trees or playing ball with the boys. The doctor had been worried about her. Passing by the school yard one day, he was watching a group of boys scrambling for a ball when the black-stockinged legs of a girl emerged from the pile. He stayed just long enough to identify Lucinda and, rather than embarrass his daughter, went home to complain to Mary. "You've got to do something about that girl, Mary. I like her spirit, but she could be seriously hurt playing rough games like that with boys." But doing something about Lucinda was not easy, and it had become even more difficult since the death of the doctor, whose mildest word had been enough to curb his adoring daughter for a time at least.

More upset than he liked to admit by what Mr. Wallace had

said, Scott found Lucinda's silliness intolerable. "I'm going to pump," he said, and left for the cellar.

The Stewart house was one of the few in the countryside with an indoor bathroom. Though they had a well for drinking, bath water was caught in a cistern and transferred by hand pump to a tank on the roof which delivered it to the tub by force of gravity. The pump was powered by a large, horizontal wooden bar which you could push back and forth or even lean into with your weight, and making it go was a chore the Stewart children hated. But it had to be done at least once a week, usually on Saturday, the night of the weekly baths. Since going into the city, Scott had begun to take a new view of pumping—it was good exercise and the once dreaded cellar was a certain refuge from his noisy sisters, allowing him peace for his thoughts.

With the soothing clatter of the pump shutting out distraction, Scott turned over the events of the day in his mind and began to worry that Mr. Wallace might be right. Hadn't Mr. Carnegie more or less made fun of his desire to be a minister? Perhaps he should destroy the note.

If he expected God's help in everything, he had to be strong enough to turn away from men who mocked belief. He had just about made up his mind when his mother came down the stairs.

"Leave that, Scott," she said. "Now that you're working, the girls ought to do the pumping. I don't want you down here alone brooding about what Mr. Wallace said . . ."

"But, Mother, I think maybe he's right . . ."

"I don't," she said. "Mr. Wallace is a good man, but he knows nothing of business. Pray over the note if you like, but use it when the time comes. Who's to say that your meeting Mr. Carnegie today isn't the leading of the Lord?"

"Well, I never thought of it that way, but . . ."

"I think it is, Scott," Mary said, and put an arm diffidently around his shoulders. "You know God works in mysterious ways His wonders to perform. You're a good boy, Scott, and I'm sure you can associate with anyone you have to without being led astray. Now let's go up to dinner."

That night in bed, Mary began to worry some about Mr. Wallace's powerful influence on Scott. She knew her thoughts were ungrateful, since the minister had proved a tower of strength to all of them in the dreadful aftermath of Doctor Stewart's suicide. Still, as the doctor had tried to hint to her in his own way, the old minister had a lot of very impractical ideas, and Scott would have to be practical, above all, to succeed in business. Not only that, but she was beginning to weary of the minister's self-righteous way of referring to her husband as if his whole life had been a dark trail of sin. Indeed, from some of the looks she was getting and remarks she overheard, Mary was beginning to fear that Mr. Wallace was spreading their secret through his unfortunate, though probably unintentional, habit of mentioning sufferers and sinners in his prayers. She couldn't help but smile a little recalling the doctor's comment that "we don't need a newspaper in this town as long as we get a chance to listen to Gordon Wallace's prayers." True, Doctor Stewart had left them in a most terrifying way, in a way that had to be condemned by almost everybody's lights. But she couldn't forget that, while he was with them, he had devoted almost every hour of every day in unselfish service to others. The doctor used to quote to her from Shakespeare that "the evil that men do lives after them; the good is oft interred with their bones," but in his case it was the other way around—at least for her.

There were still times, particularly in the night, when she couldn't really believe that he was gone. She ached for the reassurance of his warm body next to hers in bed, and sometimes she would wake up with a start, realizing that she had reached out for him in her sleep and found nothing. She had heard in girlhood of the beastliness of men, but she had never found the doctor so. When he took her, he took her with a tenderness, almost a reluctance, as if he knew too much about the agony and potential disaster this act could bring to a woman's body. They were neither of them articulate about the physical part of their love, but words were not expected. Whatever else intercourse might be, it was a duty they were commanded by God to perform to bring children into the world, and they accepted it as such. There was pleasure in the duty, too. Mary loved the feeling of the doctor's strong arms around her, his beard rough against her cheek, and even of his coming into her and filling her. She envied him his release, his deep sighs of satisfaction, his instant slumber, but she would lie awake grateful that she had fulfilled such an urgent need for him. Once she herself had the kind of stirring known to the women whom even the Bible admitted sought pleasure in sexual contact, and, though the experience had bewildered and frightened her at the time, she had, she now realized, hoped clear up to the night of the doctor's death that it might be repeated.

It had happened on their one overnight visit to Pittsburgh

47

soon after Scott was born—so soon, in fact, that Mother Shallenberger was still living with them to help with the baby. Doctor Stewart took advantage of his mother-in-law's presence to take Mary along with him to a medical dinner at the Monongahela House, and as a surprise he engaged a room for them. The dinner itself was excitement enough with ladies in silk finer than she had ever seen and men in tailored frock coats, with course after course, literally "from soup to nuts." She was concerned about the wines that were being poured freely with every course until she saw Doctor Stewart quietly turn his glass down, and she followed his example. There was a regretful look in his eye, but he was keeping, she knew, a promise he had made to her teetotalling father when he asked for her hand. She loved him for it. She was proud, too, when Doctor Stewart was introduced from the floor as "one of that noble breed of young physicians who has elected to forgo the monetary rewards of a city practice to care for the needs of our country cousins, just as his distinguished father did before him." He rose to acknowledge the applause with a graceful bow and then pulled Mary to her feet beside him. There was a new round of clapping including, this time, the ladies who well understood the sacrifices of a doctor's wife. Altogether, it was already an evening very much to remember when the doctor sprang his surprise.

Mary had scarcely ever dreamed of anything like the room they entered. Plush red drapes that hung from floor to ceiling were drawn across the windows and soft carpeting sprang under her feet. A chandelier in which the light of a dozen candles was multiplied many times over in tear drops of glass hung from the ceiling. Gilt reflected from the bedstead, the arms of the satin chairs, the mirror-fronted wardrobe in the corner. No queen, she thought, could have enjoyed more elegant quarters. Impulsively, she lifted the doctor's hand to her lips for a kiss of thanks. Instinct and her already excited heart told her something unusual might happen here.

It began with undressing. It was immediately apparent that there was nowhere to go out of reach of the doctor's eyes to take off her clothes. She had never undressed in front of him before, and she blushed when he silently handed her the nightdress he had packed in his medical bag to keep the surprise. Perhaps to help her, he casually took off his coat and vest and draped them across a chair, eased his feet out of his boots and then fell back on the bed, where he pretended to be studying one of the medical papers that had been passed out at the dinner. There was nothing left to do but to get it

48

over quickly. Her fingers shook from an odd and not entirely unpleasant excitement as she fumbled to unbutton her dress and undo her petticoats and stays. When she stood in her chemise and drawers, shivering slightly, she glanced in the mirror and saw that the doctor was watching her.

"You have the most beautiful neck, Mary," he said quietly. It was the first time since their courtship that he had ever mentioned any of her physical attributes, and she blushed so furiously that her body seemed hot all over. "Especially when you blush like that," the doctor added.

Suddenly he was beside her, holding her in his arms and covering her face and neck with kisses and letting his hands rove recklessly over the flesh under her chemise, under her drawers. A kind of giddy weakness went through her, and she flung both arms around the doctor's neck to keep from falling. One part of her kept telling her this was wickedness, the lust of the flesh against which she had been warned, and another told her something quite different. With the candles still glittering above them, they fell on the bed and came together. Now she seemed to be coming apart inside; she could feel everything in her giving way in waves of such abandon that she was literally beside herself. She could hear herself cry out, and she wrapped arms and legs clear around the doctor to keep from slipping away completely. When finally she was spent and a calm came over her, she wondered whether she had suffered some kind of fit or illness, whether she should tell the doctor about it. But she was too blissfully sleepy to care. Tenderly, he snuffed out the candles, helped her into her nightdress and laid her head onto the great soft pillows. By morning, it seemed like a dream.

It still seemed like a dream, but a dream to nurture against all her other mixed feelings about Doctor Stewart. Though she was only thirty-four, Mary Stewart doubted that she would ever know a man again. Everything she had now must be devoted to rearing her children, and she doubted that any man, however good, could ever share her fierce and unstinting concern for their welfare. More important, she was sure that no other man could ever adequately fill that abandoned place beside her in bed. Thinking of that, there was a smile on her face as she, at last, dropped off to sleep.

A Mortgage from Judge Mellon

"The thing is, Mother," Scott was saying, "I'm not just sure that it's right."

"Why not? Wasn't it Judge Mellon's idea?"

The two of them were sitting long over Sunday breakfast, a custom they had fallen into when they found that, with the younger children out of the house at Sunday school, it was an ideal time to discuss business and family affairs. In her struggle to make ends meet, Mary Stewart had come increasingly to rely not only on the money Scott brought home from the city but on the shrewd judgment he often displayed. For his part, Scott was finding in his mother a somewhat surprisingly sure instinct for what was right in a number of baffling situations. What Scott particularly liked about these Sunday mornings was that, after their talks, they would go into the sanctuary together, and he had a comforting sense that their decisions were ratified by God.

"Not exactly," Scott said. "Of course, he holds the mortgage and plans to foreclose anyway, but it's our decision about whether we take advantage of it. Like so many people these days the poor fellow who built the house is caught in economic circumstances beyond his control. You know, the papers are already calling this the great panic of '73. Is it Christian to get the house at half price under the circumstances?"

"Well, we can't afford it any other way," Mary said. "I don't suppose the judge would let the fellow live on there in any case."

"No, he doesn't have much use for people who fall into debt. As he told me, 'The motto the Mellons live by is never to be in debt.' In fact, the reason he'll let us have the place is that he admires our foresight—your foresight—in paying off the mortgage here—this is sound collateral in times like these."

"I don't know, Scott. You're always talking about the leading of the Lord, and I can certainly see it here. In the first place, it comes just when Sarah is marrying and breaking up the family . . ."

"Hardly that, she's just moving across the street into the manse. Don't you want to be around to help her set up house?"

"Nothing could be worse," Mary said. "Even though she's only eighteen, if she's old enough to marry, she's old enough to run her own household. I had just turned nineteen, and many's the time I thanked God that my mother lived a good day's wagon ride away and that the doctor's mother was clear over there in Westmoreland County. But if you want another sign, I should think you can rely upon the advice of Judge Mellon. He's certainly a godly man. You know his wife's people, the Negleys, built the East Liberty Presbyterian Church."

"That's true," Scott agreed, "it's just that God has been so good to us . . ."

"Oh, Scott, there's nothing in the Bible about not being practical, is there? Lightning didn't strike when you used Mr. Carnegie's note, did it? No, I believe, like they say, that God helps him who helps himself."

"Well, you were right about the mortgage and right about the Carnegie note, so I guess you're right about this," Scott said. "We'll do it."

"That settles it," said Mary, rising from the table. "I must rush to get my bonnet on for church. I'll speak to Dr. Jones in the morning about renting this place. I'm sure he'll take it; you know how he's always envied your father's office. He still has to receive patients in the parlor, and they have a new baby coming by January."

Though she was reluctant to leave the only home she'd known since her marriage, Mary knew the time had come to move to Pittsburgh. She was worried about Scott. Even with the new incline down the north face of Mt. Washington, the poor boy was gone from dawn until dark every day. With his new job he was sometimes staying overnight, worrying her half to death and spending money they could ill afford. Scott was still the only real breadwinner in the family, and it was up to the rest of them to do what they could to make life easier for him. Living nearer the city should help, and be an advantage to him in being on hand more easily to take advantage of opportunities. Not that he wasn't doing well already. One reason Mary was reluctant to question Scott's faith was the way in which his path seemed to be strewn with miracles.

Not a week after Mary began urging Scott to look for a new place to live, the Oakland house almost fell into his lap, as if it were a gift from God himself. In an effort to make up for the education he had missed, Scott joined an evening seminar at the YMCA. Another young man in the group, a clerk at T. Mellon & Son, the small bank the judge had opened on Smithfield Street when he retired from the bench in 1870, knew of a property they were foreclosing on. It was a sizable frame home in the Oakland district, where some of the city's finest residences, like the opulent Moorehead place, were located. The young Civil War captain who'd built it for his growing family was prospering in the giddy postwar lumber and building business until that terrible Thursday, September 18, when word came through to Pittsburgh that the great Philadelphia banker, Jay Cook, had closed his doors. Within weeks, creditors had driven the captain to the wall, and he reluctantly informed Judge Mellon he could no longer carry his mortgage. His own business staggering, the judge would be glad to pass the mortgage along to anyone with collateral, Scott was informed, and it would mean getting the almost new house at half its value.

The very next day, Scott, careful to wear his soberest clothes and solemnest expression, presented himself at the bank. Gaunt and unsmiling, the judge lived up to his reputation for severity. Though his expression didn't betray his feelings, he apparently liked what he saw in Scott. He obviously regretted not being able to hold on to the property himself, but he expressed no such emotion about the luckless captain. "He was heavy with debt," the judge told Scott, "and a man like that is bound to sink. I made my first dollars from the foolishness of men like him, and I have learned there is little you can do for such a man. I started in this city with nothing, walked all the way in from the family farm at Poverty Point, and I don't feel obligated to coddle failures. You know, I tell them if they think I'm harsh to go to the Jews and see how they're treated."

Scott, never having known a Jew, considered them as mysterious as Catholics. When he was not berating Catholics for idolatrous worship of statues, usually on the Sunday nearest Reformation Day, Mr. Wallace would be thundering at the treachery of the Hebrews who crucified Christ, usually on the Sunday after Good Friday. In the Presbyterian mythology of

52

Pittsburgh business, there was a grudging admiration which came out in the common phrase of the day, "rich as Rothschilds," but for the most part it was felt that Jews properly belonged on the fringes of trade like the Kaufmanns, who had recently opened a clothing store on Carson Street to serve their fellow immigrants who worked in the mills. Perhaps inadvertently Judge Mellon had summed up such feeling in an episode on the bench that was known about the city. Reading some papers, the judge missed the drift of a petition brought before him. Looking up suddenly, he asked an attorney. "What did you say that petition was for?" "For a charity, your honor, for a Jewish burial ground." "For a place to bury Jews?" "Yes, sir." Reaching out for the petition, the judge signed it, muttering "With pleasure."

Despite the judge's strictures, by the time Scott discussed the proposition with his mother, a nagging doubt about profiting from the captain's misfortune clouded the issue for him, and he was genuinely relieved when she'd shown him so clearly God's hand in the matter—the place in all other respects was perfect. He could get easily to his office by horse car, and there would be good schools and proper playmates for the younger children. It would mean a very different kind of life for them all, as Lucinda was first to appreciate. She'd seen Pittsburgh only once, and the experience had been something of a disaster since her excited stomach had betrayed her on the swaying horse car, much to the embarrassment of all the family. But, blessed with a blank memory for pain, Lucinda's first thought was, "Oh, we can ride the horse cars to the dress shops any day, can't we, Momma?"

Mary smiled. With her gold hair curling into natural ringlets and startlingly contrasting dark brows above the light eyes she inherited from her father, Lucinda would soon be far too pretty for her own good in any kind of clothes. "Now, Lucinda, we can't afford . . ." she began.

"But we can look, Momma, can't we? And there will be balls, won't there? And skating parties? And . . ."

No doubt there would be all of those things, but they would be of little consolation to young Reed, the only one of the family who really dreaded the move. Curly blond, like the pictures of the doctor as a child, blue-eyed, grinning, Reed was seldom alone. Even in the garden doing chores, he would be followed up and down the rows by a gang of boys, impatient for him to be free to follow them barefoot into the woods or nearest stream. He needed friends, was comfortable with the ones he had grown up with, and the thought of plunging into the unknown in a new school appealed not at all. Not only that, but he would have to give up the beloved pony that Mr. McClure was loaning him in exchange for stabling and feed. Seeing his misery, Mary did worry some about Reed, but a boy of ten was pliable clay, and she could always ease the transition for him by sending him out to newly married Sarah in the country.

Leaving Sarah here on the hilltop would be the real wrench for Mary. She had only herself to blame. She should have been more alert to what was passing between Sarah and Mr. Sharp, but then Sarah, dutiful as she was, had a quiet way of keeping her own counsel. By the time Mr. Sharp took over the church after Mr. Wallace's sudden death and announced his intentions, it was too late to do anything but bless the prospective marriage and make the best of it. Though she couldn't find much fault with Mr. Sharp, Mary felt it was a waste for Sarah's fine mind to be buried in a country manse. She had scrimped and saved to get Sarah started in the new Pennsylvania College for Women in Pittsburgh, and now she was leaving it. Worse, Mary had prodded Scott out of a job he loved—chief operator for Western Union—to get the money for Sarah's education. Fortunately, Scott took the whole thing, as he always did, as a sign that God was urging him to move, and he even consented at last to use the note from Mr. Carnegie although, as he learned more about affairs in Pittsburgh, he had come to agree that Mr. Carnegie was not a proper Christian influence.

The note proved every bit as valuable as Carnegie had predicted it would. When Scott read that Mr. Thomas A. Scott, just recently made vice-president of Pennsylvania Railroad, was coming to town on business, he knew the time had come to try it out, because this was the same Mr. Scott who had given Carnegie his start in Pittsburgh and was still associated with Carnegie in many affairs. Young Stewart presented himself at the Monongahela House at breakfast time one morning and, at the risk of losing his prize possession, sent Carnegie's note up to Mr. Scott's room. In a matter of minutes, a tall handsome man with graying hair and mutton chops, dressed in the height of fashion down to the diamonds twinkling at his cuffs, came down the stairs and directly over to Scott.

"You must be Scott Stewart," he said. "And I'm Tom Scott. Well, well. Anyone that white-haired Scotch devil of mine recommends has to be worth looking at. Come. Have breakfast with me."

Though Scott was far too excited to eat, he sat sipping coffee and answering as well as he could Mr. Scott's searching questions. He could almost literally feel the energy in the man whose very name had become part of the language of business in Pittsburgh; a stroke of fortune or a successful deal was hailed as a "Tom Scottism." While running the Pennsylvania with one hand, Thomas Scott was deeply involved in pushing other roads into the far West, in making the iron needed for rails and bridges, in developing new rolling stock like the sleeping cars that were making travel a pleasure instead of a torture. As they talked, Mr. Scott's restless eyes roved the room, and he would pause from time to time to point out to his young companion this man or that, detailing the business he was likely to be about, often in unflattering terms. It gave Scott a sense of importance, a feeling that he really would one day be able to share the secrets of business with men such as Thomas Scott and Carnegie. Before breakfast was over, Mr. Scott handed back Carnegie's note, saying, "Keep this, it's like gold in your pocket. Now I'll give you one that's at least silver." Calling for paper from the waiter, he wrote to the superintendent of the railway in Pittsburgh: "See that you find the right spot for this young man. His salary should exceed $100 a month. Please advise me of your decision. Thomas A. Scott."

Before the day was out, Scott was hired to go to work in the freight offices of the railroad in the Union Depot. Though he knew little of railroading, he was aware that it was a most sensitive spot, for here the prices and deals that could make or break the line were made. And so it proved. Though it often required working until midnight or beyond, Scott didn't mind: he felt that he was closer to the throbbing center of business activity in Pittsburgh than he had been at the telegraph office. Not only that, but the money he earned was enough so that Scott felt he finally could take Mr. Carnegie's advice and begin investing. He had his first real argument with his mother about this. A countrywoman, she insisted that they use whatever extra they had to clear the debt on their land. As Scott now admitted, she had been right, whether from instinct or vision. The panic might have wiped out any investment Scott made, but it had turned their South Hills land into a very powerful lever with which to take advantage of the depressed prices.

All of this gave Scott and Mary Stewart reason to nod proudly at the neighbors they would soon be leaving as they walked down the aisle of the old church. If any of these people had shared Mr. Wallace's dark thought about the death of Dr. Stewart, they had been forced to amend their thinking the day Don Sharp announced proudly from the pulpit his engagement to Sarah Stewart. And looking at Scott, grown as tall as his father and dignified by his city suit and a respectable mustache, only the most narrow-minded bigot could have detected the slightest shadow of sin falling across the Stewart family. Mr. Sharp had consented to installing a small pump organ in the church, and by the time the Stewarts reached their pew, Sarah, her face flushed with pride and her tongue flicking her lips in nervous concentration, was beginning to pick her way softly through the chords of "Abide With Me." The sweet music seemed to float Scott's prayer aloft, as he bowed his head and silently prayed. "Dear God, thank you for leading us once again in the right direction. Bless our new home and consecrate it to Thy service. In Jesus' name, Amen."

In view of his sister's situation, Scott found it somewhat embarrassing that he could not give the Reverend Mister Sharp the same undivided attention he had found possible with Mr. Wallace. It was, he thought, proof of the old adage that "familiarity breeds contempt." Don Sharp had simply been around the house too much. From hearing him agonize about his studies and examinations in seminary, Scott suspected that his future brother-in-law's intellect was as softly blurred as his speech. Occasionally Scott would pick up a book that Don had left behind and go through it. He was naturally curious about what he might have missed by not going to seminary himself, and was pleasantly surprised to find how easily he grasped most of the concepts in the books. More to make conversation than for any other reason, he would try to talk to Don about what he'd read. But the charming Southerner would evade him with, "Oh, Scott, I don't bother about all that nonsense. A preacher just has to preach the gospel of love. I can't wait to get out of that stupid school where they're arguin' about things like predestination, which nobody gives a hoot about and hardly anybody can even spell. I just want to preach and tell people what the love of Jesus can do for them. I just want to bind up the wounds of the war."

Talk like that tended to arouse a sense of contempt in Scott. Predestination, as nearly as he understood it, was nothing to shrug off; it was the doctrine that put teeth into their creed. If you couldn't agree that God had determined everything for all eternity, including who would be the elect and who the damned, how could you believe in God's overriding power?

How could you account for the fact that some people, even in the same family, were strong and wealthy and powerful while others were weak, poor, plagued with trouble? Scott had taken great comfort since his father's death in the thought that it was predestined rather than a willful act just as his own freedom from similar temptations might be predestined. The love of Jesus was all well and good, but without the power of God behind it the love would be wasted on sinful man.

Scott suspected that Don Sharp was getting more of his theology from Henry Ward Beecher of the Plymouth Church in Brooklyn, New York, than from the seminary. Sharp went to hear Beecher every time he lectured in Pittsburgh, and it wasn't hard to understand how a young prospective minister's head might be turned by such a spellbinder. He was then the wealthiest minister in the nation, said to be making more than $45,000 a year from his preaching, lecturing and writing, and his influence spread from ocean to ocean. Love, the same kind of muddled love Sharp seemed to be talking about, was Beecher's message, too. The man did have a way with words, though Scott had never heard him, but he remembered being impressed when Sharp quoted Beecher at the dedication of the church's little organ: "An organ is the synonym of majesty, grandeur, power and sweetness. It contains nearly all sounds —the note of the song sparrow, the sweetest singer of all birds, the voice of the thunder, the roar of the ocean waves, and almost the blast of the last trumpet."

Well, Scott had to agree with that. Though he knew little of music himself—he had never so much as touched the Stewart piano, considering it a girl's toy—he did find himself moved by hearing it in church. And, oddly, he had to admit that, if he didn't listen too hard, he could allow himself to be moved by Sharp's preaching. The sound was splendid. Something in the Southern accent seemed to turn Don's voice into a soothing musical instrument when he was in the pulpit. If you didn't let yourself sink into the quicksand of his muddy thinking, you would go away from one of his sermons with the feeling Mr. Browning caught when he wrote, "God's in His heaven and all's right with the world." They said, too, that Mr. Sharp brought the same soothing quality to his visitations, particularly at the time of death, and Scott could well believe it. When Don and Sarah were engaged, Mary Stewart felt obliged to discuss with them all the implications of Dr. Stewart's suicide so that no ugly rumor could boomerang on their marriage or Don's work. Don scarcely listened. "Why, ma'am," he said, "please don't go on about that and distress yourself. In all my time here I've heard nothin' but good about Dr. Stewart. God alone looks into all hearts, and I am sure He has taken the good doctor to heaven to live with those saintly children who lie, by his side."

Whatever the growth of his mental equipment, Don Sharp had obviously increased his physical magnetism in seven years. A hint of gauntness remaining from the War had been fleshed out, and a confident maturity gave a new strength to his grip and strut to his walk. Sarah plainly adored him. She sat now at the silent organ listening to him preach with a rapture that transformed her rather plain face. Scott envied her, envied both of them. This kind of love was so far a total mystery to him. Although he was almost twenty-one, he had not yet so much as called on a girl. With some justification, he rationalized that he was too busy to bother with such nonsense. But the fact was, as he had to acknowledge on those occasions when his young body embarrassingly reminded him of his physical needs, that he was terrified of the experience. Full to the brim with Mr. Wallace's admonitions against lust of the flesh, he literally prayed it down whenever it even mildly assailed him. How, he wondered, could a girl as innocent as his sister had to be and a professed man of God like Sharp even imagine doing the things they were supposed to do to each other? The thought was upsetting, the more so coming to him now in church. "Make me pure in heart, Lord . . . make me pure in heart. . . ."

That night Scott was on his way from the bathroom down to his bed in his father's old office when the girls waylaid him in the upstairs hall. They were going through what had become a nightly ritual in the Stewart household during cold months. Since the only source of heat upstairs was a grate in the middle of the hallway floor, the girls, wearing only nightdress, would sit crosslegged on top of it and talk while they pinned up their hair. Then, thoroughly toasted, they would make a dash across their cold room to beds they had warmed with hot-water bottles. Scott considered the whole thing a sign of feminine weakness and frivolity, and when he could hear them tittering, he felt jealous of a companionship denied him since his brother Reed was so young. So Scott tried to ignore them, to avoid the hallway at such times or to rush past with averted eyes. They were so careless and their nightdress so flimsy that occasionally he did catch a flash of white leg or the curve of a nubile breast. Since the flesh was sisterly, the thoughts such sights could stir in him were sinful beyond contemplation. As Mr. Wallace had pointed out in one of his more daring sermons, the dreadful union of Lot's daughters with their drunken father had produced Moab and Ammon, nations that caused nothing but grief for the chosen people of Israel—the clear wages of this dark sin within a family.

"Scott! Scott!" Lucinda called out to him as he headed for the stairs. "Come on over here. We're having an argument about men, and maybe you can settle it."

"Let it wait till morning. I have to go to bed."

"It *can't* wait," Lucinda said. "It's about the way we look right now, you've got to come and really look at us. I say a man doesn't want to see his wife with her hair all curled up like this, and Sarah says it shouldn't matter if he loves her. What do you think? C'mon over and take a look. *I* think we look terrible."

Even Sarah joined in trying to persuade him.

Lucinda jumped up to turn up the gas jet, causing the night-gown to fall away from one of her smooth thin shoulders. Scott, blushing with embarrassment, looked from one to the other of his sisters. "I . . . I really don't know . . ."

"You don't know much about girls, do you, Scott?" Lucinda teased. "I'll bet Mr. Sharp could tell us right away. That's what I'm afraid of. I don't want Sarah to go making herself ugly for him."

Scott struggled to reassume the command of seniority. "I don't think you should be thinking of such things, Lucinda."

"And why not? A girl's supposed to make a man happy, isn't she?"

"But you're only fourteen."

"It isn't me I'm talking about. It's Sarah. What if Don—I mean, Mr. Sharp—doesn't . . ."

"That's their business, Lucinda, and not the business of a silly girl. Marriages are supposed to be made in heaven, and if you really want to do something for them you might try praying."

"Praying—pooh!" Lucinda said. "If that isn't just like you, Scott. Gosh I pity the girl you marry—she'll get calluses on her knees."

"Lucinda!" It was Sarah's turn to be shocked. After all she was marrying a minister, and, in fact, the argument had begun when she tried to explain to Lucinda that such trivial things as hair curlers should play no part in such a marriage. Scott's reaction confirmed her. Where, she wondered, did her little sister get such silly ideas?

"Yes, Lucinda, think about what you are saying. If Mother

59

heard you, she'd wash out your mouth with soap," Scott said, and gratefully escaped.

Mother, still lying awake in bed, did, in fact, hear the whole thing. Unintentionally, Mary Stewart often eavesdropped on her daughters' nightly chatter in the hall and she found it comforting since the girls' innocence and goodness shone through every artless remark they made. Far from wanting to wash Lucinda's mouth with soap, Mary was stuffing her own with pillow to keep from betraying her awareness with laughter. That Lucinda! She would certainly bear watching, but she was so right. Mary often wished that someone had given her that kind of advice. If she could have enticed the doctor more often the way she unconsciously did that night in the Monongahela House, theirs would have been a deeper and different relationship, perhaps enough so to have provided the warmth and solace he needed when things went so terribly wrong.

Poor Sarah and Scott were too much like she had been at their age—too serious, too ignorant, too trusting. She had been putting off talking to Sarah about the physical side of mariage, but now she knew the time had come when, however embarrassing, she would have to do it. Scott was another matter. A son should have a father to go to on matters like this; she couldn't even imagine bringing it up with him. If he weren't so pious! She chuckled again at what Lucinda had said. Out of the mouths of babes. Still, piety had so far kept him out of trouble, and Mary Stewart was honest enough with herself to admit that she was not anxious for Scott to show an interest in girls. The whole family would need his help and earnings for a long time to come, and he wouldn't be twenty-one until December. She guessed there was plenty of time to worry about Scott later; a man could well afford to be thirty or so before he concerned himself with such matters as marriage. Meanwhile, the "armor of God" Scott talked so much about might well protect him. . . ."

A Meeting with Mr. Rockefeller

They took Annie with them to Oakland but left Moses in the South Hills not only to serve the new tenant, Dr. Jones, but to keep a faithful eye on the property. Though there was a barn for Old Pat, now aging but useful in an emergency if the horse cars weren't running, and a small kitchen garden at the Oakland place, Reed was deemed old enough to take care of these things in return for pocket money. While the new house was actually smaller than their old one, it had compensations. There was, for instance, an octagonal tower rising at one corner that provided a sunny nook for the living room and an odd little room upstairs that the younger children immediately appropriated with their mother's blessing. Standing in the little room with windows all around you could be, if you were Reed, the pilot of a river boat, or, if you were Lucinda, a princess awaiting rescue from her castle cell. If the tower room as they called it, was a goad to imagination, it was an even more fascinating window on reality. From it they could look out over the tall hedge that fronted their property onto the broad avenue with its gleaming car tracks that led to the heart of the city. Often of a nice afternoon, Mary Stewart would bring her sewing into the little room to join her children in the endlessly intriguing game of watching and commenting on the passing scene.

In a way, they were fortunate that their first view of the road was in winter, for snow soon transformed the otherwise dusty thoroughfare into an entrancing sheet of white glass that turned ruby red when the sun sank into the pall of smoke lying above Pittsburgh to the west. Saturday afternoons and Sundays were the best times for watching. Then their wealthy neighbors would be out with matched teams, often racing each other on the flat stretches, their sleighs swaying and screeching and striking sparks from rocks or bare spots. Most times there would be children in the sleighs, children whom Reed and Lucinda came to envy. In the heat of the race, they would be shrieking delighted taunts at each other while the long colorful scarfs that half-muffled their faces stretched like banners in the wind. "Oh, I wish we could do that. Do you think Old Pat . . . ?" Lucinda would say. Mary Stewart would catch another stitch, look up over her glasses and reply, "No, I'm afraid Old Pat isn't up to it. Besides, we don't have a sleigh." "Why not? Why not, Momma?" "We can't afford it." "Can't afford it. Can't afford it. That's all I've heard all my life," Lucinda would complain. "When I grow up, I *will* afford it." "Me, too," Reed would join in. Mary Stewart would look at her children, noses pressed against the pane, and wonder whether the move to Pittsburgh wasn't harming them in some undefinable way. Still, envy could be turned into ambition. "Well, then, you'll just have to work hard like Scott," she would warn.

Thanks mostly to the nearby Presbyterian Church, the Stewart family settled into their neighborhood rather easily. It was a pity, Scott thought, that there was no United Presbyterian Church close enough for an easy walk, but Mary, having shifted once from Methodism and having found the corset of United Presbyterianism too tight for comfort, was well content. The younger children didn't know the difference and were only glad that the Sunday School and Christian Endeavor meetings Sunday afternoons would provide a source of potential friends. One of the elders, a man named McCandless, was Scott's supervisor at the railroad, and he immediately saw to it that Scott was appointed an usher, an appointment that would get him maximum exposure to his new neighbors, as well as a teacher for a class of boys in Sunday school. Mary Stewart fitted easily into the ladies' sewing circle that met in the church every Tuesday for a few hours of work, gossip and prayer, the latter two sometimes becoming confused, as they were with Mr. Wallace. Soon, all the Stewarts were nodding at familiar faces on the street and in the local store, and by spring Reed, with his talent for friendship, had a whole crew assisting him in the construction of a tree house back of the barn.

The move had transformed Scott's life. He was able to go earlier and stay longer at the office, and results weren't long in coming. Over the years Scott had taken one bit of his father's advice to heart—to buy the best clothes. Though he owned only three suits, one of which was growing a bit shiny, they were of the finest broadcloth and all a conservative black. Nightly he would brush them, remove spots and, when Annie was otherwise engaged, heat an iron himself on the kitchen wood stove to knife edge the creases. He was just as careful with his interchangeable pair of ankle-length black boots, polishing them to a mirror shine every day. As he'd learned years before, throwaway collars and cuffs took care of the black rings that were the inevitable result of a day in Pittsburgh. At any hour of any day Scott was as ready as any man to stand before the legendary Edgar Thompson, the railroad's austere, silent president, or any other man of business. This readiness did not miss the eye of his supervisor, and Scott was soon being sent not only out into the city of Pittsburgh but on the road to deal with important clients on the delicate matter of freight rates.

The most difficult problem for the Pennsylvania, as for other railroads in the area, was the shipment of oil. In the fifteen years since Edwin L. Drake, himself a former railroad man, struck oil on the Brewer farm near Titusville some sixty miles north of Pittsburgh, the substance had turned into a river of black gold. Thousands of barrels of it were shipped daily to refineries in Pittsburgh and Cleveland, and then on to all points to be retailed for lighting the lamps and easing the machinery of the land. All along the line—at the well heads, on the railroads, at the banks and refineries in the cities—there was a fierce competition to claim a part of this steady, lucrative trade. Emerging as the man to deal with, for railroads at least, was a Cleveland refiner by the name of John D. Rockefeller, who over the last few years had quietly begun to gain control of the flow through pulling together various parts of the business into the Standard Oil Co. One of his techniques for underpricing competitors and forcing them to sell out to him on favorable terms was to negotiate rebates from the major railroads. Though the railroads didn't like it, they knew it was the price of doing business with the largest shipper, and their own competitive position was often so shaky that they had no other recourse. One of Scott's regular tasks was to cast up figures to determine exactly how far the railroad could go in meeting Mr. Rockefeller's demands. It was particularly hard now in this time of panic when Rockefeller had slashed the price of oil from $3.25 a barrel to 82 cents and was looking to the railroads to help him survive. Though negotiations for this trade were normally carried on at the highest levels between Edgar Thompson or Thomas Scott in Philadelphia and

Rockefeller in Cleveland, it was decided that young Scott Stewart go to Cleveland in an effort to provide his superiors with the best available information.

Since none of them had been outside of Allegheny County for a generation, the trip was somewhat of an event for the whole Stewart family. They all went down on the horse car to Union Depot to see Scott off. It was worth the trip, for, as an employee, he was traveling free and could afford the best overnight Pullman accommodations. Lucinda couldn't get over the plush seats that made up into berths and the mirrored glitter of the lights inside the car; Reed was awed by the hissing power of the engine; Mary Stewart, however, was most impressed by the way the porter, knowing Scott was from the front office, literally rolled out the red carpet for her son. It was no more than he deserved, she thought as she kissed him good-bye amid the clouds of steam and confusion of people on the platform. Straight, tall and dignified in the best of his three suits, aged by his mustache and the new curl of mutton chops at his ears, he did look to be a man of important affairs. She had no fears that Scott would run into trouble in a distant city. His armor of God was still well in place: when she helped him pack, the only things he wanted to take along for diversion were the Bible and the Sunday-school lesson for the following week. And from what she heard around the church, the man he was supposed to meet, Mr. Rockefeller, was himself a Baptist Sunday-school teacher. He and Scott should have a lot in common.

Scott didn't really expect to meet Mr. Rockefeller; he presumed he would be dealing with a clerk in the oil company somewhere near his own level, and so he had no anxieties to keep him awake in the snugness of his berth. Although he regretted he couldn't see the countryside to the north and west of Pittsburgh, he enjoyed the sensation of being on a mission so vital that not a day could be wasted. Most of the other men in the car were on business too, as he could tell from their chatter while they shaved in the wash compartment next morning. Not knowing Cleveland, Scott hired a carriage at the station and set out directly for the Standard Oil offices. Though less saturated with smoke, the city he rode through was flat and sprawling and far less interesting to the eye, he thought, than Pittsburgh. There seemed to be no reason for it to have captured such a great share of the oil business other than the shrewd manipulations of Mr. Rockefeller.

Greeted warmly at the oil company's offices, Scott was ushered into a room with a cheerful fire burning in the grate.

Just the sort of young man he had imagined awaited him there. He had charts and figures spread out in front of him on a table and invited Scott to enter at once into detailed discussion about feasible rates. They'd hardly begun before there was a knock on the door and a lean man of about forty, six feet tall with a full head of light brown hair, a thick reddish mustache and the bluest eyes Scott had ever seen, walked in. The young clerk seemed a bit flustered.

"Oh, Mr. Rockefeller," he said, "excuse me for using your office. I thought . . . This is Mr. Scott Stewart, Mr. Rockefeller, from the Pennsylvania Railroad at Pittsburgh. We're just . . ."

Rockefeller extended a somewhat limp hand for Scott to take and said, "Yes, don't let me interrupt. I'll just listen in."

While the discussion went on under somewhat strained circumstances, Rockefeller sat in a rocker by the fire, swinging back and forth pressing his hands over his eyes as if he were trying to sleep. Scott was explaining somewhat heatedly to his counterpart why it was utterly impossible for the Pennsylvania to lower rates to the level the oil company was seeking when suddenly Rockefeller pulled his hands away from his eyes, fixed Scott with a stare that seemed as powerful to him as the searchlight on a locomotive and said, "Very well, Mr. Stewart, we will have to find other means of transportation."

Scott was truly frightened. If he lost the Standard Oil account, he was certain to lose his job, perhaps be hounded out of business in Pittsburgh altogether. "But . . . but, Mr. Rockefeller, I'm not empowered to say we *won't* meet your figure, it's just that . . . well, you can see from what I've been saying . . ."

"I can see one thing, Mr. Stewart, you haven't calculated the future in your equation," Rockefeller said. "I'm cutting the price of oil until I'm almost giving it away to keep my customers because I know business will improve. I think you have to do the same thing. Keep our volume in mind."

"Yes, sir, I do, sir. The problem is that if the other companies get news of this . . ."

"There won't be any other companies worth the worry in a few years, I can assure you, Mr. Stewart. If the Pennsylvania wants to go on shipping oil, it will have to meet our demand. Please take that message to your superiors."

Scott felt he was jumping from the frying pan into the fire; although he had apparently not lost the oil business yet, he'd gained nothing for his own employers and might just as well have stayed in Pittsburgh. He decided that he had to take a small risk. "Mr. Rockefeller," he said, "if you would just look at these figures, you would see that just another eighth of a cent would be enough to enable me to justify the rate to Philadelphia. It's less than we need to make any kind of profit, but we could keep the trains rolling—for the future, as you say."

Rockefeller reached for the papers. For a number of minutes that seemed to Scott interminable, while the only sounds in the room were the spitting of the fire and the rhythmic creak of his rocker, Rockefeller studied the figures. "Have you ever thought of adding another car, or maybe two, to each train?" he asked at last.

"Yes, sir, it's been discussed, but our operations people say the engines don't have the power."

"Too bad. It would be the best way of cutting costs—more freight for the same labor. But if that isn't feasible, your figures add up, young man."

"Thank you, sir."

"I'm not surprised," Rockefeller said, "I took the precaution of looking into your background. I understand you have a Sunday-school class of boys—what age?"

"Thirteen, sir."

"Just the same as mine. Little devils, aren't they? Well, Mr. Stewart. I don't mind telling you I don't like this. You people are going to have to try harder on cutting costs. Meanwhile, though, because you have been honest with me, I'll go along, for a time. I'm not fool enough to sell cheap for long, and you shouldn't be either. Good day."

Scott's gamble that a man as shrewd as Rockefeller could tell at a glance that the rates were figured so closely that the railroad really would be making no profit on his traffic had paid off. He walked on air all the way back to the station, where he waited for the night train back to Pittsburgh. Though an eighth of a cent was far less than they had hoped for in Philadelphia, it was workable, and Scott had the satisfaction of knowing that he had done a good job. Even so he was surprised when, a few weeks later, he was called to the superintendent's office and told that he'd been promoted to assistant superintendent in charge of traffic with a salary of $150 a month and a cubicle of his own.

The news was greeted at home with whoops of delight from Lucinda. "Now we aren't poor, are we, Momma?" she wanted to know. Mary Stewart was more cautious. "It does help, but

66

you still have to get back to your sewing if you want a new dress for the Sunday-school picnic." Actually, with the rent coming in from the South Hills property and careful management of the increased amount Scott planned to give her, Mary could begin to see a few extra dollars at the end of each month. She knew what she wanted to do with them; the time had come, she felt, for her to help Scott enlarge his life at home to keep up with his progress in the city. She would open the house, invite promising young people in for evenings, try to put some gaiety into her solemn son's days. But first she would have to fix up the parlor. She needed a new rug and some pieces to replace those old hand-embroidered ones that had so impressed Mr. Wallace. Good enough for the country, they were out of date in the city parlors she'd seen, where shiny, tufted mohair was favored. She would need a few touches of art, too, like one of those Rogers statues that were being so widely advertised. The one she liked best, because it somehow reminded her of Lucinda, was called "The Favored Scholar," depicting a young girl getting special attention from her professor while a boy, not unlike Reed, crouched under the desk, and it was only eighteen dollars. The more she thought about what she could—and should—do in the months ahead the more excited Mary became. Maybe she ought to do something about herself—a new dress? a new bonnet? Being the mother of a rising young executive opened wide vistas.

No such thoughts were in Scott's head. He took his new promotion, as he was inclined to take most everything, solemnly. Indeed he prayed over it, asking God's blessing and promising Him to be worthy of the opportunity. He then went to work. Work. Even his family and fellow workers could never quite understand Scott's true passion for work. He had no apparent interest outside the office except for the church —no sports or girl friends or hobbies. To Scott work was everything; all else was petty distraction. Given his nature, he would have poured the same kind of concentration and dedication into being an artist or a teacher or a preacher if circumstances had not led him elsewhere.

All in all Scott was happy the way things had turned out. He recognized in himself a real talent for business that might have been wasted in the ministry, as Mr. Carnegie had suggested, and he saw that the men of business were the ones who were really shaping the future. He was proud to be among them. Being young, he was sometimes impatient with his progress, but he kept reminding himself that he was just twenty-one and that he had only been at work some seven years. He was still confident that the way up lay through diligence in whatever he was given to do—"he that is faithful in that which is least is faithful also in much," as the parable said. The real, the satisfying meaning of his promotion to Scott was that events were proving him right. Where before he'd only had to master the intricacies of freight rates, he now had to know all he could learn about the movement of every piece of equipment everywhere on the western division, and the challenge drove him eagerly to his desk every morning. At some point, he was sure, what he was learning would provide him with a break leading to wider opportunities.

It came sooner than he could have hoped. Perhaps because he brought a fresh eye to the traffic pattern, Scott soon spotted a place where the construction of a spur line would save enough money in costly shunting of cars and engines to more than pay for itself. His proposal was quickly accepted, and a few days later Schultz, the assistant superintendent for construction, dropped in to discuss details with him. Up to now Scott had scarcely exchanged a word with Schultz, just nodding at him as he passed through the office. A squat, florid, powerful man of about thirty, given to wearing dove gray pants and loud checked vests, Schultz started his railroad career driving spikes into ties along the tracks, and he liked to boast about keeping the common touch with coarse language and frequent trips to the nearest saloon. Now he tilted back in the creaking little guest chair in Scott's cubicle, hitched his feet up on the desk and said, "I gotta hand it to you, Stewart, I've been screamin' about building this spur for a year now, but nobody would listen."

"I guess the thing that turned the trick was the cost figures," Scott said mildly.

"Maybe so," Schultz conceded. Then, bringing his feet to the floor with a crash, he leaned close to Scott, bathing him in a whiskey breath so strong Scott's stomach nearly turned. "But listen, Stewart, if you've got any money, there's a good thing in this for you—and me."

Drawing slightly away from Schultz's red face, Scott said, "I'm afraid I don't understand . . ."

"Simple. Seein' this comin' I bought options on all the land for the right of way. Now if you were to buy my options, you could gobble up the land. The company'd pay you twice as much as it's worth now and be happy for the chance. What d'ya say?"

"Well, it doesn't sound right to me. . . ."

"Right? Why the hell not? The company has to buy from

somebody. You could make it a lot easier for them—one owner, no haggling, just a reasonable profit."

"Why did you come to me with this?"

"Just say I like your looks, Stewart. A fella who wears dark suits always has money. Okay? . . . No, seriously, I figure if you hadn't shoved this through, my options wouldn't be worth a damn. So one good turn deserves another, eh? . . . Still not with me, I can see by your face. You Sunday-school fellas always think a fella like me is up to no good, don't you? Well, the truth is that I need money right away. My debts are pilin' up—four kids eat like hell, you know—and the bankers don't have any understandin' in times like these. Nobody outside the company knows about this—and won't I'll betcha—so to them the land isn't worth a damn. Most of the fellas in the company who do know about it are worse off than I am. The super couldn't get involved—that would be goin' too far because he calls the shots. So that leaves you. Okay? Think it over—it's a hell of an opportunity."

"I still don't see why you don't take advantage of this yourself," Scott said.

"Like I told you, I need the money right away—tomorrow wouldn't be too soon. I'm up against a wall. There isn't a loan shark in town would give me enough cash to make good on those options, and God knows how long it might take the company to act on a proposition from me. What do you say?"

"I'll let you know in the morning. Now here are the plans."

On the way home, Scott began to get excited about Schultz's proposition. The long horse-car ride was always conducive to dreaming dreams since night transformed the city of daytime soot into a thing of wonder. Thousands of lights from offices, stores, dwellings and along the curbs blossomed like feathery flowers in the seemingly perpetual mist, and above the rivers the sky glowed angry red from the open furnaces that cooked tubs of metal around the clock. Pittsburgh never slept. Day and night, men were making, building, transporting the things a growing country craved. All an alert young man of business needed to be part of this was money, and here was his chance. Though he had nothing to speak of in the bank, he had learned that he could borrow. He was pretty certain that Judge Mellon, despite the bad times, would still trust him; the country property was clear and earning money, and he had been regular in his Oakland payments. According to Schultz's figures, he needed only five thousand dollars to make another five—a thousand for the options and four for the worthless bottom land the railroad planned to acquire. He was aware he would have to move fast. Schultz's need for ready cash would drive him soon to seek a quick sale elsewhere. But was it ethical to take advantage of the man's need and his own inside knowledge? And when the company found out he owned the land, wouldn't they doubt his motives in promoting the spur? The idea of having five thousand dollars to invest, particularly in these distressed times, was so compelling that Scott could hardly bear to entertain any doubts. He looked around him at the tired men in the car, nodding their way home with faces etched in lines of fatigue, and thought how this one stroke could lift him above the prospect of such lives —if he could bring himself to pull it off.

At home, as soon as the dishes were cleared away and Reed and Lucinda shunted off to their studies, he took the whole matter up with Mary. He had to have her consent to using the family property again as collateral, but more than that he wanted her blessing. Though she upset him once in a while with what he considered female frivolity, like ordering that statue from New York, Scott still trusted his mother's instincts. True, there were times when he thought she was less zealous than she might be about the Lord's work. He was surprised, for instance, when she didn't join the ladies of the church in the new temperance crusade that was sweeping the country. He sometimes spent his lunch hours watching the women as they sang hymns and prayed at the saloons and he'd have been proud to see his mother among them. Of all people, she should appreciate the horrors of drink. It would be one thing if the protest were fruitless, but whole towns in Ohio were said to be banning the sale of liquor and there was reason to believe that the ladies could save Pittsburgh too. Mary Stewart let it go with the explanation that she thought the activity "unladylike," and Scott had to accept it. Perhaps it was all part of her clear-eyed common sense, the very quality that brought him to her for advice at times like this.

"Why shouldn't you go through with this, Scott?" she asked. "As far as borrowing is concerned, anything I have is yours. You know that. And I think Mr. Schultz may well be right that you could save the company money and trouble. Why don't you just go in and talk to them about it?"

It was all he had hoped for—a kind of flash of sanity. The next day, having gained Judge Mellon's somewhat grudging agreement to a loan, Scott presented himself to the superintendent. He outlined the possibility of his getting the land and turning it over to the railroad at once, omitting on the grounds that he might be breaking a confidence any mention of Schultz's part in the scheme. When Scott had finished, the superintendent rocked back in his hair and stared thoughtfully at him. Finally he said, "A neat package, young man." Then he winked and added, "I suppose there's a little money in it for you."

"Well, I . . ."

"Oh, don't play innocent, Stewart. Frankly, I admire your gall. I guess you might as well profit as the next man if our real estate people think the price is fair. Confidentially, they told me they thought we'd have to pay twenty thousand or more. So I guess you've got yourself a deal."

When Scott was halfway to the door, the superintendent called out an afterthought. "Next time, Stewart," he said, "it might be wise to keep your speculations further away from the office."

Within a few weeks, Scott Stewart had five thousand dollars earning interest in Mr. Mellon's bank while he looked for the best investment for it. He was no longer a kind of glorified clerk; he was a capitalist. Once again, he thanked God for his good fortune—and prayed for further guidance. It came, as might seem appropriate, through that pillar of the East Liberty Presbyterian Church, the dour and dignified judge. This time, impressed by the speed with which Scott had repaid his loan and the evident one hundred percent profit on it, it was Judge Mellon who sent word that he would be pleased to have Mr. Stewart call on him. Scott approached the Mellons' iron-fronted bank on Smithfield Street with a new sense of assurance that he was now a man of affairs.

Not one for small talk, the judge came right to the point. "I think I've found a good place for that five thousand dollars of yours, young man. Of course, I'd like to keep it in the bank, but I've been impressed with your ability and I think you deserve every opportunity to make the most of your money. There's another young man, not a great deal older than you, by the name of Clay Frick who's building up a coke business out near Connellsville. Times are bad, as you know, and Frick is having a problem getting hold of cash to buy up coal lands. I can assure you that this is the time to buy, as you've already learned, and, in fact, we've loaned young Frick considerable sums on that basis. Once business turns the corner, coke will be very valuable—after all, it's the best fuel for making iron and steel. Now I think Frick might give you a small fraction of his business for your five thousand dollars. If you are interested, I'll make the arrangements."

While the idea of seeing his new nest egg melt away into a fraction on somebody's books rather frightened Scott, he felt that, if he couldn't trust Judge Mellon's reputation for shrewdness and solvency, he couldn't trust anybody. So he held out his hand and was rewarded with a remarkably strong grip surviving from the judge's days on the farm. On the way out, the judge stopped by a desk where a thin, pale young man was at work. "Andrew," the judge said, "I'd like you to meet Mr. Scott, an assistant superintendent at the Pennsylvania. You should know my son, Andrew, Mr. Stewart, since he's taking over more and more of the business here."

Andrew said nothing, just shyly held out his hand for a quick shake. "Andrew, I've just advised Mr. Stewart to put his five thousand with your friend Clay," the judge said. "Would you agree?"

Andrew merely nodded assent. Scott tried to ease the other young man's shy awkwardness by saying quickly, "Pleased to meet you, Mr. Mellon. I have to hurry back to my office."

Mary Stewart's plans to liven up their home didn't sit well with Scott. With busy days and nights now being given over mostly to anxious study of high finance, he felt little need for any kind of social life. Several times he pleaded business or weariness to turn away her suggestions. It was only when she hit on the brilliant notion of entertaining the group of young men he met weekly with at the YMCA that he went along. She put it on the beastly hot weather that had set in during that July of 1874. Wouldn't it be nicer to meet on the Stewarts' cool porch and perhaps enjoy a dish of homemade ice cream than crowd into a stuffy room downtown? Scott agreed, and she sent a note to each of the six young men inviting them to join the Stewarts for Sunday evening services on July 26 and a gathering afterward at their home. It was Mary's thought that the guests would find it more convenient to make the long trip to Oakland on a Sunday, rather than a working day, and Scott suggested that church attendance might help elevate the nature of their discussions.

The purpose of the YMCA group was to provide a kind of continuing education to its members, all of whom had been forced early out of school by hard circumstances but now had their feet firmly on the first rungs of the ladder to success. Their talk was wide-ranging across the fields of business, politics, religion, philosophy, art. For the most part they were in agreement: General Grant, who understood the needs of business, had made a wise president in his calm handling of the Credit Mobilier scandal and now the panic; the Reformation had rescued Christianity from the black arts of the Catholic church; though probably wrong about the origins of man, Darwin's idea of the "survival of the fittest" seemed a true description of the life they knew in business; the British novelist Wilkie Collins, now touring America, would very probably put Charles Dickens' reputation into eclipse; the murky music coming from the pen of the German composer Richard Wagner would soon die a well-deserved death. There was one young man, however, who took delight in playing a kind of devil's advocate. Perhaps because he had more formal education—two years at Western University of Pennsylvania —and had now left a secure clerkship at Carnegie, McCandless & Co. to read law, Henry Schmidt was always questioning orthodox views, often to Scott's annoyance. Though he was the son of a Lutheran minister, Schmidt was particularly cynical about the relationship of religion to business. But Schmidt's saving grace was his personality. Red-headed, freckled, beardless, grinning like a jack-o'-lantern, he had a touch as warm as the sun, and not even Scott could get really angry at him.

As luck would have it, the day of the Stewarts' first gathering was one of the worst in memory. Rain poured steadily from clouds so low that they seemed to be resting on the round shoulders of the hills above Pittsburgh. Streets turned into such a quagmire that the horses pulling the cars along their slippery tracks had difficulty keeping a footing. Since there was no way of getting messages to their guests, the Stewarts felt obliged to prepare for whomever might come in spite of the filthy weather. Mary, knowing the dripping porch would be useless, tidied up the parlor as best she could, hastily covering the worst worn chairs with some spreads she'd bought for such an emergency and making sure that the new Rogers statue held a prominent place. Though nobody would probably want it now, Reed and Annie were set to churning ice cream in the kitchen. Lucinda, as usual, was useless. Even rain couldn't dampen her delight at the idea of not only having a houseful of young men, though she had been warned repeatedly by Scott to make herself scarce, but appearing with them in church where all her friends could see her. She spent the afternoon in her room, trying on one dress after another. Occasionally she would come bounding down the stairs to seek her mother's advice. Finally, Mary Stewart said in exasperation, "Lucinda, you are only fourteen, and these men are your brother's age. I'm sure they won't even notice what a little girl is wearing."

Lucinda promptly broke into tears to match the weather,

73

and Mary quickly put an arm around her daughter, saying, "I'm sorry, Lucinda, I shouldn't have said that. Of course, you should look as nice as you can. Why don't you try the dress we were working on last week? The dark brown won't show the mud and it's cold enough with this rain for a fall color. If you bring it down, I'll stitch it up for you."

Lucinda's sun came out again. She threw her arms around her mother's neck and hugged her. "Oh, would you? Mother, that would be perfect. . . ."

By church time the weather was worse. Flashes of lightning periodically whitened the glistening grass and trees, and thunder echoed through the sky. Even so, three of the young men met them at the church, one of whom was Henry Schmidt. Though her feet and probably the bottom of her skirt were wet and muddy, Lucinda felt she looked far older than her fourteen years in her new dress. It was, in fact, her first really grown-up style, and she had to wear one of her mother's bustles under it to lift the folds high enough off her hips in back. When they started down the aisle, Henry Schmidt quickly and gallantly offered her his arm, sure confirmation to Lucinda that she didn't look her age. She held herself severely straight and tried to make her features assume the cool composure she thought suitable to a lady of sophistication. All the while, though, she kept plucking with her free hand at her long skirt to make sure she wouldn't trip and worried about how she could gracefully sit down with all that stuff sticking out behind her. Somehow she made it, but then she didn't know quite what to do. All she could think of was to sit rigidly straight and stare primly at the pulpit while Schmidt tried to thaw her out by handing her a program and whispering comments about the ugliness of the weather. She felt that if she looked at him or said anything the veneer of sophistication would crack and reveal the little girl lurking under it. When the service began, he shared his hymnal with her like a real gentleman. At first she wouldn't sing, thinking it somehow indelicate. But after a verse during which she was conscious of Schmidt's true tenor voice, she couldn't resist mingling her small soprano in harmony with him. Carried out of herself by the soft strains, and sentiments, of "Now the day is over, night is drawing nigh . . ." she dared look at her partner. His merry eyes, dancing over the rims of the half-glasses he used to read the music, met hers and one of them closed in a slow wink. She could feel a hot blush rising right up from the rim of her high tight collar and shooting to the roots of her hair. He knew! He knew! But it turned out to be all right after all. During the tedium of the prayers and sermon, Mr. Schmidt would scribble little notes on the program like "See the old bird asleep in the third row left" and pass them to her. Freed of sham, she actually giggled aloud once and subsided into a fit of choking and coughing behind her handkerchief, only too aware of the look of cold disapproval from her brother Scott at the end of the row.

On the damp walk back to the house, Schmidt held an umbrella over her and carried her reticule so that she could devote both hands to the task of keeping her skirts above the ankle-deep mud. "You know I have a sister at home about your age, Lucinda. What is it—fifteen, sixteen? Anyway, I think you two should meet. Would you like that?"

Fifteen or sixteen. Well, that was better than fourteen, she thought. "Oh, yes," she said.

"Good, we'll arrange it. Life's pretty dull for Martha out there in a country parsonage. All the other girls are hicks, if you know what I mean."

"Oh, I know. I grew up in the country myself," Lucinda said.

"So you did. I remember Scott's complaining all the time about the long drive."

In the hallway at home, in the damp confusion of people scraping mud-caked feet, discarding dripping cloaks and umbrellas, Scott took Lucinda aside. "I hope you'll go up to your books now and leave Mr. Schmidt alone. You almost disgraced us all in church, and that's enough. We've some serious things to discuss . . ."

Reluctantly, Lucinda started for the stairs—nothing now but a little girl banished. What a pill Scott could be, she thought. She wouldn't even get to say good-bye to Schmidt, who was following her mother into the brightly lit parlor. The first thing he saw was the piano, and he asked, "Do you play, Mrs. Stewart?"

"A little," she said. "But Lucinda's the good one. She's been taking lessons ever since we moved to Oakland."

"Oh, let's have a tune," Schmidt said. "Could we get her in to play?"

Before Lucinda could reach the landing she heard her mother calling and nearly fell over her skirts in her headlong rush to get back down to the party. What better stage than the piano? Two candelabra hung on each side of the music rack, and Schmidt was lighting them when she came in. "What can you play, Lucinda? Can you play this?" he asked, picking a sheet from the rack. By luck it was one she had learned, one

75

of Mr. Foster's songs that she loved. But Scott, coming up behind them, said, "Why not a hymn instead? Wouldn't it be more appropriate?"

"Ah, no, let's have a little gaiety with all this rain," Schmidt said. "Anyway, Stephen Foster was one of the true sons of Pittsburgh. You know, my father met him once when he was in his last bad days, poor fellow. Come on, Lucinda. You don't mind if I sing along?"

In a rich tenor that had been masked before by the congregation, Schmidt sang, "I love my Jeannie with the light golden hair. . . ." Could he have changed the words just for me, Lucinda wondered, and she blushed again, a happy blush. Her evening would really end with this song, she knew, but instinct told her that she would surely see more of Mr. Schmidt.

Mary Stewart had the same impression. She had been aware of Schmidt's teasing her daughter in church, and now, watching him as he sang with his eyes fixed on Lucinda's exquisite profile, she knew that he saw the woman this girl was fast becoming. It was happening all too soon, on Lucinda's very first evening in any kind of society. Lucinda's blush showed that she was fully aware of what was going on, too. At the very least, this sort of thing would turn the girl's head. How could Mary control her a year from now, two years from now, three years from now? Such beauty, combined with a willful spirit, was a powerful and dangerous weapon that could produce tragedy as well as joy. . . .

Scott, too, was fascinated by the performance, but for a reason far different from his mother's. It had to do with the music, or with some mysterious mixture of the music and the obviously warm communication going on between his sister and Schmidt. The whole thing—the beseeching melody, the candlelight, the shine in the performers' eyes—was absorbingly beautiful. Almost against his will, Scott found himself momentarily transported into an area of emotion he tried but failed to ignore. Just then he wanted desperately to have a girl, a woman, of his own, wanted to know in his own soul and body the raptures the composer must have known. Music could do this to him, he knew, and it may have been one reason why he'd asked for a hymn; hymns were safe in all their associations. Generally, Scott steered clear of music, except in church, because he was secretly ashamed of what it could do to him. Music in his experience was a plaything of women, and the emotions it stirred up in him had to be a form of weakness. But just for now, he really wanted it to go on and was sorry when Lucinda with an "aren't-I-a-good-girl" glance at him snuffed out the candles at the end of the song and left the room.

The discussion, as Scott had hoped, did gain something from the church service. Evidently Schmidt had given at least half his mind to the sermon while using the rest to divert Lucinda. He led off by saying, "Well, you all heard the dominie tell us that it's harder for a rich man to get into heaven than for a camel to go through the eye of a needle. Now does anybody here believe that?"

"I don't," Scott said. "Look how God allowed Abraham to prosper. Aren't riches a just reward for the faithful?"

"I agree with Scott," another of the young men said. "I guess the way I feel is that the Lord believes in stewardship. He puts wealth into the hands of men who've shown they know what to do with it. Look at the great benefaction you read about every day to our schools and seminaries. Daniel Drew, for instance . . ."

"Daniel Drew!" Schmidt said. "He'd make Blackbeard, the pirate, look like a saint. You know where the phrase 'watering stock' came from, don't you? Drew used to drive his animals down from upstate New York, starving them on the way. Then just before he took them to market he'd let them bloat themselves with water. I'll tell you if that old scoundrel can buy his way into heaven by endowing a theological seminary, I'd rather go to the other place—not that I'm not going there anyway."

"I wouldn't be surprised," Scott said, and they all laughed.

"Seriously though," Schmidt went on. "You all talk about the Lord, but what Lord are you talking about? Are you talking about Jesus? If so, look at what he said: 'Sell whatever thou hast and give to the poor . . . lay not up for yourself treasures upon earth where moth and rust doth corrupt. . . .' And look who he hung around with. Were they bankers? Steel makers? Not on your life. If he were in Pittsburgh tonight, I'm sure you wouldn't find him sitting high and dry in a church like the one we attended tonight. He'd be down along the rivers with all those poor hunkies who must be getting pretty wet feet by now."

Just then there was a sharp knocking at the door. Scott opened it to find a neighbor, a man who every Sunday evening went to the First Presbyterian Church in Pittsburgh. Hat dripping rain and voice loud with excitement, he told Scott, "Mr. Stewart, I've just come out by horse car. The whole

talk in town is of heavy flooding. I thought maybe the tracks
. . ."

Scott thanked the man and turned to his friends. "Please excuse me. I've got to go down and see."

"Oh, Scott, must you?" his mother asked. "It's such a bad night."

"I have to go," Scott said. "But don't let it break up the gathering. Serve the ice cream, Mother—Reed would be very unhappy if it weren't eaten after all his work."

Though it would be very wet and uncomfortable, Scott thought it would be better to hitch Old Pat to the cart than depend on public transportation. He might have to get around to the trouble spots, and walking would be almost impossible in the muddy flats. He was out in the barn harnessing the horse when Schmidt, swinging an extra lantern he'd found somewhere in the house, joined him. "Mind if I come along?" he asked. "Might take two of us to get this contraption out of the mud some places."

Scott was truly grateful . . . he'd frankly not relished the prospect of setting out alone through the flash and crash of the storm. Talking, though, was almost impossible as they huddled into their capes, hats brimmed down to protect their eyes, Scott just let Old Pat pick his own way through the mire in the general direction of town while he concentrated on trying to remember where each train was supposed to be and what tracks might be most endangered by rising waters.

Schmidt's mind was on the surprises of the evening. Somehow it had never occurred to him he might find such a girl in the Stewart household—so strikingly beautiful, so full of lively mischief. She was young, yes, but years would ripen her deliciously. Lucinda must take after the doctor, because Mary Stewart was much what Schmidt had expected—handsome, cool, dark, like her son. Thank God, though, she wasn't as somber as Scott. There were times when Henry felt like tickling Scott or wrestling him to the ground just to see him come alive. There was a mystery about Scott Stewart that Henry couldn't fathom. Except in debate, where he could be forceful enough, Scott was too quiet and withdrawn for a man of his age. And he was far too pious. Still, it was hard to dislike him. In fact, Henry Schmidt rather grudgingly admired Scott, because he felt a power in him that none of the rest of them had. He seemed to have no doubt he was one of God's elect and that whatever he did was right. What a great feeling that must be. Henry himself was still floundering. Business had proved boring and the law wasn't much better.

The only thing he'd liked was his brief stint at college, but he couldn't afford more of such a fling. Maybe later. Meanwhile, though, he wished he could dedicate himself to something, even making money, the way Scott had. Just look at how Scott bounded out into this drowning weather—and without a thought that he was profaning the Sabbath! Yes, there was a kind of iron in Scott Stewart, not unlike the stuff they were cooking over there by the river.

It was well past midnight when they reached the city. Jolting along between the dark hulks of buildings that shone like wet coal in the lightning's glare, Scott kept an eye out for some source of information. The first lights were in the offices of the *Dispatch* and, hitching Old Pat to the nearest post, Scott and Henry rushed up the stairs. A reporter had just returned from the scene of the worst flooding across the river in Allegheny, and they listened while he blurted out the story to his colleagues.

"It's not the river this time," he said. "It's those ravines over in Allegheny—Butcher's Run, Wood's Run, Spring Garden Avenue. The water's pouring down them like you wouldn't believe. One man told me it sounded just like Niagara Falls. Everything's being swept away—houses, people, carcasses from the slaughterhouses along Butcher's. The force of it! I got as far as Madison Avenue in the city, and there was a gash, I swear, thirty feet deep where the water from Butcher's Run just blew the sewer apart. Nobody knows how many are dead yet. Everybody with a boat is out trying to help, but it's hard to find anything. The gas pipes were ripped out and the whole area's so dark you can't see the back of your hand except in lightning flashes. My God, it's terrible!"

The reporter knew little or nothing about any problems the railroad might be having, but he doubted they would be too serious because he'd been able to get back and forth across the bridge to Allegheny. That was enough for Schmidt. "C'mon, Scott," he said. "We're soaked, and my room isn't far from here. Let's go and dry out."

"You go ahead," Scott said. "I guess there isn't much use in trying to go down to the river, but I think I'll go on to the depot and see if I can be of any help. There'll probably be a need for special trains or something."

"Maybe you're right," Schmidt conceded, as they went out again into the rain. "I'll just walk on home. You know, in a way I envy you, Scott."

"Why?"

"You're so all-fired wrapped up in your work, you don't

even know whether you're wet or dry. Yes, in a way I think I envy you very much."

A Centennial to Remember

Rain threatened all morning. Lucinda and Martha Schmidt carried umbrellas with them but Lucinda doubted they could raise them without poking somebody's eye out, they were so surrounded by people. There were two hundred thousand of them, according to some man in the crowd, and they were all pressing in around the platform that had been set up between the Main Exhibition Building and the Art Gallery for the opening ceremonies. There were already several famous Civil War generals sitting up there—Henry pointed them out as they came in: William T. Sherman, Winfield Scott Hancock, Philip H. Sheridan—and everybody was waiting for General Grant to appear with his guest, Dom Pedro II, the emperor of Brazil.

"Oh, this is so exciting! Imagine being right here to see the Centennial Exhibition begin! Oh, thank you, thank you, Henry for bringing us." Lucinda said.

"My pleasure," Henry said. "I only wish we could have persuaded Scott to come too."

"Oh, he's such a pill," Lucinda said. "Work, work is all he ever thinks about."

"I bet he'd love the music," Martha said.

"Except for that 'Centennial March' by Richard Wagner," Henry suggested. "You know Scott really thinks Wagner is inspired by the devil. . . . Oh, here they come."

The two-hundred-piece orchestra under the direction of the celebrated New York conductor, Theodore Thomas, began sawing away at the Wagner march as Grant—a surprisingly small, plain man in Lucinda's disappointed eyes—moved down toward the front of the platform with the emperor. When the music stopped, the President spoke, so softly and briefly they could only catch a phrase or two such as "celebrating a century of progress of this great country." Then suddenly the orchestra and a choir of a thousand voices, massed behind the President on the platform, broke out in the "Hallelujah Chorus." Everybody in the huge crowd stood silent, as if in prayer, the men with bared heads, and Lucinda promptly felt a kind of lump in her throat. At the end of the chorus the American flag was raised while a hundred guns fired from somewhere on the edges of Fairmont Park and chimes rang from all the buildings on the grounds.

The President and the emperor made their way through a path in the crowd cleared by soldiers to the Machinery Building, where they would start one of the features of the exhibition—the Corliss engine. "No use trying to get in there," Henry said. "We'll see the engine later."

"I don't care about any old engine," Lucinda said.

Henry laughed. "This isn't just any old engine, Lucinda. This is the biggest steam engine the world has ever seen. Imagine twenty-three miles of shafting, forty miles of belting. They say it has a fly wheel thirty feet—that's almost like a three-story house—in diameter."

"Oh, well, I guess we should see it then. . . ."

"I want to see everything," Martha said.

"Being from Pittsburgh, why don't we begin with the monument to steel—the Main Exhibition Building?" Henry suggested. "You know the story behind that, don't you? Your brother's friend Andrew Carnegie got himself on the Centennial Committee to make sure the main building would be an advertisement for iron and steel structure. Might be just a coincidence but the contracts for building it went to Carnegie's Keystone Bridge Company and the Union Iron Mills. So, ladies, here's a little bit of Pittsburgh in Philadelphia. I should think Scott would appreciate this even more than the music."

Through a long and footsore afternoon, they did see just about everything. The girls were particularly fascinated with one of the Japanese exhibitions—a group of almond-eyed girls in bright kimonos reeling out silk from real cocoons. Lucinda thought her mother would swoon with delight in the Horticultural Hall—a huge brick building with a whole glass top that let the sunshine filter down through a tropical forest into a reflecting pool. It was just like the garden of ferns and plants Mary Stewart cultivated in the tower alcove off their living room, only on a giant scale. Henry shook his head at the sight of the great guns from the Krupp works in Germany on display in Machinery Hall. "They could blow the world to pieces," he said. But the huge hand for the Statue of Liberty Mr. Bartholdi was making in Paris as a gift from the French people was a reassuring sign that the nations of the world could get together. About the only rest they took was when they stopped for a bite in a replica of a German beer garden. Henry gave Lucinda a taste of the foaming brown liquid in his stein. It was terrible, like the yeast her mother sometimes made her take for her complexion, but she felt nicely wicked swallowing something with alcohol in it. People around them were talking in all kinds of strange languages, and Lucinda said, "Oh, I just can't wait to grow up and see the whole world! I think I'm ruined for smelly old Pittsburgh."

The city that night was almost as exciting as the exhibition grounds. Though it was cool for May, the streets were full of people looking at the fireworks exploding overhead. It was truly a giant birthday party for the nation—a historic event Lucinda wouldn't have missed for the world, even though, by the time they'd elbowed their way through the crowds and found the boardinghouse where they were staying, her feet were killing her. Up in the bedroom she shared with Martha, she tore her boots off and began massaging her insteps and toes. "I couldn't have walked one more step," she said.

"Me, either," Martha agreed, "but wasn't it fun?"

"Oh, yes. Henry really is a dear, isn't he? I don't know any other man who would spend all that time and money on two silly girls like us."

"He's sweet on you, Lucinda."

"Really? He's ages too old for me. How do you know? Did he say anything?"

"Oh, no, but I can tell from the way he looks at you."

Lying in bed that night, Lucinda had something more to keep her awake than the kaleidoscopic events of the day. Martha was more than likely right about Henry. That was probably the reason Scott had raised a dreadful row with Mother about letting her go to Philadelphia with Henry and Martha. He had argued she was too young to take such a trip, that it didn't look right to let a man foot the bill for her even though Lucinda and Martha had become best friends and Henry was well off now. But Scott's real worry, Lucinda knew, was that he might get Henry Schmidt for a brother-in-law. Scott scarcely tried to conceal his contempt for Henry these days—calling him a "fool" for giving up the law to go back to Western University to "study philosophy, of all things," just because someone had found a little oil on the family property up near Butler, and calling him a radical for the views he expressed about business in their YMCA meetings. Once Scott went so far as to say, "I wouldn't let the fellow in the house if it weren't for Martha."

If Henry really was interested in Lucinda, he could not have conceived of a better strategy than bringing her and Martha together. The girls had hit it off right away with their contrasting personalities. While Lucinda was tall for a girl, almost regal in her grown-up moods, Martha was small, dainty, curved—a kind of dimpled doll. She was dark, too, with black hair and almost black eyes that emphasized her china-white skin. "One of the black Germans," red-headed Henry would laugh. "Don't know where we found her—probably under a toadstool in the Black Forest." Martha was as quiet as Lucinda was vocal. Brought up in straitened circumstances, Martha had learned automatically to be a help around the house, and Scott had not missed that trait. "Reminds me of Martha in the Bible," he said once after she had gone. "Yes," Lucinda agreed, "but remember that Jesus said Mary who entertained him had chose 'the good portion.'" "I didn't know you knew so much about the Bible," Scott said. "You don't know a lot about me," Lucinda retorted, "but I am glad you like Martha." "Oh, I didn't say I liked her," Scott hedged, "I just said she seemed a nice girl." But Lucinda thought otherwise as she stared into the dark and heard Martha's breathing shift into the easy rhythm of sleep.

Martha came to Pittsburgh almost once a week now for piano lessons and stayed overnight at their house, so Scott, who was too shy or busy to bother with girls, was getting accustomed to her. But the thing that really seemed to bring them together was music. It all started when Mary Stewart virtually made Scott chaperone the girls to a concert. All the way downtown, he fussed that it was silliness and a waste of time, but when the orchestra—a symphony orchestra all the way from New York under the same Mr. Thomas who was conducting at the exhibition—began to play. Scott got a rather odd look on his face, sitting there and looking almost as if he were in some kind of trance. Afterward he admitted it was a great experience, and he even hummed the opening bars of Beethoven's Fifth Symphony—da-da-da-dum—while he was driving the buggy. Martha and Lucinda dug each other in the ribs and giggled; after that, they didn't have any trouble getting Scott to go to concerts, and even paying for them. When

83

Martha would practice on their piano, Scott would sometimes idle into the room and just sit there listening and looking at her. Lucinda thought it a good deal more likely that Scott would marry Martha than that she would marry Henry, even though both Scott and Martha were too quiet and reserved to say anything about it. The most she could worm out of Martha was that she thought Scott was handsome; the most she got out of Scott was that business about Martha's being a "nice girl."

Lucinda finally fell asleep deciding she would think seriously about Henry another day. It was enough that he was showing them a good time. Just as she was drifting off she giggled a little at the thought of what Scott would say if he knew Henry had let her taste beer. That was the wonderful thing about Henry; he was always doing and saying things that shocked old fuddyduddies like Scott, not to mention her brother-in-law, the Reverend Mister Donald Vincent Sharp, who was going to be living too close for Lucinda's comfort now that he had been called to the pastorate of the Oakland Presbyterian Church.

Donald Sharp's sudden rise from his country parish in the South Hills to one of the more fashionable pulpits in the city was almost wholly the work of Mary Stewart. There were lots of reasons for Mary's wanting to have her daughter Sarah and Don closer to her, the most compelling being the arrival of her first grandson, Stewart Lee Sharp. So when old Dr. McClintock announced his retirement, Mary saw it as an ideal opportunity for Donald Sharp. She brought the matter up with Scott, who as an elder of the church was on the selection committee to find a new minister. He was shocked; his brother-in-law's name had never occurred to him. He had hoped to find a strong man like old Mr. Wallace, a man who believed in, and preached, the doctrine of God's elect; Don Sharp, as far as he knew, was still awash in some fuzzy concept of love. But Scott felt such theological objections would be meaningless to his mother. She might, though, understand that Sharp's political bias would be unsuitable to the Oakland congregation, so he brought that matter up.

"You know with his Southern background he's always talking about what a nincompoop Grant is, and I guess some of those South Hills farmers have gotten to him on the money question," Scott said.

"Oh, I don't think Donald gives a fig about politics. Anyway, he's so handsome and has such a beautiful voice. . . ."

"But, Mother, the pulpit committee is made up of men,

serious men. They aren't interested in a man's voice but what he says."

"Well, why don't you at least talk to Donald about it. They're coming to tea Saturday."

"All right, but you realize I'll have to resign from the committee. . . ."

"I should think that's the least you might do for your sister and her husband," Mary said. "You don't want Sarah and her children stuck out there in a country church when the rest of us are all doing so well, do you? I should think you might even find it advantageous to have a brother-in-law occupying such a well-known pulpit."

Mary's last words began to work on Scott in the days before he confronted Don Sharp. In Presbyterian Pittsburgh, it would be useful to have a relative well-known in the church, and he had to concede that Don Sharp's Southern charm might carry him a long way if he got a base like the Oakland congregation. By the time the Sharps came to tea, he was convinced he did want his brother-in-law to try for the post, and so he brought up politics more in the way of a warning than a challenge. "Don, if you really want to be a candidate for the Oakland church, you'll have to be more careful with your political views," he said.

"Now just what do you mean by that, brother Scott? You know I don't pay any mind to politics."

"Maybe you should. You just can't go around accusing the Republicans of 'waving the bloody shirt' and implying that President Grant is an imbecile, or worse," Scott said.

"Do I do that?" Don asked. "Well, I declare I cain't help it if your Republican people are raisin' the issue, lookin' toward this fall's campaign. Did you all hear what that Robert Ingersoll said? He said, 'The man that assassinated Abraham Lincoln was a Democrat.' Now if that isn't wavin' the bloody shirt, I don't know what is. And ah cain't help it if your President Grant surrounds himself with fools and thieves. Maybe he is honest, but with his own secretary, that fellow Babcock, involved in the whiskey ring, and now Secretary of War Belknap, no less, resignin' because he and his wife were takin' money from army tradin' posts, there isn't much ah can say that would make him look worse."

"You see?" Scott said, turning to include his mother in his remarks. "That kind of talk just won't go around our session. It's made up of prominent businessmen who believe that the Republican Party's *policy*, regardless of the bad lapses by Grant, is essential to the business and the future of this coun-

85

try. We just couldn't invite a man to our pulpit who thought otherwise."

"I don't think Donald thinks politics is important when it comes to preaching, do you, Donald?" Mary prompted.

"No, mother Stewart. You all know I only want to preach the word of God's love. I guess it just grieves me, seein' how I went into the ministry tryin' to heal the wounds of war with love, to hear these politicians talk the way they do," Sharp said. "As for business, you all know I think this country needs more of it; we wouldn't be havin' these hard times if we had more business."

"Well, if you can persuade them you think like that . . ."

"Oh, I can persuade them, brother Scott. Never you fear."

"You'll have to switch over to the Presbyterians, of course," Scott went on. "But the fact that you are a United Presbyterian now will stand well with the conservatives on the session."

"Shucks, brother Scott, there's no difference," Don said. "I just want to spread the word of God to a larger congregation. What do you think, Sarah?"

Sarah, who was rocking little Stewart to keep his whimpering from interrupting the conversation, said, "It would be nice to be nearer the family."

"Well, that settles it for me," Don said. "I do hope you'll put my name in."

Scott sighed and nodded. Sharp was really stupider than he had imagined, and he only hoped that his candidacy would not be an embarrassment. But Mary Stewart's instinct had been right again. The Oakland congregation reacted favorably to Donald Sharp's good looks and mellifluous voice. Now that the Sharps were living only a few blocks away from the Stewarts, he seemed to be in and out of the house all the time, taking what he called a fatherly interest in the younger children. It was Sharp, for example, who found Reed when, inspired by a reading of *Tom Sawyer* and aided by Lucinda, he tried to launch a raft and escape down the Monongahela, and it was Sharp who suggested that Lucinda be included in the punishment—a whole month of staying in the house after school and on weekends. Perhaps prompted by Scott, Sharp had tried to quash the Philadelphia trip too. Smiling at Lucinda in that way of his, he had said, "Mother Stewart, I'm surprised at you letting a pretty girl like Lucinda go all the way to Philadelphia without a proper chaperone." But Momma had replied with her usual good sense: "I can't keep her in a box, Donald, and Martha will be with her, you know."

Darling Momma! Lucinda was just beginning to suspect that behind her rather plain and sober country-woman facade, Mary Stewart hid a lively and mysterious spirit. Scott had known this for a long time and was, at turns, fascinated and frustrated by it. She had an uncanny feeling for money that often humbled him with all of his pride in the logic of figures. Though she went around spouting to the younger children like a page out of a copy book—"Waste not, want not," or "A penny saved is a penny earned"—it was Mary, more often than Scott, who saw the wise gamble when it came along— or, to put it more simply, knew a good thing when she saw it. The matter of their growing Frick interest was a case in point.

Not long after Scott put his $5,000 into Frick's coke business, young Andrew Mellon sought him out. The Mellons were willing, Andrew told Scott, to lend him another $10,000 on the South Hills property if he would pass it on to Clay Frick. Scott thought that this was more debt than the family should handle, but Mary said, "Something tells me we are in good hands with the Mellons, Scott, and I think we should take the chance." So they did, and good fortune, thanks be to God, blessed them beyond their wildest belief. Though times were still bad, Carnegie had been firing his mills right along on reduced prices, and they were devouring coke almost as fast as it could be shipped. The price per ton had already tripled, and it was still rising; according to Andrew Mellon, three-fifths of it was profit, owing to Frick's shrewd management. By now the Stewart share in the business had to be worth at least $50,000. With his new position as assistant to the superintendent of the Pennsylvania's western division paying $300 a month, Scott could consider himself at twenty-four a young man of substantial means.

Increasing riches, like a rising tide, were slowly changing the landscape of the Stewarts' lives. The parlor of the Oakland house was now suitably darkened by the heavy velvet drapes Mary had long admired at the Joseph Horne Company, and an oval marble-topped table with graceful bentwood legs had made its appearance in the center of the room to hold an alabaster statue of a nymph which Lucinda had described to Scott's horror as "just like me with my clothes off." Scott himself had succumbed to one indulgence—a new horse and buggy. With his present job he reasoned that he had to be able to move in an emergency just as much as his father had before him. Apart from that, he had always envied the men of business who drove themselves to their offices, like Henry Phipps, the Carnegie partner entrusted with borrowing for the firm whose horse was said to be so attuned to business that he stopped automatically in front of every bank in town.

Scott's horse, as he had to admit soon after he got it, was more for pleasure than business. Driving back and forth to town became his chief recreation, and he made the most of it. The horse was a spirited black animal named Uncle Tom that had cost Scott an unbelievable five hundred dollars. Before he made the purchase, Scott took the precaution of having Moses come over from the South Hills where he still tended the old property to pass on Uncle Tom. Moses ran a hand over the horse's sleek flank, studied his teeth, watched him walk. "I like everything but the name, Mr. Scott," he said.

Scott was honestly surprised, and suddenly embarrassed at having laughed when the original owner explained, "Named him that, because he runs as fast as that nigger."

"Well," Scott said, feeling awkward, "Mrs. Stowe's Uncle Tom did a lot to help free your people . . ."

"All the same, I prefer an Irish horse," Moses said, turning away from his examination of Uncle Tom to stroke Old Pat's nose.

Moses had proved a reliable caretaker, keeping the South Hills gardens green and the house white, but Scott always felt uncomfortable with him. Behind the old man's opaque eyes lay a world of experience Scott couldn't fathom. He could remember as a boy having the shivers run up his spine when he would hear Moses singing one of his spirituals as if keening for the whole human race. In every slow and steady gesture, Moses expressed a kind of deep, resigned sadness that belied all the possibilities of betterment and progress Scott so genuinely and firmly believed in. What religious beliefs Moses revealed seemed to have in them more the certainty of hell than the hope of heaven. He also never quite understood how his brother-in-law, who came from a slave-holding family, got along with Moses so well. When he asked about it once, Don just said, "Oh, we have a lot in common." Maybe defeat did something to people that Scott couldn't comprehend; there had been a silent bond, he now felt, between his father and Moses too.

Uncle Tom ran as well as his former owner claimed, and Scott, who had found that he loved speed on his very first train ride, took to letting him have his head on every level stretch. He would invite races with anybody else who seemed so inclined, and he equipped the harness with saucy bells that served both as a challenge and a warning to others in the flow of traffic. Neighbors were astounded to see the dignified Scott Stewart, body erect, face taut, reins expertly in hand, careening down the avenue as if the very devil were chasing him. He was so reckless that even the wild Lucinda preferred taking the horse car to riding with her brother. Reed, whose chores still included stabling and rubbing down the lathered horse when Scott came home from work, accused his older brother of being too hard on the horse. "Nonsense— running's what horses are for," Scott argued. "I'd say he doesn't work any harder in his harness than I do in mine." And, indeed, he had a point. Mary, for whom the sight of Scott's having any kind of fun tipped the scale of values, agreed. "I don't think Uncle Tom minds it, Reed," she said, "and anyway I think Scott deserves some pleasure."

When Lucinda came back from her trip East, she was hard to live with. Nothing, either in the city at large or in the Stewart home, seemed to suit her. "Ugh, what a filthy place Pittsburgh is. Now in Philadelphia . . ." "Annie, take away those dreadful sausages. What we ought to do is send to Philadelphia for some of that heavenly scrapple." "Momma, you really ought to get a new dress. Nobody in the East wears such drab colors any more. . . ." And as for the boys she used to tease when they carried her books home from school, "They're such children, such absolute hicks. . . ."

Obviously, Lucinda had been somewhat overwhelmed by the attentions of Henry Schmidt, and it was hard to blame him for it. The beauty that had been in bud at fourteen had come into full bloom at seventeen. Although he was wholly correct and brotherly in his relations with Lucinda, Schmidt had invented an elaborate game that allowed him to flirt with her safely. Years before he had taken to calling her "Princess" in a mocking way. Now he used the nickname constantly and suited his actions to the word. Every time they met, he would bow and kiss her hand. He would lift her over puddles and hand her into carriages. Exaggerating for effect and winking at Mary or Scott, if they happened to be about, he would play the obedient courtier to her every whim, picking up hand- kerchiefs, bringing a glass of lemonade, holding the yarn for her knitting, turning the pages while she played the piano. Lucinda loved the game and played it to the fullest herself. When Schmidt was around, her back straightened and her chin tilted in what she conceived, not without some justification, to be a regal bearing. Although Henry seemed to be indulging in brotherly teasing, she knew very well that he was not, for when they were alone together he performed a true act of flattery: he treated her as an adult.

Once when she complained to Henry about the way Scott was always treating her like a silly little girl, he told her, "You've got to remember that Scott just naturally has to be sort of a father to you. Anyway, there are times when I think he was born an old man."

"So do I," Lucinda sighed. "But I guess it all had something to do with Daddy's death."

"Yes, I'm sure it did," Henry agreed. There was, in fact, some mystery about Doctor Stewart's death that Henry had long tried to fathom. When he asked Scott how it happened, there was an awkward pause and an oddly halting reply: "Well, he . . . apoplexy, they said." Nothing strange about that to account for Scott's grim reticence whenever the subject of his father came up, so Henry pursued the matter with Lucinda. "How did your father die, Lucinda?" he asked.

She was perfectly open. "Oh, he died of apoplexy—out in the barn when he was harnessing the horse to go on a call," she said. "At least that's what Momma's always told me. He was a wonderful man, everyone says so."

"What was he like?"

"I don't remember too well, I was so young. He was handsome, I know that—tall and handsome. He was always reading, sort of like you, and talking about things none of us could understand except maybe Scott, who was always reading too."

"Oh, Scott was a reader?"

"He was a regular bookworm, all the time sneaking into Daddy's office when he was away."

So that accounted for one of the dilemmas in Henry's mind: why Scott Stewart seemed to have a fairly wide frame of reference now despite his lack of formal education and narrow interests. "You don't remember anything else about your father?" Henry prompted

"Yes, his eyes. There was something in them—a twinkle, maybe—that made you feel he didn't always believe what he was telling you. The more I think of it, the more I think he must have been a lot like you; you couldn't always tell what he was really thinking. Sometimes I think he would have been a lot of fun if he hadn't been a doctor."

"Why so?"

"I don't know. I think he felt he had to be dignified so people would trust him. And he felt terrible when something happened to a patient. He'd be all grumpy and quiet so you were afraid to go near him. The worst was when Mrs. Mc-Clure died, and right after that Daddy died himself. I heard mother say once that it killed him. . . ."

Dr. Stewart's personality was hard to grasp, but Henry liked what he was hearing. The fact that Lucinda, even as a little child, had sensed strange depths in him and the fact that she had so obviously loved him encouraged Henry. The doctor had obviously been as different from his open, practical-minded widow as night from day. No doubt this helped to account for the fact that Lucinda and Reed were so different in looks and temperament from their older brother and sister. Of course, he realized they'd been young enough to escape the full shock of a father's sudden death, but Henry believed strongly in the theory that a lot of character flowed through the very blood a person inherited: Lucinda was more Stewart than Shallenberger, more Scotch-Irish than German, just as he himself was more Shaw than Schmidt. This made sense of the cutting edge to Lucinda's personality, the volatile temper, the sometimes too keen wit, the willfulness. There were times when Henry thought that Lucinda could be summed up in a word—headstrong—and she exasperated and enchanted him. She could be outrageous.

"What do you want to be when you grow up?" he once asked.

"Rich," she said at once.

"Rich? Why rich?"

"Because I like nice things. I like nice dresses and riding in fine carriages. And I'd love to travel, see the whole world. Oh, wasn't it fun in Philadelphia seeing all those quaint costumes and odd people? If you don't think it's nice of me to want to be rich, you have to remember that you ruined me with that trip, Henry Schmidt."

"And if you want to be rich, that leaves me out," he said, testing.

"Why? You have all that oil. . . ."

"That's not mine, it's my father's."

"He'll die someday . . ."

"Lucinda!"

"What's so bad about that? He will, won't he? We all do."

"Ah, Lucinda, sometimes I think you have a heart of ice, like your brother," Henry said.

"Why drag him in? Scott, Scott, Scott. It seems to me we're all always talking about him. At least I'll say this for Scott, he *is* going to be rich."

"But at what price! My God, I wouldn't want to be like

him—mind churning day and night with schemes to make more money. You know he even tried to buy out my father's land when he heard about the oil? Know what he said to me? 'You people don't have any sense about money, Henry, you'd be better off with cash in the bank.' "

"He was probably right. Your father's a dear, but you have to admit his head is somewhere up in the clouds most of the time, like Martha's."

Henry had to agree, and he found it almost scary the way Lucinda could read people. As far as he knew, the Reverend Gustavus Schmidt, a balding gnomelike man, had never had a practical thought in his life. With a perpetual smile twisting his lips, he went around mulling over abstruse points of theology to elucidate in the next sermon he would send over the heads of the corporal's guard of farmers and oil men who gathered in his little church. It was clear that the Reverend Schmidt would never get a bigger or better church, but it was equally clear that the congregation loved him for his smile and would go on dozing through his sermons until death did them part. Some yearning from a peasant past had induced Gustavus Schmidt years before to buy a small farm several miles from the rectory. From Henry's point of view, it was nothing but an instrument of torture for the Schmidt children who were sent periodically to hoe out the gardens that invariably bore more weeds than vegetables. When a member of the congregation asked permission to sink a well on the property, Gustavus Schmidt almost absentmindedly agreed and when oil began to flow he struck no terms, accepting gratefully whatever his parishioner chose to give him. To the good minister, the money was as astonishing as the manna must have been to the Israelites, and he tried to follow their example of consuming it all before sundown. He staked Henry's older brother, Jacob, who was miserable in his job as a country store clerk, to a farm of his own; he urged Henry to quit work and go back to school; he encouraged Martha to pick out the most expensive college in the East; he hired two servant girls to help the long-suffering Mrs. Schmidt and took her to Pittsburgh to outfit her in the first store-bought clothes she had ever owned. He was, as they say, generous to a fault, and everybody around him loved him for it.

"Well, and what about me, Princess? Do I take after my father?" Henry asked Lucinda.

"I don't know," Lucinda said. "Sometimes I think you do, I mean, studying all that old philosophy is like your father. But then I think you don't know what you want to be yet."

"You don't believe I want to be a teacher—or maybe, if I'm lucky, a lecturer and writer like Mr. Emerson?"

"Does he make a lot of money?"

"Yes, I'd think so."

"Well, then, what's wrong with that?"

"You are certainly going to be hard on any man who asks for your hand, Princess. You'll probably want to see his bank book first."

Lucinda laughed. It wasn't a ladylike laugh, but a wild whoop and a ringing of bells. "That's not a bad idea. Why don't you bring it next time?"

Henry turned red—and speechless. That first night he had sung to Lucinda, he had made up his mind that he would one day marry her. Since she was only fourteen, he had necessarily steeled himself to wait at least four years during which time he would craftily engineer, through Martha, as many opportunities to be with her as possible. He was still counting the months before he thought it would be decent to speak to Mary Stewart and here was Lucinda challenging him, or taking him for granted, whichever it was. At the moment, there was only one way out—back to the game.

"Well, it's very flattering, but you don't think I could aspire to the hand of a princess like you, do you?"

"You've kissed it enough," she said.

"So I have, but it is as far as I dare go. I can see you're looking for a prince on a golden charger."

With a bow and a smile and another kissing of her hand just to show that he wasn't afraid to go on with the game, Henry left before the conversation could lead to statements either of them might regret. It was the most daring exchange they'd had so far, and he, at least, needed time for thought about the next step. Henry was tremendously excited to learn for sure that Lucinda understood his deeper intentions and, apparently, didn't reject them. Through the waiting years, he had tried to force himself not to think about Lucinda physically except to admire her beauty, as he might a painting. He didn't always succeed. There were those nights when the essence of her, mutilated by dreaming into a kind of floating montage of hair, eye, breast, lips, settled around him while his starved organ rose and erupted in a relieving wash. Sometimes then he would have to wait days before he could dare see her again without risking an embarrassing thrust in his loins. But for the most part, the unreality of the situation, the knowledge that she was simply too young to make his dreams come true, made it possible for him to enjoy her freely, as a doting brother would. Now that he realized that there was more than a hope that he would one day be able to caress all the secret recesses of this lovely child-woman, he knew he would find it harder and harder to resist the temptation. Being with her might well become a kind of torture instead of a delight.

Though there was no question of Lucinda's physical attraction for Henry, he was becoming concerned, especially since their trip to Philadelphia, whether she would grow up enough to make a good wife. He had laughed off her love of things, her passion for riches, as a childish yearning in the class with wanting to be a real princess. But this conversation unsettled him. The fact that she could speak so plainly and explicitly about his father's death showed a far from childish flash of cruel practicality. She really did want wealth, and with her beauty she could get it. If Henry moved fast, he might by reason of his age and her misunderstanding of the oil business convince her that he was, indeed, the prince on the golden charger. But what would happen when the well ran dry? Would she by then have learned some values, values that would enable her to stick with him in some smog-blackened dwelling while he tried to sink a well into those reservoirs of truth that he believed lay within him? The only thing he had in his favor was Lucinda's feeling for her father who, by all accounts, shared much of Henry's inquiring, doubting character. If he could make her love him as she had loved her father, wouldn't she forget frivolity? The Stewarts were, after all, serious people, and he felt he could count on Mary Stewart's steady help in the campaign. So the thing to do now was to talk to Mary Stewart.

Henry had certainly ruined Lucinda for the pimply boys her own age who cut capers in front of her at Sunday-school picnics to try to attract her attention, but his brotherly attitude had let her put off the question of whether she loved him in the way she understood love from the romances she read. She glowed in his flattery: he had proved himself gratifyingly open-handed in taking her places and buying her the best that was available in food and entertainment. While he was not darkly handsome like her brother-in-law, Mr. Sharp, the open, freckled face and dimpled smile he'd inherited from his father were appealing. She liked the way he dressed in care-less style with discreetly patterned pants and vests that blended with but didn't match his coat, with ruffled shirts and flowing ties, with a soft, western-style, wide-brimmed hat. Henry could afford to look that way, Scott told her, because he was a student and not a business man. Well, with all that oil, he would be independently rich, and it gave her a pleasant feeling of superiority to be with a man who carelessly thumbed his nose at the stern world Scott inhabited. So if she didn't love him, maybe it was just that she wasn't quite certain that he loved her. The thing to do was to provoke him into declaring himself and when he left, still blushing despite his effort to appear playful, she felt she'd achieved her objective. Time enough to decide whether she loved him when he really sought her hand. Whatever the outcome, she would be the first girl in her group who had a serious beau, and that was quite enough to think about for now.

A Visit with Mr. Frick

When the first warm days of the spring of 1877 arrived, fourteen-year-old Reed Stewart was ready for his great adventure. It was inspired by a reading and rereading of Mark Twain's *Tom Sawyer* and *Life on the Mississippi*, the first books that ever spoke to his own experience. The more Reed pored over the books the more he longed to see that great wide river that ran through the heart of America. It would be easy to do, he figured, since the Monongahela flowed into the Ohio, and the Ohio flowed into the Mississippi. Heavily laden fleets of coal barges set sail daily from the Monongahela wharves to go all the way to New Orleans, so there was no reason why a well-constructed light raft couldn't make the same voyage. Reed's first effort the spring before had failed not so much because Donald Sharp got wind of it and found him but because the hastily built raft leaked so badly that he was afraid to sail away from the shore. This time it would be different since Reed and two carefully selected companions—Tom McCandless, youngest son of Scott's old boss at the railroad, and Hiram Smith, who had ready access to planks and nails from his father's lumber yard—had spent Saturday afternoons for a whole winter building their craft.

Carrying out the construction project itself had done a lot in the way of preparing the boys psychologically for the voyage. They'd had to learn the discipline of secrecy, for if any member of any of their families found out about the raft the adventure would be aborted. Reed didn't even tell Lucinda who, since her engagement to Henry Schmidt was announced, had become an alien adult. Maintaining secrecy had involved, of course, learning to lie expertly about their whereabouts on those Saturday afternoons when they mysteriously vanished to the vacant lot along the river where they kept their growing creation well-hidden in reeds and brambles, and obtaining materials had instructed them in the arts of stealing and finding their way around quietly in the dark of night. The result of their labors was, to their minds, a triumph of nautical engineering. A platform, eight by twelve, tightly planked and braced athwart with two-by-fours was set on a dozen empty oil barrels which should not only keep them afloat but well above the lapping waters of the river. In the center was a small four-by-four shelter open to the stern, where they could store food and crawl in out of the rain. Though they counted on river currents for locomotion, they laboriously carved out of planks two long steering sweeps which could be used for rowing in an emergency. The yellow Monongahela, fouled by the effluvium of the industries along its banks and the steamboats plowing its surface, gave little promise of providing the fish Tom Sawyer and his friend Huck so easily flipped out of the Mississippi, so Reed and his friends began stocking the raft with imperishable items like biscuits, smoked bacon, turnips and potatoes they could filch in small, unnoticed quantities from their families' larders. When the weather began to turn, all that remained was the selection of a departure date, a decision the others left up to Reed, their self-appointed captain.

Scott made it easy for him. He announced at dinner one Friday night that somebody named Mr. Frick had invited him out to Connellsville for the weekend to inspect the coke business in which the Stewarts were invested. Though it meant missing church and Sunday school, Scott felt that Don Sharp would certainly understand, and he was eager to meet this Mr. Frick who had so wisely used the last four years of depression to acquire some eighty percent of the world's best coke-producing facilities. To Reed the significance of all the boring talk about coke was that Scott would be away for some forty-eight hours, increasing the likelihood that he and his friends could make good their escape. Because he was younger than the parents of the other boys and more widely acquainted in the city, Scott was considered the person most likely to find them when their absence was noted. The plan was for each boy to tell his family that he was spending the night of their departure at the home of one of the other boys—a plan they'd made feasible by doing just that on Saturday nights throughout the winter. This would give them a minimum of twelve hours or more, until church time the next morning revealed their absence, enough time to get safely onto the broad Ohio, where they could hide by day and travel by night. When Scott announced his plans, Reed's stomach began to knot with excitement and he had to labor at pushing down his food so as not to arouse suspicion. As soon as it was decently possible, he left the table and was off running in the spring twilight to spread the word—it was tomorrow night, or never.

Luck was with the boys. They not only managed to get away from unsuspecting families in the early evening but were able legitimately to carry off a small bag of extra clothes, thought to be their night shirts and Sunday-school outfits. The night was cool but as fair as a Pittsburgh night could be; stars, like candles in a wind, flashed off and on through the swirls of smoke-blackened mist rising from the river. The boys heaved and pried themselves into a sweat easing their awkward raft into the dark water. It floated high and lightly, and with the slightest pressure on the steering sweeps they were able to guide it out into the current. They were free! Like Tom before him, Reed took his place amidships, scrambling on top of the little house so as to better guide his ship. In the best nautical tradition, he would call out "labbard" or "stabbard" to Tom and Hiram at the sweeps, and then, in disgust, translated to his less literate companions, "To the left, you ninny!" or "To the right! To the right! There's a barge ahead!"

Before an hour was out, the captain was facing an unforeseen problem. Though they piled on all the sweaters and jackets they'd brought with them, the cool river wind was chilling their sweaty bodies too rapidly. Reed's teeth were literally chattering, and there were ominous mutterings from the crew. "I'm c-cold," Tom complained. "Me, t-too," Hiram said. Reed suggested stomping to warm their blood, but they gave it up quickly when the raft teetered ominously. Then they tried rowing, a clumsy business with the long sweeps that only tended to foul them with the current and set the raft to spinning. They were drifting by the clattering yard of a steel works, where the red flame of a Bessemer converter in full blow shot its reflection across the water at them in a taunting reminder of the comforts of fire and warmth. The prospect of a long, long night of deepening chill was more than they had bargained for; if only they could find a place to warm up where they wouldn't be suspected, they could set out again at sunrise and still get away.

Ahead on the right were the Monongahela wharves, where hundreds of steamers nuzzled the banks. Most were darkened hulks, put to bed for the night or weekend by crews who were undoubtedly roistering in the waterfront saloons. But one glittered like a giant chandelier, and the lights strung along its tiered decks shimmered in the river's mirror like a field of stars. The shivering sailors on the raft could see carriages pulling up to the gangplank and men in their shining top hats and ladies in glistening silk going into the boat, and they could hear snatches of gay music coming from one of the cabins that stretched the length of the hull. Showboat! None of the boys had ever seen one at night, let alone gone aboard. To their Presbyterian families, these gaudy river palaces with their saloons and minstrel shows and ladies who were said to show their undergarments when they danced were little more than floating dens of iniquity. But Reed and his friends were free now, and there was no one to tell them what they might do. "Look at that," Reed said, "I'll bet it's warm in there."

"Yeah," Tom agreed. "I w-wish we c-could get aboard."

"Why not?" Reed asked.

"It c-costs money," Tom said. He had made a good point; the one thing the boys had not been able to appropriate was money. They had less than three dollars between them, but with free transportation they figured it to last until they could hire out to someone down the Mississippi.

"Why don't we sneak aboard, tie up on the river side, aft there by the paddle where it's dark and just climb up when nobody's looking? There's so much noise they wouldn't hear us."

"I . . . I don't think my father would like that," Tom said.

Reed laughed as scornfully as his unsteady voice would allow. "Your father? You don't have a father to worry about now, Tom. Scott wouldn't like it, either, or my mother, but do you think I give a rap? That's why we left, isn't it—to do what we want to do?"

"Yeah," Hiram seconded. "Let's go. D'you think we'll see some of those ladies dancing? I hear they show their bare bottoms."

"Yeah? Who told you that?"

"Fred Shoemaker. His brother went once."

"Oh, boy!"

Reed remembered enough lore to order his crew to muffle their sweeps by tying handkerchiefs around the spot where they rested on the lock. It was a useless precaution since any noise short of a steamboat whistle would have been drowned out on deck by the music and laughter. Securing the raft to a spoke of the wheel, the boys scrambled up the huge paddles and dropped onto the main deck astern. Back in this functional part of the ship there was nobody to see them, and they grouped in the lee of the cabin already warmed by their own excitement and shelter from the breeze. The question was what to do now, and Reed reasoned aloud that, since tickets were sold at the gangplank, they would already be presumed to be paying passengers and, therefore, had nothing to worry about. The others accepted his logic, none of them stopping to consider that a trio of fourteen-year-old boys in old caps and jackets might stick out in the elegant showboat crowd like the proverbial sore thumb.

Boldly, the boys strode down the deck until they came to the door of the main salon. Inside everything was dark except for a bright rectangle at the far end where the show was going on. The boys slipped in and fortunately found some empty chairs in the back. On stage was the minstrel show, a dozen or more men, ringed in a semicircle, with blackened faces and dazzling sequined frock coats. In the middle sat a white man in fashionable formal clothes and opera cape, the interlocutor, who would provoke the others into telling jokes in exaggerated Negro dialect or prompt them to sing a song. Just as the boys sat down, he was asking, "Rastus, how did you get to Pittsburgh?" "On de Pennsylvania Railroad, ob course." "And did you have a good trip?" "Well, we had a little railway accident on de way." "Oh, my goodness, Rastus, what happened?" "We done arrive safely." The audience roared, and Reed, laughing along with them, thought how much fun he would have telling that to Scott until he remembered that he would probably never see Scott again and then he felt a little sad. He felt even sadder when the banjos struck up, and a big man stepped forward and began singing "Old Black

Joe." Reed knew all of the Foster songs because Lucinda and Henry so often played and sang them, and hearing the music now reminded him of the warmest, brightest moments in the home he'd left forever.

Reed forgot all about home when the curtain fell on the minstrels, and the interlocutor stepped through its fold to announce, "And now, ladies and gentlemen, the *pièce de résistance*. Straight from Paris, France, we bring you ten— count them, ten—lovely can-can girls dancing to the incomparable music of Jacques Offenbach played by your own showboat orchestra." Hiram nudged Reed in the ribs and whispered, "This is it." In the faint light reaching them from the stage, Reed could see his friend actually licking his lips, could see the anticipatory glitter in his eyes; Tom, on his other side, looked more scared than anything else. Hiram was the one among them who knew all about girls and what you did to them. He got most of his infomation from Fred Shoemaker who got it from his older brother who had actually, so Fred swore, been in a whore house in Pittsburgh once. When they were skinny dipping in the river or spending the night together, Hiram liked to tease his organ into erectness and challenge the others to a measurement duel. It was embarrassing, because Hiram was the first of them to have a luxurious growth of dark hair down there and had, without question, the biggest "prick," as he called it. He showed them how you could work with your hand and get almost the same effect as if you were with a girl, according to Fred Shoemaker's brother, and Reed had tried it out when he was alone in bed and liked it more than he knew he should. He wondered if Scott ever did anything like this but simply couldn't imagine it since he knew there must be something in the Bible against it. The Bible had a way of knocking most everything that was fun. Once when he was staying overnight at the Stewarts, Hiram persuaded Reed to climb into a tree outside their bedroom window so that they could get into a position to watch Lucinda undress, but fortunately she pulled the blinds before they could see anything and saved Reed from what he knew would be a kind of shame.

Looking at the girls on the stage was a different thing; that's what they were there for. In a whirl of bright color, they pranced like ponies to the exciting music, kicking their legs up and out to reveal a long stretch of stockinged thigh and alluring ruffled pants. At the end of the number they turned their backs and, with a saucy flip of their skirts, wiggled their bottoms at the audience. From where the boys sat, it was hard to tell whether they were bare or not, but you could imagine it easy with the sight of tightly stretched white pants, and that was enough. "Oh, boy; oh, boy," Hiram was saying, "I hope they do that again."

"Yeah," Reed agreed, feeling almost sticky warm now in the crowded salon and hopelessly aflame with lust.

Hiram leaned over him and leered at Tom. "Like that, Tom?"

Tom, who was actually blushing, maybe from the sudden heat after their chilly voyage, could barely manage an "Uh-uh."

"Y'aren't still worrying about what your dad will think, are you, Tom?" Hiram persisted.

"It would kill him if he ever found out," Tom said.

"Scott, too," Reed said.

"Oh, I'll bet they've been to shows like this before. I know my dad has," Hiram said.

"But he isn't an elder," Tom said.

"Well, he's a deacon."

"But deacons aren't elders," Tom argued. "They don't have to be ordained."

"Oh, shut up. You talk like a preacher," Hiram said. "Hey! They're coming back!"

But the boys weren't to see any more titillating dances. Heavy hands descended on their shoulders, and they looked up into the brass buttons of a policeman. "All right, out you scamps," he said. "I had the devil's own time finding you. I never thought you'd have the nerve to sneak in here. What would y'r mothers be sayin' if they knew you were watchin' this filth?"

It developed that the policeman had spotted their empty raft and taken the precaution of cutting it loose so that they couldn't escape by river while he searched the boat. Hearing it was gone was almost a worse blow to Reed than being taken into custody—a winter's work adrift and no hope of retrieving it. Since it was nearly midnight, the policeman thought it wisest to let the boys cool their heels in the station house until morning. If, as they said, their families didn't know they were gone, it would be cruel to wake them in the middle of the night. Though they stretched out on benches, the boys slept only fitfully if at all as they contemplated the dreaded confrontations at home. In the morning all pleadings with the police just to let them sneak back were useless. "Y'r families have to know what scalawags you are so's they can keep an eye on you in the future," they were told. They were piled into a real paddy wagon and delivered, one by one, to whoever answered the door at their homes.

In Reed's case it was Lucinda. Her first astounded reaction at seeing her brother in the charge of a policeman was laughter. "Oh, Reed," she said when the officer was gone, "now you've really gone and done it. Wait till Scott hears about this, or Mr. Sharp."

"Do they *have* to hear?"

"I don't know how you can hide it—coming up the street in broad daylight in a paddy wagon. Everybody in church will be whispering about it this morning for sure. Imagine, the preacher's brother-in-law. And Tom McCandless. Oh, won't his father be furious! But what did you do? Tell me about it."

"I don't want to talk."

"I think you'd better. Maybe we can cook up something to tell Mother and Scott that would make it easier."

So Reed talked and, as he talked, he began to take pride in what he now saw as a bold adventure, embellishing every moment of it for his sister's benefit. When he got to the part about the can-can girls, she shouted with laughter. "Oh, Reed, I don't think you'd better tell them about that. Just say you went aboard the boat to get warm and got caught right away."

"Lucinda, shame on you!" Mary Stewart's voice stopped Reed's boastful tale in midpassage like a shot across the bows. They had been so busily talking they hadn't heard her come quietly down the stairs. "Bad enough what the boy's done," she said, "without encouraging him to be untruthful. Now up with you, Reed, and into a bath and get dressed for Sunday school. . . . We'll deal with this later when Scott gets home."

It made a long, suspenseful day for Reed, who couldn't imagine what kind of punishment might be deemed fit to match his crime. The worst torture of all was at the end, at the dinner table when he was forced to squirm silently through Scott's interminable recital of his own adventures in Connellsville. Reed couldn't understand how his mother could be so fascinated with every detail of how Mr. Frick looked and how they baked coke when through all the long day she hadn't asked him a thing about a voyage as exciting as anything in one of Mr. Twain's books. Reed kept exchanging long-suffering glances with Lucinda, who was as bored with business talk as he, and both of them had all they could do not to giggle.

For his part, Scott found it difficult to convey, even to his interested mother, the excitement he'd felt on meeting Mr. Frick and seeing with his own eyes the enterprise they were involved with. Mr. Frick had met him at the station in a handsome gig, and before they exchanged any words Scott had the odd sensation of encountering at last a man he could wholly admire. Young, lean, taut to the point of strain, Frick gave the impression of a man who was both self-confident and self-contained. He had quiet brown eyes and a voice to match. Small talk interested him not at all. He drove Scott directly to see the ovens, explaining all the while with a kind of clipped enthusiasm how the business operated. While they went past row after row of small, grimy wooden houses, sullen men or occasionally a woman with a child tugging at her skirts would look out the door to watch them go by. Though one or two of them tipped their caps as to the lord of the manor, Frick looked straight ahead. "Company houses," he explained out of the side of his mouth. "We own the store over there too. We kept going during the bad times when there wasn't any money coming in by issuing our own scrip."

Scott wasn't really prepared for the massive operation Frick showed him. The whole countryside, once gently rolling farmland, was a bustling, smoke-blackened scene of feverish activity. Coal tipples scarred the hillsides, and along the Youghiogheny River valley a lacework of railroad sidings chuffed with engines shuttling long strings of gondolas bearing coal to the ovens and coke to the city. The ovens themselves, small beehives made of brick, stretched out in long smoking lines. As Frick explained, the best soft coal for cooking in the world was found in these hills, under the foreclosed farms he'd been able to buy up so cheaply. The manufacture was simple. The coal was fed into the conical top of the beehive, then fired until the sulfur and phosphorous burned out in a flaming gas. Continued baking for two or three days fused the residue into coal-coke and when the hot cake was doused with cold water it fractured into usable lumps of coke, the fuel the blast-furnace men in the city needed to mix in their furnaces with iron ore and lime.

There was nothing that Frick didn't know about making coke and nothing, as he made the rounds with Scott, that escaped his steady brown eyes—an oven ready to crack here, a gondola not filled to capacity there. "It's a solid business, Mr. Stewart, as you see. You know where you are. Not like oil, where you don't know how much you'll get or what the price will be. They say Andy Carnegie went into oil once, back in '61, made seventeen thousand dollars in the first year on an eleven-thousand investment but dropped it. The story is he went up to the fields and didn't like the smell of it, reminded him of when he used to get sick oiling the machines in the bobbin factory over in Allegheny. What I don't think he liked was the uncertainty of it; oil isn't solid like iron—or coke."

It did bother Scott that Frick had worked in the whiskey business, helping his grandfather Overholt, who made a brand called Old Overholt that Scott understood to be a favorite in Pittsburgh saloons. But when they went back to the Washabaugh House, where Frick lived alone in a simple room, Scott was offered no drink with his dinner. "I hope you don't mind, but I never touch whiskey," Frick said. "I used to sell it, you know, but I always pitied the poor fellows who used it. I've had a bad stomach all my life, and it would kill me. My only vice, if you can call it that, is a good cigar. Do you smoke, Mr. Stewart?" Though Scott hadn't tried tobacco since he once got sick sampling a chewing plug he stole from his father's office, the mood of the moment prompted him to say, "I don't mind if I do, Mr. Frick." The taste was foreign, and he grew a little lightheaded from his first encounter with nicotine, but it was worth it to sit in companionable silence with the coke king on the porch of the little hotel, rocking and watching the glow of their cigars in the gathering dark.

"Mr. Stewart, I didn't just invite you down here to look around. I hear good reports of you, particularly from Andy Mellon. I've been wasting a good part of my time these last few years going up to Pittsburgh to sell my coke, and I think the time has come for me to have a permanent agent in the city. Would you be interested in the job?"

Scott was completely surprised. His own affairs were running in such good order that he'd no thoughts of another position; indeed, he was fairly certain that his old benefactor, Schultz, who perhaps by reason of seniority had been made superintendent of the Pennsylvania's western division when Scott was named assistant, wasn't up to his job. Given a little luck, it was only a matter of time before Scott would succeed him, and in a little more time Philadelphia might beckon. Frick mentioned a figure twice what he was earning, but Scott didn't jump at the opportunity. He would have to think it over and, though he didn't mention it to Frick, whose religious attitudes were unknown to him, he'd take it to God in prayer. And to his mother.

"No hurry, Mr. Stewart. With things running as well as they are now, Andy Mellon and I are planning a jaunt to Europe this summer. You know, I haven't had a vacation in my life, and I feel a little used up. Next to cigars, I guess my vice is collecting paintings, and Europe is where I hope to find them. So really I want to make a change in the fall. Maybe you could let me know your feelings before then."

When he finished his story, Scott was hoping to get his mother's clear and sensible advice about what he should do. All the way home he had thought, and prayed, over the decision but had come to no conclusion. Logic prompted him to take the offer. It made sense not only to get into the business where most of his money was invested but also to get into a business that was showing a profit. Other businesses were still floundering as a result of the prolonged slump. As shrewd and honest a man as Henry Heinz, whose horseradish and pickles were beginning to sell all over the country, had been sucked into bankruptcy. Heinz had the courage to borrow and begin again and now seemed to be making headway, but others hadn't been so fortunate. Of course the general business inactivity had made running a railway a challenge. Rebates and kickbacks to get freight had to be balanced carefully against costs, and it was in this area of juggling figures where Scott's precise mind functioned most brilliantly. Before the contract with the workers expired in June, Scott knew he was going to have a showdown with Schultz on costs, and he was sure that he would win. If so, the sky would seem to be the only limit on his advancement in railroading, which was, after all, still the biggest, most glamorous business in the country. Would he be happy as the agent of a local coke company, however prosperous, when he might stand in line to be president of the mighty Pennsylvania Railroad?

The thing people often didn't understand about railroading was that it put a man with a sharp eye in a position to see other business opportunities, like the one Scott had going with Mr. Magee. It was certainly a factor that made him hesitate over the Frick offer, and it was one his mother knew nothing about. He'd kept it from her only because Magee, who was much more experienced in such matters, suggested a pact of secrecy. Not that there was anything wrong with it; they were, as Magee put it, simply following normal business practice. Besides, Scott truly felt the leading of the Lord in this since he had met Christopher Lyman Magee, the brilliant young former city treasurer, at a temperance meeting where they were both speakers. Having saved the city treasury some seven million dollars, Magee left office to get involved in various affairs stemming from his honorary position as chairman of the County Republican Committee, a powerful office, especially now that Congress's Electoral Count Commission had finally designated Rutherford B. Hayes as President in February, putting the White House again in Republican hands.

When they went to have coffee together after the temperance meeting, Scott was agreeably surprised to find that Magee didn't share the average Pittsburgh businessman's hatred for the Pennsylvania, which, they charged, was throttling the city by its monopolistic practices. The situation had erupted into actual battle over the handling of oil—local businessmen complained that the Pennsylvania's deals with Rockefeller were shifting the lucrative refinery business from its natural location to Cleveland. Scott and his fellow executives at the railway had to be continually alert to offset the tactics of people like Dr. David Hostetter. Having made his fortune peddling a nostrum called Hostetter's Bitters, the doctor put his money into oil up in Butler County in '74. Then he tried to escape the Pennsylvania's rates by forming something called the Columbia Conduit Company to drive a pipeline to the Pittsburgh-Connellsville branch of the Baltimore and Ohio. Up in Butler County they ran into a branch of the Pennsylvania; twice the Columbia crews tried to sneak their line under the tracks in the dead of night, and twice the Pennsylvania crews went out and dug it up again. The doctor finally found a way around the problem, but when he hit another Pennsylvania branch in Allegheny County he decided to think ahead. A stream called Powers Run ran under the tracks; the doctor bought the stream bed. When he started to lay pipe along it, the Pennsylvania sent an armed crew not only to tear it up but to round up the pipe layers and deliver them into the hands of a cooperative county sheriff. Dr. Hostetter went into the courts, where he used up his entire fortune of $400,000 and had to sell out. The buyers of Columbia Conduit set up a terminal at Powers Run and lugged the oil in a 1,000-gallon tank wagon across the tracks to a pipe on the other side. The railroad countered by parking long lines of freight cars in front of the crossing, but other inconvenienced citizens prevailed on authorities to have the cars moved. Meanwhile, with its influence in Harrisburg, the railroad kept the legislature from allowing Columbia Conduit Company to condemn the right of way, and so the oil continued to flow only in a wagon trickle through its fractured pipeline.

A man who knew well the economic value of protecting rights of way, Magee seemed to look on such jousts with cynical amusement and, indeed, admiration for the railroad's toughness. So Scott was encouraged to ask his help in securing some new local rights of way where they'd met opposition. "I'll see what I can do. I think I have some influence over the city council," Magee said. It was a masterful understatement since no councilman was nominated without his approval. In return, Magee suggested that perhaps the Pennsylvania could use an agent in Allegheny County who might do something to damp the smoldering bitterness in the business community. "If you'd let me issue railroad passes," he suggested, "I think I could do a world of good for you. Funny thing, most of these fellows around here, particularly the ones in politics, would rather be able to flash a railroad pass for a free ride than get a raise in pay. Makes them seem like big shots, I guess. Anyway I think I know just the right people to give them to."

When Scott reported his conversation to Philadelphia, the appointment for Magee came through imediately. Not only that, but Scott received a personal, handwritten letter from Thomas A. Scott, now president of the Pennsylvania, who said in part, "You have certainly lived up to my initial faith in you. For once, Carnegie was right." Scott understood the somewhat bitter allusion to Carnegie, for it had been the talk of the business world back in '74 when Carnegie and his former mentor broke up over Carnegie's refusal to sign Scott's Texas and Pacific Railroad notes. At the time, the canny little Scotchman, who was known to have made his first big killing peddling railroad securities in Europe as an agent for Thomas Scott, issued some pieties against gambling in the market that his old friend and protector couldn't swallow. But it was all of no concern to Scott Stewart, who saw in this favorable attention from top brass good reason to be hopeful about the approaching conflict with Schultz.

Magee's new association with the railroad brought him into frequent contact with Scott, and it was natural that Magee should bring up his interest in street railways. He was looking, he said, for backers in picking up some new franchises that had come his way as a result of his political activity. Would Scott be interested? Scott certainly was, for the right to lay track on a busy city street was an automatic monopoly and a nearly certain way to profit. For a number of reasons Magee thought it best to keep the deal under their hats, and so Scott had. Getting the money was no problem now that the Mellons would lend him anything he wanted within reason and with no questions asked. Now the question hanging in the air was: would leaving the railroad adversely affect his relationship with Magee? If so, he might be foolish; there was no way of telling what might fall in his lap from a man who had a grip on the public works of this whole growing industrial county.

Since he really needed advice, Scott began to think he should take his mother into full confidence. If only they could get rid of Reed and Lucinda, he would do it right now. But Mary Stewart seemed to have other things on her mind. "That's an interesting proposition from Mr. Frick, Scott," she said. "Since he's giving you time to make up your mind, I think we should all sleep on it for a while. Right now, we have a more immediate problem." Then she proceeded to outline, as well as she could, the many transgressions of a blushing Reed.

"What a disgrace!" Scott said. "Mother, this boy needs a good hiding. I'd give it to him, too, right now, if you'd let me."

"Now you know I don't believe in physical punishment, Scott. We have to work out something that will really make him think about what he's done."

Reed decided to fight back. "What did I do that was so wrong?"

"See, Mother," Scott said, "the boy doesn't even know right from wrong. Running away from home. It's a terrible thing to do to your mother. The Bible tells us to 'honor thy father and thy mother.' And watching that . . . show . . ."

"Ah, it wasn't so bad," Reed said. "They sang all the old Foster songs, and there were these fellows telling jokes with a Negro accent. There was one you would have liked, Scott. This fellow came to Pittsburgh on the Pennsylvania and said he had an accident on the way—the train arrived safely."

Lucinda exploded into her ringing laugh, and Mary, struggling a little for control herself, said, "Lucinda, this is a serious matter. You'll have to leave the table if you can't keep from laughing."

Scott was not amused. "When are you going to grow up, Reed? At your age I'd already been working for . . ."

"If I hear that again I'll throw up," Reed said, and then attacked with an instinct for the only weapon he might have —a bit of knowledge he'd held in secret embarrassment for years. "I don't know why you are all still sitting around telling me how bad I am after what Father did."

Mary was stunned. Particularly after the move to Pittsburgh, she'd decided not to burden the younger children with the facts about Doctor Stewart's death, and it never occurred to her that they might know. "What do you mean—after what Father did, Reed?" she asked weakly.

"Well, I don't know exactly, but it was something awful. . . ."

108

"How do you know?" Scott asked.

"Moses. I could see by his face every time I asked about father's death that something had happened. He'd say, 'You know all you need to know about that, Mr. Reed. Now you run along,' and stuff like that. Anybody could tell he was lying. What did happen, Momma?"

Although this certainly wasn't the time or place of anybody's choosing, Mary felt obliged to say, "I guess you're both old enough to know now. Your father didn't die of apoplexy . . . he took his own life . . . he, well, he hanged himself in the barn."

"*Why? Why?*" The questions spilled almost simultaneously out of both Reed and Lucinda.

"Well, you remember poor Mrs. McClure. She died in childbirth, and your father thought he could have saved her if he had been with her instead of taking Scott to town."

Nobody expected Lucinda's reaction. "Oh, the poor man—he must have suffered so!"

"Yes, he suffered, more than any of us will ever know," Mary agreed. "And your brother Scott has borne the burden . . ."

"Don't, Mother. It's been no burden. God has let us prosper, and I think we should all be grateful to Him for it," Scott said. "What I think is that Reed here and Lucinda, too, since she thinks everything is so amusing, should be sentenced to reading the Bible through in the next month. Maybe they would begin to understand that life is more than having fun and pretty dresses and . . ."

"Not a bad idea," Mary said. "That will be the sentence of this court for Reed. As for Lucinda, she isn't really guilty of anything, and she's going to be too busy getting ready for the wedding."

"I still think she's too young to get married, and her behavior this evening proves it," Scott said.

Jumping from her place, Lucinda stuck her tongue out at Scott. "Oh, pooh, you old fogey. You're just jealous—or scared. Martha asked me the other day when I thought you'd work up the nerve to hold her hand."

Scott flushed with anger. Before he could think up a suitable response, she flounced out of the room, calling over her shoulder, "C'mon, Momma, I need some help with that new stitch. . . ."

Left alone with his brother, Reed looked bleakly at Scott. "The *whole* Bible?" he asked.

"Yes, the whole Bible," Scott said. "And, believe me, I'm

going to question you about it. You should have been thrashed, too, especially when you brought that up about father."

"Well, I have a right to know. I'm his son, too."

"Yes," Scott said quietly, "maybe more than I am. . . ."

"That's fine with me!"

"Fine or not . . . and your mother doesn't like me to speak of this . . . our father committed a sin when he took his own life, as you'll find reading the Bible. He was a good man, of course, but there are some things you must learn not to admire—even in our father. . . ."

With that, Scott left the house and went out for a walk. Family affairs always upset him; they never seemed to yield to logic the way business affairs did. One trouble was that they were in the hands of his mother who, despite her good judgment when it came to money matters, was after all a woman and prey to emotion. No doubt with the best of intentions, she spoiled these younger children, shielding them from the truth, letting them get away with little or no work, never really punishing them. She even seemed to enjoy Reed's childish pranks; her faint smile at the boy's joke about the railroad hadn't escaped him. And that absurd marriage of Lucinda to Henry Schmidt! When Scott had voiced his objections, Mary Stewart had argued that Lucinda was only a few months younger than Sarah had been ("and look how well that is turning out") and that a decent marriage might be the best way of protecting a beautiful, high-spirited girl like Lucinda from herself. Never mind the fact that Schmidt was becoming an increasingly atheistic idler. Mary was impressed that Schmidt had insisted on delaying the wedding until September when he would be starting on a job. A job? What kind of pittance would he be getting as a professor of German philosophy at Western University? True, Schmidt's doting father had settled a percentage of the oil money on him as a wedding gift, but who was to say that the well wouldn't run dry before snow fell? The worst of it from Scott's point of view was that they were planning to live here, under the roof he'd done so much to provide, until they could find a "suitable place" of their own. It would be intolerable if it weren't for the fact that it would give him an excuse to go on seeing Martha, who fortunately was as different from her brother Henry as he, Scott, was from Lucinda.

Scott didn't know whether he was in love with Martha or not. He mistrusted that mushy word, love, which was bandied about by preachers, poets and moon-struck girls. All he was certain of was that he liked everything he knew about Martha

110

Schmidt and that her calm presence had a soothing effect on him. They could sit together in silence without embarrassment, each reading or lost in his own thoughts. With Martha, Scott felt free to indulge his growing taste for music. Her own playing entranced him. She had a preference and a touch for the bright passages of Mozart, the fragile lines of Chopin's etudes and nocturnes. With Martha's help Scott was beginning to distinguish Beethoven from Bach, Handel from Haydn. There were certainly times when, sitting in the dark of the concert hall with the music flowing around him in a cleansing bath of sound, he would steal looks at Martha's intent profile and feel that he must be in love. The fact that he hadn't held her hand did have something to do with fright, as Lucinda unsubtly suggested—a fear that any kind of physical intimacy might debase a relationship so perfectly tuned to the more lofty harmonies of the spirit. Scott simply couldn't reconcile the gross realities of what he felt to be the illicit lust of the flesh with such a delicately beautiful creature as Martha, or with his own sense of dignity. Beyond that, he'd early made up his mind to avoid marriage until the Stewart fortunes would allow for establishing two households of equal standing, and from this point of view one of Martha's greatest attractions was her age, which would allow another four or five years before a wedding seemed in order. If Lucinda were right about Martha's getting impatient, the fault lay with the way Lucinda and Henry were rushing things and probably tilting Martha's usually level head.

The light was still on in the tower room upstairs when Scott returned, somewhat calmer, from his walk, and he had a mind to stop in and have it out with Lucinda about Martha. He decided against it, however, when he heard his mother's voice mingling with Lucinda's and went on past toward his own bedroom. On the way, he looked into Reed's room. The boy was propped up on his pillows, lamp burning by his side, Bible open on his lap, fast asleep. Reed's face, hairless and rosy as a baby's with a smile of dreaming contentment curling his lips, was almost too beautiful for a boy's. Such a devilish boy for so angelic a face, Scott thought as he closed the Bible and blew out the lamp. It was high time for Scott to take Reed away from this house of women and make a man of him. He would begin this summer, right after school, by getting Reed a job in the railway yards.

A Poor Way to Run a Railroad

"Damn it, Stewart, I don't care what you say. This just isn't the way to run a railroad," Schultz said. "If we've got to cut costs, let's do it some other way than taking it out of the men's hides."

The superintendent was so agitated he was pacing back and forth across his office puffing at his cigar like a locomotive getting up steam. In the years since he'd offered Scott the land deal that was the foundation of the Stewart fortune, Frank Schultz had grown stouter, probably from swilling beer, and had taken to wearing the same dark conservative clothes as other leading Pittsburgh business men. But his language was still as blunt as a stake driver's, and he always seemed more comfortable when he was out with the train crews or yardmen talking shop than in the board room discussing policy.

"Well, they accepted the ten percent cut on the first of June . . ."

"Accepted it? For God's sake, Stewart, you should hear them talk. They're mad, and I don't blame them. Do you know what a fireman is getting now—somewhere between $1.35 and $1.58 a day. If he's lucky enough to work four days, that brings him $6 a week. How the hell can you raise a family on that? And the brakemen . . . those poor bastards get all of 75 cents a day!"

"If you'd just take time to look at these figures, Mr. Schultz, you would see there's no quicker way of getting our costs down to meet competition than reducing the cost of the labor force," Scott explained patiently. "The B. & O.'s doing it, and we've got to meet them. We're not in this alone, you know."

"Neither are the men," Schultz said. "Look what that fellow Ammon's doing over there in Allegheny, organizing something called the Trainmen's Union to take in all the railway-men from all the lines. If it gets off the ground, it'll make the old Brotherhood of Locomotive Engineers look like a chowder and marching society. They're talking strike now, and let me tell you it'll be a goddamn mess if it comes. Your idea of double-heading, as you call it—putting two engines on a train and hauling twice as many cars to cut the work force—would be like striking a match to powder. Bad enough to cut their wages without throwing more of them out of work."

"Then you won't approve it?" Scott said.

"No, goddamn it."

"Would you mind if I sent the suggestion on through to Philadelphia?"

"Yes, I would," Schultz said. "You do it, and I'll have your ass. I want you to figure out some other way of saving. We're having enough trouble keeping trains from banging into each other without making them twice as long with half as many men. Who the hell do you think keeps a railroad going anyway? A bunch of clerks with cost figures? It's those men out there on the trains—the fellow who's quick enough to flip the right signal or grab the air brake at the right time, or the guy who sweats enough coal into the fire box to keep the steam up. Starve them enough, and you won't have any trains left to play with."

For the moment Scott gave in to his superior and quietly retreated to his own office. The battle with Schultz was shaping up just as he'd anticipated. There was no doubt that the man knew how to lay rails, build bridges and run trains. When he was in charge of construction and equipment, Schultz was one of the first men in the country to appreciate the value of George Westinghouse's new automatic air brake, and it was a word from Westinghouse to Thomas Scott that undoubtedly brought about Schultz's promotion. When it came to business, however, Schultz's head was full of mush. Given his way, he would probably run the trains at a loss just to get the reputation of being a good fellow. Successful business men outgrew their past; Schultz made a point of reveling in his. He still went across the Monongahela to his old Birmingham neighborhood, now annexed to Pittsburgh as the South Side, to drink with his boyhood chums, most of whom were laborers in the mills or on the railway. No wonder he was wrong-headedly sentimental about the working man. He would do them more good if he convinced them to make a few tempo-rary sacrifices to strengthen their company's competitive posi-tion, and thereby make their own jobs and families more secure. It wasn't a very popular or dramatic message, but it was honest and the truth of the matter. Scott was convinced of it.

From where Scott sat, labor was another figure in the equation that could come out either plus or minus at the end of the year. And labor was much more of a variable than the cost of something like steel rails which had to be negotiated with the powerful Carnegie interests, and whose prices were undergirded, thanks to the U.S. Congress itself, by elaborate tariff schedules. And since labor cost was enormous, just a fraction off here or there could make the difference between profit and loss. It was Scott's primary job to see that the stockholders of the Pennsylvania Railroad got dividends from the property they owned. They were the ultimate employer—of him and the workman, who was free to take another job or go West and pick up a homestead or work his way into the white-collar class as Schultz himself had done. But this business of banding together in unions to force business to pay wages it would have to take out of honest profits was, in Scott's mind, against the best interests of the men themselves, not to mention the American basic traditions of individual freedom and rights of property; in fact, it ran counter to the laws of the divinity, who so obviously favored enterprise and initiative. If they were to give in to these misguided unionists, as Schultz seemed to think they should, there would soon be no way of keeping a business in black ink, healthy and able to employ the very men who would destroy it. Scott sincerely believed this, and that men in management agreed with him. In time he must find a way of getting his suggestion for double-heading to them.

With his mind so engrossed by business affairs, Scott had recently been neglecting his daily checks on Reed's progress through the Bible. The boy was only into Deuteronomy by the time he went to work as a water carrier for the labor crews at the depot yard, and Scott could see that the time limit he'd set was unreasonable. Most nights Reed was so exhausted he fell asleep after struggling through a few verses and had no memory of them in the morning when they set out together in the buggy for work. For Scott, the daily rides had become even more of a pleasure with Reed along. He was able to display his skill with the reins and soon had Reed responding to the challenge of speed and begging to drive himself. As they weaved in and out of traffic, often coming close enough to scrape a hub against another racing buggy, the brothers would for the first time in their lives laugh together in a shared pleasure. The prescription was working, Scott thought; Reed was becoming a man, and he had half a mind to let the Bible-reading go. Until, that is, one evening when Reed said, "Scott, what's a cocksucker?"

"A what?" Scott was embarrassed that he didn't know and was stalling for time.

"One of the men called me that today," Reed explained. "He said, 'Hurry up, you little cocksucker.'"

Scott was sure of one thing. "It's a filthy word, and don't you ever mention that in front of the ladies."

"But what does it mean?"

"You're too young to know these things. Maybe I was wrong in putting you with those rough men. Instead of listening to that kind of trash, you ought to be thinking about what you're reading in the Bible. Are you still reading it, by the way?"

"Aw, Scott, don't you ever think about anything but business and that old Bible? Don't you think about girls? That's all the men talk about in the yards."

"That's maybe one reason why they're in the yards and not in the offices," Scott said. "You don't see the men who are getting ahead in this town going around with fancy ladies or loafing in saloons. You see men like Mr. Heinz and Mr. Mellon and Mr. Magee and . . . and your brother . . . in church. Remember *that*."

Now that he was out in the world and seeing the way other men lived, there were times when Reed really felt sorry for Scott. Except on those wild buggy rides, he never seemed to have any fun at all. The way Scott talked about saloons would chill your blood, but Reed would watch men coming out of them laughing, clapping each other on the back, making excited plans and wonder if they hadn't found something more elevating for their spirits in there than the solemn-faced people he saw coming out of church. One thing sure: when he was old enough, he would try it and find out. Henry Schmidt knew about saloons, because Reed had seen him going into one near the depot. Reed ducked so that he wouldn't embarrass Henry, who pretended around the Stewart house to like lemonade better than anything else. Actually, Reed was as happy as Lucinda must be that Henry would soon be part of the family. Henry was more of a brother than Scott and, certainly, than Mr. Sharp who was always lecturing him or asking, "Well, what did little brother learn in Sunday school today?" The thing was that Henry would be able to tell Reed what a

115

cocksucker was and that's what older brothers were supposed to be for.

Even Henry was surprised by Reed's question, but he managed to explain the term, pointing out that men who were raised roughly often used such language without a thought for its real meaning. Aware that he might be confusing Reed with a novel and perhaps ugly concept of human sexual activity, Henry drew the boy out to find out what he already knew about the subject. Apparently Hiram Smith by way of Fred Shoemaker's somewhat mythical brother had provided a reasonably basic course of studies. Reed's impulses and curiosity were healthy enough in Henry's view, and, indeed, it seemed probable that Reed was more at ease about sex than Scott. Often Henry worried about the damage Scott's aggressive innocence might do when, and if, he actually married Henry's equally innocent sister, Martha. There was some hope that Martha might learn something from Lucinda after they were married, but who could ever get to Scott? Henry simply couldn't imagine himself, or Don Sharp, or anybody else having a conversation about sex with Scott Stewart. The poor fellow had gone through a lopsided kind of growth. On the level of achievement and responsibility in the city, in the church, he already seemed twice his age while on the level of personal relationships he was still a kind of shy boy, taking refuge in his mother's home.

But Scott wasn't Henry's real worry; Lucinda was. She was still half a child, and he was sure that, despite her preening and regal posing, she had not come to grips with the realities of the marriage bed. No doubt Mary Stewart, whom Henry had come to admire for her common sense, and Sarah, who, with one child and another on the way, seemed able to satisfy her flamboyant husband, would provide Lucinda with the necessary facts. But facts weren't enough, and what worried Henry was that, since they had given up the hand-kissing game for real kisses on the lips, Lucinda's response was only dutiful. He wondered if Lucinda might just be in love with love itself, with the excitement and triumph of making the first match among her contemporaries. . . .

Lucinda tossed through many a night with the same worries on her mind. After that time when she teased Henry about his bank book, he came back a changed person. First, he sought out a tête-à-tête with Mary Stewart to ask permission to become a serious beau. Lucinda was somewhat surprised and a little frightened that her mother agreed. Mary Stewart gave no reasons for her decision except to say that she considered Henry Schmidt a fine young man who would make a devoted husband if Lucinda truly loved him. So it was left up to her. Henry became more aggressive, then, playing to all her vanities. He brought flowers on every visit, sang love songs to her to the accompaniment of his mandolin, hired sleek carriages from the livery to take her to the theater or to dinner in the glittering salon of the old Monongahela House. Though he didn't actually show his bank book, he did disclose that his father, delighted with the idea of his marriage to Lucinda, had given him a fifth of the oil rights, enough to let them live in comfort and, best of all, to travel. The summer after their wedding, he promised, they would go to Germany and live in an old castle on the Rhine while he studied his philosophers. After that, there would be a different country every summer—Italy, France, England, maybe one day Japan and China. Matters like bearing children, cleaning house, cooking, balancing a budget didn't come up much in Henry's glowing prospectus of the life she would lead with him.

So she was sold. She did have passing regrets that she would miss the balls and skating parties and picnics she was just beginning to be invited to by the daughters of the more prosperous Pittsburghers who lived around them. But wasn't the purpose of these events for a girl to meet just such a man as Henry? The open admiration of her friends whenever she artfully dropped details of his courting told her as much. She also regretted, as her mother evidently did too, that she wouldn't go on to college as the family had so long planned. But wasn't that, in truth, a kind of stalling for a girl until she met her destiny in a man? With Henry as her mentor, perhaps she could read herself into an education.

The thing that bothered Lucinda now was that, whenever they were alone together, Henry seemed to lose interest in whatever they were talking about: he was always wanting to touch her, hug her, kiss her. She did experience a thrill of naughtiness from the first kisses in a dark corner of the porch or the back of a carriage, but this continual fumbling urgency Henry was displaying frightened her. It would be worse, of course, if he acted like Scott. Then she'd be like Martha, worried sick that something was wrong with her. She was confident on that score; her mirror told her that she had a body to be proud of—a bit too long, perhaps, and on the thin side with breasts small compared to those she observed on fashionable matrons in their low-cut evening dresses, but white and smooth as the alabaster statue in the parlor. She had a funny feeling about it, though, a feeling that the power of her body to attract lay somewhere in its white purity. She wanted to hang a sign around her neck like she sometimes saw in a museum or art gallery: "Look—but don't touch." Yet she knew that touching, and more, was supposed to be part of love. It was all pretty confusing.

Whenever Lucinda tried to get any information about how she ought to feel about these things, she met a blank wall. Martha, her best friend, had never been kissed and just blushed at talk of it. Other girls when they let down their hair confessed to disappointment in the gummy kisses some forward boy had managed to steal from them. Though Sarah should have been a help, she acted as if she were a hundred years old when Lucinda brought up anything about the bedroom. "Oh, that part takes care of itself with God's help," she said quickly. "It doesn't last long." Although she suspected that her mother, being a doctor's wife and all, would be of more help, Lucinda couldn't think of how to go about asking. Sex just wasn't a thing proper mothers and daughters discussed. The only time it had come up at all was when she ran crying to her mother with her first terrifying flowing. Mary Stewart held her in her arms. "Don't cry, baby, you're perfectly all right. It's just the curse of women."

The curse of women—that was the unfair part of it all, Lucinda thought. Everybody acted as if sex were a kind of curse on women. A girl was expected to flirt and attract men, like a lamp draws moths, and yet she was made to feel there was something repulsive in their getting too close. It was all right for a man to clutch and paw at a woman; in fact, he was expected to do it. But if a woman were to reach out to a man —horrors! Lucinda's head had been packed since childhood with biblical injunctions against lust of the flesh and with the subtler signals coming from older and experienced women who tended to roll up their eyes in pained and knowing resignation whenever the subject of men came up. No wonder she was a little frightened. Well, maybe, she hoped, there would be some magic in a wedding, some special blessing from God that would free her to respond.

Meanwhile, there was a lot to think about and do in the next two months. Much to Reed's annoyance, Lucinda had taken over the whole tower room, which was billowing with cloth being sewn into a trousseau for the parties and trips that were starting now that school was out. The girls of Lucinda's high school graduating class were organizing a picnic, and Henry's classmates at Western University were planning a dance on a chartered river boat. In July they were going to Chautauqua, a kind of summer cultural camp the Methodists had started in western New York State a few years before. Henry had been invited to conduct a class there in philosophy and religion, and Martha was elected to go along as a chaperone. Probably because the place was supposed to be religious, they had persuaded Scott to go too and take his first vacation in more than ten years. And after that there would only be a month to get ready for the wedding which, because of Don Sharp's position, if nothing else, would be one of the biggest events of the year in the church.

The Reverend Donald Vincent Sharp, now the Reverend Doctor Sharp since the granting of his honorary doctor of divinity by Western University this month, had become an amazing drawing card. While it was no doubt owing in part to the fact that Pittsburgh was spreading in all directions, the Oakland Presbyterian Church had gathered in a hundred new members in the first year Sharp held the pulpit. It was getting so the church—a heap of stones with a square, squat tower that Henry dubbed "coal-sludge Gothic"—could hardly accommodate the people who arrived at 11:00 A.M. every Sunday. As a result Sharp had already been taken enthusiastically into the councils of his fellow ministers and of the businessmen downtown who presided over the finances of the greater church. Men he'd admired from afar would often stop Scott in the streets and tell him what a charming brother-in-law he had, and influential members of their own church who had once been content to nod distantly at the Stewarts were now including them in invitations to tea or an evening of lantern slides. Sometimes Scott thought it was a case of the tail wagging the dog, but he was willing to concede that his mother's instinct had once again been more than right in bringing Sharp in from the country.

In his new role, Sharp was undergoing a subtle change in attitude toward the Stewarts. Out there in the country, where they occupied the most substantial house for miles around, he'd been somewhat in awe of them. Even the touch of having Moses in their service reminded him of the landed gentry of the South. When Scott's single-minded drive lifted them into one of the more sophisticated sections of the city, Sharp knew that his instinct for getting connected with a solid family was sound. Too bad Scott was so contemptuous of his gifts, but then Mary Stewart seemed to understand him. Thank God for a woman of such good sense! Sharp knew he owed not only his job but the contentment of his bed to Mary, who

119

somehow had straightened Sarah out in those awful days when she began to weep and turn her back on him and pray for deliverance from lust. It had taken Sharp only a few months in Pittsburgh, however, to become aware of how far down the incline of true social and business success the Stewarts stood. As pastor, he was invited as an equal into the gargoyled stone palaces of parishioners who had been rich for generations, who journeyed regularly to Europe and summered in Newport or Long Branch, whose sons went to Princeton and whose daughters married titled nobility. Sharp could afford now to play a kind of suave, patronizing elder brother to Scott, turning away his ill-humored thrusts with laughter. Scott seemed something like one of his own trains, scheduled to ride a designated set of rails, but there was promise in the others, particularly Lucinda, whose spectacular beauty should have Pittsburgh society at her feet. Sharp had been quietly engineering the right kind of invitations for her when the bombshell of her engagement to that weird Henry Schmidt exploded over his head.

As soon as he heard about it, Sharp went straight to his mother-in-law, who must have had a lapse in her usual good sense. "How can you let this happen, Mother Stewart?" he asked. "Why the girl's just throwing herself away. You know she'd be the belle of every ball she went to. In time she might manage to link up with a Mellon, or a Heinz, or a Thaw."

"Yes, and she might be taken over by a wastrel with a handsome face," Mary said. "When that girl is awakened, I just wouldn't vouch for what she might do. I'm content to see her married decently to man who, I know, loves her."

"But do you think he can really take care of her? One thing I agree with Scott about is that Henry Schmidt is nothing but a dreamer. If he ever runs out of that oil money, they'll be begging in the streets."

"Well, he is going to be a professor. . . ."

"Even I make more than the best paid of those, forgive me, grubby professors—and get a house to boot," Sharp said. "I'm afraid, Mother Stewart, that you're too impressed with the supposed importance of learning. I can still remember how you felt about Sarah's leaving school."

"I guess I do think there's a magic in something I never had. . . ."

"Well, if you do, why don't you insist at least that Lucinda finish college before marrying her professor."

"I'm afraid it is too late, Donald. I've given my word. Now

it's up to you to help us make it a wedding they won't forget. Oh, by the way, Lucinda has asked that Henry's father be included in the services."

"I was afraid of that," Sharp said. "Oh, well, I guess it won't hurt to let the old man read a prayer or some such."

So Lucinda was gone, and, with Scott heading for marriage with that mousy little Martha Schmidt, Reed was the last hope. He was a dreadful rascal. It had taken all of Sharp's diplomacy to patch up relations between the Stewart and McCandless households after that escapade on the river; McCandless held Reed responsible for leading his son astray and bringing shame on all their heads. Still, Reed was smart, reading all the time and coasting without any visible effort through his studies. The thing to do, Sharp explained to Sarah, was to get Reed into Princeton. Because it was Presbyterian, Princeton was drawing the cream of Pittsburgh youth, and, if he went there, Reed would automatically be among them. Sarah, who was as worried as Scott that her little brother would come to no good end, agreed. Together, she and Sharp worked on Scott and Mary and finally brought them around to transferring Reed in the fall to the Pittsburgh Academy, with Princeton as the goal. Although he wasn't consulted in the process of this decision, Reed accepted it placidly enough; any avenue of escape from Scott's domineering and moralizing seemed welcome to him just then. . . .

As June melted into hot July, tempers rose along with the thermometer among the workers sweating at the hearths of Pittsburgh's furnaces and along its molten tracks. Reed could sense the change almost daily as the men who used to kid with him good-naturedly began turning ugly. They all knew who he was. "Hey, kid, whose side are you on? You with us or them bastards in the office?" Or they'd say, "Go tell that fathead brother of yours we're going to fight this time." Some even went so far as to say, "If that brother of yours ever shows his face around here, we'll flatten his big nose with a shovel." On their rides home, Reed would pass these remarks along to Scott, who seemed to ignore them. "It's just the heat," he said. "The men are always surly in the heat. Can't say I blame them. But if you're scared, Reed, I'll have our railroad police keep a special eye on you."

"Oh, no, don't do that," Reed said. "It would only make it worse."

If the workers disliked Scott Stewart, they hated what they called the goons from the company police. These men went well-armed for good reason; any one of them who was caught unarmed and alone would likely be beaten half to death. Reed relied for his own safety on his sunshine smile and his wits. Once in a while he would surprise the men by going to the nearest saloon and lugging back a growler of cold beer instead of the tepid water furnished by the company, and paying for it out of his own pocket. Then one of them would run a rough hand affectionately through his curls and acknowledge, "You're a good kid after all, Stewart. Guess you can't help where you come from."

In truth, Reed went along with the men. He heard enough of their robbing Peter to pay Paul, of their meager meals and tired wives and sick kids to open his eyes and heart. Rough they were, but most of them seemed decent men whose greatest concern was for their families. Reed got tired enough himself to understand how most of these men after twelve hours of back-breaking labor could only care at the end of the day about easing their pain with drink and their anxiety with sleep. Only a few were gifted by nature with enough energy and intelligence that they could think about the ambitious self-improvement Scott had prescribed as the solution to their problems. Why couldn't the company siphon off some of the profits on its watered stock that were going to pay for palaces in Newport instead of taking beer and bread from these men?

"Profits are what makes business go," Scott explained patiently to Reed. "Without profits, you can't get money; without money, you can't buy more locomotives or lay track; without more locomotives and more track, you can't employ more men. It's as simple as that, but most of these men just won't understand; they want to kill the goose that lays the golden egg."

The one in the family who could best understand how Reed was feeling was Henry. "Well, Scott's right in a way," Henry said. "You do need profits to attract money. The real question is how the profits are made, it seems to me. Take steel. The big profit in steel comes from it being protected against foreign competition by tariffs. This amounts to a tax on all of us since we have to pay more for everything that has steel in it. The way the Carnegie people sell this to the working man is to argue that without the tariff, they wouldn't be in business and there wouldn't be any jobs. Well, they could be right if they're so greedy that they won't work for a five percent profit instead of a forty percent profit. But, you know, if five percent were all you could make, I'm sure somebody would be ambitious enough to come along and make steel for five percent. The thing is, Reed, and the men sense this, the lust for money is worse than the lust for sex; once a man gives in to it, he can never satisfy it this side of the grave. All these industries springing up in Pittsburgh are being built by men with a lust for money."

"But the men want money, too," Reed said. "That's all they talk about now. They don't even talk about women any more, just money."

"Oh, yes," Henry conceded, "I'm not trying to say that the heart of the man with a shovel in his hand is automatically purer than the heart of, say, the accountant pushing a pencil. It's just that he's usually powerless to do much for himself, and most men in the front office do what they can to see that he stays that way. What I can't understand is how they can call themselves Christians and not make some effort to share their wealth with their less fortunate fellow men. All this God talk by men in power makes me a little sick."

"Me, too," Reed said.

"Atta boy," Henry said, clapping Reed on the back. "I think you're learning more on this job than Scott bargained for. Say, what are you going to do when you grow up?"

"I don't know. Go to Princeton, I guess."

Henry laughed. "That's not an end, that's a means, as we'd say in philosophy class. What do you want to be? What do you want to study?"

"Oh, I don't know. I once thought I wanted to be a doctor, but everybody was against it. I guess that's because my father killed himself. . . ."

"He what?"

"Killed himself. Hanged himself in the barn because some patient died. Didn't Lucinda tell you?"

So *that* was it—the key Henry had been seeking to Scott's baffling personality. The poor fellow . . . he must have been just old enough to feel that something awful had happened, but too young to be understanding about it, and so he'd retreated into the protective shell of that all-powerful righteousness of his. But why hadn't Lucinda told him? What was that cock-and-bull story about apoplexy? "How long have you known, Reed—you and Lucinda?"

"Oh, we just found out a little while ago."

"And what did Lucinda think?"

"She thought it meant that our father must have suffered a lot. I guess it shows he worried a lot about other people, like his patients and all."

"It does," Henry agreed.

"I guess Lucinda and I were too young when it all happened to let it bother us now, the way it does Scott. You know, he thinks father committed a real awful sin."

"It's understandable, but don't let that get to you, Reed. From everything I've heard about your father, he must have been an extraordinary man. Go on and be a doctor if you want to."

"I might."

Henry decided not to worry about why Lucinda hadn't told him about her father. No doubt she would in time, but meanwhile he was satisfied with her reaction, as reported by Reed. Apparently the news hadn't tarnished the favorable, even romantic, image she carried of her father, an image Henry was counting on to help him with her. Actually, if she felt that way about her father's suicide, it might well have enhanced that image for her, as it did for him—the image of a man of depth and sensitivity who finally rejected the realities of an unjust world. (In his rush to find helpful parallels between the late doctor and himself, Henry tended to overlook the doctor's anguish at his *own* failure—at least failure as he saw it. . . .) For years now the smiling, singing, playful face Henry turned to the world was the silvered side of a mirror that reflected to his inward eye darker recesses of spirit. He often felt like a boy whistling by a graveyard in the night. In a way, he envied a man like Scott who could latch onto dogma like a floating log, while he was awash in uncertainties; he envied even more the good fellows he met in saloons, who seemed to find the pleasures of just being alive enough to satisfy their spiritual thirst. If Scott's lust for money was a consuming vice, perhaps his, Henry's, lust for understanding was even worse in bringing him endless dissatisfaction. When she scratched the silver and so turned the mirror into a window, would Lucinda be sympathetic with what she saw? Perhaps, if she saw him as she saw her father. Anyway, Henry was hoping that by possessing Lucinda's beauty he himself might undergo a sort of Faustian alteration in his outlook, find an answer to life's frustrating mysteries in a woman's warm body. He did worry still whether Lucinda was sufficiently a woman yet. He gave little thought to whether his expectations were not in any case putting too great a burden on any young woman's spirit.

• • •

"Scott, dear," the letter began, and Scott felt himself blushing at what this simple inversion of a salutation seemed to imply. He really hadn't wanted to read the letter from Chautauqua aloud, but his mother and Reed were so insistent that failure to do so would be an embarrassing admission that there was something secret going on between him and Martha Schmidt.

"You'd better read it," Reed told him, "because I'll bet we're never going to hear from Lucinda. I'll bet she's spending all her time spooning with Henry."

"Reed!" his mother said.

"Well, that's what they do. You ought to see them when they're supposed to be talking on the porch."

"And you oughtn't to see them. Shame on you for spying!"

"I wasn't spying. I was just walking through the yard."

"From now on, you should keep your eyes where they belong—straight ahead. Now go on, read, Scott."

Scott cleared his throat and began. "Scott dear . . . You should be here, you really should. Every few minutes, it seems to me, one or the other of us is saying, 'Oh, how Scott would love this!' The place is quaint as can be. We live in a little gingerbread house that looks like something in a picture postcard of the Swiss Alps. Lucinda and I share one bedroom up under the eaves, and Henry has the other all to himself. The weather is cool at night and warm enough in the daytime to go bathing in Lake Chautauqua. But the thing you would like most is the atmosphere of Christian worship that's everywhere here on the 'grounds'—that's what they call the place. Every Sunday morning, *everybody*—three thousand they said last week—gathers in the open air to sing hymns and listen to a sermon by a famous preacher (not always Methodist, there was a Presbyterian last Sunday) and on Sunday nights there are vespers. Every night of the week, chimes sing the whole grounds to sleep with your favorite hymn tunes.

"Most days there is a lecture on some subject related to religion, like Henry's. You would be amazed at your future brother-in-law, he is really interesting. Lucinda and I started out sitting in back and trying not to make faces at him and we've ended up sitting in front really listening. Although he doesn't have that honey accent, he's every bit as good at talking as Mr. Sharp. I think I should warn you that you are going to have a hard time holding your own at family dinners from now on . . ."

"That'll be the day," Reed interrupted.

Mary Stewart looked up from her sewing. "Hush, Reed. You see, Scott, I knew that young man had a talent. Go on."

"A lot of the speakers are missionaries telling about their

adventures in places like Africa and China and asking for money to help out the poor heathen they work among. When I hear them I feel proud to know a person like you that's so generous with your tithe. . . ."

"You tithe, Scott?" Mary asked. "You didn't tell me that."

"Well"—Scott flushed—"you aren't supposed to give your alms before men. I just give from my salary, not the money coming in from our investments. I didn't mean to tell Martha, but somehow the subject came up . . ."

"Oh, don't apologize, Scott. I'm proud of you, even though I wonder sometimes whether you couldn't do more good with the money right down here in the South Side than sending it off to China with some missionary."

"Yeah, I work with men right now not making as much money as that tithe you give and trying to feed six children," Reed said.

"Look, that's unfair. I'm not in the business of running a private charity. When I give money to the church, I know it is going into doing the Lord's work. The people you're talking about have heard the gospel; if they choose to ignore it, that's their business. Missionaries are carrying the Word to the heathen, who through no fault of their own have no chance at all for salvation unless they're reached in time. . . . Besides, if I gave every cent we have, it would literally be a drop in the bucket spread out among all the men."

"I just hope the heathen never find out what it's like to be saved if it means working on your railroad in Pittsburgh," Reed said. "I'd like to hear what those coolies who laid the Union Pacific would tell their friends back in China about our good old Christian civilization."

"Reed, wherever do you get such thoughts?" Mary asked.

"Probably from Henry," Scott said.

"Well, you're the one who thought working on the railroad would make a man of me," Reed came back at him.

"Now, boys," Mary said, "I want to hear the rest of what Martha has to say. Please go on, Scott."

He was glad to, if it meant cutting off Reed. ". . . When they aren't having services, they are having music. One night there was quite a good brass band from the little town of Mayville at the end of the lake. Another night they put a whole choir on a big boat and anchored just off shore. They sang Handel and all the things you like and afterwards shot fireworks into the sky. It was just beautiful.

"I'd like to come back here someday, and if I do I'll know to bring warmer clothes next time. There is no heat anywhere

126

except in the kitchens, and the chill gets into everything. I've been coughing a lot, but the cold doesn't seem to bother Lucinda. She is just scandalous, she says Henry warms her up. Tell your mother not to worry, though. I've been with them every minute and haven't seen anything improper going on. Give my regards to your mother and Reed. I do hope the strike doesn't happen, although Henry is sure that it will. He says when enough men don't get enough bread they finally pull down the granary. And do you know what that sister of yours said? She said, 'I agree with Marie Antoinette—let them eat cake.' I think Henry would have killed her if he didn't worship her. Oh, how I wish all this trouble hadn't happened so that you could be with us. Maybe another time. Your [no "s," just "your," a signal as strong as the salutation] Martha."

"Well, it does sound like they're having a good time," Mary said. "Poor Scott, you have all the worst luck."

"I wouldn't say so, Mother. This actually might be good luck for me. As I told you, Schultz is on the way out if my idea saves as much money as I think it will. . . ."

The chance Scott had been looking for came in the early weeks of July when Thomas Scott came on from Philadelphia, mainly to urge more labor economy in the western division. They were sitting around Schultz's office discussing the possibilities when Scott said, "Have you ever thought of double-heading, Mr. Scott? That way you could cut your train force almost in half."

"Well, Stewart, that's a very interesting notion. . . . What do you think, Schultz?"

Schultz was scalding Scott with such a look that he might reasonably have feared for his life if the president hadn't been in the room with them. "Stewart knows damn well what I think of that. I think it stinks to heaven. In the first place, a train that large would be a hell of a lot harder to control. I wouldn't vouch for the safety. In the second place, it'll surely bring on a strike."

"As to your first place," Thomas Scott reasoned in his quiet, commanding voice, "we won't know till we try, will we? Your longest suit has always been that you have the guts to try something new, and I don't see why you should balk at this. And as to your second place, the way we feel in Philadelphia is that nothing could be better. We've been trying for a long time to get a showdown with these union fellows and let them know just who runs this railroad. We're not going to give in like the steel people did last year."

"But I tell you, Mr. Scott," Schultz argued, "this just isn't the time for it. The feeling's damned ugly around here. I know these men—I get out among them. This time there's going to be shooting."

"You are a stubborn Dutchman, aren't you, Schultz? If there's shooting, we'll bring in the troops—federal troops, if need be. President Hayes and others in Washington won't let us down; they know which side their bread is buttered on. . . . Let's try it, Schultz—and thanks, Stewart, for the suggestion."

When Thomas Scott had gone, Schultz came raging into Stewart's office. "You son-of-a-bitch," he said, strewing ashes on the carpet as he paced back and forth. "I really ought to break your neck, but you've got me really good, with old Scott on your side. Boy, how stupid I was when I asked for you as my assistant! My assistant? My Judas would be more like it. Well, listen, Stewart, I'm telling you right now that I'm not going to have my friends' blood on my hands. If any orders for double-heading go out, you are going to sign them."

"All right," Scott said, "if that's your decision," and Schultz stomped out, probably, Scott figured, heading for the nearest saloon. He was right.

Scott let out a sigh of great relief. He'd gambled on Schultz being more bluster than bite if he stood any chance of losing his job. Despite his higher salary, Schultz's easy-come, easy-go ways still kept him so much in debt he'd once had to borrow one hundred dollars from Scott to cover his mortgage. As for telling Scott to sign the orders, Schultz's rage had unhinged his judgment: no clearer signal of the superintendent's insubordination could be sent to Philadelphia. . . .

All this occurred at about the time Scott was planning to go with the others to Chautauqua. Obviously, he now had to stay on the job. Orders were already out for the first double-header to leave Pittsburgh on Thursday, July 19, and the responsibility for making a success of it rested totally on Scott's shoulders.

A Fiery Strike

The jangle of the telephone in the Stewart hallway tensed Scott's nerves. The instrument, one of the first of its kind in Pittsburgh this year of 1877, had only been there a few days. Perhaps it would prove to be the wonder all the papers said it was last year when Alexander Graham Bell first displayed his invention, but right now it was more of a nuisance. It was awfully hard to hear very clearly what was being said on the other end, and it meant that there was no way a man could get away from his office. That was the intention, of course, when the railroad jumped on the new device and insisted, in view of the impending crisis, on having the first lines installed between the depot and the homes of Stewart and Schultz. Everybody was still so cautious about using the telephone that Scott knew before he picked up the receiver that the news would be bad.

It was Schultz. "Better get your tail down to the office, Stewart. The trouble's already started. It came in over the telegraph that the B. & O.'s been struck in a place called Camden Station near Baltimore."

Scott glanced at the clock in the hallway. It was a little after nine of a Monday evening. "That's the B. & O., not us," he said. "I don't see what can be done tonight."

"For one thing you could rescind that goddamn order about the double-heading on Thursday," Schultz said.

"I wouldn't do it until I heard from Philadelphia, and I don't think you should either. Tom Scott was pretty clear about it. I'll be in the office first thing in the morning. Good night."

Although he knew he was being openly insubordinate, Scott didn't worry about what Schultz might do; the man seemed to be losing his nerve over this whole strike situation. When Scott told his mother what the phone call had been about, Mary suggested that Reed stay home. Neither brother would hear of it. Reed, caught up in the excitement, wanted to see what a strike was like. Scott felt that pulling his brother out of the labor force would constitute a damaging and inaccurate admission from management at a critical time. Besides he was now really listening to Reed's daily reports on the temper of the men, hoping to glean some forewarning of action. But none came, and on Thursday morning the first two double-headers cleared Pittsburgh without incident. Scott was delighted as he walked into the superintendent's office. "Well, Schultz, what do you say now?"

"I say wait and see, the day isn't over yet."

Shortly before ten o'clock word came from the yards that the crew of the scheduled 9:40 double-header had refused to move the train.

The strike was on. Almost by the minute, reports of further involvement rolled into the executive offices. Crews of incoming freight trains were joining the first strikers and taking over the switches at the Twenty-eighth Street crossing. Crowds were gathering in the street to watch them and to cheer them on. Schultz seemed paralyzed; he sat smoking his cigar and muttering, "I told you, I told you. . . ." Scott realized something had to be done immediately. If the men were simply walking off the job, they could sit it out. But seizing the railroad's private property was an illegal act that demanded immediate law enforcement. Scott telegraphed Philadelphia and then went to call on Mayor Charles McCarthy for police protection.

Though Scott invoked the powerful name of Mr. Magee, the mayor only shrugged. "I'm afraid I can't help you, Mr. Stewart. There must be five hundred people or more out there by now from what I hear, and I just don't have the force to control them," he said.

"You must be joking, Mr. Mayor."

"Not at all. Where were you fellows when council voted last year to cut the police force in half to save money? You and Magee didn't give a damn then because it meant more dough for your street railways. Well, now I can't afford to have more than a few deskmen at work during the daytime. And let me tell you another thing, Mr. Stewart, the people of this city are in sympathy with the strike. You Pennsylvania fellows have had it your own way around here long enough."

Scott could see that there was no use in wasting time with a small-minded politician who was using the situation to settle old scores. He went on to the office of Allegheny County Sheriff Fife, who wasn't much more help than the mayor. "Look, Stewart, I could try to raise a force of deputies," he said, "but I don't think they'd do you much good. Folks around here think maybe the trainmen have a better break coming to them, and I don't think any deputies I could get would move in on the strikers."

"Then wire Harrisburg for the militia," Scott said. "They're already backing trains up as far as the depot, and I gather looters are breaking into the cars. You know the county's going to be held responsible for any damages."

"All right, all right," the sheriff said. "I'll try Harrisburg."

By the time Scott got back to the office, it was clear that no more trains would be running in the Pittsburgh area for an indefinite time. Reports from the east were not encouraging. Trains were still idle at Camden Station in Maryland, and new strikes were breaking out all along the lines of every railroad. Philadelphia reported that an alarmed Thomas Scott was telegraphing President Hayes every hour to plead for federal intervention. While the cars of incoming trains continued to pile up along every available inch of track, and the menacing crowds in the streets grew larger, there was little Scott and the other executives could do but wait for some kind of force to restore order. Scott phoned home to tell his mother he'd have to stay on duty indefinitely. She asked about Reed. "The boy's big enough to make his own way home," Scott said, feeling less confident than he tried to sound for her benefit. "Beside, I couldn't possibly find him out there in these crowds"—and now feeling guilty about letting Reed go in the first place.

As darkness came, strikers and their friends lit small fires along the tracks in the streets. In some places they gathered around them and drank and sang and danced. Near midnight Mary Stewart phoned to report that Reed had not come home, and Scott alerted the railway police to look out for him. He knew it was a useless gesture, because the police, outnumbered, were lurking in the safety of the depot and roundhouses. Scott couldn't know for sure, but he also began to fear that Reed was being held as some kind of hostage.

In a way, it was true. When they heard that the 9:40 wasn't going to move, the gang Reed served threw their tools into the air and cheered. One of them—a huge, fiercely bearded Irishman named O'Hara—yelled at Reed, "Okay, kid, this is where you show your spots. Go on, run to your big brother."

"Not me," Reed said. "I'm on strike too."

"Well, so you are, I guess," O'Hara said. "Stick around then and see the fun. How's about getting us some beer? Hey, you fellows, give the kid some money so's he can get us some beer."

So Reed became the official bearer of beer to a growing crowd of strikers and onlookers who moved in mass to the Twenty-eighth Street crossing. Heat and thirst and a feeling of belonging with this group of still cheery, lusty men prompted Reed to sip at the beer himself. It didn't taste as good as it looked, but before long he didn't care. A pleasant, giddy sensation floated him as free from the bonds of normal responsibility as his raft had done on the river. When the men saw Reed smiling, slurring his words, lurching on his feet, they were good-natured and even protective. . . . "Hey, look, our beer boy's got a head full of suds!" "Wouldn't that holy brother of his love to see 'im now?" O'Hara, who in a way had started it all, was moved to take Reed into custody. "Listen, kid, you really do have a snoot full. Maybe you'd better stick by me till it wears off." So Reed, full of fuzzy love for his protector and for all of these good fellows, dogged O'Hara's heels and finally curled up like a puppy against the big Irishman's sweaty body for a few hours' sleep toward dawn.

On Friday a militia contingent from Pittsburgh took to the streets in obedience to orders from Harrisburg. They were young men, hardly more than boys, many of whose brothers and fathers worked in the mills or on the railroads. They kept their rifles on their shoulders as they marched the streets at a discreet distance from the area along the tracks where strikers, beginning to grow tired and touchy now, kept tight control of the switches so that even if a blackleg crew could be recruited, no train could move. If the troops did get within hailing distance, they were likely to be undone by a taunt from a striking friend such as "Hey, Charlie, where'dya get that monkey suit?" Women and children were now joining their menfolk in the streets, bringing them food and encouragement and making evident that any use of force might result in harm to innocent bystanders.

Exasperated at the impotence of the troops and edgy from a long night's vigil, Scott set out to make another call on Sheriff Fife. "You've got to get some troops from out of town," Scott told the sheriff, who was bleary-eyed and stubbly from his own long night.

"I already have, Mr. Stewart," Fife said wearily. "Governor

Hartranft has promised us a thousand men from Philadelphia by noon tomorrow. We'll just have to wait."

"But . . . but I've got a brother down there somewhere, Sheriff. God knows what's happening to him . . ."

"A lot of people have brothers down there, Mr. Stewart. So far nobody's been hurt that I know of."

By morning the fun had gone out of striking for Reed. His stomach was queasy, his head hurt and he felt as grimy as if all the soot of Pittsburgh had settled in his pores. He had to stumble out onto the tracks and relieve himself behind the wheels of a freight car, hoping nobody was watching. He thought longingly all the while of the clean sunny bathroom at home and then, for the first time really, thought of how worried his mother must be. He decided to go home, to pick his way through the lines of standing cars that would shield him from his fellow workers and then make a break for it. But just as he was buckling his belt, O'Hara found him. "There ya are, ya little scamp. Thought I lost ya. Listen, we're supposed to head for Phoenix Hall, you and me, and see what's up and report back. C'mon."

Reed's real feelings must have shown in his face. "You're still with us, ain't you, kid?" When Reed nodded weakly, O'Hara said, "Good, I told the others you was smart and could learn more than most from the meeting."

It was a compliment to turn the head of any fourteen-year-old; apparently the men considered his presence an asset beyond the mere lugging of beer. As they walked along O'Hara explained the situation. After a night of milling around, the strikers were beginning to organize. Details had been set up to try to keep looters away from the cars—such lawlessness, they felt, would hurt their real cause; other details were assigned to man strategic points on the tracks to keep the trains from rolling; still others, like O'Hara and Reed, were delegated to join in the deliberations of the new Trainmen's Union, meeting in Phoenix Hall.

By the time they got to the hall it was already packed with weary men. The place smelled of sweat and whiskey and smoke. A few men were up on the platform and finally one, a young man who identified himself as Robert Ammon, brakeman by trade, stepped forward. He waved his arms and shouted over the restless buzz, "Men . . . we couldn't get a strike going last month but now, thanks to the men of the 9:40, we have a strike. . . ."

Cheers of "Yeah, you bet" . . . "Damn right" . . . "All right, what're we going to do with it? I'll tell you what we're going to do with it. We're going to win!"

Followed by applause, whistles, shouts of "victory to the workers!"

"We're going to shove those double-headers right up the company's caboose. . . ."

Laughter, more whistles, cheers.

". . . And we're going to get our wages back to what they were before June 1. You with us? Stand up!"

The men surged to their feet yelling affirmation. Reed found himself shouting along with the rest and vowed to himself he also wouldn't desert the cause.

"All right," Ammon bellowed over the din. "Out with you now. Out there on the lines and keep those trains from running until old Tom Scott says uncle. . . ."

In a way Tom Scott was already saying uncle—his hourly telegraphic barrage of the White House was into its second day. He wasn't alone . . . Maryland's Governor Carroll was also seeking aid from President Hayes, his militia being unable to move trains through Camden Station even after shooting down ten people. There was no reason to suppose that the Pennsylvania militiamen from Philadelphia would do any better in Pittsburgh. As the strike spread through West Virginia and on to Ohio and Illinois, politicians, preachers, and press joined in the clamor for federal intervention. A true revolution seemed at hand.

By noon Saturday, July 21, the Philadelphia Hussars accompanied by a battery of artillery reached Pittsburgh. Their train, brought west through hostile junctions only by a bristling show of force, was halted far east of the city by the backup of idle cars. They detrained and marched arms at the ready toward Liberty Avenue and Twenty-eighth Street, still the scene of major action. The crowds at first parted in angry silence to let them through. Then somebody started throwing stones. Frightened, the troops closed ranks, firing one volley and then another into the wall of people surrounding them. People fell screaming and bleeding to the streets. The noise of the firing drew more people on the run. A thousand steel workers, marching in formation from their South Side mills, moved steadily toward a confrontation with the troops. The crowd became a thing alive, a kind of headless monster, swelling and swelling until more than twenty thousand screaming people were pressing in around the militiamen. Those who didn't move forward were shoved aside or trampled. Somebody got the idea of breaking into the Great Western Gun Works and other weapon shops nearby. Guns were passed around, and snipers began picking off soldiers. The overwhelmed Hussars ran for the shelter of an engine roundhouse—a natural fort with its sturdy iron shell; the river of people broke against the walls of the roundhouse and flowed down along the tracks. Some began breaking into freight cars, others smashed into the shops lining the streets near the tracks; stolen whiskey and beer flowed from hand to hand.

By nightfall the battle was a standoff. Twenty bodies had been counted in the streets, and another twenty-nine wounded had been taken to hospitals. Frustrated, the crowd hissed and snarled at the gates of the roundhouse but was driven off again and again by fire from the troops. Somebody got the notion of burning them out. A gondola loaded with coke was doused with petroleum and set afire to become a soaring torch. Straining backs and shoulders set the flaming car to rolling toward the roundhouse; it fetched up against a wooden sand house that burst into a satisfying shower of brilliant sparks that rained down on the roundhouse. But choking in the heat and smoke, the soldiers stayed in their fort. Meanwhile the crowd, diverted and pleased by the fireworks, began spreading the flame from car to car. More than a thousand cars stood between the roundhouse and the depot at Washington Street, and the fire moved west in glowing ribbons toward the building where Scott Stewart, Schultz and their assistants still manned their offices in helpless frustration.

"Well, we're next," Schultz said.

"This building will never catch fire," Scott said.

"Wanna bet? They'll see to it. Burn us out like rats. This is no longer a strike. It's a riot."

Aroused by fire and excited by the possibilities of getting their hands on goods they'd been without during the depression years, the crowd began a major assault. While some men leaped from car to car with flaming torches, others ran ahead of them with heavy sledgehammers, breaking open the doors and heaving whatever they found to those around them. Along Liberty Avenue the tracks ran some fifteen feet above street level, and bags and boxes broke as they fell to the ground, spilling hams and Bibles, umbrellas and bacon, flour and fruit. Men, women and children dove into the plunder. Women literally waded in flour, pulled up their skirts as makeshift bags to carry it away in. Men brought carts and wheelbarrows and heaped them with anything they could lay hands on. A pall of smoke denser than usual held back Sunday's dawn in Pittsburgh, but the whole area along the tracks where the looters worked feverishly as a colony of ants was eerily lit by what rapidly was becoming a wall of fire.

Officials of the city and railroad still had hopes that the Hussars might be able to restore some sort of order, but at seven in the morning, when they broke out of the roundhouse, the mob, hundreds of whom were by now armed, attacked them. Another twenty people and half a dozen troops were killed in the running battle that continued until the Hussars had retreated across the Allegheny River to Sharpsburg. Meanwhile, some rioters had commandeered a cannon to drive off firemen who tried to reach the scene. Bolder now, they put their flaming torches to the roundhouses and other buildings of the Pennsylvania's outer depot and then headed downtown for the Union Depot and Hotel at Washington Street, a structure that was considered a marvel of modern architecture and the impressive symbol of the Pennsylvania's dominance in Pittsburgh.

By Sunday noon, the mood of panic all around him was at last getting to Scott Stewart. For a time the sustaining power of prayer had enabled him to present what he hoped was a face of calm leadership to the clerks and other executives around him. Now even that seemed to be failing. Since early morning when first reports of the militia's retreat came in, he'd been organizing everybody, including an increasingly distraught Schultz, into the task of sorting out important records in the event they had to abandon the offices. A supposedly fireproof safe was stuffed to overflowing, and the rest were assigned to each man to carry as a personal responsibility. All the while Scott kept in telegraphic contact with Philadelphia, but Tom Scott and his top lieutenants were taking their Sunday ease as usual. And as if his situation at the depot weren't bad enough, he was harried by phone calls from a frantic Mary Stewart, who reported that Reed still hadn't appeared. Sarah and Don Sharp had moved in with her to keep a prayerful watch for both sons, and a special service had been held that morning at Oakland Presbyterian Church to ask God for their safety. Where was God, Scott wondered. How could He loose such fury on a good city like Pittsburgh? He looked out the window at the crowds thickening around the depot.

It was time to go. All morning guests had been escaping the rooms in the hotel above as fast as they could pack. Ticket agents, porters, railroad police had long since deserted their posts. Except for Scott and his force, the building was an abandoned shell. Nobody seemed to care about them; they could hear voices calling for the torch and shouting, "Give them hell. . . ." Did they want blood as well as fire? Only one way to find out. "We'll all go together," Scott said. "United, we ought to be stronger than a mob." Since there were only eight of them, Scott's suggestion met with a good deal of frightened skepticism. "I think we'd do better going out one by one," a man said. "Why don't we wait till the fire really starts and maybe we can get away in the excitement?" another proposed. "What do you think?" Scott asked Schultz. "Don't ask me, you got us into this, Stewart. Now get us out."

Scott and Schultz kept hand guns locked away in their desks, as many a prudent Pittsburgh businessman did in case of robbery or violence. Though he'd never held a weapon in his life, Scott got his gun out now and suggested Schultz do likewise. The superintendent refused. "I'm not going to kill my friends," he said. "Nobody's asking you to . . . well, give it to somebody else." Sensing the mood of the men around him, Schultz took his keys from his vest and threw them out the window. "Shoot your way out if you want. I'll go alone." And he left, the others watching as he ran across the square in front of the building and into the embrace of the crowd. A knot of men seemed to gather around him, but there was no way of telling what was happening to him.

Now suddenly their attention was diverted as they saw people start to run toward the rear of the depot or strain to see in that direction. "Now!" Scott said to the rest of the men and, gun in hand, he led them in a rush. Nobody noticed them—a blazing car was being shoved under the long pine sheds built out behind the depot to protect passengers from the weather. Though the sheds broke into flame, the process was apparently too slow for the more impatient and several men with flaming torches had invaded the empty passenger agent's office and touched off everything that would burn. Mired in the mass of people that pressed in from every quarter of the city, Scott and his companions could do nothing but watch along with the rest. By midafternoon the blazing depot with its skirts of fire trailing for three miles or more along the tracks to the east was such a sight that people were packed along the heights clear across the Allegheny River and recklessly scaling buildings for miles around Washington Street to get a better view.

The mayor, meeting in emergency session in City Hall with leading citizens, was handing out arms. Five hundred citizen vigilantes began patrolling the streets around the edge of the rioting in hopes of confining it. Their services were largely unneeded. The symbolic burning of the depot seemed to exhaust the lust of the crowd, most of whom were weary in any case from more than twelve hours of frantic activity. As the flames sank and night came on, they drifted off into the alleyways and crowded gray shanties. The wounded and dying lay in streets strewn with rotting produce and flotsam from the pillaged cars. A tired Bishop Tuigg, sent to the scene by the mayor as peace envoy, walked the streets until dark to read prayers over dead soldiers and strikers alike. While Pittsburgh fell asleep that night, word of the riots going out over humming telegraph wires was waking up a whole nation.

As soon as he got free of the crowd, Scott went to look for Reed, and managed to locate him lying on a cot with half his head covered by bloody bandages, in the dim corridor of the nearest hospital, which now looked like a battlefield aide station. A black-bearded giant of a man sat beside the cot, holding Reed's hand and mumbling under his breath. He evidently recognized Scott, because he said right away, "Ah, Mr. Stewart, thank the Lord y've come. Hit bad he was by the first volley from the troops. Right through the face and neck. Missed his eye, though, praise God. I've been sayin' the beads over 'im."

"Been what?"

"Sayin' the prayer beads." O'Hara held them up for Scott to see.

"What's your name?"

"O'Hara, sir."

"A railroad man?"

"Stake driver on the yard crew."

"And you had the boy with you when he was hit? You ought to be ashamed, a man your age, not sending the boy home. Well, I'll take over now. Thank you."

When O'Hara had gone, Scott bent over Reed. The boy had a hard time talking through his bandages, and the one eye Scott could see was flushed with tears. "Why did you make him go?" Reed asked. "He's my friend."

"He's no friend, Reed. No friend would have let a boy like you get into this mess."

"I'm not a boy, I'm a worker . . ."

"We'll talk about that later. . . . I'm just grateful to God you're alive. Mother's been frantic, wondering what happened to you. I've got to go to her now, Reed, but we'll get you out of her as soon as we can. Now try to sleep."

The shock and the morphine the doctor had given him were wearing off, and the ache in his face and head was nearly intolerable. He cried and thrashed, even called out for O'Hara.

A man near him growled, "Pipe down, kid, for Christ's sake, we're all hurting." Ashamed, Reed subsided, tried to stifle his cries of pain by chewing on his thumb. He slipped in and out of a ghastly world of dreams in which crowds came tumbling down on him and shots rang out and people screamed. The helpless sense of being swept along like a chip in a torrent that he'd felt when the crowd pressed him and the other strikers toward the soldiers kept returning like the pain itself. He couldn't remember in more detail, just the feeling, the out-of-control sensation and the sound of firing and screaming and one indelible image recorded before his own brain blanked out—the face of the man next to him, frozen in the surprised shock of instant death. He couldn't remember more, and he couldn't remember less. He didn't really know, or want to know, how bad his wounds were. He couldn't know that he had been scarred for life.

By Monday the riots would have seemed a bad dream for most Pittsburghers except for the gently smoking ruins that stretched for miles along the Pennsylvania right-of-way. Not a major railway building or piece of rolling stock remained undamaged. By Scott's quick calculations they had lost 1,383 freight cars, 104 locomotives, 66 passengers cars and more than 30 buildings. Scott's telegraphed report was received in Philadelphia with surprising calm. "Don't panic," Tom Scott wired back. "File claim five million damages with county. No negotiations with strikers. Help is on way."

Indeed it was. An alarmed President Hayes had assigned General Hancock and three thousand federal troops to Governor Hartranft, who was now making his way slowly west from Harrisburg. Troops on his train, which was equipped with a Gatling gun mounted on a gondola in front of the engine, were under instructions to fire into any crowd that gathered along the way. The governor arrested strike leaders at every stop and jailed them without bail. Finally, on Saturday, July 28, the governor's armed train pulled into Pittsburgh. Thousands of troops spread out through the city, and arrests began. The Trainmen's Union lost its leadership to the county jail, and Scott and his fellow executives worked around the clock to sign up repentant strikers and eager strikebreakers to get what was left of their equipment rolling. By Monday trains were moving again, and an exultant Thomas Scott telegraphed Pittsburgh: "Well done. We've won. Scott Stewart appointed superintendent western division as of this date."

The Great Railway Strike had its effect beyond Pittsburgh. Though the carnage and damage were the worst there, terrify-

139

ing incidents erupted in Baltimore and Chicago, as well. The New York Central was kept peaceful only by the quick thinking of Commodore Vanderbilt, who promised—and paid—$100,000 in bonuses for loyalty. To some the uprising was seen as the first class revolt in a young nation's history, the first glimpse into the pit of rage beneath the sullen surface of growing city slums. To others, men like Tom Scott and his man in Pittsburgh, Scott Stewart, well deserved the praise they were getting for their courage in standing up to the pressure, and militiamen were scorned for their cowardice. Taxpayers of Allegheny County, through their county commissioners, paid more than half of the Pennsylvania's five-million-dollar bill as an admission of their failure to protect property. Whatever qualms Scott Stewart might have had about his part in the affair, particularly after he saw what happened to Reed, tended to dissipate in the aftermath as voice after voice was raised to defend his position.

In fact, when Scott came across choice items, he took to reading them aloud at the Stewart dinner table, where a kind of uneasiness had reigned ever since Reed was brought home from the hospital. "Listen to what Henry Ward Beecher said last Sunday: 'We look upon the importation of the communists and like European notions as abominations. Their notions and theories that the Government should be paternal and take care of the welfare of its subjects and provide them with labor is un-American. It is the form in which oppression has had its most disastrous scope in the world. The American doctrine is that it is the duty of the Government merely to protect the people while they are taking care of themselves—nothing more than that. God has intended the great to be great and the little to be little." On another occasion, Scott read from an editorial in *Harper's Weekly:* "If a railroad workman may justly seize the property of the company which, in his judgment, pays him too little wages, then another man may justly steal bread from the baker whose loaves he considers too small; or, to bring it home, if a railroad engineer or fireman or freight hand may rightfully take the property of the company, which is the road and the rolling stock and the use of both, then the company may rightfully take the property of each of those employes, that is, their labor. But what is all this but anarchy, the right of the strongest, the dissolution of civilized society?" It was hard to tell whether such arguments made an impression on Reed or not, but Scott felt they strengthened his position with his mother and sister, who'd been lending a sympathetic ear to the boy's stories about the big-hearted workmen. If intellectual argument failed, Scott could always point out what happened to poor Schultz, the only one of them who was soft about the strikers. He'd been beaten half to death that Sunday morning by his "friends." The railroad was generous enough to offer to pay Schultz's medical expenses and to hire him back in his old job as chief of equipment, but he went to work for George Westinghouse, who was "nice to his men." Well, Westinghouse was only running a small air-brake factory down on Liberty Avenue and not a railroad with thousands of unskilled, illiterate men from all over the world who had to be kept in line. . . .

Every time these "discussions" came up, Mary Stewart was grateful there was a wedding in prospect. At least it was a happy event, and shifting the talk around to details of the wedding, which Lucinda was only too happy to do, seemed to bring the family together again. She couldn't blame Reed for being bitter; she almost hated to look at his face, once nearly too beautiful for a boy's and now torn with a scar from just below the left eye to the ear. She was thankful for Henry Schmidt's help. . . . "That's really romantic, Reed," Henry said. "Looks just like a dueling scar. You know, in German universities, a man isn't a man until his face is scarred by the sword. That's a silly thing, but in your case you can be proud of earning your mark in real combat." After that, Reed, who had been shunning mirrors, took to studying himself again and perfecting the story he would tell friends about his heroism under fire. That forlorn, helpless feeling of being shoved willy-nilly toward a dreadful fate had been buried somewhere deep in his subconscious; Reed began, like all the heroes of battles before him, to convince himself that his place at the forefront of action was a matter of choice. And the more he did so, the more he identified Scott with the enemy. Scott seemed to have so many on his side, but Reed had the memory of a big, awkward man named O'Hara, holding his hand and praying through the long night of his pain. His case was based on experiences none of the rest of the family had shared, so he couldn't argue with his brother. He simply let his glum silences and his scar speak for themselves. But more than ever he was happy that Henry was joining the family, and he could hardly wait until he would have, if not an ally, at least a sympathetic ear at the table.

Pittsburgh was put back together in the little more than a month between the strike and the wedding. People who received invitations—and now that Scott was superintendent of the railroad they included many businessmen of prominence such as Andrew Mellon, Henry Clay Frick, George Westinghouse, William Thaw, Henry Heinz, Thomas Carnegie, Christopher Magee, William Flinn—could consider the wedding of Lucinda Blackburn Stewart and Henry Shaw Schmidt an event worthy of note. True, very few prospective guests had heard of the principals, but the prominence of the bride's brother and brother-in-law in business and ecclesiastical circles made attendance almost mandatory. Indeed, many were curious to have a closer look at the cool young man who barely escaped the raging inferno of the Union Depot with his company's most valuable records intact. Others wanted to see in action the "handsomest preacher in town." So acceptances flowed into the Stewart home, along with enough presents of crystal, cut glass, linens, silver to make the dining room look like the showroom of an opulent department store.

All this drove any doubts she might have had about marriage out of Lucinda's head. It was abundantly apparent she'd be a princess for a day at least, and she gave herself over to enjoyment of it. Mary Stewart, too, was caught up in the excitement, and mother and daughter were like two girls together as they breathed admiringly over each new gift; wrangled spiritedly about what should be served ("Not even champagne? These people are used to something"—daughter. "Liquor? Not in my house and that's final"—mother. "Oh, Momma!"—daughter.); about what music should be played ("There's that nice march from Mr. Wagner's *Lohengrin*"—daughter. "But it isn't Christian, is it? I thought something from Handel"—mother. "Oh, Momma, even Don says everybody is using it these days"—daughter. "Well, if Don says so, all right"—mother.); about what Mary should wear ("That old thing you made looks like you're going to a funeral. You've got to get something gay"—daughter. "But we can't afford . . ."—mother. "Now stop it, Momma, even Scott admits we're well off, and you wouldn't want to embarrass him in front of his business friends"—daughter. "Well, you come with me to pick it out"—mother) . . . and on and on until the very day of the wedding. What with all the arrangements for the first big gathering the Stewarts ever had—servants had to be hired to help Annie, food for the buffet and fruit for the punch had to be ordered, furniture had to be refurbished, windows had to be washed and carpets sent out for cleaning—the talk Mary Stewart knew she should have with Lucinda almost slipped her mind. But on the Thursday before the ceremony, it popped into her head after she'd crawled into bed, and she reluctantly dragged herself out and headed for Lucinda's room, wondering how to bring it all up to a girl as skilled in the arts of coquetry as her daughter.

Lucinda was surprised to see her mother's silhouette against the hall light. "Momma . . . ?"

Mary sat on the bed, grateful for the semidarkness that would hide their mutual embarrassment. "I just thought there are some things I ought to tell you about what will happen after . . . after . . ."

"Oh, Momma!" Lucinda broke out in what she hoped sounded like sophisticated laughter. "You mean about going to bed with Henry? You don't have to tell me about that. Sarah told me not to worry, it doesn't last long."

Mary Stewart sighed. "Is that really what she said?"

"Yes."

"Poor Don," Mary said, mostly to herself.

"What do you mean?"

"Oh, nothing. What I wanted to tell you, Lucinda, is that it might hurt a little—at first. There might even be some bleeding, but don't worry about that, because it's natural. I am sure Henry will be a very considerate man. . . ."

"Momma?"

"Yes."

"Is it . . . well, is it . . . exciting?"

Mary found it impossible to say what she would have liked. It would go against the grain of all her own upbringing, of all she'd dutifully tried to instill in her daughters about sexual purity. "I don't know quite what to say, Lucinda. There were times with your father . . . oh, I guess it all depends on how much you love Henry."

"What do you mean—'times with father'?"

"Oh, I can't tell you, I just can't tell you. But you do know how much I loved him. . . ."

Overwhelmed with the realization that her own happiness would never return and fearful that her daughter's might never arrive, Mary started to cry. Lucinda sat up in bed and put her arms around her mother and wept with her. Suddenly, Mary pulled herself free, stood up and said briskly, "Now, Lucinda, tomorrow we must see about the flowers. Let's not forget. Good night."

Some things just don't lend themselves to talk, Mary thought as she got back into bed. Oh, how she wished for her daughter something to compare with what she'd experienced that night in the Monongahela House—but soon, soon enough that Lucinda could know a lifetime of love instead of a moment. But maybe that was never to be possible for a decent woman. . . . She just didn't know. She would have prayed for it as a blessing for her daughter except that the God she'd been led to know frowned on such pleasures of the flesh. Someday she would like to discuss the whole thing with Don Sharp, who must still be suffering if Sarah had the attitude she expressed to Lucinda, although the fact that another baby was well on the way would indicate the poor man was at least getting some satisfaction. . . . Thoughts of the baby shifted Mary's speculations to the improbable image of Lucinda as a mother. She could easily visualize Lucinda playing wife but this high-spirited and quixotic girl enduring the drudgery of daily feedings, baths, diaper changing was almost beyond imagining. While she had honestly been happy to leave Sarah alone, Mary wondered whether it might not be well to keep Lucinda and Henry here in the house through the sobering experience of their first child. Well, she would cross that bridge when she came to it. . . .

Everybody agreed that the wedding was a wonderful occasion. The Stewarts had a "nice little house—so quaint with that tower and all that gingerbread"—and the bride—"wherever did she come from—she was simply dazzling." A number of the men spent some time surreptitiously searching the pantries and kitchen for booze, but they gave up cheerfully enough. A prohibitionist wedding in Presbyterian Pittsburgh was not unusual—just an experience to be endured until you could get away to the club. Scott, coming down the aisle with Lucinda on his arm, was everybody's idea of what the hero of the Pennsylvania should look like—tall, straight, severe. And that minister with his Southern charm! He made the marriage vows sound like a love song. The little gnome of a father-in-law was sweet, too, but it was easy to see that Lucinda Stewart was marrying beneath her. The men in the audience knew, some to their regret, that a little oil wouldn't go very far unless Mr. Rockefeller got his hands on it.

Naturally, they were going to Niagara Falls for the honeymoon. Even though it was said to be ruined these days by vendors of worthless notions who all but tripped tourists trying to see the sights, it was still the place to go unless you were rich enough for a voyage to Europe. Since the wedding was late Saturday afternoon, Henry had engaged what was represented as a "bridal suite" in the Monongahela House for the night; they would entrain for Niagara in the morning. The carriage to the hotel was still a magic coach to Lucinda who, buoyed by kisses and compliments, was in a state of flushed euphoria. Henry had never loved her more. Coming down the aisle toward him, wrapped in trailing white, she'd been so regally beautiful that he'd almost fainted with anticipation. Now, sitting near her in the carriage and only half listening to her excited babble about the people and events of the day, he could think only of the sheer physical joy it was going to be in an hour or so when he could finally claim her.

The bridal suite had the faded elegance of an aging dowager —a little musty smelling and threadbare in spots but hung with enough glitter and guilt to be impressive. Henry had thoughtfully ordered flowers and a bottle of champagne that sat icing itself in a silver bucket. Though he had never seen Lucinda take a drink beyond trying a sip of his beer in that German restaurant in Philadelphia, he had a feeling she would like this touch. He was right. Lucinda was more taken with the idea of champagne than with its sour, tingling taste, but she managed to get through the first glass with which Henry toasted her beauty and their happiness. She was too excited to feel any effect of the wine, and it did little to undo the cold little knot that was beginning to tie itself in her stomach at the thought of what waited just ahead. She hoped she wasn't going to be actually sick, and when she retired to the bedroom to undress alone, at Henry's tactful suggestion, worry over controlling incipient nausea took her mind momentarily off everything else.

Henry, meanwhile, paced the tiny parlor of the suite and finished off the rest of the champagne. It didn't do anything for him either. His palms were damp with sweat, and he seemed to have no control over his member that stiffened and strained against his tight britches. He attempted to reassure himself that he was, after all, a man of experience . . . there was the little farm girl in Butler who'd allowed him to run his hand up under her skirts during their sweaty fumblings in the hayloft . . . and there was the time when he went with some classmates to a Pittsburgh whore house, an evil-smelling warren on the wharf. He could hardly see the middle-aged woman who'd led him up the stairs, which was probably just as well. Her face was powdered to a ghostly whiteness, and he could still smell the cheap perfume she used to disguise the grosser smells of rutting. She didn't even undress, just pulled up her skirts and invited him to spend himself. He went limp with disgust, and although she made a try at helping him with her hand, he pulled away and nearly fell down the stairs in his urgency to get out into the smoggy river air which, by comparison, came clean to his lungs. Lucinda would be his first real test, and

145

now that the moment was approaching, anxiety was colliding with desire.

When he heard a rather breathless, nearly inaudible "Henry . . ." he went in to find Lucinda propped up against the pillows. Her face, so flushed all day, was marble white; her hair, unpinned for the first time in Henry's experience, flowed in a golden stream down across her breasts that were rising and falling rapidly, as if she were having trouble breathing. Her eyes, opaque, followed his every move. He sat beside her on the bed. "Dearest," he said, reaching out with the thought of touching that flowing hair.

Lucinda wriggled away.

"Sweetheart, we're married," Henry said. "We have to learn to . . ."

"I . . . I don't want to." Tears were showing now in her frightened eyes. "I . . . I don't want anybody to touch me—ever."

"Do you realize what you are saying, Lucinda? What about all those times before? We kissed and . . ."

"They weren't this . . ."

"But I love you."

"It will hurt. Momma said so . . . and . . . and I think I'm going to be sick . . ."

Henry, of course, had heard all about what happened to girls the first time, and indeed he had been warned that it would probably hurt him too. The idea was to take it easy, and he promised her he would. "It's nature's way, darling . . . now you're not going to be sick, Lucinda, you're just nervous. Please try to relax . . . maybe if we just lie together quietly . . ."

Lucinda saw the offer as a sort of reprieve. "I think I'd like that," she said, and moved over slightly in the bed so that Henry could stretch out beside her.

Henry was by no means sure that he could control himself —or that he would. Wouldn't a real man simply brush past her girlish fears and claim her? Nobody in the world would ever blame him for it; it was the acknowledged privilege of the marriage bed. Even Lucinda, who obviously knew nothing of what should happen, would in time come to accept it as right. . . . Henry reached out a tentative hand and touched something soft. Lucinda shrank away.

"Lucinda, please . . ."

"Henry, you didn't turn off the gas."

It was true. In his excitement he'd forgotten the hissing lamp against the wall. Awkwardly, trying to hide the erection that made a tent of his nightshirt, he rolled out of bed and hobbled to the light. The darkness, paled faintly by the city's night sky beyond the window, seemed kind. When he got back into bed, he asked, "Are you still feeling sick, sweetheart?"

"Not so much," she said, then sighed and added, "but I am tired. It's been such a big day. Couldn't we just sleep, Henry?"

"Soon," he murmured, "soon." He circled her lithe body with his arm and tried to bring her close to him. She didn't struggle, but her body stiffened and lay rigid as death under his arm. He bent to kiss her lips and got a face full of hair. Her head was turned away, and she was biting into the pillow to stifle her desire to cry out. Though his own body, knotted and aching, urged him on, Henry realized he needed to go slower. Relaxing his grip, he began gently stroking her, from the silk of her head, down over the small, soft pillow of her breast, down over the flat of her belly, down through the sharp pelvic cornices, down to the small mound between her thighs which even through her nightdress revealed the downy texture of its shawl of hair. Over and over he stroked her as he would stroke a frightened kitten until he could feel her relax, feel her ribbed lungs returning to normal rhythm, feel her head turn away from the stifling pillow so that his fingers could now lightly trace the curve of her cheek. He'd lost all sense of how long this had gone on, how many minutes, how many hours. Suddenly, she turned to him full face, her eyes darker than dark but fully alive. "Try it, Henry," she whispered. "Try it now."

He was caught unaware, but the fire that had been slowly banking quickly flared. Fumbling he tugged and pulled to get her long nightskirts up. The touch of her bare flesh set off a throb in him he had no control over. As he tried to enter the tight, moist place that was yielding so reluctantly to him, he erupted like a volcano being born, the lava of his manhood flowing over Lucinda Blackburn Stewart in her baptism of love.

Shuddering, sighing, Henry sank on top of Lucinda and buried his head in her neck. "I'm sorry, sweetest, sorry . . ."

"Sorry for what?" she asked. "It didn't hurt at all."

"But I didn't . . . I mean, it happened too soon."

"Henry?" she asked, trying to wriggle out from under his weight.

"Yes . . ."

"Can we go to sleep now, Henry?"

A Castle in Oakland

A maid in black with a white apron starched so stiffly that it cracked when she walked brought in a tray of tea things and set it down on a table in front of the couch where Lucinda and Martha sat. "Will that be all, madam?"

"Yes, Maureen, thank you," Martha said.

"God, how many do you have around here?" Lucinda asked.

"Well, she's the downstairs maid," Martha said. "And then there's Janey upstairs and Hannah in the kitchen and . . ."

"Enough! I can't stand it."

"I'm sorry," Martha said. "Sometimes it's hard for me to find things for them all to do."

"Send them to me," Lucinda said. "I could think of something—the laundry, the baking, the dishes. . . ."

"One lump or two?"

"Don't you have any sherry around here?"

"Oh, Lucinda, you know Scott."

"I certainly do. Well, you don't mind if I smoke as long as he isn't here to see me?"

Lucinda took a cigarette from her reticule, inserted it into a long ivory holder and lit it. Martha watched in shocked fascination. "How long have you been doing that?"

"Months, years. Your brother taught me. I think he's bad for my morals. . . ."

"Oh, Lucinda!"

Lucinda always enjoyed shocking Martha; it was her only revenge against the woman who had everything. The poor girl seemed particularly vulnerable to any hints of the fleshly delights that Lucinda and Henry shared. No wonder. Lucinda simply couldn't picture her stiff and dignified brother and this wide-eyed, paling girl romping together on the bed. Young Benjamin and little Mary, whom they called May to distinguish her from her grandmother, were proof, of course, as she used to laugh with Henry, that they had done it twice, and he would always come back with, "Jealousy will get you nowhere." Henry could get away with that, even though there was a hint of his bitter disappointment that they had no children, because they both felt that nobody of their acquaintance had ever experienced rounds of passion like theirs. They had the scars to prove it—the faint tracks on his back where once her nails had dug into the flesh, what they called the "rosebud" on her neck where his nibbling teeth inadvertently closed in the throes of climax. Lately, though, Lucinda had begun to realize that this was not enough to compensate for the dreary round of her days. Henry was a good man, no doubt. Except in between sex and his intellectual pursuits, he seemed to have little left for his darling Lucinda. So she had prepared another shock for Martha.

"I'm going to get a job," she said through a curl of smoke.

The teacup in Martha's hand rattled. "No! Oh, Lucinda, why?"

"Why? Oh, you can ask that with all your maids. But just try a day of carrying the wash down three flights of boarding-house steps and grinding it through the wringer and carrying it back and hanging it on a two-by-four porch. Try that and see if you have any energy left for anything, even bed. . . . Oh, there is one funny thing about it. There's a kind of a signal—a warning call, really—that every woman in the neighborhood knows, and when the wind's the wrong way and bringing dirt clouds from the plants, the first of us who sees them gives the signal and everybody rushes out all up and down the street, because if you don't get the clothes down fast they'll turn absolutely black and have to be done all over again. . . ."

"Oh, Lucinda, I never thought . . ."

"No reason why you should, sitting here in this place. But I've about given up on your dear brother Henry—I'm afraid he couldn't pick up a dollar if he put glue on his fingers . . ."

"Now, Lucinda . . ."

"Oh, Henry and I understand each other. He's all for my doing something on my own."

"But what?"

"I don't quite know yet. I do have some talent, it seems. Remember those little sketches I've been doing? Well, a banker—a friend of Scott's as a matter of fact, Andrew

Mellon—bought one to hang in his office. He paid me one hundred dollars. I might find someone who would hire me to draw . . ."

"Scott will be furious—the thought of his sister going out . . ."

"Let him be furious. I'm sick and tired of being poor. Oh, why did that damned oil have to run out? If it hadn't, maybe we could at least have had a decent place to live. Nothing like you have here, of course. . . ."

Although Lucinda frankly envied Martha's wealth, she had no envy for the stone dungeon Scott had given his bride as a wedding present. When Henry first saw it, he laughed and said, "All it needs is a moat." Two turreted towers stood at each corner of the facade, a stone arched porch and porte cochere effectively blocked from the bottom floor whatever sun struggled through the Pittsburgh skies, gargoyles leered from the cornice. To make it even gloomier, smoky rain had washed the stone a uniform black. Still, it was as impressive as any house in the Oakland area. Scott had got it as a bargain in '79 from the estate of one of his fellow elders whose assets had leached away in the long depression. The widow was grateful, feeling it a Christian act for Scott to take it off her hands at any price. In a way it was, meaning as it did that Scott was obliged to pass up an opportunity to buy a mansion on Ridge Avenue in Allegheny City, which had lately become the truly fashionable place for a rising Pittsburgh business man to live. Pleas from Mary Stewart, who was staying on in the Oakland house, and surprisingly from Don Sharp, who claimed his church couldn't get along without Scott's steady hand on the financial helm, were the deciding factors. Martha was not consulted, but it would have been difficult for a poor country preacher's daughter to object to moving into one of the most substantial houses in the city, no matter its aesthetics. . . .

Martha and Lucinda's tête-à-tête was interrupted by a maid —the upstairs one this time—bringing in the children. Benjamin, as prematurely solemn as his father had been in boyhood, dutifully and silently shook his aunt's hand and then began stuffing cookies into his mouth. May, still teary and cranky from her nap, hid her head in her mother's lap. Sometimes Lucinda thought that the poor girl inherited the worst features of both her parents. Despite the opulence that surrounded her, she looked at age four, in Henry's words, "like a famine sufferer."

What a difference between these two and the three lively

young Sharps! Stewart, especially, although he was only eight, showed every sign of carrying his father's dark curly hair and swarthy good looks into manhood, and was becoming what Lucinda would have liked in a son of her own. Because Sarah was still fairly housebound with her youngest, who staggered under the preposterous name of Henry Ward Beecher Sharp, and the new one on the way—"For a holy family, they're terrible, they've done it four times," Henry would tease—Lucinda often took Stewart and his sister Rebecca skating or down to the city to window shop and gorge themselves on cakes and ice cream.

Naturally Lucinda was Stewart Sharp's favorite aunt, maybe his favorite person of anybody. She wasn't at all like grown-ups. She loved to skate, or turn the first wet snow of winter into a snowball fight, or play blindman's bluff with him and Rebecca in the summer twilight instead of sitting around the yard in chairs talking, talking. She would draw funny pictures —his father with his mouth open and a halo like an angel's ringing his head, Uncle Scott so straight and stern he leaned backwards like a stick soldier, Uncle Reed with his curls sticking up in horns so he looked like a grinning devil—and she could blow smoke rings that he could stick his finger through. When she sank to the floor to hug and kiss him the way she sometimes did, she smelled good like flowers or candy.

Feeling as he did about his aunt, Stewart couldn't understand the snatches of talk he sometimes heard from his parents about Lucinda before they realized he was around and changed the subject. And now something so terrible had happened this time that his father simply ignored the fact that Stewart was still dawdling over his breakfast. "I tell you, Sarah, this is really the limit," he said. "All that smoking and, from what I hear, drinking, too, is bad enough. But going out to work! You know decent women don't do that sort of thing."

"Well, as Lucinda herself says, it is 1883 and not the dark ages," Sarah said mildly.

"She's always been a child. She doesn't realize what she's doing, putting herself in the way of men like that. She's still a beautiful girl, you know. . . ."

"But she's married, Donald, and Henry agrees . . ."

"Henry. Henry's an ass, a silly ass. Did you read that last article of his? Can you imagine—him a minister's son—saving the church was responsible for the poverty capitalism inflicts on people? He as much as called all of us Christian ministers hypocrites, even quoted from one of my sermons, though, thank God, he had sense enough not to use my name. He's nothing but a communist, or worse. . . ."

"Please, Donald, I don't know anything about such matters . . ."

"I know you don't, and I thank God for it," Sharp said. "But your family is getting to be a burden. Oh, I overlooked that business about your father, especially since your mother and Scott and you have behaved in such a Christian manner, but these other two . . . I haven't even mentioned Reed. . . ."

Stewart didn't want to hear any more. He slipped quietly from his chair and left the room. He didn't like the mean tone of his father's usually pleasant voice, and he didn't like to think that his father was angry with all the people he liked best. Uncle Henry didn't like to play with him like Aunt Lucinda, but he did smile a lot, even though there was a kind of sadness in his eyes, and he knew how to talk to a boy like he was a boy and not a baby. And Uncle Reed? What could be wrong with an uncle who knew how to build tree houses, who could change the tower room of Grandma Stewart's house of a Sunday afternoon into the pilot house of a stern wheeler, who could tell you where all the best swimming holes on the river could be found? He did have a funny scar that made his face look a little like the devil in Aunt Lucinda's sketches, but he had eyes full of smiling fun. When he dressed up to go out at night, like he did a lot, with white tie and swallow tails and white ruffled shirt and black swinging cape and shining black top hat, you forgot about the scar. Anyway, it was exciting to hear him tell about the fires and the shooting and all that stuff that happened when he was a little boy. So Stewart never liked the way they talked about Uncle Reed. There was something about "all that drinking" and "nothing but a playboy" that didn't sound good, and there was something about an "actress in his room" down in that college in the East, Princeton, that made them send Uncle Reed home before he graduated. Still, no matter what they said about him, Uncle Reed was fun to be around, which was more than he could say for Uncle Scott. The only fun about Uncle Scott was his scary house, where you could get lost playing castle and going up all those back stairs into the turrets in the dark. And there was his carriage . . .

Just before his wedding to Martha Schmidt and the move to his new house, Scott Stewart dropped into the firm of L. Glesenkamp on Penn Avenue to have a look at their line of carriages. They had models of all styles—Phaetons, Sulkies, Victorias, Rockaways. Scott finally decided on a Victoria because there would be no real need for some time to accommodate more than Martha and himself and the coachman he planned to hire and because the folding top would make it possible for them to take the sun on nice days. The buggy had been appropriate to the old house and suited to Uncle Tom, but now he had in mind realizing a dream he'd carried since his first sight of Judge Wilkins's place—he would be driven to work behind a fine matching pair. With a rig like that, there was no need to impress fellow travelers with speed; indeed, it was much more effective to busy himself conspicuously with paper work while his carriage wound its way into the city at a dignified pace. Only on weekends would he occasionally take the reins himself and indulge his surprising passion for speed. If his niece and nephew happened to be visiting, he would strap them securely in the seat and give them a real thrill. He often envied Henry's and Reed's natural ways with the children, and this was his only means of competing with them in playing uncle.

Scott could well afford both his house and his carriage. The years since 1877 had been good to him. When Frick came back from Europe in the fall and pressed him again to represent the coke interests in the city, Scott yielded. Even though it had brought him to the top, the railway strike had frightened Scott more than he'd ever admit. It wasn't just the ugly face of violence, it was the damned messiness of the whole thing. There were too many variables in running a railroad—too many things that could go wrong with equipment, with a polyglot labor force, not to mention a habitually complaining public and sly, greedy shippers. The coke business seemed, as Frick described it, "very solid" by comparison—dig an inert substance out of the earth, bake it, ship it at prices fixed well above costs to a few big customers. There was labor, of course, but Frick showed a masterful hand in keeping it under control. With his system of company houses, company store, company scrip, Frick had built-in control over his men. When the stubborn miners of English, Welsh and Scotch stock started making trouble, as they did back in their own islands, Frick scouted eastern Europe for sturdy peasants who would consider a fortune the twenty-five cents an hour they could earn at Connellsville. These eager-eyed young men with their cloth bundles and shawled wives and children were shunted safely through Pittsburgh and out to the blackened hills they would learn to call home. When Scott was describing the situation to the family soon after he went to work for Frick, Don Sharp forgot he was talking to his leading elder and commented, "Sounds like the way we used to treat the nigras before the war."

At a glance of reproval from Sarah, Don amended himself, and made matters worse. "Well, the nigras were happier then than they are now, as far as I can tell."

Scott resented the connotation of slavery.

"We are giving these impoverished European peasants a real opportunity. If there is anything in the concept of America as a land of opportunity, it rests right in the industries of Pittsburgh, where a man can make what he wants of himself, no matter his origin."

"I think so, too," Mary added mildly in an effort to smooth ruffled feathers.

"Well, when you put it that way, it does sound different," Sharp admitted. "In fact, mind if I use that thought in a sermon?"

Henry Schmidt, whose love of dissonance prompted him to add sour notes to the family harmony whenever possible, cut in. "I think you were making more sense before, Don. What kind of opportunity can you say we are offering these poor hunkies who can't speak English, have no skills, fall in debt from the minute they hit our golden shores? And that's a laugh, too. Golden shores. Most of them will be lucky ever to see the sun again."

Scott was increasingly losing patience with his new brother-in-law. "What would you have us do, Henry—just stop making things?"

"There ought to be a way of making things without breaking things," Henry said, unable to avoid admiring his turn of phrase as he made it. "I don't see why we have to foul the air and the earth and the water—and along with it the bodies of the people who have to live under this pall. You fellows are always talking about God, but what are you doing to His creation? If you were willing to forgo some profits, you might be able to make love to it instead of raping it. I know you argue that God gave man dominion over the earth and that man has a God-given right, or even duty, to do what he wants to with it, sort of like the conjugal rights of a husband in wedlock. Well, I argue that the earth and all that is therein still belong to God, and if we forget that we're in trouble. Remember how Jesus taught us to pray—'*Thine* is the kingdom and the power and the glory'?"

"I thought Don was supposed to be the minister here," Scott said.

"You don't have to be a minister or, for that matter, even

a Christian to see what a mess we're making of things. Remember when Andy Carnegie brought us his favorite philosopher, Herbert Spencer?—the fellow who's made competition's jungle intellectually respectable? Little Andy—who, incidentally, I notice moved to New York as fast as his money would take him—was proudly showing Spencer this great end product of his philosophy, this grimy beehive of unrestrained competition. And what did the great man say? He said, 'Six months' residence here would justify suicide.' So much for your land of opportunity."

"You know, Henry," Don Sharp said, "I feel sorry for you—livin' here with an attitude like that."

"I suppose I could go away," Henry said. "But even hell needs its philosophers as well as its preachers. To be honest, I find the awfulness of it stimulating. I doubt I could think in the sunshine. And in a way I've got to admire people like Scott here and . . . and George Westinghouse and Tom Carnegie . . . and the others who're still spitting cinders every day like a hunky laborer instead of using their money the way Andy Carnegie does to live like some king in that Windsor Hotel in New York."

"Well, thank you for small compliments," Scott said.

Lucinda got up from the table. "Time to end this discussion," she said. "Henry, you promised to take me to see the Alleghenies play."

"You? You're interested in baseball?" Don Sharp asked.

"Why not? I'd play it if I weren't hobbled with all these skirts."

"You know, I believe you would," Sharp agreed, shaking his head in mock wonderment and giving his sister-in-law a look of appreciation. "I envy you, Henry. No telling what this girl will do. . . ."

That was in the happy early days of the Schmidt marriage, in the days before the oil field in Butler went dry, in the days before increasing disagreement between Henry and Scott—two, in their fashions, righteous men—drove them out from under the Stewart roof, in the days before Lucinda did begin doing things that in Sharp's mind weren't suitable for telling in respectable circles. Actually, it was only a month or so after the wedding that Henry found himself thrown back on the slim resources of his professional salary. He and Lucinda had the first argument of their marriage when he insisted on moving out of the Stewart household. "I've found rooms in a boardinghouse over in the Allegheny near the university," he said. "They'll be all right for a while until I start making money with articles . . ."

"But, Henry, there's no need . . ."

"Every need in the world from my point of view. I just can't go on eating the bread of a man I disagree with, and I'm sure he'd be more than happy to see me go too."

"But this is Mother's house too, and Scott will be marrying and leaving in a few months. . . ."

"You can say it's your mother's, but you know where the money came from to get it. No, I wouldn't feel a man if we went on living here. You'll like it, Lucinda, there are lots of young people over there. . . ."

At first Henry proved to be right. Fixing up the two little rooms and kitchen was like playing house. It was awkward and smelly going down to the shack in the courtyard to perform your functions, but Lucinda got around it as much as she could by keeping a commode hidden in a corner of the little porch off the kitchen and emptying it when Henry was away. This was a sordid detail of her living she could never bring herself to discuss with anyone, even her mother. Baths, on the other hand, were rather fun. They used a big wooden tub in the kitchen, where they could heat the water and pour it right in. They would take turns in the same water, scrubbing each other's backs, and then almost always ended up—naked and crazy with excitement—in bed. This was a unique pleasure that Martha, lying back in her steaming enameled tub with a maid to lay out her towels and clothes, could never imagine, and Lucinda was not above occasionally teasing her sister-in-law with hints about what went on on those Saturday nights.

There were things about the experience that Lucinda could never really, ever, tell anybody, because they were feelings she suspected a good woman wasn't supposed to have even though Henry assured her that they were perfectly normal. It all began so naturally at the time that it was only recently she'd begun to suspect Henry of planning it. She could remember going in to take her first bath in the kitchen, primly closing the door behind her and telling Henry not to peek. He waited until she was relaxed in the hot water and sort of trapped there and then he walked right into the room, kneeled on the floor beside her and said, "Now I'm going to show you how they bathe in Japan." He took the soap and a cloth and then with his bare hands lathered and massaged her back that was already beginning to ache from toting the wash and her feet that were tired from standing at the sink and then the intimate parts of her until she thought she would jump out of her skin from the prickly sensations all over her.

When he had her all excited, he'd said, "All right—out. My turn—after all, we can't waste water." He took off his clothers while she was drying herself, got into the tub and handed her the soap. "Now be a good Japanese wife," he said, "and do my back." She started gingerly but found she enjoyed the feel of his smooth muscled back and soon was letting her hands wander around, soaping over his firm pectoral muscles and down across the ridges of his stomach. The towel she had wrapped around herself fell loose and her breasts crushed against his warm, wet back as her hands plunged to examine his stiff maleness. Suddenly Henry was out and, dabbing himself with a towel, led her to bed. She was giddy and almost sick with the sense of the forbidden as they explored each other with hands and lips. When he finally entered her there were star bursts behind her eyes, and she moaned her delight without shame.

Afterward they lay a long time in each other's arms, exchanging lazy kisses and the old, old words . . . "I love you" . . . which seemed now to have a new and deeper meaning. Finally Henry said, "You know, darling, it appears I'm probably not going to be able to take you to Japan, or even Germany, the way I once promised. Well, we don't have to go now, do we? We can make our own worlds. . . ."

She agreed. "I think we've been there, Henry." It was indeed a considerable trip from the fumblings of their wedding night.

And so it went for a year, perhaps two. Lucinda realized that, although Henry's patient tenderness had soon overcome her fears of being touched, she had been inhibited living in Scott's home. In the intimacy of their own little apartment, she learned to glory in her own physical pleasure. She'd begun to loosen up in other ways. She fell easily into Henry's habit of lying abed on Sunday morning instead of going to church. Almost in self-defense, she learned to enjoy the taste and sensation of the beer and wine Henry and his university friends used to lubricate their interminable talk. Despite what she told Martha, the smoking was her own idea. Because of her own lack of education, she often felt a wounding loss of attention when Henry and his group would fall to discussing the theories of some German named Karl Marx or debating whether Sheakspeare was better than Dante or arguing about the existence of God. Looking around for a way to demonstrate that she too was a free spirit, she practiced smoking the cigarettes Henry left about the house, and then one night, ostentatiously, and hopefully with sophistication, lit one in front of the whole company. It worked as she'd planned. When the others had gone, Henry seemed less than delighted.

"Just trying to keep up with you," she said.

"I know, which worries me. I can just hear the tongues wagging over in Oakland . . ."

"I thought you didn't care what the bourgeoisie, as you call them, think," Lucinda said.

"Yes, I suppose you're right. . . ."

"Sometimes, though, I wish you did, Henry. I do get bored here and, well, I don't mean to upset you, but I am tired of being poor . . ."

"Why do you always have to think about money? Doesn't anything we talk about over here penetrate your pretty skull? You know man doesn't live by bread alone. . . ."

"But women do. . . . And they *need* things like pretty dresses and jewelry and nice furniture. . . ."

"Not all women. Look at Mabel Grimes."

"I have, but I doubt you would."

"Touché," Henry said. "But it won't be long now. I'm sending out articles all the time, and you know I'll be good on a lecture platform, once I get the chance."

But Henry didn't get the chance. The trouble was that Henry found himself out of step with the popular mood of the day. The men who were achieving fame on the platform were ministers such as Russell Conwell and Henry Ward Beecher who extolled material success, or a humorist like Mark Twain whose satire on "The Gilded Age" allowed people to release their moral indignation in cynical laughter at the antics of Colonel Sellers, or a philosopher like Ralph Waldo Emerson whose gentle message of self-reliance left well-to-do audiences content with themselves. Henry's cry of alarm at the social cost of unbridled individualism was so far finding outlet only in obscure liberal journals that paid little or nothing and were unlikely to bring his name to the attention of either lecture managers or potential audiences. Nevertheless, it was the direction Henry felt he had to go, and he was certain his time would come.

Try as she would, Lucinda could never work up much interest in the tomes Henry would bring home for her to read. But, almost by accident, while doodling to ward off boredom during his weighty discussion sessions with the university people, she discovered her talent for sketching. Even Henry was amazed, but lavish in his praise. So Lucinda took to roaming the city, sketchbook in hand, as far as the horse cars would take her. The trip she liked best was across the Monongahela and up the incline to the top of Mount Washington. From there she could see and draw the whole smoke-belching city, and it was one of her panoramic sketches of that scene the caught the eye of Andrew Mellon when she worked up the nerve to display her work at the university. Promptly thereafter she announced she was going out to try and earn some money.

As for himself, Henry was beginning to worry he never would make a success and even more that he had somehow damaged his beautiful Lucinda. Though only twenty-four, she was beginning to show a slight bend at her shoulders and faint worry lines between her clear eyes. They grieved him, as it would grieve a sculptor to see his best work of art eroding. The irony of the game they'd played so long haunted him; she still wanted to be the princess he'd promised she'd become . . . and he was failing her. Was it fair for him to cage so rare and lovely a bird? Her beauty alone would guarantee the flight she so wanted. Letting her try her wings would certainly be better than losing her through some grinding change of character. There would probably be hell to pay from her family, but he told her . . . "Go ahead, and God bless you, I hope you make a million. At least then we can support the revolution."

"Not before I have a house and carriage," Lucinda said.

"Of course," Henry agreed. "Seriously, Lucinda, I want it clearly understood that anything you make is yours. I don't need it. I'm just sorry I can't give you more. Lovelace said it for me . . . 'I could not love thee, dear, so much, loved I not honor more.' " He smiled.

"Well, that's all right, Henry, I understand, or at least I think I do. Anyway, I'll always love the way you rub my back. . . ."

Reed was the only person in the family who wasn't shaken by Lucinda's decision to look for work. Unemployed himself, he spent much of his time sitting around the Schmidts' little apartment drinking beer and discussing life with a capital L with Lucinda and Henry. He wasn't at all sure what he wanted to do. There were times when he thought of enrolling for classes and finishing his education, but he had a yen for some kind of action. Besides, there was this girl he thought he was sweet on and he didn't want to drag her through the grubby sort of existence that was threatening to take some of the sparkle out of his lively sister. He didn't blame Lucinda for wanting to get out and do something for herself; in fact, one reason he was in love with Alma was that she had the same kind of independent spirit. Reed's trouble was that unlike Lucinda or even Henry he didn't have any discernible talent, except perhaps the rather vague one of being able to get along with people. Though it might be useful in business—"you could sell ice boxes to Eskimos," Henry had assured him—he got a shuddering yawn every time he thought about a life like Scott's, and while he wasn't as extreme as Henry on the subject, his experiences in the railway strike had left him with a strong bias against the front-office people of most successful concerns. So that summer of '83 Reed drifted through the current of idle days with an eye out for the right challenge, as he had been drifting for some time now. Steadier members of the family like Scott and Donald Sharp were concerned that Reed would come to no good end—certainly, despite all their efforts, the beginning wasn't promising.

At Pittsburgh Academy and then at Princeton, Reed had become the center of a coterie of very rich young Pittsburghers. His scar, as Henry had suggested, proved to be more a combat decoration than a disfigurement in the eyes of the sheltered boys he first met at the academy. Because of his experiences, Reed knew language they'd never heard, could drink beer and chew tobacco without getting sick, was able to describe in graphic detail the illicit delights of a high-kicking chorus line. Reed drew followers like a pie draws flies, but he began to learn that the price of such popularity was the invention of ever more daring escapades. Whatever it was in Reed that had prompted him to raft down the river and to throw in with the strikers rose to the occasion. He was the first of his group to get roaring drunk, the first to take up with the new fashion of smoking cigarettes, the first to kiss Alma Jones, the reigning queen of such youthful society as Pittsburgh boasted, the first to learn the game of tennis on the first court in the area, which he persuaded his mother to build back of the Stewart carriage house. When Scott acquired his Victoria and team, Reed took over the old buggy and Uncle Tom and began setting new speed records, usually with a girl squealing by his side. By the time he went off to Princeton, the family was rather glad to see him go.

The freedom of college went straight to Reed's head. Although his mother and Scott gave him barely enough to live on—indeed, it was the exact amount of $230 for a year which *Harper's Weekly* had reported as the cost of "necessities" at Princeton—Reed's richer friends were always glad to stake him to an escapade. Studying just enough to get by, Reed devoted most of his time to gentlemanly drinking and to becoming so adept at whist and poker that he was able to raise funds whenever he could get up a game. These usually went to financing nights in New York, where he would haunt theatrical stage doors and take off the most willing girl—or girls, depending on how good his luck had been—to Delmonico's for supper. On one of these occasions, inspirited by champagne and the taunts of his companions, Reed invited an equally bold girl to go back with him to Princeton. The next dawn a prowling campus proctor found Reed and the girl blissfully asleep in each other's arms on his dormitory bed—still fully dressed and innocent of any transgressions beyond violation of the rule against entertaining young ladies in a dormitory after certain hours. For the sake of general discipline, President McCosh found it necessary to ask Reed Stewart to withdraw from college.

Knowing how difficult it might be for Reed to return to Pittsburgh in disgrace, his classmates rallied around. The father of one, more amused than disturbed by the incident, offered him a promising job in New York; a Philadelphia boy assured him of a similar welcome in his father's business circles there. Reed turned them all down. Sobered now into a bit of uncharacteristic taking-stock, he came to a strange awareness of the hold that Pittsburgh with its blackened buildings and ashen-faced hills and mustard-colored rivers had on him. It would be there in America's crucible, he felt, that he'd have to look for whatever peace he could make with life. Though he would be lying to himself to pretend he hadn't enjoyed them, Reed knew that his last six years of rakish behavior had been a juvenile effort to escape commitment and to challenge the values his brother and associates seemed to wave like a flag. The only other way he could have followed his heart would have been to cut off all ties and join up with the labor force, but he sensed that, in the long run, such a course would not have been honest. He didn't belong there—he was, willy-nilly, part of the managing class. Through education, or at least the growing years devoted to that end, he might stumble on the right thing to do, might find new values to replace the old. But he had lost much of that opportunity too.

Back in Pittsburgh, the scene with the family was about what Reed could have expected. Mary kept her peace, and Scott raged. Sarah sighed, and Lucinda laughed. Sharp preached, and Henry took him aside. "Well, what now, Reed?"

161

"God, I wish I knew."

"I guess you've lost your chance to be a doctor."

"Not necessarily. I wasn't flunking, you know," Reed said, "I hear they're opening a medical school here at Western University this year. I could transfer, but I don't think medicine's for me. Too slow."

"What do you mean—too slow?"

"Well, there's the grind of all that studying, for one thing. Then when you're through, what can you do? Take out somebody's appendix here, cure somebody's cold there, while all the time your heart breaks for all the miserable suffering bastards in the world. I think that's what must have got to Dad."

"I suspect you really do care, Reed."

"Maybe . . . anyway, I didn't think it showed."

"No, it's a good act. Keep it up. Bleeding hearts just annoy most people, which is also why I've pasted this silly grin on my face all these years. But you can talk to me—any time."

"Thanks, Henry."

Reed did keep up the act. If he was a disappointment to most of his family, he was a returning hero to his wealthy young friends. The story about the actress, embellished in the telling and retelling, had enhanced his reputation for sophisticated daring among males and females alike. Although parents, particularly the parents of alluring daughters, took a dimmer view of the escapade, it was hard to slam the door in the face of a relative of one of the city's most established young businessmen and one of Pittsburgh's most promising clergymen. So he was invited everywhere, and when the weather grew warm enough his friends gathered almost daily at the Stewart tennis court. Under the circumstances, it was easy enough just to drift along, to spend both days and nights in play, to pretend to Scott and his mother that he was weighing offers from the parents of friends, and watching for what he wanted. Both Scott and Sharp were somewhat appeased by the quality of Reed's companions, and Scott was secretly delighted when summer came and Alma Jones, just home after her graduation from Smith College, appeared regularly at the court and seemed to be the girl Reed was most frequently calling on come evening. The Jones family had important interests in steel and other industries, and Scott felt that they might well succeed where he had failed in drawing Reed into the life of Pittsburgh's business community.

Scott, fortunately for his peace of mind, didn't really know Alma. The reason she was attracted to Reed, beyond his rather sinister good looks, was that she had detected behind Reed's playboy facade the rebellion against everything the Joneses and the Stewarts stood for. Though schooled in the classic style of flirtation appropriate to gently reared young ladies, to which Reed had so far traditionally responded (except for that stolen kiss when they were sixteen), Alma was sure that the day would come when she could break through to the Reed she wanted to know. More intrigued than put off by the gossip about the actress, Alma declined her father's offer of a graduation present of a trip to Europe that summer of 1883 and came back to Pittsburgh with high hopes. She wasn't disappointed. The first thing she asked for in lieu of the European trip was a dance in the ballroom of the family's Ridge Avenue mansion to which Reed was invited over some objections by her mother (settled when her father said, "Oh, well, if he's Scott Stewart's brother . . .").

Reed arrived attired in the evening dress so much admired by his little nephew Stewart and obtained from one of New York's leading clothiers with the proceeds of an exceptionally good night of poker on the top floor of Reunion Hall in Princeton. He also wore his best company manners, which included patient exchanges with Mrs. Jones about the temperance movement in which she was a leader and with Mr. Jones about the state of the steel industry, as well as laying claim to as many entries as possible (three, including first and last) on his hostess's dance card. Through the first of these, a sweeping waltz, and the second, a vigorous polka, Reed and Alma could do little more than grin pleasantly at each other. But when the last dance came around, Alma whispered, "My feet are killing me. There're some chairs on the terrace. Do you mind?"

Reed didn't mind. The years had been kind to Alma Jones, who had lengthened out from a butter ball of a girl into a tall, handsome woman. She had a thick cloud of auburn hair and wide-set, green-gray eyes that invited trust. The part of her figure not hidden by skirts or distorted by bustle was promisingly full; in fact, as he twirled her through the figures of the dance, Reed thought the breasts swelling above the low-cut neck of her gown might daringly free themselves. It was an alluring thought, and it was still on his mind as he followed her out to the back terrace. For Pittsburgh, it was an unusually kind summer night: from the rise where they stood, pale stars were visible, the windless atmosphere allowing the smoke to lie like a fluffy pink blanket above the fires along the Allegheny River below them. Even the smell of the gardenia pinned in Alma's hair won out over the acrid odor of burning coal that usually pervaded the air. "Nice night," Reed ventured.

Alma's personality had evidently changed as much as her looks. When she had settled herself in a high-backed chair, like a queen on a wicker throne, with Reed standing above her, she dropped all pretense of flirting. "Tell me about yourself, Reed Stewart. What are you going to do with yourself?"

"I don't know. Go to parties. Play tennis. Flirt with pretty girls like you."

"C'mon now," she said, her voice cream rich and coaxing. "You're out of college, so to speak, aren't you? Men don't just play in Pittsburgh. I'm sure Daddy would give you a job if you need one. You sure made a hit with him at the door tonight."

"Oh God, I'd say that's just about the last thing in the world I want, Alma." He fingered his scar and leaned forward so that Alma could see it more clearly in the light coming from the windows. "See this? Of course, you see it, who can miss it? I'm not saying I'm any hero or anything. But getting this I also got a little real education. A lot of the men I got it with didn't get off with just a scar. People like your father—forgive me—and my brother too are responsible—although I'm sure they'd think I was unfair to say so. We happened to be in their way, nothing personal since to them it's people who get in the way have to be knocked aside."

"My, you're bitter, Reed. I always thought your scar was kind of romantic—"

"Oh, come on, Alma, it isn't the scar, and you know it. They don't give you a diploma at Smith for being dumb. What I mean is that I feel bad about all the working stiffs who're going down the drain. . . . They talk about progress . . . ever get into a situation you can't control at all? It's the scariest thing in the world. That's the way I remember it was when I got this scar and a lot of other people got much worse. It's the way most people live all the time."

"I guess I've never felt that way, but I think I know what you mean. And I like you for it," Alma said.

"Well, thanks, Alma. But, gee, I shouldn't be boring you with talk like this."

"Boring me? And you talk about being dumb, Reed Stewart. What would you say if I told you the reason for this whole dance was for me to get you talking like this?"

"I'd say I don't believe you,"

"Don't then. That's not important. What is important is to

find something for you to do. I have an idea. Did you ever think about politics?"

"Politics! Are you out of your mind? That really would be jumping from the pan to the fire. There isn't a politician in this city or in all of Pennsylvania or maybe all of Washington who isn't on the payroll of the Joneses, the Stewarts, the Carnegies, or whoever."

"Maybe there ought to be," Alma argued. "The thing is that I think you have the personality for it. People like you. I think even Mother and Daddy are convinced that what they thought were horns are really just curls."

Reed laughed, but Alma went on seriously. "Listen, Reed, there are a lot of things that need changing in this country, and the only way to get them changed is through government. That means politics. If people like you don't get into it and do something, nothing will ever happen. God, how I wish we women had a vote! We'd set things right. That's what I'm going to fight for. Susan Anthony was up speaking on the campus, and I signed up to work for her National Woman Suffrage Association right here in Pittsburgh. Mother nearly died when I told her about it . . . she'd rather have me marching against saloons with her. Well, Miss Anthony tried that, too, but she says now that as long as you let men run the country, they'll vote for saloons. How true! But Mother just can't see it. I'm afraid she really thinks we came from Adam's rib."

"Say, you can get worked up too, can't you?" Reed said. "Maybe we ought to get into this thing together."

"Is that a proposal or a proposition?"

"What do you think?"

Alma lifted up her arms and commanded, "Come here, Reed Stewart."

Reed went down on his knees beside her chair, and Alma, taking his face in her hands, turned it gently so that she could kiss his scar. Reed was instantly and irrevocably in love. He was not surprised to find that her lips were as cream rich as her voice.

A Mr. Flinn and a Mr. Magee

Lucinda Stewart Schmidt, on knees so weak she had to hold on to the banister to keep from falling, climbed the stairs leading to the news rooms of the Pittsburgh *Call*. She had walked around the block three times trying to shore up her courage and once had almost jumped on the nearest horse car to escape the ordeal. Nobody would know the difference. She hadn't told a soul where she was going or what she planned to do, except Reed's girl Alma, who came up with the idea after she saw Lucinda's sketches. "I've got this uncle who runs the *Call*," she said. "Why don't you show them to him? I just bet he'd hire you. The name is Gillespie Jones, but don't be frightened by it. He really isn't a stuffed shirt. . . ."

So now here she was, walking uneasily into this masculine den, wondering where Mr. Jones might be and how to find him. She'd never seen such a shambles as the rooms she found at the top of the stairs. The place was choking in paper piled precariously on desks, sticking up out of those odd new machines they called typewriters, almost floating in the air as shirtsleeved men passed it from hand to hand, often ending up rumpled and strewn across the floor like a rough fall of snow. Cigar smoke hazed the air, and battered cuspidors ringed around with the ugly brown stains of careless aim stood by every chair. Evidently nobody ever washed the windows, which darkened the smoky gray skies to a charcoal hue, but it didn't matter . . . the *Call* had been one of the first buildings to install the electric lights that were everywhere beginning to push back the dark. Men were laughing and shouting, banging on the typewriters; telephones in a bank along one wall seemed always to be ringing. Nobody paid any attention to anybody else. In one corner, four men with cigars were playing cards; at another long desk, men with green eyeshades to cut the electric glare and bright sleeve garters to hold their white cuffs above the smudge of ink, were frowningly at work. Somebody always seemed running to the clanging phones and then yelling for somebody else; in the midst of it all a shriveled gray-haired man, eyeshade pulled down and lips trembling gently with his breathing, slept like a baby. Lucinda would have turned and run except that one alert young man nearly knocked down his chair scrambling to her assistance.

It wasn't every day that the men of the *Call* were visited by a slim, tall, golden-haired girl—a lady in every line. Lucinda had picked a plain brown dress, relieved only by a small white ruffle at the edge of the high collar. She wore no jewelry except for a gold pocket watch, her only legacy from her father, which hung as a pendant by a gold chain on her chest. She wore dark brown gloves and her plainest hat. Though intended to demonstrate her seriousness, the effect of this conservative costume was to set off the radiance of her natural endowments. The young man was certain that Mr. Jones would be delighted to receive her and led her through the clutter of the newsrooms to a cubicle in one corner that was protected from pandemonium only by frosted glass partitions rising halfway to the ceiling.

Gillespie Jones instantly rose to greet her. He was a man over forty, Lucinda guessed, and only because she could detect a slight frosting of gray at the edges of his sideburns and sweeping mustache. But his lean frame, his quick movements, his smile, the light timbre of his voice were all youthful. Unlike his shirtsleeved colleagues, he wore a charcoal frock coat over dove gray vest and pants—no doubt the unconscious uniform of authority. Jones took the note of introduction Alma had scribbled for her and studied it.

"Friend of Alma's, eh?"

There was a note in his voice that made Lucinda uncharacteristically uneasy. "Well . . . she's a friend of my younger brother. . . ."

"Oh, so you must be Scott Stewart's sister."

"Yes, sir."

"You don't have to call me sir, Mrs. Schmidt. Everybody around here calls me Gil. First name is really Tom, you know, but can you imagine being called after a novel—and a lewd one at that?" He said it with a straight face.

Lucinda missed the allusion, but her long training with Henry's friends had taught her how to laugh appropriately at such times.

"Well," Jones went on, "I take it then that you aren't one of Alma's feminist troopers." Seeing her affirmative nod, he added, "You know Alma's a great girl in her way, but she does get pretty carried away sometimes with her cause. You're married, I judge from your name? Your husband couldn't by any chance be Henry Schmidt? I know it's unlikely, but . . ."

"Oh, but he is . . ."

"Well . . . Well, well."

Lucinda didn't like the tone of his voice. "Do you know Henry?"

"Yes, slightly . . . comes around from time to time to get me to print his stuff. Nice fellow, I'm sure, but he can't seem to accept that even if I agreed with what he's saying, I'd lose every advertiser in Pittsburgh if I ran his copy . . ."

"Well, I don't agree . . . I mean, I'm a Stewart too and I think Henry has some important things to say and . . ."

Jones was studying her so intently she trailed off, annoyed to feel herself flushing as well. "Yes. Yes, I can see that," he said. "You have style, Miss Stewart . . . Mrs. Schmidt. And spirit, if you don't mind me saying so. . . . Well, what can I do for you?"

Lucinda spread out on his cluttered desk the portfolio of sketches she'd brought. He leafed through them. "Very nice . . . yes, quite good . . . You say Andrew Mellon bought one? . . . And you think I might want to buy some?"

Now was the moment to bring up her proposition. "No . . . I . . ."

A man rushed in and without apology pushed some papers in front of Jones. He glanced at them, put them down on his desk, made a few pencil corrections and handed them back. "All right, Johnson, let it run," he said. "Now, Mrs. Schmidt?"

The whole idea that had seemed so great when she and Alma discussed it seemed preposterous in this atmosphere. "Well . . . I . . . well, my idea was that you might allow me to work for you. I mean write stories, do sketches. Sort of a woman's-eye-view of Pittsburgh . . .?"

"I see." Leaning back in his chair he made a tent of his fingers and pressed them against his mouth. Lucinda was afraid he was trying to hide a smile.

She felt obliged to push ahead anyway. "I . . . I thought I could maybe make sketches of important people and tell what I thought about them . . . or of buildings, maybe . . . or . . ."

"Are you *sure* you aren't one of Alma's recruits?"

"Oh, yes!"

"Well, I can tell you one thing . . . if you move in Alma's circles you don't have any idea how little we pay our ink-stained wretches . . ."

"Money isn't . . ."

"Money is always important, my dear. But, all right. I admit I'm intrigued. I'll give you a try. Salary is fifty a month."

"Oh, Mr. Jones, *thank* you . . ."

"There's one condition—around here you're Lucinda, or better yet, Cindy. And I'm Gil," he said, rising to indicate an end to the interview. "We've never had anything like a girl reporter before, Cindy, so I'm going to suggest you work out your own assignments with Frank Johnson, the managing editor, the fellow who was just in here."

Jones let her out into the newsroom and introduced her to Johnson, a grumpy man who was chewing on the stub of a dead cigar. He pretended interest until Jones left them and then said to her, "I'm sure I don't know what to do with you, Miss . . . Mrs. . . . Schmidt. Why don't you just try something and let me see it? Come back tomorrow."

The usual buzz of the room had quieted, and Lucinda could almost literally feel the weight of all those masculine eyes. "Yes, sir," and fled gratefully. She thought she could hear laughter ringing her down the stairs, but it didn't really matter. She had a job.

Mary Stewart was perplexed and uncertain. "Lucinda, I just don't understand. There's no call for you to do something like this."

"Do what? What are you thinking, Momma? I'm only working. Women are doing lots of things these days. Didn't you read where a Mrs. Mary Miller was licensed to pilot a Mississippi Steamer, the *Salina*, I think it was . . . the first woman river pilot ever?"

"No, I didn't. Everything's happening so fast these days I can't keep up," Mary complained. "I must be getting old."

Lucinda looked sharply at her mother, who had always been a kind of ageless presence in her life. Though Mary Stewart was only fifty-two, gray flowed through her hair and lines were etched in her face. "Oh, Momma, I don't know anybody as young as you. What other mother could put up with my disgraceful ways? Sometimes I wonder why you do it."

"Sometimes I do, too," Mary admitted, then smiled. "You know, I think Scott and Donald blame me for . . ."

"For what, Momma? For how I turned out? Am I so bad? I'm healthy. I think I'm happy—or I will be. I know, I smoke

169

and drink a little, and now I'm going to work. But this way Henry can go on doing what he wants and I can get out and . . ."

"Now, don't go on so, Lucinda. If sometimes I worry about the things you do, it's for your sake. People with small minds just aren't ready to accept such unusual behavior."

"And I bet one of them is my sainted brother Scott . . ."

"I won't listen to that kind of talk, Lucinda. Scott has been good to me, to all of us. I don't know where we would be without him. It does grieve me that both you and Reed seem to take delight in shocking him. Hurting him, actually. . . ."

"All right, Momma, I'm sorry. But don't you worry about Scott too? Don't you wonder sometimes if he's . . . well, if he's really human like the rest of us?"

Although she didn't care to confess it to Lucinda, Mary often had a heavy feeling of concern after a visit to Scott's gloomy palace. Martha was always ailing, it seemed—nothing specific except for a recurring cough she couldn't seem to bring under control. Scott, taken up by long hours at the office and nights and weekends at the church, had, it seemed, little time for his wife and family except to see that they had everything they could desire in the way of service. True, he and Martha did share their music. Scott had been one of the first in the city to get an Edison gramophone as a Christmas present for Martha, and they would sit together listening to it on an idle evening. They attended every important concert in town, too, and they took her along. It was then, at these concerts, that Mary sensed something passing between Scott and Martha not so unlike the evident passion Lucinda shared with Henry. . . .

There had been something inevitable about the marriage of Scott Stewart and Martha Schmidt. Neither was sure of love for the other in the way people always talked about love, but neither of them knew, or even felt, they'd ever know any other possible partner of the opposite sex. So, goaded by the example set by Lucinda and Henry and after some stiff and blushing conversation about details, they elected to have a simple ceremony for families only in Pastor Schmidt's little country church, as befitted the circumstances of a minister whose oil had run out. There was an air about the whole idea of a honeymoon that appalled Scott; he couldn't imagine what they would actually do together for all the empty hours of a journey to Niagara Falls or Atlantic City or wherever. He proceeded to evade it, cleverly he thought, by putting his castle in order before the wedding and romantically carrying

170

his princess across the threshold that night.

Scott had gone in embarrassment to Don Sharp for ministerial and brotherly counsel on his proper conjugal duties. Himself embarrassed and uncertain of how much Scott already knew, Don had dealt only in the coldest physiological terms and the loftiest spiritual sentiments. He hadn't felt it necessary to discuss tenderness or wise to dwell on passion. So Scott Stewart, in ignorance darker than the shadowy darkness of their massive bedroom, took his bride. The excitement of novelty and perhaps even the sense of obeying God's commands gave him strength to persevere as Martha cried out beneath him. When it was over, she lay like a child awakened from a nightmare, and Scott got impulsively to his knees beside the bed and prayed aloud . . . "Thy will has been done. Bless this union and deliver us from shame. We pray in Jesus' name. Amen."

Neither Scott nor Martha had any idea about the expected frequency of marital relations beyond the biological knowledge that they were necessary to the production of each child. After the trauma of their first experience they instinctively avoided repeating it for days, then weeks and months. When Martha began vomiting in the mornings, and it was clear that she was pregnant, they both secretly were grateful that there would now be no call to perform the marital duty for some time to come. Though at the end he had been frightened by Martha's apparent anguish, there were times when Scott thought of the thrust and relief of that moment, but he prayed the sensation away just as he had as a boy before his marriage. Decent men used sex for procreation, and the coming of a child was sufficient proof to God and everybody else that Scott Stewart was a man.

For Martha Stewart, the memory of her wedding night was something that grew in her mind and troubled her sleep. It was not so much the pain, though that was bad enough, but the way Scott had turned into what she could only think of as some kind of heavy-breathing animal against which all of her powers of resistance had proved useless. Maybe that was the way God intended it to be—after all, she knew Scott to be a true man of God—but, if so, she could now understand the lamentation for woman that ran like a scarlet thread through the weaving of human history. Childbirth only deepened her fears. A small girl, always subject to colds and weakening bouts of coughing and fever, Martha suffered tearing agonies in delivering Benjamin. She was so weak for months afterward that she spent most of her days in bed, and her delicate health soon proved an acceptable way for both of them to avoid the obligations of the marriage bed.

Unfortunately, Benjamin was a sickly child. Though isolated like a prince in the Stewart palace, he seemed to pick up every kind of childhood ailment—whooping cough, measles, mumps—probably, it was thought, from the servants. For a time, life for Scott and Martha seemed a kind of continuing nightmare of a crying baby and doctors coming in the night. More than once they were warned that they might lose Benjamin, and Scott, who had begun already in his orderly mind to make plans for delivering his growing wealth into the hands of a suitable heir, was considerably troubled. Prudence suggested the need for at least another child. Scott had never forgotten the deaths of his own brother and sister, nor his father's disturbing admission to the limitations of medicine. Reluctant as he was to inflict further indignity or pain on Martha, he felt she would be even more devastated than he if anything were to happen to the child. And so one night after they'd kneeled together in prayer by Martha's bed, as they customarily did, Scott lingered in her room. Martha, after fluffing her pillow and getting into bed, asked him, "What is it, Scott?"

"I've been thinking, Martha . . . I don't mean to upset you . . . but have you thought what would happen if Benjamin . . ."

"Don't talk like that, Scott, I can't bear the thought."

"I know, nor can I, but don't you think . . . we should have another child?"

"Oh, no, Scott . . . no . . . I just *couldn't* again. . . ."

"I know, I know, dearest," he said, and put an arm around her, feeling her warmth under the thin nightdress. "But think about it, Martha. Pray over it," he said, and left her.

Not an hour later Martha appeared beside his bed, ineluctably pale. "Scott," she said, "be quick about it, please?" She trembled under his touch, and he would have left her then if she hadn't suddenly taken his hand, resting lightly on her breast, and kissed it. Then she turned her face up to his and he kissed her in a way he had not kissed her since the first night of their marriage.

Martha had more trouble giving birth to Mary than she'd had with Benjamin, and Scott could only thank the Lord that she lived through it. A daughter was better than nothing, so he determined to spare his delicate wife any more such agony. They drifted back naturally and gratefully into their celibate ways.

If they had been somewhat more perceptive, members of their families would have realized that they were wasting their concern about Scott—and Martha, too, for that matter. Martha's invalidism gave Scott further opportunity to strengthen the iron in his soul by exercising Christian forbearance and to show dutiful generosity by using his money to surround Martha with service and protection. More importantly, though he could not acknowledge it even to himself, it freed him from the customary bonds and duties of family life and allowed him to concentrate wholly on his business affairs—and thereby gave him a definite edge over men whose attention and loyalty were divided. Martha, for her part, was freed to retreat increasingly into a kind of musical dreamland. She spent much of what time she was out of bed at her piano or listening to the gramophone. Except for the occasions when she would dress to go out to church or a concert, she tended to move about the house, in long white robes and veils of her own designing, like some disembodied spirit. The purity of these costumes especially pleased her, and she came gradually to believe that there was something in her unsullied relationship with her husband that transcended the imaginations of crasser minds. It was as if they were living out in their lives the ethereal sweetness and harmony they found together in music, she explained to Scott, and he seemed inclined to agree.

They felt themselves fortunate to be different from people like Lucinda and Henry, for all their winking intimations about the delights of the bedroom. After all, they had proof of their love in the existence of Benjamin and Mary—Henry, at least, could not disguise his sorrow over not having children. And this business of Lucinda's going out to work—in Scott's mind it was as good as leaving Henry. The trouble was that the Schmidts' marriage really wasn't made in heaven, he thought, even though the vows were spoken in church and the union eloquently blessed by the Reverend Doctor Sharp. Both of them drifted away from the faith; they never went to church, and Henry's writings were openly atheistic, quoting that fellow Marx to the effect that religion was the opiate of the people. What worried Scott now was that Reed might be going the same way, and when it became apparent that he was thinking of marrying Alma Jones, Scott brought the matter up at a family dinner from which the Schmidts were absent.

"Reed, if you're serious about marrying, I hope you'll also give serious thought to what it means to have a true Christian marriage," Scott said. "All you need do is look at Henry and Lucinda to see what can happen . . ."

"Well, I think they love each other," Reed said.

"That kind of love isn't enough. Look at the Sharps here, or Martha and myself. We've been blessed with children and with the wherewithal for decent living. That isn't an accident, Reed. You agree, Donald?"

"Indeed I do, brother Scott. . . ." He restrained himself from adding an "amen."

"And don't forget, Reed, Alma's parents are good church people. They're Episcopalians, of course, but her father's on the board of the YMCA with me, and I know her mother through the Christian Temperance League. I think you would do well to become active in the Church again. Besides, the way you're letting mother come alone to church these days is embarrassing to Donald. Isn't that right, Donald?"

"Well, I'd rather have him stay home than fall asleep in the pew after one of his big Saturday nights," Sharp laughed. "Seriously, though, Reed, if you are having spiritual difficulties, I'd be happy to counsel with you."

"Appreciate that," Reed said.

Ever since the strike, Reed had given up trying to explain himself to either Scott or his reverend brother-in-law. He let their pieties drift unattended. He often regretted that he must have been hurting his mother and sometimes tried gently to reveal to her his true feelings. She would listen with a mother's kind of bewildered sympathy for a son who lived in a world she could never know, but he sensed he wasn't really getting through to her. He, like Lucinda, was content to depend on her love rather than her approval, and to hope that his own love and respect for her would in the end prove reward enough. In the meantime, he was determined to live his own life, at whatever cost. One important aspect of living that life was to strike off the religious blinders he felt his brother wore. Too young to remember the hellfire thunderings of Mr. Wallace that had so stirred Scott and too critically questioning to accept his brother-in-law's rolling apotheosis of sectarian Christian love (he never said very clearly whom you were supposed to love, although Jesus had spelled it out to the letter), Reed early lost interest in church. Not in religion, or even the Christian version of it, which he knew from history could inspire man to the highest sacrifices, but in a church which often seemed to him to present religion as a kind of rationalization of its members' privileged position in society.

This was especially so now that he was up to his ears in

politics. In this year of our Lord eighteen hundred and eighty-four the Republicans were for the first time since the Civil War facing an uphill presidential fight—against New York's Governor Grover Cleveland, an honest man who'd even admitted to fathering a bastard. The Republicans were running their old warhorse, James G. Blaine, who'd underscored his distance from the people by dining at Delmonico's with the likes of Jay Gould, Cyrus Field, Levi Morton and John Jacob Astor—an event headlined in the New York *World* as "The Royal Feast of Belshazzar Blaine." That had been bad enough, but a minister—a Presbyterian at that—named the Reverend Doctor Samuel Burchard had topped it off by calling on Blaine in the Fifth Avenue Hotel and telling him, "We are Republicans, and don't propose to leave our party and identify ourselves with the party whose antecedents have been rum, Romanism and rebellion." Though it was unlikely that a Cleveland victory would pry loose the Republican grip on Pittsburgh, talk like the reverend's made life difficult in the wards of Soho and the South Side, where the saloon and the Roman Catholic confessional were the twin supports of most voters' lives. Reed wasn't in the race himself, but he had a stake in many candidates as founder and president of the Young Republican Club, and he would gladly have cut the tongue out of all of those divines, including his own brother-in-law, who publicly equated Republicanism with protestant puritanism.

"I don't see why you're a Republican anyway," Henry Schmidt had said when Reed was complaining to him at one of their regular evenings of sausage and German beer at the Hotel Schlosser.

"I told you—it's because I want to be effective," Reed replied. "If politics is a game of power, then you have to go where the power is to play it right. Magee and Flinn have this town sewed up so tight a Democrat couldn't be elected dog-catcher, unless for some reason they so ordered."

"If you can't lick them, join them . . .?"

"Not join them exactly, Henry. The idea is to work for reform from the inside."

"I've heard that one before. Sell your principles to buy power and then turn around and use your power to buy your principles back. It won't work, Reed, believe me, it won't work."

"Well, I don't see that your way works, either," Reed countered. "I admire your idealism—and you know that—but it's pretty impractical."

"You sound like your sister."

"I guess I do a bit. I guess something of whatever it is that makes Scott go rubbed off on all of us."

"I'd say so. . . ."

"You sound rather bitter, Henry. What you need is another beer," Reed said, waving for the waiter.

"No, I'm not bitter." He laughed. "You know—and I'm not complaining—but it is kind of ironic . . . I'm supposed to be the writer, and my lovely clever wife is the one who gets published. Well, good for her. Besides, maybe she'll get across what I couldn't."

Reed nodded. "Did you see that sketch she did of Chris Magee? Makes him look like a grinning jack-o'-lantern. I hear he was furious, went charging around asking, "Who's this Schmidt woman?' Remember what you said once about bleeding hearts?"

"I do. I'm all right except when I'm writing, and then I tend to bleed all over the page. It must be the German in me. Speaking of the German, let's have another."

The beer's mellowing influence finally brought Reed to a confession. "What would you think if I married Alma?"

"Well, at least you won't have our problem," Henry said. "Her old man is richer than Croesus. I hope he doesn't know how you think . . . otherwise he wouldn't let you in the door."

"I'm saved by being Scott Stewart's brother. By the way, that brother of mine is all over the place. Trying to get out from under his shadow is like trying to escape God. When I first met Magee, he said, 'Oh, you must be my partner's brother.' His partner? I couldn't believe it, but it turns out Scott's been putting up the money for several of those street railway franchises Magee has been picking up. No wonder Scott could afford that castle . . ."

"I've always told you never to sell your brother short. He's got a nose for the dollar like a bloodhound does for blood."

"Tell me something, Henry. Why does the talk always get around to Scott whenever anybody in the family gets together?"

"Power, my boy, power. He has a strange power in him that comes from a kind of special purity. He's seen the light and he's following it. Whatever we may think about him, the rest of us with our weaknesses and diversion stand in awe of him."

"You, too?"

"Me, too."

The more he got around town, the more Reed found himself trying to resolve the paradox Henry had brought up: he tended to admire the very men whose works he deplored. With Alma's advice and encouragement, Reed had decided to start his political career at what amounted to the top. Using his wide acquaintanceship with the rich young Pittsburghers who were beginning to drift back from Princeton and Yale and other points east to take up promising positions in their family firms, he set up the young Republican organization. By calling themselves Republicans, they connected themselves to the dominant party; by calling themselves young, they allowed themselves leeway to take more liberal stands on issues than the Old Guard. The real beauty of Reed's scheme, however, was that he was quickly able to raise enough funds to be impressive to men like Magee and his colleague William Flinn. As a result he was given a seat on Magee's county committee and a promise from Flinn that he would have a position in the public-works office as soon as the election was over.

Of the men he'd met so far, Reed was most fascinated by state legislator William Flinn. Six feet tall, his two hundred pounds already slipping toward an impressive bay window at the age of thirty-three, clean-shaven except for a small mustache, he was the very model of what a politician should look like. Flinn knew at first hand the world of hard work most of his constituents were forced to live in. Quitting school at the age of nine, he sold papers, blacked boots, worked in a brick yard. From his contractor father he learned the rudiments of building, and at the age of twenty-six went into business with James J. Booth. Now their firm, Booth and Flinn, Ltd., was getting nearly every paving and building contract available in a city bursting its seams. It was all perfectly legal. Through his political power as chairman of the Republican City Committee, Flinn saw to it that city contracts contained specifications that would guarantee his firm as the only proper bidder—a certain color of stone, for example, which Booth and Flinn, by reason of foresight in buying it all up, alone could provide. The predictable result was that Flinn dwelt in a mansion in East Pittsburgh called Braemer that was even more impressive than Scott's, was an upstanding member of the Sixth United Presbyterian Church, despite his Irish name, and was welcome in all the best circles.

Observing Flinn, as Reed told Alma, was like watching some fine jungle beast—a tiger, maybe, or a snake—in action. He seemed wholly amoral, totally driven by an instinct for survival. If cornered, he'd strike for his opponent's jugular vein and watch him expire without emotion. His vision of the jungle was clear and unclouded by abstract speculation—around him were either the weak and submissive and therefore useful, or those competing for the same kill and therefore dangerous. He treated them accordingly, and he expected the same treatment from them. If he kept the primal commandments—that is, he didn't physically kill or steal—it was because they struck him as natural laws of survival, like keeping upwind of the prey you are stalking. Membership in the United Presbyterian Church in Presbyterian Pittsburgh or membership in the Duquesne Club, where all the moneyed businessmen gathered, were to Flinn one and the same thing —the protective coat any animal needs to move safely among its peers. William Flinn would have been as astonished to be challenged about his moral code as was Commodore Vanderbilt, who once snapped at an inquiring reporter, "Law! What do I care about law? Hain't I got the power?"

There were times when Reed felt like a spy moving cautiously through enemy territory, but in a way it made the game more exciting. If he seemed to people like Henry to be tarred with the same brush as Flinn and Magee and the others, so much the better for the success of his mission. What he was trying to do at the moment was to get the lay of the land, to learn how the processes of government worked, to put his finger on the real pulse of power. Being made welcome by Flinn was a sign that he was getting where he wanted to be. To Flinn, of course, a Reed Stewart would normally be a useless sport. He belonged to that group of rich young men who'd never done a day's honest work, who had gone East to fill their heads with a lot of nonsense at college and who were good only for the money that could be shaken out of them. Worse, this particular young man was flawed in good Presbyterian eyes by some silly scandal with a woman. The only thing going for him was his brother, Scott, who was demonstrating through his association with Magee a solid understanding of the jungle's immutable laws. So Flinn was pleasantly surprised when young Reed Stewart came up with his highly useful and remunerative organization. The idea deserved some kind of reward, but Flinn was even more surprised when Reed Stewart showed interest in what he himself contemptuously called "sucking on the public teat."

Reed could have had a job with Booth and Flinn, or Magee's traction company or, no doubt, with Frick Coke Co. It was pretty well known around town, too, that Reed was seriously courting Alma Jones, so in all probability there was a place being prepared for him in the Jones interests. Why then would he want to go on the city payroll as a lowly public-works inspector? Having observed Reed's public charm and his persuasive influence with his friends, Flinn's only conjecture was that he was dealing with a young man who, like his brother, had a natural feeling for the realities of life. From the outside only Flinn and a few other shrewd citizens like him could know that the mayor's office, the city council, even public safety were barren thickets; it was public works where the kill could be found. Well, evidently Reed Stewart knew it, and Flinn had to admire him for it. He passed the word to give the young man a job.

Scott Stewart was so happy to have his young brother gainfully employed at anything that he swallowed most of his objections when Reed told him about it. Still, he couldn't help saying, "You surprised me, I've got to admit, but you did a fine job during the elections. Too bad, only a miracle could have put Blaine over with all the fuzzy-headed Republicans that defected. The thing is, though, you could have had a much better position. If Flinn couldn't get one for you, Magee could. Why did you settle for this?"

Reed flashed a smile made rather sinister by his scar. "Tell you the truth, brother Scott, I don't want to be stuck in some office somewhere from eight to five. This way I can get around town. I figure in six months on this job, I'll know more about Pittsburgh than I could learn any other way."

"You're really that interested in the city?"

"Of course. Why do you think I came back here from Princeton instead of going to New York or Philadelphia?"

"I thought Alma Jones might have something to do with it."

"I didn't really know her then. No, there's something about this place. Everybody says I look a little like the devil, so I guess it's just natural that I'd want to live in hell."

Scott flushed. "I don't like to hear that kind of talk, Reed. I wish now that I had made you read the Bible through the way you were supposed to. Maybe . . ."

"Oh, come on, Scott, I'm twenty-one now, and I am tired of being preached at. You can think what you like about the divinity blessing all your deals, including the one with Magee . . ."

"Who told you anything about that?"

"Magee himself. He's proud of being connected with such an upstanding pillar of the church and crusader against the evils of liquor . . ."

"Reed Stewart, if you'd been old enough to understand what it did to Father . . ."

"Father! Father! From all I gather, it wasn't liquor that did Father in. He just couldn't tolerate the ignorance of man, not to mention the inhumanity of God. Well, maybe he did us both a favor. You've apparently learned to shut your eyes to them and I'm trying to find a way maybe to do something about them. . . . Forgive the speech. . . . I didn't know I had it in me. . . ."

"And I simply don't understand the way you think," Scott said, shaking his head.

Reed laughed. "I guess that makes two of us. Maybe I don't think, maybe I just feel."

"Well, I'm glad you got a job anyway. If there's anything I can do . . ."

"No. Thanks, brother. You've done enough for me already."

Reed, as he moved into the life of the city and took a more serious look around him, could begin to understand how Scott and his brethren felt that God had somehow specially blessed the Pittsburgh region for the making of money. The natural bounty was fantastic. The hills for miles around were nothing but great humps of energy in the form of coal. Turning this God-given treasure into private treasury depended on two things: acknowledgment of absolute rights to the property in which it lay and the ability to hire enough able bodies at appropriate wages to extract it at a profit. And now, of course, there was natural gas, which promised an even cheaper and brighter form of burning, and pipes and machinery, far more tractable cost factors, could be largely substituted for inefficient and often troublesome human labor. Reed recalled the way natural gas had delivered itself into the hands of George Westinghouse, a clear-eyed Yankee tinkerer who looked on the world as a machine in need of fixing. More or less on a whim, Westinghouse sent a drill down into the back yard of his estate, Solitude, in the quiet Homewood section. In May, after four months of probing, the ruptured earth responded with such hissing power that the drilling rig was scattered to the far corners of the property. Set alight, the gas stood in a flaming torch one hundred feet above the ground and drew crowds, among them a curious Reed Stewart, from all over the city, since the Westinghouse property fortuitously bordered the railroad tracks. Within weeks, Westinghouse had the well capped, and before the summer was out he'd bought something called the Philadelphia Company to turn the gushing gas, not only from his own well but others in the area, into dollars. With such events frequently happening to people in

Pittsburgh, it was difficult not to believe in some mysterious divine destiny.

True, occasionally God was less benevolent. The great rivers which had made Pittsburgh a center of trade and travel —the "gateway to the West"—long before the coming of the iron horse were not to be trusted. This very February of 1884 they had risen until people were slogging knee-deep in water at the busy corner of Sixth Street and Penn Avenue in the heart of town and cruising Federal Street over in Allegheny City in rowboats. As usual, the shanties of the poor that were clustered along the river banks within walking distance of the mills were turned into matchsticks by the water's power. In all, six thousand buildings went under and ten thousand people were left without homes. While he had a wry appreciation for what he considered the Lord's punitive reminder of His power, Reed, as the newest member of the public-works department, could not understand why some major public effort hadn't been committed to taming the rivers with dams and dikes. A little probing soon gave him the answer: the men of power, whose divine blessings allowed them to live in the hills or the pleasant valleys beyond the reach of the city's fuming and flooding, saw little sense in taxing themselves to stave off God-made catastrophes. If not filtering the water resulted in occasional epidemics of typhoid in the slums and not diking the rivers let the waters wreak havoc, weren't these acts of God and wasn't suffering as surely ordained by heaven as success?

Getting Pittsburgh out of the hands of a capricious God and his seemingly heartless servants here on earth was, Reed decided, a worthy challenge. He was schooled enough in the Bible to remember that Jesus had advised his followers to be "wise as serpents," and he intended to follow that advice. It grieved him at times that Henry considered him a traitor to the cause of justice, that Scott—and to a lesser extent, Lucinda—considered him foolish for mucking about with cheap politicians, and that his mother was simply bewildered by him—only Alma really seemed to understand. So it was with considerable unease that Reed Stewart presented himself one Sunday afternoon at the tall, square mansion on Ridge Avenue to ask Alma's formidable father, Alexander Hamilton Jones, for his daughter's hand.

Since everybody in the Jones household knew the reason for the visit, Reed was ushered by the white-aproned maid, who met him at the door, into an oak-paneled study beyond the parlor. "Mr. Jones will be with you in a minute, sir," she said, shutting the door behind her and leaving Reed to pace the small chamber, damp-palmed and dry-mouthed with apprehension. The walls were hung with hides and bristling with antlers, proof positive of the blood Mr. Jones had shed in the name of sport and not at all reassuring to an aspiring son-in-law whose one brush with violence had made him forever abhor it in any form. Reed kept reminding himself that, as a wise serpent, he should be able to handle Mr. Jones ("Oh, and where did you say you shot that, sir?" . . . "Gosh, that must have been a big one!" . . . and so on) and that, although he would hate himself for it, he could always fall back on Scott's reputation ("Yes, my brother tells me that the Frick Coke Co. is capitalized at $3,000,000. They own 1,026 ovens and 3,000 acres of good coal land. You know, Andrew Carnegie has bought into the company" . . . and so on). That's the way he would have to play it, although he longed to say only, "I love your daughter and she loves me and nobody in the world is going to keep us from being together."

The arrival of Mr. Jones interrupted his meditations. Somehow he loomed larger in the close confines of the study than he had standing quietly beside his equally formidable wife at the ballroom door. Despite a great mane of white hair and a white beard, Jones moved forcefully and quickly, as one would expect a hunter to do. He shook Reed's hand and motioned him to a leather sofa beneath a most imposing forest of antlers. "Well, young man, good to see you, good to see you. Have a cigar?" He proffered an ivory inlaid box he'd picked up from a small table in front of the couch.

"No, thank you, sir, but if you have a cigarette . . ."

"Cigarette? Not in this house, Mr. Stewart. They're an abomination, I say—a lady's smoke, if anything. By the way, I hear your sister smokes cigarettes. Alma cited her as an example when she was trying to get our consent to smoke the things. I told her not in this house, not a daughter of mine."

Having shared many a companionable cigarette with Alma, Reed didn't know what to say. He had a pack with him, but he felt it would be wrong to take one out. He was clearing his throat to launch into a safe discussion of the antlers above when Jones, having puffed his own cigar into life, told him, "I'm a businessman, young fella, and I like to come right to the point. I gather you want to marry Alma, and right now I'm inclined to say no."

When Reed tried to say something, Jones silenced him with a gesture and got to his feet. "Let me finish," he said, walking back and forth and pausing occasionally to stroke a shiny antler. "I guess I could be very conventional and say I don't want my daughter to marry any young fella who's been mixed up in a scandal with an actress. But"—and here he winked at Reed—"far as I'm concerned that just shows you've got spirit. I know you come from good folks. There isn't a businessman in town I admire more than Scott Stewart, and even though I am Episcopalian, I have to admit that brother-in-law of yours, Dr. Sharp, is one of the finest preachers I've ever heard. Now, as to you, I've got to hand it to you for turning out all those young rascals for the Republican cause. . . ."

Reed was amazed; he probably couldn't have put his own case better himself. "But then why . . ." he started to say.

Jones waved him silent again. "The thing is," he went on, "we've only got one child. She had a little brother, but he died of scarlet fever. Well, anyway, as you can imagine, Alma's likely to come into a lot of money, and whoever she marries will have to be a good steward. . . ."

Mostly owing to the building tension inside him, Reed laughed, then tried to respond to Jones' angry look with, "I'm sorry, sir. It just came out. I mean it sounded like a sort of pun—you know, steward . . . Stewart?"

"I wasn't meaning to be funny. This is no laughing matter."

"I know, sir, but I think . . ."

"No, let me finish," Jones said again. "This is very important to us, so I've been doing a little research. I've got to be honest with you. I went out to the South Hills there and asked people about your father and they acted as if there was some kind of mystery about him. I didn't like that."

Reed felt himself flushing, more in anger than embarrassment. "No mystery, Mr. Jones. My father killed himself, hanged himself in the barn when he lost a mother and baby," Reed said.

"Oh," Jones said. "Oh, well . . . I'm sorry."

"There's nothing to be sorry about, Mr. Jones. It happened a long time ago, and I was so little it didn't mean much to me. Are there any other mysteries about me I can clear up for you?"

"Matter of fact there are . . . that business about the railway strike. I've never understood how the superintendent's brother . . ."

Really angry now at the older man's prying. Reed no longer cared much what kind of impression he was making. "Simple, Mr. Jones. My brother got me a job working with a track gang, and when the strike came, I was a striker. I just happened to get in the way of a bullet like a lot of other innocent people."

"But you weren't in sympathy with those ruffians?"

"Well, I was only fourteen, but, yes, I was. The strikers were doing their damnedest to hold down the pillaging and rioting, but when the troops came in the people got mad. I did, too."

"I see. Well . . ."

"Any more mysteries, Mr. Jones?"

"Yes. For the life of me I can't understand why you're working with that gang of crooks down in city hall when . . ."

"When I could go to Scott for a job? Or come to you for a job? Is that it?"

"Yes, if you care to put it that way. Forgive me for being so frank, Mr. Stewart, but both Mrs. Jones and I love Alma, and . . ."

"I do too, sir."

"Yes, I dare say you do—or think you do. But the kind of love you're talking about, young man, isn't going to sustain a marriage for a lifetime . . ."

"But . . ." Reed started to protest, thinking that Jones was beginning to sound like Scott, except more so.

Jones held up a warning hand. "I'll plead guilty to spoiling Alma rotten. She's been pampered and sheltered and given everything her heart desired, and she's going to expect the same kind of treatment from whoever marries her. What that comes down to is that her husband is going to have to make a lot of money, because, God willing, she won't get her inheritance for years to come. Now if you were willing . . ."

"I'm not willing if you are going to say what I think you are, Mr. Jones. Matter of fact it was Alma herself who got me started off in politics, and I intend to stay in it. I can only say again that I love her and . . ."

"Frankly, Mr. Stewart, you and Alma are only twenty-one, and I think you will both come around to seeing things in a better light when you're more mature. So I'll tell you what I propose to do. I'm going to send Alma and her mother to Europe for a year. You know she passed up her trip last summer—something about this women's suffrage nonsense. Well, anyway, if you both feel the same way when they come back, we'll take another look at the situation. Is that fair?"

"Have you told Alma?"

"Not yet. I thought I'd let her mother . . ."

"Would you let me tell her, sir?"

"Well, I don't see why not. I'm glad you're being so reasonable, young fella. Go ahead, she's in the parlor."

Alma was sitting with her mother, pretending to read, but the letters were lying dead on the page before her. Her mind was on the conference that seemed to be going on too long in the other room. Though they hadn't told her directly, she sensed that her parents were not going to approve unless Reed agreed to join her father in business. Half her heart hoped he would, just to make peace in the family, and the other half hoped he would stand firm. When he came out and stood, silent and white-faced, at the parlor door, she knew things had not gone well. With a motion of his head, he summoned her to take a walk in the garden with him.

It was by now the evening of the day in the evening of the year, and gray November skies, heavy with a freight of chilling rain or snow, pressed down on them. A cold wind fingered the last few leaves, clinging like tongues of fire to the maple trees. It was altogether the proper atmosphere for Reed's gloomy report, which he delivered in word-for-word detail as he and Alma dragged their feet through the debris of the dead garden behind the house. When he'd finished, he asked her, "Are you going to do it, Alma? Are you going to go?"

"Well, I don't know what else . . ."

"There is a what else, Alma. You could come with me, with me now. We could elope. There isn't much they could do to us. We are twenty-one . . ."

Alma suddenly stopped, put a restraining hand on Reed's arm and looked up into his face. Her eyes were questioning him louder than her tongue. "Do you mean that, Reed? Do you really?"

"I certainly do."

"Where could we go? I mean on Sunday night . . ."

Reed knew just the place, and he told her about the little country church near Butler, where Pastor Schmidt was certain to be putting a handful of farmers to sleep with his theological musings. "But can you get out of the house?" he asked.

"I think so. It might surprise my parents, but I could tell them I'm going to church. You know, to pray over our problem."

"What if they go with you?"

"Oh, I can insist that I need to be alone. Anyway, Daddy always falls asleep in evening church, and it embarrasses Mother."

"Then I'll meet you at the church. I think there's a train about nine. If not, we'll hire a carriage and wake up the old man."

"Oh, Reed . . . God, this is so exciting . . . hold me . . .?"

He did, gladly. While they clung there together, the sun slipped under the skirts of cloud to the west and bathed the whole world around them in fire.

A Merry Christmas

Reed Stewart was alone in the club except for an old gentleman, pudgy hands laced across a gently heaving paunch, who slept soundly in the corner. The tall black man who brought his drink reminded Reed of Moses, long dead now, and of Christmases when life seemed simple and full of bright promise. It would have taken the wildest sort of imagination then to picture a gathering such as even now was assembling at brother Scott's Fifth Avenue pile for the annual rite to display family solidarity. Of them all, only his mother and Scott showed in their features and their talk the essence of the severely upright Stewarts of Reed's early memories. The fact that Reed was here now, sipping appreciatively the Old Overholt in his glass to fortify himself against the dry dinner to come, was evidence enough of what the years had done to most of them. The whiskey Reed felt as essential to smooth sailing as oil on troubled waters was an even more telling sign of where he was than the dark, rich atmosphere of the Duquesne Club.

Staring at the grate in the marble fireplace, where the coals sank quietly into white heat with only an occasional indecorous hiss and spurt of blue flame to disturb the room's silence, Reed kept asking himself: why am I here in this year of our Lord eighteen hundred and ninety-one? On one level the answer was simple enough. Because Alexander Hamilton Jones, for all his bluster, couldn't bring himself to disinherit his only daughter and because the old hunter's heart, crippled no doubt in the chase, gave out early, John Reed Stewart, Jr., was so wealthy by reason of sharing in his wife's estate that it would have been a kind of reverse snobbery not to belong to the Duquesne Club. But why on Christmas day when he should be with the family and why drinking whiskey alone? Not to drown some kind of sorrow or failure certainly. As a lawyer about to become one of the youngest judges in the county's history, he was looked upon as a person of consequence even by his fellow club members. As the husband of a stunning, socially and politically active heiress and father of two children, he was the envy of the ordinary citizens who read notices about his family's comings and goings—births, baptisms, balls—in the papers. Why then? He really wasn't sure.

Henry, of course, would say that he had sold out, that he was trying to drown the fires of conscience in alcohol. Poor Henry with his old-fashioned long hair turning a kind of rusty white at forty and his old-fashioned socialism turning a kind of communist pink. Henry just couldn't see that the way to social salvation might lay not in jeering from the sidelines but in playing a better game like, say, Teddy Roosevelt in New York. In his way, Reed reflected, Henry was becoming as dogmatic as Scott—the big difference was he wasn't willing to recognize goodness unless it came from the *wrong* side of the tracks, and at least Scott's preference was deep-rooted in his training and livelihood. "The only thing I agree with Mark Hanna about is that Roosevelt is nothing but a 'damned cowboy,'" Henry had said. Reed could have been drinking with Henry instead of sitting here alone . . . he was sure Henry was out somewhere loosening up his tongue for the annual lashing of the rich that had become his special Christmas pleasure. But Henry absolutely refused to set foot inside the Duquesne Club, and the idea of spending even part of Christmas in Henry's kind of intellectual saloon didn't appeal to Reed all that much.

For the sake of some kind of family harmony, Reed could only hope that Henry had not discovered Donald Sharp's role in getting him fired from the university. Reed doubted that anyone else in the family, even Sarah, knew it yet since he had been told in strictest confidence by a political friend who served with the reverend on the board of trustees. Some favor-currying student had written the trustees accusing Henry of spouting communist doctrine in his philosophy classes. The student tried to demonstrate how passages from his own class notes were paraphrases of material in Marx's *Das Kapital*.

187

Rather than remove himself from the controversy on the grounds of family interest, the Reverend Doctor Sharp backed up the student's charges by himself reading into the record antireligious passages from Henry's writings that had begun to appear in obscure liberal journals in the East. The effect on the conservative trustees was, of course, predictable, and Henry was asked for his resignation without a hearing.

It might have been devastating except for Lucinda's astonishing success. Much as he had always liked his sister, Reed had to admit to being amazed by her talent. By now she was the top star on the *Call* and probably the best-known woman in Pittsburgh. Jones had sent her everywhere to give his readers the "woman's eye view" through sketches and informal essays. In the years since she had been on the paper she had watched the unveiling of the Statue of Liberty, had an exclusive interview in London with Mary Schenley, viewed the Seven Wonders of the World, toured the White House with Mrs. Cleveland. All of Lucinda's dreams of travel and comparative wealth seemed to be coming true. With their combined income, she and Henry moved into a small but elegant Ridge Avenue house near Reed and Alma, hired a maid and butler and held almost continuous court for the artists and intellectuals of the city. Lucinda dressed with quiet elegance, with diamonds often sparkling at her wrist or throat. There was disquieting talk that her relationship with Gillespie Jones was more intimate than that of employee and employer, but both she and Henry laughed it off.

Still, Reed could detect all the signs of a marriage of convenience in the Schmidt household. Separate bedrooms for one thing—"so that Henry won't keep me awake all night with his endless reading," Lucinda explained airily. They were seldom at home together, even when Lucinda was in town. "Oh, you know how these newspaper people are—erratic, never know when they'll be out on a story," Henry explained. "And I'm not much better—classes any old time of the day." But there would be no more classes now, and Reed wondered how long Henry's pride would allow him to hold out.

"You know if it were up to me, I wouldn't live this way," Henry once confessed to Reed. "I really don't approve of it, but Lucinda works hard and deserves to do what she wants to with her money. Oh, I know people think I'm living off her, but it isn't true. I pay half—I really do. You know I give private lessons in German and then those little pieces of mine earn a few dollars—not much but some. And there's going to be a book, I swear. I'm writing it now. 'Course, I couldn't afford those baubles Lucinda wears. I wouldn't; they're the kind of conspicuous spending I don't much like, and I tell her so. Still, I've got to admit I am proud of her. And, God, she is beautiful, isn't she?"

Reed believed what Henry told him—at least the important part about being proud of Lucinda. He had to admire Henry's guts in ignoring all the tongues that were wagging about him in order to let Lucinda become the person she wanted to be, and he felt sorry that in so becoming Lucinda obviously was leaving Henry somewhere behind. When Henry was fired, Lucinda no doubt took it as another sign of his dreamer's incompetence. Even if she knew the truth of the matter, she would probably be impatient that Henry let his foolish ideas jeopardize his work. In her own writings she stayed away from politics except for an almost unconscious comment by caricature, like the sketch that so infuriated Mr. Magee. Reed still had a feeling, or at least a hope, that Henry would some-day arrive and that he and Lucinda would come together again. When he heard of the firing, he entered into secret agreements with some of Henry's New York editors to supply the money for them to pay him higher fees. Only Alma knew about this, and Reed hoped to God nobody else would ever find out. Not only would it do him no good politically to be known as a supporter of left-wing publications, but it surely would wound Henry's pride worse than anything Donald Sharp had done to him.

Maybe, Reed thought as he signaled the waiter for just one more, he was here drinking because of Sharp and all the Sharps in the world. His preaching brother-in-law was na-tionally famous now—not exactly a Henry Ward Beecher yet, but getting there. His big break had come in Chicago in '88. By a kind of reverse triple play—Scott Stewart to Chris Magee to Matthew Quay, the state chairman who was now National Republican Chairman—Sharp got to home plate, the podium of the Republican National Convention, where he prayed Benjamin Harrison toward the White House. It wasn't a difficult prayer for Donald Sharp to put his heart into—Harrison being known in his home town of Indianapolis as a "frigid Presbyterian deacon." But Reed, sitting in the audi-ence at Chicago as a delegate from Pennsylvania, nearly got sick as he listened to the Reverend Doctor intone in the sugary Southern accent that seemed to deepen with the years in Pittsburgh's Northern smog: "Oh, Lord, we thank Thee that Thou has brought forward from the ranks of this republic a certain man of God to lead us on to greater prosperity. . . ."

Reed's trouble was that, by then, he knew almost more than he cared to about politics. His stint in the city's public-works department had been a real eye-opener. The whole thing was beautifully simple. Controlling their county and city Republican committees respectively, Magee and Flinn simply picked the men who would serve in city council or go to Harrisburg in the legislature. These men would then pass ordinances or laws favoring the numerous ventures in which Magee and Flinn were involved—at one point Reed figured out that Magee was a director or controller of more than fifty companies. The men who ran Pittsburgh had cleverly persuaded the legislature to designate it a "second-class city"— the only one in the state. Which meant they could introduce legislation pertaining to "second-class cities" for which representatives from Philadelphia or Harrisburg or Erie could vote without a thought, since it was of no concern to their own constituents. To control state law with regard to Pittsburgh, then, Magee and Flinn had only to control representatives from their own district. Councilmen and legislators, of course, profited well from doing the will of their bosses. They had ventures of their own that needed civic action—or inaction, as the case might be. Attending churchmen though they were, Magee and Flinn turned a blind eye to such enterprises as houses of prostitution and saloons. Enterprising madams were left alone so long as they rented their houses from the right people and bought their furniture at inflated rates from the right stores. It was the same for saloon keepers. And then, there were jobs on the public payroll for relatives and relatives of relatives. A man with Flinn's working background understood that most voters would remain loyal to the party that catered to their vices and took care of their daily needs such as housing or jobs. If Republicans at the remote national level favored legislation that kept prices up and wages down, it had relatively little impact for the Pittsburgh slum dweller whose Republican ward boss had got his son out of jail and found a job for his daughter in the Heinz pickle plant. As long as Magee and Flinn could keep the right people in the right places, Republicans would go on being elected and reelected. Though there might be *something* to be said for this process, it was depressing to Reed to have it sanctioned by the Reverend Doctor Sharp.

Armed with the independence his father-in-law's untimely death put on him, Reed quit his city job and tried to interest some of his fellow Young Republicans in reform. A few responded. A merchant named Oliver McCormick, for example, was particularly incensed at the evidence Reed produced of sloppy work by Booth and Flinn—the surfaces of new streets, laid over weak foundations made cheaply from the rubble of old coal tar sidewalks, sank and buckled within months. The aroused McCormick went about town taking pictures of potholes and collecting facts with which he hoped to break the Booth and Flinn monopoly on public works, and so far as Reed knew he was still doing it. Another citizen inspired by Reed's revelation, David Bruce, saw beyond the potholes to the machinery that made them inevitable, and was leading a crusade for a new city charter—one bound to fail as long as Mat Quay, that half-Indian sphinx with his unreadable almond eyes, continued to control the legislature with his little card index of its vices and traded its votes for Magee's support in Allegheny County. Reed was glad these quixotic efforts by people like McCormick and Bruce were still continuing, but he was no longer as hopeful as he once had been that they really would accomplish much.

Reed had done everything he could, even studying law at Western University and passing the bars, to turn himself into an effective gadfly within the Republican organization. Using his Young Republicans as a base, he had run again and again as an independent for city council, only to lose, sometimes by a few highly suspicious votes. The last time out he'd proved in court that he'd been beaten by names copied from tombstones, and yet he had lost by an even greater margin in the court-ordered rerun. There was no way of proving that a substantial amount of Booth and Flinn money had found its way into the pockets of voters known to have previously favored Reed Stewart. But the almost comical revelation in open court of such flagrant ballot packing had stung the organization, and the bets were high that Reed just might finally make it in '92. He was laying the groundwork for his campaign when much to his surprise he was invited by Magee and Flinn to a very private luncheon at the Duquesne Club.

There were no drinks, of course, with such a prominent prohibitionist as Chris Magee in the party, but the finest Havana cigars were passed around with the coffee. What polite chit-chat they could manage under the circumstances—asking after the health of Scott, whom Reed seldom saw, and after the health of Mrs. Alexander Jones, Magee's "great comrade in the cause," and the like—having been exhausted during lunch, Magee came to the point. "Mr. Stewart," he said. "You know Mr. Flinn and I have always been impressed with the work you're doing with your young people and we're appreciative of the funds, not to mention votes, you've raised for the party. We'd like to see you get some reward commensurate with your services . . ."

"Then why don't you stop fighting me for a council seat? It should be obvious by now that's what I want."

"Ah, yes," Magee said. "But you must be aware that you're opposing a man of long-standing faithfulness to the party, Mr. Stewart. What kind of people would Mr. Flinn and I be if we were to let him down now? In any case, we have in mind something far more suited to your position and education—we need a candidate for the Common Pleas Court."

The thought of running for the bench had never occurred to Reed, partly because he was so young and partly because the court seemed rather distant from the arena where the reform battle was taking place. He was astounded that they would offer him so rich a plum—a sure seat (since the Republican nomination they controlled was a guarantee of election) for ten years on the county's highest court. Such a position was the green pasture they usually reserved for old warhorses. Reed was suspicious.

"Gentlemen, it's certainly a compliment, especially in view of the trouble I've been causing you. . . ."

"You're absolutely right, young man," Flinn said, "and I wouldn't have any part of this if it weren't that your brother and Chris here are such good friends. I can tell you right now that I have no use for your kind. I should have seen what you were up to when you asked for that job in public works. You're really nothing but a spy . . ."

"Now, Bill," Magee said soothingly, "Mr. Stewart is very young. He has a lot to learn. . . ."

"I'll say he does. If he thinks he can get a bunch of college types together and overturn the work you and I've been doing for a decade, well, he's got another think coming."

"If you feel that way, Mr. Flinn, why bother with me? Why not just let me beat my head against your stone wall?"

Flinn shrugged. "Ask Mr. Magee. This was his idea."

Unruffled as always, showing his jack-o'-lantern grin, Magee took a long puff on his cigar and blew out a rich cloud of smoke. "I'm going to be absolutely frank with you, Mr. Stewart. It's true, as you suspect, that we find your efforts to upset the council annoying. On the other hand, we do need you, or somebody like you, in an appropriate place on the ticket. I suppose you've asked yourself why a certain number of Democrats go on getting elected in a county so well controlled by our Republican party. The simple fact is that we encourage the election of the right Democrat in the right place; if we were to snuff out all opposition, why, we'd be asking for some kind of revolution. By the same token, we always need a certain number of Republican candidates of proven independence even if they give us a little trouble . . ."

"And you think I'll give you the least trouble salted away in the courthouse?"

"Chris, I told you he'd be impossible . . ."

"Just a minute, Bill, I haven't finished," Magee said, his tone still friendly but his words taking on an edge. "Mr. Stewart, I think you're overestimating your nuisance value. If you don't choose to cooperate, we can, and will, see to it that you are never elected to any office in this county. I should have thought we made that clear to you in the last rerun. We're offering you this chance to stand for the court not out of the goodness of our hearts but because we think it would be good politics to have you on the ticket and the court is an institution we feel the people must have faith in. Don't answer now, Mr. Stewart—think it over."

Reed stubbed out his cigar. "I will," he said, and left them without shaking hands.

Reed and Alma talked all through that long night. Round and round and round they went. She liked the idea of being Mrs. Judge Stewart; what a boost it would give her own woman suffrage activities. . . '. He wanted to fight the bastards, beat them at their own game. She argued he could do more good in office, bringing real justice to the people. He explained that a judge had to work within the law, and the law was rigged by the likes of Magee and Flinn through their influence in the legislature. Maybe the thing to do was forget the council and run for the legislature. On what ticket and with whose support? Be practical for once. Since when was she practical—marching around the streets with a lot of silly women screaming for the vote? Alma cried. Alma almost never cried, and Reed was shaken by it. "Please, Reed, do it for me. I know you'd be a wonderful judge, and I know you'll break your heart the other way. Please."

"But it violates everything I believe in . . ."

"Does it? Weren't you the one who talked about being a wise serpent?"

He was, indeed, and she'd suddenly hit on the perfect rationale for doing what he really wanted to do—give in to her. The truth was that Reed had found he could not deny Alma anything. In a way, her father had been right about "spoiling her rotten." Indeed, so much so that Alma wasn't even aware of it. Take money, for instance. During the months they'd been estranged from her family by the elopement, Alma went on spending so freely that Reed was soon forced to the ignominy of using his brother's name to borrow to cover their debts. It wasn't that Alma was either selfish or extravagant, it was simply that money had always existed for her in much the same way as the air she breathed. In the same way she took for granted the compliance of people she loved or people who loved her. Always at the center of her own world, Alma had developed the kind of trusting confidence in life that enabled her to be forthright and generous and fearlessly outgoing. Reed found Alma's innocent self-confidence such a charming relief after his own self-doubts that he was willing to do almost anything—including taking the olive branch extended by her relenting parents—to keep her that way.

One thing Reed Stewart did not know when he consented to run for Common Pleas Court was the way his name would be used to milk all the Stewarts and Joneses and his Young Republican followers for funds, and by the time he found out it was too late to do anything about it. A great deal of fuss was made publicly about John Reed Stewart, Jr.'s record of fighting for reform; privately, a number of people, including Scott Stewart, were informed that the young hothead was being put in his place in a very respectable way, but it would take money to do the job. Scott put up five thousand dollars at once; he couldn't imagine a better solution to the problem of Reed, who was becoming somewhat of an embarrassment to him. Scott didn't think Reed would make much of a judge with all of his drinking and wrong-headed sentimentality about the rights of workingmen and the like, but now he literally would be cloaked with respectability and at least would be a source of pride to his mother.

As for the money, Scott had simply come to regard political contributions as a necessary cost of doing business; it was a bonus this time to get some possible personal benefit out of it as well. Nobody in their right mind in Scott's circles questioned the ethics of political support. In fact, in '88, when they were facing an uphill fight against the incumbent Cleveland, the Republican Party came right out in the open to collect on its years of favors to the business community. The issue was the tariff, which Cleveland and his Democrats threatened to revise downward. New York's boss Platt thought nothing of riding downtown in a carriage, calling on such as J. P. Morgan in their offices and collecting ten thousand dollars a head. They called Platt the "begging chief," but he got the job done. Businessmen John Wanamaker of Philadelphia and Mark Hanna of Cleveland openly solicited their colleagues. In a circular letter James P. Foster, president of the Republican League of the United States, said, "I would put the manufacturers of Pennsylvania under the fire and fry all the fat out of them." Well, Scott had had some fat fried out that year, but it was worth it: a good Christian, Harrison, had won, and the McKinley tariff was passed. It might be a different story, though, this coming year. McKinley had somehow fallen out with Platt and Quay in Pennsylvania, and it looked as though Cleveland would run again. "That's why I think your brother Reed would be an asset to the Republican ticket," Magee had told Scott. "You know he does have a clean record, and people understand he's opposed to mixing business with politics. Of course we know that it's a damn healthy relationship, that nothing would get done if likeminded people didn't pull together . . . but I don't need to make speeches to you, Scott. . . . It's your brother who hasn't seen the light, but we figure it doesn't matter." Magee shrugged. "What harm can he do on the bench?"

Reed, of course, hoped he could do a great deal of harm. Mulling it over for the thousandth time this Christmas day, he was looking for ways to parry Henry's inevitable thrusts. Sure, they'd dealt from a stacked deck, but he felt they'd slipped up and left him with a couple of aces. He was not only permitted but encouraged to speak out in order to keep up his pure public image; and the very nature of the common law allowed a thinking judge to have a hand in shaping it. Better by far, as Alma had argued, to be on the inside, in the heat of the action, than out there somewhere in the cold with Henry.

Reed finished his third drink and got up to go. Dinner was set for three, and, thanks to the new cable car running along Fifth Avenue, he would just have time to make it. Outside the club the long city twilight had already set in. Lights were burning in the Christmas-emptied streets, and snow was whirling every which way through the narrow canyons between buildings. For an hour or so, before it was churned into black slush under foot and wheel, the snow would drape a mantle of white purity on the dark city, lifting every spirit. Reed walked the few blocks up Grant's hill to wait at the cable-car stop on Fifth Avenue beside the new courthouse. Designed by one of America's most famous architects, Henry

Hobson Richardson, the French Romanesque courthouse with its round arches, its battlemented stone walls, its 150-foot tower looked like something out of the Middle Ages. Reed could imagine armored guards dragging screaming wretches through its vaulted halls to a dungeon death. This time next year he likely would be sitting on one of the raised benches in one of the courtrooms that ringed the sunless courtyard, and he wondered now if the gloomy facade would lend a proper dignity to his youthful judgments. He noted that the building rose above the church spires that had for so long dominated the Pittsburgh skyline, and in his mind this, at least symbolically, tended to enshrine a human justice hopefully more reasonable than divine whim. Looking at the building in this light, it occurred to him that an intuitive fear of its symbolic meaning was what had driven dour old Judge Mellon to fight the county commissioner's $2,500,000 bond issue clear to the supreme court. The judge had tried to make fun of the building. "Strikes me and others as like a fine building with a grain elevator erected upon it," he said. But could he have been afraid of it, afraid of seeing an arm of the state physically elevated above the heretofore enshrined alliance of God and commerce? It was a kind of farfetched notion, but it gave Reed a boost as he uncertainly contemplated his new venture.

As he had been at the club, Reed was alone at the car stop. Pittsburgh was a home city on Christmas. Looking all the way down Fifth Avenue to the Allegheny River, he could see only one or two shuffling figures, and scarcely a light in the solid walls of commercial buildings. On any other dark Friday afternoon the place would have been ablaze and people would be bumping shoulder-to-shoulder along the narrow sidewalks. The only building alight was the *Chronicle-Telegraph* column that stuck up above the surrounding structures like a crooked finger. Proudly illuminated by electric bulbs, its quaint tower was, Reed supposed, meant to symbolize the light of knowledge that the paper bestowed upon its readers—of course there was no holiday for men engaged in such a consecrated task. The only dark offices in the building were those rented out to Carnegie Steel Company Limited, where Scott now labored at the elbow of his much admired partner, Henry Clay Frick. But plans already were on the drawing board for a Carnegie Building that would prove the worth and power of structural steel by rising fifteen stories and put all of the rest of the city, including the brave courthouse, into its shade. Perhaps then Judge Mellon would be happy, Reed thought; if God couldn't dominate the scene, business could, which was almost the same thing.

Reed climbed aboard the nearly empty cable car that clattered south and then swung east around a curve in the hill that opened a vista of the Monongahela and the jumbled yards of the Jones & Laughlin Steel works, where the usually blazing Bessemers squatted in dark homage this one day to the memory of a child who had been born in a stable in a distant land of thorns and shepherds. Alma, bless her, had been completely understanding about Reed's need to visit the club rather than sitting in awkward and stone-dry silence with Scott while the women and children bustled about the affairs of Christmas. The only reason the annual rite was now held in Scott's house was that it had also become the home of Mary Stewart, who reluctantly had moved in when Martha had begun spending most of her time in a sanitarium in Saranac, New York. The Jones mansion, where Reed and Alma and their children now lived with the widowed Mrs. Jones, would be adequate to the gathering but the Stewarts prevailed by weight of numbers. Reed had to admit when he stepped off the car in front of Scott's palace that the candle-trimmed Christmas tree showing through the windows of one tower room and the sugar frosting of snow on the shoulders of the black stones did give a place a softening touch of holiday cheer. Just as he started to climb the steps, laughing, jostling young people from Sharp's church around the corner tumbled past him and grouped under the porte cochere to sing carols.

Reed stood aside to listen. "God rest you merry gentlemen; let nothing you dismay. . . ." The door opened, and Scott's tall figure was silhouetted in a shaft of light. Soon Martha, ghostlike in her trailing white gown, stood beside him. A foolish thing for a woman with tuberculosis to do, Reed thought, and then another figure, Lucinda's by the shape of it, appeared and threw a wrap around Martha. "O come, all ye faithful, joyful and triumphant. . . ." A hand seized Reed's elbow, and he looked around to see Henry beside him. Henry's shaggy hair and eyebrows were frosted with snow as if he'd walked a long way. He'd obviously been in a saloon, rocking gently back and forth as he was. Tears—brought on by a mixture of the cold, whiskey and the sentiment of the moment—shone in his eyes as he confided, "It's beautiful, isn't it, Reed? You know, this is the only time of year I wish I were still a Christian."

When the young people paused between carols, Henry went over to them. "Do you know 'O Holy Night'?" he asked them.

A chorus of assent. "Hum it then while I sing. Who's got the pitch pipe? Give me the pitch." Then Henry's tenor, a little ragged now at the edges, soared with "O Holy Night, the stars are brightly shining; it is the night of our dear Savior's birth. . . ." Out of the corner of his eye Reed saw Lucinda duck back into the house. It didn't surprise him that this might be more than she could take, for this was the side of Henry that nobody could help loving. At last came "Silent Night, Holy Night, all is calm, all is bright . . ." and Don Sharp stepped forward from the little knot of people by the door to bless his young carolers with a prayer and invite them in for hot chocolate.

Reed followed them into the house and met Alma in the hall. "How's everything going?" he asked.

"Fine, fine," she said. "Lucinda's a little on edge. I guess Scott's been lecturing her again."

"I'm sure of it," Reed said. Six-year-old Alexander had run down the stairs and was clutching at him. "Daddy, Daddy, come see what I got," he demanded.

Reed followed his son up to the tower room, where the children were sprawled in a profusion of toys and books and wrapping paper around the glittering tree. Annie, enormously fat and puffing, was supervising after a fashion. Reed gave her a hug. "Merry Christmas, Annie. I don't see how you can stand all this noise."

"I'm used to it, Mr. Reed. Anyway they're no worse than you were."

"That I can't believe." Reed laughed, and then tried to show proper enthusiasm for the little cast-iron train Uncle Scott had given Alexander and the black mammy doll Aunt Martha had given his four-year-old daughter Carolyn. When Uncle Henry came into the room, dispensing the candy canes he always brought with him in a paper sack, Reed gratefully escaped to the quiet of the study, where the adults not directly involved with the general confusion were awaiting the call for dinner. Oddly, for a brief time there were only the four Stewarts— Scott and Sarah, Lucinda and Reed.

Lucinda was taking a long puff on a cigarette and visibly sulking when Reed came in. "Ah, thank God you're here, Reed," she said. "These two have been taking me apart all afternoon."

"What now?"

"Oh, the usual," Lucinda said. "Too much smoking. Too much drinking. Disgracing the family by traveling around the world alone—or worse, with my boss. Do *you* think I'm a disgrace to the family, Reed?"

"Not as long as you keep using the name Schmidt," Reed teased.

"Oh, you're all so provincial," Lucinda moaned. "Gil says I've got to be one of the most famous women in the whole United States. Well, that's what he said. . . . Do you know that papers all over the country picked up my stories and sketches about the Seven Wonders of the World? I even upstaged Nellie Bly, Gil says, though I've got to admit she was smart to come up with that idea of beating Jules Verne's eighty days around the world. 'Course she had to leave Pittsburgh and go to New York to make it, and I've apparently done it right here . . ."

"Maybe you'd be better off in New York too," Scott suggested.

"I don't know why. I was born here. This is my home . . . I do have a husband, you know."

"Nobody else would from the way you act," Scott said. "Now that there are just the four of us here, I think I should be frank with you, Lucinda. People are talking. I was approached privately the other day by a member of the Jones family—I'll not tell you his name—and asked to exert my influence with you before a nasty scandal breaks."

"Scott, you mean you think . . ."

"I'm not saying what I think, I'm saying what other people think. If there is anything going on, just please consider what it could do to the family. Henry may not mind, I don't know . . . but your family has its positions to think about. I've got some important business associations with the Joneses, Don's been put up for chaplain of the U.S. Senate by Mat Quay, Reed's running for judge. A scandal could be ruinous. What do you say, Reed?"

"I say take it easy on her, Scott. At least on Christmas."

Lucinda went across the room and kissed Reed. "Thanks, little brother," she said. "You know, I'm a little sick of all this holier-than-thou business. I wouldn't even come into this house if it weren't for Momma. Thank God *she* hasn't consigned me to hell yet. As far as I'm concerned, she's the only one around here, except maybe you, Reed, who understands me at all . . ."

A maid appeared at the door to summon Scott to carve the turkey. When he'd left, Sarah, quietly busy with her needlework as she always seemed to be, said, "I think both of you are too hard on Scott. I don't know where any of us would be

199

if it hadn't been for him. He's just trying to give you advice for your own good, Lucinda."

"Did he ever once mention my good?" Lucinda said. "No. It was his good, your Don's good, Reed's good, all those stuffy Joneses' good. I'm not going to let Scott or anybody else interfere with my life. I've worked hard for what I have, and I'm going to keep it. . . ."

The maid was back at the door. "Dinner is served," she announced.

Every board had been inserted to stretch to fullest capacity the table in Scott's ample dining room. Laid with an enormous white linen cloth that came out only at Christmas, and sparkling with silver that caught the light of the great gas chandelier that hung above it, the table almost made the room seem festive. Almost, but not quite. The heavy oak wainscoting and sideboard, stained fashionably dark, the figured red wallpaper, the leaded stained-glass windows that strained out any possible light maintained the room's somber dignity against all intrusion. Before sitting down, each member of the family stood at the chair by his nameplate. Scott, of course, was at the head of the table and Mary at the foot. Ranged on Scott's right were Martha, his children Benjamin and May, Henry Schmidt, little Carolyn, Alma, Alexander and Reed; on Scott's left were Sarah and Donald, their four children—Stewart, Rebecca, Henry Ward Beecher and Myrtilla—and Lucinda and Mrs. Jones. Instead of a blessing, by Christmas tradition they all joined hands and sang the doxology, with Henry Schmidt, again by tradition, setting the tune. "Praise God from Whom all blessings flow; praise Him all creatures here below; praise Him above ye heavenly host; praise Father, Son and Holy Ghost. Amen." Then with much scraping and shuffling of chairs and much oh-ing and ah-ing over the size and smell of the turkey in front of Scott, they all sat down. As Scott passed plates heaped with turkey, two maids followed with steaming bowls of dressing, onions, potatoes, gravy, beans, rolls. Except for a "please pass the cranberry sauce" or the wail of a child that "I didn't get a drumstick," talk gave way to hearty eating.

If the walls had fallen suddenly away from a thousand homes in Pittsburgh that Christmas afternoon, they would have revealed a scene alike in all but detail to the one in Scott Stewart's Fifth Avenue castle. It was at this time that Mary Stewart allowed herself the once-a-year luxury of feeling that her family was indeed a true family after all. She knew the dissensions among them, and they grieved her. But when she was tempted to blame herself for Lucinda and Reed turning out so differently from Scott and Sarah, she would ponder the additional fact that Lucinda was, after all, a very successful woman in her own right and that Reed, about to be one of the youngest judges in the county, was more publicly prominent than Scott, or even Donald Sharp. True, the talk about Lucinda and Gillespie Jones was worrisome, but it was hard to think evil thoughts about a girl at once so beautiful and warm. Of all the children, Lucinda was the only one who really hugged Mary and who, on the rare occasions Mary would stay overnight in her home, would crawl into bed with her and talk the night away. Particularly on Christmas, Mary rejoiced that, out of thinking about the doctor's agony, she had come to feel that it was impossible to play God with people, that love had to suspend judgment. She wished the rest of the family could learn this lesson, but then they were too young and, except for Henry Schmidt and his sister Martha, had not been dealt the kind of punishing blow that had forever shattered her sense of surety about the ways of God with man.

The feast, punctuated only by innocuous small talk, went so well that the younger members of the family would forever look back on it as a kind of last hymn of family harmony. Even Henry kept quiet. He'd stayed so long at the saloon that he'd gone beyond his argumentative phase into a mood of gentle sentimentality. Throughout dinner he limited himself to stealing looks at the incredibly beautiful woman who was still his wife, at least in name, and like an artist congratulate himself on his creation. She'd thrived in the air of freedom, coming at thirty-one into that rarest of blooms—a mature woman without blemish. Look at her now . . . her hair, still golden, twisted artfully into a high crown, pinned with diamonds, a glittering choker of diamonds enticing the eye to the graceful curve of her neck; even a modest high-necked blouse with puffed sleeves failed to hide the thrust of her full breasts, and her long skirt swung gracefully from a waist a man could circle with his two hands. Henry didn't really know where she got the money to adorn herself, and he didn't ask. From his understanding of the economics of publishing, he doubted that Jones could pay that much, even for a star reporter, and he had to accept the probability that the rumors of a special relationship with Jones were true. Though Lucinda put her gradual—but still, thank God, not total—withdrawal from the marriage bed on all sorts of practical grounds such as his habit of reading till all hours and her need for sleep, his snoring and her thrashing about, he felt it had more to do with an alienation of the spirit than of the flesh. All her success had only convinced Lucinda more that the delights of the world were something she could grasp and hold in her own pretty hands; all his failures had only confirmed Henry in his belief that there was no true delight to be found in a society that especially rewarded the strong. Ironically, though, Henry thanked God that at least Lucinda was one of the strong, that she seemed to be making her little-girl-princess dreams come true. It relieved him of the guilt of dragging her down with him, and practically, her efforts were making it possible for him to go on living and writing, though the surprising increase in his fees he was getting from New York had given rise again to the romantic hope that he might make a financial success on his terms as well and spirit her away to a new kind of life. . . . Meanwhile, he was still glad he had a princess to worship, instead of a drudge like Sarah or a wraith like Martha. Poor Martha with her sick smile and ghastly pallor and spooky white shrouds. Sometimes Henry thought of his sister as a kind of wounded spirit Scott kept about to haunt his castle in case he was tempted by the sin of cheerfulness. God, he would any day rather be a cuckold than a ghost keeper.

Dinner was scarcely over when Lucinda moved back her chair, got up and said, "Well, I've got to go to work. No rest for the wicked, or newspaper reporters, you know." Henry started to rise, too, but she said, "No, you all stay here. I'll just take the car to town. I do it all the time."

Young Stewart Sharp, however, saw an opportunity and seized it. "I'm supposed to go to this open house at the Laughlins," he said. "Couldn't I borrow the carriage and drop Aunt Lucinda on the way, Dad?"

Donald Sharp didn't much like the idea of sending his son off with Lucinda. In recent years he and Sarah had quietly done their best to discourage the old easy relationship Lucinda had enjoyed with their children. She was seldom in their home, and they were never in hers. "She can't be anything but an unfortunate influence," Sharp would say to his wife, and Sarah, as in most things, didn't argue, although she regretted being cut off from her sister. The truth was that Donald Sharp was afraid of his sister-in-law, not only for his children but himself. Whatever she might be doing, she seemed to grow increasingly fascinating, and, like Henry, he'd hardly been able to keep his eyes off her all this Christmas dinner. Unlike Henry, he was ashamed of the thoughts that rose unbidden in his mind. Still, it seemed grudging on this of all days to deny Stewart's rather sensible request.

"All right," he said, "but don't be long. Remember we all have to be at vespers by eight, and I don't want your mother walking in this snow."

Stewart was elated at the chance to be alone with Aunt Lucinda, still the most fascinating of his relatives. All his fellow Pittsburghers at Princeton envied him for knowing her, and for them the whisper of scandal going around through their families only added to her luster. Stewart would have loved to know the truth, but he knew he couldn't dare ask. He could only hope that, once they were alone together, something might come out. Thinking such thoughts, he was suddenly shy in the carriage and was glad Aunt Lucinda opened with conventional talk.

"How do you like Princeton, Stewart?"

"Capital."

"Good. I always wished Reed could have finished there. I hope you aren't carrying on the way he did."

"Oh, no. But you know, that old proctor still talks about him. He claims he was a real gentleman, says he's sorry he ever found him . . ."

"Well, that's nice to know. You'll have to tell Reed if you haven't already. Reed and I don't get much good news from your side of the family, you know."

"I know. I'm sorry. . . ."

"Oh, you shouldn't be sorry, it has nothing to do with you, Stewart. I only wish I could see you more, we used to have such fun."

"Yes, I still remember. . . ."

"What's this girl like?"

"What girl?"

"The one you're going to see now."

"Did I say I was going to see a girl?"

"Come now, Stewart," Lucinda said in mock severity, "no more games with your old aunt. What's her name?"

"Jane. Jane Laughlin."

"One of *the* Laughlins?"

"No, a poor cousin. But she'll be there. She goes to Vassar on a scholarship. We met on the train."

"How romantic!"

"Now, don't laugh at me, Aunt Lucinda. . . ."

"I'm not laughing," Lucinda assured him. "There *is* something romantic about meeting on trains or on ships, about being on a journey together."

Something in the tone of her voice caused Stewart to turn and look at his aunt. She was staring straight ahead, and her face blooming white under each street lamp they passed had a kind of dreamy expression. Of coure, he couldn't know that it was on the night train from Philadelphia to New York on the occasion of covering the unveiling of the Statue of Liberty that she and Gil . . . But he could suspect something of the kind, and it gave him a thrill to be in the presence of an authentic woman of the world.

"Yes, I guess you know all about journeys," he ventured.

"I do a bit, Stewart, and I assure you they're wonderful. Oh, I hope you go on lots of journeys too—you and Becky and Henry and Tillie and all of you kids coming along," she said. "I know the way people talk about me—well, I think maybe they're just jealous of my freedom . . . but let me tell you, there's a pretty big world out there waiting to be discovered again and again by anyone who's willing to go out and look for it. I hope you go look, Stewart . . ."

"I will, Aunt Lucinda."

"Oh, don't call me that, Stewart. You make me feel like I'm a hundred. Do you know what they call me around the office —Cindy? Try that."

"Cindy . . ."

"See, it's not so hard, is it?" They were passing a hotel, and Lucinda said, "Just drop me off here, please, Stewart. There's somebody I have to see before I go on to the office."

Stewart reined the horses to a stop, and Lucinda surprised him by leaning over and kissing him on the cheek. She still smelled like candy, and he suddenly wished he could go on talking to her instead of going over and making awkward conversation with Jane Laughlin. But she had moved away again and was collecting her packages and things so he jumped out to give her a hand down from the carriage.

"Good night, Stewart," she said. "And, Stewart, do come see me—any time. There may be some things I could help with that . . . well, good night, and thanks, Stewart."

Gil was waiting for her in the little suite he'd rented on the hotel's top floor. Dear man, he'd made an effort to make it look like Christmas, with a few sprigs of green and a red ribbon around the champagne bottle icing in a bucket. When she came in he winked and pointed above his head, where he'd hung a sprig of mistletoe from the chandelier. She went over to kiss him, and he pulled her down onto his lap. "Have a good Christmas, darling?"

"Not too bad. And you?"

"Awful," he said. "There are just too damned many Joneses in the world, and they were all there. Thank God, Reed has skimmed a couple of them off into the Stewart bucket."

Lucinda extricated herself. "My goodness, Gil, let me get my wraps off. . . ."

"Gladly, and anything else you'd like . . ."

While she was taking off her bonnet and hanging her cape, Gil brought a small package out of the pocket of his coat. She stopped in front of the mirror to straighten her hair, and he stepped up behind her, deftly unsnapped her diamond choker and tossed it carelessly aside. "I never did much like that," he said. "Looks like something for a fancy dog. Try this— and . . . and Merry Christmas, darling."

Gil then draped about her neck a diamond necklace with a pendant diamond larger than anything she'd ever seen. She turned to thank him with another kiss, and he scooped her up in his arms and carried her into the bedroom.

When the storm was over she was still wearing the diamonds. They felt deliciously cool against her hot flesh. She wished she had something to give him, but she didn't. Still holding him close, she whispered in his ear, "This was my present, darling. I hope it was all right. Merry Christmas."

Gil stirred. "All right? . . . I couldn't stand anything more all right. And now for the champagne. No, don't get up. I'll bring it."

He put on the silk robe she'd given him just to wear in the apartment, and she pulled the covers to her chin. While he sat beside her on the bed, they toasted each other and the future neither of them really liked to think about. "Darling, why don't we get married? I mean, it could be arranged; it really could," he said.

Lucinda put a finger to his lips. "Now don't start that again," she said. "You have all those children to think about and . . . and Agnes. She knows, doesn't she?"

"I suppose so, though I don't think she's really sure."

"And I have Henry."

"Yes. Does he know?"

"I think he has to. But whatever you think of him, he's a very kind man . . . he's never said a word."

In the early stages of their affair, when they had been together only on trains or ships or in New York or Philadelphia or London or wherever he'd sent her on assignment, Gil would say, "If you ever want to have an affair, get into the newspaper business. You have a perfect excuse for being away from home." Gradually they learned, or told themselves, that the excuse would work as well in Pittsburgh as anywhere else—only a newspaperman, for example, had a good reason to leave his hearth on Christmas day. It worked for expenses too, like the rent for the apartment. Who was to say the paper couldn't afford housing for guests on the nights the boss had to stay in town? Gil had the apartment telephone wired through the paper's switchboard so that he could take calls as if he were in the office. So the proprieties were more or less maintained, and, although most everybody guessed that Lucinda and Gil were having an affair, only a few people at the office and the hotel knew for certain.

Gil would gallantly renew his offer of marriage from time to time, but Lucinda knew that he didn't, or shouldn't, mean it. At fifty-one, he was in midpassage of a successful career, running a paper so widely quoted nationally that there was now talk of an ambassadorial or cabinet post for him, and with a respectable family life, raising seven children some of whom were already in college and the rest coming quickly along. For all these reasons, in fact, she had laughed off his flirtatious interest in her for two whole years until that trip in '86 to New York when he'd argued long and, he hoped, plausibly. "This statue we're going to see is all about liberty, about freedom. Why can't we be free, too? You know I love you, have loved you from that first moment you walked into my office. I realize it's a pretty rotten thing to say—a man with seven children and all—but I lost Agnes somewhere in the middle of diaper changing and music lessons and Sunday-school picnics and annual caravans to Long Beach and back. She really doesn't much care what goes on in the world or in my head as long as I'm home in time for dinner. I won't deny you're the most beautiful woman I've ever seen, but what I really love you for, Cindy, is your spunk. Just being with you makes me feel alive again. I'll cherish you, believe me, as no woman has ever been cherished, but you'll also be free, Cindy, to go where you want to, do what you want to, be with whomever you want . . ."

"And what about Henry?" she said.

"Do you still love him?"

"Yes, in a way. After all, he taught me how to . . ."

She blushed, and Gil laughed. "Good for Henry! Oh, I know you feel loyal, and I love you for it, but you know, and I know, that you don't have that much in common with him any more. I suspect if he had his way you'd be grubbing around somewhere with his masses instead of sitting here in this Pullman drinking champagne and going to New York . . ."

"I suppose so, but . . ."

"Well then?"

He leaned over and kissed her, kicking shut the door to her compartment, which he had left open at first so as not to alarm her. "Gil, oh Gil . . ." As if sitting outside herself, as if separated from the self she ought to be by the champagne and the roar of the train that seemed lost in a dark tunnel between nowhere and nowhere, she let him undress her, let him admire her in words and caresses bolder than any even Henry had managed, let him finally love her in a way that sent fire through her and set her head to spinning. Afterward, he was gently grateful as they lay together in each other's arms and planned a far more interesting few days in New York than she ever had imagined.

It would never have happened at all, she kept telling herself later, if she and Gil hadn't liked each other so much as friends, as fellow workers. He sincerely admired her work, helped her along with praise and suggestions. They had the same kind of humor, which could be pinpointed in a cartoon of a pompous stuffed shirt slipping on a banana peel. They enjoyed the same things—good food, good wine, good clothes, good gossip. They saw a lot that was wrong with the world around them, but, unlike Henry, they felt no special compulsion or obligation to change it; indeed, they suspected that the only kind of salvation truly possible in an imperfect world was individual salvation. With the detachment apparently born or bred into members of the fourth estate, they pointed to the warts on the face of progress and tended to let it go at that. Gil indulged but found it hard to take seriously dedicated Henry's and militant Alma's vision of the future perfect— indeed the only Stewart, aside from Lucinda, for whom he held real hope was Reed, and his paper enthusiastically endorsed Reed's candidacy. Sharing Gil's laughter, his feeling about people, made Lucinda feel more comfortable with her own feelings about herself and people around her. When her relationship with Gil changed from friendship to something more intimate, she found the world a warmer, more exciting place to be alive in, and it was rewarding to know that Gil did too.

Once in a while, though, as on this Christmas night when she'd plunged directly from the chill of sanctity that seemed to lie upon every gathering of Stewarts directly into the heat of Gil's love, she did experience twinges of guilt. Was she really a bad person, as virtually all of her family and most everybody else she knew in Pittsburgh thought now . . . even though they weren't sure? Was she a lost sheep, in the terms Donald Sharp would probably use? Lost from whom? Not from herself certainly. From God? From whose God? From Reverend Doctor Sharp's God, perhaps. But wasn't there a God for people like her, like Gil—a God who blessed love as much as a lucrative business deal? She hoped so, but the worst of it was, she wasn't all that worried about it. Fact was . . . maybe she was selfish . . . she liked herself the way she was. She didn't even want to marry Gil, partly at least because she knew that whatever they now had between them was very likely to get lost in the unholy mess that surely would result if they both sought divorces. . . .

"A penny for your thoughts."

"They're not worth it," Lucinda said. "I was just wondering whether I'm a fallen woman . . . I guess it's too much Christmas, too much family, too many carols."

"I know what you mean," Gil said, "but not even as a joke are you to think like that. You, my darling, happen to be one of the best people I know. No, take it back . . . *the* best."

"Why? Tell me why; I need to know. Is this terrible what we're doing? I know we're breaking at least two or three commandments right now. We're hurting other people, or could be. So how can you say I'm good when, by everybody's lights, I'm a bad woman . . ."

"Well . . ." He was teasing now, figuring the answer was self-evident.

"See? You were just trying to make me feel good. You're really like all the rest. In fact, maybe that's why I excite you, because you think you're having an affair with a wicked woman, toying with the good old fires of hell? Isn't that it?" She too was teasing . . . well, half-teasing.

"Oh, God, shut up, Cindy. Sure, you're a wicked wicked woman—that's why I keep asking you to marry me. I'm asking it again. After all, I'm a specialist in fallen women. Cindy, please . . ."

Lucinda let the covers drop and reached over to pull Gil's head against her warm breasts. "Hush, love," she said. "You know it wouldn't work—for either of us. You're just too full of Christmas, like me. And now I think it's time we showed up at the office. You go first."

Gil nuzzled into her warmth and sighed. "You know, I think they're right, you are a wicked woman, thank God. . . ."

A Plea from a President

"By God, I wish Andy Carnegie for once could learn to keep his mouth shut!" Clay Frick tossed a file of paper onto Scott's desk. "Look at that. It's Carnegie's old *Forum* article on labor that the union fellows have reprinted and are passing around Homestead. Carnegie's not only all for the right of men to join unions, but he had to go and coin a new commandment à la Carnegie . . . 'Thou shalt not take thy neighbor's job.' In translation, no blacksheep, no strikebreakers."

"It doesn't sound much like his instructions to us before he left for Scotland," Scott said.

Clay Frick was heavier now, with hair trimmed to the new fashion but still wearing the full beard of the eighties, perhaps to lend enough dignity to his forty-two years to equip him for his role as chairman of the Carnegie enterprises. He still had the same steady brown eyes Scott remembered from their first meeting in Connellsville and exuded an even stronger air of quiet command. Now he permitted himself a rare, small smile. "No, it doesn't, does it?" he said. "The old fox will never learn that you can't be all things to all men. He can give away all the organs and libraries he wants to, but he ought to have enough sense to stay out of this labor business."

"You think this will really hurt us?" Scott asked, glancing through the article.

"I couldn't care less," Frick said. "I'm running this company, and I'm going to do things my way. I think Carnegie made that clear before he left. You and me and a few close friends are the only people in this country who know where he is, thank God. If we keep our mouths shut, the press won't be able to get at him—that Rannock Lodge is in the most inaccessible part of those godforsaken highlands, some ten miles by private road from the nearest railway station, they tell me. It'll be a blessing if we have no statements issuing from there. . . . By the way, how are the fortifications coming?"

In that spring of 1892, looking toward trouble when the contract with the Amalgamated Association of Iron and Steel Workers ran out at the company's Homestead plant, Frick had directed that the whole landward side of the property be surrounded by a stout wooden stockade equipped with firing holes, like a fort on the Indian frontier. To the men of Homestead, it was an ominous gesture—and was meant to be. A bit of a threat might cool them off, but, in case it didn't, Frick had also made special arrangements with the Pinkerton National Detective Agency in Chicago to have sufficient force ready at a moment's notice to man the stockade. In Frick's mind, and according to explicit instructions from Carnegie, the negotiations for a new contract were going to be used to break the union's grip on Homestead which, ironically, had delivered the plant into Carnegie's hands. Built in 1879 by rival interests as a challenge to Carnegie, Homestead was so wracked with labor troubles that its owners had to sell out to Carnegie in 1882. Now, with hard times again and steel orders running so low that a long shutdown would be economically acceptable, the Carnegie partners had decided to bring Homestead into line with their nonunion plants like the Edgar Thompson works in Braddock and the Union Iron Mills in the Lawrenceville section of Pittsburgh. Carnegie had even drafted a notice to this effect and instructed Frick to post it at the works, which was the cause for Frick's reaction to Carnegie's public prolabor scripture. Frick didn't post the notice. He felt that a knowledge of the company's true intentions would give the workers a chance to arm for the fight, and he wanted surprise to be on his side.

Frick was a genius at organization and a man of great personal strength. Under his management, H. C. Frick Coke Co. had not only overwhelmed all competitors but had broken the mine union's back in '89 in a long and bloody struggle. It was after that victory that Carnegie prevailed on Frick to take a partnership, merging the coke company with the other Carnegie operations, and move in as chairman of them all. Frick brought Scott right along with him, partly because he needed a man of railroad experience to help in his program of literally binding all the diverse Carnegie plants together with the company's own railroad. Not only physically, but on paper as well, Frick molded various coke and iron and steel-producing units into a single colossus that was enjoying increased profits by the millions each year.

Shy and quiet, soft-voiced and clear-headed, Frick was the supreme example of the kind of self-discipline Scott Stewart himself respected and did his best to practice. Frick was at his desk every morning of the week, except Sunday, by eight and often still there by six. But Frick was no drudge. Behind his controlled clerical exterior lay the heart of a riverboat gambler. When, for example, Henry W. Oliver offered a lease on the huge ore deposits in the Mesabi Range of Minnesota, Frick unhesitatingly put up the money from the Carnegie Company's treasury. His Scotch boss was furious; he'd grown up with Oliver and seen the mercurial salesman win and lose half a dozen fortunes. There was no reason to trust Oliver's judgment now, Carnegie argued, but Frick stood firm. "I'm surprised at Andy," Frick told Scott. "I guess every once in a while his Scotch soul gets the better of him. You know, I've found in life that you never haggle over price when you see something you want. If you have the money, use it."

Though wealthy even by Pittsburgh standards, Frick lived in comparatively modest style on a hill above Penn Avenue in the fashionable Homewood section. His house, Clayton, was no match even for Scott's Oakland castle. It was a tall, narrow structure of stone, fronted by a porch, winged by a gingerbread porte cochere and topped by such a jumble of towers, railings, and juttings of different shapes and sizes that it might have been built by an imaginative child with an ill-assorted box of blocks. The only sign of Frick's true worth was the collection of paintings on the walls within. A contented family man with one small daughter and another child on the way, Frick got his only relaxation from contemplating his pictures.

In finding a wife, Frick seemed to have the same kind of luck that graced his business life. His wedding to Adelaide Howard Childs, with Andrew Mellon standing in as best man, had been the social event of 1881. Apparently it got enough publicity to reach all the way to New York, for when Frick arrived there on his honeymoon, Andrew Carnegie and his mother invited them to lunch at the Windsor Hotel. The invitation was somewhat of a surprise to Frick, who then knew Carnegie only in a business way through selling coke to his mills, and he supposed it had come about as a result of Carnegie's notorious habit of seeking out anyone in the social swim. It was surely a complete surprise to the Fricks when Carnegie rose at the end of the lunch and proposed a toast to "the new Carnegie-Frick partnership." According to reports old Mrs. Carnegie, equally shocked, leaned over and under her breath said to her son, "I know what he gets out of it, but what do we get out of it?" Soon after that Carnegie got an interest in the Frick Coke Co., and now he had Frick himself.

However different they were in personality, Frick and Carnegie were agreed on one thing: cutting costs was the surest way to increase profits. Wherever he might be in the world, Carnegie, studying the reports he got from Pittsburgh, would fire off little notes to his partners such as . . . "See nails are up an eighth of a cent a pound, pard. Any way we could use less of them?" Frick laid the same kind of lash on the men under him. As soon as Scott joined him at Carnegie, Frick told him, "Go out to E. T. and look around, Stewart. Maybe you can see a way to cut costs."

"I don't know a thing about making steel, Mr. Frick," Scott protested.

"Neither do I. That's what we have a man like Captain Jones out there for, but you and I know balance sheets, Stewart, and sometimes we can see more with a fresh eye than the experts."

By the time Scott went out to inspect the Edgar Thompson plant, its superintendent, William R. Jones—or "Captain Bill," as he was known from Civil War service—was famous worldwide as the best technician in the steel business. A spunky little Welshman with an open, beardless face, he made no bones about the fact that he didn't welcome having someone from the front office snoop about his works. Jones was always at war with the front office. When Carnegie brought him down from Johnstown twenty years before, he refused a partnership. "I don't want my thoughts running on business," he told Carnegie. "I've got enough trouble already looking after these works. Just give me a hell of a salary if you think I'm worth it." In the Carnegie version of the story, which he recounted with gusto whenever the name of Jones came up, Carnegie replied, "The salary of the President of the United States is yours." So Jones was making $25,000 a year at a time when a partner like Scott was getting only $12,000. Jones felt he could spit in the eyes of these men who came down from Pittsburgh, and, indeed, he more than once got his way from Carnegie by resigning. Once when Carnegie was leaving for his annual trip to Scotland he told Jones, "You can't imagine the relief I feel when my ship heads eastward out into the ocean." Jones snapped back, "Think of the relief *we* feel. . . ."

"So this is your first time in a mill, Mr. Stewart? I'll send a boy with you to guide you around, but look out you don't get killed," was Captain Jones's greeting. "We have enough trouble with men who're supposed to know their way around."

Within minutes of entering the works, Scott could appreciate that the warning was more than just bad manners. To his orderly mind, the whole place was pandemonium—a scene of screeching, hissing, clanking, exploding activity that numbed the senses. True, there was an awful beauty in the fire that everywhere leaped and glowed and wriggled and spit, turning the great barnlike sheds into crazy and dangerous infernos. Most fascinating to Scott was the converting mill, where the 30,000-pound Bessemers, great pots twice the height of a man, belched saffron flames from their throats as air forced from beneath refined the molten iron by burning away impurities. At the end of the blow when the flame turned blue, the pot was tilted and the metal, glowing white now, was poured into a ladle that in turn slopped it into the train of clay pots that trundled it to the molds. This process, repeated every twenty minutes or so amid a continuous rumble of overhead cranes, rattle of cars, hoot of whistles, shouts of men, clunk of machinery, would, Scott thought, drive a sane man crazy within hours. No matter what was inside his head, a man seemed puny and fragile in the face of these forces he was trying to control—one slip, a second of inattention, and he would be cooked or crushed beyond life, beyond recognition.

Looking at the men around him, their faces grimy, pale, intent, grayed to an age beyond their years, their bodies lean and bent, Scott wondered how they could endure it—and why. He knew the figures: fourteen cents an hour, for example, for the men up there with the worst job of shoveling away the hot slag that was skimmed off the top of the purified steel. Of course, some of the more skilled hands—the tonnage men as they were called because their wages were pegged by contract to the amount of steel produced—could make as much as three or four thousand a year. But for how long? The personnel records Scott had scanned indicated that there was hardly a man over fifty in the plant; they were literally burned out by the fire they handled. Here at the Edgar Thompson works, Captain Jones was trying a radical experiment that was being watched with much skepticism from the front office— eight-hour shifts. Though everywhere else steel men worked twelve hours a day, Jones argued that the cost of a larger labor force would be easily defrayed by fewer accidents, more efficiency, and perhaps a longer working life for the skilled men. No wonder Jones was so popular with the workers, but was he properly representing the interests of the owners?

On the way back to town, Scott pondered the question—the economic use of labor was the only thing he really understood about the operation. He spent the night casting up figures, comparing Homestead and rival companies where they did work twelve hours with the E. T. He concluded that the Jones system, however humane, just wasn't competitive and so informed Frick. "You see, I knew some good would come of your going out there, Stewart," Frick said. "Let's have Mr. Jones in for a talk."

Jones was furious. Without so much as looking at Scott, but speaking only to Frick, he said, "I knew I shouldn't have let this damned accountant anywhere near the plant. I . . ."

"Mr. Stewart is a partner," Frick said icily.

"I don't give a damn what he is. He don't know a thing about making steel. My job is producing, and the reason the E. T. has been busting all records is that I discovered flesh and blood ain't made for twelve hours of continuous labor. I had this all straightened out with Tom Carnegie and now . . ."

"Mr. Tom Carnegie's been dead three years, Captain Jones, and I'm the chief executive of this company," Frick said. "Mr. Stewart here has done what is, in my opinion, a remarkable job of analyzing all the figures. His conclusion, with which I agree, is that production or no production, we would save money by returning to twelve-hour shifts. After all, that's the common practice in the industry."

"If I stuck to common practice, you'd have nothing but a common plant, Mr. Frick."

"I'm fully aware of your reputation, Captain Jones," Frick said. "And I ask you to take Mr. Stewart's figures back with you and study them. We'll have another talk later."

Jones scooped up the papers Frick handed him and went out without a word. There was never another discussion. A few weeks later a furnace at the E. T. developed a hang—a block in the flow of metal—and Captain Bill went to examine it. The furnace exploded in his face. Jumping back from the scorching flame, he struck his head against the metal side of a car and suffered a fracture of the skull. It was a shock to everyone in the company, but the men said Captain Bill died where he would have wanted to—on the floor of the mill. Not long afterward, under the management of the young and amiable Charlie Schwab, who was a partner and more than a little interested in what went on in the front office, the men of E. T.

returned to twelve-hour shifts, and Scott Stewart became Frick's right-hand man.

By the late spring of 1892, Scott's position with Frick was widely known outside of the company, which was the reason Whitelaw Reid, the editor of the New York *Tribune* and Republican candidate for Vice-President, came all the way to Pittsburgh for a conference with John Reed Stewart who was on the ballot for the Court of Common Pleas in Allegheny County. The meeting was held within the thick walls of the Duquesne Club, where their words were likely to fall only on the ears of the discreet servants who brought them food and drink.

"We have a problem this year, as you know, Mr. Stewart," Reid began. "I think the chances are more than even for a Democratic sweep of such proportions that it could engulf even a candidate like yourself. It's bad enough that Platt and Quay have said they won't take part in the campaign, but now that he's a Wall Street lawyer and making loud noises against free silver, Cleveland's picking up a lot of business support."

"Yes, I know all that, Mr. Reid, but how do you expect me to help?" Reed asked.

"Well, confidentially, we hear that negotiations between the Carnegie people and the union out at Homestead are going badly. A noisy strike right now might be just the last straw for us," Whitelaw Reid said. "I've tried to get to Andy Carnegie in Scotland without success, and Frick just shuts the door in my face. He's an arrogant type, I must say."

"So I hear," Reed said.

"Oh, you don't know him?"

"I'm afraid I don't move in those circles, Mr. Reid."

"I thought with your brother Scott . . ."

"I think I should explain that my brother and I don't see exactly eye to eye on a number of things. We seldom even meet."

Whitelaw Reid was visibly disappointed. "Then you won't speak to him?"

"If I did, I doubt it would do much good," Reed said. "You'd have to understand my brother to know why. He greatly admires Frick, and he honestly regards it as his God-given duty to deliver the workingman from the clutches of the devilish unions. As far as Frick and my brother are concerned, the rest of the world can go hang when it comes to a challenge to their power to run the Carnegie company the way they see fit."

"What do you suggest I do, Mr. Stewart? The party designated me—President Harrison himself talked to me about it —to try to get this strike settled or at least put off until after the election."

"I'll talk to Scott, but I guarantee you it won't help," Reed said. "I think your best bet is Carnegie. He's supposed to be a liberal. You know they're hoisting him with his own petard out in Homestead right now—passing around a tract he wrote some years ago giving his blessing to unionism. He fancies himself such a benevolent public figure that he might be reached on grounds of embarrassment. Right now he's certainly in the public eye here. I suppose you've heard about the institute he plans to build out in Schenley Park?"

"Yes, indeed, I saw a sketch of it in *Harper's Weekly*—very impressive. Well, I'll try again, but nobody will even tell me where he is. I've been trying to communicate through the American Embassy in London, and all I got in reply was something to the effect that he's left everything in Frick's hands. Maybe you could at least get me his address?"

"I'll try."

The mission wasn't much to Reed's taste. He hated to ask Scott for any kind of help, but he'd become enough of a politician to realize that doing what amounted to a favor for the President of the United States could prove very useful indeed. And if he were to follow through in his plan to use the workings of the system to improve it from within, he'd hardly be consistent if he passed up an opportunity to have, at least potentially, a President in his debt. He decided Scott's home was a better place for a talk than the office, and so on the evening of his conference with Whitelaw Reid, he fortified himself with enough Old Overholt at the club to quiet his misgivings and set out for Oakland. He found Scott so pale and edgy that he truly felt sorry for him. Scott admitted that Frick had dumped the burden of negotiations on his shoulders and that they were going so badly he was having to work night and day. Also the news from Saranac was bad. Scott had hoped to bring his little family together during the summer at Ocean City, New Jersey, the many-steepled seaside resort he favored because of its ban against alcohol, but it looked now as if Martha wouldn't be permitted to leave the sanitarium. Reed offered his sympathies. All the way out he'd been trying to decide how to approach Scott. Now that he saw his brother's stern, eagle-beaked face, etched ever deeper with worry lines between the brows, he felt the only way to present the matter to Scott was direct and unadorned, and so he related the whole story of Whitelaw Reid's visit.

Scott didn't respond immediately. He'd long since fallen in with the universal habit of Pittsburgh businessmen, cigar smoking, and so he selected one from a humidor on his desk and pushed it toward Reed. "Very good Havanas—seventy-five cents apiece," he said. "Clay Frick put me onto them. Oh, I forgot that you smoke those abominable cigarettes."

Scott used the ritual of carefully clipping the end of his cigar and then lighting it to gain time to meditate about his response. Finally, he said, "I can well understand how this might mean a lot to you, Reed, but I can't tell you a thing—particularly Mr. Carnegie's whereabouts. My first loyalty is to Mr. Frick and the Carnegie company."

"Ahead of the President of the United States?"

"He may be President now," Scott said, "but when Mr. Harrison runs again in November, he's just another politician. He's only interested in this for political reasons."

"But I always thought it was important to people like you and Frick to see a Republican in the White House. The way you've talked for as long as I can remember, the Republican Party has been right up there next to God."

"Ordinarily you'd be right, but Cleveland seems a sound enough man. . . ."

"Even with his talk of tariff reform? Doesn't that scare you a little? You must know by now that it's a high tariff that's been keeping out competition from British and German steels all these years and pouring money into the Carnegie treasury," Reed said.

"Oh, I think we can take care of that in Congress. But in any case, in the long run we'd be in more trouble if we ever let these union fellows dictate their terms than if we lost a fight on the tariff for a few years."

"What are they asking for?"

"Well, I guess that's no secret," Scott said. "We have the usual problem of money even though there are fellows there making as much as $7.60 a day. Frick wants to amend this tonnage business—cut it by about fifteen percent. Every time the company pays for new and more efficient equipment it means an automatic increase for those fellows who haven't done anything to deserve it. I think we might get together on money—the men know as well as we do that orders are falling off and it may get down to a matter of no work at all."

"What's holding it up, then?" Reed asked.

"A small thing, I guess, to anyone outside the business," Scott said. "The men want the new contract to terminate in

July of 1895, and Frick insists it should run only until December 31, 1894."

"Why?"

"Can't even you see what these union fellows are up to? They want a summer expiration date because it's a lot easier to get the men out on strike when it's warm."

"And harder when it's cold."

The sarcasm in Reed's voice caused a spot of color to rise in Scott's pale cheeks. "Don't tell me you're still with these fellows. I should have thought you'd learned enough about strikes in that railroad mess. . . ."

Right now Reed wished mightily that Scott was a drinking man. Perhaps if they could share a friendly cup they could have one more go at trying to reconcile their differences. Just as he'd suspected when he was younger, he had discovered that there was some truth to the old adage—*in vino veritas*. He had got closer to more different kinds of people in saloons than in churches or offices or even homes, where people seemed to be compelled to wear the proper mask for whatever role they were playing. How could Scott stand being forever sober, forever clear-eyed in a world of such appalling sights? Henry once said that Scott wore his own special kind of blinders that protected him, as they might a high-strung thoroughbred, from confusion on the track. A thoroughbred . . . yes, he guessed Scott was that. He just didn't much like his track. . . ."

"Oh, I learned a good deal, Scott," Reed said, coming out of his reverie to answer his brother's question. "I learned what it feels like to be caught up in something you can't control. Unions are the only way those men can have any share in the power that controls their lives. I can tell you if I were in their shoes I'd be the first to sign up."

Scott shook his head as if he didn't believe what he was hearing, and Reed decided it was pointless to carry the argument further. If only Scott had been just a bit venal, or at least a cynic, he might have been more flexible, more open to other sources of self-interest. As it was, his undeniable rectitude and sureness made him impervious to another truth.

Going home, Reed continued to reflect on Scott and his loyalty to principle. Principle . . . or princi*pal*? For Scott and the excellent company he kept they were certainly intertwined . . . and, in their convinced view, with divine blessings. Take a true believer, like John D. Rockefeller who, on one of the rare occasions he ever opened his mouth, was quoted as saying, "A man should make all he can and give all he can."

For Reed, it sounded all right until you asked: was giving enough to make up for the means of getting? Scott honestly thought so. Carnegie thought so. But what was the use of building a library on the hill in Braddock when the men in the mills below sweated to such exhaustion they couldn't stay awake to read? Carnegie's answer would have been that the man who wanted to get ahead would make himself stay awake—let the rest sleep. If Reed could have heard Frick inveigh against the way Carnegie was always opening his mouth, he might very well have agreed, but for a somewhat different reason. He remembered something he'd once read by Carnegie . . . "I am a firm believer in the doctrine that people deserving necessary assistance at critical periods in their career usually receive it. As a rule, those who show willingness to help themselves need not fear about obtaining help from others. . . ." The key word was "deserving"—nothing there about a man broken on the wheel, or in the mill. . . . That newspaper fellow in Chicago who was always putting cracks into the mouth of a fictional Mr. Dooley probably had it about right when he made Dooley say of John D. Rockefeller, "His heart was pure seein' that he never did wrong save in th' way of business."

Reed was thankful there were a few people on the horizon like Teddy Roosevelt. Sure, they laughed about Roosevelt's high-pitched voice and the way he parted his hair in the middle and his foppish clothes, but somehow Roosevelt had managed to help clean up New York, and he was proving effective nationally on the Civil Service Commission. The fact that Roosevelt was a Republican may have been the only good reason to hope for Harrrison's reelection. Now Reed was faced with reporting his failure to Whitelaw Reid; about the only thing he could add to what the candidate already knew was that the sense he got of company intransigence from Scott made trouble a virtual certainty. The deadline for the end of negotiations was only weeks away, as Reed understood it, on June 24, and it seemed unlikely anybody could do much in the meantime to stop the collision. If the thing turned out to be as bad as everybody was predicting, Reed could only hope that the country's voters would prove more discriminating than the nation's top politicians in separating him from his brother.

Alma was waiting up when Reed came home. She was reading in the den of the Ridge Avenue house, which had been transformed into their favorite room with some white paint on the paneling and Pittsburgh sketches by Lucinda Schmidt in place of antlers on the walls. Reed kissed his wife and went right to the corner, where he kept a small bar in a gutted sewing-machine stand that had been refinished to match the white of the walls. He poured a brandy for each of them, lit two cigarettes, and handed one to Alma. By tacit agreement, this room was considered out of bounds to Mrs. Jones so that she wouldn't be obliged to endure the hurt of seeing her daughter smoking and drinking under her own roof. But, unlike the dens in other homes up and down Ridge Avenue or in any other fashionable part of the city, it was as much her room as his—Reed and Alma shared everything. Reed often blessed his inspiration to elope—that one daring act had so thoroughly cut them both off from their roots that they'd been forced to seek nourishment in each other.

Reed hadn't been able to warn Alma he would be late, but she didn't reproach him. She was perhaps more interested in politics than he, and she understood the vagaries of a politician's day. She could tell by the expression on Reed's face that this had been a bad one, and she encouraged him, as she put it, to "spit it out in Momma's hand." He did, sparing her nothing of his bitterness at the high-handed way the men of business around him operated. When he'd finished, Alma said, "Reed, I love you for the way you think, but you've just got to stop eating yourself up about things you can't change. Just wait till you get on that bench, and for ten years, at least, *you* can call the shots the way *you* see them."

"That is, *if* I get on that bench. Whitelaw Reid wasn't joking about the outlook this fall. He wouldn't have come all the way out here unless . . ."

"I know that's true nationally," Alma said, "but I haven't seen any signs of the Magee-Flinn machine losing its grip, have you?"

"Well, no . . ."

"All right, then, stop worrying, Reed Stewart, and come over here and kiss me like you mean it."

On his way over to the couch where she was sitting Reed took the precaution of turning the key to lock the door. Late as it was, he didn't think they ought to take a chance on Mrs. Jones looking for her perpetually misplaced glasses or a child, wandering in its sleep, stumbling into the room. He knew from the tone of her voice, from the look in her eye that a touch was going to set her off. It was a recurring miracle he would never understand, and nobody else would ever suspect. Though the heritage of flesh and bone from her mother, the bearing of two children, the over-consumption common among the wealthy had turned Alma into a woman who would be described as statuesque by her friends and formidable by her enemies, she turned into a ravenous female animal in Reed's arms. She liked to make love on impulse and almost anywhere but in bed—in the carriage, in the barn, in the study, in an open field on a summer afternoon. "It makes me feel . . . I don't know . . . wicked, and I like to feel wicked," she once told him. So did he, and each coupling, like their elopement, took on the added excitement of flaunting respectability. . . .

Having spent themselves now, they lay naked in each other's arms, trading languorous caresses, listening to the cicadas in the June night outside the open window. "I don't know how I was lucky enough to get you," Reed said.

"You won't feel that way long. I'm getting fat—feel this," she said, and pulled his hand over her swelling abdomen.

"All the more of you to love."

"You're just too sweet, Reed. I hate getting fat, but I hate worse doing anything about it. I wish I could have a figure like Lucinda's."

"She probably gets more exercise like this."

"Reed, you're terrible. . . ."

"Well, it's the truth. You notice your uncle has a pretty good figure, too, for a middle-aged man."

Alma put her fingers to his lips. "Reed, hush. We aren't supposed to admit anything like that is happening."

"Why not, for God's sake? What's so wrong in their loving each other?"

"Well, they *are* married. . . ."

"Yes, but marriage and love don't always go together, do they? I think we're just plain lucky."

"Me too . . ."

"But I don't think lucky people like us have any special right to sit in judgment on other people and say their only problem is not being like us. I guess that's what upsets me so much about Scott's friends. Most of them have had one good fortune after another and pretty soon they get to thinking they deserve it, that they're the elect of God or . . ."

"There you go again. I thought I took your mind off all of that. I guess I'm losing my charms."

"Never, never," Reed murmured, covering her ample body with kisses until they came together again, just as a summer thunderstorm broke in and about them. When they could be aware of anything beyond their own passion, they heard the whimper of a frightened child at the door. Alma got up and quickly dressed while Reed just lay there, wondering if life could ever again present him with such a gift.

A Death at Homestead

For weeks now, May Stewart had been tiptoeing around the house as if somebody were dying. It was on account of Daddy's "nerves," as Grandmother explained it. She couldn't even practice the piano when Daddy was in the house, although in the past it had been the thing she did that seemed to interest him most. He hardly talked to her. At breakfast it was a "good morning" and peck on the cheek, and if he talked at dinner at all, it was stuff about business that only Grandmother could understand. Sometimes May worried that her father didn't love her, but then she guessed from the way the other girls talked that her daddy was pretty much like all the other busy fathers. It was her mother who was truly different, and although she hated herself for it, she was glad when her mother had to go away and wouldn't be around to embarrass her in front of friends with her continual sighing and those awful white muslin draperies she wore.

Sometimes she thought life would be better if Benjy were home, but he hardly ever was since they started sending him East to prep school and then to camp all summer. They told him it was to broaden him and prepare him for college, but May knew from hearing them talk that it was to get him off their hands now that Mother was sick all the time. She secretly wished they would get her off their hands, too, but they said she was too young and that it wasn't right for girls to be away from home. May didn't know why girls were all that different from boys; in fact, until a year or so ago she could beat Benjy up even though he was more than a year older than she was. Whenever she did it, they all landed on her about Benjy's "delicate health." When they would get letters from Benjy saying he was in the infirmary with a cold or something, her father would frown and say to Grandmother, "I worry about the boy. Takes after his mother, unfortunately. Do you suppose he could have it, too?" She didn't know why her father always talked about "it" when everybody knew that what her mother had was tuberculosis, which the doctor said was a very common disease that nobody should be ashamed of. Still, she was embarrassed that her mother was different from other mothers, and she didn't like it that her brother was "delicate" and always away when other girls' brothers were around to show them how to skate and swim and play ball and everything.

It was hard for a sheltered twelve-year-old like May, whose forays into the world were mostly limited to carriage rides to church and the exclusive girls' day school she attended a few blocks from home or an occasional trip downtown in the cable car to go shopping with Grandma, to know just how different her life might be from that of a normal girl, but she suspected it was considerable. For one thing, there was the house itself. Nobody else she knew lived in a castle. She might have taken it as a matter of course if it hadn't been for her cousins. They always said it was spooky, and whenever they came over that devil Stewart Sharp would organize all of them into games of "ghost" and "dungeon" that would leave May trembling with fright long after they'd gone. Even now there were parts of the house, like the attic tower room, that she would not visit alone, and she knew she was lucky that they could afford to have a maid like Tracy who slept in the room next to hers with the door open and kept away the spooks at night.

Then there was the music. For as long as she could remember there had been music around her most of her waking hours—her mother playing the piano, the gramophone. . . . Even before she could read she was picking out tunes of her own on the piano, and long before she started to school an enormous, perfumed lady by the name of Madame Lutz began coming to the house, as she still did, every Thursday afternoon to give her lessons. It was far and away the best time of her week, of her life. For half an hour or more before Madame Lutz was due, May would sit impatiently on the little seat below the stained-glass window in the hall so that she could open the door herself. Invariably, Madame Lutz would sweep her into her arms, hold her against an ample bosom where she nearly suffocated in the waves of sweet perfume or sneezed from the tickle of the feather boa the teacher always wore. Madame Lutz would caress her with "my precious . . . my genius . . ." Nobody else ever said anything like that to her, but she knew that Madame Lutz meant it. When May played, Madame Lutz would sit beside her, tapping time against the music rack with her lorgnette and emitting "oohs" and "aahs" of pleasure. Time after time she assured May, "You are my best pupil, my little genius . . . a female Mozart."

Aware that she was not pretty and that she was awkward in classroom or Sunday school, May unconsciously turned more and more to music, the only thing she was really good at, as the support, almost the reason, for her existence. It provided a kind of triumph, too, because she was always being asked to accompany the school chorus or play the hymns for Sunday school or give a little concert for visiting parents. Her father was proud of her on these occasions, and he let her know it in his odd, shy way with an extra pat on the back or a few clipped words such as "very good, May." Though her mother had first suggested the lessons and had sat by her side encouraging her through the beginning exercises and children's tunes, her attitude oddly began to change when May moved on to playing Liszt and Chopin and Mozart with a kind of flawless grace that Martha could not match. Maybe it was her sickness or something, but toward the end, just before she went away, her mother would often scream at her to stop playing, saying it made her head ache. And Martha stopped playing herself. She refused even to listen to the new Victrola Daddy brought her one Christmas even though the records sounded much better than the old cylinder thing she once loved. Maybe it was this reaction to the music that made May secretly glad her mother went away, more than the embarrassment about her clothes and everything, but now even Daddy was getting touchy about her playing. It looked like it was going to be an awful summer. . . .

Caught up between a son who seemed on the verge of nervous collapse and a granddaughter turning sulky with bewilderment, Mary Stewart would have agreed with May's feelings about the summer. She was disappointed that the plans for going to Ocean City had collapsed. Nobody really understood what the annual respite at the shore meant to her except Lucinda, who remembered how the doctor had always wanted to take her to view the sea. When she was there, Mary would just sit on the boardwalk by the hour and stare out at the heaving, ever-changing water and indulge herself in memories. At sixty-one she was not really so old, and Martha's illness had brought her unexpectedly back into the arena of life. Still, she knew she would never again experience that sustaining sense of shared adventure, of moving toward unknown future delights that were hers in those years of marriage to the doctor. This knowledge was with her always like a kind of lump in the throat that allowed her to swallow but threatened to choke her at any time. She didn't know whether it helped or hurt to realize, as she did now, that the lump might be there, though smaller, even if the doctor were still at her side, that it really was a symptom of time, of life ebbing rather than the consequence of some single event like the doctor's tragic death. Probably everyone of her age and experience had the same sensation, but that was no solace. They passed each other on the boardwalk with eyes shuttered by a lifetime of learning to conceal the truth from each other, instinctively aware that opening them now might reveal a reality too painful to bear. Sometimes Mary wondered if the doctor had not come to feel this particular and yet common lump earlier than most, and if his dreams of the sea weren't an instinctive yearning for the limitless horizon it seemed to provide.

Mary was grateful that her children were still too young to share this intimation. Scott, she was sure, truly believed that, with God's help, he was in control not only of himself but the forces that had been put into his hand by reason of his wealth and position. Mary had once felt that way too, but whatever it was that snapped in her on that morning when she saw the doctor hanging in the barn had never come taut again. She guessed she still believed in God, but He bore little relationship to Scott's God, who seemed forever to be separating saints from sinners; He was more the kind of God who let rain fall on the just and unjust alike. She still went through the forms of worship, still found a kind of balm in the sonorous words of the scripture and hymns, but she found, too, the longer she lived, the less certain she was about anything. Mary had come almost to envy Sarah, who once she became reconciled to the physical facts of life found the daily business of her role as wife and mother completely satisfying; there was no evidence of unanswered questions in her placid mind. But Lucinda was, as Mary had always known she would be, still a loving vexation. Grieved as she was over the rumors and gossip about Lucinda, Mary stood in awe of the driving force in her younger daughter that might, just might, sail her to some strange shore of contentment that none of the rest of them could perceive. In any case, Lucinda had a kind of steel in her, a belief in herself as strong as Scott's in his God, that she felt would protect her. It was Reed who, despite his new wealth, his obviously happy marriage, and his growing public fame worried Mary the most. She felt he had been scarred more deeply by his accident, as she liked to think of it, than any of them would ever know. There was a kind of gentle cynicism in most everything Reed said or did that was too close to her own to be quite healthy in a young man of twenty-eight. She sensed it had something to do with his drinking, which couldn't help but upset her with the memories she bore. And yet in the end Reed always seemed to do the right thing, or at least the sensible thing, like casting his lot with the Republicans instead of waging a frustrating, quixotic battle like Henry's.

When Mary compared her own family with people like the Schmidts, she had to acknowledge that the Stewarts were made of good stuff. Poor Henry. Poor Martha. Both of them had retreated from life's realities in different ways. She was glad that Lucinda had had enough sense to make a life of her own, and she wished now that Scott's piety had not sentenced him to bear with Martha "as long as we both shall live." True, tuberculosis, as the doctor explained it, was a contagious illness that might strike anyone down, and the seeds of it were in Martha long before their marriage. Perhaps Scott, or she herself, should have detected it then; she could still remember Martha's complaints about cold and coughing on her long-ago trip to Chautauqua. But Mary was sure that it was Martha's own drifting away from life, symbolized in those dreadful white shrouds she wrapped herself in, that had brought her to her present state. Mary simply could not discuss Martha with Scott, who became silent and took on that terrible tight look about his mouth whenever she tried. If God really had mercy, Mary thought, He would take Martha soon before Scott— and, worse, the children—sank under the weight of her illness too. Meanwhile, Mary felt that she had to do everything possible, however unfair it might seem to May, to help Scott through the crisis that was developing at Homestead.

Usually reticent about his business affairs, Scott talked incessantly over the dinner table about the Homestead negotiations and even prayed over them while he was saying grace. Mary listened as sympathetically as she could, since she felt that this was perhaps his only release from the strain. Although Scott, his nerves and temper frazzled by long negotiating sessions, predicted serious trouble with the recalcitrant workers, he could not foresee the tragic consequences this would bring on his own family. It never occurred to him that his impractical, fuzzy-minded brother-in-law, Henry Schmidt, would involve himself in what was just a business problem—more grievous than usual, perhaps, but of no concern to anyone else—of the Carnegie company.

It might not have occurred to Henry either, except for the recent and surprising liberality of his New York editors. One of them wired him and offered expenses and an interesting fee for an on-the-spot color story about Homestead. "What luck!" Henry told Lucinda, flashing the wire in front of her. "I've wanted to go down there, and now I've got a good excuse."

"Do you think you should, Henry?" she asked. "From what I hear around the office, people in Homestead are in an ugly mood. It's dangerous for newspapermen . . ."

"Maybe for your people, but not for me. Everybody knows whose side I'm on."

"Are you sure? I hate to say it, but you're not so widely read in Pittsburgh and . . ."

"But I will be now . . . don't you see?—this is really my chance. Maybe there will be two famous writers in this family."

"Henry, please. I wish you wouldn't."

"Why not? Nothing keeps you from your job, even Christmas night."

"Touché," she said, blushing slightly and hoping he wouldn't notice. "But, Henry, please be careful. . . ."

So on Friday, July 1, 1892, Henry Schmidt boarded a train in the city for the short trip to Homestead, which lay on the south bank of the Monongahela some six miles to the east. He was full of exciting expectation. Although he'd written a backgrounder on the dispute, he had never seen the place nor met the steel workers he so admired. Despite Lucinda's warning and accounts in the press of reporters being turned back by angry mobs, Henry hoped to rent a room in the town and stay on as an eyewitness to further developments. Something was sure to happen. Henry knew that men like Henry Clay Frick and his brother-in-law, Scott Stewart, would not long tolerate a situation in which the workers had taken over the whole town and would not permit company officials to enter their own fortified works.

On the train ride, Henry reviewed the situation. The town of Homestead was virtually new, laid out in '72 on the old Amity Homestead farm John McClure had cleared two generations before in a broad bend of the Monongahela about a mile below Braddock's Crossing. Because of the panic of '73, the place didn't prosper until six years later when Andrew

Kloman, the disgruntled ironmaster on whose technical skill the whole Carnegie enterprise was founded, broke away from Carnegie and, backed by a number of other businessmen who formed Pittsburgh Bessemer Steel Company, selected the river flats at Homestead as the site of the most modern steel mill in the country. As a result of Kloman's artistry, the mill was a wonder, but the men who came to work it proved difficult from the first. They not only fought management, they fought each other, carrying their national and ethnic rivalries with them into the plant where the Welsh dominated the rail mill, the Irish the converting works, the Germans another section, and the Slavs still another. It didn't help matters when Pittsburgh Bessemer engaged tough William Clark, a noted strikebreaker, as manager. In the next three years, the Amalgamated Association of Iron and Steel Workers, grown to 70,000 nationally, flexed its muscles continually at Homestead until Clark was forced to resign and Bessemer Steel had to sell out to Carnegie at a loss. As late as '89, just before Frick was in full command, the Amalgamated, which represented only 800 skilled workers out of the 3,800 labor force at Homestead, won a round against Carnegie and earned the contract Frick so deplored.

On June 23, 1892, the day before the deadline ran out on negotiations for a new contract, Frick met with representatives of the Amalgamated in his *Chronicle-Telegraph* building offices. Although they were close on the money issue, Frick was adamant on the need for a new expiration date. The union was equally adamant; June 24 passed with no concession from either side. On June 25, the company posted notices at the plant that it would deal only with individual workers, and Frick informed the already alerted Pinkerton agency to have a force of at least three hundred men ready in Ashtabula, Ohio, by July 5. The plan was to bring this force by train to McKees Rocks, a community some ten miles west of Pittsburgh on the south bank of the Ohio River, and then transport them by boat up the Monongahela to the Homestead plant. This was one thing Henry didn't know for sure, nor did the workers of Homestead. Frick had insisted on absolute secrecy in his dealings with the Pinkerton people, and only a few reliable executives like Scott were aware how far it had gone. Still, everybody with eyes to see knew something was in the wind—the board stockade at the plant had recently been topped by barbed wire, several strands of which were kept continually charged with electricity by the plant generator.

By the time Henry set out for Homestead, several skirmishes

had already taken place. In one, angered workers had hanged Frick and plant superintendent J. A. Potter in effigy and then had turned a hose on the men Potter sent to cut them down. Leaders of the Amalgamated had set up a Union Advisory Committee under the chairmanship of Hugh O'Donnell, a skilled roller, and had virtually taken over control of the town with the cooperation and blessing of Burgess John McLuckie, another skilled roller. The committee, fearing that the company would import "blacksheep" strikebreakers posted guards and patrol boats to keep any unwanted strangers, in-including newspapermen, out of town. But Henry knew that County Sheriff William H. McCleary had gone down to Homestead on a train a few hours ahead of his and figured he'd by now probably opened the place up.

As the train chugged across the river and then lurched eastward under the shoulders of the steep hills on the south bank, Henry began to understand how a town not much more than a good walk away from the city could be turned into an isolated fortress by its citizens. The land between Homestead and Pittsburgh, sheering from narrow valleys up wooded hillsides to peaks of two or three hundred feet, was forbiddingly wild and rugged. Henry could easily imagine Indians still coursing its torturous paths. The river itself, whipped by wind and eddied where the current swept around bends and snags, was as forbidding as the empty wall of forested hills on the far bank. Homestead, when the train jerked and hissed to a stop beside a little brick station house, seemed as remote from the city of banks and cathedrals and office buildings Henry had just left as a frontier mining town in the West. A few fairly solid saloons and churches and stores flanked Amity Street, leading up the hill from the station, which stood just south of the gates to the plant, but the rest was a collection of grubby frame dwellings, many of them jutting precariously from the hillside like outcroppings of dirty rock. The streets were unpaved, except where they were roughly cobbled at the crossings, and rickety wooden stairs laced the hills. The day was relatively clear because of the work stoppage, but the gray-sided buildings and the grime everywhere testified to the pall that habitually engulfed the little community when the plant was spewing smoke and cinder into the trough between the hills that flanked the river.

Hundreds of people—men, women, and children—were eddying aimlessly about the area between the station and the plant stockade when Henry detrained. The only passenger to get off the train, he was immediately surrounded on the platform by a group of men. Unshaven for the most part, dressed in work shirts and pants of corduroy and denim, several of them armed with shotguns or pistols, they were a menacing sight even to Henry's sympathetic eyes. Their words were also no comfort. "Who are you, fellow? What are you here for? You one of them sheriff's boys? If you are, you'd better get your tail back on the next train. We run McCleary out of here an hour ago—him and Potter, too."

Henry held out a hand to the nearest man, who refused to take it. "I'm Henry Schmidt," he said.

"Henry Schmidt?" one fellow said aloud to the crowd now pressing in close behind the ring of men. "He says he's Henry Schmidt. Now who in the hell is Henry Schmidt? Anybody know a Henry Schmidt?"

"Oh, nobody here would know me," Henry said, trying one of his broadest smiles. "I've never been here before. . . ."

"Never been here before, he says," the self-elected spokes-man echoed, and then turned to Henry. "You one of them newspaper fellows? You look like one of them newspaper fellows."

"Well, not exactly . . ."

"Not exactly. Not exactly, he says. He's not exactly a newspaperman," the spokesman called out, obviously enjoying his role. "He's just like a woman who says she ain't exactly pregnant."

This earned appreciative snickers from the crowd. Henry, misunderstanding, laughed too. Just as he'd suspected, they were good fellows, full of earthy humor. As soon as he could get a few of them together in a saloon he'd get along with them just fine. . . . Singling out the spokesman, he said, "That's good—like a woman who 'ain't exactly pregnant.' Say, I'd like to buy you a drink and . . ."

"And go to hell—I don't drink with no 'not exactly' news-papermen. You're all nothing but a bunch of damned spies . . ."

"But I'm not a newspaperman. I write for magazines— labor magazines in New York. Somebody here must have heard of me. Where's Mr. O'Donnell?"

"O'Donnell don't have time for the likes of you," the spokesman said. "Nobody here's heard of Henry Schmidt. You heard me ask, didn't you?"

The day was hot. The faces closing in around Henry were glistening with sweat, and Henry realized he was sweating too. Trickles of it ran from his armpits down along his ribs. He reached for a handkerchief to mop his face, and a hand grabbed his arm. "Watch it—no guns, buddy," a voice said in his ear.

"But you don't realize I . . . I'm for you. . . ."

At that, a man who had been silent up to now spat at him, and a dark blob of tobacco juice hit the front of his shirt and slowly trickled down. "For us? Nobody outside's for us," the man said to the crowd at large. "Funny this fellow showed up same day as the sheriff, ain't it? I say let's teach him to stay out of this town."

Somebody behind Henry grabbed the neck of his coat and wrenched it so tight his arms were pinned to his sides. The man who'd spat on him struck a stinging blow to his face and then doubled him with a punch in the stomach. Fighting now for his life, Henry struggled, wrenched free of his coat but went down under the weight of several men, all of whom were pummeling him. Lying on his back, he saw a great heavy boot descending directly on his face. With the impact, there came a searing flash of light and then the merciful dark.

Henry Schmidt was dead before the crowd really knew what it was about. When the men pulled themselves away from his smashed, lifeless body, a curious hush settled over everybody. Those who could see just stared at Henry; the others tried to squeeze forward for a look. Then the argument began. Some wanted to take him off and bury him somewhere on the hill. Others thought they should go tell O'Donnell and McLuckie. But the self-appointed leaders, the men who'd actually done this, had to save face. To hell with all that, they argued, let's send him back to Pittsburgh to show we mean business down here. And so they did. They stuffed the remains of Henry Schmidt into a burlap bag, attached a crude note—"This is what happens to spies in Homestead"—and delivered it to the crew of the next westbound train.

At the depot in Pittsburgh the body was put on a cart and trundled across town to the morgue. There, after notifying the sheriff, the attendants did their best to patch and powder Henry's cuts and bruises so that his face could be recognized by friends or relatives if they came to view him. Then they stretched him out on a slab in the cooler beside the still unclaimed body of an aged black man who had died quietly of drink beside a piling on the Monongahela wharf.

The news, of course, was going to be sensational in the next morning's papers, and one of the first to hear about it was Gil Jones. Managing Editor Johnson brought it to him as soon as the *Call* man phoned in from the morgue. Lucinda was due in the office any minute, and Johnson felt that it was up to Jones to handle the situation. Jones agreed and asked that some-body be stationed at the door to bring Lucinda directly to his office. Then he put his head down on his hands and tried to prepare himself for the ordeal. Gil Jones was aware that in her way, Lucinda still loved Henry, and he'd come to respect her for it. That poor bastard Schmidt, always a loser.

Lucinda was prepared for almost anything when she was rushed into Gil's office, except what she heard. "You sent for me, Gil?"

He looked up at her, and there was such a confusion, such a look of warm sympathy in his eyes that she was abruptly unsettled. "I'm afraid I have bad news for you. . . ."

Lucinda decided to be light. "I know—I'm fired."

"No, Cindy. This is very serious." He got up and moved around his desk to be near where she sat when he told her. "Henry is dead, Cindy. He was . . ."

The gasping cry she gave surprised even Gil. "Oh, God, *no!*" Then after a disbelieving pause, "How?"

"A mob in Homestead . . ."

She began to cry then, the first time she'd ever cried in his presence. The beautiful, the gay, the sometimes haughty face Gil loved splintered like a mirror struck by a stone. Gil handed her his handkerchief and looked away. She buried her face, and her shoulders shook. The thin white curve of the back of her neck looked peculiarly vulnerable to Gil, and he moved closer to caress it while she wept. "I just can't believe it, where is he now?"

"In the morgue . . ."

Lucinda straightened up. Her eyes were still wet but drying fast. "In the morgue? My God, doesn't anybody . . ."

"Cindy," Gil said gently, "I suspect you're the first in the family to know about this. I had to tell you right away because they're writing the story out there now and I knew you'd hear about it. And . . . and Cindy, I love you—you know that. Anything you want me to do . . . Do you want me to go with you?"

"No . . . No, it wouldn't be right . . . I'll get Scott."

"Scott?"

"Why not? Henry's his brother-in-law—double brother-in-law, in fact."

The idea of getting Scott had been a kind of spur-of-the-moment reaction, but back out on the street Lucinda decided to go through with it. She didn't like the idea of going to identify Henry's remains alone, and there were probably lots of practical things to be done that she would know nothing about. So, for the first time in her life, she went to Scott's office. Scott said nothing at all when she first told him the news; the only sign that he'd heard her was a deepening of the frown lines between his dark eyebrows. She rushed on . . . "But don't you see, Scott? You've got to come with me to get him . . . we're his family. . . ."

Scott got up from behind his desk. "Wait here, Lucinda. I have to tell Mr. Frick and then we'll . . ."

"I'll not wait, Scott. I can't bear to think of him lying another minute in that morgue. Go tell your precious Mr. Frick—and don't forget to tell Martha too . . ."

Scott, who'd already been moving in the direction of Frick's office, turned around. "About Martha. I don't want her to be told. She's too ill."

Lucinda stamped her foot so loudly in her fury that all the clerks in the outer office turned to stare. As they watched this enraged but still stately blonde woman take her leave, banging gates in the office dividers behind her, they developed a new interest in the cool and correct Mr. Stewart. Apparently unaffected by whatever had passed between him and the striking woman, he moved among them, erect and unseeing, and disappeared behind the opaque glass walls of the chairman's office. Minutes later before this excitement had time to subside, reporters began arriving and demanding to see Mr. Frick. A clerk was instructed to show them in, and he lingered in the confusion at the door, hoping to bring back to his fellows an explanation for the strange goings on.

"Gentlemen," Mr. Frick told the reporters in a voice so quiet they had to crowd nearer to hear him. "This senseless killing demonstrates more clearly than anything we can say what the company is up against. These are not workingmen seeking their rights, but an unruly mob. The company extends its sympathy to the family of Mr. Schmidt. That is all. Thank you."

Lucinda, on the way to the morgue, was almost grateful to Scott, whose seeming detachment had turned her crippling grief to an enabling rage. She would need all the grit she could muster not only to look at Henry but to think clearly enough to make all the right arrangements. She was furious that Scott's first thought was for the company. At least his concern for Martha was more human, but didn't make much sense, she thought. Even ill as she was she'd be bound to hear about it sometime, maybe read it in the papers, and then how was she going to feel? . . . Lucinda thought she probably ought to be cursing the men who killed Henry, but strangely, she had no feelings about them at all. She knew how Henry would explain it—or Reed. They were a mindless force, like the crowd that had once pushed Reed in front of the guns. Cursing them would be as useless as cursing God. She'd save her fury for others.

In an irony he might well have appreciated, Henry Schmidt the next day became the darling of a press that would never print his writings. "REPORTER SLAIN BY RIOTERS," "NEWSMAN BEATEN TO DEATH BY MOB" went the headlines. The kind of reporting Henry Schmidt might have done at Homestead played no part in the stories; he was a sterling citizen who had been cruelly done to death. Frick's statement was used along with an irate outburst from Sheriff McCleary, who told how he himself had been driven out of town by the lawless crowds. Though Hugh O'Donnell sent word to the newspapers that his committee equally deplored the incident, his side of the story got little notice. The men who committed the act were steel workers, weren't they? Editorials demanded the sheriff establish the rule of law in Homestead and return the company property to its rightful owners. As in the railroad strike of '77, the good burghers—the bankers, the businessmen, the ministers, the shopkeepers—were seized with the fear of revolution.

Sheriff McCleary, like Sheriff Fife before him, was nearly powerless in the face of several thousand aroused and united citizens. He could not find people in Pittsburgh willing to be deputized to force their way into Homestead. But he was on the spot: the Carnegie attorneys were reminding him that the county would be held responsible for any damage or loss of property. O'Donnell and his crew had actually had the effrontery to suggest to the sheriff that *they* be deputized, but he turned them down flat—"like setting a fox to guard the chickens," he said. So on July 2 McCleary sent his whole office force of twelve men to Homestead. One look at the situation, and they turned tail. When the sheriff reported this to the company, word went out to Chicago to proceed as planned, and the Pinkertons began moving.

A Fourth of July

Whatever her uncertainty about the religion of her fathers, Lucinda Stewart Schmidt always felt a sense of awe in the sanctuary of the Oakland Presbyterian Church on a bright day. The pews were ranged in a great open square that was topped with a stained-glass skylight through which the sun fractured itself into rainbow shafts of warm light. Sitting there, adrift in color, Lucinda could almost believe in the goodness of God, could almost recapture the wonderfully clean Sunday-morning feeling she had as a child of going off to church in shiny boots and starched dress and believing with all her heart that "Jesus wants me for a sunbeam." Her feelings had nothing to do with the service; indeed, they were stronger when she was completely alone as now, without the distraction of what had become to her a largely meaningless ritual and the sight of people she knew too well to associate them with her deep craving for true sanctity. She tried to believe that she had been drawn here almost against her will to pray for Henry, but she knew that she was really praying for herself.

The day was Monday, July 4, 1892, and the world Henry had left behind was heartlessly celebrating a holiday. Flags fluttered from poles or windows of nearly every house she passed in her short walk from the trolley stop on Fifth Avenue to the church; small boys were popping cherry bombs or strings of firecrackers behind the hedges; whole families obviously bound for gay picnics were setting out in their carriages. It was a good day to find sanctuary in the church; nobody else would think of going there.

Henry was already underground—"ashes to ashes, dust to dust"—lowered into the grave yesterday. Mary Stewart had agreed to let him be buried in the little cemetery in the South

235

Hills near Doctor Stewart who, Lucinda thought, would probably have liked him. She hadn't been able to bear the thought of having Donald Sharp conduct a service, but it turned out to be no problem since the Reverend Doctor pleaded the press of business, the day being Sunday, to avoid attending at all. Lucinda located an old retired Lutheran pastor from the South Side who'd been a friend of Henry's father and asked him to do nothing but read the liturgy; a eulogy would have been an insult to Henry. Perhaps even the liturgy was too much. Toward the end, Henry had insisted he really didn't believe in the God of Christian ritual. But the others who came—her mother, Scott, Stewart Sharp and his sister Becky, Reed and Alma and their children—probably did, and it was for them she had the prayers pronounced. And herself? What about herself? She was here trying to decide about herself.

Why here? It still was her church. In deference to Scott and the minister, the session had not been able to bring itself to striking her name from the rolls, and Lucinda had not gone so far as to offer a resignation. Now she was glad she could claim it as hers, if just for this day . . . the whole atmosphere evoked those memories of childhood innocence she sought, needed. Though in her mind she knew she was in no way to blame for Henry's death—hadn't she tried to keep him from going?—she'd nonetheless suffered ever since she'd stood there in the shadowy morgue looking down at his face. In the harsh electric light dangling only inches above it, it was a white, cold, joyless mask; Henry was most definitely gone. Staring at the mask, she felt the awful realization that there would never come another time for them. She knew then that somewhere, back in her mind, she'd been anticipating that her passion for Gil, or his for her, would finally spend itself, and that somehow Henry might eventually realize his dreams and she would be there to share in them. While he'd been alive, condoning her behavior with his silence, she'd felt more deliciously errant than sinful, and felt, despite her misgivings with Gil, that one day she would make it all up to Henry and . . . but now he was gone, and, the hurt she'd given—and she knew she had, regardless of what Henry pretended—would go with him into the grave.

Lucinda, as never before in her sunny life, felt the need of a sanctuary. Even Henry had said recently, "There's the one thing I miss about Christianity—that escape hatch of repentance and forgiveness. It's a hard thing to live with, a purely rational notion of cause and effect. We aren't really rational creatures. Like naughty children, we're driven by

236

something we don't understand to chalk dirty words up there on the board, and we need some kind of eraser to save our hides before teacher gets back." Lucinda smiled to herself, thinking of the way Henry had put it. Could she make the eraser work, she wondered. She felt foolish trying to pray in the old "Now-I-lay-me . . ." way of childhood, and even more embarrassed trying to phrase her thoughts in the Biblical language that came easily, and naturally, to people like Scott and Don Sharp. She would just sit here, hoping for some peace.

Although Lucinda was not aware of it, the ecclesiastical light bathing the sanctuary was working a special kind of wonder on the pale gold of her hair and the clear skin of her cheeks and neck. The Reverend Donald Sharp, who had come over to the church to escape the bedlam of his holiday house and work on the series of prayers he one day hoped to deliver to the nation from the Senate floor, was thoroughly startled, as well as enthralled, to see Lucinda sitting there. Apparently she hadn't heard or seen him, and he stood for a long time just delighting his eyes. The beauty he had struggled to force himself to ignore all these years stirred him now as never before. There was, indeed, a kind of radiance around Lucinda now that seemed incongruous in the light of all that he knew about her. . . . What would bring her to his church—to him? —under such extraordinary circumstances? It was almost like some strange gift from God. . . . He felt himself beginning to tremble a little, and tried to force himself to go away without disturbing her. He could not; he felt bewitched . . . .

"Lucinda." As softly as he tried to speak her name, his voice was a shout in the silent church, and Lucinda jumped with surprise.

"Oh, it's you," she said. "I thought maybe I'd have the place to myself today. Aren't you supposed to be at a picnic at Scott's?"

"Aren't you?"

"I wasn't invited."

"Yes . . . well, I'm sorry we couldn't get out to Henry's . . ."

"Never mind, Don. You really didn't like him much anyway."

"Now, Lucinda . . ."

"Don't 'now Lucinda' me, Don Sharp. I'm in no mood for your big-brother treatment. You've made it clear all these years what you thought of Henry, not to mention me. His death doesn't change anything . . ."

"I'm sorry if you feel that way, Lucinda. But I am your brother and my concern has been for your good—"

"You have a peculiar way of showing it."

"Did you ever think that you have never given me a chance? Do you realize that this is the first time you have come to the church in years? What does bring you here, Lucinda?"

"I don't know, I don't really know. . . . In any case, certainly not you."

"Please, Lucinda. Forget I'm your brother, if you like, but think of me as your pastor. Can't I help you?"

"Yes, by leaving me alone now . . ."

He knew he should go, but her tartness, which stood in such contrast to her almost ethereal beauty, now bedeviled him even more. Whatever had prompted her to come into the church had brought no changes in her spirit; she was still the woman who could carry her head high through an adulterous affair that was a shock to the whole city. Perhaps in her there was a different order of sin . . . perhaps she was one of those women so fashioned by God that she craved men the way others craved drugs, and now that Henry was gone . . . My God . . . his temples began to pound as he attempted a new tone.

"All right, Lucinda, I'm sorry for your feelings, but for the sake of Sarah and Momma, let's try to get along. At least come back for a moment to my study and we'll smoke a pipe of peace, so to speak. As family."

She decided that, however clumsily, he was making a genuine effort at least to be tolerant, to acknowledge her habit of smoking cigarettes, which he so publicly deplored. Perhaps he *had* changed a little since he took up smoking a pipe to go along with the black vest and reverse collar he'd recently adopted to the dismay of the more conservative Presbyterians in the congregation. ("Next thing you know he'll be burning incense," Scott had said.) Since Don's intrusion had broken the spell of the sanctuary for her anyway, she shrugged and got up to follow him.

Outside the sanctuary, they walked along a deeply carpeted hall and into a chamber straight out of an English novel. A fireplace with a coal grate was set into the middle of one book-lined wall; another wall was made up of nearly floor-to-ceiling casement windows in the shape of ecclesiastical arches and fitted with leaded diamond panes. "This is all new, isn't it?" Lucinda asked, taking a cigarette and holder from her purse while Don, with the air of a kindly British vicar, busied himself with packing his pipe.

He lit her cigarette and then, between puffs to get his pipe going, said, "Yes—a kind of fifteenth-anniversary present from the congregation. Some people thought it looked too Episcopal, but I think it goes with the rest of the church, don't you?"

"I suppose so. You must really be upsetting them—with that dog collar and everything."

He laughed. "You never change, do you, Lucinda? You've never taken me seriously, have you?"

"Well, pardon me, but you know what they say—familiarity breeds contempt . . ."

"Must it, Lucinda? It doesn't for me. When I saw you sitting there in the sanctuary, well, and please pardon *me*, but I thought you were about the most beautiful sight in the world."

Such words were somewhat of a shock, even coming from the lips of the Reverend Donald Sharp, whom she derisively thought of as the apostle of love. Lucinda tried to read the expression on his face, but she could hardly make it out since he was seated against the great bank of windows. "Why, Don Sharp!" The faint indignation sounded about right.

"You know what I mean, Lucinda. After all these years . . . well, seriously, something must have brought you here. It couldn't be guilt about Henry's death . . . you couldn't blame yourself for that."

"No . . ."

"Of course not. Henry was, forgive me, a fool to go out there. I have no doubt you told him so yourself."

"Yes, as a matter of fact I guess I did, though I'm not proud of it. . . ."

"Yes, well, but . . ."

"Well what?"

"Why are you here?" Don asked again.

"I told you I don't really know." She rose, tossed her half-smoked cigarette into the coal grate, and turned to go. Don got up from his chair, came between her and the door, and took both her hands in his.

"Wait, Lucinda. I'm convinced there's something on your mind . . . remember, I am your brother, your pastor, you can tell me anything. . . ."

Lucinda could feel a trembling in his hands that gripped hers too tightly. Sophisticated as she was supposed to be, she could hardly believe what she was beginning to suspect. "Let me go, Don. Please, I don't have anything to tell you . . ."

He held on. "Not even about Gillespie Jones?"

She could see his face clearly now, and what she saw thoroughly frightened her. His eyes now seemed to glitter like blue glass in the light streaming through the Gothic windows.

"Don Sharp, let me go—right now," she commanded. "Don't be crazy . . ."

He let go her hands but put his arms around her. "Can't you see, Lucinda, I'm trying to comfort you . . . I . . ."

Putting her hands against his chest and trying to pull free, she looked him full in the face and tried laughter. "Really, Don," she said, "if you weren't my holy brother-in-law, I'd think . . ."

He was losing control, tightening his grip. "Lucinda . . . can't you understand now? . . . all these years . . . God help me . . . I'm just a man and . . ."

Laughter obviously hadn't worked. Lucinda brought the heel of her boot down against his shin, hard as she could. He broke away with a cry of pain.

"Don Sharp, you're a . . . you're a . . ."

She couldn't find words strong enough, and she turned and ran out of there. He followed her, back through the hall, down the aisle of the sanctuary. "Lucinda, please, I don't know what got into me"—he was almost gasping—"I'm *sorry*, Lucinda, please don't tell anyone, you won't tell anyone? Lucinda . . . Please . . .?"

He had sense enough not to follow her out into the street. Still, she ran all the way to the trolley stop, conscious of people staring at her from their yards and porches. There, out of breath, she sank on a bench set out for waiting passengers, and shivered in the July heat. She wondered if she could get home before she would have to throw up. God, was there really no sanctuary, no sanctuary at all for her? On the trolley, she realized that she didn't want to go home, didn't want to wander those rooms alone with the ghost of Henry. She got off downtown and went to the offices of the *Call*. Gil was there, as she had hoped, going over copy. One look at her and he jumped up from behind his desk to lead her to a chair.

"My Lord, Cindy, what's wrong?"

"I don't know, I mean I can't tell . . . I just want to cry. Do you mind if I cry, Gil?"

He did. He never wanted to see her face again the way it was after he'd told her about Henry's death. "Not at all," he said as he gave her his large handkerchief and turned away.

After a few long minutes, she managed to control the tears. "Gil, would you take me home?"

"Do you think it's all right?"

"Why?"

"You know what I mean."

"Well, then couldn't we go to the apartment? I need you, Gil."

Later, much later, lying in bed, spent, at sweet ease despite the heat, she was able to talk . . . in fact, had to talk. But not about Don Sharp. Because of him partly, but not about him. He had terrified her, and then saddened her when she thought about it. She supposed she should feel sorry for him, but that saintly she wasn't. Still, it was better she keep it to herself, because what, really, could be gained by telling Gil, or anybody else, for that matter? Of course, if he ever even *seemed* as though he might bother her again . . . Meanwhile, she could be grateful for what she had, for Gil, lying here with her. . . .

"I guess this is what really matters," she said.

"What?"

"Loving . . . being together like this."

"Well, it's enough for me, Cindy, more, by far, than I'd ever hoped for . . ."

"Is it? . . . Gil, do you believe in God?"

"Why . . . I'm not sure . . . yes, I guess so"—he smiled—"after all, I *am* a vestryman—" And cut himself off, seeing that she was quite serious.

"I mean," she said—and then she smiled—"with all the . . . well . . . bad people there are? I know that's a sort of little-girl way to put it, but you know I'm not so profound, and you know what I mean."

"I'm not so sure about either of those statements. And I'm certainly not sure about who these 'bad' people might be . . ."

"Well, sophisticated and wicked as I'm supposed to be—"

"Ah, not supposed to be, my dear, but deliciously so, so don't ruin it . . ."

"All right, Gil, but please, I'm trying to be serious. I am serious. And I'm talking about me, and you and. . . ."

Gil propped himself up on an elbow and looked down at her. "Cindy, unaccustomed as I am to quoting from the Bible, I have read it and I'd like to remind you that there's nothing in there that I can remember *except* bad people. And as I get it, the whole message is that God loved them anyway."

She pulled his head down and kissed him. "Gil, I don't know what I'd do without you . . ."

"Or I you . . ."

241

"Oh yes, you do. You'd still have somebody—a whole family of somebodies if anything . . ."

"I know, darling, I'm sorry . . . and I know it's too early to say this, it isn't right, but you are alone now and . . ."

She put a restraining finger on his lips. "Hush, no more of that talk."

"You can't stop me, Cindy. I love you, and I am going to propose to you every day until you say yes."

"And I am going to turn you down every day—unless your proposal is indecent."

They both laughed and, damply intertwined, began teasing each other until they came fiercely together again. "I don't have to see the fireworks," Cindy whispered in his ear. "You're giving me my own."

As she had hoped, Gil's warmth and love bathed away the ghastly crawly feeling Lucinda had had when she escaped from Don Sharp's study. Love between lovers still was sweet no matter how others might profane it. But when Gil left her, she felt edgy, restless, empty.

No reason now to get out of bed, rush into her clothes and go back home to pretend she wasn't deceiving Henry. She could lie here all afternoon, all night. Nobody would care. Where was she going? She felt adrift. All this time, she realized, she'd been reassuringly anchored to Henry, securely tied however long the mooring line from which she danced and circled. The security of Henry for her was that he really did believe in something—not God, maybe, but the possibilities of people—believed enough to die for it. She'd argued with him, laughed with Gil about him but felt always that the goodness in Henry—however humorless and even preachy at times—might one day be . . . well, the salvation of all of them. . . . Funny she should think of it that way, but she did . . . and now Henry would never be able to tell her he understood, and she would never be able to tell him what she really counted on being in his heart. This secret feeling about Henry was something Lucinda couldn't talk about with anybody, even with Gil—even, apparently, with God.

There was still a long, blazing holiday afternoon and a long, empty twilight to live through before she could hope for the little death of sleep to quiet her thoughts. Suddenly inspired, she got up, dressed and headed for the South Hills, for the grave, fresh-mounded with earth, where Henry lay. All the long ride—by trolley, by incline, by hired carriage (the driver drunk with independence but the horse sober)—she composed the speech she had to make. It was silly, she knew,

242

but she had to do it. She hoped, was sure, the cemetery would be emptier on the Fourth of July than the church. She was right. She stood over the grave with the explosions from the community picnic in the nearby schoolyard of her youth puncturing her loneliness. And she talked to him.

"Henry, I need you to forgive me, for not telling you what you really mean to me. And for the other, too, even though it would probably embarrass you to hear me ask. I tried to ask God to do it, but you were right about God, Henry—He wasn't there. You wouldn't believe who was. I'd call him the Devil, but you don't believe in the Devil either. Anyway, Henry, what I really wanted to tell you is that I think I am growing up, and I thank you for that. You showed me—and I'd bet some others—what it was to love somebody else more than you love yourself, and I'm only beginning to understand . . . it wasn't just me . . . you loved everybody more than you loved yourself, maybe even those people who killed you. I'm sure I'm not capable of that, but I do think I can do something more, well, useful with my life, something you would be proud of. I don't know what it is yet, but somehow I think I'll find out, and when I do, Henry, it will be thanks to you . . ."

Drained, she stumbled back to the carriage. She felt she owed some kind of explanation to the driver, who'd been watching her curiously; no doubt he'd seen her lips moving. "My husband," she said, "buried yesterday."

"A shame on a holiday, ma'am."

"Yes."

"Must have been a young fella, too."

"Yes, he was killed at Homestead."

"Ah, that newspaper fella? Meaning no disrespect, ma'am, but I thought he was a damn fool to go out there. I told the missus when I read . . ."

"Please."

"Sorry, ma'am . . ."

No use going on with it. She leaned back against the seat and closed her eyes to indicate her desire for silence. Apparently this was the way the world would always remember Henry—as a damned fool. Though he held his tongue out of respect for her, even Gil felt pretty much the same way. Reed was the only one who seemed moved at the graveside yesterday, but Lucinda suspected he was mourning more for the Henry who'd once been a big brother to him than the Henry who'd gone to Homestead. Well, she knew now there was only one Henry—the same heart that beat in the breast of the brother, and lover, also beat for the "fool." And knowing it, she already felt the hard knot of regret begin to dissolve somewhere inside her, as if Henry actually heard her and answered her. Perhaps it was her reward for beginning to understand him, for being the one person in the world for whom Henry Shaw Schmidt would never be a fool.

It was just sunset when the carriage dropped Lucinda at the Duquesne Incline on Mt. Washington. Looking out over the view, she had a lifting feeling that even the city had been remade a little that day. The air was as nearly smokeless as it could ever be. For two days, a Sunday and a holiday, the factories had lain idle, and since it was summer no home fires smudged the jumbled rooftops of the slums on the Point. The whole panorama—the hillsides, the rivers, the windows of the blackened buildings, the hulls of steamboats nosed up to the wharves, the spires of churches, the courthouse tower—glowed golden in the setting sun. It really *was* a golden triangle, and Lucinda felt a curious surge of love for this city with which, at this moment, she was sharing something so personal and new. . . .

Lucinda had never seen the ticket shed or the little cars of the incline so packed. But then she had never made the trip on a holiday before. At a penny a ride, going up the incline was cheap family entertainment for the workers who lived at its foot. The ride itself was a thrill. The car, perched on a platform that conformed to the thirty-degree slope of the tracks, jutted straight out into the air so that you felt you were falling the whole four hundred feet to the bottom even though it was secured by steel cables more than an inch thick that wound around drums powered by a steam engine. The view was spectacular, as good, some claimed, as anything in the mountains of Europe, where many had come from. All day long, the ticket agent told her, people kept coming and going as in an amusement park. Traffic was especially heavy this time of Fourth of July evening when rockets were beginning to arch and burst into the air above gatherings all over the city.

Lucinda squeezed herself into a car. The smell of sweat and whiskey and garlic was almost overpowering, but strangely exciting too. It was, after all, the smell of life. Around her were people of all ages, shapes, sizes, laughing and calling back and forth to each other in an incomprehensible babble of tongues. It occurred to her, with a start, that from families like these came the men who'd killed Henry not three days ago, and yet they seemed incapable of anything but joy now in their holiday mood. They were flirting, bouncing babies, shrieking in mock terror as the car shuddered down. Seeing them like this, she realized how little she really knew about *people* . . . out for a day from under the Presbyterian thumb, they were not wearing the confused, sullen look she so often saw on their faces in the street or going to work. They seemed to have pride and to take real pleasure in themselves. She wanted to know more about them, know where they came from, know what they believed in, what they dreamed. . . .

By the time the car reached the bottom, Lucinda had an idea that somewhere here was the new challenge she'd been looking for. She *would* get to know these people—*people*—do sketches and write stories about them. It was time that the native-born people of Pittsburgh got to know about the newcomers among them, got to see them, as she just had, as individuals instead of part of a threatening mass of foreigners. Gil would let her do it, he'd let her do anything within reason. And Henry would be proud of her for it. She probably wouldn't get into politics the way Henry would have, but she suspected he'd be pleased with her. She stood for a while watching people pour on and off the cars and forcing herself to pick out faces, to imagine particular lives. She felt so excited she could hardly wait until morning. She would begin here in the South Side, where the minarets of strange religions were transforming the skyline into a place as exotic, she suspected, as the sights at the end of the Orient Express. When she got home at last to her empty house, she felt far less empty herself. Life did indeed renew itself. Thank you, Henry . . .

A Cargo of Pinkertons

Scott Stewart stood apart from the other men in the darkened pilot house of the tugboat *Little Bell* as she strained into the Monongahela current with two heavy barges, each carrying 150 men, in tow. He felt foolish to be involved in such a melodramatic episode at his age and station in life. He didn't even know how to dress for the occasion, and so he wore his customary business garb complete with vest and watch chain and hard straw hat. At the last minute before leaving the office, he had stuck the small revolver he kept in his desk drawer—the same revolver he had brandished but never fired in '77—into the inside of his suit coat, and the clumsy weight of it gave him an odd sensation of being slightly off balance. Not being a drinking man like the others who passed a bottle around just before boarding, Scott's only concession to the nerves that were knotting in the general area of his stomach was the cigar, mostly unlit, which he kept clamped between his teeth.

"I wish I could go myself, Stewart," Frick had told him. "But Mrs. Frick is expecting a child any moment, you know and . . . well, I guess a commander's place is at headquarters anyway. Potter is going to be aboard, of course, but I'd like to have somebody with a wider view of company policy along, just in case."

The "just in case" seemed to be developing rapidly. Even before they passed under the Smithfield Street Bridge an argument broke out in the crowded little pilot house. It was so dark—no lights, not even running lights, an obviously nervous Captain Rodgers had decreed—that Scott could only identify the speakers by voice.

246

The first was Potter's: "I think you should deputize them right now, Colonel Gray."

"Those aren't my orders," Colonel Joseph H. Gray said. He himself had been deputized to represent the law by Sheriff McCleary.

"Why not?" It was Captain Heinde of the Pinkerton force. "I can't see the harm . . ."

"The way I understand it, this is purely a peaceable occupation of company property by men hired by the company," Colonel Gray explained. "You've still got those arms locked up, haven't you, captain?"

"Yes."

"Good. There's no need for deputizing unless we find some open violation of the law down there."

"Oh, we will, I can assure you," Potter said. "I've been in Homestead, you know, and seen the way those mobs are acting. You gentlemen haven't. What do you think, Mr. Stewart?"

Scott struck a match to relight his cigar and give himself some thinking time.

"No lights, Mr. Stewart."

"Oh, yes, sorry, Captain Rodgers. I'm afraid I have to agree with Colonel Gray, Mr. Potter. I think Mr. Frick's hope is to keep this as much within the company as possible. We're not to enforce order in the town; we're to protect our property."

"So be it," Potter said, "for now."

Unseen by the men on the boats as they slid under the bridge, a figure detached itself from the shadows, ran to a horse tethered at the south end of the span and set off at a gallop for the borough of Homestead. By 4:00 A.M. on July 6, 1892, he was clattering down the dark streets of the little town like a modern Paul Revere, yelling that the Pinkertons are coming. A man, detailed by the committee for this specific job, tied down the factory whistle, whose continuous wail brought people rushing into the streets. Calling to one another to head for the river, the crowd flowed down and around the empty stockaded plant. The committee's own patrol boat, *Edna*, came first around the bend, her whistle screaming alarm. *Little Bell* and its tow—dark lumps against the river's reflection of the early-morning light—appeared. "They're going to land at the plant—let's stop 'em!" With axes, rams, rifle butts, bare hands, they began tearing at the stockade.

Aboard *Little Bell* there was, at Captain Rodgers' request, total silence in the pilot house. He needed all his concentration to get his tow into position alongside the landing flat of the plant long enough to put the gangplanks down and secure

247

his lines. Scott, standing by a window with Potter at his side, watched the dark mass of the crowd apprehensively. It was perfectly obvious that they were trying to break into the plant, and that it was all a question of time. . . . "How long before we land, Captain?"

"Long enough if you don't let me tend to my job," he said, deftly spinning the big wheel to meet an eddy in the current.

"We're never going to make it," Potter whispered to Scott. "This is a job for the law now. I think we'd better get Gray over here and tell him so."

Scott agreed, and they pulled Gray into a corner where they could exchange whispered conversation without disturbing the captain. Gray still refused. "I'll not preside over a slaughter, which is what it'll be if you try to shoot your way in there. Anyway, I say we've still got a chance. . . ."

The boat was now only about two hundred yards from the landing. Suddenly, in the gathering light, they saw a figure, then another, and another streaking around the great empty sheds and heading for the shore. A hundred yards more to go. Men were beginning to pile up now all around the landing flat and down the bank. The captain, still steering full speed forward, called over his shoulder, "What the hell do I do now?"

Everybody looked at Colonel Gray, who deferred with a gesture to Scott. "Land," Scott said, reacting, uncharacteristically, more from instinct than thought—the sight of the strikers wantonly seizing company property was like a personal assault.

By the time the barges were in place with the planks run out, a crowd of more than two thousand men, women and children faced the landing party. Nobody made a move. "Talk to them," Scott told Potter. "Go on, talk to them."

Potter shouted from an open window of the pilot house. "We're not here to harm you. These are not blacksheep. These are just guards to keep the plant secure. Now please clear away and let us land!"

"Not on your life, we don't want any Pinkertons here," someone yelled back from the crowd.

"That's right, no dirty Pinkertons," another shouted.

"We don't want trouble," Potter told them. "These men are not even armed."

"Ay, they've got arms enough"—a voice from the crowd. "We've heard all about it. Let's go get the guns . . ."

A young man stepped onto the gangplank. Captain Heinde, jumping from tug to barge to gangplank, called out over his shoulder to his Pinkerton colleague Captain Kline, "Break out the weapons."

Heinde grappled with the young man, pushing him back. A shot cracked out, and Heinde went down, a bullet through his thigh. More men moved toward the gangplank, but a volley from the barges drove them back, leaving several men twisting on the ground. Under protection of this fire, several Pinkertons managed to get the wounded Captain Heinde into the pilot house of the tug. Shots were popping all around now, ironically sounding like a string of Fourth of July firecrackers. One smashed a window in the pilot house, showering those inside with glass. More wounded Pinkertons limped or were carried aboard the tug, where they thought there might be a doctor. Through it all, Scott pressed himself against the after bulkhead of the pilot house and watched. He was immobilized not so much by fear as by sheer astonishment. It never occurred to him to draw the gun sagging his coat so uncomfortably.

When a second bullet embedded itself in the pilot-house roof, Captain Rodgers shouted, "I'm getting out of here," and then ordered his deck hand to "cut the line to those barges."

The *Little Bell* was soon chugging straight across the river toward the safety of the wild, unpopulated hills on the other side. There were half a dozen wounded aboard, most of them in pain.

Once he was safely out of range and close to the north bank of the river, the captain turned the *Little Bell's* nose eastward and soon was engulfed by a welcome blanket of smoke laid down by the company's normally functioning Edgar Thompson works at Braddock. The acrid smell was comforting to Scott—somehow a sign of normalcy out of the nightmare he'd just witnessed. Captain Rodgers steered his boat into Port Perry, just beyond Braddock, where there was a convenient railroad station, and Scott, Potter and Gray debarked with the wounded. "I'm going back and try to pick up them barges. They belong to me, you know," Rodgers said. "I think there might be less excitement if they see there's no law or company men aboard."

The captain made sense, Scott thought. Clearly the outnumbered Pinkerton men could never land; the only hope was to retrieve them with as few casualties as possible. When *Little Bell* maneuvered in toward the stranded barges, shore fire drove Rodgers clear out of the pilot house, but he managed to go back and man the wheel long enough to keep his boat from grounding and head her back to safety. While the

Little Bell had been gone, the men in the barges had huddled below decks, despite the rising July sun that was turning the cramped hulls into furnaces. They exposed themselves only long enough to drive the crowds back with gunfire, but even so, several more of them were wounded. Seeing the tug leave again, they tried running up a white flag. It was promptly shot to pieces. The crowd, angered by its dead and wounded, began pumping oil onto the surface of the water and trying to set it on fire. Because it was lubricating oil, every effort to make it burn failed. The crowd was frustrated.

For Hugh O'Donnell and his committee, this was going too far. Roasting Pinkertons alive would surely turn the American public against the strikers. While members of the committee fanned out through the crowd to advise moderation, O'Donnell pushed through to the landing to see what he could do. A white handkerchief was again hanging from a window of one of the barges—the Pinkertons apparently had had enough. After telling those nearest him to put up their arms, O'Donnell called to the men in the barges that he would come aboard and personally guide them to safety if they would give up their arms. The Pinkertons agreed. Boarding the barges, O'Donnell found a kind of hell: hundreds of thirsty, sweating, terrified men; eleven wounded, one dead. With nothing to lose, they left their arms and followed O'Donnell down the gangplank.

From the landing, the path to the town jail, where O'Donnell planned to stash the Pinkertons for safety against the mob, led up an incline, across the mill yard and the tracks and on to Amity Street, approximately a mile. Even with their own leader in the van, shouting and cursing for room to pass, the crowd converged on the path and parted only wide enough for a single file. They were in a far uglier mood than O'Donnell had anticipated. Six workers had been killed and another seventeen wounded in the long exchange of gunfire. They wanted revenge. As the Pinkertons staggered through them, the people of Homestead—women and children as well as men—threw stones, struck out with clubs, grabbed coats, hats, satchels from them. By the time O'Donnell managed to get his prisoners within the protective walls of the jail and the nearby Eintracht Saenger Halle, two more of them had been killed, another badly injured, and the rest badly roughed up. One Pinkerton, deranged by the experience, killed himself as soon as he broke free. Back at the landing, the crowd turned the empty barges into a victory bonfire.

In Pittsburgh meanwhile, the ever cool Mr. Frick, after listening to a full report from Scott and Potter, called the press and issued this statement: "Homestead is now in the hands of a lawless mob. Since the Carnegie company's best efforts to control the situation have been frustrated, we will no longer have anything to do with the matter. We now hold the County of Allegheny responsible for the restoration of law and order and the protection of our property. And I can add with greatest emphasis that under no circumstances will we have any further dealings with the Amalgamated Association as an organization. This is final."

Somewhat to his surprise, Scott found himself being privately congratulated by Frick for his good sense in withdrawing early from the scene. "The fact that you and Potter were driven off," he said, "gives us a better case in dropping the whole mess in the lap of the county, where it belongs now. But I still can't understand why that fool Gray didn't deputize those men when he had a chance and march ashore and make a few arrests."

"He was worried about bloodshed," Scott said.

"Worried about bloodshed? Those people have been *asking* for bloodshed ever since they killed Henry Schmidt. When we settled matters up in the coke fields, I learned you have to be able to stomach a little blood if you want to keep things in line."

Sure of his cause, Frick stood firm under fire from the press for his use of the Pinkertons and frantic bombardment from Whitelaw Reid and other high-ranking Republicans who wanted him to bring the strike to a quick end. Only a direct order from Scotland might have moved him. It didn't come. Still hidden away in the highlands, Andrew Carnegie, who everybody—including the workmen of Homestead—thought would want to make peace, remained uncharacteristically silent despite the fact that the once friendly press was now calling him a coward and worse. Nor could any personal consideration keep Frick from his post of command. On the evening of Friday, July 8, Henry Clay Frick, Jr., was born at Clayton. He was a sickly baby, and Frick was up all night while doctors struggled to keep the child alive. At his desk the next morning at eight, Frick passed out the customary cigars—the famous 75-cent Havanas—and received congratulations without letting one of his colleagues know of the uncertain battle taking place behind the stone walls of his home. It was only when he heard of it later that Scott could further appreciate the chairman's iron self-control.

Without such an example, Scott himself might well have snapped. The strike added on to an already enormous load of work Scott was carrying. Frick had taken to entrusting Scott with detailed supervision of just about everything he had a particular interest in, the newest project being the planned construction of the company's fifteen-story headquarters building. Since Frick was a man who demanded instant and accurate answers to any question, Scott was continuously immersed in reports, figures and conferences to keep on top of everything going on. Further, Andrew Carnegie, remembering —or at least being reminded of—Scott's long ago visit to him as a messenger boy, took an instant shine to Scott on his first visit to Pittsburgh after Scott had joined the company. Pausing by Scott's desk one day, he gestured toward Frick's office and said, "Thank God we have a good Scotsman like yourself here to keep an eye on the German." Though Carnegie, whose loyalty to Frick was then unquestioned, laughed heartily at his own little joke, he had since been troubling Scott with personal and pointed little notes from all over the world, like, "Don't you think Frick's paying too much for coke, pard? You know the business. Give me your honest opinion." These notes had to be handled instantly, and delicately. Feeling his loyalty was to Frick, Scott would pass them along for comment, invariably getting them back with a penciled jotting, such as, "Do what you think best" or "Tell him the truth, I have nothing to hide." Quite apart from his duties at Carnegie, Scott Stewart had become a much-wanted man about town. He was, of course, a director of the traction company in which he had invested with Christopher Magee, and at the personal invitation of Andy Mellon he not only served on the board of the Mellon Bank but was a director of a little concern called Pittsburgh Reduction Company that was turning out the new and promising lightweight metal called aluminum by a process invented by its young manager, Charles M. Hall. Scott had put money into this venture too, and by now, keeping track of his own investments kept him at his desk at home for many a long evening.

As well as he was doing, Scott still found the figures he periodically cast up somewhat disappointing. At nearly forty, he was not yet worth a million, a kind of magical figure in Pittsburgh circles that seemed to separate the truly wealthy from the highly paid such as Scott. Viewing material prosperity as a crucial sign of God's favor, Scott was determined to pass that magical line. There were times when, pressed by some members of his family whose attitudes toward money truly baffled him, Scott worried whether he was in the grip of greed. He seriously thought of it in such terms, and occasionally went so far as to pray about it, getting for the most part a very satisfactory answer. During one period of doubt, for example, he went to hear Russell H. Conwell give the "Acres of Diamonds" speech that had made him famous on the Chautauqua circuit, and Scott felt the preacher was directly responding to his prayers when he declared, "Get rich, young man, for money is power, and power ought to be in the hands of good people." Amen. Money should be in the hands of good people, Scott agreed.

Three and often four times on the Sabbath and every Wednesday night at prayer meeting, Scott went before the Lord in his temple to confess his sins and offer prayers of praise and thanksgiving. He supported the work of the Lord with a tithe of his $12,000 salary, though not his investments, whose yield would remain uncertain until they were harvested. He not only publicly professed his faith but propagated it from the platform of his Sunday-school class. He not only did not commit adultery but he did not look upon women with lust; he not only eschewed drunkenness but tried to save others from that sinful trap by his temperance work; he not only did not steal but had twice put his own body in jeopardy in the cause of law and order. He seldom uttered an oath stronger than "pshaw!" and he coveted no other man's wealth, being content with struggling for his share of the new wealth he was helping to create with the sweat of his brow. If all this couldn't be counted goodness, he didn't know what could, and so he was genuinely hurt and disturbed when those closest to him often seemed less impressed with his rectitude than colleagues who were among Pittsburgh's leading men of affairs.

It was especially aggravating now, during the tension of the strike, to have this attitude displayed by his own daughter. Once when he was trying to concentrate, May forget herself and began playing the piano. Scott stomped into the parlor and told her, "Keep quiet, please. I'm *trying* to work."

May slammed the cover over the keyboard. "Work. Work. That's all you do, Daddy. I'm *sick* of it."

"You're sick of it? You haven't worked a day in your life, young lady."

She was only going on fourteen, as his mother always reminded him, but then he had been at work a year or more at that age. There were boys in the mills no more than fourteen, and the girls who packed pickles for Mr. Heinz mostly started at that age. He had met Mr. Heinz, a jolly little fellow with old-fashioned mutton chops, at a Sunday-school meeting, and now he wished he'd arranged for May to have a job there this summer. The twelve cents an hour she could earn wouldn't mean so much to her, but at least it might do the girl some good to get out of this house and away from the piano, and they said Heinz provided the finest conditions for working girls of any business in the country.

"Oh, pooh," May said, "you're going to tell me again how you started working at thirteen. . . . you didn't do that because you wanted to, it was because Grandfather died. I know . . ."

"May . . ." It was a warning note from Mary Stewart, who had been sitting silently by, paying scrupulous attention to her sewing.

"Daddy, do you know everybody in the family says you're a stuffed shirt?"

"May!"

"But they do. And now even my friends are saying, well, bad things about you. . . ."

"May!"

Scott quieted his mother with a gesture. The muscles in his cheeks were working with the effort to control himself as he asked quietly, "What are they saying, May?"

"Well, you know, that you work for Mr. Frick, and you know what the papers are saying about Mr. Frick, and that you led the Pinkertons into Homestead, where they killed all those people, and . . ."

"And how do you feel about it, May?" Scott asked.

"Well, it doesn't sound right. . . ."

Mary Stewart thought it was time to intervene. "May, you run along to your room. Your father's had a very hard day . . ."

This time Scott didn't interfere. He was simply too weary to try to explain to his daughter about the rights of private property, the basic need for law and order. . . . But he realized, with regret, that he had rather hoped his being under fire would be a source of pride to his family.

"Don't pay any attention to her, Scott. She's only fourteen," Mary said when the girl had left them.

"Mother, I'm weary of this 'only fourteen' excuse. Why, I . . ."

"I know. I know, Scott. But they don't grow up as fast these days, and maybe it's just as well. And you have to remember, she has been sheltered. But May is right about one thing—you do work too hard."

"Now, Mother, don't start on that again. Why, compared to Mr. Frick . . ."

"Why must you always compare yourself to Mr. Frick? He has more reason to . . ."

"No, you're wrong about that. I'm the one who has reason to work harder. He has made his million, and more besides. Is it wrong that I want to make mine too?"

Mary looked at her son. He was still rigidly straight but so thin and drawn and white that she wouldn't have been surprised to see him fall flat on his face. So that was what drove him? But why? They had long since achieved not only security but, compared to anything she had ever expected in life, true wealth. Still, it wouldn't do to argue with him now when he had so many troubles on his mind; besides, she could never win an argument with Scott, who always stood on his rock of faith.

"No," she said. "No, I suppose not but . . ."

"You were with me, Mother, when we heard Mr. Conwell. Remember he said, 'I say you have no right to be poor!' "

"But, Scott, we aren't poor. We've got all this Frick stock, and you've got your share with Mr. Carnegie. And don't forget the South Hills place. It's going to be valuable when they put that tunnel through for the electric cars they're talking about. . . ."

"I know all that, Mother, but I'm not rich yet, and I agree with Mr. Conwell that wealth is power that ought to be in the right hands. Please don't laugh at me when I tell you that when I decided I couldn't be a minister I made up my mind to serve the Lord in a worldly fashion, by earning as much of His power in the form of money as He would allow me . . ."

"I'd never laugh at you, Scott, you know that," Mary said. "I'm eternally grateful to you. . . ."

"Now, Mother . . ."

"It's just that as your mother I worry about your health. You're looking so miserable and acting so jumpy lately . . ."

"I feel fine," Scott lied. "Anyway, things should ease up some now that the soldiers are here. . . ."

After the battle of Homestead, Sheriff McCleary, harassed by the press and the Carnegie attorneys, had managed to round up some sixty citizens as deputies, just enough to go in and escort the battered Pinkertons to a train. But there was no way that his little force could take over the town or plant, and so he left it all in the hands of the committee, who restored order of a sort by organizing their own patrols. After several days of frantic appeals to Harrisburg, McCleary finally succeeded in convincing Governor Pattison that it was time to call out the militia. On July 12, some 8,000 militiamen under the command of Major General G. R. Snowden marched into Homestead and took over the borough without firing a shot. Now they were encamped on the heights above the town with field guns in perfect position to cover every street and building. Though the streets of Homestead were quiet, the strike not only continued, but spread. On July 13, more than five thousand men in Carnegie's nonunion Upper and Lower Iron Mills in Pittsburgh and at the Beaver Falls works down the Ohio walked off the job in sympathy with their brothers in Homestead.

This action did not faze Mr. Frick. The company's order books were so empty that, in fact, it could even be considered a Godsend. He would teach the union a lesson they'd not forget. "We'll fight this one out if it takes all summer," he told the press, and then turned to implementing his battle plan. It was a simple plan, one that had worked before in the coke fields. Now that the troops were maintaining control, Potter was sent back to his job and the company began quietly signing up men who were willing to work and shipping them into the plant by water. To protect them from the angry strikers, the stockade was repaired and manned. Temporary housing was set up for them within the plant. Predictably, their village was called Pottersville.

The press continued to inflame passions as far away as London, where one newspaper said: "Here we have this Scotch-Yankee meandering through Scotland in a four-in-hand opening public libraries, while the wretched workmen who supply him with ways and means for his self-glorification are starving in Pittsburgh." In St. Louis an editorial declared, "Say what you will of Frick, he is a brave man. Say what you will of Carnegie, he is a coward. And gods and men hate cowards." Such notices brought a thin smile of appreciation to Frick's usually impassive face, Scott noticed, but they worried him, too, since the mercurial Carnegie was perfectly capable of emerging at any moment and calling for a settlement. "He'd get it over my dead body," Frick told Scott one day when they were discussing the matter. It was Friday, July 22, and both of them were then unaware that within twenty-four hours Frick's comment would stand as near prophecy.

About two o'clock the next afternoon Scott was sitting in his office, eating lunch at his desk. His door was ajar, and he saw Frick returning from the Duquesne Club with John Leishman, the company's vice-chairman. The two were deep in conversation as they went together into Frick's office, letting the swinging door in the oak-and-glass partition close behind them. Moments later a stranger, a thin young man, clean-shaven and with pince-nez glasses glittering at the bridge of his nose, appeared at the oak partition that separated the clerks' desks from the hall and elevator. He handed a card to a young clerk, who turned and started for Frick's office. Evidently too impatient to wait for a reply, the young man pushed through the gates in the railing, brushed by the clerk and entered Frick's office. A shot rang out, then another, then another. Scott was on his feet at once, heading along with everybody else on the floor for the chairman's office. A clerk named May, a deputized sheriff, had drawn his gun; a carpenter working on a repair job in the office had his hammer in hand.

They came on an unbelievable scene. Leishman and Frick were rolling on the floor and grappling with the young man, who was stabbing at Frick with a knife. Frick's beard and collar were already covered with blood. Beyond the floor-to-ceiling round window that formed a corner of Frick's office in this strange *Chronicle Telegraph* building, a crowd, alerted by the shots, had gathered in the streets to watch the struggle just one floor above them. They had no doubt who was involved, because the windows were heavily lettered "The Carnegie Steel Company Limited," and Frick's bearded features had recently been on every front page. They were so stunned that nobody even called for the police until they saw the flash of the knife.

The carpenter, wielding his hammer, got into the fight and the others, Scott included, went to his assistance. When they disarmed the young man and dragged him to his feet, May threatened him with his gun. Frick, who'd hauled himself erect and was leaning against his desk, said, "Don't shoot, don't kill him. The law will punish him. Hold his face up and let me see it." May put his hand under the man's chin and jerked his face up. He was chewing something. May forced his jaws open and found a capsule of what was identified as fulminate of mercury. Another second, perhaps, and the whole room might have blown up.

Responding to the crowd's belated call, police now arrived on the scene. They took the man in custody and, with difficulty, escorted him through the thousands of people jamming Fifth Avenue just below the office. Meanwhile Frick, bleeding from the neck, was carried to a couch in Scott's office, where he could be out of the way of the curious. A doctor arrived and offered anesthetic. Frick shook his head. "I can help you better if I'm alert," he said. While Scott looked on in true awe, the doctor began probing for the bullets, Frick guiding him through clenched teeth with "I think you're getting close. There, that feels like it, Doctor." Two of the three shots had passed through each side of Frick's neck, missing by less than half an inch vital nerves and arteries; the third, deflected by Leishman, had embedded itself in the ceiling of Frick's office. The knife wounds, seven in all, were miraculously superficial. When the doctor had retrieved the bullets and bound Frick up, the man insisted on sitting up. "I still have work to do," he said, "and I don't want anybody to bother Mrs. Frick with this. She's still ill, you know. I'll tell her myself when I get home tonight."

The piecing together of what actually happened began. Frick recalled that the young man had approached him earlier when he was getting out of the elevator after lunch. The man had asked for the office of someone else in the firm, and Frick had directed him upstairs. The card the man had given the clerk read, "A. Berkman, representing The New York Employment Agency." That rang another bell with Frick. Somebody had sent a note the day before offering to recruit strikebreakers and requesting an immediate audience, but Frick hadn't had time to see him then. Reports flowing in from the Central Police Station where the man was being grilled confirmed that his name was Alexander Berkman and that he was from New York. Far from being in any kind of business, he was an unemployed, Russian-born anarchist. He insisted he'd acted wholly alone and that his motive was his belief that Mr. Frick was the embodiment of all the evil forces suppressing the world's working classes. He had only one regret—that his mission might have failed.

"I guess I have to thank God, if it did," Frick said. "You know I had my back to him and my leg cocked up over the arm of my chair so I really couldn't move fast. Luckily I heard the little scuffle when he pushed his way in and turned to look. He was already in the act of firing, and my turning must have thrown off his aim. Of course I ducked then and diverted the second shot. Then Leishman knocked his arm up. How is poor Leishman, by the way?"

"He was pretty badly shaken up," Scott said, "and the doctors insisted he go home."

"Good." Frick sank back somewhat wearily onto the couch, then ordered, "Get my secretary in here, Stewart. I still have letters to get out. We have two more hours of business today."

Frick waved away all arguments by Scott and the doctors that he should go home or, better yet, to a hospital. He did consent, however, to allowing Scott to talk to the press. "Give them this statement," he said. "I do not think I shall die. Whether I do or not, the company will pursue the same policy and it will win."

Scott went to deliver these fighting words to the reporters in the outer office, and was even more impressed by what he heard about Frick's next few days. Taken home by ambulance and into the house on a stretcher at the doctor's insistence (though not until after the 6:00 P.M. closing time), Frick was being carried past his ailing wife's door when he called out cheerfully, "Don't worry, Ada, I'm all right. I may come in later to say good night. How's the baby?" But after that, the adrenaline that had carried him through the crisis drained off enough so that he was persuaded to stay in bed. He was down but not out; he worked regularly by telephone or with his secretary, who came to the house. While Frick gained strength daily, in another of the mansion's thirty rooms his tiny namesake was losing his. On Wednesday, August 3, Frick was summoned from his bed to watch the baby die. He sat up all that night with his distraught wife, rested a little the next day and on Friday, August 5, arose as usual, walked down to Penn Avenue, firing the guard who had been posted at his home on the way, and took an open streetcar to the office, where he promptly fired another guard before he sat down at his desk and called for Scott.

"I don't like this guard business, Stewart," he said. "It creates a bad image for the company. It looks like I'm afraid of somebody, have reason to be afraid of somebody. I'm not and I don't. Now let's get down to business. I've had a thought: it might be a good idea to get Potter out of Homestead and put Schwab in charge. He seems to get along better with men —he's never had this kind of labor trouble at E.T."

Still only thirty, Charles Schwab had been manager at Edgar Thompson since the horrible death of Captain Jones and, before that, at Homestead for a brief time. The son of a livery-stable owner in the mountains near Cresson, Schwab went to Braddock at the age of seventeen as a clerk in a grocery store. He met Captain Jones, who took a liking to Schwab's cheerful personality and offered him a job as a stake driver at the E. T. for a dollar a day. It was better than clerking, so Schwab took it. Catching on fast, Schwab so impressed Jones that within six months he was put in charge of installing and operating the plant's new blast furnaces. Like Jones, Schwab preferred to be on the floor of the plant, where he was always joking and teasing the men on to greater efforts

259

in their own earthy language. They liked him and called him "Charlie," just as they had always called Carnegie "Andy." Some said, in fact, that Schwab was another Carnegie in the making.

Knowing all this, Scott could see at once that Frick's idea of putting Schwab at Homestead was exactly right. With Schwab at Homestead, and a recovered Frick not only back in command but enjoying the full confidence of Carnegie, who had been very upset by the shooting, Scott was certain that the company would win out.

It was no longer necessary to be apologetic for the company's stand. Berkman's bullets had backfired; they had transformed Frick from a villain into a kind of hero, not only in the eyes of his colleagues but of a public that, discriminating little between a single anarchist and the unionized workers of Homestead, reacted against sinister foreign influence.

That Friday Scott Stewart went home and asked his astonished daughter to sit down and play his favorite Chopin etudes for him.

A Deal by Mr. Schwab

"Oyez. Oyez. Oyez. All present in the court arise," the tipstaff sang out. "His honor, Judge Stewart."

Though he was thirty-eight now and almost ten years on the bench. Reed Stewart still felt a bit embarrassed by this fanfare. Gathering the skirts of his black robe to sit down, he nodded absently at the faces of the lawyers ringing the tables in front of him and noticed rather gratefully that, through familiarity with the court, they only half rose before settling back to an examination of their papers and whispered conversations. The case today was an interesting one, and Reed knew that he would have to pay sharp attention to see to it that the plaintiff's attorneys didn't run away with the sympathies of the jurors without benefit of law. The defendant, eighteen-year-old Wilbur Curry, the son of one of Pittsburgh's new millionaires, had run his automobile into a drayman, killing the horse, shattering the wagon and seriously injuring the man himself. The drayman, Callahan by name, was suing for the very substantial amounts of $500 for the horse, $250 for the wagon and another $1,000 for personal injury.

What made the case especially interesting, not only to Reed but to the reporters who swelled the audience in the little courtroom to the point where people were standing around the walls, was the automobile. Few people had yet seen one, and fewer still had any idea of how one of these gasoline-powered contraptions was operated or what it might do at such terrifying speeds as twenty or thirty miles per hour. There were, in fact, only fifteen of these machines in all the city of Pittsburgh, and Reed remembered hearing that when an effort was made to call a meeting of automobile owners in the Duquesne Club, only three men showed up. Young Curry was, unfortunately, the first of this daring, little band of drivers to be involved in an accident and the first to show up in court. The fact that Curry's father was, like his own brother Scott, one of the forty men who had been made instant millionaires when Carnegie sold out to U.S. Steel would, Reed knew, hurt him with the jury.

Gallivanting about in an expensive toy and running down a poor working man was just the sort of behavior the public had come to expect of the newly rich and their families. No wonder. Many of them had indeed gone silly in the head with sudden wealth. Reed hadn't been there, but could well believe the story friends told him about what happened during the recent visit of the Metropolitan Opera Company when one of these fellows rose up during intermission and ostentatiously draped a pearl necklace over his wife's head. Almost all of them were buying or building new homes that would have made Louis XVI jealous. Scott appeared to be following suit. Though he had never like Scott's gloomy Oakland castle, Reed at first thought it rather foolish—and uncharacteristic—for his brother, now that poor Martha was dead and Benjy and May away most of the time, to move over to East Liberty, to swap twenty rooms for forty, three servants for six, Romanesque for Renaissance. Mary, however, explained Scott's special reasons. At seventy-one, she was having a hard time getting around because of her arthritis, and Scott felt the new place with its elevator would be much easier for her.

Of course, the two of them would rattle around in such a big house, but Scott was secretly hoping it would entice May home from Paris once she heard about the music room with its perfect acoustics and its own pipe organ. Then, too, it was convenient to Belmar, the new golf course that had been laid out in Homewood. Would Reed believe it—Scott was actually taking nice Saturday afternoons off to play a round with Mr. Heinz and other men in the neighborhood. The wonderful thing about his mother, Reed thought, was that she never gave up on them. She had always wanted to see Scott loosen up and have some pleasure, and here he was at nearly fifty learning to play a game. Well, better late than never. Next thing, Scott would have an automobile when he found out they could go faster than any horse alive. . . .

"If it please your honor . . . if it please your honor," the lawyer for the plaintiff was trying to get his attention, and Reed tipped his head slightly to show he was now giving full attention. "I would like to call Mr. Matthew Callahan as first witness."

Callahan was sworn and instructed by the lawyer to tell the story in his own words. "Well, here I was your honor, mindin' me own business, just swingin' me load around the corner when this . . . this thing . . . comes out of the blue, y'might say, and hits me. Well, I went ass over teakettle, if y'll excuse the expression, your honor, and here was me wagon and me load scattered all over the street. . . ."

"What was your load, Mr. Callahan?" Reed interrupted.

"Whiskey, your honor, barrels of whiskey. Them that wasn't broken was bein' stolen fast as people could pick 'em up. And the poor horse, she was breathin' her last—moanin' and pantin' with a wild look in her eye like . . ."

"Objection, your honor. This description is irrelevant," the defense attorney said.

"Objection sustained," Reed said. "Please try to be less emotional, Mr. Callahan."

"While we're on the subject, Mr. Callahan, would you tell the jury why you valued your horse so highly?" the plaintiff's attorney prompted.

"Oh, yes, I'll tell you, she was one of them Heinz horses— you know, all black she was with only a little white star on her forehead. Maybe she was a little over-age, else they wouldn't a sold her to me, but you ever see how Joe Hite takes care of them horses over there at the plant in Allegheny? Why, they got cork floors to walk on and foot baths to ease their hooves and electric fans to cool 'em and a Turkish bath to sweat 'em if they got a cold. I'll tell you, she was sure in good shape when she come to me. I'll tell you . . ."

"Thank you, Mr. Callahan. Now you say you were injured —you were knocked unconscious?"

"Yes, sir. I was out for minutes, don't rightly know how long. My head ain't been right since. And you saw how I limped comin' up here; my leg ain't been right either. And I can't lift no more whiskey barrels. . . ."

"Thank you, that will be all, Mr. Callahan," his attorney said and, turning to the defense table, "Your witness."

"How much did you pay for the horse, Mr. Callahan?" the defense asked.

"I don't rightly remember. But it wasn't the money, ya see, it was that ya can't get a Heinz horse for love nor money unless you're lucky .You know, Mr. Heinz picks 'em all himself, goes clear to Kentucky—"

"I think we all know enough about Heinz horses, Mr. Callahan," the defense attorney interrupted. "Now could you tell me, did you visit a hospital or a doctor for your injuries?"

"No, sir, I don't hold with doctors, I . . ."

"I see. Thank you, Mr. Callahan. No further questions."

Three or four people who had happened to be on the corner and seen the automobile rush by at speeds they described variously as "terrific," "ungodly" and "hell-for-leather" were paraded by the plaintiff before young Curry had a chance to take the stand. It was unfortunate, Reed thought, that Curry was attending Harvard, where he seemed to be shedding his good honest Pittsburgh twang for a marbles-in-the-mouth accent that was sure to set the jurymen's teeth on edge. Though he seemed suitably nervous on the stand, he couldn't help sounding superior, as if he had been wafted out of the ordinary circumstances of life on a cloud of his father's money. In a way, of course, he had.

"Would you please describe for the jury the vehicle you were driving, Mr. Curry?" his attorney asked.

"Well, there's been a lot of talk here about Heinz, and it just so happens that my car is like the one Mr. Howard Heinz drives—a Panhard-Levassor from France. You know, Mr. Heinz made forty miles an hour in the Century Run with his 'Red Devil.' It's got a two-cylinder, six-horsepower gasoline engine, chain drive and . . ."

"Thank you, all those details aren't necessary. The point is that this machine normally travels twenty miles an hour or more. Is that correct, Mr. Curry?" the attorney asked.

"Yes, sir."

"And you were going approximately that speed when Mr. Callahan pulled out of a side street without looking in your direction . . ."

"Objection! The witness has not so testified," the plaintiff's lawyer shouted.

Reed sighed. "Objection sustained. Go ahead."

The defense lawyer nodded. "Tell us what happened, Mr. Curry."

"Well, I was driving along about twenty or so, looking out for people crossing the street and the slow wagons and buggies in front of me when suddenly this wagon just pulled out across my path. As far as I could tell, the driver didn't even look my way."

"And you did what, Mr. Curry?"

"I honked the horn, you know, and then I put on the brakes. But at that speed I just couldn't stop. I went right into him."

"In your opinion, could any automobile have been stopped under the circumstances, Mr. Curry?"

"No, sir, none that I know of."

"Thank you, no further questions. Your witness."

"No questions," the plaintiff's lawyer said.

The real gist of the case would come in the lawyers' summation to the jury, Reed decided. He picked up his gavel, banged it on the desk. "Court stands adjourned until two-thirty."

Going out on to Grant Street on his way to lunch at the Duquesne Club, Reed was again confronted by the slab of the new 21-story H. C. Frick Building rising across the street from the courthouse. Perhaps because the morning case had got his mind going on the problems presented by change, he began playing with all the symbolism involved in what he considered Frick's monstrosity. Naturally it had to be, like the Carnegie building before it, a monument to the structural powers of steel. But what about the lobby—three stories high, sheathed entirely in marble and graced with a huge, stained-glass window, "Fortune," by John La Farge, that more appropriately belonged in a cathedral? Maybe it was meant to be a kind of cathedral. Certainly it dwarfed the churches whose spires formerly were the city's skyline and, as old Mr. Wallace said, pointed the citizens toward God; it also shaded the now puny courthouse tower which must have been a comfort to crotchety Judge Mellon in his extreme old age. After all, he'd himself deserted the temple of justice for the altar of finance. Men built cathedrals to celebrate what they worshipped, and in this sense Frick's building, honeycombed with offices where the commerce of the city could go forward, was entirely fitting, as was, Reed reflected, his brother Scott's being in charge of the project. He doubted, though, that Scott would much care for the humor he saw in it: shooting his building higher than the old Carnegie offices was surely Frick's way of spitting in the little Scotchman's eye.

That Frick-Carnegie case had been one that Reed would have savored. Although he'd been on the docket for it, he had to disqualify himself because of his brother's position with the Carnegie company. His disappointment was mollified when the matter was settled down in Atlantic City and didn't go to trial, but the depositions in the case had blown the lid, so to speak, right off that canny little Scot's secret money-making machine. No doubt the figures that came out—net earnings of $40,000,000 in 1900 alone—had quite a bit to do with J. P. Morgan's eagerness to form U.S. Steel. But what a wealth of testimony was lost! Reed had been able to piece most of the story together from gossip at the club, where tongues had been loosened both by money safely in the bank and liquor in the stomach, though God knows he heard none of it from brother Scott, who kept his mouth shut and managed to walk a tightrope between both sides. You had to hand it to Scott— like that business down in Homestead, he could wade right into the middle of the firing and somehow not get hit. Maybe God *was* on his side. Anyway, Scott surely wouldn't appreciate Reed's finding the whole story pretty hilarious.

When you looked at it in retrospect, the whole affair had more to do with the characters of the men involved than with the specific details of the dispute. Whatever else you might think about him, Frick was straight—that is, if he called a spade anything, he called it a spade. Carnegie was a real corkscrew, twisting this way and that until he had a grip on you. The way he treated the partners was unbelievable: low, low salaries with promises of profits to come. When they became restless, he'd pat them on the head, call them "my young geniuses," point to the astounding books that proved the business was getting richer by the day—and then spend the profits on some new piece of equipment that would yield even more money by cutting costs. When one of them might be thoughtless enough to get tired or sick or die, he would buy him or his heirs out at "book value," according to the terms of what Reed considered to be a spurious "iron-clad contract" he'd made them sign. One instance involved a partner who'd died while Carnegie was abroad. Carnegie wrote anguished letters to Frick, extolling the partner's contributions to the business and insisting that no settlement be made with the widow until he could get to Pittsburgh. Everybody was afraid, as Reed heard it, that Carnegie's sentimentality was going to lead him to give away too big a slice of the pie. Not so; he wanted to make certain the widow got book value only. Another angry partner wanted to get out, received the same kind of offer and accused Carnegie of making him a "slave." Andy, according to the story, blandly replied, "Well, that's the idea. I contracted for your services for life." Even partner Henry Phipps, so old a friend that Carnegie's mother had mended shoes on piece work for Phipps's father, a cobbler in Slabtown, got so tired of waiting for his money that he joined in Frick's court action.

The way it all came about was predictable by hindsight although there was a time, right after the Homestead strike, when nobody would ever have believed that Carnegie would argue with the man who'd so courageously carried the brunt of the fight for him. In February, '93, some four months after the workers had been forced into submission by their need to eat and gone back to nonunion jobs, Carnegie actually stood on a pile of steel at the Homestead plant and told them that Mr. Frick was "one of the foremost managers in the world." No doubt he was, and it may have been Frick's consciousness of this fact that made him tired of doing the dirty work while Carnegie flitted around the world, making friends with emperors, kings, presidents and philosophers and writing polemics on democracy and peace. Peace . . . Reed smiled to himself as he thought of Scott's own account of how Carnegie reconciled his self-interest with his proclaimed ideal.

Although now Scott rarely had a good word for Reed's idol, Teddy Roosevelt, he was feeling quite differently back there just before the Spanish-American War when Roosevelt was assistant secretary of the Navy and trying to build up the fleet. Reading about this at the time, Scott had gone in to Frick one day and asked, "Why aren't we bidding on the armor plate for all these new ships? I was just doing some figuring and found we could underbid any competitor and still turn a profit. Look at these figures."

Impassive as usual, Frick studied the jottings Scott had put before him. "I'm not surprised it works out that way," he said, "but you must know Mr. Carnegie doesn't believe in armaments. He thinks the world ought to be beating its swords into ploughshares."

"But this is to strengthen the United States," Scott argued.

"That fellow Roosevelt talks about 'speaking softly and carrying a big stick,' and I have to agree with him. Surely, Mr. Carnegie wants to see this country strong."

"He's an odd kind of patriot, Stewart—got one foot in Scotland and one here. Always cozying up to the Kaiser. I just don't know," Frick said. "I do know he'd find those figures interesting. I'd like to have the business. Why don't you go up to New York and talk to him?"

So for the second time in his life Scott Stewart was ushered into a Carnegie home. The one on Fifty-first Street in New York was far grander than the one in Homewood, and the man who met him was far older. His hair and his square spade beard were truly white now, but his complexion was pink and his eyes were still lively. He was full of good humor and apparently not at all anxious to get down to business.

"Say, I've got to tell you something that happened the other day, Stewart," he said. "You know my sister-in-law, Lucy—Tom's widow—has a son she named Andrew after me. Well, the young scoundrel's in college now and he never writes his mother. I bet Lucy ten dollars I could get an answer out of Andrew by return mail. What do you think I did? I wrote the boy a letter and added a P.S. saying I was enclosing ten dollars—but I left the money out. Well, sir, two days later that boy wrote back, politely informing me that no check had been enclosed. Lucy's a good sport, and she paid me the money—which I sent on to Andrew. Fruits of a lifetime of handling men, Stewart. . . ."

Somewhat embarrassed, Scott chuckled politely. While Carnegie was telling his story, Scott's eye had been roaming about the room picking up bits of Carnegie scripture. Carved above the mantle was "Let There Be Light" and below that: "He that cannot reason is a fool; he that will not is a bigot; he that dare not is a slave." On another wall was "Thine Own Reproach Alone Do Fear." Nothing there about patriotism or profit, the motives Scott was counting on to carry his argument. Well, nothing to do but begin.

"Mr. Carnegie, you've written many times that you are a firm believer in American democracy. . . ."

A little jarred at the abrupt shift in the course of the conversation, Carnegie said impatiently, "Yes, yes, so I have."

"Our government, particularly Assistant Secretary of the Navy Roosevelt, believes that democratic principles are being threatened all over this hemisphere by the royal imperialism of Spain," Scott went on.

"I agree, I agree. I never could abide royalty in any form,"

Carnegie said. "Why, do you know when I was a boy in Dunfermline we weren't allowed to set foot on the laird's property. No, sir. Well, I've bought the whole thing now and made it a park so any good Scots lad can enjoy it."

"Then how would you feel, Mr. Carnegie, if you could help return a whole hemisphere to the people?"

"What are you getting at, Mr. Stewart?"

"The Carnegie Company has been asked to bid on armor plate for the Navy which, in Mr. Roosevelt's view, is the necessary weapon to enforce the Monroe Doctrine. Now, we all know in Pittsburgh how you feel about weapons of war. . . ."

"Quite right. Quite right, pard. I want nothing to do with them."

"Yes, but wouldn't you agree, Mr. Carnegie—a strong navy is ultimately a weapon of peace? It could keep America free of the old rivalries of Europe that have caused so many conflicts." Scott had studied and rehearsed carefully.

"Well, well, perhaps, but I think our company has enough on its hands without getting into this, Mr. Stewart."

"The thing is, Mr. Carnegie, the Carnegie Company, because of its efficiency, is in a position to provide our country with what it needs at a much lower price than our competitors —and still make a profit. Look at these figures," Scott said, handing over the notes that had impressed Frick.

Carnegie took them in with a practiced eye. When he looked up at Scott, he was grinning. "Well. Well, well. You certainly know how to appeal to a Scotch soul, Mr. Stewart— but then I guess you come by it naturally. So we can have patriotism and profit, too?"

"That's about it, sir."

"It's a bargain that's hard to refuse. I guess it wouldn't be fair to let our country pay more for something we can provide. Tell Frick to go ahead."

Tacking into such continuous wind shifts from New York and Scotland was more than Frick, basically a power-boat man himself, could stand. So in '99 he and Phipps and a few others got the idea that it was time to try to buy Carnegie out. After all, the old Scotchman was sixty-four, and he had been talking and writing about quitting and devoting his life to philanthropy for thirty years. Obviously Carnegie wasn't really interested in his Pittsburgh operations; he spent most of his time abroad and was bemused by his new role as the father of a two-year-old daughter. Still they were surprised when Carnegie accepted an offer from a syndicate which included Frick, Phipps, the Moore brothers of Diamond Match and National Biscuit fame, and John (Bet a Million) Gates. The price was $320,000,000 with $1,700,000 option money, the option to run out in August '99. The option money wasn't difficult to raise—Frick and Phipps put up $170,000 of it themselves—but the Moores and Gates could not get the rest by August. Carnegie not only gleefully pocketed the option but told a friend when they were discussing the $1,000,000 cost of Skibo, the estate of the Roman Catholic Bishop of Caithness he'd bought for a permanent Scotch summer home, that "the whole thing is just a nice little present from Mr. Frick."

The remark got back to Frick, as Reed heard the story, and the chairman was in a testy mood, to say the least, in November '99 when Carnegie came to Pittsburgh to settle the matter of coke prices. Carnegie claimed he had a three-year contract with the Frick Coke Co., of which Frick was also chairman, to deliver at $1.35 a ton, although the market price had risen to $3.25. This would clearly be robbing Peter to pay Paul, and Frick, who claimed there was no such contract, did not want to see the company bearing his name sacrificed in that way. Unfortunately, on his Pittsburgh visit, Carnegie picked up the news that Frick had offered to sell the Carnegie Company some land he owned along the Monongahela for $3,500 an acre. Annoyed at Frick's intransigeance about the coke prices, Carnegie went about telling the younger partners that Frick's land deal was questionable, if not improper. At a board meeting on November 26, Frick exploded: "I have stood a great many insults from Mr. Carnegie in the past, but I will submit to no further insults in the future."

After that, events went quickly. By December 5 Carnegie had managed to get Frick's resignation as chairman of the Carnegie Company. He then used his stock ownership to appoint several new members to the board of the Frick Coke Co. On January 9, 1900, the Frick board voted to authorize the $1.35 price to the Carnegie Company, and Frick resigned as chairman. With Frick off both boards, Carnegie pushed a resolution through the Carnegie Company board to buy Frick out at "book value"—some $4,900,000, or a sixth share of the company's ridiculously low book capitalization. Armed with the resolution, Carnegie went in to confront Frick, who was still cleaning up his affairs at his desk in the Carnegie building and who, of course, had more reason than most to know that Carnegie's own valuation on the company was more than ten times the book capitalization. Frick glanced at the resolution and then told Carnegie—and Reed had reason to believe these were the exact words because he had heard them from a man who was standing right outside in the hall at the time—"For years I have been convinced that there is not an honest bone in your body. Now I know that you are a goddamned thief. We will have a judge and jury of Allegheny County decide what you are to pay me."

Imagine being the judge on such a case! Imagine testimony such as that coming out in court! Ah, well, Reed acknowledged, it was inevitable that Carnegie wouldn't allow it, especially after Henry Phipps, the long-time borrower for Carnegie interests, joined Frick's suit. From what Reed understood, the deal all the parties reached when they met in Atlantic City in March of 1900 was that Frick would get $15,484,000 in stock and $15,800,000 in bonds of a new Carnegie Company, which absorbed the Frick Coke Co. It was enough, at any rate, for him to build his skyscraper, retain a sizable interest in U.S. Steel and move to a fine and fancy house in New York City. God knows what Scott profited from the whole U.S. Steel merger, but it surely was over a million, and Schwab, who arranged the entire sale, asked Scott to stay on the U.S. Steel board.

Charlie Schwab was a man Reed thought he could like. He seemed to enjoy his money. He always brightened up the bar of the Duquesne Club with the latest joke he'd heard in the mill or some story about how he'd taken Duke So-and-so or Lord So-and-so (complete with accent, of course) at the tables in Monte Carlo. When Schwab had a drink or two under his belt, it wasn't difficult to get him to reveal details on the big deal that was the formation of U.S. Steel. He was, in a way, a new Carnegie. None of the tight-lipped secrecy of people like Scott and Frick and Mellon for him. The livery boy from Cresson, not yet forty, like the immigrant from Slabtown, seemed always to have to pinch himself to make sure he wasn't dreaming, and one way of pinching was telling.

It all began when Schwab, who had taken over from Frick, made what he thought was a rather routine speech at the University Club in New York on what now seemed fittingly the first December of the old new century. It was a kind of a blue-sky speech in which Schwab told the overstuffed and sleepy diners in front of him what the steel industry could do if it weren't for all the ragged competition. To some of the more alert minds at the meeting, young Schwab's words were a surprise. The Frick confrontation had stirred old Andrew Carnegie into a new burst of action. Taking command of the company with Schwab as his first lieutenant, he had suddenly ordered the construction of a large tube plant at Conneaut, Ohio, to compete with J. P. Morgan's National Tube Company and a new railroad east from Pittsburgh to break the galling Pennsylvania Railroad monopoly. Now here was Schwab, the action man of this new competitive battle, talking about how much better it would be if there were less competition.

One listener, a large man with a great bulbous red nose who had expected to be thoroughly bored, came awake with a start. J. P. Morgan, representing the investor's point of view, had spent much of his time over the past several years trying to make sense out of America's overcapitalized and overly competitive industries. He had labored long and hard, for example, to get the railroads consolidated and pared down to the point where they could make a profit, and now this ass Carnegie was talking about building a new one. But here was Carnegie's own man sounding like Morgan himself. What was going on? Immediately after the dinner Morgan, whose tomb-like silence under normal conditions made Henry Clay Frick seem a raconteur by comparison, pushed his way through the men gathered around Schwab, fixed the young steelmaker with his searchlight eyes and began to ask pointed questions. What companies ought to be brought together? How much money could be saved by this move, by that move? Schwab answered easily and openly until the tough one came—was he speaking for Carnegie? No, Schwab had to admit.

Schwab went back to Pittsburgh and forgot the whole thing until he received an invitation to a private meeting in Morgan's home on Madison Avenue in January. Please keep it confidential, make some excuse for the trip, the invitation urged. Schwab couldn't resist going if only to have a look inside the great library, which Morgan was packing with art treasures from all over the world. It turned out to be a select group—Morgan himself, his handsome partner Robert Bacon, Schwab, and surprisingly in the home of so cautious a banker, the famous "Bet a Million" Gates. Cigars were passed, but no drink; serious business was obviously in the air. While Morgan sat at a table dealing himself a hand of solitaire, Schwab was asked to repeat the gist of his December speech. Then Gates was encouraged to speak out on the vision he'd shared with the others in the abortive effort to buy Carnegie out. "The real trouble was those Moore brothers," he said, "Carnegie never did trust them, and he was only too glad to back out and pick up the option. If Carnegie ever does sell, it will only

271

be to somebody he trusts to keep the company going. That's where you come in, Mr. Morgan." Not a word from the solitaire player. The talk went round and round with Bacon asking the sharp questions and Schwab and Gates supplying the answers. Dawn was graying the windows when Morgan at last spoke. "Mr. Schwab, you obviously think this all makes sense. Would you be willing to ask Carnegie if he would sell?" "When?" "Now—today."

Too excited to be tired, Schwab went back to his hotel, breakfasted and then proceeded to Number Five, West Fifty-first Street. Mr. Carnegie was not at home, he was told at the door, but Mrs. Carnegie would receive him. What good luck . . . Louise Carnegie, Schwab knew, would be a valuable ally. She'd been trying for years to get her husband out of business, and she might give him advice on how to approach the matter. He was right. "Mr. Carnegie's up at St. Andrews in Westchester playing golf. Yes, golf in this kind of weather. He's gone wild about the game—calls it 'Dr. Golf.' I think he may be right. He looks so fresh and healthy when he's been out playing. It also puts him in a good humor, and if I were you, Mr. Schwab, I'd go right up there now and play a round with him, and I think he might listen to you. I certainly hope so."

Schwab took the advice. The golf was a trial, because his hands shook so from cold and excitement that he could scarcely grip a club. Perhaps fortunately, this caused him to lose, and so Carnegie was in an especially jovial mood when they sat down to lunch in the little cottage he maintained near the course. Schwab simply blurted out his story about the meeting with Morgan, and Carnegie listened attentively. "You know, Charlie, I'd like more time for golf, and Mrs. Carnegie is always hounding me to get out of business. I've never met Mr. Morgan, but I guess he can raise the money if he says so. Here is my price." Carnegie took a piece of paper and jotted down a figure that nearly made Schwab faint when he saw it—$485,000,000. "Oh, and there's one other thing you might tell Mr. Morgan, Charlie. I want my share, and my uncle George Lauder's share, and Lucy's share in five percent gold bonds. No stocks for me." Odd, Schwab thought, for a man whose fortune was built on selling railway stocks to European investors, but then, consistency had never been Andy Carnegie's long suit.

That very afternoon, Schwab went to Morgan's Wall Street office and handed him the slip of paper in Carnegie's handwriting. Morgan merely glanced at it. "Sold," he said. . . .

How did they like *that?* Oh, there was one more amusing thing, Schwab added to those assembled around him at the Club. Morgan decided he ought to meet Carnegie and phoned him to come down to his Wall Street office. It's as far one way as the other, Carnegie told him, why don't you come to see me? So, as Louise later told Schwab, Morgan got in his carriage, rode up to Fifty-first Street and disappeared into the study with Carnegie for about fifteen minutes. Just as he was leaving, he held out his hand. "Mr. Carnegie," he said, "I want to congratulate you on being the richest man in the world."

Talk of figures such as that tended to make Reed's head reel. Compared to them, the $500,000 or so Alma had, now that her mother was dead, seemed peanuts. It was money enough for a lifetime of comfort, but there was something about Pittsburgh that put the yen for real money, for the kind of big money that bought power, into your blood, just the way the soot got into your lungs.

And thinking of the soot, Reed laughed aloud at the memory of young Stewart Sharp's story. When he was in medical school over at Western University cutting up cadavers, Sharp and a classmate were working on the body of a Chinaman when the classmate, who was carving into the chest, suddenly called for the professor. The lungs were red instead of the usual dirty gray, obviously the sign of a rare disease. But the professor, who had studied in Philadelphia, assured them that they were only seeing normal lung tissue for the first time. . . . Then why did people stay on in this place—the lights were already burning at noon of this November day in 1903 as Reed pushed his way down Sixth Avenue through the lunchtime crowds toward his club—until their lungs blackened or their hearts stopped? The blunt answer was money: they either were making so much they couldn't afford to leave or they were making so little they couldn't afford to leave.

But why then did he stay—he and Alma and their kids? Well, a frivolous answer was that there was almost as much good whiskey as money in Pittsburgh. Frick might not be Reed's favorite, but his grandfather had known what he was about when he cooked up Old Overholt. Reed could hardly wait to get a glass of it in his hand, even though he knew the talk about town was that you'd better get to Judge Stewart before noon if you wanted him to pay attention to a close argument. He'd have to be careful today—no more than two —since he was sure he'd have to straighten out the jury after

273

the lawyers got through in this Curry case. . . . Come to think of it, though, was this really frivolous? Did he stay because he drank, or did he drink because he stayed? All he knew for certain was that he would find life intolerable, as well as less pleasurable, without the soothing dimension of booze. With it he could see and indeed admire the strong qualities of the Fricks and Scotts and Mellons of this world; without it, he would tend to be overwhelmed by their—for him at least —less tolerable sides. True, he tended to yawn on the bench after lunch, but he had also managed to achieve a judicial temperament for which the wrangling attorneys ought to be grateful.

Reed knew his drinking was an abomination to Scott, which in a way was one good reason for keeping at it. It did trouble him that he might be causing his mother some pain too, but he suspected she could forgive him as she surely had forgiven his father. And it pleased him greatly that the two women he cared most about, Alma and Lucinda, seemed to understand as well as tolerate him. Maybe they though that if he didn't dampen his fires with alcohol, he might commit something wild, as in his early years. Maybe they were right, although Henry's death had just about dissuaded him from believing in the efficacy of noble acts in a world that seemed so indifferent to them. Not that he seriously saw himself in either role, but at least with the perspective of an enabling glow he was able to convince himself that he was doing more good in the world as a would-be Solomon than a Christ.

It was really a matter of having the right attitude. Laugh and the world laughed with you, cry and you cried alone. Henry was certainly right about not crying: when you taught yourself not to cry, you could also begin to teach yourself not to care quite so much. Too bad Henry couldn't take his own advice. All of Henry's public crying in those dreadful articles of his didn't save him when his caring brought him down to death. What was wanted by a man of wisdom was balance—perhaps more the Greek middle way than the Christian cross. So you couldn't change the world; well then, enjoy it—laugh at it, use its tested pleasures to make it more tolerable. Humor, a sense of humor—that was it, that was what was wanting in the Henrys and Scotts of this world. But Reed needed it, needed it like drink, if he were to go on presiding over the struggles of humorless men. Affected permanently by his long-ago experience on the showboat, Reed often went to the theater now, particularly if there was a comedy playing. His favorite was Gilbert and Sullivan, and he never missed a performance that came to Pittsburgh. Often while on the bench he would have to restrain himself from chuckling aloud while he pretended to ponder a sentence with the Mikado's sage advice to "Make the punishment fit the crime" singing in his ear:

All prosy dull society sinners who chatter and bleat and bore
Are made to hear sermons from mystical Germans who preach
    from ten till four . . .
And amateur tenors whose vocal villainies all desire to shirk
Shall during off hours exhibit their powers to Madame Tussaud's
    wax works . . .

Oh, what he wouldn't give to be able to pass such perfect sentences! Just thinking about it brightened Reed's mood as he entered the club and made his way to a round table in the upstairs dining room where he lunched with whomever turned up. Scott, as usual, was eating alone in a corner, and they exchanged nods. There was a fellow judge holding forth when Reed sat down and signaled the waiter for his usual dram of Old Overholt. The other judge broke off his story and said, "Well, here he is now—the man with the landmark case. Tell me, Stewart, do you think the automobile's here to stay? A body isn't safe in the streets with those things snorting around."

"I guess we'll just have to learn to control it like we've learned to control everything else that's come along," Reed said. "I can predict one thing: there will be a lot less horse shit in the world if it catches on."

Everybody laughed, and another man, one of the city's largest glass manufacturers, turned the subject. "Say, tell me, Stewart, what do you think about your friend Teddy Roosevelt now—going around and talking about 'malefactors of great wealth' and threatening suit to break up all the trusts?"

"I think he's just about what this country needs," Reed said.

"Well, I don't," the other man replied and, nodding toward the corner, added, "and I'm sure your brother would agree with me. For my money he's no Republican, and that fellow who shot McKinley did this country a disservice we'll never live down. I don't think the government has any right to mess about with business, and even the Supreme Court agrees with me. You ought to know your law . . ."

"Oh, I do, I do," Reed said. "But fortunately the law isn't a static thing. You know, there's such a thing as the Sherman Anti-Trust Act on the books, but nobody's really tested it in the courts. The thing I'm going to enjoy is watching old

Philander Knox waffle around. Imagine the counsel for the old Carnegie Company having to lead the fight against big business now that he's T. R.'s Attorney General! Politics surely does make strange bedfellows in the law."

"You bet it does," the other judge said. "For example, I'm just waiting to hear how you talk when you're up for re-election next year, Reed, with damn near everybody in Pittsburgh out for Roosevelt's skin."

"Everybody in this club perhaps," Reed said. "But I'll wager most other people in town think differently. Anyway, I'm willing to trust the public. You'll remember I managed to squeak through in 'ninety-two when everybody in the country was singing, 'Grover, Grover, four more years of Grover; in he goes, out they go, then we'll be in clover.'"

"Sure, but you had Magee and Flinn with you then—God knows why. Now that old Chris Magee's dead, Flinn's a toothless tiger," the other judge put in.

"Ah ha," Reed said, "but I at least was smart enough to get behind Steele Bigelow's movement for a new city charter. I remember you warned me to stay out of it then, and Chris Magee was sore because Bigelow was playing the rift between him and Mat Quay, who'd do anything—and did by swinging the state power to Bigelow—to get back at Magee. And thus do thieves fall out. . . ."

"Quiet, dammit," a doctor at the table said. "You'll make me lose my lunch. Remember, I've got to work in the hospital Magee's money built."

"Yeah, and we wouldn't have a zoo if it weren't for Magee's mo—" another man began, but Reed cut him off.

"No, but we might have clean water and pure air for us human animals to drink and breathe. That's another thing I like about T. R. He thinks we ought to do something about saving this God-given earth. . . ."

"With the taxpayers' money," the glass man said. "I tell you we'll all be in the poorhouse before we know it."

The panic the older business men were showing at the antics of the young man in the White House was at least ironic to Reed. After all, Teddy was a true patrician of comfortable personal wealth and a lifelong Republican. If anything, Reed thought, Roosevelt was trying to save these capitalists from having their wealth appropriated in a bloody revolution by forcing some social responsibility on them. They couldn't or wouldn't see it that way. They longed for the good old days under high-tariff McKinley, the man who'd made his whole political career out of protecting profits. They were heady

276

days, all right, with business booming and the American flag being raised in Cuba and the Philippines. Reed's favorite newspaperman, Finley Peter Dunne, summed up the mood when he had Mr. Dooley say about the Republican Convention in 1900 that renominated McKinley: "Th' proceedin's was opened with a prayer that Providence might remain under th' protection iv th' administration." It was the kind of prayer Don Sharp might have given before he went queer in the head.

"Well, I've got to get back," Reed said, rising. He had stuck to two drinks, somewhat to the dismay of the doctor who usually counted on Judge Stewart's going along to make his own consumption seem less noticeable. An ear-nose-and-throat specialist, he argued that "you don't have to be sober to take wax out of a kid's ears."

Back in the courtroom, the case went on almost exactly as Reed had imagined that it would. The attorney for the plaintiff pulled out all the stops in the organ of legal oratory, picturing his client as the poor, honest workingman whose body and means of livelihood had been crushed by a young playboy carelessly indulging himself in the pleasures of a new and dangerous toy. He even went into the imagined feelings of the horse, an aging but still lustrous queen of the equine world with whose terror at the unknown the jury could easily sympathize.

At first, Reed thought, the defense lawyer struck rather too dryly to the facts, but then he grew quietly eloquent. "Gentlemen of the jury," he said, "I hope you will bear in mind that this is truly an historic case. In rendering your verdict, you will be telling the world"—a gesture toward the newspapermen with their busy pencils—"whether twelve good men and true of Allegheny County, Pennsylvania, are willing to march boldly forward into the future or will fearfully recoil into the safety of the past. I contend that the day will come when each and every one of you sitting in that jury box will own your own automobile. I contend that the day will come when you will be driving your own vehicle not at twenty, not at thirty, not at forty, but at fifty or sixty miles an hour. But I contend that that day will come only when all of us are willing to look forward and make way for the future and not, as this unfortunate drayman did, throw ourselves blindly across the path of progress. I thank you."

Reed could tell from the skeptical looks on their faces that the jurors were not particularly sold on this point. In his charge to them he urged that they ignore the oratory and concentrate on whether the defendant had been operating his vehicle in a reckless manner and whether the plaintiff had given due allowances for the oncoming automobile when entering the road on which the accident had taken place. He suggested that the speed at which the automobile was traveling, however astonishing or even frightening, was a factor inherent in the operation of this new kind of vehicle and not necessarily pertinent to the issues of responsibility involved in this case. The feelings of the horse, he said with as straight a face as he could muster, were, as he had ruled earlier, irrelevant, since it was to be assumed, particularly in the case of a horse so ably trained, that the horse was obeying her master's commands. Then he dismissed them and retired to his chambers, where he kept a bottle of Old Overholt in the lower left-hand drawer of his desk, to await a verdict.

It wasn't long in coming. Within the hour the jury returned and announced that it had voted damages not of $1,750 but of $2,000 for the plaintiff. Though it announced no other findings, the jury clearly expressed its belief that such a dangerous machine had no place on the county's roads. The verdict was wrong, Reed knew, both as to the actual facts of the case in hand and as to its broader implications. But the law had been served, and the twelve good men and true had reacted exactly as most people could be expected to react in the face of a phenomenon they didn't understand. Hold back the clock. That's what we all want, Reed thought, and what we'll try to do whenever we are given the chance. The defendant could appeal, of course, but Reed doubted that he would. Two thousand dollars wasn't much to a newly minted millionaire, and there were no obvious legal loopholes in the case as grounds for overturning the verdict. The people had spoken; so be it.

A Lesson from Matthew 10

Even those people who should have known better often said they felt sorry for Judge John Reed Stewart, Jr.—who would want to live with a woman like that wife of his? As the leading Pittsburgh representative of Susan B. Anthony's National American, she was always marching in the streets or talking at the top of her lungs in some hall or other for woman suffrage. Because she had continued to expand to statuesque proportions, newspaper cartoonists had an open season with her, using her size to depict overpowering womanhood. With a public image like that, what must she be like at home? No doubt at all that Reed Stewart was henpecked. Why, he was even living on her money, as everyone could plainly see, since they stayed on in the old Jones mansion on Ridge Avenue.

Reed bore these clearly discernible thoughts of his fellow citizens stoically. There was no way of telling them they were wrong without revealing the sort of thing a man wouldn't share with his own children. Reed alone knew that this stately woman so often seen in caricature behind a podium—great expanse of flowered silk across her bosom heaving with every breath, pince-nez she wore for reading glittering in the light, hat brim flopping with each emphatic nod—could still be turned by a touch into a creature as fierce as a tigress in heat. The exciting thing was that he never knew where and when it might happen.

The last time it had been in the barn. Reed had gone round with the carriage to pick Alma up from one of her afternoon meetings. He was still somewhat annoyed from being nagged at lunch by a couple of cronies who were irritated that their own wives were going to hear Alma speak. "I don't know why you don't keep her home, Stewart," one man told him.

Reed had tried to turn it away lightly with, "Because I only have one wife to give for my country," but Alma could sense the edge to his voice as he pretended to be amused in telling her about the incident. "You know that isn't true, Reed," she said.

"How?" he asked.

"Just wait till we get home," she said, giving him an intimate pat.

Reed was slowing the carriage to drop her at the house when she said, "I'll ride on to the barn with you."

"Now, Alma, we do have a bed."

"Yes, but the children are still up."

"Won't they wonder what we're doing down there in the barn all that time?"

"It won't be that long if you're still the man I think you are. I'll tell them you wanted to wipe down the horse, and I wanted to talk. They think we're crazy anyway."

It was true. Alexander and Carolyn, now entering their sensitive teens, were embarrassed by their mother's public image. They made up all kind of excuses, including pretended illness, to avoid attending any of her meetings or marching with her in parades. And they were puzzled by their father. They were proud that he was a judge but, frank to say, somewhat embarrassed that he didn't go to church like other fathers and drank too much whiskey and had that bad scar on his face. When they talked about their parents, as they did by the hour, Alexander and Carolyn also had to agree that nobody could be nicer to them. They were never punished or even yelled at, like most of their friends, but maybe that was the problem. Their parents were different, and it was a difficult thing to have different parents. They began asking to be sent East to school, where nobody would know them, and right now Reed wished that he and Alma had agreed.

While Reed was putting the horse into his stall, Alma scrambled up the ladder to the hay loft, calling, "Last one up's a rotten egg."

Reed followed her, and they wrestled and rolled and laughed together like children in the warm, soft hay. Just when they were finished, just when Alma, lying quietly in his arms, asked, "Do you think you still have a wife, Reed," and he answered, "You bet," they heard a sound below. Alma was scrambling to arrange her clothes when they saw Alexander's head poke up the ladder. "Mother, Dad . . .?"

"We're just finishing our chat from the ride in, Alexander," Alma said. "Run along now; we'll be right there. . . ."

"Well, it was your idea," Reed said. "God knows what he'll make of this." He was smiling, in spite of himself, as he said it.

"Oh, I don't think he really saw anything," Alma said. "Anyway, I wouldn't have missed it for the world. . . ."

And it was more, much more than their deliciously spontaneous sex lives that made Reed happy to be married to Alma instead of some mousy, motherly lady like his sister Sarah. It was also—maybe most especially—the extraordinary friendship they shared. After nearly twenty years of marriage they could still hardly wait to talk to each other at the end of each day. He chatted about everything with her—cases, conversations at the club, thoughts about life and politics—and she was equally open with him. They didn't always agree, but more often than not they had it out on a person-to-person, man-to-woman basis rather than husband-to-wife. This was also something you couldn't talk about; it was more shameful than sex in the company of men whose jokes and casual conversation revealed their scorn for the female mind and the pitiful apartness they accepted in their own homes as the normal condition of marriage. But Reed was most content with his unique relationship, and the night of his first automobile accident case, he naturally told Alma about it as soon as he arrived home.

"You know if there'd been women on that jury, it would have been a different story," she said.

"I doubt it," Reed argued. "Women are more conservative than men, you know that. Protection of hearth and home and all that."

"You just don't know what goes on behind the masks we wear to fool you men," Alma said. "Speaking of women, I've asked Lucinda to dinner."

"Good, we can break out the drinks," Reed said.

"How many have you had today, Reed?"

"Oh, God, you too. I don't know that it matters."

"It matters to me," she said. "I'm not worried about your morals, Reed, but your health. . . . And then there's the why . . . why?"

"I don't know why. Not in a way to tell you. I only know it gets me through the day, lets me keep my mind off things I can't *do* a damn thing about. Besides, I've got some good company, you know. Stephen Foster was fond of the bottle, died of it, matter of fact, and Edgar Allan Poe before him and even, they say, Tom Carnegie, an evidently reluctant operator for his cheery big brother. Certainly no Frick."

"But, Reed, if you had something to commit yourself to the way I do, something you could really get your teeth into . . ."

"Maybe it's an excuse, but I'd be worse, I can tell you. I'd drink out of frustration."

"Yes, I'm afraid I believe you," Alma said. "I'm sure in the back of my mind when I'm working for what I believe is the feeling that if women had more to say the world would be a better place for decent people like you."

"Not if it's a place where you have to account for every drink. First thing women would do is push through prohibition. That's why I can't understand why Scott isn't one of your strongest supporters."

"Oh, Reed, that isn't what I had in mind at all. Actually, in spite of the crazy few charging into saloons, I think women are a lot less fanatical than men. There's a practical streak in them that doesn't go for simple-minded solutions. Women are more interested in people than in causes, and in that way you're right about the instinct for the protection of hearth and home. But it isn't so much an instinct for safety as an instinct for nurture—for the nuture and growth of human beings—"

"Hey, can I get in on this? Sounds interesting." It was the voice of Lucinda, who'd been let into the house unnoticed.

"Certainly. I need your help," Alma said. "I'm trying to explain to Reed how letting women in on the process of government will help to make the world safe for sensitive souls like himself."

"Sorry, I can't help you with that," Lucinda said. "I doubt if the world will ever be safe for sensitive souls. Phew, what a day! Fed a hundred and fifty. On my feet the whole time. Give me a drink, Reed. I need it."

"Gladly," Reed said, pouring one for all of them.

Lucinda sat down, kicked off her pinching boots and lit a cigarette. Her informality was taken by both Alma and Reed as the best kind of tribute to their efforts over the past ten years to make her feel at home with them. At forty-two, Lucinda was still trim, still stunning, but there was a kind of special quality to her beauty now, enhanced perhaps by her reputation as a somewhat unconventional angel of mercy. She did dreadful things, for a lady—smoked cigarettes, drank whiskey, rode a bicycle through the city streets . . . and got away with it. After all, her art work was appearing in the prestigious international exhibits at the new Carnegie Institute in Oakland and her book, *The New Americans*, compiled from the series of articles she wrote about the families on the South Side, had become, all unexpectedly, a national best seller.

She had long ago sold the Allegheny house and installed herself in a suite at the Schenley Hotel, a new and palatial edifice in the heart of an Oakland that was being turned into a cultural center by the presence of Carnegie's imposing institute. Rather quixotically, in the view of the rest of the family, Lucinda had opened a kind of home-away-from-home soup kitchen in an old store on the verge of the Point slums, where she ladled out nourishing meals three times a week to any hungry man, woman or child. It was a regular beat for the sob sisters of the Pittsburgh papers such as Willa Cather, and they had made Lucinda Stewart into one of the city's foremost characters. Too independent to seek the sponsorship of any church or organization, Lucinda raised funds for her project by shamelessly hounding friends and relatives, including brothers Reed and Scott and Ambassador T. Gillespie Jones, now a kindly white-haired grandfather and Episcopalian vestryman of impeccable morals.

"How long are you going to keep this up?" Reed asked Lucinda as he handed her a drink.

"Forever—or until the money runs out. Which reminds me I need another hundred to get through the week."

"It's yours," Reed said, and then asked, "Tell me, does Scott contribute too?"

"Oh, yes, through Mother. Scott claims to be worried about me associating with all those rough characters. Little does he know that my morals are in much more danger from the people hanging around his beloved Carnegie Institute."

"Funny thing," Reed said, "I've always wondered why they put Scott on that board since he's so obviously a Frick man."

"And you call yourself a politician," Alma said. "Your brother Scott practically single-handed the Symphony Society into being, and Andy Carnegie's gilded music hall would be an empty barn unless the orchestra played there. Simple, right?"

"I guess so. I keep forgetting about Scott and the symphony. Somehow it doesn't go with his character, especially now that they have that fellow Victor Herbert leading it. He appears to be quite the cosmopolitan man-about-the-world."

"That's what I mean about Scott's new friends," Lucinda said. "Maybe they'll make him human. You think so?"

"I wouldn't exactly count on it," Reed said.

"You two! You're impossible," Alma said. "You'd both be hay seeds living on some farm in the South Hills if it weren't for Scott. I used to think Jones was a pretty big name, but when I go downtown now it's 'Yes, Mrs. Stewart this' and 'Yes, Mrs. Stewart that,' and I hate to tell you, Reed, but it usually turns out they have me linked up with the wrong Stewart."

"Why do we always end up talking about Scott?" Lucinda asked.

"I don't know. I guess because, like Alma says, he's *the* Stewart," Reed said. "Did you hear he's going to have Benjy's child living with him?"

"Poor thing . . ."

"Now, listen . . . you two, that's enough of that. Let's go to dinner and leave off back-biting my brother-in-law. . . ."

David Scott Stewart was a two-year-old bundle of ferocious energy when a missionary worker from far-off Siam deposited him in the ornate hallway of his grandfather's Renaissance mansion in the East End of Pittsburgh. There had been little forewarning. A letter from the father, Dr. Benjamin Shallenberger Stewart, had reached them only a week or so before the baby himself.

"Dear Dad," it said, "Joan and I are being sent from Chiengmai to a village up country to open a new medical facility there. It's a wild area, and we don't know exactly what we'll run into. We do know, though, that we both will be working night and day to get the station started and we're afraid that taking a child as young as our David might be dangerous. Fortunately, Mrs. Anderson is going home on furlough and has agreed to bring David to you, where we know he will be safe with you and Grandmother. We won't be gettng back ourselves for another five years, and by then we would be wanting him to start his education in the States anyway. It's not easy to give up your child like this, but we look upon it as one of the sacrifices demanded of the Lord in our work. Nobody should appreciate better than you the need to do God's will. The new assignment will be an exciting challenge to both of us, and I hope you will be able to see your way to supporting it generously. Give my love to Grandmother and May, if you ever see her—why doesn't she write me? Your loving son, Benjamin."

Mary Stewart was immediately excited by the letter. She looked forward to having a child in the house again, and the attention he would need would no doubt help take her mind off the arthritis that was plaguing her more each day. There were enough maids—of course they would hire a special nurse—to relieve her of any physical burden. Scott was less certain. He'd always been uncomfortable around young children, even his own, and he couldn't imagine what it would be like to have one under foot after all these years of quiet order in his home. It was typical, though, of Benjamin to shove another problem at them without a by-your-leave. Once again Scott wondered where he had gone wrong with his son, how he had managed to raise a child without a practical bone in his body. If it weren't that Benjamin was such a staunch Christian, he'd have to believe it was the Schmidt influence. The boy was devilish clever in his way; he'd wielded his poor health like a weapon, not only in avoiding the things Scott thought would be good for him, such as working in the mills summers, but in explaining his interest in medicine. And then when it came to entering the mission field, Benjamin had simply recited everything Scott had told him about serving the Lord.

What battles they had had! Scott hated to recall them, because he'd been bested every time by this sweet, peculiar son of his. They began not long after Martha had left him alone to deal with the problems of their children. One night at dinner, Benjamin had said casually, "Dad, I was talking to cousin Stewart today, and he said they have a very good premed course at Princeton, so if you want me to go there . . ."

"You're not thinking of becoming a doctor?"

"Why not? Grandfather was a doctor, wasn't he?"

"And it killed him."

Mary Stewart couldn't restrain herself; she saw no reason to carry the story into the third generation. "Now, Scott . . ."

"I'm sorry, Mother," Scott said, "but I've heard you talk to the children about Father. It's all right for you to remember him the way you want, but I have a responsibility to my children to see that they don't make the same mistakes. I had always taken it for granted that Benjamin was going into business with me . . ."

"Business! I'm not the least bit interested in business, Father."

"And why not?"

"I want to *do* something with my life."

"And you don't think I've *done* something?"

"Oh, yes, you've made a lot of money, but I want to do something for other people . . ."

"You don't think building businesses, creating jobs, is doing something for other people?"

"Not the way I mean. . . . I don't know how to say it, but I don't want all this," Benjamin said, indicating with a sweep of his hand the vast dining room in which the three of them at the table seemed almost lost.

"That's only because you already have it. If you'd been left the way I was . . ."

"Dad, please, don't tell me all over again about going to work at thirteen and . . ."

" 'How sharper than a serpent's tooth it is to have a thankless child.' "

"I didn't know you read Shakespeare, Father."

"I read a lot in my youth. I had to educate myself. There was no Princeton for me . . ."

"Now, Scott," Mary Stewart interrupted again.

"I think it's high time this boy understands money doesn't grow on trees, Mother. And I think he ought to realize, too, that money is a trust. You know the parable of the talents, Benjamin—'For to every one who has will more be given, and he will have abundance; but from him who has not, even what he has will be taken away.' You see, the way I look on it, Benjamin, is that God gave us this wealth; he commanded us right in that parable to put it with those who best handle it, bankers. It will be yours someday, and you must learn how to use and multiply it."

"I thought Jesus told us to sell everything and give it to the poor."

"That's nonsense," Scott said. "He wasn't talking then to His disciples, but to a man who wasn't a Christian."

Knowing from experience that it was almost impossible to get the best of his father on a reading of scripture, Benjamin tried to turn the argument. "I still want to be a doctor," he persisted. "If there were better doctors, maybe I wouldn't have been sick the way I have all my life, maybe Mother wouldn't have died. . . ."

"Nothing could have saved her, Benjamin," Scott said. "It was God's will. When I was a boy my father told me how little a doctor can really do for people. It would only frustrate you."

"But they didn't know much then. They're learning more every day. Cousin Stewart says he could have helped Uncle Don . . ."

"Fiddlesticks. The best people in the country don't even know what happened to your Uncle Don. I don't want to hear any more of this talk of medicine."

Benjamin saw to it that his father didn't hear more of the matter, but he went right ahead and took the premedical courses anyway, tacking them onto a regular academic curriculum. When Scott tried to persuade him to work summers in the office to get a feel for business, Benjamin cleverly evaded him by signing up as a counselor for a religious camp sponsored by the Oakland Presbyterian Church. Elder Stewart could hardly object. Then Benjamin pulled the trumping ace from his hand. Even before he graduated from college, he signed up with the Board of Foreign Missions to go into the field upon completion of his medical studies. They accepted him, and before Scott really knew what was happening the Reverend Mr. Timmins, who'd replaced Don Sharp in the Oakland pulpit, was planning a special consecration service for Benjamin—the first of the church's young men to elect a missionary life. Elder Stewart, who was obliged to appear proud of his son, was furious.

"Why didn't you consult me about this?" he thundered when Benjamin came home from college for the service.

"Well, the board is located in New York, you know," Benjamin explained, "and I just went up there and talked to them. I didn't know they would tell Mr. Timmins about it."

"You can't do this without my permission. You're not twenty-one."

"I'm afraid I took your permission for granted. I prayed about it, you know, and I thought you would be proud of me."

"Proud of you? I think it's a fool thing to do. This business of being a doctor is bad enough, but why in the world would you want to go out to a godforsaken part of the world with a lot of barbaric Chinese . . ."

"They want me to go to Siam."

"Even worse—a lot of heathen Buddhists."

"But, Dad, that's where we're needed to spread the Word, isn't it? You've always told me you gave money to missionaries because Jesus commanded us to go out to the ends of the earth."

"Yes, well . . . well, it may be all right for some people. But I thought I made it clear to you that you have an obligation here, a fortune to use wisely. When you have it, you can send fifty missionaries out if you want instead of just . . ."

"You don't."

"I don't have that kind of money yet, but I will—and you will too. Son, you cannot leave here (he could not bring himself to say "me"), don't you understand?"

Scott looked hard at his boy. He'd never thought he would stoop to pleading. Slim and straight, taller if anything than Scott, but delicately pale like Martha, Benjamin stared directly into his father's eyes and said, "I have to, Dad. It's God's will. If you refuse permission, I'll wait until I am twenty-one and leave home. I know it hurts you, but I've prayed and prayed and searched the scripture. Here, let me read you this. .. ."

Taking out a pocket testament, Benjamin flipped through it to a dogeared page. "Listen, Dad—Matthew 10:37-39. 'He who loves father or mother more than Me is not worthy of Me; and he who loves son or daughter more than Me is not worthy of Me; and he who does not take his cross and follow Me is not worthy of Me. He who finds his life will lose it, and he who loses his life for my sake will find it.' There's no other way you can read that, is there, Dad?"

Scott knew he was finally beaten . . . and later, standing at the church door beside Benjamin and receiving the hearty congratulations of other members of the congregation, Scott was chagrined at the irony of being robbed of a son by the very faith he had so zealously practiced and preached.

Scott saw very little of Benjamin after that. Pushing himself year around as if the very devil were after him, the boy got through his medical studies at Johns Hopkins in half the regular time and set sail at once for Siam. Within months he had married a missionary nurse and fathered the son who was now being placed in Scott's lap. Although Scott had tried to feel proud of his son and to pay attention as Mary read aloud at table to the long letters full of unpronounceable names and dreadful diseases like leprosy and malaria, he was mostly aware of a sense of emptiness whenever he thought about Benjamin. For all practical purposes, the boy might as well be dead, and his hopes of finding someone to take on the burdens he would one day have to surrender had shifted somewhat uncertainly to May.

The girl was very nearly as exasperating as Benjamin. Ever since she'd been in Paris she had barely written a line to any of them, even Benjamin, except when she needed money. Well, in Scott's mind two years was quite long enough for any kind of study, and he'd decided to bring her back by the simple expedient of cutting her allowance. Her response had been immediate, and strange. "I'll come, but you won't like it," she wrote. "I'm not nearly through here, and you are going to have a most unhappy girl on your hands unless you begin to realize that I'm as deadly serious about my music as Benjamin is about his medicine or religion or whatever. I can't understand why you want to keep us all under your thumb. If you have any hopes of marrying me off to one of those oafs in Pittsburgh, I am afraid you're in for a disappointment because I am no better looking than I ever was—and totally uninterested in living the rest of my life in a cultural desert."

Though Mary Stewart cautioned that he might be doing the wrong thing, an infuriated Scott sent a one word message to

Paris over the new wireless: "Come." Having a son assert his independence was understandable and tolerable, however sad it made him feel. A daughter was simply obliged to be obedient, just as a father was obliged to see that a daughter was guided through the treacherous enticements of sin and danger to the safe harbor of marriage. Thinking of the problems May was presenting, Scott recalled the comment old Judge Mellon made in his autobiography about the death of one of his children: "Daughters who die young need not be greatly lamented." Of course, he had no such feelings toward his spirited May, but she *was* a problem. Very well, he would handle it.

A Fruit of Love

It was supposed to be morning, and supposed to be spring. But the gray light, filtering through the overhead railway that shielded the grimy window of their bedroom, was without time or season, as if all the human artifacts through which it bounced and twisted to reach them strained out God. It was rather like the light in Pittsburgh, and it made her actually shiver with apprehension at what lay ahead. This slight movement must have awakened him, because even before she turned to look she could feel the morning caress of his deep brown eyes. For a while she simply lay there looking into those eyes, wanting and not wanting what she knew was coming next. Neither of them spoke.

Still quiet and seemingly half asleep, he began fondling her small breasts. She could feel the nipples rising, stiffening to the touch of fingers made sensitive by years of searching out the right frets on the violin. Deftly his nimble hand eased her nightdress off one shoulder, then off the other, baring her risen breasts to the play of his lips. Her whole body was tingling now, sandpapered with the same gooseflesh that had made a thrill out of scary childhood games. Now there was no need for words. She played with the tangles in his tight curled head while he inched her dress down, following it with his lips across the curve of her swelling belly and down, down until she was arching and opening to his inquiring tongue all the recesses of her body.

She was beyond words, almost beyond thought, when his face came over hers, came down in a blur of white to kiss her lips to force them open till their tongues met and danced and toyed. She inhaled in frantic draughts the pungent smell of him—sharp sweat of love and fading sweetness of his familiar scent. Her hands swept down his lean back, muscled now with springs of steel, around cool buttocks and on to seize his throbbing member and guide it up, up until her aching emptiness was filled.

And just at that moment a train hurtled by, rocketing its hiss and screech around the room and shaking the building till the bed under them quivered. He whooped. "By God, a real New York salute! It's even better here than in Paris."

"Oh, oh," she moaned and pulled his spent body down on hers and rocked him in her arms. "Don't wake me up, please . . . don't wake me up."

"Oh, but you are awake, May darling. Good morning," he mumbled into the pillow by her ear.

"Is it morning? I can't tell. And is it really spring?"

"That you should be sure of. 'In the spring, a young man's fancy . . .' Did you like this, sweetheart? Did you mind?"

"Loved it. Oh, loved it. You can do anything with me—any time. You know that. I'm all, all thoroughly yours . . ."

Ira gently untangled himself from her arms, sat up on the side of the bed and stared out the little window at the blank, thousand-eyed face of the dirty building across the street and under the tracks. What a hole, he thought. God, what a hole . . .

"Darling," he said, "it really is time to get up now. I think the train leaves in less than an hour."

May curled into a ball and pulled the covers over her head. What he heard was something like, "I don't want to go, I don't want to leave you. . . ."

Maybe there was such a thing as being too good a lover, Ira thought immodestly as he gently pulled the covers away from her. Looking at her now that he was wider awake and it had grown just a bit lighter, he suffered once more that small twinge of regret that May Stewart was not also beautiful. The too-white skin of her face with its stubby nose and jutting jaw, its pale brows and lashes, was blotched with red from the heat of love as if she suffered from some rare disease. Her breasts, despite the child, were small, almost nothing but the excitable nipples, and her hips were spread and soft from a lifetime of sitting. It was his own fault, of course, that her stomach was bulging now too. When she got up, he knew only too well, she would slouch around with that curious stoop of the shoulders that came from hunching over a keyboard. But "beauty is as beauty does," Ira told himself. After years of experiencing biddies of every age and shape from the streets of Paris, Ira could truthfully, wonderingly admit that he had never been treated to such ecstasy as he found with May. It was her response, of course—not only the way she opened her flooding self to him but the greed with which she examined and claimed every pulsating inch of his own body. And to think she was also a genius, and an heiress—incredible —*incroyable* . . . and people still wondered why he had packed up his violin to carry her music case.

"Well, you've got to go, May," he said now. "We can't live very long in this flea bag where there's no morning and no spring. This is old stuff to me, but you're a sensitive soul."

May sat up, struggling back into her gown. "I wish you would go with me, we could get it all over at once."

"Now, May dear, we've gone over that a hundred times. It would be too much of a shock for your father."

"We could *say* we're married."

"That might be even worse. No, I think you've got to go alone."

"Oh, God, how I dread this . . . isn't there some other way?"

"Well, I could fiddle in saloons, and you could play in churches—until the baby comes, that is. Maybe we could get a room with a view of an air shaft instead of a railroad. Be sensible, May. How many times do I have to tell you that you really are a genius, another Clara Schumann? I've meant it and I still do. But you just aren't ready yet. Not quite. We need time—a year, perhaps two. . . ."

"I know . . . I mean I realize what you've given up and I'm not overwhelmed with false modesty, but . . ."

"Why, I should think your father would be proud of you —he must be already. Why else would he send you to Paris? Why else would he buy a house with a music room and a pipe organ, for God's sake?"

"And why would he suddenly cut the money off?"

"Love, I guess—mistaken, of course. But he is your father,

and he probably wants you back," Ira said. "In a way I can't really say I blame him—I mean, I love you, too."

"And I love you, Ira. Oh, God, how I love you. I still don't see why we can't just get married now and go out and . . ."

"Darling, sweetheart, we've been over it and over it. You go out there as Mrs. Ira Goldberg and that will be the end of it. The shock would be too much. But if you let him *hear* you . . . you told me one of his few passions is a love of music. . . . Darling, it's not because of me. It's *you*. You simply can't afford to take chances now. You owe it to yourself . . . to people, to *me* . . . you really do, to go on and give your glorious talent. . . . It's what I want most. It's what our whole relationship is about, really, and I would walk out of this door right now if I thought that I was hindering . . ."

"Oh, Ira. I couldn't . . . I couldn't play a note without you . . . or do anything else for that matter."

He took her into his arms. "I know, darling, and I need you just as much as you do me—I don't fool myself. . . . But how could we ever convince your father of that? To him I'd seem some sort of fortune hunter from the East Side, out to latch on to his precious heiress. No, May, I'm afraid this one you'll have to handle alone. All I could contribute would be an ugly scene and your permanent disinheritance. It'll only be—what?—a few weeks, a month. Then when you come back. . . ."

All the long ride to Pittsburgh the chugging train pounded a rhythm in her head—"I have to do it, I have to do it, I have to do it." She scarcely saw the flat and fertile fields of eastern Pennsylvania, greening delicately with the spring that the bricks of New York had shouldered back from her window, or the blue and rugged mountains, white dimpled with snow reluctant to withdraw. There was too much to think about, too much that had happened in the last three years since she'd left the old castle in Oakland, shy and frightened, to go to Paris under the loose chaperonage of an aging Madame Lutz. Oh, what a time she—or she and Ira, really—gave poor "Lutzie," as they called her now. Deaf as a post she was, thank God. Though she pretended to hear music, her old ears thankfully missed what went on in the music room while she nodded by the fire in her bedroom. The first time was quite incredible. She was backed up into the curve of her grand piano while Ira, on his knees, teased and teased until she couldn't stand it, and then he took her right there on the floor, her head so cocked against a stack of Mozart sonatas that her cricked neck hurt almost worse than . . .

than down there. It couldn't have happened any other way, she realized, because she would have been afraid, would have been tightened into a shrieking witch by her long-conditioned Presbyterian conscience. But he played her well: sitting by her on the bench, flipping the pages while she read, leaning nearer until he was kissing her ear, her neck; sliding from the bench, allowing his practiced fingers to play up her skirts until she had no wish, or will, to resist. It was . . . it was *incroyable*, in any language. She hoped she would never forget it . . . she was sure she would never want to.

The thing was—and May Stewart was honest enough to admit it to herself—she had given up, as early as her sixteenth birthday, even the possibility of knowing a man in the biblical sense. Though she looked for it daily in her mirror and in the reflections from the eyes of people around her, she could see no signs of the expected spring—not a bud to indicate she might bloom from a blotched and awkward spring into the much read about but never witnessed desired flower of womanhood. She didn't know why this had happened to her. Sometimes, dreaming of Paris, Vienna, Rome, the cities where the music she loved was born, she blamed it on the acrid atmosphere of Pittsburgh itself. But this was romantic nonsense: her girl friends, living under the same pall, were blossoming by the minute. More likely it had to do with the bleak, echoing halls of the old castle in which she felt imprisoned. How could a flower bloom there? It could die easily enough, and she could remember too well how her mother was brought back by special train from Saranac to gasp her last breaths in the sunless, stuffy front bedroom while her father, seemingly wound like a clock, departed for the office every morning at precisely seven-fifteen. As if to make up for what she had somehow been denied in life, Martha Stewart was stretched out—artificial blooms in her cheeks, courtesy of Pittsburgh's most expensive mortuary—on a couch in the parlor that was so heavily banked with flowers (sympathies from the William Thaws, the George Westinghouses, the Henry Heinzes, the Andrew Mellons, the Andrew Carnegies, the Henry Clay Fricks, the Richard B. Mellons, the George Mestas, countless Joneses, Laughlins, Olivers, Magees, Flinns) that forever after May hated the smell of more than one flower at a time. The real going of this mother who had never quite been a mother might have fertilized her own flowering but it didn't, and she gradually came to terms with the fact that music was, would have to be, her life.

It was Madame Lutz herself, unconsciously growing deaf,

who said that May had gone far beyond her ability to teach her anything more. Marching up and down the study, her feather boa rustling with every deep breath she took to fuel her impassioned oratory, Madame Lutz explained the whole thing to a stone-silent Scott and a busily sewing Mary Stewart. This was a genius they had on their hands, and she deserved the very best training she could get—in Paris, where Madame Lutz herself had studied. Surely Mr. Stewart could see his way to this. She knew how they might feel about sending a young and sheltered girl to Paris, but she, Madame Lutz, was getting on, you know, and she was weary of listening to scales by the hour being played by young people who had no more ear for music than a brass monkey. She would herself agree to give it all up and go with May, if they could see their way to it, because what more could a teacher ever want than a pupil, just one pupil, who could play in the heavenly choir? Though Mary Stewart was a bit skeptical of Madame Lutz's hyperbole, she was sadly aware of the fact that there seemed little else in store in the way of excitement for her unattractive grand-daughter. Scott had a better grasp than his mother of the true grace of May's playing, but the idea that his only daughter might be heading toward the frivolity of the concert stage troubled him. Still, she could improve herself and stop short of that when the time came. In any case, she needed to do something between now and whenever, if ever, she got married, and the attempt to interest her in regular academic work at the Pennsylvania College for Women had been a sorry failure. So, for different reasons, Scott and his mother agreed to let her go. It was a kind of miracle, and a kind of a scary one, since she would never have thought of going as far away as Paris on her own.

Ira was in one of her harmony classes at the conservatory. They were thrown together simply because they were the only two Americans in the class, and he took pity on her struggling efforts with French. An aspiring violinist of twenty-three, Ira was lean to the point of emaciation but blessed with dark, curly hair and the deepest, darkest eyes she had ever seen. But, like all the other eyes she had ever studied, they reflected back to her only the image of an awkward, plain Jane who deserved the same kind of sympathy any decent man would bestow upon a lost puppy. Still, he was kind about the language problem, a problem he had mastered in the two years he had been subsisting in Paris on the thin gruel of on-and-off cafe engagements, and before long they began walking together and talking about the music they were studying.

One day, as they reached the apartment she shared with Lutzie, they were still deep in argument about one note in a difficult harmonic transition. She claimed it was a B-flat, he insisted it had to be a B-natural. She invited him up to prove her point on the piano. He won, and perhaps as an act of sportsmanship asked her to play something for him. It was the beginning of everything, of a life she'd taught herself not to hope for, even to pray for. From the very first few passages she played he became so excited he kept bouncing about the room, calling for "more! Play more, for God's sake, more." When at last she was too tired to go on, he told her flatly— and meant it—"You're a genius—do you know that, May, a genius!" He was so loud that even Lutzie, beaming from the doorway, heard him. "You see, May, there you are," she said. "Haven't I always told you?"

She had to listen to them, to believe them, and the reaction to her few small recitals in Paris rather confirmed their judgment. She knew, knew without question, that given a little more work and study, she could play the piano, perhaps like no woman—and few men—before her. And she wanted to do it, for at the keyboard she was wholly transported into that wonderful sky of sound, where she left behind her all the mundane measurements of worth and beauty. And it was the same when Ira made love to her, maybe because he'd taken her so by surprise, taken her almost literally in the midst of music, as if transposing one trance into another. She knew she should have felt wicked about giving in to such physical passion, but she didn't—couldn't, really, since reason told her she had no normal claims to what might be regarded as normal love. She didn't even raise the question of marriage until it was obvious that she was pregnant, and she was surprised at how easily she accepted Ira's reasoning against it. Actually, he had Lutzie on his side. Pretending to be hurt and shocked when the coming of the baby could no longer be denied— she began throwing up so much that an alarmed Lutzie wanted to take her home—Lutzie quickly shifted to more concern over the fading of her own dream of seeing the name of at least one of her own pupils up in lights (now that she could no longer hear) than over any outrage to conventional morals. Actually, in the view Lutzie took as she endlessly discussed it with May, Ira was being more truly a gentleman by letting her stay free to claim the inheritance she would need to carry on her work than by marrying her at uncertain risk. Perhaps he was. Perhaps he was simply in love with her "genius," but was that less meaningful than being in love with a beautiful face or a rolling bosom or a twitching bustle? It belonged to her as much as any of those things belonged to another girl, and she had every right to offer it for love—and every need to nuture and protect it, at whatever cost. . . .

Her father met her at the station, as promised, with Mac, their old coachman, in tow to carry the bags. The meeting went off as awkwardly as all meetings and partings of Stewarts—a stiff handshake and then a trading of fumbling pecks to the cheek. Three years had almost completely grayed Scott Stewart, but he still stood lean and erect; the line between his brows, still dark like his now neatly trimmed mustache, had deepened. He didn't know what to say, so he pulled his watch from a vest pocket, glanced at it and observed, "Well, right on time. Have a good trip?"—and then, with just the slightest wisp of a smile, "We've a surprise for you—right outside."

The surprise was a new Pierce-Arrow. As he had with all his various carriages, Scott showed his daughter the only glimpse of boy she was ever to see in him as he took her around to exhibit all the wonders of this new machine that twinkled back from every brass fitting in the lights from the station's great, arched rotunda, which itself was new since she had left the city. Though she had seen many automobiles in Paris, May quickly gathered that this was still something rare for the streets of Pittsburgh in this spring of 1902, and she was happy about it if for no other reason than that it gave them something to talk about. Her father proudly got up behind the wheel and fiddled with switches and levers while Mac grunted and jerked on the crank. When the engine began exploding and the machine shimmied into life, Scott handed May up into the back seat and joined her there. An obviously nervous Mac got the car underway with a neck-snapping jerk and started careening down dark streets that were only dimly lit by the car's bouncing kerosene lamps. May wondered why they didn't hit something, and she was actually shocked to see her father laugh aloud with nervous excitement as they overtook everything in their path, including the lighted streetcars, whose windows flashed by them in a yellow blur. It took both of her hands to hold her hat against the wind, and her father apologized, "I should have brought you a motoring scarf, but we'll soon be home."

"That's all right. Do you know, Daddy, this is my very first ride in one of these things, though I saw lots of them in Paris."

"So I heard from Madame Lutz."

"Oh, you've seen her already?"

"Yes. Matter of fact she's at the house now. I still don't see why you didn't come on with her instead of staying in New York."

"I wrote you I wanted to look into a new teacher."

"I don't see any sense in going to New York. Mr. Herbert himself said he'd teach you here."

"He's a cellist, Daddy, not a pianist."

"Well, well. Well, we'll talk about it."

"Did Madame Lutz tell you anything else about Paris?"

"Tried to, but I can't talk to her. She's deaf as a post, you know. Don't know how she keeps thinking she can hear music," Scott said.

"Beethoven was deaf too."

"That's right. Maybe some special thing in the ear. Well, here we are."

May had seen the finest buildings in Paris and environs— Le Louvre, Versailles, L'Opéra, Les Invalides. They had to be bigger than the house they were approaching, so it must have been an illusion created by the setting that made her think they weren't. The Renaissance facade of her father's house stretched a full block and rose four stories into the air. Every window was alive with electric light, and great wrought-iron lanterns shone at each side of the heavy door. It swung open as if by magic, and a new maid she had never seen bowed them in. "This is Miss May, Carla," Scott said. "You'll see to her things." Then with some of the same delight he had shown when he was exhibiting the car, he held out his hand to his daughter. "Come, see the music room."

"I want to see Grandmother first," May said.

"Oh, she's in there. They'll all be there."

"All?"

"Yes, the whole family. They came to welcome you back."

She couldn't remember the whole family's being together since the last Christmas her mother had been able to come home, the Christmas before Uncle Henry died. It had been so long, and so much had happened to her, that she'd almost forgotten that there was a family. Now she was truly glad that Ira had insisted she go alone; she couldn't imagine dragging him before such a court. She followed her father down a hall past a parlor. They paused before double mahogany doors, which her father opened to reveal a room like nothing she had ever seen in a private home before. Fully forty by twenty feet, it rose two stories to a vaulted ceiling, embossed with alabaster angels blowing golden horns and strumming golden harps. In the middle of one wall was the console of a four-manual organ, its golden pipes fanning out on either side. In the middle of the opposing wall was a great marble-faced fireplace, and at the far end of the room, sitting like a toy on a raised platform in the curve of an enormous bay window, was a winged-open grand piano. The parquet floor shone like checkered glass in the light of the great icicle of an electric chandelier that dropped from the ceiling. The room would probably seat a hundred, and the massed family she had expected to find so overwhelming seemed lost in it.

Struck shy by the chorus of "Hello," "How are you," "Wonderful to see you back," May hurried to her grandmother, who was sitting in a winged-back chair near the empty fireplace. At seventy-two, Mary Stewart had finally aged: her thinning hair was pure white; the welcoming smile she gave May seemed to illumine rather than lift the lines around her eyes and mouth. "Excuse me for not getting up, my dear," she said. "It's the arthritis, you know."

"That's all right, Grandma. Oh, it's good to see you," said May, kneeling to kiss the old lady and then, turning to the room in general, "to see all of you."

Lucinda was there, looking enviably chic. Uncle Reed, somewhat red-faced and a bit puffy about the eyes, was also going a little soft in the middle, but he looked considerably less like the devil now that his gray-tinged hair was close-cropped in the new fashion. Aunt Alma was imposingly enormous. That tall, somewhat stout boy had to be their Alexander, and the gawky-looking girl who apparently inherited the Stewart frame, their Carolyn. The others were easily recognizable—all but Uncle Don. His proud mane of hair had disappeared almost completely, leaving him with a dome that shone like marble in the light from the chandelier, and his eyes, protruding from a bland soft face, seemed curiously dull. May never had understood what had happened to Uncle Don, and she had scarcely seen him in ten years. It wasn't drink or anything like that. In fact, she was in the church the Sunday he froze right in the middle of a sermon and had to be led out of the pulpit by one of the more alert members of the choir. If her father and grandmother understood any more than she what happened to Uncle Don, they wouldn't tell her. "It's just a sad, sad case. Poor Sarah," was about all they would ever say.

Uncle Don, who shook her hand but never spoke, was led away by Aunt Sarah, now a prune of a woman, the moment the greetings were over. The rest left as soon as they decently could, and it was quickly obvious that this was no party— rather a duty call more on account of Grandmother Stewart than her arrival. Well, none of them, she felt, had ever liked her much, and the feeling was fairly mutual. The only one she'd ever liked was Stewart Sharp, on whom she'd had a cousinly "crush" for years. She had to admit he was as handsome as ever, and he had a new look of authority about him, probably from being a doctor. Maybe he would help her now; maybe as a doctor there was something he could do for her so she wouldn't feel the way she did. . . . The baby . . . how *did* she feel about the baby? Well, right now she felt strangled by her corset, a warning that she had little time, perhaps only a matter of weeks, to somehow win over her father before her secret would be obvious to anyone with eyes to see.

Lying in bed that night she wondered whether she should have made Ira come with her, but she quickly decided that his instinct had been right after all. She simply couldn't imagine him fitting into that group of people who were, after all, her family. Her family . . . good God . . . There was her father —to her a sort of quietly humming money-making machine that seemed to be wound up by God every Sunday. There was Don, gone crazy; Lucinda, an adulteress; Reed, a drinker. Who else? Everybody would probably agree that Grandmother Stewart was wonderful, but she seemed as out of place as a well-worn antique from the last century in a modern drawing room. No doubt little Henry Ward Beecher Sharp, who was living up to his name by studying for the ministry, would pass for respectable in public, but May could also remember his not so pious little-boy antics that included stringing up kittens and flushing toads down the toilet. Becky Sharp McCandless, as far as May could tell, was a graceless girl who seemed to say all the wrong things but had been lucky enough to marry well before the McCandless family realized what had happened to her father, the Reverend Doctor Donald Vincent Sharp. She simply didn't know the teen-agers—Alexander and Carolyn Stewart and Tillie Sharp—well enough to fit them in. As she ticked them all off in her mind, including her poor dead mother and Uncle Henry, she suddenly realized something that had never occurred to her before: while other families died out, were lost sight of, broke up, or whatever, the Stewarts seemed somehow to hold together, regardless of their lacks and vices. Was it something in the blood, the way Uncle Henry always argued? She could remember him shaking a finger under her father's nose and saying, "Scott Stewart, you've got nothing but steel, bloody cold steel, in your veins." Or was it, as her father might claim, that they were of good stock, and the elect of God? It was all a little frightening to think about. Ira—thank God—had not a trace of steel in his veins and was clearly beyond the pale of her father's God. No, Ira would never, never fit in, and, as a result, she could never, never stay. In fact, another day seemed too long.

The very next day May surprised Stewart Sharp by appearing in his office. For long minutes they fenced awkwardly with idle words about the weather and the health of their respective families until, blushing, May managed to get her story out. Stewart listened with astonishment. It would never have occurred to him that this plain and shy little cousin would have a lover; indeed, when they were younger he had teased her out of pity, knowing that she had no boy friends and an odd, serious brother who was away most of the time. Now he felt real pity and a sense of helplessness. "May, are you telling me you don't want the baby . . . because if you are I'm afraid there's nothing I can . . ."

"Yes . . . no . . . oh, I don't know . . . but what am I going to do? . . . Daddy doesn't think I need any more lessons, he wants me to stay here and . . . and find a husband. It's almost funny. . . ."

"Almost, but not really," Stewart agreed. "I can see your problem, all right. I just can't imagine what Uncle Scott would do if he knew. I don't think he's quite forgiven Benjy for turning out the way he did and leaving his child with him . . . and now this . . ."

"He can't know . . . he just *can't*. . . ."

"May, what would happen if you just went away again? You're twenty-three. Nobody can legally hold you. Would this fellow marry you, support you?"

"I think so . . . but even so it would mean I'd have to stop studying and give up playing . . ."

"Are you that good, May? I mean, I haven't heard you for a long time."

Stewart was somewhat surprised at the way the lines in May's face, crinkled with worry, straightened, the way her Stewart chin came up now. "Yes, I *am* that good. I'm not sure of anything else about myself, but I am about that. Stewart, I'd kill myself if I had to stop playing. I *mean* it."

It was clear she did, and suddenly he had great respect for this young woman—no longer just another girl in familiar trouble. Matter of fact, in spirit, if not in flesh, she reminded him of Aunt Lucinda—Cindy . . . "Tell you what, May, I think the best medicine I could prescribe would be a good talk with Aunt Lucinda."

"Why? She never seemed to have much use for me. . . ."

"I wouldn't say that. It's more that she never had a chance to know you—your father's pretty much seen to that. She'll understand, that I promise you, and she might think of some way to help."

They found Lucinda at home in her Hotel Schenley apartment—a pleasant shambles—an easel set up where it would catch the best light, drawings and paintings in various stages of completion stacked carelessly around the walls, bits of clothing everywhere, two Siamese cats slinking through the debris. It was like a bit of Paris, and May felt right at home, particularly when Lucinda brought out a bottle of sherry, though it was only midmorning, and offered her a cigarette. "Well, you are in a fix, poor child," Lucinda agreed when Stewart Sharp outlined the problem. "The only person who might really be able to help you is Mother—she's the one who has the most influence with Scott."

"Grandmother, Oh, I wouldn't want her to know . . . it would hurt her. . . "

"Yes, I suppose it would, but she's absorbed more than a few shocks in her long life, mostly from me. Let me go down and telephone her. Mac can bring her over. She likes to come here for a nip anyway."

"For a *what*," Stewart asked.

"Well, the doctor told her she ought to have some sherry once in a while, and she says she won't profane Scott's house by keeping it there, so she drops in on me whenever she can."

Both Stewart and May laughed, and when Lucinda had gone, May shook her head. "What a family!"

"And you don't know the half of it," Stewart said.

"Well, I do know I've always been afraid of this family. In musical terms, they kind of remind me of 'Onward Christian Soldiers.' Especially father . . ."

"Your father, you may be right."

When Mary Stewart hobbled into Lucinda's apartment, gasping for breath a little after the long walk from the elevator, she knew she was going to hear some bad news. It was a strange summons and an odd little gathering. But she put off the bad moment with some motherly fussing. "This place is messier every time I come into it, Lucinda . . ."

"Now, Mother . . ."

301

"I should think you could at least pick up your clothes. Sarah's house is neat as a pin."

"But she doesn't paint, and you can't get this in her house," Lucinda said, handing her mother a glass of sherry. "Now, Mother dear, I'm afraid we have a problem for you. Why don't you tell her, Stewart? It might be difficult for May."

On the surface Mary listened calmly enough, but Lucinda noticed that her mother took down her wine in two rather quick gulps. Quietly, she filled the glass again. As she'd hoped, Mary Stewart proceeded straight to the heart of the problem: "Do you really love this man, May?"

"Yes, oh yes, more than I can tell you . . ."

"And he'll marry you?"

"Yes, if he's sure it won't ruin my opportunity to study and play. He's like Lutzie—he thinks I'm very good, and I . . . I feel it, too."

"That does complicate things," Mary said. "If I had the money I'd . . ."

"No, Grandmother, *no*," May protested. "We only thought you might know how to help explain it all to Daddy. I really don't want to hurt him."

"I know, child, and if he knew about your condition, it would more than hurt him," Mary conceded. "I'm afraid I just couldn't vouch for what he might do. Under the circumstances, I think you are just going to have to bring your young man on here to ask for your hand and hope for the best. I'll help all I can and perhaps we can persuade your father that it's 'better to marry than to burn,' as St. Paul says."

Lucinda clapped her hands delightedly. "I was sure you'd think of the right note, Momma."

Mary Stewart sighed. "I can make no promises. You know your father puts certain principles above everything . . ."

"Why is he like that?" May asked. "I mean, so . . . well, so *right* about everything . . .?"

"I don't expect you to understand all this, May. And I'm not sure I do. But I can tell you that your father had a terrible blow as a young boy when your grandfather died. He was always a serious boy, even then. He looked to God for help, and he found it. Now I believe he feels the Lord has blessed him, and who's to say he is wrong? I think he also may feel that if he does not follow every commandment as he understands it, he will have betrayed the Lord's trust and all he's gained will be taken away from him . . . that it then *should* be taken away from him. . . . You've been studying about the way people think, Stewart. What do you say?"

"I say I think you're right, Grandmother. It may be a little more complicated than that, but in general I agree with you. I also feel that in a way you have to admire him. I know I do—"

"I do too," May said. "That's the trouble. I even think I love him, and that's why I don't want to hurt him. I think what I hope is that if I can just get through this all right, I'll make him proud of me one day. He really does like music, you know."

"Well, that may be our salvation," Mary said. "I do hope your young man also plays well."

And so it happened that one soft, blue spring evening when Scott Stewart arrived home from the city in his dashing Pierce-Arrow, he heard the sounds of a violin, accompanied by a piano, spilling out of the open windows of the music room. He stood silently for a while on the path from the garage, listening. It was good music, gay music—a lilting Strauss waltz. Scott hurried into the house, where he found his mother sitting in her chair by the music-room fireplace, and a slim, dark young man leaning into the curve of the piano and playing a violin while May accompanied him. Neither of the young people, who were looking into each other's eyes, saw Scott as he walked quietly over to his mother, his eyebrow lifted in silent query.

"May has a caller—a young man she met in Paris," Mary whispered. "Isn't it nice?"

When the music stopped and they were aware of him, May jumped up and pulled Ira by the hand over to where her father stood by the marble mantle. "Oh, hello, Daddy. May I present Mr. Ira Goldberg?"

Scott took Ira's hand. He found it soft and somehow foreign, but then it did belong to a musician and . . . he hoped there was nothing but music between this young man and May.

"I believe my mother said something about your coming from Paris."

"Yes, sir," Ira said. "That's where we met. I was studying there too."

"Oh, and you came all this way . . ."

"To see your daughter. Yes, sir."

May didn't like the way things were going—not so much the words but the tone of voice, the looks the men were exchanging. Both of them seemed to be struggling to ignore an unpleasant odor. She took Ira's hand. "Come on Ira, let's play father's favorite—'My Rosary.' Did you know

Daddy knew Ethelbert Nevin before he left Pittsburgh? I hear the poor man died last year—and so young too. Sit down, Daddy, I want you to hear Ira play."

The young man did play reasonably well, but through his work with the symphony Scott had developed a practiced enough ear to realize that he was not listening to a real virtuoso. Still, "My Rosary" called for the cafe vibrato Ira put into his playing. As the violin throbbed, the words began running through his head, words that always evoked memories of Martha with whom, as he was more certain every year she was gone, he had shared a unique and truly undying love. It was a love that was best articulated through music, and there were many times in the midst of a concert or recital when the austere Scott Stewart could be seen blowing his nose and repeatedly wiping his glasses in a vain effort to clear the blur in his vision. It was that way now as his mind sang,

"The hours I spent with thee, dear heart,
Are as a string of pearls to me;
I count them over, every one apart,
My rosary, my rosary."

If there was just a hint of the sacrilegious in the last phrases—"to kiss the cross, sweetheart, to kiss the cross"—Scott would not allow it to bother him, just as he would try not to allow himself to be upset by this Mr. Goldberg. . . . Perhaps there was nothing more between them than a musical friendship, though he doubted it. There was really no mistaking the way they looked at each other, and why would a mere friend, who must be impoverished by the look of his clothes, come all the way from Paris to see her?

Dinner was difficult. Ira tried hard to ask inteligent questions about the steel business and other matters in which he felt Scott might be interested. Scott, preoccupied with apprehension over what was obviously to come, hardly listened and spit out answers short and hard as melon seeds. When Mary got around to trying to save the day by questioning Ira on the sights and sounds of Paris, he turned sulky as well. He had expected not to like May's father, and he wasn't disappointed. The man made him damnably uneasy. . . . There was an imperiousness about him—the hawk nose, the hard flat cheeks, the solemn dark eyes, the clipped voice . . . the casual way he moved through the high-ceilinged gilt rooms of this mausoleum of a house, the absentminded manner with which he handled the Sèvres plates, the cut-glass goblets, the heavy silver at dinner. When Scott bowed his head and said, "Bless this food in the name of the one and only true God, our gracious Lord and Savior, who died upon the cross to save us from our sins, Christ Jesus," Ira felt even more uneasy before such relentless piety. May must have taken after her late mother, he decided, although one did have to admit that Mary Stewart was most gracious in her somewhat antique fashion.

The mandatory meeting of the two men took place in the study immediately after dinner. The feeling of mutual antagonism and distrust was hanging so heavily between them that any effort at pleasantries would have been absurd. After waving away a proffered cigar, Ira plunged right in. "I'm sure you realize, Mr. Stewart, that I would not come this long way on an idle mission. I have come to ask for your daughter's hand."

While listening to this opening speech, Scott bit off the end of his cigar and spat it out with such force that the gleaming brass cuspidor by his desk sounded with the impact. Ira thought it an incongruous gesture in these elegant surroundings, but in a way comforting—the man had a human dimension, after all.

"I'd say this is pretty sudden, Mr. Goldberg—May I ask what your profession is?"

"I play the violin, as I believe you . . ."

"But not very well . . . am I right?"

Ira flushed, but tried to turn the insult to his advantage. "You have a good ear, Mr. Stewart," he said. "As a matter of fact, from the moment I first heard May play, I gave up my own aspirations in order to serve her. I'm convinced she's a genuis, Mr. Stewart, and, as they say, genius must be served. She will be another Clara Schumann if . . ."

"But she needs your help?"

"Yes. I honestly believe that, sir. An artist like May shouldn't be distracted by the routine things—bookings, travel arrangements, where to live, what to eat. I can do this for her—and more. A violinist must have a good ear, you know, and I am her best critic."

"You haven't mentioned supporting her. It seems to me your hope is that she will support you. Do you think she's ready for that?"

"I hope we will do well together. She needs perhaps another year of training, two at the most . . ."

"And in the meantime I'm to support both of you . . . I'm afraid not, Mr. Goldberg. I also don't want my daughter making a fool of herself on any stage, and I think you—and possibly that deaf old lady, Madame Lutz—have filled her head with utter nonsense."

"No, believe me, Mr. Stewart, she's really . . ."

"I *don't* believe you. Oh, she plays well enough, but she doesn't come from the kind of people that make artists. We are serious people who believe in getting along with the Lord's proper work . . ."

"But I thought you liked music, Mr. Stewart."

"Oh, yes, in its place as a relaxation, but it isn't a fit career for a serious man—or woman either who ought to be settling down to raise children. And as for that, I must tell you frankly that I would never consent to my daughter marrying out of her faith. She was baptized and raised in the Christian faith, and I as her father took my own vows to see that she and her children remain in that faith. Do you understand that?"

"Yes, sir, I believe I do, but we love . . ."

"What you call love has nothing to do with this. Human love is an abomination if it isn't right with God. . . . In any case, I think I have something here you will fully understand."

Rummaging through his desk, Scott pulled out a thick checkbook. "I won't deny you have me in a bad position. Somehow you've managed to turn May's head—I could see that tonight. She won't be right until she can forget about you, as she will soon enough if you behave as a gentleman and leave her alone. Obviously you are without means, so I am prepared to write you here and now a check for one hundred thousand dollars if you will leave this house and this city tonight and never return or communicate again in any way with May."

To Scott's surprise, Ira Goldberg laughed—not just a chuckle but a real, hearty laugh. "I don't believe it . . . I don't believe it . . . ," he spluttered.

"I don't find this amusing," Scott said as he uncapped a pen he'd drawn from his vest pocket and poised it over the checkbook. "Well?"

"Mr. Stewart, this is like a scene out of a nineteenth-century novel," Ira said, regaining control.

"I don't find it so. I'm waiting for your answer."

"My answer, sir, is *no*. I meant it when I said I love your daughter, and she loves me. Whatever you think of love, we think it is very real. It's too late for your bribe in any case. She's carrying my child. . . ."

"Your what?"

"I believe you heard me—my child, your grandchild, Mr. Stewart."

"Then you're already married? Why . . ."

"No, sir."

"Oh, my God." The words were both prayer and exclamation. Scott flung the pen like a dart, raising a blue wound on Ira's shirt front. "Out, get out of here. . . ."

To Ira's eyes the man had gone mad. His marbled face had turned red; the muscles along his jaw, the veins of his forehead stood out in ridges of steel. He was fumbling in his desk—for a gun? Ira left as fast as he could, shutting the door solidly behind him against this suddenly unpredictable figure of wrath.

Scott's immediate regret was that he had left his gun in the office. If it had been there in his drawer, he would have used it. Knowing himself to be capable of this was an odd, almost comforting, feeling. The fellow had spoiled his daughter. And how could she, reared in the faith, bring herself to live in sin such as that? It must be the Schmidts' blood running in her veins. He had always known it was weak. Oh, God, give me strength and wisdom to do the right. . . .

Even as he prayed, Scott felt a cooling wind of rational thought. It was soon quite clear that he could make only one correct response to the situation. Since May was an adult for whom he had no legal responsibility, he would turn her loose without a cent. Let that damned adventurer take care of her. Her and her—he couldn't think it. He would never see either of them again. If he did, he was certain he could not trust what he might do. They had outraged everything he believed in. Well, he would stand by what he believed—even if it meant losing his own daughter. There was simply nothing else he could do. Scott rang for the girl Carla and told here to see that Miss May was moved out of the house that night.

The news spread rapidly through the house, and Mary Stewart, who was preparing for bed, wearily put her clothes on again to go down and plead with her son Scott at least to allow some time to pass before he took such drastic action. It was no use. Her quotation from Paul only brought from Scott, "As far as I'm concerned, she's burned already."

"But the child, Scott. She's going to have a child. If you offered him a hundred thousand dollars, as I hear you did . . . that's a good deal of money. . . ."

"That was to get rid of him. I learned from Clay Frick not to be careful with money when you want to accomplish something. But I will not support them in sin . . ."

"But they plan to marry."

"I don't want to set eyes on them again. I don't know what I might do. If I'd had a gun tonight . . ."

Mary turned angry. "Scott Stewart," she said, "you listen to me. I have a little money, thanks to you, and if you don't do something about them, I will. I don't intend to see my granddaughter and great-grandchild turned out in the cold. I admit what they did was wrong, but if there is anything our religion preaches, it is forgiveness."

Scott knew that his mother meant what she said. She had always been too easy, he felt, when it came to discipline, and the results were usually disastrous. Witness Lucinda and Reed. Still, he also had a deep respect for his mother's instincts that made him hesitate now. The important thing, really, was to get May and her paramour out of his sight, out of the city.

"All right, Mother," he said. "I accept what you say about the child. It is certainly innocent. I'll set up a trust of a quarter of a million dollars, the income to go to May—not that . . . until the child is twenty-one, if they both sign an agreement never to return to Pittsburgh. They can see my attorney, Mr. Shaw, tomorrow. Good night, Mother."

Mary Stewart left without speaking again. It grieved her deeply that this son, who had helped her so much and on whose strength she so gratefully relied, could at the same time be so uncompromisingly harsh. There was nothing really that she could say without hurting him, and nothing in any case that would change his mind. At least May now would be taken care of in a material way, and perhaps time and curiosity about his grandchild might eventually soften him. She found May and Ira in the hallway ready to leave with all their baggage. Lucinda was going to take them in for the night. When she told them the news, Ira declared that he never wanted to see the place again. May, though, began to cry, and she continued to do so as he guided her away.

Scott was as good as his word. By the time they went to the station the next night to catch the train to New York, May had in her hands a check for $1,040, the first monthly installment on the trust. With it, Ira told her, she would at least be free to hire a nurse for the child and work as much as she wished. Inwardly he was still seething, but would not let her see it. Like her father, he did not trust what he might do if he ever should come back there again. . . .

Lucinda was also trying to comfort May. "Ira's right, you know. I envy you, May. Don't worry so about your father. Wait'll he sees your name up in lights—he'll be begging you to come back, believe me. . . . By the way, did I ever tell you about Mary Schenley? You know I went to interview her in London back in 'eighty-nine after she'd given all that land for the park in Oakland. . . ."

Thinking to divert May while they waited for the train to be made up, Lucinda recounted the scandal that had truly rocked Pittsburgh in 1842. It all happened when Mary Croghan, a granddaughter of General James O'Hara, one of Pittsburgh's largest land holders, was attending Mrs. McLeod's fashionable boarding school on Staten Island in New York. Her father, William, widowed a year after her birth, had sent his only daughter to the school expressly because he was given to understand that a motherless young lady would not only learn the proper female graces but be sheltered from contact with the opposite sex. He had reckoned without knowledge of Captain Edward Wyndham Harrington Schenley, Mrs. McLeod's 43-year-old twice-widowed and penniless brother-in-law. During a visit to the school Schenley fell in love with fifteen-year-old Mary—and she with him. With Mrs. McLeod's connivance, he managed to take her away to a vessel heading for London.

When the news reached Pittsburgh, William Croghan was heartbroken—and furious. He persuaded other Pittsburgh parents to remove their daughters forthwith from Mrs. McLeod's, thus ruining the school. He implored Washington to have the U.S. Navy stop the boat on which the elopers had sailed; that failing, he was more fortunate in Harrisburg, where he got the legislature to pass a special bill putting Mary's large inheritance into his hands and, after his death, into the hands of trustees. The newspapers had a field day with the story, always emphasizing Captain Schenley's age. "The bill," wrote one, "places the property of Miss Croghan, the young lady that married Captain Schenley, out of the hands of that juvenile Lothario of forty-three." Another described Schenley unflatteringly in verse: "His eyes had the hard glint/of new dollars from the mint." The couple, effectively exiled from Pittsburgh, went first to Dutch Guiana, where Captain Schenley was serving as Her Majesty's representative on a mixed court for the suppression of the slave trade and where he was proved to have a heart ahead of his times by being forced out of the country for his efforts to free the blacks. After that, they returned to London, where Mary settled down to bearing a family of six daughters and a son.

They apparently—however improbably—not only lived happily ever after, but a lonely William Croghan relented. He visited his daughter in London and built an addition to his Pittsburgh mansion so that she and her family, including a reluctant Captain Schenley, could spend long periods in Pittsburgh with him, but the law he had so hastily sought had to be broken in the courts. "There, you see, that's how it will probably end up for you," Lucinda finished triumphantly. "Old Mary Schenley told me she never did regret running off with her captain, and I don't think you'll regret this either. Take good care of her, Ira. She seems to have grown up to be quite something, my little niece."

Lucinda was pleased to see that May was now smiling up at Ira as they turned their backs and walked off through the cones of light along the dark platform leading to the train. She really didn't think Scott would prove as soft as old William Croghan, but it wouldn't hurt May to hope. Meanwhile, she envied May and Ira their love—she truly did. She could tell by just being around them, even if for only a few days, by watching them touch each other, that they had something of what she had known with Henry . . . with Gil. She wondered what Scott might be like now if he'd ever known this kind of love, had ever come as close—just once—to another human being. Going home from the station, she was startled to realize she was feeling sorrier for Scott than for May.

A Puritan Named Harry Thaw

Sitting in a front pew of the Oakland Presbyterian Church with the rest of the family, and listening to the new young minister struggle to achieve a proper tone of sincerity in his eulogy, Dr. Stewart Lee Sharp tried once more to come to grips with the tragedy of his father's life. Except for his mother, who sat, head down, dabbing futilely under her veil at eyes that would not cease watering, this funeral was not a sad affair. Anything that could reasonably be considered the Reverend Doctor Donald Vincent Sharp, the preacher who had briefly stood in the national limelight on a Chicago political platform, had in effect departed this earth fifteen years previously. The fact that the church out of politeness kept his name on its bulletins as Pastor Emeritus maintained enough of a ghostly presence for his son, Doctor Sharp, to account for the full house rustling and coughing behind them through this hymn to "a great man of God." Stewart felt physically and spiritually ill at ease, unable to stop himself from wondering what was going on behind the composed features of his Aunt Lucinda, who sat proudly erect at the end of the pew. You had to hand it to these Stewarts, he thought—they could get through anything.

Stewart could remember every vivid detail of that awful Sunday when they led his father out of the pulpit. As luck would have it, it was his last Sunday at home before going back to college, and he had brought Jane to church with him, with the plan of taking her home to Sunday dinner—her first meeting with his family. Years of enforced experience had taught Stewart to endure his father's sermons by letting his mind drift pleasantly to livelier subjects. That Sunday, while his father's mellifluous voice droned from the pulpit like background music, he was toying with speculations aroused by Jane's nearness. They were so jammed into the pew that he could feel the softness of her hips and shoulders against his own, breathe in the subtle perfume that drifted upward from some secret recesses of her bodice. He was, in fact, having difficulty avoiding an embarrassing arousal when suddenly the voice in the background stopped and a soft gasp, or sigh, seemed to rise from the whole congregation. Looking up from his surreptitious study of Jane's pink ear lobe, Stewart saw his father, white-faced and slack-jawed, being led down the pulpit stairs by a black-robed man from the choir. Before anybody could think much about what was happening, the organist broke into the strains of the final hymn, "A Mighty Fortress Is Our God," and Dr. Booth, the little, round Sharp family physician, hurried importantly down the side aisle toward the door leading to the pastor's study. Sarah Sharp started forward too, and Stewart, whispering to Jane to stay with the younger children, followed his mother.

Donald Sharp was slumped in the big chair behind his desk staring, as if they were all total strangers, at the little group crowding into his study. He said nothing and paid scant attention as the doctor took his pulse, thumped him, went

311

over his chest with a stethoscope. Sarah's frantic, "Don! Don! What's the matter?" brought no response. Though wide-open, his eyes were glazed; his lips were so slack that a rivulet of saliva trickled down his chin. The doctor straightened up from his quick examination.

"My first thought was stroke," he said. "But I can find no evidence of it. His pulse and heart seem a bit weak and irregular but nothing really alarming. I just don't know. For the time being, I suggest we get him home and in bed and keep a watch on him."

Stewart helped the doctor get his unresisting father to his feet. Each of them draped a limp arm over his shoulders and walked him slowly out to his carriage. Stewart was surprised to find how thick and heavy his father's body was—and how alien. With no words, no smile or even look of recognition coming from him, the man was suddenly an awkward body, a body that could have belonged to anybody. Fortunately he was so docile that they had no trouble getting him home, undressed and into bed, where he fell almost immediately into a snoring sleep.

"Best thing for him," the doctor said as they walked cautiously away. "Let him sleep all he wants. Feed him broths and such—anything he'll take. I'm going to guess at the problem—some form of exhaustion or fatigue. But we'll wait and see. I'll look around again this evening."

Thus Jane's introduction to the family was awkward at best. Nobody felt much like eating or talking. Several times during dinner a distraught Sarah went upstairs to "look in on father," each time reporting him still asleep. "Poor dear," she announced to the table, "I guess he's been overdoing. He's been working on prayers for the Senate. Oh, I do hope the Republicans get in, though they say Mr. Cleveland is sure to win. But maybe they'll call him anyway. It would be sure to revive him."

By the next day it was clear that something more than fatigue had overtaken Donald Sharp. He began grunting to indicate a desire for food or a need for the commode, but otherwise he showed no interest in life, dozing off and on around the clock. Though Dr. Booth did not want to alarm the rest of the family with his suspicions, he took Stewart aside, since he understood the boy was studying to be a doctor. "I'm very much afraid we have some kind of mental or nervous breakdown here," he said. "Would you know any reason for something like that?"

"No, sir," Stewart replied. "What can we do about it?"

"Nothing I know of, except wait and see what happens, unless of course he should get violent and then . . ."

"You wouldn't send him to an asylum, would you?"

"I hope we don't have to. I'll put it out around the church that it's a case of extreme exhaustion and tell them Dr. Sharp needs a long, long rest. They'll have to start looking for another man to fill in. . . ."

Disturbed and puzzled by his father's condition, Stewart returned to Princeton a young man with a mission. If his father were suffering from mental disease, why couldn't it be treated as easily as a disease of the body is treated? He began to read everything he could about the mind—and found precious little of value. There was, however, a new book out by a Harvard scholar named William James, *The Principles of Psychology*, that made some sense, arguing as it did that the mind could be studied the way you might study anatomy, and one of his professors, just back from Europe, told him of encountering a young Viennese doctor, Sigmund Freud, who was doing exciting work on hysteria, which sounded very much like what his father might have. Stewart decided not only to go to work on his father's case but to join the pioneers who were struggling to turn psychology into an effective medical instrument.

By midfall letters from home indicated to Stewart that the rest of the family had reluctantly come to the same conclusion as Dr. Booth. His father, they reported, had regained some powers of speech but no desire to communicate. Then came what to Stewart was an alarming announcement: in desperation and in hope of some form of treatment, Sarah Sharp had decided to send her husband to an asylum in New Jersey, which would be far enough away to keep their secret in Pittsburgh but close enough to Princeton so that Stewart could keep an eye on his father.

Each Sunday Stewart would go to find his father sitting in a large room with other inmates, staring at nothing. Beyond grunting hello and complaining about the food, Doctor Sharp seldom said a word to his son. For the permissible hours of visiting, Stewart would strain to go on brightly about his studies, the state of the world and anything else that might strike a spark of interest—to no avail. The asylum's doctor, if the fool could be called a doctor, was no help at all. "We just try to keep them from hurting themselves," he said. What about the work of Freud? Never heard of him. James? Never heard of him. "Can't do much with them when they go round

313

the bend, lad." . . . At Christmas recess Stewart took his silent father back home.

Since there was no direct communication with Dr. Sharp, Stewart set about searching for every clue he could find to what might have triggered the breakdown. He spent hours questioning his mother, pressing to evoke memories of any useful detail. Yes, she did recall a change in Father—nothing you'd think about really at the time. It began in early summer. He was unnaturally quiet, spent longer hours than usual alone in his study. She thought it had to do with the Senate possibility, though he never did explain himself. This was an embarrassing thing to ask your mother, but Stewart felt he had to: what about—love? She blushed, but she was honest. There hadn't been much of that for a long time, they had all the children they wanted, and, well, when you got older . . . nothing at all like that since summer. "He even stopped kissing me, and he grew so absentminded. I tried teasing him about it once, but he got angry—I don't know why. . . ."

Stewart came away from his talks with his mother with little to go on. The other children were no help at all, each being farther removed from their busy father as they descended in age. He seemed all right to them, though he had turned a bit grumpy through the summer—probably the heat, they thought then. Trying a new tack, Stewart went through all the sermons his father had preached in the three months preceeding his September breakdown. There he stumbled on an odd fact: they had all been taken from "the bottom of the barrel"—many from the old South Hills days. And there was no evidence in his father's papers of the prayers he was supposed to be composing for the Senate. So he hadn't been working at all? What about the last sermon, the one Stewart hadn't really heard? Nothing special: a more or less routine exegesis of the Ten Commandments, closely parallel to Christ's own comments on the law. Stewart thumbed through it, and he was almost ashamed of himself to find out that he was concentrating on the Seventh. But it was natural, he thought, since so much of the new thinking about the mind had to do with sex and since the passage came along about halfway through the sermon, where he thought his father might have broken down . . . "In this matter of adultery, I can only say to you what Jesus said to his followers: 'You have heard that it was said, You shall not commit adultery. But I say to you that every one who looks at a woman lustfully has already committed adultery with her in his heart. If your right eye causes you to sin, pluck it out and throw it away;

it is better that you lose one of your members than that your whole body be thrown into hell. And if your right hand causes you to sin, cut it off and throw it away; it is better that you lose one of your members than that your whole body go into hell.' Hard words, my friends, hard words—particularly from our gentle Master. But the meaning is clear, nothing less than hellfire itself awaits not only the adulterer but the man with lust in his eye and heart."

Reading these words in a new light and with a new purpose Stewart realized that the words were, indeed, hard and the meaning was, indeed, clear. For the first time he had a dreadful feeling that he might be getting somewhere. To anybody who grew up in the church, it was almost a standing joke that adultery was the minister's sin, much like embezzlement was the sin of the bank teller. Temptation was always at hand for a popular and handsome minister like his father, obliged as he was to deal daily, and often privately, with hundreds of impressionable women. Now that he thought about it, Stewart recalled that everybody always spoke of his father as "warm-blooded"—an obvious euphemism for an excess of sexuality—and some of the more forward men actually would joke and kid with him about all the opportunities he must have had. Sometimes they were even indiscreet enough to mention a woman by name, like the widow McCandless, who batted her eyes at him through every service and was always calling on him for the advice she had once sought from her dead husband. If Stewart had stumbled on the truth, who could it be? Not the widow McCandless, certainly; his father had better taste than that. Ticking off the ladies of the church one by one, Stewart couldn't think of any that seemed remotely possible.

The more he thought about it, the more Stewart felt compelled to discuss his suspicions with somebody. Not his mother, of course, it would be too cruel. Not the other children. His grandmother was a possibility . . . there was a comfortable, unshockable quality about her. Often Stewart had detected a smile in Mary Stewart's eyes even when she scolded him for some horrendous offense, like the time he locked his cousin May in the dreaded tower room. But Grandmother didn't need this kind of grief. Finally, he hit on Aunt Lucinda —Cindy. He hadn't seen her since Henry Schmidt's funeral, but hadn't she told him then to come to her anytime? And being a, well, a woman of the world, so to speak, she just might have more insight into the situation than anybody else.

Stewart found his aunt warmly receptive. She hugged and

kissed him, asked about school and his girl friend and then inquired politely about his father's condition. "That's what I really came to see you about, Cindy," Stewart said. "He's not good, not good at all. You know he's, well, crazy, don't you?"

"Well, I . . . no, Mother keeps saying he's suffering from exhaustion, although it seems to me he ought to be over it by now."

"That's just for the public," Stewart said. "He's really out of his mind, and I *think* I know why."

"Oh?"

Stewart decided to break it to her gradually, going through all of his own thought processes, beginning with his new interest in psychology and continuing through his search for clues to his father's case. Lucinda was genuinely fascinated. By the time he reached his conclusion, she had reached one too.

"Stewart," she said, "you've grown up faster these last few months than anybody I've ever seen."

"Thanks, Cindy . . ."

"No thanks necessary, Stewart. I'm not flattering you; I'm just trying to explain why I'm about to tell you something that I don't want another living soul, especially your mother, ever to know." And then Lucinda told Stewart, as delicately as possible, about what had happened at the Oakland Presbyterian Church that Fourth of July. Her story dropped into Stewart's mind like the last piece of a jig-saw puzzle. Of course! Stewart's sudden surmise showed in his face, and Lucinda said, "Honestly, Stewart, if you feel like crying, go ahead, I'll understand. . . ."

He hadn't cried then, or since. He wasn't even crying now while the minister mumbled his last prayer over his father's remains. Nor, he noticed, was Lucinda. It was now the year of our Lord nineteen hundred and seven, and his father's fall into lust was nothing compared to what was actually appearing in the papers about such esteemed citizens as Harry Thaw and William E. Corey—except, of course, for the fact that his unfortunate father was a "man of God." Everybody was rising now to sing the last hymn, a favorite of his father's, which was to be sung softly as the casket was borne down the center aisle. Stewart rose along with the rest and sang.

"Abide with me; fast falls the eventide;
The darkness deepens; Lord with me abide.
When other helpers fail and comforts flee,
Help of the helpless, Lord, abide with me."

Stewart hoped that whatever God there was would abide with his father, who had proved so helpless against the contradictions of his own nature. If he had any strong feelings about what had happened to his father, they were sorrow and regret. Though it was only fifteen years ago that his father had plucked out his mind rather than have it give offense, it seemed almost a demonic dark age in the light of the new twentieth century. If the same thing had happened today, the poor man might have been able to get some professional help —or at least compare himself not too unfavorably with other men who had succumbed to the temptations of the flesh. The whole change in attitude was symbolized for the world by the passing of the British crown from the publicly proper Victoria to her publicly wanton son, Edward. In Pittsburgh, the puritanical lid that had made the place a sort of emotional pressure cooker had been sufficiently lifted to let off quite a bit of steam when the secretive Carnegie went out of business. The distribution of the huge profits of the city's principal business revealed the human clay beneath the steel facade of the men who made them.

The more he studied the problems that came to him in his practice as a psychiatrist, the more attention Stewart paid to the Pittsburgh brand of puritanism. By heritage as well as training, he felt uniquely equipped for this task. All he needed to do was reflect on his own relatives, sound the depths of his memory for the echoes of fire-and-brimstone assurance of hell on earth and assured promises of heaven hereafter. While his Uncle Scott stood firmly above all floods upon the rock of Presbyterianism, his own father had been swept down upon it and broken. The others, like his grandmother, mother, Lucinda, Reed and most of his own generation, were testing the currents of life to various degrees but staying within safe swimming distance of the rock. In Stewart's mind, none of them—though not surprisingly—were truly free to come to terms with their own humanity. The pulpits of Pittsburgh, his father's not excepted, preached a God perhaps too tough for frail human flesh to obey. Each person standing naked before the mirror of this God was likely to feel embarrassed by his own inadequacy, driven to hide his eyes or clothe himself with propriety. Sensing all this, Stewart, whose practice included counseling employees in some of the more forward-looking concerns, had come to be interested in the Roman Catholic Church, which tended to be feared, and indeed in some quarters despised, by the Protestant hierarchy of Pittsburgh.

At least with regard to religion, he found many of the Catholic workers healthier in their attitudes than their bosses. Their church knew them to be sinners—and provided the confessional to ease the pain; their church understood an ordinary mortal needed the priest as intermediary between himself and his God. But for the Pittsburgh Protestant, there was, as the old hymn put it, "no hidin' place down here."

Perhaps it was Stewart's understanding of how puritanism, even when filtered through a fine screen, could muddy the emotional waters that caused him to act as he did in his most sensational case. Just a few months before his father's death —in early January 1907—he'd been summoned to the Beechwood Boulevard mansion of old Mrs. William Thaw. He had been to the house many times before on social occasions, but he knew this time it was business. Hardly an American alive was not aware that Mrs. Thaw's son, Harry Kendall Thaw, as about to go on trial in Supreme Court of New York for the sensational murder of architect Stanford White. All through the past summer and the long fall, while Harry waited in the Tombs of New York City for his trial, the papers had been full of salacious stories about Harry, his showgirl wife Evelyn Nesbit and White. Stewart took it all in, because Harry, just five years older than he, had been one of the "big boys" around the East End while he was growing up. There was almost nothing Harry wouldn't do—and get away with. When he didn't like a drink served to him in a bar, he would break the place up—and send a check later to cover the damages. When he thought a place was stuffy, he would insult it outrageously, like the time he rode a horse up the steps of New York's Union League Club. But all of these had been in the nature of pranks. When on June 25, 1906, Harry shot and killed Stanford White, Stewart was as shocked as the rest of Pittsburgh.

The details of the murder were as public as the act itself. Harry had taken his wife Evelyn to the opening of a new musical, *Mamzelle Champagne*, at the rooftop theater of Madison Square Garden. Unhappily, the building's architect, Stanford White, who had enjoyed a much publicized affair with Evelyn Nesbit before she met Harry, was there too. Harry spotted him, of course. While the audience's attention was riveted to the stage, where a famous sextet known as the "Big Six" were singing "I Could Love a Million Girls," Thaw made his way to White's table, pulled a revolver from his pocket and shot the architect. Harry made no effort to get away. Surrendering himself to the first policeman on the scene, he merely said, "He deserved it. He ruined my wife and then deserted the girl." The papers went wild. It was, they claimed, the most stunning crime since a man named Ed Stokes shot the flashy financier Jim Fisk on the steps of the Grand Central Hotel years before in another love triangle. To the New York press, Thaw's action was only what you could expect from an uncouth Pittsburgh millionaire. Already notorious for his scrapes in bars and for his unorthodox courtship of the beautiful Miss Nesbit, he was tagged a wastrel son, ruined by inherited wealth, whereas White, America's most famous architect, was depicted as a kind of national treasure, cut down in his prime. Admittedly White was a man of the world, known for squiring showgirls (he and Evelyn had been ejected from a New York hotel in a headlined incident a few years before), but this was regarded as an artist's privilege. Moreover, at fifty-three, White was considered little more than a kindly uncle to young stars, a man whose love for the theater had led him to furnish support for retired and indigent actors.

The reaction in Pittsburgh, particularly in circles frequented by Stewart Sharp and the other Stewarts, was far more complicated. If Harry Thaw himself was somewhat of a maverick, the Thaws *were Pittsburgh*. Old William Thaw, Harry's father, who had perhaps fortunately died in '89 before his son was old enough to get into real trouble, had made a $40,000,000 fortune in river freighting long before Carnegie turned steel into gold. He had been generous with it too, supporting the Allegheny Observatory and the Western University of Pennsylvania, among other causes. The Thaws were more than pillars of the Third Presbyterian Church—they were its steeples. Mrs. Thaw was as noted for good works as her husband, having been one of the founders, as early as '75, of the Pittsburgh Association for the Improvement of the Poor. Most of their ten children had turned out well, as would be expected in the light of such a background. One daughter, Alice, may even have inspired the classical role for daughters of Pittsburgh wealth by becoming, through marriage, the Countess of Yarmouth. As to Harry, old William Thaw must have had some premonitions, because he directed in his will that Harry receive only $200 a month until he could be trusted with his $12,000,000 share of the inheritance. But Harry, handsome and winning in his reckless ways, charmed his aging mother into giving him a yearly allowance of $80,000, enough to enable him to woo Miss Nesbit in a manner grander by far than White's.

The Nesbit liaison caused more of a stir in Pittsburgh than

it might have otherwise, since Evelyn Nesbit was also local, though her people were unheard of in the world of Thaws. Moreover, her life was truly scandalous in a day when nice girls were still doubtful about the propriety of working in an office. After she broke into show business in New York in 1901, her beauty attracted such famous artists as Charles Dana Gibson, who persuaded her to pose for him. Indeed, no matter what they thought of her morals, almost everybody agreed about her beauty. Newspapermen strained their vocabularies in efforts to describe her. One, Irvin S. Cobb, called her "the most exquisitely lovely human being I ever looked at—the slim, quick grace of a faun, a head that sat on her faultless throat as a lily on its stem, eyes that were the color of blue-brown pansies and the size of half dollars, a mouth of rumpled rose petals." While playing a flower girl in *Floradora*, Evelyn's beauty caught the artistic eye of Stanford White. She traveled openly with him through a Europe more tolerant of such affairs until she met the younger, richer Thaw. They, too, indulged in an illicit and widely reported affair, mostly on the continent. Rumors were that White tried to get her back. He spread stories that Harry Thaw was a pervert and sadist—that he had once put a girl in a bathtub and poured scalding water on her, that he enjoyed tying young girls to bedposts and beating them. He implied that Thaw was engaging in such unnatural acts with poor Evelyn and even went so far as to send to Paris a Pittsburgh girl who had grown up with Evelyn to spy on the relationship.

At this point all the weight of Pittsburgh came down on Harry and Evelyn. Mrs. Thaw, who held the purse strings and who had tried to break up the affair, now insisted that they marry. So on April 4, 1905, a quiet wedding took place in the parsonage of the Thaw's pastor, the Reverend Doctor W. L. McEwen. Not content, the imperious Mrs. Thaw set about transforming what she regarded as an ugly duckling of a showgirl with no family to speak of—Evelyn's mother had remarried and was now a Mrs. Holman—into a social swan. Tutors were engaged to teach her French and German; leaders of the Pittsburgh Symphony were brought to the Thaw mansion to school her in music. Actress that she was, Evelyn was blooming so fairly in the hothouse of the Thaw wealth that some said Harry shot White only because the architect knew too much about the poor soil from which Evelyn had sprouted. . . .

Stewart Sharp thought otherwise as he was ushered under the ivied portico of the square-towered Thaw fortress. Though he didn't know Harry well enough to be sure, he suspected that the shadow of special home-grown Presbyterianism had fallen across the whole affair—from bed to bullet.

Mrs. Thaw was in the parlor in conference with a man she introduced to Stewart as Mr. Delphin Michael Delmas of San Francisco. Stewart had, of course, already seen the name in the papers. Known as "the Napoleon of the western bar" for winning nineteen acquittals in nineteen murder cases, he had been engaged as a special attorney by Mrs. Thaw for a reputed fee of $100,000. Mrs. Thaw, a steel-haired lady with the unconscious graciousness confirmed by a lifetime of having more money than she could possibly spend, said to Delmas, "Dr. Sharp's the young man I told you about. He grew up as a friend of our family, you might say, mightn't you, Stewart?"

When Stewart assented with a nod, she went on. "Quite fortunately, under the circumstances, he's a specialist in mental disease—an alienist, or whatever you call it these days. I think if he could see Harry . . ."

The lawyer rubbed his hands together and began pacing around excitedly. "Splendid! You see, Dr. Sharp, since Harry's admitted his crime, the only defense we have is that he wasn't in his right mind at the time. I know—and I'm sure you know even more than I, being a friend of the family and all—that a young man raised like Harry Thaw couldn't just murder a person in cold blood unless he had taken leave of his senses. I don't know what you'd call what happened to him, but we're calling it, for the sake of the laymen on the jury and the press, emotional insanity."

"But I've read that Harry still claims he was completely sane," Stewart said.

"Well, he is now and maybe was just before it happened," the lawyer said. "What we're going to try to prove is that just for a split second there he lost his power to reason. That's possible, isn't it?"

"Yes, I suppose it's possible. . . ."

"Good. Then it's likely you'll agree with Dr. Britton Evans of the mental hospital at Morris Plains, New Jersey—you've heard of him, I'm sure—who has examined Harry and says he'll testify for us. Dr. Evans has coined a wonderful phrase to describe what happened to Harry: he calls it a 'brain storm.' It'll make all the headlines. The thing is, though, we need some corroboration—and what better than from a doctor who more or less grew up with Harry, who knows in his guts that a good Presbyterian boy wouldn't be capable of such an

321

act in his right mind. I was suggesting this to Mrs. Thaw when she came up with your name. . . ."

"Well," Stewart said, "I can't promise anything until I've at least seen Harry."

"Naturally, naturally," the lawyer agreed. "I've taken the trouble to book us both on tonight's train to New York if you can arrange your affairs. . . ."

Encountering Harry Thaw in the bleak visiting rooms of the Tombs was to stand out in Stewart's mind in all the grotesqueries of a dream. Handsome as ever, Harry was clean-shaven, well-groomed, dressed conservatively except for a pearl-gray vest and spats. Against a background of massive walls, bars, shadeless bulbs, battered furniture, he stood out like a bird of rare plumage trapped in a pet-shop cage. Deprived of drink for a long time, he was leaner and clearer of eye than Stewart remembered, but he also was excessively nervous. He refused to sit down, pacing back and forth, back and forth, and occasionally kicking at the walls or rattling the barred door with his hands as if to test the reality of his incarceration. At Stewart's insistence, the attorney left them alone together, and Harry immediately began raging. "Goddamn them all, Stew, they're trying to make a madman out of me. I suppose you're in on it, too, but you know me, you know I'm not crazy. I'd rather be hung than crazy."

"Then why did you do it?" Stewart asked in his most professional manner.

"Because that son of a bitch was evil—that's why. The world's well rid of his kind. He took this little girl from Pittsburgh—you know the type as well as I do, Stew, bred on a slag heap, no background, no education, but pretty as a rose—and seduced her, ruined her reputation without ever so much as offering to marry her. And she wasn't the first—for twenty-five years that famous studio of his was a deflowering factory—"

"C'mon now, Harry," Stewart said. "From what I've read in the papers, you . . ."

"I what? I what?" Harry ranted. "What I did was marry the girl. Get that straight—I *married* her."

"Why?"

"Why? Why? My God, you, the son of a minister, ask me that question! Because it was the right thing to do, Stew. For God's sake, it was the right thing to do. You know that as well as I do."

"It didn't have anything to do with your mother?"

"Of course it had something to do with my mother. My

mother *stands* for something in Pittsburgh, and I was hurting her. I didn't want to go on hurting her, and I wanted to give Evelyn my name."

"You know what?" Stewart said. "You're a real honest-to-God puritan, Harry—a perfect Presbyterian puritan."

For the first time Harry stopped his pacing and shaking and looked curiously at Stewart. "That doesn't sound like a doctor talking," he said, "but maybe you're right. I guess I am a puritan, though I've tried to get away from it. God, how I've tried! You wouldn't believe all the ways I've tried. It makes me sick to think of what I've done, but I can't get away . . . You know, that's funny—Harry Thaw, puritan. Is that a disease, Doctor?"

"In a way, you might say it is . . . especially in advanced stages," Stewart said. "Harry Thaw, puritan, thought he was doing the world a favor shooting down Stanford White, whom he held to be guilty of deflowering young maidens without benefit of parson, albeit with their consent. It's sort of like my own uncle, Scott Stewart, who I'm sure felt he was on the side of the angels when he moved with the Pinkertons into Homestead. It seems to be a characteristic of us puritans to see things as black and white and take on ourselves the job of turning black to white, never mind how. It was something like that in your case, wasn't it, Harry?"

Harry, calmed somewhat by this strange and interesting reflection, scratched his chin thoughtfully. "You might have something there," he said. "Yes, you just might be right, if I understand what you're getting at. . . ."

At this point the guard interrupted. "Time," he said in a voice that sounded like a flat gong. Stewart got up to go. "Harry," he said, "I'm sorry I'm not going to be able to testify at your trial. I think you were sane. . . ."

Harry, a look of gratitude on his face, grabbed Stewart's hand like a drowning man clutching at a lifeguard. "You do? Really? Oh, God bless you, Stew. But why can't you tell the court that?"

"Because they'd hang you," Stewart said.

"Why? Why should they do that when I was doing the right thing? I was doing the right thing, wasn't I?"

"I didn't say that, Harry. I just said you were sane—at least in the way the world you and I came from often reckons sanity. I'll say good-bye now, Harry. And good luck to you. . . ."

Despite his own opinion, Stewart wasn't surprised that Thaw, after two trials, was remanded to an asylum for the criminally insane at Matawan, New Jersey, still protesting he had been sane, sane, sane! Star witness in the trials was Evelyn, who reportedly had been paid $200,000 by her mother-in-law to testify for Harry. Actually, dressed like an innocent schoolgirl in a plain navy-blue suit with a shirtwaist and stiff collar tied with a black bow, she somehow managed to testify for both sides at once—first by acknowledging the blackest rumors about Harry's sexual perversions, and then by demurely denying that he had shown any such side of his character to her. Throughout the trials Harry's staunch old mother and several of his sisters, including the Countess of Yarmouth and Mrs. George Carnegie, sat prominently in the court to proclaim their faith in him. It was a grand show in the best tradition of the prevailing belief that people with enough money could never really be guilty of anything serious. Stewart was fairly certain that as long as there was life in old Mrs. Thaw and her son Harry, and as long as there was money in the bank, the world had not yet heard the last of Harry Kendall Thaw. . . .

Unhappily not so for the Reverend Doctor Donald Vincent Sharp, whose single sin of the spirit had proved far more tragically destructive than all of Harry's sins of the flesh. They had decided to lay Donald Sharp to rest on the hillside below the first church and among departed Stewarts. Ironically, his grave would be only a few feet from that of Henry Schmidt, the man he'd so disliked in life. Riding out in the same car with Reed and Alma, Lucinda said, "I wonder who's going to start rolling in his grave first—Don or Henry?"

Reed smiled, "Not to mention Father."

"You two!" Alma said. "I should never let you get together. You've got no respect, even for the dead."

"You're right there," Reed said. "I never could understand why dying was supposed to confer automatic virtue. Shakespeare put it well . . . dying is 'a necessary end.' My God, look at the statues and solemnities that greeted the departure of old Chris Magee, who devoted a lifetime to rigging the public weal to his private profit. Well, maybe it was all to prove how glad they were that he was gone."

Alma shook her head, but had to suppress a smile in spite of herself.

From a pocket beside the seat in their new Packard, Reed extracted a silver flask. He unscrewed the top, filled it and offered it to the ladies. "Something for the nerves?"

Both of them declined, and Reed had just raised the cup to his lips when there was a loud bang, followed by a swerving jolt that sent the whiskey splashing down over his chin and collar. "Goddamn," he said, forgetting his manners.

The chauffeur, a stolid man accustomed to handling the caprice of horses, got the car to the side of the road and announced redundantly, "I'm sorry, sir. Flat tire, sir."

They were third in the line of cars bumping and grinding their way over Mount Washington. Reed got out and waved the others on while his chauffeur prepared for the ritual of changing the tire. "Well, so much for progress," Reed said to the ladies who had got out on the road beside him, lifting their skirts to avoid the dust. "I told Scott he'd never get a fleet of five cars all the way out there to the South Hills without something breaking or boiling over."

"We couldn't have done it any other way," Lucinda said. "There wouldn't have been time with horses . . ."

"We could have put the body on a streetcar and gone through the tunnel."

"Reed!" Alma said, and then asked, "where is that nerve medicine—or did you lose it all in the jolt?"

"Oh, no, only what I was trying to drink."

"Well, bring it. I think Lucinda and I could use some now. We'll sit over there on the grass until James gets this fixed. I wonder if they'll have sense enough to go on without us."

"I hope so," Lucinda said. "Funerals really depress me."

Reed agreed. "I'd say we ought to turn around now except that I would like to see what's happened with the old property."

"Me, too," Lucinda said. "Can you believe it—a store right on the corner and two new houses down where the apple orchard was?"

"Progress," Reed said. "Civilization follows transportation. As the railroads opened the great West, so the streetcar is opening the South Hills."

"Well, I think it's nice for Sarah," Lucinda said.

"For Sarah?"

"Yes, the money's all Momma's, and she's sure to get some of it someday. I don't know how much it will be, but I did hear Scott managed to get five thousand dollars for that lot with the store on it. Poor Sarah's been living such a grubby life since the church cut them off."

"I know it, and I still don't see why they couldn't have given him a little salary along with that empty title," Alma said. "After all, they support missionaries and Chinese orphans and God knows what else."

"The way I heard it," Reed said, "my brother took the

position in session that, especially because he was a Stewart relative, Don should not be a burden to the church. He said the denomination's ministerial pension plan was set up for such contingencies."

"I don't see why Scott didn't help out himself," Alma said.

"To give him his due, he tried to," Reed explained. "Sarah was just too proud to take anything except for what they could filter through Mother in the form of tuition for the children."

The chauffeur did a remarkable job of changing tires quickly, and they were on their way in time to reach the cemetery while the graveside ceremonies were still in progress. And so now all the Stewarts in the area were once more brought together by death within sight of the home—now dwarfed by a yellow brick building next door that housed a meat market, a drugstore and a real estate office—from which they had all set out to take their places in Pittsburgh. The Reverend Henry Ward Beecher Sharp, who with his smooth round cheeks and heavy glasses looked more like a wise old owl than a 27-year-old seminary graduate, was reading prayers over his father's grave. Pressed in around him were Mary Stewart and Sarah Sharp, looking as a result of Sarah's troubles more like sisters than mother and daughter; Becky McCandless with three bewildered children clutching at her skirts and a fat baby in her arms; Jane Sharp with her two small sons; and Tillie Sharp, a dark willowy girl who seemed to have inherited the best features in both the Sharp and Stewart lines. In an outer circle, where they could move around a bit to relieve their nervous embarrassment at the tears, were the men—Scott Stewart with little David, Benjy's son, firmly in hand, Byron McCandless, Dr. Stewart Sharp and Tillie's current "young man," a foppishly elegant blond fellow whom Reed recognized at once as Wilbur Curry, the luckless defendant in the automobile suit that had been tried before him years ago. Seeing Reed's party approach, Stewart Sharp moved back quietly to enlarge the circle. Impulsively, he took his Aunt Lucinda's hand in his own and squeezed it tightly. It was his way of telling her that he bore her no ill will over the secret they alone shared. Her response was to allow herself to cry over all the misunderstandings human beings like the late Reverend Donald Sharp—not to mention her late husband—managed to torture themselves with. In some cases right into the grave.

A Scandal in Steel

"Grandy, are they all my cousins?" David Scott Stewart asked when he was alone in the new Cadillac riding back home from the Sharp funeral with his tall, severe-looking grandfather and the little old lady he called "Granny."

"Yes," Scott said.

"Then why don't they come play with me?"

"That might not be a bad idea, Scott," Mary Stewart said. "I almost forgot how many there are of an age. Young Tom McCandless may be a little old—I think he must be eleven now—but Sarah's just David's age, and Stewart's older son, Laughlin, can't be more than a year younger. It grieves me to see us all getting so far apart."

"We don't have much in common, Mother. . . ."

"Why not? Why not?" David wanted to know. "I'd like to play with them. I never have anybody to play with."

"You have your pony Mitzie," Scott said, "and that puppy —what's his name?"

"George."

"An odd name for a puppy."

"But they're not people, Grandy," David protested.

"Less trouble than some people . . ."

"Scott, what a thing to say!" Mary Stewart chided. "David needs friends."

Mary was increasingly worried about the boy, growing up in isolation with two old people like Scott and herself. Somehow it hadn't been so bad before the boy's parents died. Even far away as they were, they bore a kind of primary responsibility for David. They wrote little messages to him all the time in their letters, detailing the more exciting parts of their lives, such as encounters with tigers and elephants, and holding out the promise that David would one day share their adventures when he grew up. Though David was, of course, too young to understand, in Mary's mind his living in Oakland was always a temporary thing, and she had the consolation that, if anything happened to Scott or her, his parents would certainly take over. Then came the letter that was still hard to believe. It was from the Board of Foreign Missions and couched in the same kind of impersonal, formal terms the government used to notify families of a death in combat. It was all very distant.

"We regret to inform you," the letter said, "of the death last month of Dr. Benjamin S. Stewart and his wife, Joan, in the course of performing their duties at the Siam station. Since there were no other missionaries in the area where they worked, we can unfortunately supply few details. According to word from Chiengmai, news of their deaths was brought there by a runner who could only describe their last illness in a way that was unmistakably diagnosed by our medical staff in Chiengmai as a severe attack of malarial fever. We extend our deepest sympathies to you and to the family of Mrs. Stewart, whom we are informing by separate letter. These fine young people were true soldiers in the army of Christ. May the Lord bless you and keep you. Sincerely . . ."

Mary found Scott's strength in accepting this news amazing even for him. He sat dry-eyed through the memorial service held for young Dr. Benjamin Stewart at the Oakland Presbyterian Church, though inside was a turmoil—both his children lost to him now . . . well, they would *not* separate him from David, and thinking this he worried that his sons-in-law might make some claim on David. Scott had his attorneys draft an official-looking agreement that he would be responsible for David and mail it out to Kansas, where the in-laws were known to live on a farm. Blessed with other children and grandchildren and struggling with an inadequate income, they were happy to sign and to see the boy in the care of a man of "such noted Christian principles as yourself." In view of the distance he had seemed to keep between himself and his own children, Scott's interest in little David was almost baffling to Mary, but she put it down hopefully to some kind of middle-aged mellowing. The problem now was that Scott couldn't seem to see that the companionship of a busy grandfather wasn't enough for a seven-year-old boy.

"Well, he'll be going to school this fall, and the whole thing will be solved. I don't want to get mixed up with relatives any more than we have to," Scott said. "All we seem to get from relatives is grief, and I don't need any more grief, what with this business about Bill Corey at the steel company and the organization of the aluminum company. . . ."

Mary put a hand on her son's knee. "I know, Scott, I know. When are you going to ease up? Next thing, son, we'll be burying you out there too."

Scott said nothing; it was no use. After all these years, his mother still couldn't understand that indeed he might as well be buried as to give up his business interests. They were his passion, his dedication, his *responsibility*. He wasn't like so many others who'd taken their money and run—to Newport, to Europe, to Florida. He was one of the solid men, like Westinghouse or Heinz or Mellon or Frick, who knew that money would soon get away from you if you didn't watch over it every day and who had a real sense of the trust and responsibility involved in handling money. If God gave you this responsibility, what kind of a man would you be if you shirked it? Back in '02 during the union troubles in the anthracite fields, some people snickered and others raged when George Baer, president of the Reading Railroad, wrote to a friend that "the rights and interests of the laboring man will be protected and cared for—not by the labor agitators, but by the Christian men to whom God in his infinite wisdom has given the control of the property interests of this country. . . ." Scott neither snickered nor raged when he read that; in fact, he sat down and wrote Mr. Baer a letter of appreciation. Now there was a man who really understood the basis of wealth and who, like Frick, was willing to stand firm against all the fuzzy-minded people bent on throwing a wrench into the money-making machine that was turning America into the wonder of the world. Only a few insiders like Scott understood how Frick's obstinate stand at Homestead had finally paid off for every stockholder in the United States Steel Corporation. Usually silent as the tomb about his affairs, Frick told Scott all the details this time, because he thought his loyal lieutenant might appreciate the way Homestead had echoed down the years.

There was one missing link in the great steel chain J. P. Morgan tried to forge from mine to manufactured product— the Rockefeller ore properties in the Masabi range. Though he had no intention of entering the steel business, Rockefeller, now an aging man who'd turned over active control of Standard Oil to his son and other associates to retire to a life of golf and Sunday-school rallies, seemed reluctant to part with the ore. Efforts to deal with young John D. Rockefeller,

Jr., failed, and the Morgan interests, seeking the right emissary to the old man, chose Clay Frick because Rockefeller had been heard to express admiration for Frick's handling of the Homestead affair.

"I didn't know Mr. Rockefeller well," Frick told Scott. "I'd met him once or twice, but you know neither of us are noted for being garrulous on such occasions. In matters like this, I always believe in the direct approach, so I went up to Westchester and hired a carriage to take me out to Pocantico Hills. I got there about ten o'clock in the morning, I guess, and told the carriage to wait in the street while I walked up the long driveway to the estate, trying to think what might persuade the old fellow. Well, the answer was simple: money. Luckily I found Rockefeller out walking around and looking at his estate—you know, having trees and bushes moved around is as much a hobby with him as buying paintings is with me, and it seems to put him in a good mood. So I fell in step beside him while we exchanged the time of day. He would make a great bridge player, I can tell you. He has a face expressionless as a blank sheet of parchment, but his eyes—they're just like Morgan's—look right through you. But you met him years ago, didn't you? Anyway, I could see there was no use to jolly him along. 'Mr. Rockefeller,' I said, 'I'm here about those ore lands. As one director of the steel company, I think we've offered you too little money.' I think you could say his eyes twinkled, but he didn't smile. 'So do I,' he replied. 'I'm prepared to press for five million more if you will sell,' I went on. He held out his hand, and I took it. 'Mr. Frick, I think you and I see eye to eye,' he said. 'As far as I'm concerned, it is all in your hands. I'll speak to my son. Good day.' Well, that's how it was—fifteen minutes at the most. I was back in town before the day was out. Of course, I found Morgan a man of my stripe, too—never quibble about price when you are putting together a major deal."

Scott could remember there had been some muttering in the board about Frick's generosity in offering Rockefeller an additional five million, but, as Morgan pointed out, it was only a drop in the bucket of the country's first billion-dollar corporation. People in Pittsburgh who didn't see the inside plays like this often spoke as if Frick, by moving to New York and spending more of his time collecting paintings, had somehow opted out like Carnegie. Not so, as Scott knew only too well. He shared so many of his former boss's interests, including management of the Frick Building, that he was obliged to go down to New York several times a month for conferences in the old Vanderbilt home Frick had rented on Fifth Avenue.

The one worrisome period for Scott was when Frick began unloading U.S. Steel to invest in other stocks, mostly railroads —"the Rembrandts of investment," he called them. With some six million dollars in seven roads, including the Pennsylvania, of which he was a director, Frick became the largest individual holder of railway stock in the world. Fortunately Morgan knew Frick too valuable—or dangerous—to let him go. Along in '04 when U.S. Steel fell to its lowest point —8¾ for common and 50 for preferred—partly because of Frick's unloading, Morgan held one of his famous meetings aboard his yacht *Corsair*. While the big vessel steamed around Long Island Sound, these two silent men reached an almost wordless agreement whereby Morgan bought out the Union Steel Co., in which Frick and Andy Mellon held an interest, and Frick went back into U.S. Steel for 100,000 shares of common and 50,000 of preferred. The stock began rising at once, and, much to the relief of Scott and other holders, reached 50¼ for common and 113¼ for preferred by the end of 1906. They all felt more comfortable with a man like Frick aboard again. . . .

When the time came for a vote, Scott figured, Frick probably would join him and the others in deposing President Bill Corey just as he had not resisted the decision to get rid of Schwab. Nonetheless, Scott regretted that Frick probably didn't share his reasons for the action; during all their time together he'd found Frick reticent about his religious convictions, if any. Not so some of the other members of the board, who were as morally incensed as Scott that the president of U.S. Steel would divorce his wife of twenty years to marry a showgirl. Whatever he thought about the morals of the thing, Frick would agree, Scott was sure, that such an act demonstrated an unsteadiness, a fatal flaw of character in a man with so much responsibility. The same had been true for Schwab's gambling at Monte Carlo. A lot of people tried to excuse it on the grounds that Schwab was young and that all the money he got when Carnegie sold out went to his head. But Scott had been glad to see that Mr. Morgan, as steady a vestryman as Scott was an elder, had taken a different view of it. As reported in the press, Schwab told Morgan, "I didn't do anything to be ashamed of. I didn't do anything behind closed doors." They said Morgan, laconic as ever, replied, "That is what doors are made for." In any event, Schwab had sense enough to resign, and maybe he had learned a good lesson—at least his success in bringing little Bethlehem Steel along would indicate he had.

Mulling all this over in blessed quiet—since David had subsided into a pout and his mother was lost in the kind of musing usually brought on for her by funerals—Scott determined to keep pressing to get Corey out, no matter what the consequences. Maybe he would run up to New York and see Frick; he was sure a wavering Judge Gary would go along if Frick said the word. Most important, Scott was sure he was right. He didn't know what the world was coming to—first that business with Harry Thaw and now this. You could write young Thaw off as a spoiled playboy, but not Corey. One of Carnegie's "young geniuses," Corey had started in the Braddock mill and followed Schwab up the ladder, rung by rung. In the process, he put his name forever on the records of steel manufacturing by inventing a new method for the manufacture of armor plate called the "Corey reforging process." But from Scott's point of view his moral perceptions did not keep pace with his worldly progress. Instead of staying in Pittsburgh and sticking to business, he bought a big house in New York and began squiring showgirls about. This galled Scott not only on a moral but practical grounds. It was one thing for an owner like Carnegie or a director like Frick to operate out of New York, but the president, the man in charge of day-to-day affairs of the company, ought to be home breathing smoke. As a result of Corey's absenteeism, Scott found himself called upon to look into matters that weren't properly a part of a director's business.

He'd brought the whole matter into the open at the last board meeting. It was a surprise to the other directors, who'd expected the usual quick session—a rubber stamping of Corey's reports and recommendations. However when the routine business concluded, Scott quietly said, "Gentlemen, I think we have to face the fact—and face it now—that however much we may not wish to intrude upon anyone's personal life, the marital affairs of our president are bringing very unfavorable publicity on the company."

Corey, a man with the toughness of a life in the mills still visible in the lines of his body and the set of his jaw, turned crimson. "Why, you . . . that's damn well none of this board's business. I move the meeting be adjourned . . ."

"I differ with you, sir. Anything that affects the welfare of our company is of concern to this board. How you conduct your affairs in New York may be up to you, but when you set aside your wife of a lifetime by divorce it did not go unnoticed by the Christian businessmen of this city."

There were a few murmurs of assent, but Corey said, "Mrs. Corey was agreeable to the settlement. As to my 'affairs in New York,' as you put it, Mr. Stewart, I intend to marry Miss Gilman as soon as I get my decree, which should satisfy even you."

"No, I'd say that makes it worse, Mr. Corey. I suppose there will be a great deal of publicity, since I gather the young lady is an actress?"

"Why not? I'm proud of her, and I don't care if the world or you gentlemen know it. I'm not going to sit here and listen to any more of this. I'll tell you one thing—if you want my resignation, you'll have to ask for it."

When Corey slammed out of the room, the other directors looked at each other in somewhat embarrassed silence. Finally the affable chairman, Judge Gary, said, "Well, I thank you for clearing the air by bringing this matter up, Mr. Stewart."

"I don't," another man said. "Corey's a good steel man, and we're in the business of making steel, not making morals. We damn near lost a good man right there."

"Well, I agree with Stewart," another man said. "This is the kind of scandal that in my opinion doesn't speak well for the man's personal integrity, and at least here in Pittsburgh, business is built on integrity."

Not liking the way the discussion was developing, Judge Gary said, "I'm going to rule this business out of order at the moment. Corey's a pretty sensible fellow and when he calms down, I think he may realize that it would be a good idea at least to keep this all quiet. Let's wait and see. Meanwhile, meeting adjourned."

Obviously Gary hoped the whole matter would blow over, but now Scott was determined that it wouldn't. Since that meeting not only a number of fellow directors but many of their wives had come to see him and urge him to keep up the fight. The women, particularly, were indignant. They'd come to like Mrs. Corey, even though she had been no more than an unpaid mother's helper in the Coreys' Braddock home when eighteen-year-old Bill eloped with her. It didn't help that Corey was said to have settled three million dollars on Laura; the best years of a woman's life were without price. Though the Coreys had already obtained a quiet Reno divorce, it wasn't too late for a reconciliation if he could be prevented from marrying Mabelle Gilman. But it seemed unlikely. Scott had heard that Charlie Schwab cornered Corey for two hours in the Waldorf-Astoria in New York and tried to talk sense into him—to no avail. The man was incorrigible.

But Corey was only one matter on Scott's busy mind. Another, as he had told his mother, was helping to draw up the incorporation papers for the Aluminum Company of America, an organization that had become necessary to handle the ever-growing business of the little Pittsburgh Reduction Company he'd invested in at Andy Mellon's suggestion. They now owned in addition to their facilities in New Kensington, north of Pittsburgh, bauxite mines, fleets of ships and generating stations. Their product went into everything from cooking utensils, peddled door to door, to superstructure for Navy vessels, and it now appeared that the limit would literally be the sky. It was more than probable that the new heavier-than-air craft the Wright brothers had succeeded in getting off the ground would need the lightest possible metals if they were to develop into practical machines. Fortunately, the Mellons had not only stayed with this product, but Andy's younger brother, Richard B. Mellon, had consented to act as chairman of the new corporation.

Scott, who sat on the boards of the Union Trust Company and the Mellon National Bank, had good reason to trust anything the Mellons touched. They had noses like hound dogs for ferreting out the smell of a good thing. Take oil, for instance. Scott had been one of the skeptics when Colonel J. M. Guffey ran out of money trying to cap Spindletop and came to the Mellons for help. Schooled by Carnegie and Frick, Scott regarded oil as an illusive thing; too many Pittsburghers he knew had seen the money they put into oil blow into the air or seep into the ground. Though it was the biggest strike since Drake's first one at Oil City nearly half a century before, this Spindletop in Gladys City, Texas, seemed nothing but an unruly phenomenon of nature. When Anthony Luchick's drill tapped oil on January 9, 1901, it began spewing 100,000 barrels a day 200 feet into the air. Trying to cap it, Luchick—who was now calling himself Lucas—ran quickly through all the money he could get from Pittsburgh—John Gady's, then Guffey's. Why wouldn't the same thing happen to the Mellons, Scott argued. Just a hunch, Mellon insisted. The result was that a once-skeptical Scott Stewart was now sitting on the board of Gulf Oil Corporation, which gave promise with its great Texas reserves of giving even Rockefeller a run for his money.

Oil, aluminum, coal, steel, glass, gas, food, finance—virtually everything upon which a mighty America fed and grew—were centered in the tight, smoky triangle across which Scott's

Cadillac crawled homeward from Donald Sharp's funeral on the bumpy, potholed streets. In another few months when the annexation of Allegheny City would become a fact, Pittsburgh would become the nation's sixth largest city with a population of more than 500,000—a growth of nearly ten times since Scott first looked down on it. How could one doubt that this city and the men who managed it were blessed of God? It was the only explanation for the amazing Mellon foresight, in which he had fortunately participated, that made any sense to Scott. With his mind for figures, he understood very well what had been happening over the forty years he had been in business in the city. The men who had property and money to lend at the time when the Civil War inflation had cut the dollar's value in half—like old Judge Mellon and to some extent Scott himself with his "found" five thousand and his mother's South Hills land—had seen their fortunes grow as if by magic when tighter currency forced creditors either to forfeit goods and property or repay in what amounted to double the money. It was simplest to think of money in terms of the labor it would buy. Put that way, you could, say, buy a day's labor for a dollar in 1870 and two days' labor for a dollar in 1900. This meant that the man who bought labor for a dollar in advance, as, in effect, anyone did who loaned money to an enterprise, was over the years getting increasing value for his dollar without lifting a finger. This, of course, was what had fueled the fiery oratory of such as William Jennings Byran, who wanted to go back to the old inflated dollar by coining silver. It was obviously worth every political contribution the business community could make to keep idiots like *that* out of office. Better a trust-busting Roosevelt who didn't understand money well enough to fool around with it than a Bryan. Though, as Rockefeller had demonstrated with Standard Oil and Morgan was demonstrating with U.S. Steel, monopolistic organization made economic sense, there were hundreds of ways in which business could somehow be put together, but money obeyed laws of God as ancient and immutable as gravity—and as simple to comprehend. Just as an apple will surely fall, so money will surely grow if you buy cheap and sell dear. The businessmen of Pittsburgh, reared in the fear and respect of God's laws, understood this instinctively and so, in Scott's view, not only deserved every penny that came their way but were, in fact, elected by the Lord to supervise the development and use of creation's resources, including the labor of decent, however less deserving, men.

Looking now at the little boy David, Scott wondered if he could ever get across to him the excitement, indeed the glory, of this concept. He felt sorry for people who could think of the challenge of business—of tearing open the land and firing its elements into iron and steel, of boring into earth's heart and converting its black blood and gases into useful flame, of channeling its waterfalls and tides into dynamos to send energy crackling across the country, of laying rails across deserts and over rivers and through mountains, of making pots and stoves and automobiles and sewing machines and elevators to ease the lot of man—as mere work. Certainly too pious to allow himself the image of playing God, Scott could nevertheless live with the feeling of helping God in the remodeling of His creation as he went to his office in the Frick Building six mornings every week. It was a corner suite on the top floor, approached through a door on whose glass paneling was the simple, gold-leafed legend: "Scott S. Stewart, Esq." In a large outer office sat two stenographers—although he deplored women in business, Scott had succumbed to hiring young ladies when he found their fingers were more nimble on typewriter keys and their desires in terms of wages considerably more modest than those of men—and two clerks, one a young lawyer to look into legal matters and the other an accountant. As in Scott's own inner office, which was flanked by windows on two sides, giving a view of the Monongahela and Mount Washington to the south and, on a clear day, the Point and the Ohio to the west, the furnishings were simple oak desks and chairs in the dark mission style and banks of austere, metal filing cabinets.

No product issued from the offices of Scott S. Stewart, Esquire. The daily work consisted of studying reports of the many enterprises of which he was a director, of keeping abreast with the money markets of the world, of meeting or corresponding with men who had ideas to sell or money to loan. Fascinating as Scott found these affairs, he knew it would be difficult to make them exciting, or even comprehensible, to a young boy such as David. Still, remembering bitterly his failure with Benjamin, he'd decided to try. Nearly every Saturday—which was gradually becoming a half day in Pittsburgh largely as a result of George Westinghouse's mistaken (in Scott's view) idea that people would profit from more leisure—Scott took David to the office with him. For these occasions he had had his tailor fashion a miniature business suit for David, complete with high collar, cravat and vest, and he had a small desk installed in a corner of the

336

outer office where the boy could draw or pretend to write and cast up figures the way clerks did. The stenographers thought David was "cute"—a word Scott deplored—and wasted a good deal of time amusing him, but Scott felt it would be worth the waste if the boy developed a good feeling about business. At noon Scott would take him to lunch at the Duquesne Club where, by having to be on his "good manners," David would learn something about the ways of the world. Then after lunch, Scott indulged in behavior which most of his business friends and family would have regarded as truly quixotic: he took the boy to the nikelodeon on Smithfield Street.

To Scott's mind there were all sorts of good reasons for going to see the motion pictures with a seven-year-old boy. First and foremost was the fact that the promise of going to the nickelodeon made the rest of the long day tolerable to David. Not far behind that was that Scott was keeping an eye on one of his more unlikely investments. When in 1905 a man named John P. Harris had come to see him with the idea of opening the world's first all-motion-picture theater, Scott had experienced what he told himself was a typical Mellon hunch. Though his only knowledge of the entertainment business came from the musical world where, except for the performers, it was a cultural charity, he could appreciate at once that the technical ability to multiply labor—the actor's performance—cheaply on film had a great potential for profit. So it was proving. In only two years nickelodeons were being opened all over the district and offering cheap entertainment more wholesome than the saloon to laboring men and their families, who had little time and less money to spend in regular concert halls and theaters. Aside from that, though, Scott Stewart *liked* the movies. He found himself laughing along with David at the antics of the frantic cop who couldn't get out of the way of the fast car or the burglar caught in the revolving door. The whole thing was quick, fast, clean—not weighed down with a lot of lugubrious dialogue that most playwrights passed off as thinking. A man with his problems didn't need that kind of palaver in the guise of entertainment. And then there was that secret joy that always came when, riding home with David and discussing the films they'd seen, Scott felt that he had at last a person to whom he could relate, a grandson, indeed a son. . . .

It was fear of cluttering up these Saturdays, of losing this special relationship with the boy, as much as anything else that prompted Scott to resist the idea of drafting David's cousins as playmates. If his mother argued, as she sometimes did, that David was being denied a normal childhood, Scott reminded her that there was nothing especially productive about a normal childhood. Princes, he said, were trained from the cradle for their role on the throne; short of being a Rockefeller or a Mellon, David was as close to being a prince as an American boy could be. Did Mary Stewart realize that the way things were going the boy might well inherit a hundred million dollars? . . . In any case, by the time the Cadillac crunched up the gravel driveway that arched in front of the Stewart residence, the subject had long been closed. A great, awkward Irish setter puppy came bounding around the corner of the house. With a joyous cry of "George!" David jumped out of the car and let the dog paw him and lap at his face. Scott hurried out, too, and pulled the dog away. "Don't let him do that, David," he said sternly. "He'll ruin your good suit. We can't afford that."

Still sitting in the car and watching the scene, Mary Stewart laughed for the first time in a long, long while. Somehow it was the perfect antidote to the melancholy reflections she'd been nursing about Don Sharp's mysterious breakdown and all the other incomprehensible buffetings of life. Can't afford it! A hundred million dollars or no, Scott Stewart was one person who never changed.

A Morgan Miracle

It was said to be the greatest building of its kind in America, if not the world. Sprawling over some five acres of land, it housed a library, a museum, an art gallery, a music hall. It cost six million dollars and took, in all, sixteen years to build. The first section, opened in 1895, was Italian Renaissance in design; the second section, being dedicated on this April day in 1907, was neo-Baroque of the École des Beaux Arts. But it all blended splendidly into a great temple to the arts and sciences. Huge, seated statues of such immortals as Bach, Shakespeare, Galileo guarded it gates; a frieze into which the names of nearly all the rest were carved crowned its walls. Within, gilt and marble prevailed. Great echoing halls housed paintings, sculpture, skeletons of dinosaurs, models of engines, stuffed samples of the world's fauna, stacks upon stacks of books. It was free to the public, and there was virtually nothing in the known history of mankind that a curious wanderer through its maze could not discover. In this, it perfectly fulfilled the intention of its donor, a man who had first found the world through books loaned to him by a generous neighbor in the slums of Slabtown, Allegheny City, Pennsylvania. It was Andrew Carnegie's most spectacular gift to Pittsburgh, the city that had made him the richest man in the world.

Of all the twenty thousand people attending these dedicatory ceremonies and craning for at least a look at the diminutive Scotsman with the white spade beard and merry eyes, none had more mixed feelings than Judge John Reed Stewart, Jr. It was a mandatory performance for nearly every public official in the county. Reed was far enough up the line to be seated in bleachers within easy viewing distance, but he considered himself fortunate that he was not required to share the central platform with Carnegie like his brother Scott, who represented the all-important Symphony Society. Reed noted that Carnegie went out of his way to say a special word to Scott, as well he might since everybody was aware that steel-blooded men like Scott Stewart had made this occasion possible. Reed had not yet settled in his own mind—perhaps never would—the nagging question as to whether a thing like this Carnegie Institute, good in itself, had not been bought at too dear a price. It had been paid for not only by the gold bonds of the U.S. Steel Corporation that had come to rest in a special vault of the Hudson Trust Company in Hoboken, New Jersey; it had also, after all, been paid for by the blood of the men killed at Homestead and of the men dying daily—fifty a year in just one plant—in the mills where tongues of fire licked always at the weary or unwary. True, Carnegie had established a fund to pay subsistence recompense to U.S. Steel workers for loss of life or limb, but he'd also literally shot down the union which might have won universal benefits and safety regulation for all the men in the industry. Reed remembered ruefully hearing that

339

Carnegie set the price of $1,500 a head on importing "hunkies," because that was the going price of a good slave just before the Civil War. Yet here was Carnegie beaming like a sunburst, speaking of freedom and opportunity, of peace and prosperity, of commerce enhancing culture. It was all a bit hard to take, and Reed did not join in the general applause when the little man handed the deed of gift to Mayor Guthrie.

While the mayor responded with the obligatory platitudes, the judge next to Reed leaned over and whispered in his ear. "Did you hear about the statues in there? Bill Frew was telling me about a big argument over whether to put some clothes on 'em or not. You know, they came over as naked as the day they were born—gods with their dinguses hanging out and what not. Saint-Gaudens and the artier types were all for preserving the purity of art, but the others on the board were shocked. Seems they put it up to old Andy who, after all, was shelling out for the whole thing. He voted for fig leaves, told Bill, 'I do hope that nothing in gallery or hall will ever give offense to the simplest man or woman. We should begin gently to lead people upward. . . .'"

Reed laughed aloud and found a number of astonished faces turned toward him. Apparently laughter was not in key with phrases rolling from the platform. But humor had once more rescued Reed from a morose state of mind when the Old Overholt with which he'd fortified himself for an ordeal was wearing off. Reed imagined that Scott had heard him, although it was impossible at this distance, and that the frown that was becoming the habitual expression of Scott's face even in repose was meant for him. The only time Reed ever saw his brother smile these days was when he was with David. He could hardly believe it, but a reliable friend had told him that he'd seen Scott and the boy in the nickelodeon and that Scott was laughing his head off. It almost sounded too human to be true, especially in light of what his mother told him about Scott apparently doing his utmost to turn David into a very proper little man ahead of his time. Imagine dressing up a seven-year-old like a banker and taking him along to lunch at the Duquesne Club! Reed's friends there thought Scott had gone a little strange, and he couldn't much blame them.

Maybe the fellow actually was snapping. Losing Benjy had to have been a blow, no matter how Scott had felt about his going over there to Siam. And this ridiculous business with May! Oh, he understood Scott's reasons, but still, if it weren't for his brother's unyielding attitude, she would be here right now, reflecting glory on all of the Stewarts. Several people had told Reed that the committee for the celebration had invited May, as the most famous artist from Pittsburgh, to give a concert in the Carnegie Music Hall. All they got by reply was a frosty and somewhat mystifying note from her manager, a Mr. Ira Goldberg, to the effect that "Miss Stewart declines to appear in Pittsburgh under any circumstances." They approached Scott, who was equally elusive. "I know nothing about it; my daughter manages her own affairs." One music critic for a Pittsburgh paper got so huffy about the situation that he devoted a column to it: "The leading female pianist in America—and possibly the world, judging from reports sent back from her recent European tour—is a young lady from this city named May Stewart, daughter of one of the famed 'Pittsburgh millionaires.' Ironically, Pittsburgh is the only place in the country where she refuses to appear. Neither she, nor her manager, a certain Mr. Ira Goldberg, will offer any explanation for this snub. We can only conclude that Miss Stewart, like so many of our industrialists, has taken her money and fled, leaving the smoky city to us black-lunged barbarians whose ears for music are supposed to be dulled by the roar of blast furnace and the jangle of the cash register. What makes this a double irony is that Miss Stewart's father, Mr. Scott S. Stewart, has for years been the leading light of the Symphony Society. But in matters musical, as in matters of business, Mr. Stewart has 'no comment.' When, oh when, will Pittsburgh's native sons, and daughters, get over their inferiority complex? When, oh when, will they come to realize that this city—birthplace of Stephen Foster, birthplace of Ethelbert Nevin, birthplace of Mary Cassatt, home of the great Carnegie Institute, home of the International Art Show, home of the Pittsburgh Symphony —is as preeminent in the arts as it is in the production of iron and steel and glass and oil? Come back, May Stewart, and test our ears!"

But May Stewart did not come back, even though she wanted to, according to Lucinda, the only person in the family who saw her regularly on her trips to New York to sell her art works. "I'd love to see Grandmother and little David and, well, Daddy too, but I won't give him the satisfaction; he's got to ask me to come, and Ira too," May told Lucinda repeatedly. Reed wished he knew the girl better, because he admired that kind of pride. After the first six months or so, May's attitude had nothing to do with the money; unfortunately she aborted, and Scott's trust fund was automatically revoked by one of its fine-point clauses. By then May's talent was so apparent to her teacher in New York that he and Ira together found backers for her, including Mary Stewart and Lucinda. Everybody but Scott was profiting from the investment now—in pride, if not in dollars. Though she and Ira were married, she played under the name of Stewart, at Ira's insistence, and friends of the family all over the country, even abroad, were writing back glowing notices of her performances. If Scott got them too, he never acknowledged them in any way.

Reed continued to be appalled at the human carnage wrought—and sincerely so—in the name of principle, and indeed had begun to consider himself fortunate to have more or less stumbled into a judicial career—at least the common law he helped to administer was not, like the Ten Commandments, carved in stone. It was a living thing, and its truths were relative. Often he could see emerging from a battle in court a kind of truth wholly different from that on which either of the parties would have staked their lives before the case evolved. Watching this process was always rewarding, whether the issue was as simple as an accident or as complicated as a contract. Occasionally Reed had been driven to try to make Scott understand the relativism of truth in terms of a case in court, and always ended up getting precisely nowhere. "A lot of legal mumbo-jumbo," Scott would say. "You should know as well as I do there's a right and wrong in every situation. Of course, if your lawyer friends admitted that, they wouldn't have any business."

Well, he did have a point there. Reed thought, but still, if only Scott weren't so certain about his positions May would probably be sitting proudly up there beside him the way Lucinda, one of the institute's better-known artists, was sitting beside another prominent member of its board, Ambassador T. Gillespie Jones. During their intimacy over the years, Lucinda had revealed to Reed and Alma nearly everything that mattered about that celebrated affair. The part Reed liked best was the ending, because it proved to him that Lucinda had indeed "grown up," as she liked to put it, and that, as the bard and his imitators put it, it was "better to have loved and lost than never to have loved at all." Feeling in a small way responsible for the events that led up to the termination of the affair, Reed was profoundly grateful for his sister's understanding attitude.

In the years immediately following Henry's death, Lucinda

continued to see Gil, rather more freely than before. They weren't exactly indiscreet, but he did begin visiting her at the Hotel Schenley. Under the circumstances—her articles on the immigrants of the South Side having been such a success, not only for her but for the *Call*—it was natural enough for the boss to be doing business with his star reporter, who now was entitled to work out of her home rather than the office. Still, people talked: the idea of a married man visiting an attractive widow was scandalous on the face of it. Once the hotel manager, already upset by the Siamese cats, tried to persuade Mrs. Schmidt in his most deferential manner that it might be pleasanter to meet Mr. Jones in the public rooms, where everything would be provided, but he was told in no uncertain terms to mind his own business. There was little else he could do since Mrs. Schmidt's brother, Mr. Scott Stewart, was an elder of his own church and a director of Carnegie Institute, and the Mr. Jones in question was the owner of one of the city's most influential newspapers. So, giving up with a sigh, the hotel manager dined out on his whispered reports of the frequency and duration of the visits Mr. Jones made to Mrs. Schmidt.

Whatever the affair did for Lucinda, it certainly made a new man out of Gil Jones. Long a caustic critic of his niece Alma's militant stand for suffrage, Gil's appreciation of a truly independent woman like Lucinda gave him new insight. His paper, much to the disgust of managing editor Johnson and his hard-boiled news staff, began supporting Alma's cause. Reed's house on Ridge Avenue was one of the few neutral spots where Gil and Lucinda could meet openly, and so they were often there. Also, as a result of long argument, Gil found himself persuaded by Judge Stewart that Theodore Roosevelt was the hope of the Republican Party, and so his paper began to push the Rough Rider long before Mark Hanna conceived the idea of putting "T.R." on ice by giving him the vice-presidential nomination in 1900. When McKinley's death brought Roosevelt into office, a grateful young President offered T. Gillespie Jones the post of Ambassador to Spain, and Lucinda never hesitated.

"Do you really want it?" she asked Gil one afternoon while they were lying in bed, relaxed by the fulfillment of their love-making.

"Well, it's new," he said. "It's a challenge—an honor to the paper and, in a way, the whole damn city."

"Then you shall have it, but you won't have me," Lucinda said.

"Why? I don't understand what you're talking about . . ."

"Really, Gil, don't be naive. It would hurt you, the party, the President, everybody, if it came out that his newest nominee for ambassador is a philanderer. Now wouldn't it?"

"It may be too late for that. Our secret isn't very well kept, you know. . . ."

"Suppose I resign from the *Call*. We could make that public enough. Then you stop seeing me. With this gossipy manager here, that would instantly get around. Then start going to church with your wife, and everybody'll know our affair—if it ever really existed—is over, that you've repented."

"Ah, Cindy, Cindy, don't talk that way. It's crazy . . . I love you. . . ."

"I love you, too, Gil, enough to want you to do this for me. I want the whole world to know what kind of a man you are—not just me, not just Pittsburgh . . ."

"But Cindy . . ."

She leaned over and closed his mouth with a slow, long kiss. "Hush," she said. "I didn't want to—but you're making me say this. If you don't take that appointment and leave me, I'll leave you. Don't you see it would be so much easier on us both with you away . . ."

"I just don't understand, Cindy. I thought you really loved me. . . ."

"Love knows when to let go, Gil. Henry taught me that. We ought to be grateful to have something good like this come along and push us . . . it's really time for you to begin acting like the grandfather you are and for both of us to realize that nothing lasts forever just because we want it to."

". . . But what will you do?"

"Oh, don't you worry about me. I've wanted for a long time now to try myself out on doing some real art. And I have another idea—one you can help me with."

"What's that?"

"I want to open a soup kitchen."

"A *what*?"

"A place, down near the Point probably, where people without enough to eat can come in and at least get a good meal—no questions asked."

Gil sat up in bed and looked at her. "For God's sake, Cindy, do you realize you'd have bums and thieves and prostitutes and Lord knows whatnot to deal with?"

"I don't care. It happens to be something I want very much to do. When I was writing that series, I saw so many hungry people. . . ."

"You can't feed all the hungry people in the world."

"No, but I can feed some of them. I'm going to do it anyway whether you help or not, Gil."

"Well, of course, I'll help. . . ."

"Good . . . and, Gil?"

"Yes?"

"Can we be friends—really good friends?"

She was too honest, and too much woman not to let down her defenses now that she'd managed the hardest part, and suddenly she sobbed, as he took her in his arms and rocked her back and forth. "Cindy, Cindy, we'll always be more than friends, my God, you know that. . . ."

Both Ambassador Jones and Lucinda Schmidt welcomed the dedication ceremonies for the institute; after more than five years it was not only possible, but even necessary, for them to meet in public and thus show the world they had nothing to hide. Mrs. Jones was there too, and although her acknowledgment of Lucinda was somewhat frosty, it was open enough to quiet any rumors that might still be floating about. Altogether a remarkable performance, Reed thought, watching them, and he wondered if Scott's frown might not have more to do with the sight of Gil and Lucinda shamelessly enjoying each other's company than with his own inappropriate laughter.

Actually Scott was scarcely aware of the presence of either his brother or sister, nor was he dwelling on the conspicuous absence of his famous daughter May, whom he'd determinedly steeled himself not to think about these past five years. He was, in fact, thinking about Henry Clay Frick. All the directors of U.S. Steel, with the notable exception of Frick, were here at the ceremonies as a polite showing of honor to Carnegie. When they were filing into their seats, Carnegie, as Reed had noticed, went out of his way to greet Scott. Then, his lively eyes searching the faces around him, he asked, "Isn't Clay Frick here, Mr. Stewart?"

"No, sir, I hear he was detained in New York on business," Scott lied. Actually, a fellow director from New York had told Scott that Frick wanted "no part of honoring that old fraud Carnegie."

"Too bad, too bad," Carnegie said. "I'd like to see him again. You know he was the best man I ever had. Wouldn't you agree, Mr. Stewart?"

"Yes, sir . . ."

"Too bad, too bad," Carnegie murmured again. "I understand you still see Mr. Frick regularly. Please give him a message that I'd like to meet with him. We live only a few blocks apart, you know, and I always believe in letting bygones be bygones."

"I'll do that, sir," Scott promised as Carnegie turned away.

He would, too; it was a commission Scott valued. While he'd agreed with Frick on the business matters that brought about the split between the two men, he did not share Frick's personal dislike of Carnegie. Scott was sure that Carnegie's amazing generosity with the money he'd made was doing as much to redeem the good name of business in the minds of the American public as his astute salesmanship had done to promote the use of Carnegie steel. True, to a coldly logical mind like Frick's Carnegie's philanthropies would appear as crazy as his business methods—a multi-million-dollar institute here, a three-hundred-dollar church organ there, a statue to peace at The Hague, a lake at Princeton University.

Scott had heard details of the last gift from his brother Reed, who kept abreast of Princeton affairs. Princeton's new president Woodrow Wilson quickly demonstrated his fitness for the job by inducing the college to give the little Scotch grammar school dropout an honorary degree in the hope that Carnegie would settle some of the millions he was giving for educational purposes on the ivied campus in New Jersey. But, much to Wilson's astonishment, all Carnegie wanted to talk about during and after the ceremonies was what he regarded as the brutalizing effects of college football—a game which had originated in a contest between Princeton and neighboring Rutgers and in which Princeton teams, along with Yale and Harvard, were still excelling. When the scholarly Wilson diplomatically avowed his sympathies with Carnegie's views, despite the fact that he had coached the "brutal" game at Wesleyan, the little steelmaker pulled a surprising rabbit out of his hat. "What you need here, Mr. Wilson," he said, "is water so that the boys can row. Rowing in my observation is the most beneficial sport for young men. If you'll permit me, I would like to give you the funds to accomplish this." So Princeton acquired an artificial lake, immortalizing Carnegie's name (mispronounced *Car*negie) for generations of her sons—and went right on playing football.

It proved to be a long time before Scott could actually deliver Carnegie's message to Frick. First, there was the long summer to get through. In a moment of weakness he'd yielded to his mother's pleading and promised to spend two whole months at Ocean City. She was content that he was doing it for his own health, but he knew that he was doing it for hers. He could never understand why, but there was something about being down by the sea that seemed to ease her arthritis—or at least lift her spirits. Unlike his mother, Scott found gazing at an empty ocean a totally unrewarding pastime, but he usually made himself stroll the boardwalk every afternoon for the sake of his liver, or whatever organ it was that benefited from light exercise. About the only thing he enjoyed was the evening or two a week when he could get a foursome together to play auction bridge. Raised as he was in the Wallace school of morality that equated card playing along with dancing and drinking as a sinful diversion, Scott came to this engrossing game late in life. In fact, he would never have touched cards at all if he hadn't been caught in the embarrassing situation of being a guest in Clay Frick's New York home when his host needed a fourth for the table. The mathematics of the game entranced him at once, and he quickly became quite good, although he could never be induced to bet—a temptation which fortunately seldom arose in the religious atmosphere of Ocean City.

In the summer of 1907, Scott insisted on one arrangement to make the Ocean City trip more interesting for him. While his brother and the maids went down as usual by train, Scott and young David and Mac, the chauffeur, drove east in the Cadillac over the newly laid-out Lincoln Highway. People told him he was crazy; an automobile might be all right around the city where there was paving, however poor, but who knew what he would run into in the rugged Alleghenies or across the long stretches of farmland in eastern Pennsylvania? After all, when a Packard called "The Old Pacific" made the first transcontinental crossing only three years before, the feat had been reported as an act of daring just short of Peary's efforts to reach the North Pole. Indeed, there were times on the trip when Scott wished he had listened to his friends. The Cadillac wheezed up the mountains at almost a walking gait, guzzling water every few miles like a thirsty horse. Tires blew out with monotonous regularity. Though they carried two spares, a patching kit and a pump, there was one awkward time when only two tires could be kept full of air, and they were embarrassingly towed to the nearest small town by a team of horses, the crippled Cadillac's nose trussed up to the rear of a wagon. There they spent two fuming days as paying guests in a farmhouse while they waited for new tires to be shipped east from Pittsburgh by rail.

But David's reaction made the whole trip worthwhile.

Every moment was a wonder to him, especially on the farm where he got his first closeup look at cows and pigs and chickens. Seeing David's fascination with animals that had simply been part of the normal scenery of his childhood, Scott realized for the first time that there was a generation, perhaps two, of city-bred Americans for whom the farm had become exotic territory. He wondered what, if anything, it might do to their thinking, for he was conscious that, undergirding all of his own adventures into the unseen and uncertain world of business and finance, was the certainty that, given a few acres, he could live off the land. But David was a boy for a new age, as he demonstrated to Scott's delight every time they went down the other side of a mountain. For these stretches of the trip, Scott would take over the wheel himself and put David beside him in the front seat. While the old chauffeur prayed under his breath, Scott would satisfy his appetite for speed. Jumping from excitement in his seat and clinging to the windscreen until his little fists turned white, David would cry, "Faster, Grandy, faster!" When they reached the bottom, man and boy would grin at each other in what to Scott was the sweetest possible form of wordless communication. . . .

Somehow the summer passed, and by the time Scott got back to his desk in September, he realized that it was none too soon. The great American money machine that had been roaring wide open ever since the turn of the century had begun to cough and sputter like his Cadillac mounting a steep grade; now it showed signs of stalling out altogether. Stocks had been falling all summer, and bonds were going begging to the extent that only $4,000,000 of a September issue of $75,000,000 by Union Pacific was subscribed. To Scott's eye, the situation seemed quite clear: like a giant blotter, something was drying up the worldwide pool of money needed to slack the thirst of the nation's ever-expanding industries. As usual in time of economic crisis, everybody had theories as to what went into the composition of the blotter. Internationally minded financiers thought it might be a delayed reaction to the expensive Russo-Japanese war; others blamed the weather, which had delayed crops that year and tied up farmers' money; still others said it had something to do with the enormous cost of rebuilding San Francisco after the earthquake. Though any or all of these could have been contributing factors, Scott was inclined to go along with his friends in the Pittsburgh business community who blamed it all on that idiot in the White House.

With his lawsuits against big business and his irresponsible statements about Wall Street, the popular Theodore Roosevelt was probably driving the money of the average American out of the market. Using the presidency as what he called a 'bully pulpit," he was preaching a sermon in which business was depicted as the devil. Railing against the "dull, purblind folly of the very rich men," Roosevelt blamed the shaky money market "upon the railway and corporation people—that is, the manipulators of railroad and other corporation stocks—who have been guilty of such scandalous irregularities during the last few years." He openly accused businessmen of having "no moral scruple of any kind whatever." With a President who talked like that, how could anyone expect the American people to display cash confidence in the economy?

Scott Stewart felt he personally had little to fear from the turn of events, sharing as he did the President's distrust of speculation—though for different reasons. Having lived through and learned from the panics of '73 and '93, he agreed with Andrew Carnegie's view that "the man who has money during a panic is the wise and valuable citizen." Indeed, over the years, Scott had listened rather carefully to Carnegie's utterances. He'd not forgotten from twenty years ago, attending commencement exercises at the Curry Commercial College in Pittsburgh, where Carnegie told the young men, "I beseech you avoid liquor, speculation and indorsement. Do not fail in either, for liquor and speculation are the Scylla and Charybdis of the young man's business sea, and indorsement his rock ahead." Scott had been laying away a good part of his fortune in savings, gold bonds, real estate, and using stocks more to keep his hand on the power throttle than as a means of personal wealth. The one piece of Carnegie advice he ignored was the little Scotchman's often quoted explanation for tying all his money up in steel—"Put all your eggs in one basket and keep an eye on the basket." In Scott's view, Carnegie had been lucky to pick the right basket. He preferred to follow the practice of his friends, the Mellons, by spreading his money widely in a variety of promising ventures. Unless the whole ship of state sank, carrying every lifeboat with it, Scott Stewart figured he was likely to remain afloat. The trick for a man sailing safely across troubled financial waters, as Scott well knew, was to keep an eye out for foundering ventures that might prove worth the effort of salvage.

By October, the storm broke with full fury. Overextended brokerage houses began closing their doors, as did some of the shakier trust companies which, permitted by law to operate on as little as two to three percent cash reserve, were unable to meet withdrawal demands from their depositors. Lines of terrified people, frantic to get their hands on their cash, formed at banks in major cities all over the country, including Pittsburgh, where the stock exchange suspended operations indefinitely. Even the solid George Westinghouse was forced out of control of his electric company, weakened by years of competition with Edison's General Electric, and now staggering under the new burden of panic. Although President Roosevelt showed supreme confidence—or indifference, or ignorance, depending on how you viewed it—by setting off to hunt bears in Louisiana, an aging J. Pierpont Morgan cut short his visit to the Episcopal Convention in Richmond to return to New York—to Scott the most disquieting sign of all. His suspicion was right, for within days the $67,000,000 Knickerbocker Trust Company went under, and the Trust Company of America was teetering. Newspapers carried reports of round-the-clock meetings of all the financial wizards of New York at the new marble library Morgan had erected on East Thirty-ninth Street to house the art treasures he'd collected in his sweeps through Europe. Daily, almost hourly bulletins were issuing from Morgan headquarters to the effect that enough money had been found to shore up this bank or that bank—and on two occasions the whole stock market. Treasury Secretary George B. Cortelyou virtually took up residence in New York to be near Morgan, and it was said that Roosevelt, back with a bearskin trophy, was at last showing real concern. It was also said that Morgan's terse comment on the President's hunt was, "I hope the first bear he meets does his duty."

On Saturday afternoon, November 2, just as Scott and David were getting back from their weekly visit to the nickelodeon, the phone rang in Scott's study. It was Henry Clay Frick calling long distance. Could Scott take the night train to New York and bring with him copies of certain papers from the steel company's files? It was a most urgent matter, of vital importance not only to the company but the country —and it was secret, so secret Frick could not risk telling him more by phone. The call couldn't have come at a worse time for Scott. The next morning the Oakland Presbyterian Church was launching its annual drive for pledges, and as the senior member of session he was scheduled to give a major address. More important, perhaps, was the fact that it was a bad time to be away from his desk, the salvage business having just begun to pick up. Only yesterday he'd managed to acquire a small building-supplies business in the South Hills when its owner, one of the McClure boys whom he'd known slightly in childhood, came to him in distress. With building at a standstill, McClure simply couldn't meet his debts, but Scott's accountant assured him that the inventory on hand, not to mention the good will of the old McClure name, was worth far more than the money at issue. So Scott owned another business and was able to do a good deed as well by hiring the distraught McClure back on salary to run it. Any moment something bigger of the same nature might come along.

"I hate to drag my feet, Mr. Frick," Scott said into the phone, "but it seems to me that Corey could bring you what you want. I . . ."

Frick exploded with what for him was a long speech. "Stewart, you don't understand how important this is. Judge Gary, who is here with me, insists that you come. We simply couldn't trust that exhibitionist Corey with a job of this kind. This isn't a matter for an iron puddler but for a diplomat; we need a man who can keep his mouth shut."

Scott knew all too well what Frick was talking about. Despite the warnings from the board of directors, Corey had not only gone ahead and married Mabelle Gilman last May but had spread every vulgar detail of the event over the press. It was a midnight ceremony in New York's Gotham Hotel, so well publicized that special details of police had to be rushed to the scene to cordon off the curious crowds. The roses for the affair alone cost $5,000, the supper $6,000. Corey paid the minister $1,000 and let everyone know that his wedding gift to his bride was a $200,000 chateau in France and that he had set aside another $250,000 to pay for their honeymoon. The press gobbled it all up and closed nearly every story with the beautiful irony that Corey's runaway marriage to Laura twenty years before had cost exactly five dollars. Well, at least from the tone of Frick's voice, Scott felt he would have another ally on the board if he took up the Corey matter again. Perhaps even Judge Gary was tilting his way. Furthermore, Frick was not a man to plead with anybody, as he seemed to be doing now, unless the matter was truly vital, so Scott said, "All right, Mr. Frick, I'll be there."

Instead of standing before his fellow church members that Sunday, November 3, Scott found himself closeted with Frick and Judge Gary in the study of Frick's Fifth Avenue home, listening to the most unbelievable financial tale he had ever heard. Moore & Schley, a prominent brokerage firm, was facing bankruptcy; if it went under, the whole stock market might collapse. Moore & Schley's problem was that it had financed the Tennessee Coal & Iron Company, taking TC & I stock as collateral and then using this stock, in turn, as collateral for its own loans. Now Moore & Schley's loans were being called. They had no money to meet them and could find no market for the TC & I stock. In this crisis, Moore & Schley, like so many other New York financiers through the past weeks, had turned to J. P. Morgan with a proposition which Morgan had relayed on Saturday to Gary, Frick and such other members of U.S. Steel's finance committee as could be rounded up in New York. The idea was for U.S. Steel to exchange $25,000,000 of its sound stock for the TC & I stock. This would shore up Moore & Schley and all the banks holding their collateral and prevent another panic on the market—if the deal could be consummated before the market opened at 10 A.M. on Monday. Though Morgan and some of the U.S. Steel directors seemed to favor it, both Gary and Frick were skeptical: if nobody else wanted TC & I, why should U.S. Steel? They wanted Scott on hand for this afternoon's meeting with Morgan not only to produce the figures to show what a bad $25,000,000 bargain might do to U.S. Steel but also to support them, if necessary, with what they knew to be his conservative skepticism.

Scott had never seen a more unlikely place for a financial conference than the famous marble library where old J. P. Morgan held court. They gathered in a great room, lined with red silk and embellished with priceless Oriental vases and statuary. But Morgan himself, arrestingly ugly with his disfiguring red nose, fixed them all with those commanding eyes and made it clear at once that business was the only order of the day. At Morgan's nod, an aide ticked off for the steel men the values of TC & I; 500 million tons of iron ore, a billion tons of coal, a Birmingham plant that could make pig iron for two dollars less a ton than its competitors. Worth $25,000,000? Morgan thought so, particularly since this was the only way he could see to shore up the market. Another failure in the market could take U.S. Steel along with it—and perhaps the country. If—but only if—the steel company would do its bit, Morgan planned later in the day to gather the trust-company presidents in this very library and demand of them a joint pool of another $25,000,000 to keep each of their banks in business. He felt certain that $50,000,000 available to both the market and the banks would blanket the fire of panic. Well gentlemen?

Scott could tell by their questions that both Gary and Frick were weakening. But he had one of his own. "Mr. Morgan, what do you think the government's attitude might be? We've been lucky so far in escaping President Roosevelt's trust-busting, but wouldn't the acquisition of such a property spur him to action?"

Several of the steel men, particularly Frick, applauded the question. Morgan seemed to agree. "Good question, Mr. Stewart," he said. "But I gather from Mr. Cortelyou that the President might be amenable to anything to stop this panic."

"I wouldn't trust Roosevelt unless I heard it from his own lips and with my own ears," Frick said.

"And frankly," Judge Gary added, "as chairman I don't think the company should pledge so much money unless we have assurances that it won't backfire. . . ."

"May I remind you, gentlemen," Morgan said, "that the deal *must* go through before 10:00 A.M. tomorrow?"

"How can we move that fast?" another asked. "I agree with Mr. Frick and Judge Gary that we ought to have some direct assurances from Roosevelt himself. I won't vote for the deal otherwise."

Morgan sighed like a schoolmaster dealing with stupid pupils. He was old, and he had a cold that caused him to be dabbing continually at his bulbous nose. He pulled a fine gold watch from his vest pocket. "It's only six P.M., gentlemen. You have sixteen hours. Go to Washington and see the President. I've done all I can."

Scott didn't know how the others felt, but he had a sudden feeling of sympathy for this ill old man who several times before, by the sheer force of his presence, had pulled the country out of financial disaster. It must indeed, Scott thought, be the power of God working within him, and he was glad when Judge Gary said, "Very well, Mr. Morgan, unless my colleagues object, we'll go through with the deal tomorrow morning, provided we can get Mr. Roosevelt's consent. We'll make every effort to that end, I assure you."

It was ten o'clock that night before Judge Gary could get through to Roosevelt's secretary, William Loeb, begging for an appointment first thing in the morning to discuss a vital but confidential matter. Loeb agreed and, by midnight, Gary, Frick and Scott were en route to Washington in a special one-car train. They were chosen as company spokesmen, partly because their own reluctance to go into the deal might prove persuasive to a skeptical President. On the train they huddled over the best way of presenting the case to Roosevelt. A great deal of the talk concerned T.R.'s mercurial personality. Though a wrong word could send Roosevelt off on a tirade about business, inevitably some of his closest associates were men of business. If Roosevelt scorned the process of making money, he apparently admired the power that came in its wake. "I wish the fellow were consistent," Frick said. "I just can't understand how he can scream about the very rich and then hobnob with the worst of the lot, Andy Carnegie, the way he does."

"I think you're a little harsh on Andy, Clay," Judge Gary said. "You know the old boy *is* good company with all of his jokes and good humor. Matter of fact, there's a Carnegie story we all ought to keep in mind when we meet the President tomorrow. The way he tells it, a visitor comes to a house and a large, barking dog rushes out at him. Just in time, he closes the garden gate against the dog, but the owner of the house calls out, 'He won't touch you. You know barking dogs never bite.' The visitor replies 'I know that, and you know it, but does the dog know it?' "

Even Frick cracked one of his small smiles at the story, and Scott was suddenly reminded of the commission Carnegie had given him. "I agree with Judge Gary, Mr. Frick," he said. "I think you would find Mr. Carnegie quite mellowed these days. The last time I saw him in Pittsburgh he asked especially to be remembered to you—in fact, he went out of his way to tell me he would like to see you again."

Frick's smile faded. "Stewart," he said, "you can tell your friend Carnegie that I will see him in hell, where we are both going."

Judge Gary laughed. "Well, nobody can accuse you of not being consistent, Clay. I just don't know, though, how you can be so sure of your destination. Now let's get back to this presentation. . . ."

They finally climbed into their berths about two in the morning, but as their special train car thundered and bounced through the night with all switches opened to its passing, Scott tossed and turned with an excitement unseemly in a 55-year-old man of affairs. But he had never yet met a President of the United States, and to do so under such tense circumstances would be an experience beyond any of his youthful dreams. He could hardly wait to get back to Pittsburgh and tell David all about it. Like millions of other boys. David idolized the Rough Rider in the White House, often pretending he was storming San Juan Hill when he rode his pony up the inclines of Schenley Park. Whatever he personally thought about Roosevelt's ineptitude, Scott was not above using this adventure as another lure in his long campaign to convince David of the rewards of serious business.

The three steel men reached the White House as soon as the gates were opened at nine and were ushered into an empty oval office by Mr. Loeb. Scott couldn't help but note in passing that this dwelling that had become a symbol of American might and prestige was far less elegant than even his own Pittsburgh home, not to mention the marbled Morgan library from which they'd just come. The impression eased his tension about meeting the President who, if he matched his surroundings, should prove far less formidable than the men he was with. Mr. Roosevelt, they were told, would join them in an hour or so, as soon as he was free. Too late, Judge Gary protested; they needed a decision before the market opened at ten. Impossible, Loeb warned, but he disappeared to take the message.

Within minutes, Roosevelt literally burst into the room. All Scott had heard and mistrusted about the Roosevelt magnetism seemed to flow through the firm grip and toothy smile with which the President greeted him. A young man in a hurry, glasses flashing as he looked from one to the other of the men before him, Roosevelt listened intently while Judge Gary gave him a version of the story they'd so carefully edited the night before: no mention of Moore & Schley by name or the fact that it was a brokerage on the grounds that T.R.'s hatred for Wall Street might influence his judgment, just their assurance that it was "an important business" in peril; heavy emphasis on how the three of them thought it was a bad bargain for U.S. Steel but were willing to take the chance for the good of the country; the vital figures brought and produced by Scott to convince the President that, even with control of TC & I, U.S. Steel's share of production wouldn't rise above sixty percent. Nonetheless it still obviously sounded fishy to the President who, in the absence of his Attorney General, sent for Secretary of State Elihu Root, one of the few corporation men in his cabinet. The steel men could almost hear the ticking of the clock as Gary repeated the whole story to Root. It was obviously a tricky business, and Root proved his fitness for diplomacy by hemming and hawing a noncommittal reaction. As tactfully as possible, Gary reminded the President of the time—9:50.

Roosevelt jumped up from behind his desk and for several

seconds stared out in silence across the White House lawn. Finally, he turned and in a voice quite unlike the tone of high, excited glee with which he normally announced decisions, said, "I don't like it. I don't like it at all, but I do not believe anyone could justly criticize me for saying that I would not feel like objecting to the purchase under the circumstances. Good day, gentlemen." And he strode out.

Within minutes, Gary was on Loeb's phone talking to New York. The news was leaked just as the market opened. Added to an agreement by the trust-company presidents that had been worked out during an all-night session in the Morgan library, it was enough to work the miracle Morgan had been hoping for. The market held steady, and the lines at tellers' windows disappeared. The panic was over. Knowledgeable financial writers gave Morgan due credit for saving the country, and Roosevelt invited this greatest of all "malefactors of great wealth" to a White House dinner. U.S. Steel was bigger than ever, and people in Pittsburgh who heard soon enough about Scott's part in it showed him a new deference. Little David Stewart was disappointed, however, to learn that the President was shorter than his Grandy.

A Roller-Coaster Ride

It was a day that had to be recorded. Tired as she was and a little more than half sick from the gallon of lemonade she must have drunk, the clouds of spun-sugar candy she had eaten, the stomach-dropping roller-coaster rides, she simply couldn't go to bed without putting something down in her diary—but what? She sat by the open window, hoping the fresh air, cooling as the June night deepened, would ease the queasiness she was trying to ignore, but the wind from the west perfumed the breeze with the rotten-egg smell of burning coal. Oh, if she could only get out of this smelly place—spend the summer again in Newport, where the stars shone every night and the wind off the sea was like a cool bath. But no . . . "We're all in the front lines, Ann," her father insisted. "If our boys can breathe poison gas, we can breathe smoke to give them the guns they need." So it would be a hot, boring summer—Mondays rolling bandages in the church basement with her mother's old cronies, Thursdays standing all day in Mrs. Schmidt's crowded little canteen down by the Point and smiling at gawky boys in uniform until her cheeks hurt, Saturdays riding all over town in that silly hay wagon with Judge Stewart's enormous wife to collect pots and pans and scraps of iron. But it all might just be bearable now that she had met the elusive David Scott Stewart, and that's why it was so important to put something down about today.

"Class picnic at Kennywood," she wrote. "Met *the* David Scott Stewart. He drove me home in his Packard. He goes to Harvard." Pen poised, she paused. Should she write more, put something in about the kiss? No need. She would remember that, and it might be too revealing if anyone ever found her diary even though she kept it locked and hidden in the jumble of underwear in her bottom drawer. If her mother ever knew about the kiss she'd have a tantrum twice as bad as the one when they got home. It was awful—right in front of David yelling and screaming about leaving the other girls (Miss Blankship had called the house to see whether she was safe, and they were about to send for the police) and about riding alone in an automobile with a boy she hardly knew. Her mother's tirade probably had more to do with the state of her stomach than anything she'd eaten, and the more she thought about it the worse she felt. What if they wouldn't let her see him again? She locked the diary, jammed it away in the drawer and ran to the bathroom to throw up.

Tooling homeward in his open car, sucking in great gulps of the Pittsburgh air that suddenly was perfumed just because she breathed it, David Stewart sang as loud as he dared. "There's a long, long trail awinding, into the land of my dreams, where the nightingale is singing and the pale moon beams. . . ." Fortunately, he could not imagine how the evening was ending for the girl whose sweet lips he had just kissed, since in David's mind girls like Ann Gillespie didn't even possess any part as crude as a stomach. All he could think of was how soon he might see her again, how early the next morning would be too early to go calling. Her mother had been pretty upset, but David had a feeling she'd settle down. After all, Grandy Stewart owned more than half of the airplane-parts factory that wore George Gillespie's proud name. Twelve o'clock would be just right, he decided, right after church. He'd go with a dozen roses—no, two dozen, one for Mrs. Gillespie. He'd polish up the Packard, wear his best blazer and ice-cream pants, and the new boater with the Harvard crimson band. They couldn't turn him away then— ". . . Till the day that I'll be going down that long, long trail with you." Oh, how he hoped that song would come true!

The only thing wrong, if there could be anything wrong with a perfect night, was that he owed it all to Howie Timmins. The whole thing had been a typical Timmins show-off trick, but at least he'd gotten even by stranding Howie out there. He smiled now at the thought of how mad Howie must have been riding back in the streetcar with all those giggling girls and knowing that he, David, was making time with Ann, the prettiest of the lot. Still, he owed Howie something—he would never in the world have gone out to Kennywood if Howie hadn't almost shamed him into it.

"Listen, you're in Harvard now. You can't be afraid of girls all your life," Howie had said. "C'mon, it's Saturday night, and you've got that swell car. Let's go and pick up a couple of babes."

"Where? You can't just roam the streets."

"Kennywood," Howie said. "There's always a lot of girls on the loose out there."

So David gave in, mostly because it was easier than arguing with Howie. For all of his life, or all of it he could remember, Howie had been his friend, almost his only friend, not so much because they really liked each other but because Howie, being the son of the minister, was acceptable to Grandy Stewart. What David had to offer Howie was obvious—a taste of the princely life: horses, and later cars, to ride; silk sheets to sleep between; a court for tennis and a pool for swimming; chauffeured trips downtown to the nickelodeon and, later, the burlesque. What Howie had to offer David was the exciting bustle of a house full of children—Howie was the oldest of five, two boys and three girls—and a vicarious sex life. A blond giant who would have been handsome except for the nose he broke playing fullback on the Shadyside team, Howie was, by his own account, irresistible to females. He had matured far earlier than David, getting fuzz down there and being able to masturbate by the time he was twelve. When he was fourteen, Howie was whetting David's appetite with tales of "going all the way" with Katie, the Stewarts' upstairs maid. Though David didn't know whether to believe him or not, he did notice that Katie giggled and blushed a lot whenever Howie was around. At school dances where David literally hid behind potted palms or smoked cigarettes in the boys' room to avoid having to ask some haughty girl to stumble through a tango with him, Howie was always the star of the show, doing the sinuous steps with the best-looking girl as if he'd been born in Rio. Shy David at once envied and hated Howie, and he was glad when Howie decided to go to Princeton instead of Harvard so that at least he could be left at peace with his non-existent love life.

It wasn't that David was not interested in girls—indeed, at times his interest was almost consuming. For years he had actually enjoyed going to church, because the Stewart pew was just two rows behind the one in which a lovely creature with piles of dark hair and long dark lashes by the name of Mary Louise McIntire was forced to sit, as he was, every Sunday. While the service droned on, David would study every detail of every part of Mary Louise he could see and imagine most vividly the rest. Too slight and too solitary for football or baseball, David elected track as his compulsory sport, and on soft spring evenings he would run through the neighborhood, ostensibly to get into condition but actually to pass the McIntire house in hopes of getting a glimpse of Mary Louise. But the idea of ever talking to her paralyzed him; he could just tell from the lift of her chin and the tilt of her nose and the knowing smiles she exchanged with the girl friends who often accompanied her to church that she would have nothing but scorn for a pudge of a boy who, until a sudden spurt of growth hit him in senior year, barely came up to her nose. When occasionally they were thrown together while Granny and Grandy Stewart stopped to chat with the McIntires at the church door, David would stand in furiously blushing silence, looking everywhere but at her. So, aside from Howie's tales, what little he knew, or thought he knew, about girls came from voracious reading. Bright and precocious, David had learned to read for want of anything better to do on those long, dull Saturday mornings in Grandy Stewart's office. He devoured everything he could get his hands on from the classics to the latest dime novel, but his particular treasure was a thick volume on anatomy inscribed, "Property of Dr. John Reed Stewart," which he found in Grandy Stewart's library and which he kept hidden under the mattress of his bed. The language was turgid, but it contained neat and explicit diagrams of all those female organs.

What David didn't know was that he had become an object of considerable interest and pique to most of the girls who had a chance to see him. Tall enough by the time he was sixteen, with the lithe body of a runner, dark curly hair and brows, nearly black eyes and the square Stewart jaw, he could have modeled for the clean-cut, handsome young men Charles Dana Gibson had depicted as a kind of American standard. Not the least of his charms was a shy aloofness that was naturally mistaken for an air of proud superiority. He was widely thought by both boys and girls to be "stuck up," but it was conceded that he had a right to such an attitude what with his good looks and all that money. As if that weren't enough, he had the highest grades in his Shadyside class and could play the ukulele and sing like a professional. As the star in the senior show, he broke every feminine heart in the audience with his rendition of "Indian Love Call." This was the boy Ann Gillespie so tersely described in her diary as "*the* David Scott Stewart," the attractive young man every girl in the area was dying to know.

A great deal of David's shyness derived from his long, secret shame at being an "orphan." He first heard the word under the worst kind of circumstances when he was four or five; his shrill little cousin, Sarah McCandless, thinking it was bad, used it to taunt him. "A poor little orphan, that's what you are," she hissed at him. "I know because Mother says you are." By the time he got old enough to look the word up in a dictionary, it was too late to undo the emotional damage of worrying about being odd. Anyway, the sad fact was that he didn't have parents like the other children, and the way his old grandfather dressed him up and took him downtown for years before he was old enough to wriggle out of it was considered funny by them. So David crawled into himself. Hidden in his drawer was a box of letters—all the letters his parents had written home, which his great-grandmother had saved for him. When he was feeling blue he would read them over and over and try to imagine what they had been like, and what their life had been like out there in the jungles of Siam. It sounded romantic, but it was hard to boast about them since most of the boys he knew thought of missionaries as little old ladies who made boring talks in Sunday school. For the longest time he wished his father had stayed home and made money like other fathers so he wouldn't have to be different.

Then there was that business about his Aunt May. For

years he didn't know exactly what had happened—people stopped talking about her if he was around—but he was aware that everybody in town thought it queer the way she'd suddenly left home and refused to come back. When he was old enough to realize how famous she was, David too thought it strange that Grandy, who was so interested in music, never even talked about her, and he was frightened the way the old man's face flushed and the muscles in his cheeks stood out when he once asked about her. "Don't mention her name to me again, David," was all Grandy said. Even when she died, Grandy didn't want to talk about her, although David briefly became a hero in school when the news was spread all over the papers about how his Aunt May and her husband or manager or whatever he was, a man named Ira Goldberg, acted when the *Titanic* went down. The Pittsburgh papers sent reporters all the way to New York to interview survivors and get all of the details. May and Ira were coming back from a concert trip in Europe that spring of 1912 in what was supposed to be the finest, safest ship ever built. When she struck an iceberg and began to list, panic started spreading rapidly. Although they were only booked as passengers and not entertainers, May and Ira went to one of the salons where there was a grand piano and commenced to play. Some remembered the lilt of Ira's violin as the most bitter-sweet sound they'd ever heard. Through all the milling and screaming and struggle to get into boats, their music went on— not sad music, but gay Strauss waltzes and tender love songs. Even after the lights went out, the sound continued, drifting eerily out to the boats that were pulling away across the cold, dark water. Some few others had gathered there in the salon to listen—how many, nobody knew for sure. It was certain, though, that May and Ira had done all they could to take the sting out of death for themselves and for whatever other souls responded to their playing. Even the bitter music columnist who once had so berated May for not coming to Pittsburgh wrote feelingly, "All is forgiven, May Stewart. May the good Lord bless you, and keep you."

Somebody suggested a memorial service for May and Ira in the Oakland Presbyterian Church, but elder Scott Stewart vetoed the idea, refusing to give an explanation. When the news got around, many in the congregation were shocked by Elder Stewart's intransigence, though nearly all, admiring him as a man of principle, accepted that he must have his reasons.

Only David knew, or felt he did, what that principle might

have cost his grandfather. He made the discovery much later, just the summer before he left for Harvard, when he was rummaging around for something in his grandfather's desk in the study. In the very back of one drawer he found a packet, tied tightly in the frayed twine his grandfather was always saving from packages that came to the house. It was a collection of programs for concerts featuring May Stewart and a sheaf of clippings about her heroism on the *Titanic*. The string had been tied and untied, the papers fingered many times. Though David was surprised, he was pleased, too, by such a trove. Like most people, he felt a sense of awe, almost fear, at his grandfather's rigid, silent presence. All those Saturdays at the office and the movies, all those wild automobile rides and the barking golf lessons Grandy was now giving him, all those Sundays when they sat silently side by side in church had not really made him feel at ease with the old man. Knowing he was heir to all Scott Stewart was amassing only made it worse because it meant living up to the image of shrewdness, sobriety, piety and self-control Grandy Stewart projected by example more than words. But there was hope in that little packet in the old man's drawer; perhaps behind his grandy's austere facade there was a man nobody really knew.

When he thought about it, David had to admit that he had always been able to get nearly anything he wanted out of his austere grandfather. It went all the way from little things like keeping George in his bedroom even though Grandy, raised on a farm, thought the place for a dog was the stables, to really big things like going to Harvard, which Grandy declared a "godless place" compared to Presbyterian Princeton. Sometimes he thought other people could do just as well with the old man if they tried hard enough; it always amused, and depressed, him to see how the clerks and girls in the office kept their heads down and hustled around like mice whenever Mr. Stewart appeared. Of course, David had learned almost instinctively that you had to lose battles to win the war with Grandy—by sitting quietly through those hours at the office, he could get to the movies; by going along to all the services on Sunday, he could get permission to ride his horse in the park in between; by wearing a hat, he could go downtown . . . he had come out bareheaded one hot summer day to get into the car and ride into the city with his grandfather. "Don't move," Grandy told Mac, "We're not going anywhere." "Why not, Grandy?" "A gentleman doesn't go to town without a hat." "But it's hot." "You have

362

the straw I bought for you, don't you?" David sighed, went back and got the hat, and that was the end of it; Grandy didn't even force him to lie about where he was going—to meet Howie and take in the matinee of the new burlesque. Now David was following the same pattern this summer by taking the job his grandy had found for him at the steel company as a kind of quid pro quo for the permission to go to Harvard.

It was a pretty unexciting thing to have to do at a time like this. As soon as Howie jumped into his car and they started for Kennywood, they began talking about the war. It was almost the only subject of conversation for everybody that summer of '17. "I'm going to enlist," Howie said. "I got my old man to agree to sign my papers at dinner tonight."

"How?"

"Easy, I just told him if he didn't I'd run away and join the ambulance service like a lot of other guys at Princeton. Well, he shrugged and said he thought I'd be better off getting some training as a soldier than doing that. Why don't you come with me, Davey?"

"Oh, I can't. My grandfather would never sign my papers. . . ."

"You could lie about your age."

". . . And anyway I'm working for the steel company this summer, which everybody says is as good as being in the front lines. . . ."

"Doing what, for God's sake—learning to be a salesman? You call that war work?"

"Well, that's the way I thought, too," David said, "but they did a pretty good job of convincing me how important it is. You know the mills have been going all out for three years now, sending stuff to the Allies, and now that we're in, the orders are piling even higher. The thing is, if a company invests all that money in building new capacity, it'll go under after the war unless it sells more stuff. So, you see, by selling we're really making it possible for the company to do its part. . . ."

"I don't understand all that," Howie said. "All you're telling me is that the company wants to have its cake and eat it, too. Okay for all those dumb bohunks to go out and get gassed and shot, but we're not going to risk a dollar of profit."

"Have it your own way," David said. "At least I'm doing *something*. If I were just old enough . . ."

"You're as old as me, buddy. Maybe you just don't have the guts . . ."

That hurt. Howie was always accusing him of not having guts. First it was football; then it was chasing girls; now it was going to war. They rode on in silence until they raised the fairyland of lights that was Kennywood Park. As they went through the gates, it was easy enough to leave the war behind. The only sign that America had been locked since April in the struggle to "save the world for democracy," as President Wilson put it, was a scattering of uniforms among the gay crowds and the new tunes like "Over There" and "You're in the Army Now" that the organist at the skating rink was weaving into his medley of old favorites. There were a lot of girls in their white summer dresses, and all of them looked pretty in the kaleidoscopic effect of the whirling colored lights from the merry-go-round and the great white circle of the ferris wheel. But Howie, the great lover, disdainfully passed most of them by, commenting on a thick ankle here, a pimple there, a fat rear end yonder, until he spied a group of girls waiting at the ticket gate of the roller coaster.

"Now, there's some good lookers," he said to David. "Which one d'you like? You pick her out, and old Uncle Howie'll see that you get her."

The girls did look good, but then it was darker where they were standing, with only the weak bulbs above the ticket booth and a faint yellow light where you went into the roller coaster cars to cut the blackness. To David, one girl seemed to stand out, maybe because she was so petite. Everything about her was almost doll-sized, from the tiny ankles revealed by the new short skirt she was wearing to her daringly bobbed ash-blonde head. But if she were a doll, she was obviously wound up with a powerful spring. She seemed to be in continual motion, gesturing with her hands, turning inquiringly from this girl to that, tapping impatiently with her little feet, changing her expression from frown to smile to pout to ponder like a blinking light. Instantly, David decided that if he had to go through with it at all, that was the girl—at least she was comfortably shorter than he, and it looked as though she was the kind who would do all the talking.

"The blonde," David said, "the little one with the bobbed hair."

"Shucks, that's the one I wanted," Howie grumbled. "But all right, I promised. Stay here—I'll be back with the goods."

While David watched, Howie sauntered up to the girls and

began talking to them. It was only when a girl whose back had been to them turned her head that David knew he was a victim of one of Howie's tricks. Even by her dim profile, he could recognize the girl at once as Howie's younger sister. So this must be the Ellis senior picnic, and Howie had known the girls would be there all along. Howie was back in minutes with the little blonde, whom he introduced as Ann Gillespie, and another stranger to David, Frannie Armbruster. No mention of his sister or Ellis—just a couple of "babes" he had picked up for them. David went along with the gag and, not knowing quite how to respond when Ann asked, "Are you really *the* David Scott Stewart," proposed a roller-coaster ride. The roller coaster was the one thing in the park David loved, indulging as it did his delight in speed, though from time to time some foolish rider who stood up in a car was pitched to his death and an occasional faulty mechanism had been known to send a whole train hurtling to destruction.

"Oh, but I'm afraid," Ann said, running through several contradictory changes of expression in seconds. "We were all just standing there arguing whether to go when Howie came up. I thought I could get out of it by meeting you."

David didn't have to act too much to seem crestfallen. "Oh, so that's the only reason. . . ."

Ann seized his hand, and suddenly David felt as though all the electricity in her small dynamo of a body had shot up his arm and across his chest. "Oh, no, David. I didn't mean that. I was just kidding," she said, "but I thought maybe you'd want to skate or something. . . ."

"No, I really like the roller coaster," David said. "C'mon, you'll like it, too. You aren't really scared, are you? I'll see that you don't fall out."

"Well . . ."

"Oh, c'mon," he urged, and taking her hand, began leading her back toward the ticket booth. She resisted just enough, not too much. Howie and Frannie hadn't followed them and that seemed to worry her most, once they were strapped into their seat. "I wonder where they are," she kept saying. "I wonder where they are. . . ." From the look on her face and this kind of chatter, David realized that she really was scared. As the car started chugging up the first grade, he managed with uncharacteristic bravado to put his arm around her thin waist and say, "Don't worry, Ann, I'll hold you. . . ."

The car went over the first rise, down an easy grade and a jerk around the curve at the bottom to climb the next hill. David's arm automatically tightened around her waist. Ann shot him a glance with just a hint of "this *could* be fun" in it as they went up and over the first big drop and the car seemed to fall right out from under them as their bodies strained into the strap and their stomachs rose to their throats. Down, down, down and the whip around and up, up, up and over and down, down, down again. No time now to talk or laugh or do anything but scream with the rest, David holding her so close he could feel her whole tense body along the length of his. And then the last big dip, the pause at the top and the great slide down into the unknown dark and the slow coast back into the yellow light where they had started. When the ride was all over and he could really look at her, David saw that Ann's eyes were shining and realized that he was still holding onto her for dear life. "Oh, David," she said, "let's do it again."

Then and there, David fell into love, as surely as the roller coaster fell over the next hill. They rode it for hours, shifting forward until they were in the first car where they would get the biggest thrill. Finally, when the man who managed the ride asked them to get off and give other people a chance, they did—staggering away, a little sick and dizzy, but deliciously happy. By then they didn't know where Howie was or the rest of the girls or the harried Miss Blankship. When they were trying to decide what to do next, David said, "C'mon, I'll drive you home in my car." Ann was a little worried: What about Miss Blankship? What about the other girls? What about Howie? David, exhilarated by the rides and by the fortuitous closeness to Ann, said, "To hell with them all, c'mon." And she went.

All through the ride home Ann bubbled about how swell the car was, how great a driver David was, how much fun it was to give the other girls, not to mention Miss Blankship and Howie, the slip. Then, out of the blue, she asked the question that was everywhere in the air. "What are you going to do about the war, David?"

Not knowing her sentiments but suspecting that all girls loved a hero, he had an inspiration. "Well, I'd like to be a flyer. . . ."

"Oh, David, that's you all over. I can just see from the way you loved that roller coaster and the way you drive . . ."

"Except I'm too young," he interrupted.

"But lots of boys your age—I mean, Howie's going in, you know—you just get your father . . . Oh, I forgot . . . well, your grandfather, I guess he is . . . to . . ."

"He never would."

"Well, you can lie about your age. Lots of boys do."

"You think I should do that?"

"Well, I'd be—I mean, everybody'd be—so proud of you. And wouldn't it be fun—up there in the clouds and diving down?"

"Yes, I guess it would . . . I guess that's why I want to . . ."

"Oh, do, David! I just wish I were a boy and could do it too. Oh, that roller coaster was so much fun, except I feel a little sick. . . ."

David choose to ignore her last remark. He didn't like the idea of Ann's feeling sick when all he could think about was how to kiss her, and the idea of Ann's being human enough to be sick and girl enough to be kissed just didn't go together in his mind. He knew he shouldn't even think about kissing her. After all, he'd just met her and she came from good people, but he was determined not to go back to Howie, ever again, and have to confess that "nothing happened." When they pulled up in front of her house, she didn't scramble to get out but just sat there, and her face like a milky moon against the darkness around them just seemed to swim up and swim up until it was meeting his—unhappily nose to nose. "Not that way," she giggled and wriggled until their mouths were coming together, warm on warm. Then, abruptly, she pulled away. "I've got to go in—I think Mother's up," she said.

Mother was, indeed, up, meeting them at the open door as David escorted her up the path and screaming maledictions over what they had done to Miss Blankship, to the class and to Ann's honor. On his way home, David was relying upon the fact that Mrs. Gillespie, in her excitement, had not quite got the drift of his name, which did seem to have its advantages. Especially, in this case, with Ann's father. At the Gillespie breakfast table next morning, while waiting for his daughter to appear, George Gillespie said to his wife, "Be reasonable, Maggie. As far as we know he's a perfectly nice boy, and his grandfather is our . . ."

"I know, you're going to say boss, George, and I hate to hear you talk like that. Just because he's the major stockholder doesn't mean he's your boss. Without you, there wouldn't be any company. After all, you invented . . ."

"All right, all right, that isn't the point. In fact, I don't know what the point is. So the girl rode home instead . . ."

"Now, George, stop trying to act stupid," Maggie said.

"You know very well what the point is—it's our daughter's reputation."

"Well, if she has to lose it, it couldn't be with a better boy. Do you know what that young fella's worth?"

"No, it can't be so much. Scott Stewart has a big house but . . ."

"So much? Ye Gods, it's got to be fifty million he stands to inherit now, and with the way things are booming in this war, who knows how much more?"

"Oh . . ."

"Yes, oh . . . What's more he's a darn good-looking kid. I don't blame Ann for . . ."

"Now, George, they aren't married yet."

"I know, I know. I'm just saying you ought to stay the hell out of their way."

"That's all right for you to say, but I'm her mother, and I'm responsible for . . . Well, what if this boy is like his aunt —you know, the one that got mixed up with your cousin Gil?"

"Oh, for heaven's sake, Maggie, that was a whole generation ago."

"But you know they say it sometimes runs in the blood. I wonder if we should be letting Ann spend so much time down at the canteen—the woman's probably a bad influence."

"You can't keep the girl under lock and key. How do we know all that stuff about cousin Gil wasn't just gossip? Anyway, they say Mrs. Schmidt's doing a bang-up job for our boys . . ."

"Hush, George, she's coming down now."

The Gillespies didn't actually welcome David with open arms, keeping the stiff formality considered proper between generations and between the parents of a pretty, vulnerable girl and the boy who was out to do God knew what to her, but they did offer him the hospitality of the house. Mrs. Gillespie was really touched by the roses, and impulsively she invited him to stay to Sunday dinner. He was a handsome boy, she realized as she watched him, his dark skin— evidently inherited from his grandmother, who'd died so young, poor thing—glowing with the blood that excitement brought to his face, his dark eyes attending every move Ann made. Ann deftly kept the conversation going by playing on her father's interest in airplanes—he made the parts— and David's passion to fly. "Gosh, you know," her father said, "I don't mind making a dollar giving them what they need, but I sure wouldn't go up in one of those kites. I admire your nerve, young fella."

David ducked his head and muttered, "Well, they haven't taken me yet."

"What's your grandfather think about it?"

"I . . . I haven't asked him. I just made up my mind . . ."

"Well, if I know old Scott Stewart, he wouldn't have any truck with anything as foolish as flying. Didn't he tell me you were working at the steel company?"

"Yes."

"Good. If I were you, young man, I'd stick to it. As I tell Ann, we're all in the front lines here."

David caught a "you-know-these-old-fogies" wink from Ann that made him feel good all over. After dinner he proposed a ride. Mrs. Gillespie started to object until she saw her husband's frown. Out in the car Ann said, "Phew, I'm glad that's over. I think they like you, David. Those roses were a wonder."

"I hope so. Where shall we go?"

"There's a little place up in Schenley Park I know. I'll show you."

Following her directions, David brought the car to a rest on a spur off the main road, where they were alone in a green bower of trees. Ann turned to him with an odd little smile that revealed teeth white and perfect as pearls to his eyes, and said, "I hope you don't think I'm forward if I ask you to kiss me again. I thought I liked it last night, but I was a little sick, you see . . . and I . . . I want to be sure."

Though he was already sure, David was only too happy to oblige again—and again and again. In between kisses they mostly sighed, neither of them certain of what the occasion demanded in the way of speech or other activity. For David, kissing was enough, almost too much. He inhaled her powdery fragrance, felt the bones of the corset at her waist and, above them, accidentally as they twisted for a more comfortable position, the yielding cone of her breast. He was embarrassingly aroused, and he kept thinking, if only Howie could see me now. Finally when they broke for air, David had the courage to ask, "Are you sure now?"

"Oh, yes," Ann said. "Oh, yes."

She stretched and settled back against her side of the seat with the grace of a small kitten. "Do you smoke cigarettes, David?" she asked.

"Sometimes . . ."

"Would you have any with you? Would it shock you if I smoked a cigarette?"

"Oh, no, my Great-aunt Lucinda smokes them all the time," he said, searching his pockets and then the pockets of the car.

"Yes, I know. I work down at the canteen sometimes," Ann said. "She's sort of a wild one, isn't she? But she's the nicest Stewart I've met—until now."

Luckily, David found part of a pack and lit one for both of them. They sat back, puffing away contentedly, David feeling he was at last a true man of the world.

Suddenly Ann giggled and said, "I bet I do shock you, David, don't I?"

"Why?"

"Oh, with my bobbed hair and smoking cigarettes and asking you to kiss me. I do shock you, don't I?"

"No, I like you. I like you this way. You're the first girl I've ever . . ."

"Are you going to say I'm the first girl you've ever kissed?"

"Well, truthfully, yes . . ."

"Why, David Stewart! I'd call you a liar if you didn't look so honest—and if you hadn't bumped my nose last night."

"Is it bad that I . . . ?"

"Oh, no, I love it! You're so cute and, well, pure."

"But I'm not your first . . ."

She went off into a tinkling laugh. "Oh, no. The first in Pittsburgh . . . But in Newport . . . those Eastern men are so fast. . . ."

David was consumed with instant hatred for "those Eastern men." He knew the type. They disgusted him at Harvard when they talked as if they had marbles in their mouths, like this silly Uncle Wilbur Curry who had married Tillie Sharp, and they boasted about the French girls they'd had when they were on the "grand tour" with their families and about the fat strippers from the Old Howard who'd go around the world for a fiver and a bottle of champagne. Hearing them talk tarnished all his bright dreams of sex—dreams of finding and cherishing a girl as intricate and jeweled and clean and precious as a Swiss watch. Now that he had found her, he was terrified that some heavy-handed lecher had already toyed with her delicate works. He had to know.

"Did they? I mean . . . did you?"

Ann's mobile face assumed a defiant pout, eyes away and downward. "Why, David Stewart, how could you? Whatever is in that mind of yours? I just said I was kissed. I am seventeen, you know."

David was instantly contrite. "I didn't mean anything, Ann. Honest, I didn't. I just had to ask, because . . . well, I don't want anybody else kissing you . . . I . . . well, look, Ann, would you be my girl?"

The pout evaporated, and Ann was all bright teeth and dancing eyes again. "Oh, David, this *is* so sudden. But Daddy won't take us back to Newport, and I'm stuck in this town. . . ."

"Then you will?"

"I didn't say . . . how can I promise when you're going off to be a flier . . . ?"

"I don't have to," he assured her quickly. "I'm doing essential work, you heard your father."

"Oh, but David, I wouldn't want to stand in your way. You'd hate me for it. And, besides, I think I could love a flier, especially one . . . who can kiss like you. . . ."

David skinned into the house just in time to go to evening service with Grandy. He thought it was the politic thing to do since he had made up his mind to endure one of those man-to-man conferences in the study right after church. What had begun as a spur-of-the-moment invention to impress a pretty girl had become in less than twenty-four hours a burning conviction. He had thought from time to time of flying, more for the possible fun of it than as a way of service. Now he had to go, or become a fool—or, worse, a coward—in the eyes of the girl with whom he had fallen head over heels in love. He needed to get Grandy, his legal guardian, to sign his papers, and all through church he kept rehearsing possible arguments. He might begin with their shared love of speed, but he doubted that it would prove convincing. Maybe it would be better to lean on patriotism, although Grandy's terse comments on the war didn't offer too much hope in that direction. Indeed, Grandy had voted Democratic in '16 for the first time in his life because he thought Wilson was doing his utmost to keep America neutral. He fumed about the nation's most prominent Republican—"that damned cowboy"—who was going around making bellicose speeches. But now that America was in it, Scott S. Stewart, as the leading businessman in the Liberty Bond drive, had been issuing public statements that could be set to an Irving Berlin tune. Other Stewarts were doing their part too. Aunt Alma with her big hats and a bust like the mainsail of a square-rigger had given up marching for women's rights to ride around in her hay wagon to dramatize the need for scrap; though he was over age at forty-two, cousin Dr. Stewart Sharp had chucked his lucrative practice to sign on as an army doctor because "the boys will need more help with their heads than their bodies once they get to those trenches"; Great-aunt Lucinda had expanded her three-day-a-week soup kitchen for the poor into a seven-day-a-week canteen for traveling servicemen stranded in the city; cousin Tom Mc-Candless, who was twenty-one, was already in officer-candidate school. . . . Wouldn't it look bad if David took shelter in the steel company? Surely Grandy could see that.

The Reverend Doctor Timmins was a big help. Maybe because he had just been forced to sign Howie's papers he chose that evening for a ringing sermon about the heroic young men going forth on a Christian crusade against the devilish Huns. Forgetting that a quarter of his congregation were German or part German like his leading elder, Scott Shallenberger Stewart, he waxed eloquent about the atrocities committed in Belgium and elsewhere by steel-helmeted swine who skewered little girls on their bayonets. In this fateful hour, he declared, no true Christian could stand aside. He himself would go, he announced, if it weren't for his age and responsibility for so many young Timminses, but he was proud to announce that his oldest son, Howard, though only seventeen, had elected to enlist in "the armies of the Lord." At the close, Dr. Timmins brought the congregation to its feet with a rousing rendition of "Onward Christian soldiers, marching as to war, with the cross of Jesus marching on before; Christ, the royal master, leads against the foe; onward into battle with His banners go. . . ."

David blessed the minister. No use waiting for a conference in the study. On the way home in the Cadillac he said, "Did you hear Howie is enlisting, Grandy?"

"Yes," Scott replied. "I told that fool Timmins I could get Howie a job in the steel company, same as yourself."

"But I want to go too."

Scott swerved the car over to the curb, shut off the engine and turned to David. "I don't want to hear any such nonsense from you, young man."

"But you heard Dr. Timmins. He said a Christian had to . . ."

"And I just said he's a fool. He forgets that this country wouldn't have any strength at all if it weren't for people like ourselves right here in Pittsburgh who make the weapons, not to mention pay the bills. Why, did you know your Uncle

Clay Frick is the biggest subscriber to war bonds in the country—a million and a half, they say? No, old Judge Mellon had it right when he made his sons stay out of the Civil War —and that was a war with a real cause, freeing the slaves. Why, even Andy Carnegie bought himself a substitute then and thought nothing of it. I want you to understand this, David—I'm not raising you to be cannon fodder."

"But the rest of them—cousin Stewart and cousin Tom . . ."

"I don't care what the rest of them do," Scott said. "You are the one who stands to inherit all that I have built, and you are the one who must acquire the sense of responsibility that such a legacy demands. There are plenty of penniless young men who can go out and get themselves shot if they want to. There is only one David Scott Stewart."

"I wish . . . my dad were still alive. I bet he . . ."

"David! Don't talk like that. You're all fired up by that sermon. I've a mind to talk to Timmins—"

Desperately, David tried the other tack. "Really, the thing is, Grandy, I want to learn to fly. You know yourself how great it is to go at top speed . . ."

"That's worse than joining the army. Get yourself killed for nothing in one of those flimsy machines. I won't hear of it. Now, you get your mind on business, young man. In fact, if you really want to be patriotic, you could forgo Harvard until—"

The box was closing tighter than he'd imagined. "Oh no, I couldn't do that, Grandy, you said yourself I need an education these days to . . ."

"Well, I suppose you're right. Maybe now that we're in it this will all blow over by the end of summer."

With a grinding of gears, Scott thrust the automobile into action and drove the rest of the way home at a speed so breakneck that in itself it was threat to life and limb, though David didn't think it tactful to mention it. He told Ann all about the interview and promised he would run off and lie about his age as soon as he got back to Boston, where nobody knew him. Meanwhile, as Ann herself admitted, it did give them a summer together . . . a summer full of picnics and kisses and hungrily exchanging thoughts made even more exciting to both of them by the fact that they'd grown up as "only" children. One night when Ann's parents were out, they got tipsy on some gin she found in her father's cabinet and poured into their lemonade. She let him unbutton her blouse and slip a hand in under her chemise and fondle the tiny breasts that stood rigid to his touch. They both felt

deliciously wicked and sighed about how terrible it was that
they were so young and couldn't . . . shouldn't . . .
When he left for Boston, they promised to write every day.
Her mother, who couldn't bear to lose her "only" was using
the war to make her stay home and go to Pennsylvania
College for Women (PCW) instead of East to college the
way she wanted to. But David swore that once he got his
wings and money of his own, he would take her away from
this smelly old town.

A Night Train to New York

"Only at weddings and funerals—it's the only time we ever
see your family," Alma said as they were dressing. "I thought
maybe as we all grew older . . . You know, I miss those
Christmas dinners. Being an only child, I rather thought it
would be fun marrying into a big family. . . ."

"Speak for yourself," Reed said. "I'm just as glad it's
worked out this way. We still see Lucinda and Mother, and
that's all I care—"

"Oh, come now, Reed, Scott isn't the ogre you all make
him out to be. If he were, this boy couldn't have possibly
turned out the way he has. We wouldn't even be going to
this wedding."

"I wouldn't say that exactly. . . ."

"What?"

"Well, I didn't want to say anything," Reed began, grunting
as he tried to make the end of the striped pants he hadn't
worn for years meet across a growing paunch. . . . "Dammit,
why did they have to go and stipulate morning dress?"

"Because that's proper for a daytime wedding, and this is
a *very* proper wedding. It's Maggie Gillespie's only child, you
know, her only chance. But what were you going to say?"

"Well, as I understand it, Scott actually marched down to his attorney's office the day after he heard David signed up and damn near disinherited him. Old Shaw denies it—after all, he's his lawyer—but the gossip at the club is that Shaw had a time persuading Scott to hold off."

Alma, who liked Scott's crustiness, reminded Reed that his older brother had, after all, already lost one son to a war of sorts, not to mention a daughter whose death must have left him feeling guilty whether he admitted it or not. And now the thought of losing David, who was more a son to him than Benjy had ever been, obviously angered and terrified him and he was showing it the only way he knew how. Reed acknowledged that she might indeed have something there.

"I might indeed," she said, "and now, I'd appreciate it if you'd hook me up." As he proceeded to fumble his way to compliance, she said, "Reed, I want you to promise me . . ."

"I know. I know. Don't drink too much," Reed said impatiently. "When have I ever embarrassed you? I will say, though, I thank God the Gillespies are Episcopalians. There at least ought to be champagne."

Alma was fitting a helmetlike hat to the hair she had cropped short to prove she was still in the front of the women's movement. The effect wasn't exactly a success; a smaller head tending to emphasize the formidable size of the rest of her. "Hurry up," she said, "a wedding's one thing you can't be late to."

"Right with you, love," Reed said. "Just one last crack at the crock." He disappeared into the bathroom, where he fished out a flask of Old Overholt he kept hidden behind his shaving things and took a couple of ample swallows. He didn't much like the looks of the face he saw in the mirror. Now that his hair had turned white, which was probably all right in a man of fifty-five, there was a perpetually ruddy cast to his skin, and a little booze seemed to turn the old scar into a near scarlet gash. Oh, to hell with it. If Alma could get fat, he could get flushed. He wished, though, she'd stop being after him about the drinking. He didn't embarrass her or anybody else except in the eyes of the WCTU or his brother Scott, who reacted as though a single drink was enough to grease the gates of hell. A great deal of experience had made him very adept at knowing just how far he could go, had to go, to ease the perpetual knot in his belly without actually losing control. Everybody knew that at least one reason Reed Stewart was returned to the bench again and again was because he was such a "good fellow" despite some of his unorthodox rulings, and wasn't it drinking with other good fellows that made you a good fellow? Actually, Alma was a good enough politician herself to understand this, and it was really only when they were going out to mingle with church people or his family that she nagged him. And Reed never teased her about her public appearances, even that time back in '12 when she rode in the special women's cavalry group at the head of the suffragette parade right down Fifth Avenue in New York.

That was one the kids absolutely refused to go to, and he couldn't blame them. He was secretly amused, in fact, at the way his Carolyn had turned into a little earth mother with four kids already and another on the way and seemingly content that they would all bear the impossible name of Schermerhorn, by way of her husband, Augustus John Schermerhorn, D.D.S. Carolyn could never march with her mother because she was always pregnant or just getting over being pregnant, which didn't seem to be the right condition for proclaiming women's rights. "Keep 'em barefoot and pregnant, heh, heh!" Gus liked to say to his father-in-law when they'd toast a new grandchild. The irony was that Alexander had only one son—one would think by marrying a good Irish Catholic girl with a name like Mollie Mulvihill—that dreadful Becky McCandless was supposed to have commented at the wedding, "Well, at least none of us has married a hunky . . . yet"—things would have gone the other way. But, of course, Mollie agreed to meet Alexander halfway by turning Episcopalian if he would leave the Presbyterian church and join her. Sometimes Reed thought Mollie was just too clean a woman to have children—in fact, he had never seen so *clean* a woman—every curl in place, every ruffle ironed, not a speck of dust in her house though they moved all the way to Sewickley to get out of the smoke. Or maybe the trouble was Alexander. Maybe he'd been frightened about sex ever since that time he'd surprised his father and mother out in the barn. Reed was sure he hadn't actually seen them doing it, but Alexander was old enough to figure it out himself. After all, Reed had never been able to bring himself to discuss sex with his son—or much of anything else. By the time he finished Princeton, Alexander had stretched out of his Jones fleshiness into too near a facsimile of his Uncle Scott, and it wasn't at all surprising that he chose to go to work for the Union Trust Company, of which Scott was a director. Although he didn't like to think so, Reed sometimes wondered if the boy who came along six years after Alexander's marriage when things were looking rather bad in '16 wasn't perhaps a kind of draft insurance. In any case, probably because of missing the war, Alexander was already a vice-president, and he guessed he should be proud of him. Thinking about the children and grandchildren, some of whose names he kept getting mixed up, made Reed feel old and irritable as he followed Alma out to the car. They would, of course, all be there at the wedding.

As he got into the car Reed said, "I wish I hadn't brought that up about Scott's will. . . ."

"I wish you hadn't, too," Alma agreed. "It certainly isn't the appropriate kind of thing to be thinking about on a day like this."

"Right," Reed said. "The fact is that you've got to hand it to the old buzzard. When you think about it, he's had some pretty fantastic offspring—and as you said, dreadful luck with them all dying off. But, you know, the way they died ought to make a lot of us ashamed about the way we live. . . ."

"Now please don't go getting moody on me, Reed," Alma warned as their chauffeur-driven car threaded its way toward the East End from their old Ridge Avenue home that seemed as out of place these days as an elephant in a herd of donkeys, what with all the tiny houses going up on the properties being abandoned by a new generation of North Siders fleeing to Sewickley. "Scott's finally going to have his day, and let's just be happy that the war is over. I hated all those wartime marriages . . . somehow they seemed so frantic. But I guess David will still be wearing his uniform."

"Why not? It's the only real use he'll ever get out of it," Reed said. "I feel sorry for the poor kid never getting overseas, although I understand he did learn to fly."

"I wonder if Grandma Stewart will make it. . . ."

"I hope so," Reed said. "God, she's earned a real flowers-and-champagne wedding for one of Scott's descendants. But I heard she wasn't so well yesterday. . . ."

"A woman of eighty-six is never well," Alma said. "It's just a question of how bad she feels. Some days she's so bent up with that arthritis, according to Lucinda, she can't move at all. Others she still gets down to dinner. I think the weather has something to do with it. It's crisp today, but it's clear. I think they should be able to get her into a wheelchair."

"I hope so."

They were just in time to duck through the bridesmaids clustered in the narthex and slip into seats reserved for the groom's family before, at exactly four, the organ modulated into "Here Comes the Bride." David was already standing at the altar beside the white-robed minister with Howie Timmins, the best man, on his left. Both of them were in uniform, both wearing lieutenant's bars but David boasting wings and Howie the crossed rifles of the infantry. With the armistice still only two weeks behind them, everybody was moved to see such young soldiers; all the ushers were officers too, and everybody knew the bride and groom would leave the church under an arch of crossed sabers, which would make a swell picture for the society pages. Each girl came slowly down the aisle in cadence to the music, each with her eyes severely strained ahead and down, as if her next step might be her last. Then the organ really opened up, and everyone turned to watch the tiny, doll-like bride move slowly, one hand clutching her father's arm, the other holding a prayer book to her breast, toward her Stewart destiny. Looking back at her, Reed could scan the other guests. No wonder the wedding was getting such play in the papers; nearly everybody who mattered in Pittsburgh seemed to be there. In a row directly behind the Stewart family he spotted Andrew Mellon, who looked like a retired general with his lean erect figure, his severe expression, his trim mustache, and his daughter Ailsa; next to them was the family of Andrew's brother, Richard B. Mellon, whose rounder features and softer frame gave him the appearance of a genial country squire. Behind the Mellons stood Henry Clay Frick, making a rare Pittsburgh appearance with his wife and his daughter Helen. Still sporting an old-fashioned full beard, now gone completely white, the terror of Homestead bore an ironic resemblance to Santa Claus. Across the aisle were Gillespies and Joneses too numerous to count. The whole affair was taking on the aspect of one of those marriages between royal houses in Europe. The attendance was, Reed had to admit, a great tribute to Scott, and he was sorry to note that Grandma had not been able to come after all.

Reed wished he didn't know quite so much about these people. It would have made it easier to work himself up into appropriate sentimentality about the flowering of love, like the women he saw all around him. Half a lifetime on the bench had turned him into something of a cynic . . . albeit a compassionate one; which probably accounted for that knot in his stomach . . . about most aspects of human relations —and none more so than that between man and woman. He'd heard testimony on the grossest physical violations, from sodomy to whipping to attempted murder. But worse to him were the far greater number of cases lumped together under the broad categories of mental cruelty or incompatibility. People came before him nursing wounds of the spirit they could not find words to describe. Reading the misery in their eyes, he would often grant decrees with the merest formality of a hearing, thereby acquiring a reputation for being an easy judge on divorce. No doubt that was the reason Andrew Mellon's high-priced attorneys maneuvered to bring that sad case before him . . . He'd been tempted to turn it down because he didn't like the way the Mellon millions had been used to buy the special treatment of a private hearing. In the end, though, he took it as a favor to brother Scott, who for the first and only time in their lives came to him in chambers, no doubt swallowing a large lump of pride, and begged him to do this for such long-time friends of "the whole Stewart family."

According to his custom Reed never did probe into the details; he didn't need to, because the open history of the marriage was enough to convince him that it should be dissolved. What he wondered about, as he always did, was where the seeds of such failures were planted. Did Andrew inherit, along with his business acumen, the chill blood of old Judge Mellon, who actually published a memoir in which he wrote of his own "romance" with Sarah Negley that "there was no love-making. Had I been rejected, I would have left neither sad nor depressed nor greatly disappointed, only annoyed at the loss of time." Or had shy Andrew been so shattered when the fiancée of his youth died of tuberculosis that no woman could match his dream? Or had Norah McMullen, improbably the daughter of a Dublin distiller, who had brought Andrew to the altar when he was a rich and cautious 45-year-old man, proved a frivolous fortune hunter? No matter, the grounds were desertion, and there was no question about the fact that Norah had left him in '09 to go back to Ireland.

As it always did in such cases, what saddened Reed was the plight of the children. Though by agreement their time was divided between parents, an unseemly struggle ensued in the summer of 1910 when Norah came over from Ireland on the *Oceanic* to pick them up. Andrew dutifully took them clear to the dock and then, changing his mind, took them back to Pittsburgh on the night train. Norah left the ship and followed them to enforce the agreement. It was then that Andrew put the matter in the hands of his lawyers, requesting a secret divorce. It took a while. The Mellon attorneys, working through Pennsylvania's Republican boss, Boise Penrose, whose coffers were filled with Mellon money, got a divorce bill enacted by the legislature, permitting a private hearing. But it was the summer of 1912 by the time they could get the case before Reed in chambers. He signed the decree and, playing Solomon, halved custody of the children on a six-month basis. The whole process galled him, and he was secretly glad when a nosy Eastern press got hold of the story anyway and broke it to a public apparently still avid for scandal about Pittsburgh millionaires.

One would have thought the public appetite would have been sated by Harry Thaw, who kept emerging back into the limelight like a bad vaudeville act. Escaping from Matawan in '15, he managed to get a court to declare him not only sane but not guilty. Reed had been intrigued by the reception accorded him by Presbyterian Pittsburgh. More than a thousand people met his train and escorted him to his mother's home like a returning football hero. Newspapers told how Harry bounced up the stairs from the porte cochere to greet his faithful mother who, standing in the open door, put out her arms and cried, "My boy!" For days Thaw's every act —how he slept, how he exercised, what he ate—was recorded. While the New York *Sun* thundered that "in all this nauseous business we don't know which makes the gorge rise more, the pervert buying his way out, or the perverted idiots that hail him with wild huzzas," a Philadelphia minister proclaimed that "Thaw had the courage to free the world of a moral hypocrite." Reed felt the adulation of Thaw was probably just a simple case of a lot of self-righteous people doing a little vicarious sinning, and reveling in its repentance. Their judgment seemed confirmed when Harry settled down at home with Mother, busied himself with affairs of the Third Presbyterian Church and talked of business plans in California. Harry would probably be right here at this most proper wedding, Reed reflected, except for the unfortunate fact that a year or so before he'd been arrested again—this time for allegedly kidnapping a young boy and whipping him in a hotel room. Though the Thaw money got him off once more, Pittsburgh had finally had enough. *Nobody* knew where Harry was now. . . .

Everybody thought that in a way it was too bad to hold such a big wedding in November when the Gillespies couldn't spread the reception out over their spacious grounds. But they did a very ingenious thing. They had all the flowers and plants removed from the big glass conservatory back of the house and stored in a local nursery; then they had the place converted into a ballroom with a temporary floor and bright paper streamers hung from the glass ceiling to give the effect of a colorful tent. With that and the big parlor and dining room that could be joined together by opening the sliding oak doors between them, they had enough space to "entertain an army," as George Gillespie had put it when he argued against holding the affair in the impersonal atmosphere of some club or other. There was champagne; waiters passed through the crowds so continuously with trays of filled glasses that nobody could possibly count how much anybody else had, and Reed gradually began enjoying himself. He started looking about for somebody he really felt like talking to and spied Stewart Sharp, still dressed in the uniform of a major in the medical corps. Reed often considered it a miracle that Stewart had turned out the way he had and put it down to the influence of Lucinda in the days before scandal made her *persona non grata* in the Sharp household. The others— that Becky Sharp McCandless with her waspish tongue, and pompous Henry Ward Beecher Sharp (he was here in a reverse collar, turning champagne away with a near-theatrical get-thee-behind-me-Satan flip of his plump hand), and Tillie with the fruity accent she'd cultivated to match her husband's Harvard "a's"—had been too young to benefit from the breath of fresh air Reed was sure Lucinda had let into the stuffy parsonage.

When Reed had worked his way over to Stewart, he held out his hand. "Good to see you back, Stewart. I thought you'd be out of that monkey suit by now."

"I'm afraid it will be a while, Uncle Reed, if ever. I guess the surgeons are through with their gory business, but mine's just beginning. You wouldn't believe what's happened to the minds of some of these poor fellows."

"Yes, I'd believe it. So you're going to stay in?"

"For a while at least," Stewart said, and then, putting a hand on Reed's arm, led him out into the hall away from the crowd. "Say, Uncle Reed, I stopped in on the way to the wedding to see Grandma, and I don't like the way she looks. She's listless and a bit feverish, and with all this flu going around I'm worried."

"Isn't there anything you can do?"

"Not much if she's got it, especially at eighty-six. I did call a young doctor I know who's pretty good with flu and asked him to look in on her. But the poor fellow's got so many desperate cases he's running his legs off, and I don't know when he'll get around to her. I didn't think this was a good time to mention it to Uncle Scott, but if you could manage, maybe you ought to go over."

"That bad?"

"I just don't know, but . . ."

"All right, thanks, Stewart. Do me a favor and look up Alma and tell her where I've gone."

Not long after Reed had left, the bride and groom cut the cake, each feeding the other a piece while the bridesmaids and more sentimental older guests emitted a collective sigh of appreciation. The band then struck up a waltz. Scott Stewart was looking solemnly on in silent but companionable company with his old friends Andrew Mellon and Clay Frick when the bride surprised him by coming up to him, holding out her hand and saying, "C'mon, Grandy Stewart, you get the first dance." David was already sweeping gracefully around the floor with Mrs. Gillespie in his arms. For Scott it was a moment of social terror he thought he had forever left behind him. Though he had taken up cards and cigars, he had never so much as danced a step in his life. But there was no way out. Ann, a willful little thing if he ever saw one, had him firmly by the hand and was leading him to the floor. "I can't dance, you know," he whispered to her. To which she just gave him her pearliest smile, put her arms up and told him where to put his and said, "Follow me. Just pretend." Luckily, as soon as they started, other couples began moving onto the floor, and Ann took pity on him. "Come, get me a glass of champagne, Grandy, I'm parched," she said. "I don't drink," he said irrelevantly, though from habit. "But I do, Grandy, so please?" Scott dutifully set off looking for a waiter to get wine for his newly crowned daughter-in-law and wondering what it was about that mite of a girl that made him do her bidding against his will. . . .

Scott would never forget as long as he lived the first night he met Ann Gillespie. It was a stormy evening the previous winter, and she had come uninvited. She'd flounced in, shaking wet snow off her furs like an angry terrier, and thrust a letter under his nose. "From your grandson, sir," she said. "Read it."

Somewhat flustered, Scott invited her into his study, put on his half glasses and glanced at the letter. He got as far as the salutation—"My darling Ann"—looked up over his glasses at the girl whose eyes were burning like blue fire and asked, "Are you sure you want me to read this?"

"Yes."

Scott's eyes ran rapidly down the page: "Grandy Stewart says he is going to cut me off because I have 'betrayed his trust' by joining the air corps. Well, I don't mind, and I hope you don't either. We'll get along. I just hope your parents will understand, but even if they don't you and I will have each other. The sad thing is that I really love that old son-of-a-bitch, and if he goes through with this, it will hurt him more than it will hurt me, but there is no way I can tell him this. As everybody says, Grandy Stewart is a 'man of principle,' and there's no way you can argue with a man of principle. The only thing I regret is that I probably won't be able to give you what I'd like to give you. I'd give you the moon and the stars and the earth, if I could. Maybe you'll just have to take me. . . ." There was more, some detail about his training and the like, but Scott knew he had read enough.

"Why did you bring this to me, Miss Gillespie?" he asked.

"Because I don't think you understand, Mr. Stewart, that David did what he did because of me."

One of Scott's still black brows shot up toward the line of his white hair. "Oh?"

"Well, you know, he told me how you felt and all that, but I guess I let him know he wouldn't be much of a man in my eyes if he didn't do what he thought he ought to," she said. "He really loves me, Mr. Stewart—and I . . . I love him. . . ."

"Yes, I imagine you do, but . . ."

"Well, then, couldn't you? . . . I mean, you can see how he feels about you, and the poor boy is going out risking his life every day . . . Mr. Stewart, couldn't you write him and tell him it's all right, or something . . . I mean, he hasn't done anything really bad, has he?"

What an astonishing thing, Scott kept thinking. By his standards, by the code he felt to be ordained, no girl of eighteen would even go out alone on a night like this, let alone intrude boldly on the most sacred relationships of a family she hardly knew. Nor would any girl of his time wear a skirt so short it revealed half a calf when she sat down or rouge on her lips or a helmet of curls instead of a "crown of glory." She had to be well-reared; he had known George Gillespie since before she was born. It had something to do with the generation, a second generation beyond him and almost totally beyond his understanding in their way of thinking. Still, there was something providential about her surprise appearance since he had been praying nightly for guidance ever since his lawyer Shaw refused to change the will. Could this whole bizzare experience be an answer to his prayers? Was God sending him, in the form of this forward little girl, a message that, for once, his convictions were wrong? Her question—"He hasn't done anything really bad, has he?" —was difficult to answer in any way but one. With a sense of relief that he was now about to do what all his human desires prodded him to do, Scott got up from behind his desk, handed the letter back to Ann and said, "Thank you for coming, Miss Gillespie. I'll write David tonight."

Nobody could ever quite figure out what made Ann Gillespie the way she was. Her parents were very conventional people—her father a big, stolid, level-headed man with an engineering mind, and her mother a small fluttery woman given to punctuating her conversation with "heavens to Betsy," "goodness me," and "well, I never." She went to the Episcopal church every Sunday and attended the most conventional schools. Going to Newport in the summers was a bit exotic, because she got to bathe in the sea, go sailing and learn to play tennis before such strenuous pursuits were considered quite ladylike in Pittsburgh. But on the whole there was nothing to account for why she bobbed her hair, smoked cigarettes, drank gin, asked boys to kiss her and generally took her life into her own hands by the time she was seventeen, unless it was that being alone a good deal, she also read a good deal. In her mind she was all the spirited women she encountered between covers or on the stage—Joan of Arc, Queen Elizabeth, Portia, Jo in *Little Women*, Nora in *The Doll's House*. She couldn't abide either swooning heroines or militant feminists. As she grew up, the only woman she met in Pittsburgh who seemed to have the qualities she most admired was the artist Lucinda Stewart Schmidt, and after she started working with her in the canteen they became very good friends. It was, in fact, Lucinda who advised her to take David's letter to Scott, and it was Lucinda who urged her to go ahead and get married—even though they were only eighteen and everybody thought they were too young—when David wrote from Texas that he had his wings and would be getting a few weeks leave in the East in November before going overseas. "Don't miss a chance at love, but take my word for it, it's easier when you're married," Lucinda said.

It was easier, too, Ann found, to bring her parents around to the idea of a wedding than she had feared. Although her mother clucked about how young they were, her father's practical thinking carried the day when he said something to the effect of, "Well, I guess he can afford you." David was more of a problem. "What if I get killed?" he wrote. She replied with a long letter on the "better to have loved and lost than never to have loved at all" theme, and he finally agreed. It was thought that Scott Stewart might object, but George Gillespie approached him directly on the very practical grounds that such a marriage might have a settling effect on two very restless young people. When Scott's terse comment in agreement—"Anything to get David back here at work with me in Pittsburgh"—was passed along to the Gillespie women, Ann smiled to herself: Pittsburgh was the last place in the world either she or David wanted to live.

The date was set for just two days after David was scheduled to reach Pittsburgh, so that they would have as much of his leave as possible for a honeymoon. By November 1, 1918, two hundred and fifty expensively engraved invitations were in the mail, bridesmaids had been sent patterns and swatches of material to have their dresses made, flowers had been ordered, and the renovation of the observatory was begun. Wartime or no, Maggie Gillespie was not about to stint on the most important event in her life since Ann's birth eighteen years before. Then came the Armistice. While everybody else was almost literally flinging his hat in the air, Ann Gillespie worried: had David only agreed to marry her as sort of a last fling before leaving for France? Better to know. Although her mother would have fainted away at the mere thought of calling off the show, Ann sent a wire to Texas: HAPPY ARMISTICE DARLING PLENTY OF TIME NOW STILL WANT TO MARRY ME LOVE ANN. Back came what she wanted to hear: WE HAVE A DATE IF YOU DON'T BREAK IT I WON'T MORE LOVE DAVID.

They had not seen each other for more than a year—since the day David left to go back to Harvard. While they hadn't written every day, they had exchanged letters often enough so that they felt they knew each other's minds inside out. Somewhat to her own surprise and despite the opportunities presented to her by her work in the canteen and the parties her friends were always giving for brothers and cousins going off to war, Ann remained totally faithful to David; no other boy interested her. Happily she could read between the lines of his letters, which often reflected loneliness, that he was faithful, too. His temptation was of a different sort. The men and boys who went up in the stick-and-glue crates they called airplanes soon developed a "today we live and tomorrow we die" attitude. Successful flights were usually followed by joyous drinking bouts and, if possible, a visit to the nearest whorehouse—in Texas, an old adobe hotel populated by Indian and Mexican girls as well as the usual hollow-eyed white women whose luck had run out. David lived under the constant whiplash of taunts from his buddies when he would peel off after the last toast had been drunk "to the next man to die" and go back to his quarters to compose a letter to Ann. Once he let himself be carried along with the crowd as far as the hotel's lobby. Nervous and sweating, he sat on a sofa with a couple of other cadets and ordered a drink from the madame and watched the girls who moved through the room, choosing partners. A dyed blond twice his age came over, leaned down so that her open bodice revealed all of her pendulous breasts, put a hand on the inside of his thigh and said, "Come to Momma, baby." He could think of nothing but Ann's firm, electric flesh he had so fleetingly touched, and bolted out into the night. After that David never went back, but his friends stopped pestering him because he was the most hell-for-leather flier of them all, scaring the beejesus out of everybody the way he'd roll and twist and pull out of a dive so close to the ground that he sometimes would actually spin his wheels. "No Hun's going to stay on my tail," he explained, but all the time he was really glorying in his love of speed. The only person he felt truly understood this was Grandy Stewart, to whom he began writing long letters about the techniques of flying once he got the old man's astonishing confession that he had been wrong in getting so angry about David's signing up; all he prayed for was to get him home in one piece. Once the wedding was set, David began to be more careful—after all, if he survived there would finally be a certain release to the tensions of frustration he suffered on those long hot nights he lay twisting on his bed and knowing that his roommate, unburdened by either a Christian conscience or the fastidiousness imparted by the conditioning of wealth and propriety, was getting his manly relief.

Ann, who had taken driving lessons to surprise him, borrowed David's Packard to go down and meet him at the station. She waited on the platform as the train rolled in, saw him through a window and was at the bottom of the steps when he swung down. They kissed long and passionately right there with the steam from the brakes rising around them and the other passengers jostling them. She was every bit as tiny and full of lively vibrations as he'd remembered; he was thinner, leather-tan from the Texas sun and a lot older looking than eighteen, she thought, with his clipped mustache that looked a bit like his grandfather's. They stepped back, smiled at each other a bit shyly until she said, "Oh, David Scott Stewart, you *are* handsome!" In response he hugged her again, picked up his bag and they headed for the car, where she did surprise him by jumping in behind the wheel. "Now look," he said, "let's get this family off on the right foot—I wear the pants." She stuck her tongue out at him, flicked her skirt and teased, "Oh, you don't know what I've got on under here." He climbed in beside her, kissed her on the ear and whispered, "But I'll soon find out." And they laughed together in delicious anticipation of what was in store if they could only get through the next few days, and he let her drive home, admitting grudgingly, "Say, you're not bad. Maybe I can teach you to fly someday."

As the stars of the show, they forced themselves to do everything right and proper through the dinners, rehearsal, the comings and goings of bridesmaids and ushers and relatives, through the ceremony itself and the reception. Whenever they had a minute or two alone in a dark hallway, in a car rushing between appointments, they could hardly keep their lips and hands off each other. In crowds, their eyes kept trading kisses.

By the time they were able to break away from the Gillespie home and go off to the bedroom he had reserved on the night train to New York, where they were spending their honeymoon because it was still hard to travel anywhere else with the war so recently over, they were in a froth of desire. In the car that drove them downtown, they'd kissed and kissed, and he'd let his hands roam freely all over the fitted traveling suit she wore so that by the time they reached the station he felt he knew every curve of her body except under the armor of the corset that covered those unmentionables she said he would find. The porter who got them settled in their compartment was smily and winky, and David overtipped him when he asked him to bring ice and some ginger ale. Locked in the small compartment, where the berth was already made and turned down and they almost bumped together when they moved, they were suddenly shy with each other, and quiet. Ann took off her hat and carefully hung her fur and the coat to her suit so that it wouldn't get wrinkled, while David sat back on the berth to give her room to move around and wondered just how to proceed next. He was glad when the porter came back with the ice—it gave him a chance to pull out of his pocket the silver flask Great-uncle Reed had presented him as a wedding present and say, "Gin?"

Ann, remembering, laughed and said, "You dear. You thought of everything."

So he poured a drink for both of them and then lit two cigarettes the way he used to when they were dating and handed her one. The train started with a jolt, and Ann said, "I'm glad we're on the train. I think it's so much more romantic doing . . . doing it . . . the first time when we're going somewhere. Oh, I always want to be going somewhere, David! . . . When are you going to teach me to fly?"

"How about right now?" he asked, and leaned over to kiss her while he commenced to unbutton her blouse.

"Do you think we should, with all the lights on?" she asked, and he reached across her and pulled the shade, although all you could see outside was a blur of lights streaking the dark.

"There!" he said. "Now I want to see who's wearing the pants in this family."

"Oh, no you don't!" she said, and catching him off balance, pushed him flat on the berth. Suddenly her wiry little body seemed to be all over him, touching him in points of fire. They rolled over and over, wrestling, kissing, nipping like puppies and discarding bits of clothing in the process. Finally he sought her out, trying to be gentle, while she laughed and cried at the same time, "It hurts, it hurts, but don't stop, don't stop!"

Twice more during the night when the train bumped them awake at Altoona and again at Harrisburg, they came together, and each time she said it was better for her. And they couldn't get over telling each other how much they loved each other and what a wonder each strange little thing they found on each other's body was and how glad they were that nobody else but them had ever known, or would ever know, these wonders. By morning when they went into the dining car between Philadelphia and New York for breakfast and tried to act like a dignified married couple, they were both glowing so pinkly from excitement and exertion that strangers all over the car exchanged knowing smirks. Neither of them cared. Between orange juice and coffee, they dropped the charade and had eyes only for each other. They were just sorry they would have to wait all the way through most of the morning while they went through the bustle of getting off the train, getting a taxi, getting settled into their hotel, before . . .

All that long night while love was being joyously requited on the Iron City Express, a small, worried group of people held vigil over the struggling frame of Mary Shallenberger Stewart, who lay propped up to ease her lungs and heart in a corner bedroom of Scott's palatial residence. Twice the young doctor came and went, looking more concerned each time after he'd gone over her chest with his stethoscope, checked her pulse and blood pressure, taken a rectal reading of temperature. He would confer for a few minutes in a corner of the room with Dr. Stewart Sharp, who would translate gloomily for the rest of them. "He doubts that she will live out the night."

At the doctor's suggestion, only one member of the family at a time—and Dr. Sharp, of course—stayed in the sick room. The others gathered in a little upstairs parlor nearby that Mary Stewart had turned into an island of her own identity in a sea of marble and French provincial furniture. Nearly everything in the room came either from the South Hills or the first Oakland house, including the Rogers statue of "The Favored Scholar," which still sat on the same little marble-topped table she'd bought especially to support this eighteen-dollar extravagance. The room was made homier by a coal fire hissing and sputtering in the grate that once long ago had heated Dr. Stewart's office. It was the perfect setting for nostalgia, but the people sitting there tried hard to avoid it by engaging in chitchat about the wedding they had just left, the Armistice—anything to keep their minds off the meaning of the battle going on across the hall. It didn't always work. Once when Alma, who had come to love her mother-in-law as much as the rest, was in the sick room, the four Stewarts for the first time in years were left alone together. Sarah, bent with the beginnings of the same arthritis that had afflicted her mother, was hunched over one of the patchwork quilts she seemed eternally to be sewing for one grandchild or another; Reed, who had just returned from the bathroom where he'd fortified himself from the flask he always carried to any family gathering that might wind up in either the Stewart or Sharp household, was sprawled on the couch; Scott sat in a wing chair by the fire, immobile as a statue, except for the jaw muscles that worked while he chomped on a dead cigar; Lucinda paced, smoking cigarette after cigarette in a long ivory holder.

"Oh, God, I only hope she lasts long enough so that it won't spoil everything for those kids. . . ."

Scott took the cigar out of his mouth. "Don't talk like that."

"Don't talk like what? As far as I'm concerned, this is

389

Mother's room we're in, and I'll say what I *damned* well please. . . ."

"You sound like you don't care whether she lives or dies. All you apparently can think of is the convenience of a couple of kids—"

"To tell you the truth, I believe I hope she does die," Lucinda replied. "She's been wanting to for years. You could read it in her eyes, if you bothered to look. . . ."

There was an odd choking sound coming from Scott. The others all turned to look in astonishment when they realized he was crying. The great stone face had cracked into deep fissures. His shoulders were shaking. Lucinda was the first to react. She went to her brother's side and for the first time in her life was allowed to touch him with affection. Putting a consoling hand on the back of his neck, she was surprised to feel how thin and fragile it was, how iron tight with tension.

"God, Scott, I'm sorry," she said. "I really am. . . ."

Scott was busy fussing with his handkerchief, wiping his eyes, blowing his nose. His neck seemed to cringe from her touch. "Please leave me alone," he said. "All you ever did was cause her grief, you and Reed there. Now . . ."

"That isn't fair, Scott, and you know it," said Reed. "What Lucinda says is true. I was with her this afternoon, the last time she was able to talk, and what she kept saying was, 'I'm so tired, so tired.' Once she actually smiled and said, 'I'm coming, Doctor.' I thought she was gone then. . . ."

"Stop it," Scott said. "Stop it. I don't think any of you knew her. *None* of you . . ."

Blinking back tears, Sarah said, "Please . . . why can't we all . . . you know how she hated so to hear us bicker. . . ."

In control of himself again, Scott got up and said, "You can find me down in my study."

When he had left, Lucinda plopped herself down in his chair, lit another cigarette and said, "Dammit, Reed, he is human after all."

Reed agreed. "I began to suspect it when he changed his mind about David's enlisting. I wonder what got into him?"

"Mortality," Lucinda said at once. "It gets to us all. I think he realized that there would be no future if he lost David. Scott's too good a Bible student to think he can take all those stocks and bonds to heaven."

"If he gets there," Reed said.

"Please, you two . . . ," Sarah implored.

"Scott himself told the story about where his friend Frick

thinks they're all going," Reed said. "I'll say this for Frick: he is a realist. My only worry is that I'm sure to be joining them."

"Well, I know somebody who's going the other way for sure—the lady across the hall," Lucinda said.

Sarah jumped up and fled the room with a cry of "Oh!", scattering pins and thread and patches behind her.

Reed half smiled. "Well, old girl, now that we've gotten rid of the Christians, we can cry too, without losing our reputations." He got up and came over and took hold of Lucinda's hand, and they were like that, together, when Alma came in with her report: "She's sleeping easier; Stewart even thinks she just might make it. . . ."

Mary Stewart did make it, through the next day and into the next night, when her great-grandson, David, and his wife, Ann, in faraway New York were dressing to go out to a dinner both of them felt was an annoying interruption to their fascinating game of mutual exploration. "Well, Uncle Clay's getting to be an old man, and I'm sure he likes to fold things up early. He never has anything to say anyway," David said as he buckled himself into his best dress-uniform jacket. "I hope so," Ann mumbled around the hat pins she was holding in her teeth. "I'm ready for another flying lesson, Mr. Instructor." David came over and kissed the top of her head. "Likewise. And may I say you're some cadet. . . ."

In the excitement of the wedding reception a dinner invitation to the Fricks had seemed a good idea. David had never seen their new home at Seventieth Street on Fifth Avenue, which had been designed expressly to show off Frick's art collection, now valued at more than thirty million dollars. David thought that Ann, whose family connections fell somewhat short of the Fricks, might be interested. Now, as the taxi dropped them in front of a low stone building facing Central Park that looked more like a small museum than a home, he knew Ann couldn't care less, and he wished he'd made excuses. A butler ushered them through the iron gates and into a marble foyer. Up a few steps on a landing was the console of an organ, which a young man as stiffly dressed in white tie and tails as a concert artist was playing softly. While the butler took their wraps, they had just time enough to recognize the tune he was coaxing out of the stops as "Silver Threads Among the Gold."

"How appropriate!" Ann whispered. "Nothing but precious metals in this place."

David had a hard time looking solemnly respectful when

they were ushered into the Fragonard room, where the Fricks were receiving their guests. It was a small but elegant chamber; the walls were entirely "paneled" with the artist's large paintings. There was only one other guest, Sir Joseph Duveen, an art dealer who proved as ebullient and talkative as his host was silent. After introductions, Sir Joseph insisted on guiding them around for a before-dinner view of the rest of the treasures in the house. The dealer immodestly admitted that he had been in overall charge of the design of the building as well as the supplier of most of the art he pointed out—bronzes by Giovanni de Bologna and Benvenuto Cellini, black hawthorn vases of the K'ang and Hsi period, paintings by Rembrandt, Watts, Corot, Millet.

"You know it took a while," Sir Joseph confided to the young people, "but I finally made Mr. Frick realize that when he wanted the best he had to come to me. Now take that one," he said, gesturing toward Gainsborough's "Hall in St. James's Park," and lowering his voice. "I'll tell you something if you'll promise not to repeat it. I heard Mr. Frick was dickering to get it through Knoedler's, so I had my agent in London buy it right out from under their noses for three hundred thousand dollars and then sold it to Mr. Frick at cost. He was pretty shocked about the price, but I told him, 'Look here, Mr. Frick, what else in the world can you get for three hundred thousand dollars that won't require a dime of upkeep? Anyway, you can always make more money, but you'll never get another picture like this, for it's truly unique.' Mr. Frick appreciates that kind of thinking."

At the table, the talk, almost exclusively by Sir Joseph, was all of art. The figures made even David's head swim, and Ann was literally open-mouthed. When they were discussing one of Mr. Frick's most recent acquisitions—Velázquez's "Philip IV of Spain"—that cost $400,000, Frick motioned to the butler to bring him pen and paper. While Sir Joseph rambled on, Frick made some quick calculations. Then he looked up, broke into his thin smile, cleared his throat and spoke for the first time in the evening. "It might interest you to know," he said, "that, as Sir Joseph says, Philip IV paid the painter six hundred dollars in 1645. I have just computed that sum at six percent interest, compounded numerically, down to 1918 and find I paid less than nothing for the painting."

They all laughed, and David understood more why his grandy so admired Mr. Frick.

"With all this talk of figures," Sir Joseph said, "I think I ought to tell you young people something Mr. Frick would be too modest to say himself. He plans to leave all of this—the whole house and collection—to the American people. You know that's the glory of your country—the fact that its men of wealth have the good sense and the good taste to bring the world's art treasures to its people."

"But what about the people we buy them from? Isn't it sort of . . . sort of plundering?" Ann asked.

David gave her a look, but Sir Joseph was unruffled. "My dear young lady," he said, "through all history the spoils of the world have gone to its conquerors. The conquerors of the twentieth century are not the European kings and lords with their foolish little armies but the American industrialists like Mr. Frick, whose works are changing the face of the globe. The fortunate thing for us all is that they, unlike the hereditary rulers of the past, have risen from the soil of democracy and feel an obligation to the people."

Ann, still blushing from David's sharp look, murmured, "Oh, yes, I see."

On the way home she apologized. "I'm sorry if I embarrassed you, David, but he seemed such an oily salesman. . . ."

"I know," David agreed. "Still there was some truth to what he was saying. You know, someday we too may have the problem of getting rid of a lot of money."

"Why not just stop making it?" she asked.

"Are you crazy?"

"Maybe—crazy over you but not your money. Oh, I wish this driver would hurry; we have unfinished business," she said, and turned up her face to be kissed.

Going into their hotel room, they found a telegram that had been shoved under the door. It read: GRANDMA STEWART DIED OF INFLUENZA EIGHT TONIGHT PLEASE RETURN PITTSBURGH AT ONCE GRANDY. In her passing, Mary Shallenberger Stewart, the source of so much life, became part of a deadly statistic, one of the 2,052 people of Pittsburgh who that fall died in an epidemic more destructive of American lives than the great war just ended.

A Drink in a Speakeasy

The Kit-Kat was just across the Highland Park Bridge in Aspinwall, and if they knew you, you could get honest-to-God scotch or British gin. Even though he had his own cellar, David Scott Stewart took to dropping in at the road-house for a quick one almost every night on his way home to Fox Chapel, partly to save the drain on his private stock but mostly to talk to the proprietor Frank Shaughnessy, whom he described as "my parish priest" when the young people in the Stewarts' crowd were talking about their favorite speakeasies. In this year of 1925, Shaughnessy stuck up like a hard rock of reality in the shifting currents of an unsettled world. The old Irishman had been through everything— two years riding the rails west in fruitless search of a fortune; twenty years in the mills working twelve-hour shifts and twenty-four-hour swing shifts (it was a wonder he'd had the time and energy to spawn eight kids); organizer at the Edgar Thompson works in the long strike of '19, when he got clobbered twice by hired goons, and bearing thereafter a permanent egg above his right eye to prove it. It was then, after the strike was broken, that Shaughnessy decided to go into business. He picked the selling of booze because, as he joked, he had "an Irishman's natural understanding of the product" and, of course, the right connections—a brother Pat on the city police force and a cousin Gerald Fitzgerald on the force in Aspinwall. But if you could get him in a serious mood, as David sometimes did, you would find that under-mining the Eighteenth Amendment was in the nature of a sacred calling for Frank Shaughnessy.

On a particular evening when David stopped by he found Shaughnessy alone behind the bar, reading the newspaper. He could tell there was something on his mind the way he shoved his glasses up so that they hung crookedly on the bump. "So it's you, Mr. Stewart. I was hopin' y'd come by."

David had learned from past experience not to rush Shaughnessy, and so stuck to ritual. "Got anything to cut the phlegm, doc?"

"Sure thing. Best medicine the good Lord ever made," Frank said, as he splashed whiskey on ice and pushed the glass across to David.

In the Kit-Kat, if you understood Frank, you didn't just ask for a drink. Frank's view was that whiskey was God's special grace to the working man. Anyone who'd ever done a twelve-hour trick in hell would understand, he argued. A man couldn't swallow when he came out unless he opened his throat with a couple of stiff ones. Why in hell'd Pittsburgh get the reputation as "the drinkingest place in the West"? People were no different here; it was what they had to live through, Frank contended. He knew: hadn't he gone all the way to 'Frisco and back with never seeing a place with more saloons? Nothing made Frank madder than the suggestion that he was doing something immoral or illegal in running a speakeasy. Hell, there were five hundred or more of them operating wide open—so many on Sixth Avenue in town they called it "The Great Wet Way." Frank and those other fellas were doing a service for the people, and it was time the people in Washington realized it. He'd been waiting for a chance to bring it up with young Mr. Stewart, who knew all those birds, and now he had just the right thing to get started with—this story in the paper. But, first, the ritual.

"Here's to the Pirates," David said, lifting his glass.

Frank didn't often drink with customers, but there was still nobody in the place, so he poured a small one for himself and joined the toast. Besides, nobody in Pittsburgh that summer of '25 could afford to turn down a toast to the Pirates, headed as they surely were for the World Series. Frank, however, had another toast in mind.

"Now, here's to your friend, Andy Mellon. Looks like he's got his tail in a sling, which is right where it belongs," he said, shoving the newspaper toward David with his big thumb on a story headlined: ANTI-SALOON LEAGUE ATTACKS MELLON.

David had read the story earlier in the day with a good deal of pleasure. Some enterprising reporter had turned up the fact that Secretary of the Treasury Andrew W. Mellon held Overholt stock, probably as a result of his long friendship with Frick, and now the Philadelphia Federation of

Churches and the Anti-Saloon League were objecting to having a "distiller" in charge of enforcing the Volstead Act. David laughed and raised his glass to Frank's. "I'll join you."

"You know, it ain't funny, Mr. Stewart," Frank said, thrusting a once muscular torso, gone softly heavy since leaving the mills, halfway across the bar so he could lower his voice. "These hypocrites who take booze away from the workingman while they got plenty for themselves—you got enough, don't ya?—are gonna bring on a revolution one day, mark my words. They're always worryin' about Commies and Wobblies and what not, but it's their own damn stupid laws that're gonna have men marchin' in the streets."

"Maybe you're right, Frank."

"No maybes. I know I'm right. The thing is, smart young fellas like yourself have got to start usin' y'r influence. . . ."

"What influence?"

"Chrissakes, Mr. Stewart, anybody who reads the papers knows y'r grandfather is thick as thieves with Mellon. Why couldn't he . . ."

David had to laugh again. "Oh, Frank, if you only knew my grandfather! He thinks prohibition is the finest law since the Ten Commandments; he's been working for it all his life."

"Is he crazy?"

"No, not crazy," David said. "And he isn't a hypocrite either. He's never touched a drink in his life. He's a man of principle. You know what a man of principle is, Frank?"

Frank fingered his jaw. "Yeah, I think so—a guy with money."

David roared. "God, Frank, talking to you is good for the soul. But seriously, you're wrong if you think a word to Mellon would do any good. I don't think he likes the law any better than anyone else. The thing is, there are a lot of people in this country who don't agree with you—with us. Take most of the women, now that they've got the vote . . ."

"Yeah, thanks to dizzy types like that Judge Stewart's wife. Say, is she any relation to you?"

"My great-aunt."

"Boy, you've certainly got some beauts," Frank said.

"But don't blame her. Aunt Alma likes a drink herself, and her husband, you know . . ."

"Yeah, too bad about the old judge. Now there was a guy with balls," Frank said.

David made a mental note to carry Frank's flattering description back to Uncle Reed, who needed all the good news he could get these days. What some called an act of courage and others, notably Grandy Stewart, an act of folly had cost Reed his seat on the bench. Early in the days of prohibition he'd directed a verdict of acquittal in the case of a saloon keeper who was charged with wounding a revenue agent on the grounds that he, Judge Stewart, considered the Volstead Act unconstitutional and that, therefore, the agent was entering upon the defendant's premises illegally and that the defendant had a right to protect his property against such invasion. The ruling hit the headlines and was, of course, reversed on appeal. Judge Stewart, criticized by the Bar Association and all the God-fearing hard-drinking Republican leaders of Pittsburgh, couldn't even get his name on the ballot in '22. Now, slightly crippled by a mild stroke that followed on the heels of his political collapse, Reed commuted between a small law office he had opened in the Oliver Building and the Duquesne Club, where he still entertained his luncheon cronies with outrageous opinions. Some said he was kept alive on a large retainer from a grateful bootlegger who also supplied him with unlimited quantities of Old Overholt. The part about the whiskey might have been true, but David knew that, far from accepting fees, Reed had actually sent all prospective clients in trouble with the Volstead Act to other lawyers whose personal facade of righteousness would give their case a better chance in the courts. Reed was, in fact, subsisting on what was left of Aunt Alma's inheritance and taking what pleasure he could from watching, in his words, the world go mad. He was definitely one of David's favorite people.

"There you've got it, Frank. Look indeed at what they did to Judge Stewart. . . . No. the mood of the country is against us. And it isn't just the big people. I'll bet you a cookie a lot of the votes for prohibition came from the wives of your workingmen. You see, they weren't smart enough to take the girls along to the saloons the way we do now."

"Well, I gotta admit you may be right about that, Mr. Stewart." And then, lifting his glass, Frank added, "Well, here's mud in your eye. I guess it's just a cockeyed world."

One of the most cockeyed things in Frank's mind was the way women behaved these days. The first time he had seen them come into his speakeasy he had been shocked; they were profaning his church. The worst thing was that they were good girls, people whose names he read in the paper. But business was business, and Frank soon realized he had been luckier than he knew in picking his location. Like a watering place for horses in the old stage days, it lay at just about the right distance along the route between the city's East End, still fashionable but aging, and the new rich suburb of Fox Chapel, where a lot of the younger people were settling. At the suggestion of some of the swells, Frank took to hiring a band Saturday nights so they could do the bunny hop and Charleston while they were downing his bootleg gin. It was a sight to watch those sleek ladies twitching their little rears and kicking so high you could see all the naked white above their rolled stockings. There wasn't one of them with a sexier shimmy than that little one David Stewart was married to. If it had been him, Frank would have wiped up the floor with all those guys who threw her around till you could see her panties and patted her on the fanny when they had her out there on the floor. Stewart, though, would just sit back there and grin as if he were enjoying it. Well, they were a different generation, or maybe rich types had always behaved that way and Frank just didn't know about it.

Until recently, watching Ann have a frantic good time had been one of David's favorite recreations. Not much on dancing himself because of his boyhood shyness, he was content to let others do the honors, even at the expense of a stolen pat or peck, on the theory that it drained off some of her excess energy. Besides, it excited her, and he knew that when he got her back home, exhilarated by gin and flattery, she would be all over him in her uniquely energetic fahsion. After seven years and a baby, they still had an insatiable appetite for each other, which was one of the wonders of what Frank Shaughnessy quite rightly called a cockeyed world. But recently Ann was showing signs that this was not enough, that nothing they had—and they had a good deal—was quite enough. She would turn moody in the midst of a party, stop dancing and drinking and ask to be taken home, where she would shrug him off and pace the house restlessly or sit up reading the remainder of the night.

One night she lay rigidly straight beside him, staring at the ceiling and ignoring his tentative caresses. "David," she asked, "where are we going?"

It was a question with no real answer, but hardly a frivolous one. "I don't know," he said. "To hell, along with the rest of the country, I guess."

"Oh, David, that's what I'm afraid of. I really am."

Abandoning his efforts to arouse her, David sat up, turned on the bed lamp, lit two cigarettes and handed her one. "All right, come on," he said, "spit it out."

"That's just it. There isn't anything to spit out. It's just a feeling," she said.

"I suppose you're going to say it would be better if we'd stayed in Cambridge. . . ."

"Yes . . . no . . . I've grown up enough to know that a place doesn't make any difference."

"Then what?"

"I don't know what. . . . Tell me, David, are you happy?"

"With you, yes."

"I didn't mean that. I mean with everything."

"I don't know. I don't know that a person's supposed to be happy. . . ."

"Well, that's the wrong word too, I guess. I mean, don't you think we ought to be going somewhere, doing something, standing for something instead of just drinking lousy gin and playing tennis and making love and wondering what we'll do with all your grandfather's money if he ever dies?"

"Sometimes," David admitted. "But what—?"

"Oh, hell, I don't know what, and neither do you. Maybe we ought to have a real religion. . . ."

"Great, let's join a synagogue."

"That isn't so funny. . . ."

"I could have myself circumcised, and then we really would have a cause, especially in Fox Chapel."

Suddenly she started to cry, a rare performance for peppy good sport Ann Gillespie Stewart, tennis champion of the field club. She buried her head on David's chest. "David, please, where *are* we going?" And then they did make love, which relieved the moment but didn't answer the question.

If you wanted to know where you are going, as David had learned in navigation courses, you had to know where you'd been, and where you were at the time. Even this was hard to determine. Looking back, it seemed to him that they had been drifting since the war like a plane in an updraft, a boat in a tide, without compass or bearings. The decision to go back and finish at Harvard, while Ann transferred to Radcliffe, had been easy and sensible. The old folks were delighted and put them both on an allowance just large enough to afford a little apartment on Harvard Square, where they spent most of their time sitting around on the floor and drinking wine and talking endlessly with fellow students, many of whom were disillusioned veterans of the "war to end wars." For a while there they had lots to talk about. Things seemed to be happening. The nation was writhing in pain as if trying to give birth to a new order. There was the coal strike, the steel strike, the Boston police strike, the New York cigar-makers strike, the national buyers' strike and all the rest. The revolution was at hand, and Ann and David, putting out of mind the money piling up for them back in Pittsburgh, joined the poets on their Cambridge floor in cheering from the sidelines. (It was only later David learned what it was really like when he listened to Frank Shaughnessy's graphic description. "Ever see one o' them fellas comin' at you atop his horse—you know, there was horses trained to bite a striker, grab him and bite him and hold him—swingin' that goddamn club like an axe—ever see that and you'll know what it is to shit your pants, I can tell ya.")

Perhaps because of his burning, almost inexpressible, love for Ann, David had begun to show a talent for fragile verse, and Ann had begun making grand plans for him to be another Rupert Brooke while she put her courses in social work to use in the ghetto. Then came 1920—not the year so much as the feeling of the year. A nation, yearning for "normalcy," enthroned Warren Gamaliel Harding and his businessman cabinet, and the poets of Cambridge began skulking shamefacedly off to Wall Street, where the action was. Ann, who was expecting a baby, and David, who was still underage and living off an allowance from Grandy Stewart, were getting heavy pressure from Pittsburgh—long and pleading letters from Mrs. Gillespie who simply couldn't live without her baby (not to mention her baby's baby) and curt queries with every check from Grandy Stewart as to when David would be ready to "go to work." David could still remember the real turning point—November 2, 1920 . . . sitting on the floor as usual listening on an MIT friend's crystal set to history's first broadcast of election returns from history's first licensed radio station, Pittsburgh's KDKA.

"You know what, darling?" David said to Ann. "I think I hear Pittsburgh calling."

"So do I, dammit," she said. "Is there any more wine?"

So it wasn't a thing they really decided . . . they simply drifted back on the current. It had already been arranged for David to "learn business" by moving in as treasurer of the George Gillespie Company, in which Grandy Stewart held a controlling interest. It had been a thoughtful decision, based on the feeling in Pittsburgh that David, as a trained pilot, would have more of a natural interest in Gillespie's aircraft business than some of the other Stewart enterprises. In fact, the only thing that made the job tolerable for David was that he persuaded his father-in-law to allow him to function as test pilot of the two-cockpit Tiger Moth biplane the company had acquired from war surplus to try out new devices and instruments. Once a week or more when the weather was favorable he would go out to Bettis Field and put the old ship through all the shuddering gymnastics he could think of, more to reassure himself that he was truly alive than to test performances. He also took Ann with him whenever possible, she loving it as much as he did. "It's the granddaddy of all roller coasters," she would scream as they came out of a dive. He actually did begin to teach her how to fly and would let her take over the dual controls on routine landings and takeoffs. But flying didn't really seem to be getting them anywhere, any more than making whoopee was. . . .

In maudlin moods David even took to thinking of himself as a "poor little rich boy." Because of his probable inheritance, even the joy of pursuing money that seemed to drive most of his acquaintances throughout the days was denied him. And because Grandy Stewart played his cards close to the vest, David had no real idea how much it was, though there were hints. When Clay Frick died in '19 and his will was probated at $143,000,000 Grandy Stewart declared, "I should have thought he'd be worth more than that." So there was no telling, except that the amount was obviously beyond normal dreams of avarice. Once when Ann read him a passage from Scott Fitzgerald to the effect that the rich are different from you and me, David said, "You bet. They don't know where they're going."

Ann was delighted. "Now you're getting the message," she said.

It helped a little, but not enough, to understand the question, to get some sense of what lay beneath the restlessness that drove Ann and him and most of their friends from one fad to another. It was possible, of course, to attribute their plight to the grim realities of the Great War which tended to belie all the platitudes about progress and a beneficent deity by which their elders had lived. With a draft that could not be evaded the way it had been in the Civil War, millions of men—the rich as well as the poor, the educated as well as the illiterate, the brave as well as the cowards—had been tumbled together like tickets in a giant lottery, and the lucky numbers won a chance at an impersonal, muddy death that seemed forever to make a mockery of the notion of individual will and power. Only the old men, who stood aloof by reason of age and watched the profit figures climb on the ledgers of their mills, could any longer think of war and national purpose in terms of challenge and opportunity. The young men felt they knew better. And, along with the flag, what was left of God was machine-gunned to tatters. What man could believe in a God who would permit such horrors to be inflicted man on man in His holy name? Even those who had escaped the actual experience could hardly fail to hear the siren alarm being rung in book after book, play after play—*All Quiet on the Western Front, Journey's End, What Price Glory?, Three Soldiers*. With the absolute north of its ideals demagnetized, the compass of the whole country in which David and Ann Stewart were trying to find their way was spinning wildly. If nothing was worth dying for, what was worth living for except the next drink, the next roll in the hay, the next buck—anything you could actually get your hands on? Somewhere along toward the wee hours of any gathering, someone rendered poetic by synthetic gin would sum it all up by invoking Edna St. Vincent Millay— "My candle burns at both ends; It will not last the night; But ah, my foes, and, oh, my friends—It gives a lovely light. . . ."

Of course there was more of this mood of despair in Cambridge than in Pittsburgh. There they found it only among their contemporaries, the second- and third-generation rich who had been to war, who had been to college, who had maybe even visited the Paris salon of that old Pittsburgh girl turned arty, Gertrude Stein. Even though the first American doughboy killed in the war was an unfortunate Pittsburgher by the name of Thomas F. Enright, a good number of people, tending the furnaces of war, didn't find things so bad. Talk to Frank Shaughnessy, and he'd say, "Those were pretty good times. Lots of money rolling in and a man could still get a decent drink. Hardly a one of us couldn't buy himself a Ford and put a chicken in the pot every Sunday." Talk to Scott Stewart and he'd comment dryly, "Well, they say we met more than two hundred million in government contracts." When the postwar "revolution" was put down, the city's machinery was retooled to turn out steel for cars and buildings, aluminum for airplanes, electronic components for radios; her pitchmen were on the road selling the good life any American should be able to buy. If there was a theme song for Pittsburgh, it had to be "My God How the Money Rolls In," and at least the men who managed her affairs knew exactly where *they* were going—up.

Almost symbolically, Pittsburgh's richest citizen, Andrew W. Mellon, had been summoned to Washington to preside over the nation's monetary affairs as Secretary of the Treasury, though at first there had been a slight problem when Mellon's backers proposed his name to President Harding. Although Mellon owned more money than any other American with the possible exception of Rockefeller, Harding was supposed to have asked, "Who's he?" He soon learned. At a cabinet meeting, according to a story that went around, the subject of the Chinese Eastern Railway came up, and Mellon said, "Oh, yes, we had a million or a million and a half of the bonds." An amused Harding suddenly decided that he now knew who Mellon was. "He's the ubiquitous financier of the universe," he said.

Judge Reed Stewart with his penchant for dwelling upon the symbolism of Pittsburgh buildings endeared himself to David when he discussed the Mellon phenomenon in what he called "concrete terms." They were walking down Sixth Avenue to one of the periodic lunches at the Duquesne Club that David had begun to share with his great-uncle when Reed suddenly swept the skyline with his cane and said, "Look at this place. It's a collection of tombstones, each higher than the last. First Carnegie, fifteen stories; then Frick, twenty-four stories; then Harry Oliver, twenty-five stories. The smart one, though, is Mellon. He keeps a low profile even in memorials. Look at his bank building—only four stories, though there are, suitably enough, a couple underground. Still, he's managed to stick enough fluted columns around to make it an impressive cathedral of earning."

David knew his uncle was punning on the projected fifty-two-story Cathedral of Learning to be built on the University of Pittsburgh's Oakland campus. "Say, Uncle Reed, why do you suppose Grandy Stewart hasn't built anything?"

"Oh, he's the smartest of them all," Reed said. "No Stewart park, no Stewart building, no Stewart institute. He not only still has his money, but there aren't a dozen people in town who have any idea of how much he has. They all think of him as a fussy old Sunday-school superintendent. You've really got to know Scott Stewart to envy him."

David was accustomed to such talk from Reed, and it was the reason he enjoyed being with him. Nearly everyone else took Scott Stewart so seriously that it was almost frightening, particularly now that he was known to be Secretary Mellon's right-hand man. He had no official title, but everybody knew that Scott Stewart was summoned down to the Treasury, and even the White House, almost every week. Explaining to David, Scott said, "Andy Mellon told me he wouldn't do me the unkindness of asking me to take an official position. 'I wouldn't want you to make that kind of sacrifice, Stewart,' he said. 'Why, do you know that I have to pay twenty thousand dollars a year for a decent apartment down here in Washington—five thousand more than they pay me?' " Still, anybody who knew him well could detect Scott Stewart's fine hand in the writing of what had become known as "the Mellon plan." As Reed put it to David when they were discussing the plan, "Everybody says you can't take it with you, but I've got to hand it to Andy Mellon and your grandfather—they're going to try anyway."

As part of the "return to normalcy" after the war years, the plan called for repeal of the excess-profit tax and a cut in the income tax and surtax. (Mellon's explanation was that the businessman needed more monetary incentive, adding that "when that incentive is crippled by legislation or by a tax system which denies him the right to receive a reasonable share of his earnings, then he will no longer exert himself and the country will be deprived of the energy on which its continued greatness depends.") The plan also included a reduction in inheritance taxes. (Without such a cut, Mellon explained, "private ownership of property would cease to exist. Estate taxes, carried to excess, in no way differ from the method of the revolutionists in Russia.") The tax bill Mellon put before Congress in 1925 lifted the tax load of the rich by some $700,000,000, and Secretary Mellon himself would save $828,349 as compared to his 1924 taxes. But it was sure to pass since, in these roaring days of rising markets, *everybody* planned to get rich. . . .

Although at the age of seventy-three Scott Stewart, like the seventy-year-old Secretary himself, might have been expected to ease up, he was only too happy to increase his work load by his voluntary services to Washington. He felt that, at last, the nation was coming to its senses and recognizing by its votes and the appointment of sound men like Mellon and Hoover the rightful place of business in American society. For Scott Stewart it was a kind of golden age, and he simply would not have understood the midnight where-are-we-going despair of David and Ann, even if they had chosen to share it with him. He was making money as he never had before, and he could scarcely wait until David was seasoned enough to help him shoulder the burden. Meanwhile he would go on doing whatever he could to see that the laws of the land favored the enterprises his grandson would inherit.

Scott was, however, a bit concerned when David once asked him point-blank, "Why don't you start giving away some of your money, Grandy?"

"Well, it's all tied up. . . ."

"You could liquidate like Carnegie," David argued. "Why wait the way Uncle Clay did and never get any pleasure out of what you give?"

"I don't expect to die right now, David. Never felt better in my life. And this is just the wrong time to sell out, with everything going up the way it is. If you're so inclined to give money away, David, you'll have a good deal more when . . ."

"Don't talk about that, Grandy," David said. "I was just curious. . . ."

Scott was happy to drop the conversation. He really didn't like to talk about *that*. Intimations of mortality had been encroaching ever since his mother's death. While she was still alive he'd felt himself a member of a younger generation, however old he was. It didn't help that so many others also went in 1919: Henry Heinz, dead at seventy-five, in May; Andrew Carnegie, dead at eighty-four, in August; Henry Clay Frick, dead at sixty-nine, in December. And then came the shock of his own sister Sarah's death early the next year. She'd been down shopping at Horne's with her daughter, Becky McCandless, when she "felt faint." They stretched her out on the floor of a ladies' room, but before they could find a doctor she was dead of a heart attack. She was only sixty-six, but she'd been looking twenty years older ever since that trouble with Don. Reed looked poorly these days too— somewhat blue-veined and wheezing a bit when he walked— and somebody had told Scott that Lucinda was taking digitalis. Despite what he told David, Scott himself suffered a little stiffening of the joints mornings and seemed to be going a bit deaf the way his mother had. The only way Scott knew to keep his mind off the melancholy prospect of the inevitable was to keep as busy as possible.

Even so, having passed the biblical limit of "threescore years and ten," Scott realized that David had a point when he pressed for some decision as to what to do with his assets. Andy Carnegie, by giving away some $350,000,000 before he died, and now Rockefeller, busy in retirement with establishing foundations for health and education, had established a tradition no conscientious rich man could ignore. David had been wrong about Clay Frick, who had, in fact, distributed some $60,000,000 while he was still alive, although more attention was given to the $20,000,000 of his estate that was earmarked for Pittsburgh institutions, not to mention his gift to the people of his New York home and art collection. Scott had already gone far beyond his cautious tithe of earlier years in support of church-related institutions, particularly the medical work in Siam. He was planning a significant gift to Chancellor Bowman's Cathedral of Learning, and might well participate in efforts to revive the Pittsburgh Symphony if the leaders of the movement would stop insisting on profaning the Sabbath with their concerts. But he was still a long way from either getting rid of enough money or memorializing the Stewart name.

Well, he would worry about that when he knew his time was coming. For all her lack of tact in bringing it up at the wrong time, Lucinda had been quite right about Mary Stewart's wanting to die, knowing she was going to die, and Scott supposed he would too. At the moment, though, he was more concerned about David's drinking than about the young man's seeming reluctance to inherit so much money. David and Ann thought they had him fooled because they didn't drink in front of him, but they didn't realize that people told Scott Stewart things. David would have to learn that you didn't run large enterprises without reliable sources of information, built up over the years with a job here, a gift there. . . . Scott even knew about the Kit-Kat and that fellow Frank Shaughnessy, who somehow had been mixed up in the strikes of '19. With anybody but David, Scott would have put the matter right on the table, but he was afraid that David, backed up by that strong little wife of his, might walk right out on him the way he'd done during the war. He couldn't stand that.

Drinking was bad enough in itself—Scott had seen what it did to his father, to Reed. Now it was illegal, and Scott lived in dread that any morning's newspaper might report that the heir to the Stewart fortune had been apprehended in a raid. If there was anything that made Scott Stewart feel a sense of disappointment in this golden era of the businessman, it was the way the prohibition laws for which he had worked so long and hard were failing in practice. He'd been truly shocked one of the first times he went to Washington and attended a gathering in the Mellon apartment where Old Overholt was served and wine appeared with dinner. Sensing Scott's disapproval, Mellon had taken him aside and offered an apology of sorts. "You know the kind of program we're working for, Stewart, and I must say a bit of spirits goes a long way in this town, particularly now, in influencing legislation. When in Rome, you know . . ." Even more shocking was a session at the White House when, after the meeting, President Harding led them into his own bedroom and poured drinks. "Under the circumstances, gentlemen, Mrs. Harding and I feel that we cannot openly serve alcohol, but what we do in the privacy of our own bedroom is our business." And then there was that silly business about his own brother Reed, making himself the laughingstock of the Pittsburgh bar with his absurd ruling.

With people who should know better acting that way, it wasn't so difficult to understand how young people like David and Ann might be led astray. Perhaps if they went to church more often . . . except instinct had made Scott uneasy when David joined his wife's Episcopal church; those people didn't take their religion seriously enough. Why, he'd seen a rector not a month ago taking sherry at a wedding without a thought for the prohibition laws, not to mention the biblical injunctions against strong drink. "To take a little wine for thy stomach's sake," he heard the rector laughingly quote St. Paul when he picked up a glass. Yet anybody who had studied the matter knew that people called fruit juice wine in those days. Perhaps he ought to send young Henry Sharp out to Fox Chapel to talk to David and Ann; he still remembered that young Henry was the only person besides himself who'd turned away the champagne at David's wedding. A good thing, too, now that they were talking about calling him to the Oakland pulpit when Mr. Timmins retired. Dwelling on the image of sober, serious Henry Ward Beecher Sharp, who was already presiding over a rapidly growing suburban church, made Scott feel that at least some of the good Stewart blood was flowing in the next generation. And surprisingly that young Alexander, Reed's boy, was making a name for himself; according to what Andy Mellon told him, Alexander was well in line for the presidency of the bank. Why couldn't David . . . ?

Whenever he began thinking along these lines, Scott would end up sighing aloud and shaking his head before he realized what he was doing. It was a symptom of age more frightening than stiffening of the joints. By such a gesture he felt he was admitting to himself the time was passing when he could shape his grandson into the image he'd so long held before his inner eye. He would have to content himself that the boy was at least here in Pittsburgh, and working, which was more than most of his wealthy friends could boast about their own sons or grandsons. According to George Gillespie, David was smart as a whip with figures and, through his flying, was making valuable suggestions about modifying their products. It would soon be time to call David into the office as his assistant; perhaps in a closer relationship more of Scott's example would rub off. And there was, of course, the possibility that David, too, might have a son; after all, he and Ann were still only twenty-five, although all that running about she did on the tennis court troubled Scott, who thought it was probably bad for delicate female mechanisms. He could remember how his father fretted over Lucinda's strenuous antics, and Lucinda had never had a child, though—the Lord forgive him for such thoughts—she had given herself enough opportunties. Still, Ann had Martia—a pretty little thing, perhaps too pretty for her own good. But Scott had learned through bitter experience that you couldn't rely on women when it came to anything as important as the future of the Stewart fortune.

The older he became, the more satisfaction Scott Stewart took in his growing holdings of cash, real estate, bonds, stocks. Not one to probe too deeply into himself, he nevertheless was aware of his feeling of relief when he turned from mulling over the affairs of people, or even the affairs of state, to the cool figures he understood so well. If he had been more self-analytical, he might have admitted that his reluctance to give money away had much to do with his sense of satisfaction in handling it. He did regard himself as a good steward in what he held to be the Biblical sense of that term, and the climbing figures in the assets columns of his ledgers simply confirmed that feeling. People, on the other hand, were elusive; they had a way of escaping you. The roll call in his own life was almost too long to contemplate—his father, through weakness and suicide; Martha, through illness; Benjamin through misguided religious zeal (partly his own fault?); May, through what despite himself he still unhappily viewed as sin; his mother, through age; Donald Sharp, through madness; Sarah, through grief and shame. Lucinda and Reed still endured, though sometimes they seemed more acquaintances than family. And now, despite all of his efforts, the boy David was showing disquieting signs. Would there never be someone upon whom he could rely absolutely, someone who caught his own vision of wealth as a sacred trust, someone who put obedience to the divine law above self-indulgence? No woman, certainly; a great-grandson, possibly. Well, he would continue accumulating in hopes of that ultimate blessing the Lord had so far denied him.

What had got him thinking this way? Oh, yes, David's question about giving, and the worry it evoked about the boy's attitudes. Suddenly he literally shook himself into action, repudiating his own resigned sigh, and asked one of the girls to put through a call to his grandson. Why wait any longer? He'd bring the boy into the office right now and perhaps things would start working out. Once David got a real grasp of what his responsibilities were likely to be, he might well turn his life around. "Mr. Stewart, David is on his way to the airport," the girl reported back. Scott drew the watch with the embossed gold cover that Martha had given him as a wedding present—the Lord knows where she got the money —from his vest pocket. Three-thirty. Like as not David wouldn't go back to the office. "Call his home and leave a message for him to call me—tonight."

Although he knew he shouldn't do it, David Stewart dropped into the Kit-Kat for a cooling gin fizz on his way to the airport that hot July afternoon. He'd had another where-are-we-going session with Ann that morning, and later, a battle with his father-in-law about increasing safety inspection on the new altimeter they were putting into production. He felt he needed something to relax him before he took the plane up—not so much alcohol as a session with his "priest." Frank Shaughnessy was, as David had hoped, all alone. With the venetian blinds drawn against the glaring sun, the place was soothingly dark, and a clicking electric fan struggled bravely to stir the heavy air into a semblance of a breeze. Frank was scrutinizing a newspaper under the small light above the cash register.

"Anything for heat stroke, doc?"

"Coming right up—the Shaughnessy special," said Frank, reaching for the gin.

When David had taken an appreciative sip, Frank asked, "Now what do you think, Mr. Stewart—are we descended from apes or not?"

"You've been reading about that Scopes trial again."

"Yeah," Frank said, "they've got old Bryan on the stand."

"Bryan? I thought he was one of the prosecuting attorneys."

"He is, but Darrow got the idea of calling him as a witness, so the paper here says, to make him look silly. You know, the old fellow actually believes Jonah was swallowed by a whale and Joshua made the sun stand still. Sounds like a nun I had back in school, and we all knew she was crazy."

David laughed; he was getting the real medicine he wanted. "Obviously you're on the other side, Frank. You think Scopes was right teaching evolution, don't you? So why ask me?"

"Well, I seen enough apes right in here, present company excepted, to prove it to me," Frank said. "I just thought, bein' your grandfather is such a big church man and all . . ."

"My grandfather and I don't agree on a lot of things," David said, lifting his glass in example.

"The way of the world." Frank sighed. "One of me own kids is studyin' to be a priest, and now he wants me to get out of this business. Can you imagine that?"

"Are you going to do it?"

"Not on your life, Mr. Stewart. I told the kid he can confess me if he wants, but he can't reform me."

"Thank God for that," David said, and smiled. "I don't know what we'd all do without you. Personally I think you do more good than a monastery full of priests."

"Well, thanks for them kind words, Mr. Stewart. Another?"

"Not today. I'm going flying."

"Oh. Well, they say you can't fly on one wing."

"I know, but I think I'd better try."

Out in the sun again, with the top down on his little roadster, David was beginning to feel the pleasant tension of anticipation he always had before a flight. Though the day was still bright, great white tiers of clouds were rising on the horizon. David could hardly wait to get up among them and frisk through what looked like fields of soft cotton snow. It might be a little risky today since there was likely to be a thunderhead or two, but on the other hand a bit of tossing around would be a good test for the instruments. He wished he could have persuaded Ann to go with him; maybe she would have been shaken out of her dark mood. This morning for the first time little Martia begged to go along, and he'd promised her a ride for her sixth birthday, just a little more than a year away. From the way she rode her pony he could tell that his daughter had considerable grit, and he was beginning to think about turning her into what surely would be one of the first women pilots. The more he thought about it, the better he liked the idea; it was at least *some* answer to where he might be going.

At the field, his plane was already out of the hangar and ready. He gave it a quick once-over with his eye and patted the fuselage before he climbed into the cockpit. A sturdy little beast. He knew Jake, the mechanic, who had learned his trade in France during the war, gave her good care and feeding. He struggled into his parachute harness, strapped himself down, pulled his goggles over his eyes and signaled to Jake to turn the prop over. She roared and buckled against the blocks until Jake yanked them away. He wheeled her down the runway, turned into what wind there was and let her go wide open until he felt her lift into the wonderful freedom of the sky.

David nosed his little Moth up, up, up in wider and wider spirals, coming ever closer to the edge of the clouds. Now that he was up here he could see a huge black mass moving rapidly from the west and shoving and scattering the puffy white clouds like a bull in a fold of sheep. Whether it was the gin in him or just the vague urge to do something meaningful, he decided to challenge it. He had put the Moth through every possible strain and there was no reason to suppose she wouldn't hold together. There was some doubt, however, about what might happen to those instruments that the Gillespie Company was assembling too rapidly and too sloppily for David's taste. It would give him immense satisfaction to be able to go back to his father-in-law with proof positive of the argument the old man had rejected earlier in the day on the grounds of costs.

Keeping his eye on the instruments, David flew straight into the cloud. Turbulent air rocked and tossed the little plane and then suddenly snatched the bottom out from under it. It was like dropping off the edge of a cliff. The plane bottomed out with a slam several hundred feet down—David couldn't tell how many hundred, because the altimeter had gone haywire—and threw him with such force against his belt that he thought something inside him must have ruptured. Before he could worry much about that, there was a great tearing noise. The two port wings broke away, and the plane nosed into a crazy spiral. David fought with his seat belt, cursing and tearing his fingers in his effort to get loose. When he did, he literally was tumbled out of the cockpit, clawing at the ripcord of his parachute. It broke open a fraction of a second too soon, and the tail of the gyrating plane hooked the shrouds.

Unlike most men, David Scott Stewart knew he was going to die, and it was what this knowledge might have done to him that would haunt for many years the minds of those he left behind. Frank Shaughnessy gave his own summation to the regulars in the Kit-Kat that night. "Poor bastard," he kept saying over and over again. "Poor bastard . . ."

A Promise to Keep

Reed Stewart stood in front of the bank of tall windows in the parlor of the old Ridge Avenue house watching the rain carve streaks of light into the gray stuff that perpetually dimmed the countless leaded panes. They rarely were washed now unless Alexander or Carolyn sent a grandchild up to do a day's work. Alma was too heavy to take a chance on climbing ladders, and she had simply refused to let Reed lift a finger ever since he'd had his stroke. Well, it didn't matter so much. Somehow the dirty windows went with the rest of the house that was slowly crumbling around them. The worst of it at the moment was that place in the dining-room ceiling where the plaster was cracking and flaking so badly it would snow right into your food when the boys were making too much ruckus upstairs and jarring the floor. Some untraceable leak from above was eating away at that ceiling. The boys said it was from the roof, but Reed doubted it since you couldn't see any dampness there, even on a day like this. His guess was that these heedless young men were just slopping water all over the bathroom floors; he'd heard them running the shower half an hour at a time. No point fussing about it, though; these days you were lucky to find boarders who could pay the rent and didn't mind doing their own housekeeping.

"I wonder which will fall apart first—us or this old pile of bricks," Reed said to Alma one evening when they were sitting in the little study and enjoying their one indulgence, a tot or two of Old Overholt.

"I don't know, but it makes an interesting race," she said.

God love her! Alma had been a real brick through the

whole nightmare of losing everything they had in the '29 crash. While other people were jumping out of windows, she turned coolly practical. "All we have left, Reed, is this house," she'd said. "It's been too big for us for a long time, but we wouldn't get anything from it now. Why don't we put in a bathroom in that big old closet under the stairs and turn the pantry into a bedroom for us? We could live down here and rent out the upper floors."

Reed liked the idea. What clients he had never paid much, and as the financial crisis deepened he was taking in barely enough to cover his office rent and the pittance he paid his secretary, a widow with two small children whom he couldn't bear to fire. Their children were, of course, aghast. As president of one of the biggest banks, Alexander was doing better, if anything; he'd been able to pick up a Sewickley estate with stables and tennis court and pool for a song in '30. "Why don't you come live with us? With the boy in college we'll rattle around down there," he argued without actually coming out and saying that he was also embarrassed to have his parents running a boardinghouse. "At your age, you shouldn't be living here in all this smog anyway." Alma, bless her, wouldn't listen. "I was born here," she told her son, "and I'm going to die here." With all those children still at home, Carolyn couldn't make the same kind of offer, but, Depression or no, people's teeth were still getting cavities, and Dr. Schermerhorn took his father-in-law aside and said, "If you and Mother would like to get yourselves a little house somewhere out in the suburbs, I just want you to know that I could see my way to a loan." Reed shook his head; it was too embarrassing to explain that he'd reached a stage in life when he couldn't see his way to repaying a loan.

So they stayed on—and somehow made do. It hurt a little that the kids never came to see them—"I just can't bear watching the old place fall apart," Carolyn once told them in a moment of too much candor—but they did send their cars around to take Alma and Reed down for visits to their well-kept Sewickley homes. Without quite saying it, the children somehow implied that they felt all of this would never have happened if Alma had been more of a regular wife instead of parading about the streets for women's suffrage which, God knows, hadn't done the world much good, and concentrated on making Reed into more of a regular kind of husband who put taking care of his wife and business affairs ahead of playing with a lot of strange ideas and drinking whiskey in the Duquesne Club.

As it turned out, Alma's idea of taking in boarders turned out to be more of a psychological than a financial blessing. In fact, during those low times in '32 and '33, they didn't even ask for rent for months at a time from those young fellows, who were literally wearing their shoes out looking for jobs; one of them kept a pair going almost a year by making inner soles out of newspapers. But even though they were sloppy and noisy, the kind of young men they took in—they had a newspaper reporter and a seminary student and a resident doctor now—were pleasant and even fun to have around. Unlike their own children, this succession of young men seemed to find Reed and Alma stimulating. They were forever dropping into the little study before dinner for a snort and advice about their jobs or love lives or just a chat about the general sorry state of the world.

"God, I'm glad I'm not young now," Reed said to Alma when one of the boys had left them after agonizing over troubles down at the plant. John L. Lewis's new Committee of Industrial Organization was putting on an organizing drive, and the boy didn't know whether to go along with them as he wanted to—at the risk of losing his job and having to drop out of seminary—or be a safe company man.

"And why not?" Alma responded. "At least he seems to to have a choice. In the good old days there wasn't any choice, was there? I'd love to be young now. Look what women are doing these days. Look at Eleanor Roosevelt, going all over the country, saying what she pleases. . . ."

Reed laughed. "If the boys at the Duquesne Club could only hear you now. . . ."

Alma, quick as ever to catch her husband's moods, said, "That's the only thing I'm really sorry about, Reed. You miss it so much, don't you?"

"Why should I? The whiskey's just as good right here," he lied.

Giving up his membership in the Duquesne Club had been Reed's hardest sacrifice. He'd held on, even after all the servants had been dismissed, after the car had been sold, after the house was opened to boarders. His greatest pleasure, especially after Roosevelt's New Deal got underway, was his lunchtime baiting of his fellow members. It was kind of a cruel sport, he had to admit, like shooting fish in a barrel. All you had to do with some of them to produce a rise in blood pressure was to mention that man in the White House. . . . "Say, did you see what Roosevelt said today . . .?" Whereupon at least one of his table-mates was sure to fling down his fork and say . . . "That son of a bitch! What's he up to now? He'll ruin this country yet, you'll *see*."

The joke was that the very same man had said the very same thing about F.D.R.'s cousin Teddy even though he was a Republican; yet here he sat, richer than ever despite the Depression, and was surer than ever that the country was going to hell. It was only the people out there, the people who had lost everything, or had never had anything, who gathered around their radios, hanging on Roosevelt's words, who began to have hope that they really might get a new deal. Reed had joined them, had voted Democratic for the first time in his life in '32, and was enjoying the show. Hot-blooded types like the tycoons who gathered in the Duquesne Club had, it seemed to him, such a faulty sense of history. For them, everything hung on the current year's annual report. It was useless to point out to them that, barring a Communist revolution, they were likely to come out of this Depression in better shape than ever, as men of real property always had survived such times. Even Scott, who was far older than most of these men—indeed, a kind of living relic in the Pittsburgh business world—and, in Reed's opinion, should have known better, was heard to say about Roosevelt that "the fellow's a fool, just like his cousin—must run in the blood."

Fool or not, Roosevelt had managed to get things going enough so that, by this March of 1936, smoke from the factories was once again beginning to smudge the windows on Ridge Avenue, and their tenants were more able to pay. It was an irony, Reed thought, as he looked out at the mournful skies, that the good Lord had picked just this time to try once again to wipe this city of steel right off the face of the earth. . . .

The flood was a truly frightening thing; they'd been able to watch it from the top of the house, see the whole point gradually sink under the rising waters like a ship going down at sea, see the fingers of water probe along the streets and claw above the first stories of the tightly clustered buildings. By the previous Wednesday, March 18, when the water crested at forty-six feet, the whole triangle was awash. Power was out, water was turned off. News was hard to come by, but people reported the water had washed clear over the tops of street-cars stalled in the middle of Penn Avenue; automobiles had simply vanished. Fires raged untended, and people panicked; state police and National Guard units were brought in to keep order. Nobody yet was able to count all the dead and homeless. It was the worst flood in the city's recorded history, but there was no assurance that it was the last. Again Reed, who'd brooded over these matters so long ago when he was a young man watching the city's public-works funds line private pockets, had to shake his head in amazement at his fellow man's perversity in ignoring his history. True, some Pittsburgh citizens had awakened to the necessity of trying to control floods, but nothing much had been done beyond beseeching Washington for help.

Reed's immediate problem, as he watched the rain, was getting up enough courage to sneak downtown as soon as Alma went out to shop; she would surely prevent him if she knew his intentions. Though the waters had receded, chaos was still endemic. For the most part, power was still out, and Reed knew he would probably have to walk five flights up to his Oliver Building office, might even have to walk most of the way to town. He wouldn't have contemplated going except that he'd promised to meet Mrs. Elkins, and he knew he would have to file her petition for support today or the statute of limitations would run out. He could kick her now for waiting so long to come to him, but then he knew a thing or two about pride himself. She would be there, no doubt, since unless they could get some money out of Elkins, she and her children would be obliged to go on relief, a humiliation worse for a proud woman such as Mrs. Elkins than to admit her husband had left her. Reed shivered a little at the thought of venturing forth in all that rain and muck. At seventy-three a man ought not to have to work at all. The worst of it was that he knew there wasn't a hope for a fee from a woman like Mrs. Elkins. He didn't know why he was mixed up in so many messy and unprofitable cases of people whose personal lives had become a tangle. Most of them came to him from other lawyers, and he guessed it had something to do with the reputation he'd made on the bench for being easy on divorce. And he had never mastered the technique for turning people away.

Alma bustled in now, kissed him on the forehead and said, "Don't worry about those windows, Reed. First nice day I'll try to get Carolyn to send one of the youngsters to wash them. I'm going shopping now. It may be a little difficult so don't worry if I'm gone a while."

"I won't," he said. "Be careful."

As soon as Alma had gone, Reed wrote a little note, telling her he had been called to town for an emergency, and set out himself. Fortunately, the streetcars were running and he was able to get within a few blocks of his office before he had to get off and walk. The sidewalks were jammed with people—mostly rubber-necking, he guessed—and men in boots and slickers were shoveling mud and debris into trucks and washing it off the face of buildings. Power was still spotty, and a number of buildings, his own among them, were looming dark hulks with only an eerie flickering of a candle here or a flashlight there to betray human occupancy. Here was this city—prouder than ever since the building boom of the twenties shot the Koppers Building thirty-five stories, the Grant Building forty stories, the Gulf Building forty-four stories into the sky—turned overnight into a helpless, muddy shambles by the silent, relentless forces of an early spring thaw. The papers were screaming disaster in their headlines, but Reed wondered if, in the long run, it might not be a healthy reminder to some people who tended to forget the impermanence of things.

Reed's office was five flights up. No elevators were running yet, and he wished he'd thought to bring a flashlight himself as he began slowly, pausing on each step as the doctors had warned him to do, ascending the gloomy passage of the fire stairs. The climb seemed endless. He was conscious of having a harder time catching his breath with nearly every step, but then what could a man his age and out of condition expect? At the third landing he stopped and lit a cigarette, but it tasted rank and he ground it out under his heel. He would have been smarter to bring along a flask. Then he remembered he usually kept a bottle tucked away in his desk, and he began mounting the last flights with a new sense of purpose. Once he got a good drink inside him he'd be all right; going down again would be no trick. But he began to think he had been clearly, certifiably insane to come down here at all. Surely Mrs. Elkins would have yielded to the inevitable and stayed home like any sane person should.

When he finally made it through the fire door into the strange, shadowy hallway outside his office, he saw her leaning against the wall. Well, perhaps his effort had not been so pointless after all.

"Oh, Mr. Stewart, I was so afraid you wouldn't come," she said while he fumbled with his keys to find the right one for the office door.

Reed nodded as he opened the door, started to step in, and realized, in a kind of detached amazement, that he was falling, as if he had put a foot into an empty elevator shaft instead of on the familiar floor of his office. He would never know the difference, since a merciful God had switched off his power in the second it took his body to pitch headlong across the threshold. . . .

"Damned fool thing to do, going downtown on a day like that, a man in his condition," Scott said to Lucinda while they waited uneasily in the parlor of the North Side funeral home, where Alma had elected to have the services.

Lucinda, struggling for control over her own devastating sense of loss, found a kind of comfort in Scott's gruff, seemingly irritated (how much was camouflage for grief?) reaction to their brother's death; at eighty-four, Scott still showed the world that hard surety that a sensible, God-fearing man could hang onto things, even life itself. True, Scott was somewhat bent now by the arthritis—"stiffness in the joints," he called it—that he had evidently inherited; his hair and brows and mustache were wispy white; he was a little deaf and had a habit of cupping an ear with his hand when people didn't "speak up" the way he thought they should. Still, his eyes were bright—in fact, a kind of second sight had enabled him to dispense with the half glasses he used to put on for reading—and his voice was firm. Though his thin neck seemed to wobble inside the old-fashioned stiff collars he insisted on wearing summer and winter, and his dark suits and vests hung loosely on his contracting frame, he continued to "step out," as he put it, to move with the purpose of a man who knew where he was going. Every time she saw Scott, Lucinda was reminded of Reed's wry comment on the passing of Judge Thomas Mellon in '08 at the age of ninety-five: "They say absolute power corrupts absolutely, but I say that absolute wealth preserves absolutely."

"We all have to go sometime," Lucinda said to Scott.

"Maybe so," Scott replied and then, crinkling his nose in distaste at the sickly sweet aroma of embalming fluid and dying flowers that reminded him painfully of the way the old Oakland place had smelled for months after Martha was laid out there, he said, "I don't see why they didn't have this in a church."

"Reed hasn't darkened the doors of a church for thirty years, and Alma thought it would be in poor taste," Lucinda explained.

"Well, I don't know where they are going to put all these people."

There was a surprising number of people filing into the stuffy little parlor, standing awkwardly around and talking in low voices as if they might awaken the deceased. Most of the sitting judges were there as well as a lot of old political figures who had long been presumed dead, and a handful of relatives—only Dr. Stewart Sharp came for his branch of the family. Most of the people were unrecognizable, poorly dressed strangers who likely were Reed's clients paying their respects instead of their bills. For a few more minutes the doors of the chapel were closed against them while the immediate family viewed the remains. When they were opened, there was not enough room, as Scott had surmised, to seat all the people, but he and Lucinda were ushered to chairs behind the row occupied by Alma and Alexander and Carolyn and their families. The flower-banked coffin was open. Reed was laid out in the cutaway and striped trousers he had last worn to David's wedding, and his face had been delicately turned to hide the scar that had become his proudest mark in life. Death and the mortician's deft hand had erased the lines of quizzical concern and paled the angry, alcoholic flush of his features; a smile was frozen on his lips. To both Lucinda and Scott, it was like looking at a ghost of the boy who had once seemed almost too innocently pretty to be a boy. Lucinda had to duck her head and bite her lips. Scott busied himself with blowing his nose.

There was no eulogy. A young rector from Alexander's Sewickley church, looking rather uncomfortable, read soothing passages of scripture: ". . . Though I walk through the valley of the shadow of death, I fear no evil . . . ," while an electric organ murmured soft hymns in the background. Alma wept uncontrollably. Her great body shook so that it threatened to collapse the spindly funeral chair she was sitting in. Scott turned away to pay attention to the passages the minister was reading. The closer Scott got to his own grave, the more he liked to listen to the majestic roll of promises—"in my father's house there are many mansions"—in the burial service. He thought of Reed and Alma's life together these last years and couldn't imagine it had been anything but difficult. . . . He'd tried to help out, had himself driven on a Sunday over to that old house they should have left years ago and put the offer—diplomatically, he thought—on the basis that he had just discovered an error in Mary Stewart's estate which meant Reed hadn't been given a fair share out of the disposal of the South Hills property.

"My goodness, Scott," Alma said, "you're just finding out after all these years? You should have had a good lawyer like Reed handle the estate."

"Don't be silly, Alma," Reed said. "It was handled perfectly. I went over it with Shaw at the time. No thanks, Scott, we're not charity cases—yet."

Pride. Foolish pride. And yet Scott had gone away feeling more impressed by his brother than he had in a long time. Just as he was feeling now about Lucinda, who sat beside him bearing her grief with stoic dignity the way a real Stewart should. When he was having trouble with his nose, he had seen her eyes mist, seen her bite her lips, but she had her head up now, higher than his own, in fact, since she didn't suffer from stiffening joints. Glancing sideways at her profile, Scott had to admit that Lucinda was still a remarkably handsome woman; her white hair, which she wore long and coiled into a bun instead of frizzled like Ann and the other young women these days, gave her more distinction than age. . . . Thought of Ann reminded him of a worry he'd had while they were waiting to get into the services—he hadn't seen her or Martia. He twisted around in his seat as much as he dared and got a glimpse of them standing near the door and felt relieved, although it was such a long drive from Fox Chapel he'd told her not to bother coming. She had insisted. "You know, David loved his uncle Reed, Grandy."

David. Just thinking of him again, particularly in these surroundings, brought Scott far closer to losing his own self-control than the death at hand. That was one funeral where he'd found no comfort in the scripture, where shock alone had carried him numbly through the necessary paces. More than a decade had passed, but he realized this minute that his sense of loss was as grievous as ever. Secretly, in the loneliness of his big, empty house, he had wept over David months, years, after the event, and it unnerved him to feel that he could do it again unless he kept a tight grip on himself. Scott could not get over that the accident had happened the very day he had put a call in to summon David at last to his side. It was as if the Lord rose up and said, "You can't have him . . . you can never have anybody."

In his agonized search for comfort, Scott read the book of Job over and over again and prayed for understanding. For the first time in a long life of asking God for strength and guidance, of thanking God for bountiful blessings, he found himself berating God, demanding, "Why didn't you take me instead of him?" There was no sure answer, of course, and a tormented Scott was driven to humble himself to the extent of taking the question to his pastor, Mr. Timmins. Ever since that business about the war—indeed if Timmins hadn't let his own son go and preached that fiery sermon about it, David might never have learned to fly, might never have been killed—Scott had little respect for the minister's thinking. Still, who else could help? In Scott's experience preachers sometimes had a feeling for the Word even when they didn't understand it. Timmins proved no exception. "Why, Elder Stewart," he said, "I should have thought that you, of all people, would see what the Lord is trying to tell you. You're not ready yet." "Not ready?" "Yes, not ready to go. He still has business for you—what, I don't know, but I'm sure you'll find out."

So Scott went on, taking that part about business rather literally. People were always asking him when he was going to retire, or ease up, but they didn't understand that he was happiest, as ever, in the office, in the midst of affairs he could manage and manipulate. Besides, Andy Mellon, who wasn't much younger than he, was still at the helm of the Treasury, and Richard Mellon was still on top of business in Pittsburgh. During those last years of the twenties, they were all reaping the harvests they had so laboriously sown, and Scott, watching his granary fill to overflowing, waited patiently for the Lord to tell him what to do with it.

An answer came, in part, with the Depression. Scott, who had taken the biblical lesson of the seven fat years and the seven lean years to heart as a child in Mr. Wallace's Sunday school and applied them through a long life of financial crises, was in better shape than most of the people around him. Though his fortune dwindled on paper, he hardly had need to panic; he could hold on, and he could keep his head clear to give advice to the younger men on the various company boards who were terrified by their first experience with a receding economic tide. It will come back, he kept telling them, and he agreed with then President Hoover and Andy Mellon that the wise thing to do was to let nature take its course. In a personal way, the Depression thrust on Scott an obligation that was even more meaningful. For years, independent little Ann Stewart had refused all help from Scott beyond casual presents. David had accumulated enough stock in the Gillespie Company, she explained, to take care of her and Martia and, of course, she would one day inherit her father's interest. But the company went down like David's Moth after the crash. Gillespie himself, wiped out and in debt, died of a heart attack in '31, and Scott stepped in to rescue Ann and Martia and Mrs. Gillespie, who had moved in with her daughter. Leery of long-term trust arrangements at a time when banks were closing their doors, he simply began sending Ann a generous monthly check and was still doing it. Now that things were looking up some, he would have to consider a more permanent arrangement; the old hopes he'd thought were buried in the grave with David were beginning to live again in the girl Martia.

Going on sixteen, Martia was, everybody agreed, a "spitting image" of her father. She had the dark hair and dark eyes that came down through Scott, to Benjamin, to David, to her, and a softly blurred version of the sharp, patrician features of the Stewarts, but she was also small like her mother. It didn't seem to matter, since she could ride and play tennis and swim with the best of them; she was, for example, girls' champion at the club in the backstroke when she was twelve. Scott still grumbled to Ann about letting the girl get involved in all those strenuous sports, but he had to admit they gave her an agile little figure and a comforting glow of good health. Once when they were talking about it, Dr. Stewart Sharp assured him that his fears about athletics damaging a girl's "mechanisms" were pure nonsense, but it was hard to be certain how much Sharp really knew about medicine. After such a promising beginning, he'd been content to stay out there at that veterans' hospital working with those poor fellows who would never be right in the head, and he was still a major, making only three thousand dollars a year. Good his wife Jane came from the poor branch of the Laughlins.

. . .

Scott didn't realize his thoughts had wandered so far from the ceremony until Lucinda gave him a dig in the ribs. It was all over, and people were getting up to go. Alexander was leading his mother past them, and she was still so distraught that she barely gave them a glance. There would be no graveside rites. Reed himself had asked to be cremated—"Graves are a waste of good land," he would argue—and Alma, they said, was planning to keep the ashes in the Ridge Avenue house. The thought of the whole thing made Scott shiver; somehow it seemed heathen. One thing sure: he didn't want to go back there and sit around with Alma in this condition. He wondered if Lucinda didn't either.

He turned to her and said without explanation, "I'm not going to the house. Can I give you a ride home?"

Lucinda didn't think she could stand to go to Ridge Avenue either. There were too many ghosts; besides, Alma might be better off with just her own family. Unlike her brother's,

422

Lucinda's reaction to Alma's open grief had been an odd kind of jealousy that Alma had been able to enjoy such love almost to the end and to exhibit her loss without shame. She couldn't help remembering her own muffled anguish when she sat shyly in a corner of the great, arching cavern of the Trinity Church downtown, the only suitable theater for the final accolades to a citizen as distinguished as Ambassador T. Gillespie Jones. Ex-President Coolidge himself had come to lead the silent procession of distinguished honorary pallbearers who followed the ambassador's flag-draped coffin down the aisle to the triumphant strains of "The Battle Hymn of the Republic." What would they think, Lucinda wondered, if they all knew that she had right there in her purse a note scribbled in a shaky hand not three days before, saying, "Dearest girl. They tell me my heart won't hold out much longer, but I just want you to know that, as long as it does beat, part of it beats for you. Good-bye and God keep you. Gil." She got it out and held it against her own heart and bit her lips until she could taste the blood. She would rather have wept like Alma. . . .

"Thanks, Scott, I'd like that," Lucinda said briskly. "Oh, there's Ann and Martia. Don't you want them to come along?"

"No, she drove herself, and I expect they'll be wanting to get back for dinner." Scott said.

Scott accepted pecks on the cheek from his granddaughter-in-law and his great-granddaughter and fussed over getting them to start back . . . it was such a long way. Ann, who was now president of the artists' group Lucinda had started when she gave up the soup kitchen and canteen after the War, promised to come up to town the next day and go over plans for the annual meeting.

Then, at last, Lucinda and Scott were alone, sinking back into the cushions of his limousine and shielded from the chauffeur's red ears by a wall of glass.

"Couldn't stand being with that woman," Scott grumbled as the car pulled away from the mortuary. "Made a real display of herself—"

"I know, but that's just Alma," Lucinda said. "She and Reed were . . . well, I happen to envy her. She'll get it all out of her system. The trouble with you and me, Scott, is that we never really did learn how to cry. But then we're survivors, aren't we?"

"Survivors? What do you mean? You're only—what is it?—seventy-seven."

"And still going strong. . . ."

"Somebody told me you were taking digitalis."

"Oh, yes, now and then, but the doctor tells me not to worry."

"They always say that," Scott said. "One of them told me I ought to be taking whiskey."

"You should. It's the only thing that keeps me going—helps with the pain."

"Huh! It didn't do much for Reed."

"Didn't he look peaceful, though?"

"Hardly recognized him without that scar. . . ."

Fumbling through her purse, Lucinda took out a cigarette and a long ivory holder. "Mind if I smoke? I shouldn't, but it's one of my pleasures. . . ."

Scott nodded and took a cigar out of the breast pocket of his suit. He struck a match, held it rather shakily to Lucinda's cigarette, started to light his cigar and then blew it out again. He was only allowing himself two a day now, and if he smoked this one he would have to forgo the pleasure after dinner. But he kept the dead cigar clenched between his teeth.

"I don't know why the good have to die young," Lucinda said, more to herself than to Scott.

Scott leaned forward, cupped a hand behind his ear and asked, "What? Speak up."

"You *are* going deaf, just like Momma."

"Nonsense. People don't speak up the way they used to . . . they mumble all the time."

"Why don't you get a hearing aid? And please don't tell me you can't afford it."

"No need for it. I hear when I want to."

"You always have . . ."

"What's that?"

"Nothing. I was just saying that I don't understand why the good die young—your children, David, Henry, Sarah, now Reed. . . ."

"Seventy-three isn't young."

"Compared to you and me it is. Funny thing, Scott—and you probably wouldn't agree—but you and I are a lot alike under the surface. Somehow we've always managed to get what we wanted. . . ."

"What have you got?"

"My art. Enough to live on. Memories—mostly memories."

"Huh! I should think regrets would be more like—"

"Now listen here, Scott Stewart," Lucinda said, straightening so that he had to look up to her. "I'm not ashamed of *anything* I've done. . . . And I guess there's no use asking what you've got, is there? You've got money. Well, I'd rather have made love with two good men than all your money."

Scott reddened. His jaws clamped down and bit a piece off the end of his cigar. He opened the window and tried to spit it out. It wasn't a success; a dribble of juice ran down his chin. Taking a handkerchief from her purse, Lucinda dabbed at it. "I really didn't mean to upset you, Scott," she said. "But you and I are the only ones left. Isn't it time we understood each other?"

Scott was strangely moved by his sister's fussing over him. Yet why would she bother after the way he'd treated her all these years? Suddenly he turned suspicious. Lucinda was always up to something. "What do you want from me?" he asked.

Lucinda laughed. "Oh, Scott, you poor man. There's nothing you can give me—absolutely nothing. I thought maybe I could give you something."

"What? What's that?"

"Friendship—sistership—whatever you want to call it. You don't have many people left—"

"You haven't been talking to Ann, have you?"

"Certainly. I see her all the time; you know that."

"I hope she hasn't been giving you a lot of foolishness about me being a lonely old man. I'm busier than ever."

"I know that. But why?"

"What else would I do with myself? You just said that you're still painting or drawing or whatever. Why don't you quit?"

"Now you're really making sense, Scott. I was afraid you were going to tell me you were God's steward or something. Yes, I'm still drawing—and learning something new every day. I guess that's what we share, Scott. We're not quitters. . . . Well, here's the Schenley. Thanks for the ride."

As Lucinda started to get out of the car, Scott impulsively reached out and took her hand. "Wait a minute," he said. "I . . . well . . . why don't we see each other now and then?"

Lucinda flashed him a smile that seemed to sponge the marks of age from her still lovely face. "I'd like that, Scott," she said. "Come to tea Sunday if you don't go out to Fox Chapel."

A Trip to the Rose Bowl

They had wonderful seats, as Bud had promised, on the
fifty-yard line and about half way up, right in the middle of
the University of Pittsburgh cheering section. They were
lucky, because the whole circle of the stadium was a solid
wall of people—forty thousand tickets sold, according to the
early editions of the afternoon papers. Nobody who cared a
thing about football would want to miss this game between
Pitt and their rivals across Schenley Park, Carnegie Tech. If
the Pitt Panthers won, they would surely be going to the Rose
Bowl in January, but the Tartans were always tough; last year
the two teams had played to a scoreless tie. They were late
getting started from Fox Chapel, and it was almost kick-off
time when they picked their way over knees and blankets and
picnic baskets to their seats. The Pitt band had just broken
formation, and they were all scrambling off the field and into
seats just below them.

There was a tangible feeling of excitement all around them.
People were jumping up and down, pounding their hands
together, yelling. As soon as she sat down Martia got the
feeling that it had almost as much to do with the weather as
the game. A cold November wind teased up her skirt and
down her neck; when people talked, little puffs of mist formed
in front of their lips like the balloons in cartoons. Martia
huddled down into her fur coat—her very first, a sixteenth-
birthday gift from Grandy Stewart. It was only muskrat, but
she thought it looked thicker and warmer than the mink her
mother was wearing. She wished now that she hadn't fought
so hard against her mother's insistence that she wear long
stockings, but she would never admit it; she'd rather die of
the cold. They had bought a big, thick program, and the first

thing Martia looked for, of course, was Bud's picture. She showed it to her mother. "Doesn't he look fierce?"

Ann Stewart laughed. She had to agree that the solemn young man in the picture with his shoulders and thighs padded to grotesque proportions hardly resembled the easygoing boy they knew. He was big enough, goodness knew, without the uniform—six feet two and 210 pounds—but he looked enormous in the picture. "I'll bet he'll scare the other team," Ann said. "He almost scares me."

"Not me," Martia said, and she took the opera glasses out of her purse and tried to find his number—sixty-seven—among the players who were warming up on the field. When she did see him, Bud was flexing his knees, running in short spurts, rolling over. He must be cold, too, she thought. "You'll have a hard time trying to find me after the game starts," Bud had warned. "I'm always at the bottom of the pile." He had tried to explain to her how his job as a guard was just to butt up against the other line to open a hole or try to catch one of the opposing runners. "Goldberg's the one you want to watch," he had said, so she looked for Marshall Goldberg and found him along the sidelines tossing a ball back and forth with another player. He didn't have his helmet on yet, and she thought he was rather cute, although he looked too slim and sensitive to be a football player. Studying him through her glasses, she didn't like to remember what she thought was the implication in something Bud had said . . . "Goldberg's sort of a grandstander, but what can you expect . . . ?" It reminded her of some of the whispers she'd heard about her Great-aunt May and somebody named Goldberg that nobody would talk about. "I'll tell you all about it when the time comes," her mother had once said. Maybe now was the time.

Pointing out Marshall Goldberg's name in the lineup, Martia asked her mother, "Do you think he's some relative of Aunt May's?"

"Oh, no. See, it says he's from Elkins, West Virginia, and Ira Goldberg was from New York."

"What did he do that was so terrible, Mother?"

"It's too long a story. . . . Look, they're starting the game."

It was a game to take your mind off anything, even the weather, with each team scoring one touchdown and then another, seesawing back and forth and bringing the fans to their feet again and again. It gave the cheerleaders with their pink-raw legs flashing out from under their short pleated skirts plenty of opportunities to try to bounce a little warmth back into their bodies. It was difficult to watch Bud, but occasionally Martia would get a thrill when the loudspeaker would blare, ". . . Brought down for a two-yard gain by number sixty-seven, McClure." Martia worried as she watched them running around down there that Bud would be too tired for the fraternity party, which she was determined to enjoy. After all, she'd actually had to pull a tantrum—sobs, tears, fist pounding, the whole dramatic gamut—to get her mother to agree to let her go. At that, her mother was staying in Grandy's big house for the night, as if being that much nearer would somehow keep Martia safer, and she had made Bud promise to bring her home there by twelve on the dot.

As Bud had predicted, Goldberg was the star. Even though he was only a sophomore like Bud, they were always giving him the ball. Once he went right through the center of the Tech line for a touchdown, probably through a hole Bud had made. Another time he broke loose off tackle on the forty-five and snake-hipped his way across the goal line. He ran as if he were scared, and no wonder. Martia thought those big men were trying to kill him, the way they hit him if they could. In the third quarter Pitt's Bobby LaRue caught a kick-off way down near his own goal line and threw it off to Goldberg. Dodging, weaving, running like a streak, Goldberg carried the ball eighty-seven yards for another touchdown. People were jumping up and down the whole time, pounding each other on the back and screaming. A man next to Martia, who acted like he'd been drinking an awful lot from a flask he kept taking out of his coat pocket, began to sing, "California, here we come . . . ," and almost the entire cheering section joined him. He was right—Goldberg's run was the last score; the game ended Pitt—31, Tech—14. Fans rushed out onto the field and mobbed the Pitt players. Martia could see her friend bobbing on a sea of shoulders and wondered whether going out there to California to play in the Rose Bowl would change him some way. She hoped not, because mostly she liked him the way he was.

In some ways—especially his interest in money—he reminded her of Grandy, which wasn't too surprising. It was Grandy who'd sent him out to Fox Chapel in the first place to help around the yard and gardens. Grandy felt sorry for him, and "with good reason," as her mother once said. Martia wormed the whole story out of Bud once she got to know him better. His father had run a small building-supplies business in the South Hills that was mostly owned by Scott Stewart. When the Depression came along, and people stopped building houses, Mr. Stewart as a matter of course sold the business. Of course, Bud didn't blame Mr. Stewart; business was business, and you didn't get to be a rich man by carrying losses on your books. Actually, Mr. Stewart had been pretty decent, setting up a pension for his father, though it wasn't sufficient to send Bud to college. Fortunately, he was a good enough football player to get a scholarship, and Mr. Stewart was helping him earn pin money by giving him work around his own house in the East End and sending him out here Saturdays. Next summer he'd promised to take him into the office and teach him accounting. Luckily for Bud, something had happened between Mr. Stewart's father—"old Doctor Stewart," they still called him in the South Hills—and his own great-grandparents that made Mr. Stewart take a special interest in anybody named McClure. "It's almost as if we were cousins," Bud told Martia, "but thank God, we're not. . . ."

For a while there, after she and Bud had begun to get friendly, Martia was afraid her mother was going to send him away. Even though he was only nineteen, Ann Stewart kept saying that Bud was too old for her. But Bud was smart in his own way. He kept playing up to her mother, always politely calling her "ma'am," flashing her that engaging, boyish smile he usually wore when he wasn't playing football, doing little things she didn't ask, such as polishing her car just before she went out. Once he told Martia—and he meant it—that he couldn't understand why a woman as beautiful as her mother had never married again, knowing full well the remark would get back to the right ears. . . . And another time: "Say, I was watching your mother play the other day. I wouldn't dare pick up a racket against her. . . ." Which was too much for Martia. "Or me either," she said. "Why, you little pip-squeak. C'mon." He was still a football lineman on the court, stumbling and lunging and flailing away, and Martia made a proper fool of him. Confident enough in his own athletic prowess, Bud took it rather well, though he did grumble, "Growing up poor, I didn't have time for sissy games like this, but you wait and see. . . ."

"What should I wait to see?" Martia asked.

"Me make a million."

"Is that all?"

"Well, if it isn't enough, how about two million, three million, a hundred million like your great-grandfather? I'll tell you, I'm sick and tired of being poor, of hanging around in front of drugstores too embarrassed to go in because I don't have a dime for a soda, of waiting by the back door to the movies for somebody to come out so I can sneak in, of wearing shoes that've been resoled and reheeled a dozen times, with tops as cracked and wrinkled as an old man's face. You don't know anything about that kind of stuff, Martia, and, if you stick with me, I swear you never will."

It was funny . . . Bud never told her he loved her or asked her if she loved him or anything like that, but after she started letting him kiss her, he often seemed to talk as if they were just sure to get married. He was very warm and affectionate and playful. Sometimes when she didn't know he was around, he would hide behind a hedge or corner of the barn and jump out at her and tackle her like he would some halfback, except he wouldn't let her fall too hard. The only way she could get even was to start tickling him. He just couldn't stand it and would always end up on his back, helpless with howling laughter. "Please, pip-squeak," he would gasp. "Stop it. I surrender. You've got me in your power, but then you've always had me in your power. You *know* that, don't you?"

She did know it, and she didn't know what to make of it. As far as she was concerned, there really was nothing she'd ever done, except let him kiss her, to account for a boy as handsome as Bud, who could probably have any girl he wanted, especially liking her. She knew she was fairly good-looking, but in a sort of old-fashioned way; people were always saying she was a dark miniature copy of her Great-aunt Lucinda, with her straight nose and high cheekbones and long jaw. But there were lots of prettier girls, like all of those Pitt cheerleaders with breasts that bobbled inside their thick sweaters every time they jumped or waved. She didn't really know or care much about football, or cars, or business, or any of the things Bud seemed to be interested in; like her mother, she spent much of her time reading. She got A's in English and was going to play Portia when the school put on *The Merchant of Venice*. She didn't yet know whether she would go out to Hollywood and be an actress like Norma Shearer or go to New York and live by her wits like Dorothy Parker. None of her dreams included being a housewife, unless it was a penthouse somewhere with a great big living room in which she and her husband would dance every night away like Ginger Rogers and Fred Astaire. Her English teacher was always telling her she could do anything she wanted to, she was so bright and precocious. But that certainly wasn't what Bud liked about her. In fact, any time she tried to talk to him seriously about something she'd read, he'd say, "Ah, why bother your pretty little head with stuff like that?"

It nearly killed her the time she heard her mother and Grandy Stewart talking about her and Bud. "A nice enough boy," Grandy said, "but I wouldn't let him get too thick with Martia."

"Why not?" her mother asked.

"I don't know but what the boy's a fortune hunter. You know his people were farmers, poor as churchmice. His father was no more of a businessman than yours . . ."

"Now, Grandy, that isn't nice. My father was a good engineer, you said so yourself."

"Well, maybe if David had . . ."

Ann, who had been getting angry over the old man's interference about Martia and his reference to her father, subsided. She'd always had a soft spot for him, and their relationship was cemented by their mutual love and respect for David. "Maybe if David had . . . lived"—she finished his thought, which haunted her more than it did the old man. More people than Bud wondered out loud why she hadn't found another man, and she always laughed it off with, "David spoiled me." But it was no joke; the only person who seemed to understand how you could go on living and living with the memory of a perfect love was Aunt Lucinda, God bless her. The one thing David's death had done for her was to answer that question of where she was going. She was left alone to do her best at turning Martia into a successful human being, and she always resented it when other people tried to tell her how to do the job.

"Don't worry, Grandy," she said. "They're only youngsters after all. I don't think Bud would even know what a fortune hunter is. Anyway, that kind of thing went out with the last century."

Martia wasn't so sure. It did bother her that Bud always had money on his mind. When she'd chide him about it, he'd say, "It's all very well for you to talk. You people who've got it go around acting as if money was a dirty word. Maybe I'll feel the same when I get it, but right now money's the most important thing in the world to me." Martia tried to make herself understand and put that side of Bud out of her mind, because it was too terrible even to contemplate that he might just be after her money. . . .

Martia told herself she wasn't really serious about Bud. For the moment it was enough for him to be around to have a good time with and make her feel, well, important. All the girls at school thought he was absolutely sensational, and they were simply dying with jealousy that she was going out with him after the big game. Some of them even went down to Pitt and bought programs the day before and gave them to her and asked her to get Bud's autograph and Bobby LaRue's and, of course, Marshall Goldberg's if she should be lucky enough to meet them.

Bud came for her promptly at seven. Her mother and Grandy made her wait with them in the stiff, gilded parlor and let the maid show him in. He didn't look much the worse for the game except for a slight bruise on one cheek. Polite as always, Bud took her mother's hand, then went over to Grandy, who began to push himself rather creakily to his feet. "Don't get up, Mr. Stewart," Bud said.

Grandy sank down again with obvious relief and held out a bony hand. "Well, young man, I hear you won the game."

"Yes, I'm sorry you missed it."

Martia smiled. She had heard Grandy go on endlessly about the foolishness of football. "Can't see why any young man would want to go out and get himself banged up like that." When it was pointed out that Bud was earning his way through college by playing, Grandy would say, "Plenty of better ways to make money. When I was his age . . ." It was almost a game, and either Ann or Martia would finish for him, ". . . I was the best telegraph operator in Pittsburgh." Grandy didn't think it was funny. He would say, "Well, I was. None of you young people know anything about work." Now, though, he was surprisingly gracious.

"I'm sorry, too, but I suspect an old man like me would have caught his death of cold out there today. So you're going to California? Ought to do some good for the name of Pittsburgh."

"I hope so, sir. Are you ready, Martia?"

"Remember—back by twelve," her mother said as they went out the door.

Far from being tired, Bud was strangely keyed up. All the way to the fraternity house in the little Ford he'd borrowed from a buddy for the evening, he went on and on about the game, describing plays in detail she couldn't begin to understand. When they got there he warned, "Be ready for a real blowout, pip-squeak. Jock Sutherland said we could break training just for tonight."

He was right. The old house was ablaze with light and vibrating with noise. The aroma of beer and cigarette smoke assailed them as they opened the door to go in, and they quickly were swallowed up by a swirling crowd of laughing, chattering, drinking, smoking, hugging, kissing young people. Within minutes Martia lost track of Bud, and was glad she'd brought her friends' programs along; it gave her something to do. The boys were happy to sign and some even gave her a playful kiss. She got some odd looks when she kept asking for Marshall Goldberg—it seemed he didn't belong to the fraternity. Everybody tried to get her to drink some beer, and she found it easier to take a glass than argue. It tasted terrible but made her feel very grown up and sophisticated, so she managed to get one down and then another before she found Bud back in the study of the old house. He was standing in the middle of the floor with a kind of a silly grin on his face, and a lot of boys and girls were ringed around the walls. One of the boys was saying, "Hey, Bud, show us again how you opened up that hole for Goldberg." Another boy put an old, overstuffed chair in the middle of the floor, and Bud crouched, charged and sent the chair crashing against the wall with his shoulder. "Atta boy, Bud," everybody shouted. "Now go out and do it to the Huskies . . ."

Martia didn't quite know whether to be proud or embarrassed. Bud spotted her at the door and came rushing over. "Hey, everybody," he shouted, "here's pip-squeak. Isn't she terrific?" He grabbed her and swung her up on his shoulder with his hand running right up under her skirt along her bare thighs and staying there while he marched her around the room. Now she *was* embarrassed, and could feel her face burning. She pulled at his hair and told him, "Let me down, let me down this minute. . . ." He did let her down, but he kept an arm around her and kissed her right there in front of everybody. "What's wrong, pip-squeak? I'm proud of you. Can't you see that? . . . Hey, let's have another beer."

"We've had enough, Bud," Martia said. "I need some air."

"Okay, okay," he said. "Let's take a drive."

Walking to the car through the cold, silent night, they too were suddenly quiet. Something in the air seemed to have sobered Bud. He held the door for her and helped her very formally into the car, then got in himself. "Let's drive up to Mount Washington and see the sights."

"Are you sure you can drive, Bud?"

"Oh, sure. I was just showing off in there. You don't know what it's like to get all tensed up for a game like this, and then have it over."

Along the road at the top of Mount Washington, Bud found a place to park where they could look out over the city. Veils of smoke dimmed its thousands of winking eyes, but it was still a sight. "Just think, Martia," Bud said. "Why, right at this very minute you are with one of the eleven most famous men in this whole city—"

"If you don't watch out, Bud McClure, you won't be able to get your head back into your helmet for the Rose Bowl game."

"You just don't know how lucky you are, pip-squeak. There isn't a girl at Pitt who wouldn't change places with you right now."

Bud had turned the engine off and was fiddling with the radio. He stopped when they could hear a man singing ". . . a cigarette that bears the lipstick traces, an airline ticket to romantic places. . . ." Martia shivered a little as the chill got to her, and Bud put his arm around her and pulled her close. "Cold, honey?" he asked. "You shouldn't be in your fur coat. You feel like a teddy bear." He leaned over and kissed her. While he was kissing her, she could feel his hand working in under her coat, feel his fingers fumbling with the buttons of her blouse. She knew she ought to stop him, but then, maybe because of the beer, she was kind of curious. She knew other girls who had let boys they didn't even know get to first base. She tried to concentrate on the music. A girl was singing . . . "Oh, you push the first valve down, and the music goes round and round, whoa, ho, ho . . ."

His hand was finally inside, slipping under the straps of her brassiere, hot against the flesh of her breast. She felt a queer, tingling sensation all over and was afraid, not so much of Bud as of herself. She tried to push him away. "Bud, Bud . . ."

He shut off her protests with kisses, trying to open her lips with his own, flicking them with his tongue. She felt flushed all over, flushed and scared and at the same time excited. His hand was moving again, down and under her skirt and up the inside of her thighs. ". . . I am only human, but you are so divine. When did you leave heaven, angel mine?" a man was now singing, and Bud was saying . . . "And you're *my* angel, angel. . . ."

Irritated that he'd even begun listening, that he couldn't say anything more original, she really began to squirm now, began pushing at him, trying to tickle him. For once it didn't work. It was awfully cramped in the car, and he kept crowding over on her, pushing, and sort of crooning, "Martia, please, you don't know what you do to me . . . please . . ."

He was too big for her, too strong. It was happening, and

it was terrible, and there was nothing she could do but moan some and whimper. And then Bud was saying something he had never said before. "I love you, Martia. Love you, love you . . . oh, God, Martia . . ."

Like a bomb exploding, light flooded the car. It blinded them. They could hear knuckles rapping against the window and a harsh voice saying, "All right—out, you two."

Bud shielded her for a second with his body while they straightened their clothes and whispered, "You stay here."

He rolled out his side of the car and towered over the two policemen, who examined him up and down with their flashlights. "What do you think you're doing, boy? This ain't no lovers' lane," one of them said. "Let's see your driver's license."

When he produced the license from his wallet, one of the policemen studied it under his flashlight. "Walter E. McClure . . . say, you're not Bud McClure . . ."

"Yeah."

"Jeez, I saw you out there today. You guys were terrific."

The policeman started to aim his light into the car to have a look at Martia, but Bud deflected it. "Okay, Bud," the officer said. "I guess I can't blame the little lady after what you did out there today. But, listen, do me a favor and move along. Okay, Bud?"

"Sure thing."

Now the other officer was thrusting a paper and pen in front of him. "Could you give me your autograph, Bud? My kid would really be tickled pink."

Bud signed and climbed back into the car. Martia was crying, her face buried against the seat. A man on the radio was saying, "And now we take you direct to the Glen Island Casino, where Benny Goodman, the King of Swing, is playing for your dancing pleasure. Come in, Benny," and they cut right into the middle of a number, with a girl singing, ". . . A little love, a little kiss, on Miami's shore . . ."

"Shut that damn thing off, Bud McClure, and *talk* to me," Martia ordered.

"What's the matter? We got out of that all right, didn't we?"

"Oh, Bud, oh, God, Bud, do you know what you've done . . ."

"It had to happen sometime, Martia—a pretty girl like you. Better with somebody who loves you, don't you think? I do love you, Martia, really . . ."

"Even after . . ."

435

"More than ever. . . ."

They got in right on the dot of twelve. Ann Stewart was a little disturbed at the sight of her daughter's disheveled hair and red eyes, even more disturbed by the way the girl brushed past her, saying, "I'll talk about it in the morning." Probably a fight, she thought. No doubt Bud was feeling a little too big for his breeches on a night like this, and Ann knew that Martia wasn't one to put up easily with conceit. Too bad when the girl had been so looking forward to having fun at the party. Well, maybe the trip to Washington would take her mind off it.

A Dinner with Mr. Mellon

When the invitation from Andrew Mellon had come earlier that fall, Scott had taken it down with him to Fox Chapel on one of his regular Sunday visits. Knowing from experience the weaknesses and reluctances of old age, Andy Mellon had written far ahead—the dinner party wasn't until early December—and had suggested that Scott bring along with him "that charming young Mrs. Stewart and her daughter." It was clever of Andy, because Scott would never have considered such a long trip without company. Although, except for the morning ache in his joints, he felt perfectly fine, he never knew when something in his aging body might let go. When, and if, that happened, he wanted to be near familiar things or people. It was at least partly this feeling that had led Scott into the custom of picking Lucinda up every Sunday after church and taking her with him to Fox Chapel, even though their conversation in the back of the stately if ancient Packard that Scott refused to trade in (another familiar object) was at times more like a sparring match than conversation.

On this particular blue and gold October Sunday, Scott opened with, "You really ought to come to church with me. This man in East Liberty is good and . . ."

"No doubt. They probably pay him enough," Lucinda said.

"He's worth it."

"Nothing's too good for 'Mellon's fire escape,' I suppose. . . ."

"Lucinda, I'll not have talk like that. Dick Mellon was a friend of mine."

"Is that why you moved over to East Liberty after all those years in the Oakland church? I never could understand it. . . ."

Lucinda had heard all about the move from some of her church-going friends. It had been startling as a scandal to have Scott Stewart, an elder for sixty years and the uncle of the pastor, the Reverend Doctor Henry Ward Beecher Sharp, suddenly request a letter of transfer to the East Liberty Presbyterian Church. In keeping with the habits of a lifetime, he offered no word of explanation to anybody. It wasn't possible to believe that Scott Stewart, who'd struggled all his life against every form of ostentation in the church, was suddenly enticed by the new building in East Liberty that had been erected by Richard B. Mellon and his wife at a cost of some four million dollars. Ornately Gothic and replete with stained glass and such elaborate carvings as John Angel's "Last Supper," the East Liberty church was meant to be a kind of St. Peter's of Presbyterianism, the very thing anyone who knew him would have thought Scott Stewart would shun.

"Dick's been dead nearly three years," Scott said. "I just couldn't take young Sharp. . . ."

"I'm not surprised. I always thought he was a pompous little ass—takes after his father. But they told me you brought him to Oakland."

"I didn't know he was a socialist then."

"A socialist? Come now, Scott."

"Every service he prays by name for that fellow Roosevelt, and once he preached a whole sermon on 'The New Deal Is a Christian Deal.' "

"That doesn't sound very socialistic to me."

"You wouldn't understand, you never have. If it weren't for the Supreme Court setting aside all of Roosevelt's crazy schemes, this whole country would be socialist by now. Bad enough seeing all this in the newspapers without hearing it in church. I go to hear the gospel."

"According to Saint Scott?"

With that, Scott lapsed into grumpy silence. You'd think a woman of Lucinda's age would have better sense. Why, it was plain as the nose on your face that Roosevelt and his "brain trust" were out to get every honest businessman in the country. The way those people in Washington had treated the Mellon brothers, Scott wondered why Andy continued to spend so much time down there. He had no doubt that the grilling a congressional committee gave Dick Mellon during the labor troubles of '34 hastened his death at only seventy-five. Dick was just telling the plain truth when he testified that the Pittsburgh Coal Company kept machine guns trained on the workers because "you cannot run a mine without them." If those woolly-headed professors down there had lived through the railway strike and the battles in the coke fields and Homestead the way Scott had they might have understood what Dick was trying to say. Now, of course, Roosevelt was egging this fellow Lewis on in his efforts to organize the mines and the steel industry, and younger fellows at U.S. Steel like Ben Fairless were actually talking about playing ball with Lewis instead of waiting for the court to deal with the Wagner Labor Relations Act. Maybe Scott would have to resign from the steel-company board the way he had left Oakland Presbyterian Church just to show that there were some men of principle left.

There weren't many. Besides himself, Andy Mellon was almost the only one, and that was the only reason Scott was really considering going down to see him. Poor Andy had taken a worse beating than Dick from those socialists. Imagine —a man who had served his country for eleven years as Secretary of the Treasury and two more as ambassador to Great Britain being put on trial for evading income taxes! It was nothing but harassment. When that fellow Duveen testified that ever since '31 Andy had been planning to build a national art gallery and give away his paintings, the whole government case fell apart. It was just that Andy was like himself—he didn't see any sense in going around and talking about matters that weren't anybody else's business. A good thing, too, because he might have got in worse trouble if that seven-million-dollar deal he made in '30 to buy a bunch of paintings from the Bolsheviks had come to light at the time. He was still Secretary of the Treasury then and telling people not to exaggerate the Depression, which was sound advice, as anybody who'd lived through '73 and '93 and '07 and all those other panics as he and Andy had done could testify, but certain wrong-headed people wouldn't have understood then that a man had a *right* to do what he wanted to with his own money. Of course Scott personally thought that this business of buying paintings addled the heads of otherwise sound men like Frick and Mellon. They said Mellon hid all those paintings from The Hermitage in the basement of the Corcoran Art Gallery in Washington and would go down there and brood over them. One of them—something called "Venus with a Mirror," which had cost Andy more than half a million—was said to be such a disgraceful exhibition of a naked woman that he wouldn't dare hang it anyway. Now there was talk that Andy had made an even bigger deal with that fellow Duveen, maybe out of gratitude, and one thing Scott didn't like about going to Washington was that he would probably have to pretend he thought all that stuff was worth the money.

Andy argued he'd rather buy paintings and give them away than lose the money in taxes, and maybe he was right the way things were going. Instead of getting rid of this infernal income tax as Hoover might have done to stimulate business investment, they were making it worse. Now with this Social Security business they would be taxing everybody in the country to take care of people who didn't have enough gumption and self-control to set aside anything for their old age. When they started paying out, the whole country might go bankrupt. Over in Germany, from what Scott heard, the leaders were listening to businessmen like Schacht and Krupp, and they seemed to be pulling the country together. Yet here in Washington the doors were closed to men like himself and Andy who, after all, had done a fair amount to build the wealth of this country. That Roosevelt was a fool about money, just like his cousin before him, and the galling part was that they both had lived a life of ease on the fortunes their businessmen ancestors had made—why, Nicholas Roosevelt had been one of the first to see profit in putting steamships on the rivers and had, in fact, come out to Pittsburgh to get into the business. It made a man wonder whether he should pass money along, and Scott was increasingly concerned about the boys Martia might be going out with, although he tried to hide it when he was with any of them, since whatever he said seemed to make them snippish.

By the time they reached Fox Chapel, his brooding had put Scott into a distinctly testy mood. As he always did when he got out onto the circular driveway in front of the modest Tudor-style house David had willed to his widow, Scott let his eye roam critically over the building and grounds.

He noted a few cracked panes in the second-story casements, a place on the roof where the tiles had torn away, weeds choking out the last chrysanthemums blooming in the garden by the drive. The whole place had begun to look rather seedy since that McClure boy got too busy weekends with his football to come down and do his proper work. He'd have to find somebody else; Ann, an otherwise fairly sensible woman, didn't seem to realize that letting property deteriorate was as bad as letting money stand idle. Well, spunky as she was, she'd of course never worked for anything—what David hadn't given her, he was giving her now—so her attitude shouldn't be a surprise. And while it was perhaps fortunate by way of keeping Ann busy that she and Lucinda got along so well, he sometimes thought Ann was too much like his sister for comfort . . . the only time he'd ever seen Lucinda's Schenley Hotel apartment it was such a jumble he hadn't been able to bring himself to sit down. Matter of fact, he wondered that the hotel didn't say something to her. . . .

As soon as Ann opened the door to them with a "Grandy! Lucinda! Isn't it a lovely day?" Scott took the whole property in with a wave and told her, "This place is falling apart."

"I know, Grandy, ever since Bud . . ."

"He's not the only boy in the world. We'll have to find another one. Anyway it's good he isn't seeing so much of Martia . . ."

"Now let's not go into that again, Grandy."

"Well, well . . . where is Martia?"

"Still not back from church."

"Must be the Episcopal—noon masses like the Catholics. . . ."

"Well, it's where David . . ."

"Never did understand that with a perfectly good Presbyterian church . . ."

"He liked the ceremony. I hear you're going to East Liberty now. It can't be so much different."

"Lot of tomfoolishness, but the preacher is good. I was just telling Lucinda . . ."

"Can you imagine, Ann? He's still trying to get me to go to church," Lucinda interrupted.

"That's what we love about Grandy," Ann said. "He never changes."

"What's that?" Scott asked, cupping his ear.

"'I said you never change, Grandy. You're just like the Rock of Gibraltar."

"That's so? . . . Well, where's your mother?"

"She has a little cold. She's taking dinner in her room, but I guess that won't break your heart. . . ."

Lucinda smiled, but Scott quickly said, "That's nonsense. Too bad. I'm sorry."

It was disgraceful the way young people talked these days, saying things right out loud that you weren't even supposed to think. Scott could remember that Dr. Stewart Sharp once had had the effrontery to tell him that he, Scott, would be happier if he didn't bottle things up so much. But letting your tongue wag seemed to him as improper as wearing a collar without a tie or going without a hat—no true gentleman would do it. The older you got the more you realized you had to be particularly careful about those hurtful truths you couldn't do anything about. Better not even admit them, if possible, and certainly there was no use talking about them. Mrs. Gillespie was in that category. She seemed a heavy, alien presence in the house whenever Scott was around. She blamed him for her husband's collapse and made no bones about it. She'd keep rubbing his nose in it with tactless phrases like . . . "before George was ruined" . . . "when George still had his health" . . . "about the time George was sold out. . . ." Sometimes Scott wondered how Ann could stand the woman, even though she was her mother. Talk about *his* fussing over Martia, Mrs. Gillespie was always nagging at the girl to pull her skirts down, stop chewing gum, speak up and the like. Though she was a generation younger than Scott, Mrs. Gillespie was always ailing, always complaining about heart palpitations and headaches and constipation. The only good thing about the situation from Scott's point of view was that taking care of her probably kept Ann too busy to think about getting married again. At first he'd been prepared for that, but now he honestly didn't think he could stand it. He was conscious of being the man in all their lives, and he knew it had a good deal to do with keeping him going. It was, in fact, the important reason he continued giving Ann direct support rather than setting her up with more independence, and at times he felt guilty about it, depending on Ann's pride to keep her from asking for another arrangement, and he knew her embarrassment over her mother was a factor in that pride. Perhaps she was only trying to make him understand that she didn't agree with her mother, but she needn't bother—he knew that in his heart.

Before David's death Ann Gillespie Stewart had held her grandfather-in-law in understandable awe. Indeed, she often found it difficult to understand what had gotten into her that wild night when she went to Scott Stewart with David's letter in her hand, because for all the years she'd been old enough to read between the lines of her parents' conversation, she'd been aware of their fear of the somewhat mythical "Mr. Stewart." Of course she really hadn't known him then and had supposed him to be pretty much like the only Stewarts she did know—David and his Aunt Lucinda. The only other time she'd tried to thaw him out was at the wedding, and she knew what had gotten into her then—champagne. It wasn't exactly a success; even in her excited state she realized she'd done little more than embarrass him in front of his distinguished friends. After that she was content to leave the old man alone, to follow David dutifully on what he considered obligatory visits to the palace in East End and to keep her mouth closed. It was a trial, since Scott Stewart usually sat quiet behind his frown, letting David ramble on with the kind of monologue he must have practiced all his growing years. She even gave up taking the baby, because, although Grandy Stewart made all the right noises, she could tell he was disappointed in Martia's sex and that he was tense in the presence of such an unpredictable force as an active, small child. He would be forever jumping up to move things out of Martia's reach or telling Ann such things as "Don't let her touch that vase." After the first courtesy call when they bought the house, David resisted any suggestion of inviting his grandfather out to Fox Chapel. "It's my house, and I'm not going to have anybody, even Grandy, telling me I can't enjoy a drink when I want to. I'll respect his way of life in his house, as I always did, but until he shows signs of respecting mine in my house, I'd just as soon forget it." Since Ann felt the same way, there had been no argument about it. Grandy Stewart became a kind of distant institution in their lives, like the church, that you visited on ceremonial occasions and knew you would have to do something about "when the time came." In this case, the time was to have been David's entry into his grandfather's office. It turned out to be David's funeral.

Ann would never forget Grandy Stewart's face at that funeral. Although he held himself as rigidly under control as an old soldier facing a firing squad, every muscle along his lean jaws and around his thin lips stood out. By protocol, she rode with him in the car to the cemetery, and he fussed and fumed the whole way about the fact that David was the first Stewart not to be buried in the South Hills. She let him go on, because she knew it was a grief-covering anger. When at last they left the graveside and got back into the car, Ann heard a strange, frightening, strangling noise coming from the old man. It took her a few seconds to realize that he was crying, but when she did she actually put her arms around him and pillowed his head on her breast. In a few minutes he was pulling free, blowing his nose loudly, getting out a cigar and puffing it into angry clouds. When she got out of the car he said, before signaling the driver to go on, "You needn't tell anybody about this." She never did, but the very next Sunday she invited him out to Fox Chapel for dinner.

Grandy Stewart still acted proprietarily with her, still sniffed the air each time he came into the house, as if searching for traces of alcohol or cigarette smoke or *something* to disapprove of, still fussed over Martia ("You shouldn't be letting that girl get into all those plays; she'll be getting some silly notion about the stage like my . . .") and still fretted about everything from the condition of her car to the leaky tap in the downstairs bathroom, but Ann, who had been so brutally disoriented by her beloved David's death, came to appreciate his changeless ways. She would have endless arguments about him with Lucinda, whose experiences with her brother were too personal to let her share Ann's somewhat casual feeling that he was "an old dear." It was nice that Reed's death had somehow thrown Scott and Lucinda together again, but Ann knew they probably were both too proud and stubborn to agree on anything beyond that strange and silent bond of blood. So Ann was the only one who cared enough, or had nerve enough, to tell Scott Stewart that he ought to have his old suits taken in, ought to take a tonic (the one she got for him had more alcohol than sherry) for his blood, ought at least to resign from a few Sunday-school committees and civic boards if he wouldn't quit working. When she talked to him that way Scott usually retreated into his deafness, cupping an ear and saying, "What's that? Speak up. . . ." But by the next week Ann would notice signs that he had heard her well enough. Once she even sneaked into his bathroom and checked the medicine closet, where she found a half-consumed bottle of the potent tonic.

It was natural then that Ann should take charge when Scott put the Mellon invitation into her hand at the dinner table and said, "Of course I won't go. Those people have ruined Washington—"

"Oh, but you ought to, Grandy," Ann said. "Mr. Mellon's

such a good friend, and I think it would do you good to get out."

"Good?" Scott said. "I can't see any good in riding all the way down there. Trains aren't what they used to be—they're either too hot or too cold these days, and they shake so much my bones ache."

"We could fly," Ann said. "It only takes a few hours. You've never been up, have you?"

"No, and I never will," Scott said. "I don't know what it would do to my heart—"

"You've got a heart like an ox, Scott Stewart," Lucinda said.

"Grandy, we've just got to go. Martia's never seen Washington. You'd like to go, wouldn't you, Martia?"

"I'd love it!" the girl said, and her face was so full of excited anticipation that Scott couldn't refuse her.

"No flying, mind you."

"All right," Ann agreed. "I'll book sleeper accommodations. That way we'll have all day to look around the city before the dinner."

As he'd predicted, an overwrought air-conditioner kept him shiveringly awake most of the way to Washington. Still, he was glad they'd decided to go, because even he could see that Martia needed some sort of distraction. Ever since the Pitt-Tech game she had been pale, sullen and withdrawn— not at all her usual lively self. Ann explained that there must have been some argument with that McClure boy—he'd been calling every day, but Martia refused to see him. Scott should have been happy, but actually he was beginning to be rather impressed with the boy. Although he didn't as a rule think much of football, all the publicity about the team's going to the Rose Bowl was beginning to get through to him. These boys were the best in the field, and they were holding Pittsburgh's banner high. Maybe the kind of spirit that made a good football player would also make a good businessman. Well, Scott would find out this summer—the boy had agreed to come into the office and learn the rudiments of accounting. Even if young McClure was somewhat of a fortune hunter, couldn't that be to his credit as long as he learned that the burden of a fortune was stewardship? Well, Scott would see. The mere thought of finding a young man with the proper background—the McClures were still active in the old South Hills church—and the gumption to take up the challenges he would give him was cheering enough to make the sleepless

444

ride tolerable. Scott rather hoped this little trip would get Martia over her peeve.

Andy Mellon thoughtfully sent a car with a young assistant to meet their train and show them around. Scott begged off and had himself dropped at the hotel, where he could read and rest. He'd seen enough of Washington in his time, and he was afraid that his feeling that the place was occupied by a bunch of aliens would lead him to spoil their fun with his grousing and grumbling. Like most young people, Ann and Martia couldn't seem to get very excited about what was going on; in fact, they actually liked Roosevelt's wife—*la bocha grande*, as that fellow Westbrook Pegler called her—and were always worrying about the rights of black people and such. If they had been men, Scott would have been upset with them, but he put it down to the silliness of women; even his sensible mother had distressed him from time to time with her soft-headedness. They should never have given women the vote. True, they did help put across prohibition, but like as not they had turned around and supported this cocktail-drinking fellow in the White House who got it repealed. Women just weren't consistent, and most of them had no more understanding of proper conduct than . . . well, look at the trouble Lucinda and May got themselves into. Yet people nowadays thought the story of Eve and the apple was just a fable. As Ann and Martia drove away, waving back at him, Scott sighed wearily. The fellow who said "You can't live with 'em and you can't live without 'em" certainly knew what he was talking about.

The Mellon dinner party turned out to be a very intimate affair; the only other guest was Sir Joseph Duveen. Ann had a dizzy feeling that the movie in her mind had suddenly been reeled backward to that night in New York when she and David, so full of hope and passion, had forced themselves to sit politely through a Duveen monologue in Uncle Clay Frick's house. The memory was still vivid, but she could tell that Duveen had only the faintest recollection of having met her. He was full of halting sympathy about the death of her "so attractive young husband" but delighted at last to meet the famous Mr. Stewart from Pittsburgh and, of course, the charming young Miss Stewart who looked "just like her father." That last was almost uncanny, but then, of course, Duveen did make his living with his eye.

To Ann the dinner was a kind of high comedy. Old Mr. Mellon was frail, thin, distinguished—so much like Grandy they could have been brothers. He was even more silent than

Grandy or Mr. Frick; indeed, the two old men displayed their mutual respect not by talk but by an almost palpably companionable silence. Aged and grayed by an illness he almost cheerfully admitted was a terminal cancer, Sir Joseph rattled on with the same unabashed enthusiasm for this picture and that, this statue and that, he had exhibited twenty years before. In Ann's eyes there was still a touch of the oily salesman about him, and it soon became apparent that the purpose of the dinner—at least in Duveen's mind—was to interest Scott Stewart in buying some paintings to be hung in Mr. Mellon's National Gallery of Art. It was an uphill fight. After describing one work of art in elaborate detail, including its full history, price and availability, Duveen turned to Scott and asked, "Don't you find that interesting, Mr. Stewart?"

Ann watched Grandy closely. He'd been contentedly chewing away with a rather distracted expression in his eyes, and it was the cessation of noise more than anything else that seemed to alert him. With a hand back of his ear, he asked, "Eh? What's that?"

Undaunted, Duveen went on, "This is a painting—well, actually, there's a whole collection if you would consider it— Mr. Mellon thought you might be especially interested in because the artist is American and you are a well-known patriot, if I may say so, Mr. Stewart. Nobody will forget the funds you raised in the last war. . . ."

"A picture? I don't know anything about pictures," Scott said. "You know that, Andy."

Andrew Mellon smiled and spoke for the first time. "I told you, Duveen. Stewart here is the last of the great old Pittsburgh Philistines."

"Now, Mr. Mellon, I can't believe that," Duveen said. "Why, I've seen Mr. Stewart's home. I was driven by it last time I was in Pittsburgh just because it is the best example of Renaissance style in the country. A man with taste like that . . ."

Ignoring Duveen, Scott turned to his host. "You didn't tell this fellow I wanted to buy pictures, did you, Andy?"

"I distinctly told him you *wouldn't* want to buy pictures, but he insisted on meeting you. I thought it might be a good show to watch. I've never seen Duveen beaten."

Scott turned to Duveen. "You're wasting your time, young man. I don't know a thing about pictures. . . ."

"Ah, but that's where I come in, Mr. Stewart. I'm sure Mr. Mellon would agree that when you get a work of art from Duveen you get the very best."

"What would an old man like me want with pictures, anyway?"

"They make a wonderful gift to the world, Mr. Stewart. Look at your friends Mr. Frick and Mr. Morgan and Mr. Mellon here. Their names will go down through all time for their generosity in bringing culture to their people. Who was it said, 'All else passes, art alone endures'? How true, Mr. Stewart, how true! I tell my clients that I don't sell 'pictures,' as you call them. I sell immortality."

"You sell *what*? What's that?"

"Immortality, Mr. Stewart . . ."

"Young man," Scott said, "there is only one kind of immortality—that conferred upon us by our Lord Jesus Christ."

Mellon had covered his mouth with his napkin and was making rather odd sounds behind it. He pretended to dab at his lips and said, "I think we had better have our coffee and cigars in the study. If you ladies object to smoke . . ."

Duveen, crushed into momentary silence by Scott's last remark, came alive again. "If you don't mind, Mr. Mellon, I'll take the ladies downstairs and show them around."

Mellon nodded, and Ann and Martia followed Duveen out to the foyer. While they waited for the elevator, he shook his head. "An amazing man, your grandfather."

"Yes, isn't he? Where are you taking us, Sir Joseph?" Ann asked.

"To see the largest single sale of art in all history. It is my own collection—forty-two items—that took a lifetime to amass, and Mr. Mellon has agreed to purchase it all for twenty-one million dollars," Duveen told them as they descended one flight.

Ann laughed, and Duveen asked in a hurt tone, "You find that amusing, Mrs. Stewart?"

"Not really. It's just that the last time I met you, you told David and me about selling Mr. Frick one of the most expensive paintings in history. I remember you explained to us how you had tricked . . ."

"Mrs. Stewart! I do not trick clients. Sometimes, though, you have to lead them to understand . . ."

They entered an apartment almost identical to the Mellon apartment just above them. But as Duveen went from room to room flicking on light switches, it was apparent that the place had been turned into a kind of informal art gallery. The sheer mass of statuary and paintings was impressive. While they wandered through it Duveen continued to ramble on.

447

"You see Mr. Mellon, like your grandfather, is very cautious. (With a resigned sigh.) All wealthy men are very cautious. And silent. He is like the tomb. You can't tell whether he likes a picture or not until he reaches for his checkbook. I would try to sell him one good thing here, another there. Then when the doctors told me . . . well, I realized time was running out for me as well as him. So I had this idea. I rented this apartment and put everything I thought he ought to own into it and gave him the key. Well, you know his servants told me he used to come down here at night in his bathrobe and slippers and just wander about for hours. Sometimes when he had guests he would bring them down and show them around. Before long he began to think it was all his and . . . well . . . the rest is history, as they say."

"And Sir Joseph Duveen became a wealthy man," Ann said.

"Mrs. Stewart, would you believe me," Duveen said, "if I told you that all I really did was get out of debt for the first time in my whole life? Money means nothing to me—these things do. I bought them even when I didn't have money because I knew they were unique and one day . . . well, and now they are going to the people through Mr. Mellon. . . . That Frick house, you know, I had it designed not as a home but a museum, and now people can go there . . . most of my clients . . . Mr. Kress, for example, all of his paintings are going into Mr. Mellon's gallery . . . dear lady, what is money to me in my condition? The important thing is immortality, as I tried to tell your grandfather."

"He has old-fashioned ideas about that," Ann said.

"Ah, yes, well," Duveen said, and then brightened. "But if he leaves his money . . . well, there haven't been many great lady collectors. . . ."

"Don't look to me," Ann said. "I'm afraid I have only a passing interest in art."

"But what about the young lady?" Duveen asked, turning to Martia.

Ann could tell that Martia, who had remained polite and silent all evening, was churning with the same desire to throw a brick through the show window that she'd had that night at Frick's. Now she did. "The only kind of pictures I like are moving ones," Martia said.

"A pity," Sir Joseph sighed. "A real pity. People don't understand wealth anymore. . . ."

A Giant's Burial

In that summer of 1945 Ann Stewart moved bag and baggage from Fox Chapel to the Scott Stewart place in East End. Even though the war in Europe was over, she still could not get enough gas to make the round trip daily, and she knew that Grandy Stewart counted greatly on seeing her. A good many people told her she was foolish—he had a house full of servants and nurses around the clock—but Ann was aware that those people were as interchangeable and uninteresting to him as the sheets on his bed. He seemed to be totally deaf now and could never hear a thing the nurses told him, but, oddly, though she never raised her voice, Ann could get through to him. He could hear Lucinda, too, and Dr. Stewart Sharp, who had personally taken charge of the case after Grandy outlived or fired a dozen other doctors. "It's a little out of my line," Stewart, himself seventy, told Ann when she came to him in distress after Grandy's last blowup with a doctor, "but I guess I can hold his hand as well as anybody. There's nothing wrong with him except old age, and the only cure I know for that is . . ."

But death refused to come, and even at ninety-three Scott Stewart showed few signs of welcoming it. Although he was dizzy and a bit disoriented much of the time from the small strokes that had been exploding in his brain for years, he insisted on getting up and walking to the bathroom several times each day. In the evenings of good days he would dress, make his way unsteadily to the elevator on his nurse's arm and ride down to eat with Ann in the echoing splendor of the big dining room. He could still read, and somebody over at Westinghouse had thoughtfully brought him one of those new-fangled gadgets called television. He grumbled that he didn't like it—the picture was fuzzy and he couldn't hear anything—and he predicted it would be a failure. "Don't put a dime into that," he told Ann.

It was gratuitous advice. Ann was still just getting along on the checks Grandy signed with a shaky hand once a month when the attorney who helped manage his affairs came to the house. The attorney, a close-mouthed bespectacled young man, paid the nurses, the utilities, the taxes, the food bills and everything else, no doubt including himself, and Bud was furious about the situation. He kept urging Ann to use her influence to get Grandy to make other arrangements, warning, "You'll all be left without a cent. You watch, that shyster will get it all. The old boy's just about incompetent, and I think we ought to go into court if you can't get him to do anything." But Ann could never bring herself to broach the subject of money with Grandy, who had been unfailingly generous with her and who, she felt, was still far from incompetent. The furthest she went was to ask the attorney once if she could afford to hire another nurse. He smiled faintly and said, "I don't think money will ever be a problem here."

Perhaps money wasn't a problem in terms of meeting daily expenses, but Ann could tell that it was a ceaseless worry to Grandy; he just didn't know what to do with it. There was a time before the war when he'd clearly made up his mind to pass the bulk of his estate along to Martia and Bud, who had become his "right-hand man." Ann never knew exactly what went wrong there, but she held Bud to be as responsible for the break as Grandy, perhaps more so. Bud just wasn't her kind of person, and try as she would, she could never quite forgive him for getting Martia pregnant. They had covered it over with a wedding out in California in January '37, right after Pitt won the Rose Bowl game, which seemed a natural enough thing for the kids to do in the excitement of the moment. They all prayed that Grandy wouldn't think of counting the months when Scott Stewart McClure came along, and their prayers were answered. The old man was delighted with a namesake great-great-grandson and even more delighted that Bud felt compelled by fatherhood to leave college and to work with him full time. "Never saw much sense in college anyway. I did all right without it," Scott said.

In memory the first five years or so after that were golden ones for Ann. Bud and Martia really did seem to love each other, and within a year or so there was another baby, little Ann. At work, Bud drove himself the way he once did on

450

the football field. He was in the office hours before the old man, Saturdays included, and burned the lights until six or later. By '41, when he was only twenty-four, Bud was beginning to replace the old man on various boards of directors and was making enough money to buy a substantial home in Mount Lebanon, not far from the old McClure farm, but far enough, Ann noted with wry approval, from the East End and Fox Chapel to keep Grandy and her and particularly Mrs. Gillespie from looking over their shoulders. Not that they had much to hide. With a name like McClure and his football fame still echoing down the sports pages, Bud was an instant candidate for the role of upstanding citizen. He was admitted easily to the Duquesne Club, the St. Clair Country Club, even the University Club, and the moment he set foot in the Presbyterian church nearest his home, he was asked to join the session. . . .

Ann drove out with Grandy to attend Bud's ordination service. It was the first time they'd been in the South Hills in years, and she could see the old man was having a difficult time getting his bearings. In the years since the Liberty Tubes had been thrust through Mount Washington, the rolling farmland in which Scott Stewart had grown up had been covered as far as the eye could see with small houses on small lots. High-rise apartments were beginning to sprout along the mainstream of traffic; where the old Stewart homestead had stood there were two such edifices in yellow brick with storefronts below. Across the street a new building replaced the old church, and the little cemetery full of Stewarts, where the headstones had once been fired by every setting sun, now lay like an embarrassing anachronism in the perpetual shadow of a picture-windowed apartment house. Disconcerted and a bit embarrassed as he tried to identify landmarks for Ann, Scott said, "Doesn't look like much now, but it made a tidy estate for Mother. Keeps Lucinda going."

Seeing young Bud, handsome and grave in a formal dark suit, being accepted into the fold of elders improved Scott's humor. Ann thought she saw tears in the old man's eyes during the service, and on the way home he told her, "A fine boy. He's going to make a first-rate business man. . . ."

The only time Bud and the old man had a falling out in Ann's presence was on December 7, 1941. They were all out in Fox Chapel—all except Lucinda, who was nursing a cold —for Sunday dinner when the news of Pearl Harbor came to them. The maid, who'd had the radio going in the kitchen, heard it first and came running in. They left the table and went into the living room, where there was a big old radio, and just listened for a while in stunned silence. Bud got up and started excitedly pacing back and forth. "Oh, my God . . . oh, my God . . . ," he kept saying as the news got more and more specific about the damage to American ships. Finally he said, "I'm going down tomorrow and sign up—for the Air Corps. I've always wanted to fly."

Ann loved Bud then for the first and only time; the echo of her David's voice was so strong she wanted to cry . . . Grandy must have heard it, too, because he stirred himself and scarred the leg of her best Hepplewhite table with a vicious rap of his cane. "You'll do *nothing* of the sort, young man."

"Why not? You don't expect a healthy young man like myself to sit around here when our country's been attacked, do you? We've got to teach those bastards a lesson . . ."

"There'll be enough for you to do here," Scott said. "Pittsburgh isn't called the arsenal of democracy for nothing, and you are in a position to make that name stand for something."

"But there are plenty of people too old to fight who could take over my job . . ."

"You don't have any idea what you're saying. Just *because* Martia's father was a hot-headed young fool like you I had to carry the whole burden in the last war and . . ."

"But you let him go, didn't you? Didn't you?"

"No, I didn't. He ran off behind my back. You know what happened. So let me tell you, young man, you are not going to go—and that is final. I know Stimson—he's a good Republican and understands these things. I'm going to get in touch with him tomorrow and make sure you are not acceptable to the armed forces . . ."

"I'll just bet you will. . . . You're going to use your goddamned power like you've always done to make other people do what you want. But this time it won't work . . ."

Bud slammed out of the house and got into his car, leaving his family to find their own way home. In a few minutes Scott was ready to go too. "Come along, Martia, and bring the children," he said. "I'll have Alexander drive you home. Don't worry, Bud will come to his senses by tomorrow."

"I'm not sure I want him to, Grandy," Martia said. "You go along. We'll stay here with Mother."

That evening Ann and Martia had their first open talk since the marriage, and Ann wondered why it took nothing less than the outbreak of war to jar open the doors that proper Pittsburgh families kept closed against each other. It all started when, as soon as the children were bedded down, Ann said, "I'm happy to have you here, Martia, but don't you think you ought to be getting back to Bud?"

"Oh, no, he's out getting drunk—I know it."

"Does this happen often?"

"Too often."

"Does Grandy know about it?"

"Oh, no, Bud's clever that way. It wouldn't do for a Presbyterian elder to be getting loaded all the time, would it? He finds places where nobody knows him."

"Well, I must say that I was proud of Bud today," Ann said. "He sounded just like your father—"

"But he isn't like Father," Martia protested. "Bud may be anxious to go to war, but one of the reasons is to get away from me and the children and . . . and Grandy."

"Come now, Martia, you're just upset."

"No, I'm not that upset, Mother. I've known for a long time that Bud felt trapped by the . . . well, it was his fault, but he feels trapped all the same."

"You told me yourself, Martia, that what Bud wanted most was to make money. Well, now he—and you—stand to get more money than you'll ever know what to do with."

"Yes, but Bud didn't understand then what went along with getting money, particularly from Grandy. You know what he told me once? He said, 'Your great-grandfather is absolutely impossible. He's a bone-smart business man who knows that you buy cheap and sell dear, but he thinks everything he's got has come from God. Maybe that's why he's more interested in what goes on in the session of our dinky church than the deals I'm making every day over lunch at the club. He's driving me crazy.' . . . So you see, Mother? I just don't know what's going to happen now."

"Don't worry, baby," Ann said. "If I know Bud, he will, as Grandy put it, come to his senses."

He did, and the first years of the war were not only personally good ones for Bud McClure but extremely profitable for the Stewart holdings. Framed and mounted on the wall of Scott S. Stewart, Esq., in the Frick Building was a "Dear Bud" letter from Secretary of War Stimson, dated a few days after Pearl Harbor and saying in part, ". . . I am aware that a young man like yourself, of proven courage on the athletic field, would feel a compulsion to serve in the front lines of this great battle. But I want to assure you that we, at the highest levels of government, are aware that the protection of our democratic way of life lies as much in the blast furnaces of Pittsburgh as on the battlefields of Europe and Asia. It is my

453

judgment, therefore, that the greatest contribution a young man of your knowledge and experience can make to the nation in this hour of crisis is to stimulate the production of those materials without which we would be defenseless. . . ."

This was pretty heady stuff, and so Bud McClure stayed on, voting as a board member of U.S. Steel for the seven-hundred-million-dollar expansion and conversion program, even though the government was picking up only two-thirds of the tab, and for the Aluminum Company's decision to put two hundred fifty million up against a government guarantee of four hundred fifty million. As Bud said to Martia in the privacy of their home, "You know, I can't believe some of these guys—they actually think the government ought to pay for all of it; they just don't realize what we're making out of it at cost plus. But I'll say this for old Grandy Stewart—*he* does."

Bud's best moment came as a result of his suggestion that American Bridge Company, a subsidiary of U.S. Steel, could do as well as the Dravo Corporation in making LST's and other shallow draft naval vessels—there was a lot of vacant land down there at Ambridge near the plant that could be converted into a shipyard. It not only worked out all right from a business point of view, but when Secretary of the Navy Knox, another good Republican, came to Pittsburgh in 1943, Bud McClure was one of the people he wanted to see. At a news conference Knox glowed, "Every time I approach Pittsburgh, I get a sense of tremendous power, a sense of accomplishment. Pittsburgh thrills me," and then the Secretary threw his arm around Bud's shoulders and added, "It's young men of inventiveness and spirit like Bud McClure here who make this possible."

What with trips to Washington and official dinners, Bud was seldom home. Because of their connection with essential industry, both Grandy and Bud had almost unlimited gasoline, and they would continue to drive out to Fox Chapel for Sunday dinners. But, increasingly, Martia and the children would come alone. Grandy began fussing. "Where's Bud?" he'd ask.

"He had a golf date," Martia would explain.

"On Sunday? An elder? I suppose he's drinking, too . . ."

"It's 1943, Grandy," Martia would say. "Everybody drinks, and Bud is working so hard. . . ."

"Nonsense. I haven't had a drink in my life," Grandy would say, making it obvious he had never read the label on his tonic.

But what really galled Scott Stewart was the way his great-grandson-in-law was blithely ignoring the essential business of taking care of the Stewart investments. It didn't seem fair that a man nearly ninety should have to take himself to the office every day through the choking smog of a city almost literally on fire. Of course, Bud always had the best excuses. Pittsburgh industries were going through spasm after spasm to belch out more ships, tanks, shells and armor plate each month than the month before. This took incessant prodding of the men and women on the lines and, as a personable football hero, Bud McClure turned out to be one of the best at delivering inspirational talks. Naturally he was tapped, too, for the war-bond drives among the city's wealthy. "They still remember what you did in the last war, Grandy; you couldn't expect me to do less, could you?" he'd say as he left the office for a long Duquesne Club lunch, where he was scheduled to meet "this fella who ought to be buying more bonds." So Scott would send out for a sandwich and turn back to his figures, worrying more all the time whether Bud really had the character to command a fortune that was growing almost as fast as the city's production—up more than one hundred and eighty percent in the first year of the war alone.

No doubt it was his own fault. Because his time was inevitably so short, he had probably brought the boy along too fast and too far. That little ploy with Stimson that was meant simply to keep the boy by his side had done nothing but turn Bud's head. He seemed to think he was winning the war single-handed. He would have called him down for it except that he knew Bud was getting daily offers of big jobs in Washington and finding them more and more difficult to resist. If they had a confrontation, Scott might lose him entirely, and then he really didn't know what he would do—he couldn't, after all, leave all this in the hands of a couple of women, and the boy Scott was just too young to consider. Of course, he could give most of it away, set up some kind of trust or other, but Scott had never liked the kind of people who seemed to get hold of those things. They forgot, if they ever knew, where the money came from, and threw it around to people and causes that were like as not out to undermine the very principles that produced this kind of wealth. It was a sore thing for an old man to have this feeling of having nowhere to turn, and even prayer brought him no certain answers.

All of Scott's efforts at self-control collapsed the day Bud McClure came to him for more money. It was late one afternoon after everybody else had left the office. Bud as usual had been gone most of the day and Scott could smell whiskey on his breath when he marched in and said, "Glad to find you alone, sir. I've been meaning to talk to you about an increase . . ."

The boy was making ten thousand dollars already, not including what he was getting from directorships. How could he need more? Was he gambling? With all these questions hanging in the air, Scott simply said, "You've been drinking."

"Sure, I've had a couple. So what? We had a big luncheon meeting with the War Production people; all those fellows from Washington expect a drink. But the thing is, with all these club dues and the entertaining I have to do and the place in Mount Lebanon, I'm in a little over my head. . . ."

"I never had any need to behave like that."

"But you're from another generation—*two* other generations. People do business differently now."

"No reason why they should—business is business. See here, I don't understand how you can come around asking for more money when you aren't even paying attention to where it's coming from. If it weren't for me, you'd be out there somewhere, very fortunate to be getting a hundred and fifty a month in the army. . . ."

"Yes, and feeling like a man while I was doing it."

"A man? A man does what he has to, not what he wants to," Scott said, and then, watching Bud pacing nervously in front of his desk, added, "Sit down, Bud, if you've got a minute. Actually I'm glad you've come to see me. I've been meaning to speak to you for some time. . . . You know when you married into this family you assumed an obligation . . ."

Bud, who had sat down gingerly, jumped up again. "But . . ."

"No, let me finish." He picked up the Bible he always kept on his desk. "I want to read you a bit of scripture that has always been a guide to me in my affairs. Since you're an elder you should be able to see that it applies to you as well. Here it is—Romans: 28—'We know that in everything God works for good with those who love him, who are called according to his purpose. For those whom he knew he also predestined. . . . And those whom he predestined he also called; and those whom he called he also justified; and those whom he justified he also glorified.' Do you see?"

Bud, still pacing, shook his head. "I don't get it, I really don't . . ."

"Well, I'm not surprised. You young people are not taught

456

the Bible the way we were. But it's all plainly there. I was against it, I don't mind telling you—thought you were probably a fortune hunter—but when you married Martia, I came to the conclusion that it was predestined that you . . ."

Bud started to laugh. "Oh, my God, if you only knew."

"Knew? Knew what? What's that?"

"Listen, sir, I married your precious great-granddaughter to save what you would call her honor . . ."

"What's that? What do you mean?"

"I mean she was pregnant."

"You . . . why *you*—"

"Now wait a minute, no questions asked. I at least did the right thing by her, and I think all of you owe me something for it."

Scott tried to speak, but nothing came out. Looking at him, Bud was suddenly terrified. Instead of reddening, Scott's face went white, and every vein and muscle seemed to bulge and tremble under the taut skin. He was going to have a fit, a stroke. Bud turned and ran out. Nobody had seen him come in here, and, if anything happened nobody would blame him for it. Outside, he realized he'd had one drink too many and had gone one step too far. He felt like he had the time he'd recovered a fumble and in the heat of the game actually ran it across the wrong goal line. There was no way of taking the play back then, no way of saving the game, and there was no way now. He was through with Scott Stewart. What he needed immediately was another drink. . . .

After Bud left, Scott Stewart sat immobile at his desk for an hour, perhaps more, until a worried chauffeur finally came up and helped him out. He had been afraid to move, feeling overcome by the first of those dizzy spells that those doctor fellows now insisted were strokes. It was scary.

From that day on, Scott would not leave his house lest he fall in a strange place. When Martia came to see him a few days later to tell him that Bud was going into uniform as a major in the Pittsburgh Ordnance district, he was strangely curt and brusque with her, but it was put down to illness and his understandable irritation over Bud's desertion. He didn't even want to see her children, but then he had always been nervous around little children. It was that day that Ann discovered, somewhat to her dismay, that she was the only person in the family, with the possible exception of Lucinda (who at eighty-six was going deaf herself), who could get through to Scott Stewart. He asked her to call his law firm and have them assign for an indefinite period a discreet young man to his affairs—he would make it worth their while.

Scott didn't tell anybody about his talk with Bud. He couldn't trust himself to speak of it, could hardly think of it, for fear of bringing on another spell. Anyway, he suspected they all had known and had been keeping it from him. At least it explained why a sensible woman like Ann had allowed her daughter to marry at sixteen. How it must have hurt her . . . but in a way it was her fault—she'd never listened to him about that boy. And Martia? How could she do such a thing? No wonder the Bible called women the weaker vessels. Lucinda. May. Martia. Did it run in the blood? Where was the goodness and glory promised by God to His elect? As the seemingly timeless days came and went and his powers failed despite his every effort to get up and move about and regain his self-confidence, Scott Stewart brooded incessantly. He had to make some decision about his will, as the young lawyer politely reminded him each time they met, and yet he felt paralyzed. He could tie everything up indefinitely, tie it up until young Scott McClure reached maturity or beyond, but what assurance could he have that the boy, especially with such parents, would be worthy of the trust? As he had so often in the past, Scott kept asking God for an answer. But God was strangely silent: could it have something to do with his being deaf?

Scott Stewart took more and more to his room and his bed, and a kind of death watch began. In Dr. Stewart Sharp's opinion the end could come any day, any hour, which was one reason why Ann had felt compelled to move into the house. Lucinda came as often as she could, but she couldn't be relied on. Like any person her age, she had her inevitable "bad days," and at such times Ann felt obliged to go over to the Schenley with soup or some excuse to make sure the old lady hadn't passed away in her sleep. Once in exasperation she tried to get Lucinda to move into one of the ten or so empty bedrooms in Scott's house so that she could keep an eye on both of them. She was somewhat surprised at the vehemence with which Lucinda replied. "Never. I could never live under that roof. It's just something I owe Henry's memory. Anyway, you don't want to turn the place into an old folks' home, do you?" One of the ironies of the situation that seemed to bemuse Dr. Sharp was, as he said, "With all of its death and destruction this war has produced penicillin, so we can no longer rely on the old man's friend, pneumonia. I'm obliged by my oath to use the stuff every time he gets the sniffles, so he could last indefinitely."

"Do you think he's competent?" Ann asked. "Bud's afraid . . . but you're a specialist in that."

"Oh, yes, he's competent enough," Stewart Sharp said. "Fuzzy at times, no doubt, but he knows what's going on."

"I'll say he does," Ann agreed. "You know the other day Lucinda brought Alma over here. They're all deaf and can't hear each other, you know, and they were having a rough time at conversation when I saw Grandy making frantic signals to me. I went over, and he whispered, 'Get that woman out of here, never could stand her.'"

Stewart Sharp laughed. "That's Uncle Scott all right. You know there was a time there when I used to think he was a sick man, but I'm beginning to wonder if he isn't the healthiest of us all—mentally speaking. . . ."

"How do you mean?"

"He never seems to worry about being loved, or that even more illusive thing, being happy. As long as he thinks he's right with God, as he understands it, he just marches straight ahead. And of course being right with God in his terms kept him out of the flesh pots that undo so many of us. Sometimes I wonder who's going to be more impressed when they meet—God or Uncle Scott. But there is something worrying him now, and I gather from that tight-lipped lawyer it has to do with what he's going to do with all that money. . . ."

"It's worrying most everybody else, too."

"I know. I once suggested that he put some of it into medical research, in Benjamin's name, and do you know what he said? . . . 'A lot of tomfoolishness. You doctor fellows never realize you are dealing with the will of God. If my father had known that, he wouldn't have killed himself.'"

"Really? Well, in that case he ought to give it to the Church."

"Not much chance. I mentioned that too, and he said that people like my brother would just give it away to a bunch of undeserving malcontents."

"The poor man . . ."

Stewart Sharp laughed again. "Ann Stewart, I do believe you are the only person in the city of Pittsburgh who would ever call Scott Stewart a 'poor man,' but I love you for it," he said. "Call me any time of the night or day if you see any change at all."

When people became aware that Scott Stewart was no longer appearing in his office or at the Duquesne Club or at

459

church, calls began coming in, a large portion of them from highly placed men in the businesses in which Ann knew that her grandfather-in-law held large blocks of stock. None of them was so blunt, of course, as even to hint at what must really have concerned them; they only made polite inquiries about the old gentleman's health in a tone one might use to ask about the weather. Newspapers began to call, too, some of them every day, and Ann began to take notice of a man who stopped his car every morning along the curb and stared curiously at the house. It annoyed her, and she arranged to be out clipping roses from the front garden one morning so that she could get a better look at him. His car window was open when he stopped, and she stepped out to the sidewalk to challenge him. "Could you tell me what you are doing here every day?" she asked.

"Excuse me, ma'am, it's my job," he said. "I'm a reporter for the *Sun-Tele* and the city editor just asked me to stop by every morning and take a look in case . . ."

"Well, I don't see that it's any of your business."

"Mr. Stewart's an important person, ma'am. The city editor says since Andy Mellon died, he's the last of the giants, and, forgive me, but it will be big news when . . ."

"Please stop bothering us," Ann said. "Give me your name, and I promise to call you when, or if, anything happens."

"Oh, would you do that? Thank you, ma'am," the reporter said, scribbling off his name and number on a piece of copy paper.

On Sunday morning, August 5, 1945, while across the world the *Enola Gay* was leading a flight of American bombers toward Hiroshima to unleash the most awesome power man had yet gathered into his hands, a fretful Scott Stewart fussed and fumed at his nurses until they brought Ann to his bedside. "Get me some paper and a pen and call that young lawyer fella and tell him to get over here," he said.

"I was just getting ready to go to church, Grandy," Ann said. "It's Sunday. You don't want to work on Sunday, do you?"

"Sunday? Sunday? Well, get me the paper—and tell the lawyer he can come after church. Keep those nurses out of here. They're a nuisance."

Disturbed by the old man's peevishness, Ann put in a call to Dr. Stewart Sharp on her way out to church. When she got back, he was walking restlessly around the gilt living room, picking up objects and turning them idly in his hands as if evaluating their worth.

When he looked up and saw Ann, Stewart hesitated, then said, "Well, he's gone. . . ."

"*Gone?* I can't believe it."

"I know . . . when I got your call I came as soon as I could. The nurses told me they'd been ordered to stay out of his room, but I went in and found him propped up in bed, pen still in hand. . . . He left this."

Stewart gave Ann a piece of paper on which there was scrawled in the spidery hand she'd become so accustomed to seeing on checks:

"August 5 (and then the date scratched out and changed to 6, as if he had some doubt that a document dated on Sunday would be valid), I, Scott S. Stewart, being of sound mind, do hereby commend my soul to the mercy of our only Lord and Saviour, Jesus Christ, and, bearing in mind His prayer to our heavenly Father acknowledging that '*thine* is the kingdom and the power and the glory forever and ever,' do hereby bequeath whatsoever earthly goods of which I may now be possessed t" The stroke of the "t" trailed downward and faded off the side of the page at the point where, according to Dr. Sharp, the pen had come to rest.

"What a perfect way for him to . . ."

"Yes, isn't it? But I don't imagine the lawyers will like it. I guess you'd better call them right away . . ."

"Oh, Grandy already told me to call the lawyer. He's coming right after church. He ought to be here any minute. . . ."

Lucinda, who, under the circumstances, was unfortunately having one of her good days, arrived almost at the same time as the lawyer. An old hand at coping with the news of deaths, Lucinda seemed to take it better than the attorney, who after a glance at the paper Scott had left, said, "Oh, my God, what a mess! A week or so ago when we were doing the July bills Mr. Stewart made me bring out his old will and destroy it in his presence. He said he would draft a new one right away, but this . . ."

"What does it really mean?" Stewart Sharp asked.

"Well, it really means he died intestate. To put it bluntly, all of it will be up for grabs. Of course, Mrs. Stewart, your daughter and her children as the only blood relatives should have the best claim, but others like Mrs. Schmidt here could . . ."

"Let me see that paper," Lucinda said. She put on her

glasses and studied it for a full minute and then said, "Well, of course, I don't want any money. But I'm fascinated at what he was getting at . . . reminds me of something Henry said years ago to Scott about *Thine* is the glory. . . . Do you think he finally got the idea, Stewart?"

"I couldn't say, Aunt . . . Cindy."

With her voice now trembling a little, Lucinda said, "I wonder if Scott will put in a good word for me with God."

There was a kind of embarrassed silence. The attorney cleared his throat and gently extracted the paper from Lucinda's hand. She took off her glasses, looked up at them all with her head still held regally erect and said, "Well, I guess there's no use asking for a glass of sherry in this house, but if anybody has a cigarette . . . oh, I know, Stewart, you doctors don't think I should smoke but . . ."

Relieved that a difficult moment seemed to have passed, the lawyer took out a pack of cigarettes and lit one for Lucinda. "I'm sure your attitude will make it easier for everybody, Mrs. Schmidt. And . . . I presume you'll handle the matter of the obituary."

Which reminded Ann of the reporter she had promised to call. Surprisingly, she found him at his office on Sunday. There was a lot of commotion in the background, and his voice seemed distracted. "Oh, yes, Mr. Stewart. Oh, yes, thanks for calling," he said. "Say, there's something big breaking right now, do you mind if I get back to you?"

He never did. The next day's banner headlines screamed: SECRET ATOM BOMBS TO WIPE OUT JAPAN. The whole front page of the paper was taken up with the news of the terrible new weapon and with all the side stories, such as HUGE FIRES SET BY B-29 RAID, and ATOMIC BOMB PARTS MADE HERE BUT SECRET KEPT WELL. Far inside, under a one-column headline reading SCOTT S. STEWART; INDUSTRIALIST, 93, was a notice of the passing of the last of Pittsburgh's industrial giants.

There were not enough people still alive who had ever really known him to fill more than a few of the acres of pews in the East Liberty Presbyterian Church, and all of those who followed to the little cemetery in the South Hills were able to arrange themselves around the open grave.

As they did so four young matrons were settling themselves down to an afternoon bridge game behind one of the picture windows overlooking the cemetery. One of them said, "Would you look at that—they're still burying people out there."

"I thought they were going to move all those old bones and build a decent parking-garage," another said.

"I read all the papers and nobody who's anybody died around here that I could see," a third commented. "I wonder who it could be?"

"Probably one of those old farmers out in St. Clair Township. There still are a couple in the church, you know. Isn't it your bid, dear?" . . .

Postlude

The Pittsburgh Scott Stewart and his associates built has changed. Thanks to a postwar alliance between a Democratic boss named David L. Lawrence, whose machine stood in about the same relation to the Magee-Flinn operation as a jet to a buggy, and the Republican descendants of old Judge Mellon, skies are mostly clear above the golden triangle, and citizens whose unions have seen to it that they no longer slave away the twelve hours of daylight in mines and mills are taking to the sparkling rivers in canoes and cruisers and white-winged sailing craft. Sit above the city any evening in the cozy lounge of one of the fine restaurants on Mount Washington, and you will look out over a dazzle of lights and fountains and natural wonders to rival San Francisco or Rio or Hong Kong. It is not hard to imagine Judge Reed Stewart joining you there and, glass in hand, playing on his favorite symbolism.

"Somewhere along the line old John Knox lost this place—hardly a church spire to be seen," he would doubtless say. "And he was pretty smart in not building himself a temple. Carnegie's is gone entirely, and you can hardly see, even with all this clear air, those little things Frick and Oliver and the others threw up. But look at what you do see now—Gulf,

Koppers, Alcoa and, biggest of all, that 64-story edifice of U.S. Steel. I'd take it *these* people have new gods—the organizations they serve—wouldn't you? Well, who knows, maybe it makes for a better world. I hope so. In any case, I'm just glad they haven't changed Old Overholt."